13
SHORT
DETECTIVE
NOVELS

ABOUT THE EDITORS

BILL PRONZINI, creator of the "nameless detective" series, is one of America's finest mystery/suspense writers, as well as one of its leading critics. He has published more than thirty novels and 280 short stories, has edited or co-edited more than forty anthologies, and, with Martin H. Greenberg, has co-edited *101 Mystery Stories, Baker's Dozen™: 13 Short Mystery Novels, Manhattan Mysteries,* and others. A longtime resident of San Francisco, he possesses one of the larger collections of pulp magazines in the world.

MARTIN H. GREENBERG has justly earned the title "king of the anthologists," as he now has more than two hundred to his credit. He is editor of *In the Ring: A Treasury of Boxing Stories* and co-editor of *Manhattan Mysteries, Detective A to Z, 101 Mystery Stories, 101 Science Fiction Stories, A Treasury of American Horror Stories,* and many more. He is professor of regional analysis and political science at the University of Wisconsin–Green Bay, where he also teaches a course in the history of science fiction.

BAKER'S
DOZEN

13
SHORT
DETECTIVE
NOVELS

Edited by

Bill Pronzini

and

Martin H. Greenberg

BONANZA BOOKS
New York

Grateful acknowledgment for permission to reprint material is hereby given to the following:

Finger Man by Raymond Chandler—Copyright 1950 by Raymond Chandler; copyright © renewed 1978 by Helga Greene. From *The Simple Art of Murder*. Reprinted by permission of Houghton Mifflin Company.

Death Stops at a Tourist Camp by Leslie Ford—Copyright 1936 by Leslie Ford; copyright © renewed 1964 by Zeneith Brown. Reprinted by permission of Brandt & Brandt Literary Agents, Inc.

The Saint in Palm Springs by Leslie Charteris—Copyright 1943 by Leslie Charteris. Reprinted by permission of the author.

Puzzle in Snow by Philip Wylie—Copyright 1937 by Philip Wylie; copyright © renewed 1964 by Philip Wylie. Reprinted by permission of Harold Ober Associates Incorporated.

The Case of the Crimson Kiss by Erle Stanley Gardner—Copyright 1951 by Erle Stanley Gardner. Reprinted by permission of Curtis Brown, Ltd.

The Room with Something Wrong by Cornell Woolrich—Copyright 1938, 1950 by William Irish. Reprinted by permission of the Estate of Cornell Woolrich and its agent, the Scott Meredith Literary Agency, Inc., 845 Third Avenue, New York, NY 10022.

Murder for Money by John D. MacDonald—Copyright 1952 by Popular Publications, Inc.; copyright © renewed 1980 by John D. MacDonald, Inc. Reprinted by permission of the Estate of John D. MacDonald.

The Morning of the Monkey by Robert van Gulik—Copyright © 1965 by Robert H. van Gulik. From *The Monkey and the Tiger*. Reprinted with the permission of Charles Scribner's Sons.

Maigret's Christmas by Georges Simenon—Copyright 1951 by Georges Simenon. Reprinted by permission of the author.

Withers and Malone, Brain-Stormers by Stuart Palmer and Craig Rice—Copyright © 1958 by Davis Publications, Inc. First appeared in *Ellery Queen's Mystery Magazine*. Reprinted by permission of the authors and authors' agent, the Scott Meredith Literary Agency, Inc., 845 Third Avenue, New York, NY 10022.

Death Flight by Ed McBain—Copyright 1954 by Evan Hunter; copyright © renewed 1982 by Evan Hunter. Reprinted by permission of John Farquharson, Ltd.

Who's Calling? by Bill Pronzini—Copyright © 1982, 1983 by Bill Pronzini. Reprinted by permission of the author.

City of Brass by Edward D. Hoch—Copyright © 1959 by Great American Publications, Inc. Reprinted by permission of the author.

First published in 1987 by Bonanza Books, distributed by Crown Publishers, Inc., 225 Park Avenue South, New York, New York 10003, by arrangement with Bill Pronzini and Martin H. Greenberg.

BAKER'S DOZEN is a trademark of OBC, Inc.

Printed and bound in the United States of America

Library of Congress Cataloging-in-Publication Data

Baker's dozen.

1. Detective and mystery stories. I. Pronzini, Bill.
II. Greenberg, Martin Harry.
PN6120.95.D45B35   1988   808.83′872   87-8082
ISBN 0-517-64103-8

h g f e d c b a

CONTENTS

INTRODUCTION

Baker's Dozen™: 13 Short Detective Novels brings together for the first time in book form thirteen outstanding mystery and detective novellas by some of the most accomplished writers in the field, both past and present.

These stories span more than sixty years of mystery fiction writing in the United States, Great Britain, and Europe, and they feature a wide variety of heroes, villains, settings, story types, and stylistic approaches. Taken all together, they demonstrate how the mystery/detective story has evolved in form, structure, and content over more than half a century and how succeeding generations of authors have invigorated it through thematic variation and ingenuity. The stories also reflect the times in which they were written so that they can be enjoyed from a historical perspective and as pure adventure.

The investigator of crimes is as old as the work of Edgar Allan Poe and Sir Arthur Conan Doyle. The investigator can be a policeman, a private citizen, or a professional private eye. All three types have enjoyed enormous popularity in many cultures, and all have starred on television and in the movies. The media have given us teams such as Simon and Simon, hardboiled types like Mike Hammer and his kin, and complex characters such as Magnum. These detectives represent numerous nationalities from the Orient (Charlie Chan and Mr. Moto) to Europe (Inspector Maigret and Eric Ambler's Dr. Jan Czissar of Czechoslovakia); and ethnic sleuths including Blacks (John Ball's Virgil Tibbs), Native Americans (Tony Hillerman's Corporal Jim Chee), Jews (Harry Kemelman's Rabbi Small), Chicanas (Marcia Muller's Elena Oliverez), and even a Gypsy (Edward D. Hoch's Michael Vlado). Their popularity has been so great that literally hundreds of them have made repeat appearances in several stories, making the series detective tale one of the most popular forms of writing in the world.

In this book you will read the creations of such masters of the form as Raymond Chandler, perhaps the greatest exponent of the hardboiled school; Leslie Charteris, with one of his best tales of Simon Templar, "The Saint"; Erle Stanley Gardner, one of the best-selling authors in history, the creator of the immortal Perry Mason; and Cornell Woolrich, the Poe of the twentieth century, and perhaps the greatest suspense writer of all time.

Other treats await you here: the late, great John D. MacDonald; a wonderful Inspector Maigret story by Georges Simenon; that wonderful pair Withers and Malone, created by the team of Stuart Palmer and Craig Rice; Ed McBain (Evan Hunter), master of the police procedural mystery; and Edward D. Hoch, the most prolific mystery/short fiction writer of all time.

In sum, we feel this volume provides something for every mystery taste, as well as a capsule course in mystery-making in the twentieth century. And we hope you derive as much pleasure from reading these thirteen short novels as we did in selecting them for you.

BILL PRONZINI
MARTIN H. GREENBERG
1987

RAYMOND CHANDLER
Finger Man

1

I GOT AWAY from the Grand Jury a little after four, and then sneaked up the back stairs to Fenweather's office. Fenweather, the D.A., was a man with severe, chiseled features and the gray temples women love. He played with a pen on his desk and said: "I think they believed you. They might even indict Manny Tinnen for the Shannon kill this afternoon. If they do, then is the time you begin to watch your step."

I rolled a cigarette around in my fingers and finally put it in my mouth. "Don't put any men on me, Mr. Fenweather. I know the alleys in this town pretty well, and your men couldn't stay close enough to do me any good."

He looked towards one of the windows. "How well do you know Frank Dorr?" he asked, with his eyes away from me.

"I know he's a big politico, a fixer you have to see if you want to open a gambling hell or a bawdy house—or if you want to sell honest merchandise to the city."

"Right." Fenweather spoke sharply, and brought his head around towards me. Then he lowered his voice. "Having the goods on Tinnen was a surprise to a lot of people. If Frank Dorr had an interest in getting rid of Shannon who was the head of the Board where Dorr's supposed to get his contracts, it's close enough to make him take chances. And I'm told he and Manny Tinnen had dealings. I'd sort of keep an eye on him, if I were you."

I grinned. "I'm just one guy," I said. "Frank Dorr covers a lot of territory. But I'll do what I can."

Fenweather stood up and held his hand across the desk. He said: "I'll be out of town for a couple of days. I'm leaving tonight,

3

if this indictment comes through. Be careful—and if anything should happen to go wrong, see Bernie Ohls, my chief investigator."

I said: "Sure."

We shook hands and I went out past a tired looking girl who gave me a tired smile and wound one of her lax curls up on the back of her neck as she looked at me. I got back to my office soon after four-thirty. I stopped outside the door of the little reception room for a moment, looking at it. Then I opened it and went in, and of course there wasn't anybody there.

There was nothing there but an old red davenport, two odd chairs, a bit of carpet, and a library table with a few old magazines on it. The reception room was left open for visitors to come in and sit down and wait—if I had any visitors and they felt like waiting.

I went across and unlocked the door into my private office, lettered *"Philip Marlowe . . . Investigations."*

Lou Harger was sitting on a wooden chair on the side of the desk away from the window. He had bright yellow gloves clamped on the crook of a cane, a green snap-brim hat set too far back on his head. Very smooth black hair showed under the hat and grew too low on the nape of his neck.

"Hello. I've been waiting," he said, and smiled languidly.

" 'Lo, Lou. How did you get in here?"

"The door must have been unlocked. Or maybe I had a key that fitted. Do you mind?"

I went around the desk and sat down in the swivel chair. I put my hat down on the desk, picked up a bulldog pipe out of an ash tray and began to fill it up.

"It's all right as long as it's you," I said. "I just thought I had a better lock."

He smiled with his full red lips. He was a very good-looking boy. He said: "Are you still doing business, or will you spend the next month in a hotel room drinking liquor with a couple of Headquarters boys?"

"I'm still doing business—if there's any business for me to do."

I lit my pipe, leaned back and stared at his clear olive skin, straight, dark eyebrows.

He put his cane on top of the desk and clasped his yellow gloves on the glass. He moved his lips in and out.

"I have a little something for you. Not a hell of a lot. But there's carfare in it."

I waited.

"I'm making a little play at Las Olindas tonight," he said. "At Canales' place."

"The white smoke?"

"Uh-huh. I think I'm going to be lucky—and I'd like to have a guy with a rod."

I took a fresh pack of cigarettes out of a top drawer and slid them across the desk. Lou picked them up and began to break the pack open.

I said: "What kind of a play?"

He got a cigarette halfway out and stared down at it. There was a little something in his manner I didn't like.

"I've been closed up for a month now. I wasn't makin' the kind of money it takes to stay open in this town. The Headquarters boys have been putting the pressure on since repeal. They have bad dreams when they see themselves trying to live on their pay."

I said: "It doesn't cost any more to operate here than anywhere else. And here you pay it all to one organization. That's something."

Lou Harger jabbed the cigarette in his mouth. "Yeah—Frank Dorr," he snarled. "That fat, blood-suckin' sonofabitch!"

I didn't say anything. I was way past the age when it's fun to swear at people you can't hurt. I watched Lou light his cigarette with my desk lighter. He went on, through a puff of smoke: "It's a laugh, in a way. Canales bought a new wheel—from some grafters in the sheriff's office. I know Pina, Canales' head croupier, pretty well. The wheel is one they took away from me. It's got bugs—and I know the bugs."

"And Canales don't . . . That sounds just like Canales," I said.

Lou didn't look at me. "He gets a nice crowd down there," he said. "He has a small dance floor and a five-piece Mexican band to help the customers relax. They dance a bit and then go back for another trimming, instead of going away disgusted."

I said: "What do *you* do?"

"I guess you might call it a system," he said softly, and looked at me under his long lashes.

I looked away from him, looked around the room. It had a rust-red carpet, five green filing cases in a row under an advertising calendar, an old costumer in the corner, a few walnut chairs, net curtains over the windows. The fringe of the curtains was dirty from blowing about in the draft. There was a bar of late sunlight across my desk and it showed up the dust.

"I get it like this," I said. "You think you have that roulette wheel tamed and you expect to win enough money so that Canales will be mad at you. You'd like to have some protection along—me. I think it's screwy."

"It's not screwy at all," Lou said. "Any roulette wheel has a tendency to work in a certain rhythm. If you know the wheel very well indeed—"

I smiled and shrugged. "Okey, I wouldn't know about that. I don't know enough roulette. It sounds to me like you're being a sucker for your own racket, but I could be wrong. And that's not the point anyway."

"What is?" Lou asked thinly.

"I'm not much stuck on bodyguarding—but maybe that's not the point either. I take it I'm supposed to think this play is on the level. Suppose I don't, and walk out on you, and you get in a box? Or suppose I think everything is aces, but Canales don't agree with me and gets nasty."

"That's why I need a guy with a rod," Lou said, without moving a muscle except to speak.

I said evenly: "If I'm tough enough for the job—and I didn't know I was—that still isn't what worries me."

"Forget it," Lou said. "It breaks me up enough to know you're worried."

I smiled a little more and watched his yellow gloves moving around on top of the desk, moving too much. I said slowly: "You're the last guy in the world to be getting expense money that way just now. I'm the last guy to be standing behind you while you do it. That's all."

Lou said: "Yeah." He knocked some ash off his cigarette down on the glass top, bent his head to blow it off. He went on, as if it was a new subject: "Miss Glenn is going with me. She's a tall redhead, a swell looker. She used to model. She's nice people in any kind of a spot and she'll keep Canales from breathing on my neck. So we'll make out. I just thought I'd tell you."

I was silent for a minute, then I said: "You know damn well I just got through telling the Grand Jury it was Manny Tinnen I saw lean out of that car and cut the ropes on Art Shannon's wrists after they pushed him on to the roadway, filled with lead."

Lou smiled faintly at me. "That'll make it easier for the grafters on the big time; the fellows who take the contracts and don't appear in the business. They say Shannon was square and kept the Board in line. It was a nasty bump-off."

I shook my head. I didn't want to talk about that. I said: "Canales has a noseful of junk a lot of the time. And maybe he doesn't go for redheads."

Lou stood up slowly and lifted his cane off the desk. He stared at the tip of one yellow finger. He had an almost sleepy expression. Then he moved towards the door, swinging his cane.

"Well, I'll be seein' you some time," he drawled.

I let him get his hand on the knob before I said: "Don't go away sore, Lou. I'll drop down to Las Olindas, if you have to have me. But I don't want any money for it, and for Pete's sake don't pay any more attention to me than you have to."

He licked his lips softly and didn't quite look at me. "Thanks, keed. I'll be careful as hell."

He went out then and his yellow glove disappeared around the edge of the door.

I sat still for about five minutes and then my pipe got too hot. I put it down, looked at my strap watch, and got up to switch on a small radio in the corner beyond the end of the desk. When the A.C. hum died down the last tinkle of a chime came out of the horn, then a voice was saying: "KLI now brings you its regular early evening broadcast of local news releases. An event of importance this afternoon was the indictment returned late today against Maynard J. Tinnen by the Grand Jury. Tinnen is a well-known City Hall lobbyist and man about town. The indictment, a shock to his many friends, was based almost entirely on the testimony—"

My telephone rang sharply and a girl's cool voice said in my ear: "One moment, please. Mr. Fenweather is calling you."

He came on at once. "Indictment returned. Take care of the boy."

I said I was just getting it over the radio. We talked a short moment and then he hung up, after saying he had to leave at once to catch a plane.

I leaned back in my chair again and listened to the radio without exactly hearing it. I was thinking what a damn fool Lou Harger was and that there wasn't anything I could do to change that.

2

IT WAS a good crowd for a Tuesday but nobody was dancing. Around ten o'clock the little five-piece band got tired of messing around with a rhumba that nobody was paying any attention to. The marimba player dropped his sticks and reached under his chair for a glass. The rest of the boys lit cigarettes and just sat there looking bored.

I leaned sidewise against the bar, which was on the same side of the room as the orchestra stand. I was turning a small glass of tequila around on the top of the bar. All the business was at the center one of the three roulette tables.

The bartender leaned beside me, on his side of the bar.

"The flame-top gal must be pickin' them," he said.

I nodded without looking at him. "She's playing with fistfuls now," I said. "Not even counting it."

The red-haired girl was tall. I could see the burnished copper of her hair between the heads of the people behind her. I could see Lou Harger's sleek head beside hers. Everybody seemed to be playing standing up.

"You don't play?" the bartender asked me.

"Not on Tuesdays. I had some trouble on a Tuesday once."

"Yeah? Do you like that stuff straight, or should I smooth it out for you?"

"Smooth it out with what?" I said. "You got a wood rasp handy?"

He grinned. I drank a little more of the tequila and made a face.

"Did somebody invent this stuff on purpose?"

"I wouldn't know, mister."

"What's the limit over there?"

"I wouldn't know that either. How the boss feels, I guess."

The roulette tables were in a row near the far wall. A low railing of gilt metal joined their ends and the players were outside the railing.

Some kind of a confused wrangle started at the center table. Half a dozen people at the two end tables grabbed their chips up and moved across.

Then a clear, very polite voice, with a slightly foreign accent, spoke out: "If you will just be patient, madame . . . Mr. Canales will be here in a minute."

I went across, squeezed near the railing. Two croupiers stood near me with their heads together and their eyes looking sidewise. One moved a rake slowly back and forth beside the idle wheel. They were staring at the red-haired girl.

She wore a high-cut black evening gown. She had fine white shoulders, was something less than beautiful and more than pretty. She was leaning on the edge of the table, in front of the wheel. Her long eyelashes were twitching. There was a big pile of money and chips in front of her.

She spoke monotonously, as if she had said the same thing several times already.

"Get busy and spin that wheel! You take it away fast enough, but you don't like to dish it out."

The croupier in charge smiled a cold, even smile. He was tall, dark, disinterested. "The table can't cover your bet," he said with calm precision. "Mr. Canales, perhaps—" He shrugged neat shoulders.

The girl said: "It's your money, highpockets. Don't you want it back?"

Lou Harger licked his lips beside her, put a hand on her arm, stared at the pile of money with hot eyes. He said gently: "Wait for Canales. . . ."

"To hell with Canales! I'm hot—and I want to stay that way."

A door opened at the end of the tables and a very slight, very pale man came into the room. He had straight, lusterless black hair, a high bony forehead, flat, impenetrable eyes. He had a thin mustache that was trimmed in two sharp lines almost at right angles to each other. They came down below the corners of his mouth a full inch. The effect was Oriental. His skin had a thick, glistening pallor.

He slid behind the croupiers, stopped at a corner of the center table, glanced at the red-haired girl and touched the ends of his mustache with two fingers, the nails of which had a purplish tint.

He smiled suddenly, and the instant after it was as though he had never smiled in his life. He spoke in a dull, ironic voice.

"Good evening, Miss Glenn. You must let me send somebody with you when you go home. I'd hate to see any of that money get in the wrong pockets."

The red-haired girl looked at him, not very pleasantly.

"I'm not leaving—unless you're throwing me out."

Canales said: "No? What would you like to do?"

"Bet the wad—dark meat!"

The crowd noise became a deathly silence. There wasn't a whisper of any kind of sound. Harger's face slowly got ivory-white.

Canales' face was without expression. He lifted a hand, delicately, gravely, slipped a large wallet from his dinner jacket and tossed it in front of the tall croupier.

"Ten grand," he said in a voice that was a dull rustle of sound. "That's my limit—always."

The tall croupier picked the wallet up, spread it, drew out two flat packets of crisp bills, riffled them, refolded the wallet and passed it along the edge of the table to Canales.

Canales did not move to take it. Nobody moved, except the croupier.

The girl said: "Put it on the red."

The croupier leaned across the table and very carefully stacked her money and chips. He placed her bet for her on the red diamond. He placed his hand along the curve of the wheel.

"If no one objects," Canales said, without looking at anyone, "this is just the two of us."

Heads moved. Nobody spoke. The croupier spun the wheel and sent the ball skimming in the groove with a light flirt of his left wrist. Then he drew his hands back and placed them in full view on the edge of the table, on top of it.

The red-haired girl's eyes shone and her lips slowly parted.

The ball drifted along the groove, dipped past one of the bright metal diamonds, slid down the flank of the wheel and chattered along the tines beside the numbers. Movement went out of it suddenly, with a dry click. It fell next the double-zero, in red twenty-seven. The wheel was motionless.

The croupier took up his rake and slowly pushed the two packets of bills across, added them to the stake, pushed the whole thing off the field of play.

Canales put his wallet back in his breast pocket, turned and walked slowly back to the door, went through it.

I took my cramped fingers off the top of the railing, and a lot of people broke for the bar.

3

WHEN LOU came up I was sitting at a little tile-top table in a corner, fooling with some more of the tequila. The little orchestra was playing a thin, brittle tango and one couple was maneuvering self-consciously on the dance floor.

Lou had a cream-colored overcoat on, with the collar turned up around a lot of white silk scarf. He had a fine-drawn glistening expression. He had white pigskin gloves this time and he put one of them down on the table and leaned at me.

"Over twenty-two thousand," he said softly. "Boy, what a take!"

I said: "Very nice money, Lou. What kind of car are you driving?"

"See anything wrong with it?"

"The play?" I shrugged, fiddled with my glass. "I'm not wised up on roulette, Lou . . . I saw plenty wrong with your broad's manners."

"She's not a broad," Lou said. His voice got a little worried.

"Okey. She made Canales look like a million. What kind of car?"

"Buick sedan. Nile green, with two spotlights and those little fender lights on rods." His voice was still worried.

I said: "Take it kind of slow through town. Give me a chance to get in the parade."

He moved his glove and went away. The red-haired girl was not in sight anywhere. I looked down at the watch on my wrist. When I looked up again Canales was standing across the table. His eyes looked at me lifelessly above his trick mustache.

"You don't like my place," he said.

"On the contrary."

"You don't come here to play." He was telling me, not asking me.

"Is it compulsory?" I asked dryly.

A very faint smile drifted across his face. He leaned a little down and said: "I think you are a dick. A smart dick."

"Just a shamus," I said. "And not so smart. Don't let my long upper lip fool you. It runs in the family."

Canales wrapped his fingers around the top of a chair, squeezed on it. "Don't come here again—for anything." He spoke very softly, almost dreamily. "I don't like pigeons."

I took the cigarette out of my mouth and looked it over before I looked at him. I said: "I heard you insulted a while back. You took it nicely. . . . So we won't count this one."

He had a queer expression for a moment. Then he turned and slid away with a little sway of the shoulders. He put his feet down flat and turned them out a good deal as he walked. His walk, like his face, was a little negroid.

I got up and went out through the big white double doors into a dim lobby, got my hat and coat and put them on. I went out through another pair of double doors onto a wide veranda with scrollwork along the edge of its roof. There was sea fog in the air and the wind-blown Monterey cypresses in front of the house dripped with it. The grounds sloped gently into the dark for a long distance. Fog hid the ocean.

I had parked the car out on the street, on the other side of the house. I drew my hat down and walked soundlessly on the damp moss that covered the driveway, rounded a corner of the porch, and stopped rigidly.

A man just in front of me was holding a gun—but he didn't see me. He was holding the gun down at his side, pressed against the material of his overcoat, and his big hand made it look quite small. The dim light that reflected from the barrel seemed to come out of the fog, to be part of the fog. He was a big man, and he stood very still, poised on the balls of his feet.

I lifted my right hand very slowly and opened the top two buttons of my coat, reached inside and drew out a long .38 with a six-inch barrel. I eased it into my overcoat pocket.

The man in front of me moved, reached his left hand up to his face. He drew on a cigarette cupped inside his hand and the glow put brief light on a heavy chin, wide, dark nostrils, and a square, aggressive nose, the nose of a fighting man.

Then he dropped the cigarette and stepped on it and a quick, light step made faint noise behind me. I was far too late turning.

Something swished and I went out like a light.

4

WHEN I came to I was cold and wet and had a headache a yard wide. There was a soft bruise behind my right ear that wasn't bleeding. I had been put down with a sap.

I got up off my back and saw that I was a few yards from the driveway, between two trees that were wet with fog. There was some mud on the backs of my shoes. I had been dragged off the path, but not very far.

I went through my pockets. My gun was gone, of course, but that was all—that and the idea that this excursion was all fun.

I nosed around through the fog, didn't find anything or see anyone, gave up bothering about that, and went along the blank side of the house to a curving line of palm trees and an old type arc light that hissed and flickered over the entrance to a sort of lane where I had stuck the 1925 Marmon touring car I still used for transportation. I got into it after wiping the seat off with a towel, teased the motor alive, and choked it along to a big empty street with disused car tracks in the middle.

I went from there to De Cazens Boulevard, which was the main drag of Las Olindas and was called after the man who built Canales' place long ago. After a while there was town, buildings, dead-looking stores, a service station with a night-bell, and at last a drugstore which was still open.

A dolled-up sedan was parked in front of the drugstore and I parked behind that, got out, and saw that a hatless man was sitting at the counter, talking to a clerk in a blue smock. They seemed to have the world to themselves. I started to go in, then I stopped and took another look at the dolled-up sedan.

It was a Buick and of a color that could have been Nile-green in daylight. It had two spotlights and two little egg-shaped amber lights stuck up on thin nickel rods clamped to the front fenders. The window by the driver's seat was down. I went back to the Marmon and got a flash, reached in and twisted the license holder of the Buick around, put the light on it quickly, then off again.

It was registered to Louis N. Harger.

I got rid of the flash and went into the drugstore. There was a liquor display at one side, and the clerk in the blue smock sold me a pint of Canadian Club, which I took over to the counter and opened. There were ten seats at the counter, but I sat down on the one next to the hatless man. He began to look me over, in the mirror, very carefully.

I got a cup of black coffee two-thirds full and added plenty of the rye. I drank it down and waited for a minute, to let it warm me up. Then I looked the hatless man over.

He was about twenty-eight, a little thin on top, had a healthy red face, fairly honest eyes, dirty hands and looked as if he wasn't making much money. He wore a gray whipcord jacket with metal buttons on it, pants that didn't match.

I said carelessly, in a low voice: "Your bus outside?"

He sat very still. His mouth got small and tight and he had trouble pulling his eyes away from mine, in the mirror.

"My brother's," he said, after a moment.

I said: "Care for a drink? . . . Your brother is an old friend of mine."

He nodded slowly, gulped, moved his hand slowly, but finally got the bottle and curdled his coffee with it. He drank the whole thing down. Then I watched him dig up a crumpled pack of cigarettes, spear his mouth with one, strike a match on the counter, after missing twice on his thumbnail, and inhale with a lot of very poor nonchalance that he knew wasn't going over.

I leaned close to him and said evenly: "This doesn't *have* to be trouble."

He said: "Yeah . . . Wh-what's the beef?"

The clerk sidled towards us. I asked for more coffee. When I got it I stared at the clerk until he went and stood in front of the display window with his back to me. I laced my second cup of coffee and drank some of it. I looked at the clerk's back and said: "The guy the car belongs to doesn't have a brother."

He held himself tightly, but turned towards me. "You think it's a hot car?"

"No."

"You don't think it's a hot car?"

I said: "No. I just want the story."

"You a dick?"

"Uh-huh—but it isn't a shakedown, if that's what worries you."

He drew hard on his cigarette and moved his spoon around in his empty cup.

"I can lose my job over this," he said slowly. "But I needed a hundred bucks. I'm a hack driver."

"I guessed that," I said.

He looked surprised, turned his head and stared at me. "Have another drink and let's get on with it," I said. "Car thieves don't park them on the main drag and then sit around in drugstores."

The clerk came back from the window and hovered near us, busying himself with rubbing a rag on the coffee urn. A heavy silence fell. The clerk put the rag down, went along to the back of the store, behind the partition, and began to whistle aggressively.

The man beside me took some more of the whiskey and drank it, nodding his head wisely at me. "Listen—I brought a fare out and was supposed to wait for him. A guy and a jane come up alongside me in the Buick and the guy offers me a hundred bucks to let him wear my cap and drive my hack into town. I'm to hang around here an hour, then take his heap to the Hotel Carillon on Towne Boulevard. My cab will be there for me. He gives me the hundred bucks."

"What was his story?" I asked.

"He said they'd been to a gambling joint and had some luck for a change. They're afraid of holdups on the way in. They figure there's always spotters watchin' the play."

I took one of his cigarettes and straightened it out in my fingers.

"It's a story I can't hurt much," I said. "Could I see your cards?"

He gave them to me. His name was Tom Sneyd and he was a driver for the Green Top Cab Company. I corked my pint, slipped it into my side pocket, and danced a half-dollar on the counter.

The clerk came along and made change. He was almost shaking with curiosity.

"Come on, Tom," I said in front of him. "Let's go get that cab. I don't think you should wait around here any longer."

We went out, and I let the Buick lead me away from the straggling lights of Las Olindas, through a series of small beach towns with little houses built on sandlots close to the ocean, and bigger ones built on the slopes of the hills behind. A window was lit here and there. The tires sang on the moist concrete and the little amber lights on the Buick's fenders peeped back at me from the curves.

At West Cimarron we turned inland, chugged on through Canal City, and met the San Angelo Cut. It took us almost an hour to get to 5640 Towne Boulevard, which is the number of the Hotel Carillon. It is a big, rambling slate-roofed building with a basement garage and a forecourt fountain on which they play a pale green light in the evening.

Green Top Cab No. 469 was parked across the street, on the dark side. I couldn't see where anybody had been shooting into it. Tom Sneyd found his cap in the driver's compartment, climbed eagerly under the wheel.

"Does that fix me up? Can I go now?" His voice was strident with relief.

I told him it was all right with me, and gave him my card. It was twelve minutes past one as he took the corner. I climbed into the Buick and tooled it down the ramp to the garage and left it with a colored boy who was dusting cars in slow motion. I went around to the lobby.

The clerk was an ascetic-looking young man who was reading a volume of *California Appellate Decisions* under the switchboard light. He said Lou was not in and had not been in since eleven, when he came on duty. After a short argument about the lateness of the hour and the importance of my visit, he rang Lou's apartment, but there wasn't any answer.

I went out and sat in my Marmon for a few minutes, smoked a cigarette, imbibed a little from my pint of Canadian Club. Then I went back into the Carillon and shut myself in a pay booth. I dialed the *Telegram,* asked for the City Desk, got a man named Von Ballin.

He yelped at me when I told him who I was. "You still walking around? That ought to be a story. I thought Manny Tinnen's friends would have had you laid away in old lavender by this time."

I said: "Can that and listen to this. Do you know a man named Lou Harger? He's a gambler. Had a place that was raided and closed up a month ago."

Von Ballin said he didn't know Lou personally, but he knew who he was.

"Who around your rag would know him real well?"

He thought a moment. "There's a lad named Jerry Cross here," he said, "that's supposed to be an expert on night life. What did you want to know?"

"Where would he go to celebrate," I said. Then I told him some of the story, not too much. I left out the part where I got sapped and the part about the taxi. "He hasn't shown at his hotel," I ended. "I ought to get a line on him."

"Well, if you're a friend of his—"

"Of his—not of his crowd," I said sharply.

Von Ballin stopped to yell at somebody to take a call, then said to me softly, close to the phone: "Come through, boy. Come through."

"All right. But I'm talking to you, not to your sheet. I got sapped and lost my gun outside Canales' joint. Lou and his girl switched his car for a taxi they picked up. Then they dropped out of sight. I don't like it too well. Lou wasn't drunk enough to chase around town with that much dough in his pockets. And if he was, the girl wouldn't let him. She had the practical eye."

"I'll see what I can do," Von Ballin said. "But it don't sound promising. I'll give you a buzz."

I told him I lived at the Merritt Plaza, in case he had forgotten, went out and got into the Marmon again. I drove home and put hot towels on my head for fifteen minutes, then sat around in my pajamas and drank hot whiskey and lemon and called the Carillon every once in a while. At two-thirty Von Ballin called me and said no luck. Lou hadn't been pinched, he wasn't in any of the Receiving Hospitals, and he hadn't shown at any of the clubs Jerry Cross could think of.

At three I called the Carillon for the last time. Then I put my light out and went to sleep.

In the morning it was the same way. I tried to trace the red-haired girl a little. There were twenty-eight people named Glenn in the phone book, and three women among them. One didn't answer, the other two assured me they didn't have red hair. One offered to show me.

I shaved, showered, had breakfast, walked three blocks down the hill to the Condor Building.

Miss Glenn was sitting in my little reception room.

5

I UNLOCKED the other door and she went in and sat in the chair where Lou had sat the afternoon before. I opened some windows, locked the outer door of the reception room, and struck a match for the unlighted cigarette she held in her ungloved and ringless left hand.

She was dressed in a blouse and plaid skirt with a loose coat over them, and a close-fitting hat that was far enough out of style to suggest a run of bad luck. But it hid almost all of her hair. Her skin was without make-up and she looked about thirty and had the set face of exhaustion.

She held her cigarette with a hand that was almost too steady, a hand on guard. I sat down and waited for her to talk.

She stared at the wall over my head and didn't say anything. After a little while I packed my pipe and smoked for a minute. Then I got up and went across to the door that opened into the hallway and picked up a couple of letters that had been pushed through the slot.

I sat down at the desk again, looked them over, read one of them twice, as if I had been alone. While I was doing this I didn't look at her directly or speak to her, but I kept an eye on her all the same. She looked like a lady who was getting nerved for something.

Finally she moved. She opened up a big black patent-leather bag and took out a fat manila envelope, pulled a rubber band off it and sat holding the envelope between the palms of her hands, with her head tilted way back and the cigarette dribbling gray smoke from the corners of her mouth.

She said slowly: "Lou said if I ever got caught in the rain, you were the boy to see. It's raining hard where I am."

I stared at the manila envelope. "Lou is a pretty good friend of mine," I said. "I'd do anything in reason for him. Some things not in reason—like last night. That doesn't mean Lou and I always play the same games."

She dropped her cigarette into the glass bowl of the ash tray and left it to smoke. A dark flame burned suddenly in her eyes, then went out.

"Lou is dead." Her voice was quite toneless.

I reached over with a pencil and stabbed at the hot end of the cigarette until it stopped smoking.

She went on: "A couple of Canales' boys got him in my apartment—with one shot from a small gun that looked like my gun. Mine was gone when I looked for it afterwards. I spent the night there with him dead . . . I had to."

She broke quite suddenly. Her eyes turned up in her head and her head came down and hit the desk. She lay still, with the manila envelope in front of her lax hands.

I jerked a drawer open and brought up a bottle and a glass, poured a stiff one and stepped around with it, heaved her up in her chair. I pushed the edge of the glass hard against her mouth— hard enough to hurt. She struggled and swallowed. Some of it ran down her chin, but life came back into her eyes.

I left the whiskey in front of her and sat down again. The flap of the envelope had come open enough for me to see currency inside, bales of currency.

She began to talk to me in a dreamy sort of voice.

"We got all big bills from the cashier, but makes quite a package at that. There's twenty-two thousand even in the envelope. I kept out a few odd hundreds.

"Lou was worried. He figured it would be pretty easy for Canales to catch up with us. You might be right behind and not be able to do very much about it."

I said: "Canales lost the money in full view of everybody there. It was good advertising—even if it hurt."

She went on exactly as though I had not spoken. "Going through the town we spotted a cab driver sitting in his parked cab and Lou had a brain wave. He offered the boy a *C* note to let him drive the cab into San Angelo and bring the Buick to the hotel after a while. The boy took us up and we went over on another street and made the switch. We were sorry about ditching you, but Lou said you wouldn't mind. And we might get a chance to flag you.

"Lou didn't go into his hotel. We took another cab over to my place. I live at the Hobart Arms, eight hundred block on South Minter. It's a place where you don't have to answer questions at the desk. We went up to my apartment and put the lights on and two guys with masks came around the half-wall between the living room and the dinette. One was small and thin and the other one was a big slob with a chin that stuck out under his mask like a shelf. Lou made a wrong motion and the big one shot him just the once. The gun just made a flat crack, not very loud, and Lou fell down on the floor and never moved."

I said: "It might be the ones that made a sucker out of me. I haven't told you about that yet."

She didn't seem to hear that either. Her face was white and composed, but as expressionless as plaster. "Maybe I'd better have another finger of the hooch," she said.

I poured us a couple of drinks, and we drank them. She went on: "They went through us, but we didn't have the money. We had stopped at an all-night drugstore and had it weighed and mailed it at a branch post office. They went through the apartment, but of course we had just come in and hadn't had time to hide anything. The big one slammed me down with his fist, and when I woke up again they were gone and I was alone with Lou dead on the floor."

She pointed to a mark on the angle of her jaw. There was something there, but it didn't show much. I moved around in my chair a little and said: "They passed you on the way in. Smart boys would have looked a taxi over on that road. How did they know where to go?"

"I thought that out during the night," Miss Glenn said. "Canales knows where I live. He followed me home once and tried to get me to ask him up."

"Yeah," I said, "but why did they go to your place and how did they get in?"

"That's not hard. There's a ledge just below the windows and a man could edge along it to the fire escape. They probably had other boys covering Lou's hotel. We thought of that chance, but we didn't think about my place being known to them."

"Tell me the rest of it," I said.

"The money was mailed to me," Miss Glenn explained. "Lou was a swell boy, but a girl has to protect herself. That's why I had to stay there last night with Lou dead on the floor. Until the mail came. Then I came over here."

I got up and looked out of the window. A fat girl was pounding a typewriter across the court. I could hear the clack of it. I sat down again, stared at my thumb.

"Did they plant the gun?" I asked.

"Not unless it's under him. I didn't look there."

"They let you off too easy. Maybe it wasn't Canales at all. Did Lou open his heart to you much?"

She shook her head quietly. Her eyes were slate-blue now, and thoughtful, without the blank stare.

"All right," I said. "Just what did you think of having me do about it all?"

She narrowed her eyes a little, then put a hand out and pushed the bulging envelope slowly across the desk.

"I'm no baby and I'm in a jam. But I'm not going to the cleaners just the same. Half of this money is mine, and I want it with a clean getaway. One-half net. If I'd called the law last night, there'd have been a way to chisel me out of it . . . I think Lou would like you to have his half, if you want to play with me."

I said: "It's big money to flash at a private dick, Miss Glenn," and smiled wearily. "You're a little worse off for not calling cops last night. But there's an answer to anything they might say. I think I'd better go over there and see what's broken, if anything."

She leaned forward quickly and said: "Will you take care of the money? . . . Dare you?"

"Sure. I'll pop downstairs and put it in a safe-deposit box. You can hold one of the keys—and we'll talk split later on. I think it would be a swell idea if Canales knew he had to see me, and still sweller if you hid out in a little hotel where I have a friend—at least until I nose around a bit."

She nodded. I put my hat on and put the envelope inside my belt. I went out, telling her there was a gun in the top left-hand drawer, if she felt nervous.

When I got back she didn't seem to have moved. But she said she had phoned Canales' place and left a message for him she thought he would understand.

We went by rather devious ways to the Lorraine, at Brant and Avenue C. Nobody shot at us going over, and as far as I could see we were not trailed.

I shook hands with Jim Dolan, the day clerk at the Lorraine, with a twenty folded in my hand. He put his hand in his pocket and said he would be glad to see that "Miss Thompson" was not bothered.

I left. There was nothing in the noon paper about Lou Harger of the Hobart Arms.

6

THE HOBART ARMS was just another apartment house, in a block lined with them. It was six stories high and had a buff front. A lot of cars were parked at both curbs all along the block. I drove through slowly and looked things over. The neighborhood didn't have the look of having been excited about anything in the immediate past. It was peaceful and sunny, and the parked cars had a settled look, as if they were right at home.

I circled into an alley with a high board fence on each side and a lot of flimsy garages cutting it. I parked beside one that had a For Rent sign and went between two garbage cans into the concrete yard of the Hobart Arms, along the side to the street. A man was putting golf clubs into the back of a coupe. In the lobby a Filipino was dragging a vacuum cleaner over the rug and a dark Jewess was writing at the switchboard.

I used the automatic elevator and prowled along an upper corridor to the last door on the left. I knocked, waited, knocked again, went in with Miss Glenn's key.

Nobody was dead on the floor.

I looked at myself in the mirror that was the back of a pull-down bed, went across and looked out of a window. There was a ledge below that had once been a coping. It ran along to the fire escape. A blind man could have walked in. I didn't notice anything like footmarks in the dust on it.

There was nothing in the dinette or kitchen except what belonged there. The bedroom had a cheerful carpet and painted gray walls. There was a lot of junk in the corner, around a wastebasket, and a broken comb on the dresser held a few strands of red hair. The closets were empty except for some gin bottles.

I went back to the living room, looked behind the wall bed, stood around for a minute, left the apartment.

The Filipino in the lobby had made about three yards with the vacuum cleaner. I leaned on the counter beside the switchboard.

"Miss Glenn?"

The dark Jewess said: "Five-two-four," and made a check mark on the laundry list.

"She's not in. Has she been in lately?"

She glanced up at me. "I haven't noticed. What is it—a bill?"

I said I was just a friend, thanked her and went away. That

established the fact that there had been no excitement in Miss Glenn's apartment. I went back to the alley and the Marmon.

I hadn't believed it quite the way Miss Glenn told it anyhow.

I crossed Cordova, drove a block and stopped beside a forgotten drugstore that slept behind two giant pepper trees and a dusty, cluttered window. It had a single pay booth in the corner. An old man shuffled towards me wistfully, then went away when he saw what I wanted, lowered a pair of steel spectacles on to the end of his nose and sat down again with his newspaper.

I dropped my nickel, dialed, and a girl's voice said: "Tele-grayam!" with a tinny drawl. I asked for Von Ballin.

When I got him and he knew who it was I could hear him clearing his throat. Then his voice came close to the phone and said very distinctly: "I've got something for you, but it's bad. I'm sorry as all hell. Your friend Harger is in the morgue. We got a flash about ten minutes ago."

I leaned against the wall of the booth and felt my eyes getting haggard. I said: "What else did you get?"

"Couple of radio cops picked him up in somebody's front yard or something, in West Cimarron. He was shot through the heart. It happened last night, but for some reason they only just put out the identification."

I said: "West Cimarron, huh? . . . Well, that takes care of that. I'll be in to see you."

I thanked him and hung up, stood for a moment looking out through the glass at a middle-aged gray-haired man who had come into the store and was pawing over the magazine rack.

Then I dropped another nickel and dialed the Lorraine, asked for the clerk.

I said: "Get your girl to put me on to the redhead, will you, Jim?"

I got a cigarette out and lit it, puffed smoke at the glass of the door. The smoke flattened out against the glass and swirled about in the close air. Then the line clicked and the operator's voice said: "Sorry, your party does not answer."

"Give me Jim again," I said. Then, when he answered, "Can you take time to run up and find out why she doesn't answer the phone? Maybe she's just being cagey."

Jim said: "You bet. I'll shoot right up with a key."

Sweat was coming out all over me. I put the receiver down on a little shelf and jerked the booth door open. The gray-haired man looked up quickly from the magazines, then scowled and looked at his watch. Smoke poured out of the booth. After a moment I kicked the door shut and picked up the receiver again.

Jim's voice seemed to come to me from a long way off. "She's not here. Maybe she went for a walk."

I said: "Yeah—or maybe it was a ride."

I pronged the receiver and pushed on out of the booth. The gray-haired stranger slammed a magazine down so hard that it fell to the floor. He stooped to pick it up as I went past him. Then he straightened up just behind me and said quietly, but very firmly: "Keep the hands down, and quiet. Walk on out to your heap. This is business."

Out of the corner of my eye I could see the old man peeking shortsightedly at us. But there wasn't anything for him to see, even if he could see that far. Something prodded my back. It might have been a finger, but I didn't think it was.

We went out of the store very peacefully.

A long gray car had stopped close behind the Marmon. Its rear door was open and a man with a square face and a crooked mouth was standing with one foot out on the running board. His right hand was behind him, inside the car.

My man's voice said: "Get in your car and drive west. Take this first corner and go about twenty-five, not more."

The narrow street was sunny and quiet and the pepper trees whispered. Traffic threshed by on Cordova a short block away. I shrugged, opened the door of my car and got under the wheel. The gray-haired man got in very quickly beside me, watching my hands. He swung his right hand around, with a snub-nosed gun in it.

"Careful getting your keys out, buddy."

I was careful. As I stepped on the starter a car door slammed behind, there were rapid steps, and someone got into the back seat of the Marmon. I let in the clutch and drove around the corner. In the mirror I could see the gray car making the turn behind. Then it dropped back a little.

I drove west on a street that paralleled Cordova and when we had gone a block and a half a hand came down over my shoulder from behind and took my gun away from me. The gray-haired man rested his short revolver on his leg and felt me over carefully with his free hand. He leaned back satisfied.

"Okey. Drop over to the main drag and snap it up," he said.

"But that don't mean trying to sideswipe a prowl car, if you lamp
one. . . . Or if you think it does, try it and see."

I made the two turns, speeded up to thirty-five and held it
there. We went through some nice residential districts, and then
the landscape began to thin out. When it was quite thin the gray
car behind dropped back, turned towards town and disappeared.

"What's the snatch for?" I asked.

The gray-haired man laughed and rubbed his broad red chin.
"Just business, The big boy wants to talk to you."

"Canales?"

"Canales—hell! I said the *big boy*."

I watched traffic, what there was of it that far out, and didn't
speak for a few minutes. Then I said: "Why didn't you pull it in
the apartment, or in the alley?"

"Wanted to make sure you wasn't covered."

"Who's this big boy?"

"Skip that—till we get you there. Anything else?"

"Yes. Can I smoke?"

He held the wheel while I lit up. The man in the back seat
hadn't said a word at any time. After a while the gray-haired man
made me pull up and move over, and he drove.

"I used to own one of these, six years ago, when I was poor,"
he said jovially.

I couldn't think of a really good answer to that, so I just let
smoke seep down into my lungs and wondered why, if Lou had
been killed in West Cimarron, the killers didn't get the money.
And if he really had been killed at Miss Glenn's apartment, why
somebody had taken the trouble to carry him back to West
Cimarron.

7

IN TWENTY minutes we were in the foothills. We went over a
hogback, drifted down a long white concrete ribbon, crossed a
bridge, went halfway up the next slope and turned off on a gravel
road that disappeared around a shoulder of scrub oak and man-
zanita. Plumes of pampas grass flared on the side of the hill, like

jets of water. The wheels crunched on the gravel and skidded on the curves.

We came to a mountain cabin with a wide porch and cemented boulder foundations. The windmill of a generator turned slowly on the crest of a spur a hundred feet behind the cabin. A mountain blue jay flashed across the road, zoomed, banked sharply, and fell out of sight like a stone.

The gray-haired man tooled the car up to the porch, beside a tan colored Lincoln coupe, switched off the ignition and set the Marmon's long parking brake. He took the keys out, folded them carefully in their leather case, put the case away in his pocket.

The man in the back seat got out and held the door beside me open. He had a gun in his hand. I got out. The gray-haired man got out. We all went into the house.

There was a big room with walls of knotted pine, beautifully polished. We went across it walking on Indian rugs and the gray-haired man knocked carefully on a door.

A voice shouted: "What is it?"

The gray-haired man put his face against the door and said: "Beasley—and the guy you wanted to talk to."

The voice inside said to come on in. Beasley opened the door, pushed me through it and shut it behind me.

It was another big room with knotted pine walls and Indian rugs on the floor. A driftwood fire hissed and puffed on a stone hearth.

The man who sat behind a flat desk was Frank Dorr, the politico.

He was the kind of man who lived to have a desk in front of him, and shove his fat stomach against it, and fiddle with things on it, and look very wise. He had a fat, muddy face, a thin fringe of white hair that stuck up a little, small sharp eyes, small and very delicate hands.

What I could see of him was dressed in a slovenly gray suit, and there was a large black Persian cat on the desk in front of him. He was scratching the cat's head with one of his little neat hands and the cat was leaning against his hand. Its bushy tail flowed over the edge of the desk and fell straight down.

He said: "Sit down," without looking away from the cat.

I sat down in a leather chair with a very low seat. Dorr said: "How do you like it up here? Kind of nice, ain't it? This is Toby, my girlfriend. Only girlfriend I got. Ain't you, Toby?"

I said: "I like it up here—but I don't like the way I got here."

Dorr raised his head a few inches and looked at me with his mouth slightly open. He had beautiful teeth, but they hadn't grown in his mouth. He said: "I'm a busy man, brother. It was simpler than arguing. Have a drink?"

"Sure I'll have a drink," I said.

He squeezed the cat's head gently between his two palms, then pushed it away from him and put both hands down on the arms of his chair. He shoved hard and his face got a little red and he finally got up on his feet. He waddled across to a built-in cabinet and took out a squat decanter of whiskey and two gold-veined glasses.

"No ice today," he said, waddling back to the desk. "Have to drink it straight."

He poured two drinks, gestured, and I went over and got mine. He sat down again. I sat down with my drink. Dorr lit a long brown cigar, pushed the box two inches in my direction, leaned back and stared at me with complete relaxation.

"You're the guy that fingered Manny Tinnen," he said. "It won't do."

I sipped my whiskey. It was good enough to sip.

"Life gets complicated at times," Dorr went on, in the same even, relaxed voice. "Politics—even when it's a lot of fun—is tough on the nerves. You know me. I'm tough and I get what I want. There ain't a hell of a lot I want any more, but what I want—I want bad. And ain't so damn particular how I get it."

"You have that reputation," I said politely.

Dorr's eyes twinkled. He looked around for the cat, dragged it towards him by the tail, pushed it down on its side and began to rub its stomach. The cat seemed to like it.

Dorr looked at me and said very softly: "You bumped Lou Harger."

"What makes you think so?" I asked, without any particular emphasis.

"You bumped Lou Harger. Maybe he needed the bump—but you gave it to him. He was shot once through the heart, with a thirty-eight. You wear a thirty-eight and you're known to be a fancy shot with it. You were with Harger at Las Olindas last night and saw him win a lot of money. You were supposed to be acting as bodyguard for him, but you got a better idea. You caught up with him and that girl in West Cimarron, slipped Harger the dose and got the money."

I finished my whiskey, got up and poured myself some more of it.

"You made a deal with the girl," Dorr said, "but the deal didn't stick. She got a cute idea. But that don't matter, because the police got your gun along with Harger. And you got the dough."

I said: "Is there a tag out for me?"

"Not till I give the word. . . . And the gun hasn't been turned in . . . I got a lot of friends, you know."

I said slowly: "I got sapped outside Canales' place. It served me right. My gun was taken from me. I never caught up with Harger, never saw him again. The girl came to me this morning with the money in an envelope and a story that Harger had been killed in her apartment. That's how I have the money—for safe-keeping. I wasn't sure about the girl's story, but her bringing the money carried a lot of weight. And Harger was a friend of mine. I started out to investigate."

"You should have let the cops do that," Dorr said with a grin.

"There was a chance the girl was being framed. Besides there was a possibility I might make a few dollars—legitimately. It has been done, even in San Angelo."

Dorr stuck a finger towards the cat's face and the cat bit it, with an absent expression. Then it pulled away from him, sat down on a corner of the desk and began to lick one toe.

"Twenty-two grand, and the jane passed it over to you to keep," Dorr said. "Ain't that just like a jane?

"You got the dough," Dorr said. "Harger was killed with your gun. The girl's gone—but I could bring her back. I think she'd make a good witness, if we needed one."

"Was the play at Las Olindas crooked?" I asked.

Dorr finished his drink and curled his lips around his cigar again. "Sure," he said carelessly. "The croupier—a guy named Pina—was in on it. The wheel was wired for the double-zero. The old crap. Copper button on the floor, copper button on Pina's shoe sole, wires up his leg, batteries in his hip pockets. The old crap."

I said: "Canales didn't act as if he knew about it."

Dorr chuckled. "He knew the wheel was wired. He didn't know his head croupier was playin' on the other team."

"I'd hate to be Pina," I said.

Dorr made a negligent motion with his cigar. "He's taken care of. . . . The play was careful and quiet. They didn't make any fancy long shots, just even money bets, and they didn't win all the time. They couldn't. No wired wheel is that good."

I shrugged, moved around in my chair. "You know a hell of a lot about it," I said. "Was all this just to get me set for a squeeze?"

He grinned softly. "Hell, no! Some of it just happened—the way the best plants do." He waved his cigar again, and a pale gray tendril of smoke curled past his cunning little eyes. There was a muffled sound of talk in the outside room. "I got connections I got to please—even if I don't like all their capers," he added simply.

"Like Manny Tinnen?" I said. "He was around City Hall a lot, knew too much. Okey, Mister Dorr. Just what do you figure on having me do for you? Commit suicide?"

He laughed. His fat shoulders shook cheerfully. He put one of his small hands out with the palms towards me. "I wouldn't think of that," he said dryly, "and the other way's better business. The way public opinion is about the Shannon kill, I ain't sure that louse of a D.A. wouldn't convict Tinnen without you—if he could sell the folks the idea you'd been knocked off to button your mouth."

I got up out of my chair, went over and leaned on the desk, leaned across it towards Dorr.

He said: "No funny business!" a little sharply and breathlessly. His hand went to a drawer and got it half open. His movements with his hands were very quick in contrast with the movements of his body.

I smiled down at the hand and he took it away from the drawer. I saw a gun just inside the drawer.

I said: "I've already talked to the Grand Jury."

Dorr leaned back and smiled at me. "Guys make mistakes," he said. "Even smart private dicks . . . You could have a change of heart—and put it in writing."

I said very softly, "No. I'd be under a perjury rap—which I couldn't beat. I'd rather be under a murder rap—which I can beat. Especially as Fenweather will *want* me to beat it. He won't want to spoil me as a witness. The Tinnen case is too important to him."

Dorr said evenly: "Then you'll have to try and beat it, brother.

And after you get through beating it there'll still be enough mud on your neck so no jury'll convict Manny on your say-so alone."

I put my hand out slowly and scratched the cat's ear. "What about the twenty-two grand?"

"It *could* be all yours, if you want to play. After all, it ain't my money. . . . If Manny gets clear, I might add a little something that *is* my money."

I tickled the cat under its chin. It began to purr. I picked it up and held it gently in my arms.

"Who did kill Lou Harger, Dorr?" I asked, not looking at him.

He shook his head. I looked at him, smiling. "Swell cat you have," I said.

Dorr licked his lips. "I think the little bastard likes you," he grinned. He looked pleased at the idea.

I nodded—and threw the cat in his face.

He yelped, but his hands came up to catch the cat. The cat twisted neatly in the air and landed with both front paws working. One of them split Dorr's cheek like a banana peel. He yelled very loudly.

I had the gun out of the drawer and the muzzle of it into the back of Dorr's neck when Beasley and the square-faced man dodged in.

For an instant there was a sort of tableau. Then the cat tore itself loose from Dorr's arms, shot to the floor and went under the desk. Beasley raised his snub-nosed gun, but he didn't look as if he was certain what he meant to do with it.

I shoved the muzzle of mine hard into Dorr's neck and said: "Frankie gets it first, boys. . . . And that's not a gag."

Dorr grunted in front of me. "Take it easy," he growled to his hoods. He took a handkerchief from his breast pocket and began to dab at his split and bleeding cheek with it. The man with the crooked mouth began to sidle along the wall.

I said: "Don't get the idea I'm enjoying this, but I'm not fooling either. You heels stay put."

The man with the crooked mouth stopped sidling and gave me a nasty leer. He kept his hands low.

Dorr half turned his head and tried to talk over his shoulder to me. I couldn't see enough of his face to get any expression, but he didn't seem scared. He said: "This won't get you anything. I could have you knocked off easy enough, if that was what I wanted. Now where are you? You can't shoot anybody without getting in a worse jam than if you did what I asked you to. It looks like a stalemate to me."

I thought that over for a moment while Beasley looked at me quite pleasantly, as though it was all just routine to him. There was nothing pleasant about the other man. I listened hard, but the rest of the house seemed to be quite silent.

Dorr edged forward from the gun and said: "Well?"

I said: "I'm going out. I have a gun and it looks like a gun that I could hit somebody with, if I have to. I don't want to very much, and if you'll have Beasley throw my keys over and the other one turn back the gun he took from me, I'll forget about the snatch."

Dorr moved his arms in the lazy beginning of a shrug. "Then what?"

"Figure out your deal a little closer," I said. "If you get enough protection behind me, I might throw in with you. . . . And if you're as tough as you think you are, a few hours won't cut any ice one way or the other."

"It's an idea," Dorr said and chuckled. Then to Beasley: "Keep your rod to yourself and give him his keys. Also his gun—the one you got today."

Beasley sighed and very carefully inserted a hand into his pants. He tossed my leather keycase across the room near the end of the desk. The man with the twisted mouth put his hand up, edged it inside his side pocket and I eased down behind Dorr's back, while he did it. He came out with my gun, let it fall to the floor and kicked it away from him.

I came out from behind Dorr's back, got my keys and the gun up from the floor, moved sidewise towards the door of the room. Dorr watched with an empty stare that meant nothing. Beasley followed me around with his body and stepped away from the door as I neared it. The other man had trouble holding himself quiet.

I got to the door and reversed a key that was in it. Dorr said dreamily: "You're just like one of those rubber balls on the end of an elastic. The farther you get away, the suddener you'll bounce back."

I said: "The elastic might be a little rotten," and went through the door, turned the key in it and braced myself for shots that didn't come. As a bluff, mine was thinner than the gold on a

week-end wedding ring. It worked because Dorr let it, and that
was all.

I got out of the house, got the Marmon started and wrangled
it around and sent it skidding past the shoulder of the hill and
so on down to the highway. There was no sound of anything
coming after me.

When I reached the concrete highway bridge it was a little past
two o'clock, and I drove with one hand for a while and wiped
the sweat off the back of my neck.

8

THE MORGUE was at the end of a long and bright and silent
corridor that branched off from behind the main lobby of the
County Building. The corridor ended in two doors and a blank
wall faced with marble. One door had "Inquest Room" lettered
on a glass panel behind which there was no light. The other opened
into a small, cheerful office.

A man with gander-blue eyes and rust-colored hair parted in
the exact center of his head was pawing over some printed forms
at a table. He looked up, looked me over, and then suddenly
smiled.

I said: "Hello, Landon. . . . Remember the Shelby case?"

The bright blue eyes twinkled. He got up and came around the
table with his hand out. "Sure. What can we do—" He broke off
suddenly and snapped his fingers. "Hell! You're the guy that put
the bee on that hot rod."

I tossed a butt through the open door into the corridor. "That's
not why I'm here," I said. "Anyhow not this time. There's a fellow
named Louis Harger . . . picked up shot last night or this morning,
in West Cimarron, as I get it. Could I take a look-see?"

"They can't stop you," Landon said.

He led the way through a door on the far side of his office into
a place that was all white paint and white enamel and glass and
bright light. Against one wall was a double tier of large bins with
glass windows in them. Through the peepholes showed bundles
in white sheeting, and, further back, frosted pipes.

A body covered with a sheet lay on a table that was high at

the head and sloped down to the foot. Landon pulled the sheet down casually from a man's dead, placid, yellowish face. Long black hair lay loosely on a small pillow, with the dankness of water still in it. The eyes were half open and stared incuriously at the ceiling.

I stepped close, looked at the face, Landon pulled the sheet on down and rapped his knuckles on a chest that rang hollowly, like a board. There was a bullet hole over the heart.

"Nice clean shot," he said.

I turned away quickly, got a cigarette out and rolled it around in my fingers. I stared at the floor.

"Who identified him?"

"Stuff in his pockets," Landon said. "We're checking his prints, of course. You know him?"

I said: "Yes."

Landon scratched the base of his chin softly with his thumbnail. We walked back into the office and Landon went behind his table and sat down.

He thumbed over some papers, separated one from the pile and studied it for a moment.

He said: "A sheriff's radio car found him at twelve thirty-five A.M., on the side of the old road out of West Cimarron, a quarter of a mile from where the cut-off starts. That isn't traveled much, but the prowl car takes a slant down it now and then looking for petting parties."

I said: "Can you say how long he had been dead?"

"Not very long. He was still warm, and the nights are cool along there."

I put my unlighted cigarette in my mouth and moved it up and down with my lips. "And I bet you took a long thirty-eight out of him," I said.

"How did you know that?" Landon asked quickly.

"I just guess. It's that sort of hole."

He stared at me with bright, interested eyes. I thanked him, said I'd be seeing him, went through the door and lit my cigarette in the corridor. I walked back to the elevators and got into one, rode to the seventh floor, then went along another corridor exactly like the one below except that it didn't lead to the morgue. It led to some small, bare offices that were used by the District Attorney's investigators. Halfway along I opened a door and went into one of them.

Bernie Ohls was sitting humped loosely at a desk placed against the wall. He was the chief investigator Fenweather had told me to see, if I got into any kind of a jam. He was a medium-sized blond man with white eyebrows and an outthrust, very deeply cleft chin. There was another desk against the other wall, a couple of hard chairs, a brass spittoon on a rubber mat and very little else.

Ohls nodded casually at me, got out of his chair and fixed the door latch. Then he got a flat tin of little cigars out of his desk, lit one of them, pushed the tin along the desk and stared at me along his nose. I sat down in one of the straight chairs and tilted it back.

Ohls said: "Well?"

"It's Lou Harger," I said. "I thought maybe it wasn't."

"The hell you did. I could have told you it was Harger."

Somebody tried the handle of the door, then knocked. Ohls paid no attention. Whoever it was went away.

I said slowly: "He was killed between eleven-thirty and twelve thirty-five. There was just time for the job to be done where he was found. There wasn't time for it to be done the way the girl said. There wasn't time for me to do it."

Ohls said: "Yeah. Maybe you could prove that. And then maybe you could prove a friend of yours didn't do it with your gun."

I said: "A friend of mine wouldn't be likely to do it with my gun—if he was a friend of mine."

Ohls grunted, smiled sourly at me sidewise. He said: "Most anyone would think that. That's why he might have done it."

I let the legs of my chair settle to the floor. I stared at him.

"Would I come and tell you about the money and the gun—everything that ties me to it?"

Ohls said expressionlessly: "You would—if you knew damn well somebody else had already told it for you."

I said: "Dorr wouldn't lose much time."

I pinched my cigarette out and flipped it towards the brass cuspidor. Then I stood up.

"Okey. There's no tag out for me yet—so I'll go over and tell my story."

Ohls said: "Sit down a minute."

I sat down. He took his little cigar out of his mouth and flung it away from him with a savage gesture. It rolled along the brown linoleum and smoked in the corner. He put his arms down on the desk and drummed with the fingers of both hands. His lower lip came forward and pressed his upper lip back against his teeth.

"Dorr probably knows you're here now," he said. "The only reason you ain't in the tank upstairs is they're not sure but it would be better to knock you off and take a chance. If Fenweather loses the election, I'll be all washed up—if I mess around with you."

I said: "If he convicts Manny Tinnen, he won't lose the election."

Ohls took another of the little cigars out of the box and lit it. He picked his hat off the desk, fingered it a moment, put it on.

"Why'd the redhead give you that song and dance about the bump in her apartment, the stiff on the floor—all that hot comedy?"

"They wanted me to go over there. They figured I'd go to see if a gun was planted—maybe just to check up on her. That got me away from the busy part of town. They could tell better if the D.A. had any boys watching my blind side."

"That's just a guess," Ohls said sourly.

I said: "Sure."

Ohls swung his thick legs around, planted his feet hard and leaned his hands on his knees. The little cigar twitched in the corner of his mouth.

"I'd like to get to know some of these guys that let loose of twenty-two grand just to color up a fairy tale," he said nastily.

I stood up again and went past him towards the door.

Ohls said: "What's the hurry?"

I turned around and shrugged, looked at him blankly. "You don't act very interested," I said.

He climbed to his feet, said wearily: "The hack driver's most likely a dirty little crook. But it might just be Dorr's lads don't know he rates in this. Let's go get him while his memory's fresh."

9

THE GREEN TOP GARAGE was on Deviveras, three blocks east of Main. I pulled the Marmon up in front of a fireplug and got out. Ohls slumped in the seat and growled: "I'll stay here. Maybe I can spot a tail."

I went into a huge echoing garage, in the inner gloom of which a few brand new paint jobs were splashes of sudden color. There was a small, dirty, glass-walled office in the corner and a short man sat there with a derby hat on the back of his head and a red tie under his stubbled chin. He was whittling tobacco into the palm of his hand.

I said: "You the dispatcher?"

"Yeah."

"I'm looking for one of your drivers," I said. "Name of Tom Sneyd."

He put down the knife and the plug and began to grind the cut tobacco between his two palms. "What's the beef?" he asked cautiously.

"No beef. I'm a friend of his."

"More friends, huh? . . . He works nights, mister. . . . So he's gone I guess. Seventeen twenty-three Renfrew. That's over by Gray Lake."

I said: "Thanks. Phone?"

"No phone."

I pulled a folded city map from an inside pocket and unfolded part of it on the table in front of his nose. He looked annoyed.

"There's a big one on the wall," he growled, and began to pack a short pipe with his tobacco.

"I'm used to this one," I said. I bent over the spread map, looking for Renfrew Street. Then I stopped and looked suddenly at the face of the man in the derby. "You remembered that address damn quick," I said.

He put his pipe in his mouth, bit hard on it, and pushed two thick fingers into the pocket of his open vest.

"Couple other muggs was askin' for it a while back."

I folded the map very quickly and shoved it back into my pocket as I went through the door. I jumped across the sidewalk, slid under the wheel and plunged at the starter.

"We're headed," I told Bernie Ohls. "Two guys got the kid's address there a while back. It might be—"

Ohls grabbed the side of the car and swore as we took the corner on squealing tires. I bent forward over the wheel and drove hard. There was a red light at Central. I swerved into a corner service station, went through the pumps, popped out on Central and jostled through some traffic to make a right turn east again.

A colored traffic cop blew a whistle at me and then stared hard as if trying to read the license number. I kept on going.

Warehouses, a produce market, a big gas tank, more warehouses, railroad tracks, and two bridges dropped behind us. I beat three traffic signals by a hair and went right through a fourth. Six blocks on I got the siren from a motorcycle cop. Ohls passed me a bronze star and I flashed it out of the car, twisting it so the sun caught it. The siren stopped. The motorcycle kept right behind us for another dozen blocks, then sheered off.

Gray Lake is an artificial reservoir in a cut between two groups of hills, on the east fringe of San Angelo. Narrow but expensively paved streets wind around in the hills, describing elaborate curves along their flanks for the benefit of a few cheap and scattered bungalows.

We plunged up into the hills, reading street signs on the run. The gray silk of the lake dropped away from us and the exhaust of the old Marmon roared between crumbling banks that shed dirt down on the unused sidewalks. Mongrel dogs quartered in the wild grass among the gopher holes.

Renfrew was almost at the top. Where it began there was a small neat bungalow in front of which a child in a diaper and nothing else fumbled around in a wire pen on a patch of lawn. Then there was a stretch without houses. Then there were two houses, then the road dropped, slipped in and out of sharp turns, went between banks high enough to put the whole street in shadow.

Then a gun roared around a bend ahead of us.

Ohls sat up sharply, said: "Oh-oh! That's no rabbit gun," slipped his service pistol out and unlatched the door on his side.

We came out of the turn and saw two more houses on the down side of the hill, with a couple of steep lots between them. A long gray car was slewed across the street in the space between the two houses. Its left front tire was flat and both its front doors were wide open, like the spread ears of an elephant.

A small, dark-faced man was kneeling on both knees in the street beside the open right-hand door. His right arm hung loose from his shoulder and there was blood on the hand that belonged to it. With his other hand he was trying to pick up an automatic from the concrete in front of him.

I skidded the Marmon to a fast stop and Ohls tumbled out.

"Drop that, you!" he yelled.

The man with the limp arm snarled, relaxed, fell back against the running board, and a shot came from behind the car and snapped in the air not very far from my ear. I was out on the road by that time. The gray car was angled enough towards the houses so that I couldn't see any part of its left side except the open door. The shot seemed to come from about there. Ohls put two slugs into the door. I dropped, looked under the car and saw a pair of feet. I shot at them and missed.

About that time there was a thin but very sharp crack from the corner of the nearest house. Glass broke in the gray car. The gun behind it roared and plaster jumped out of the corner of the house wall, above the bushes. Then I saw the upper part of a man's body in the bushes. He was lying downhill on his stomach and he had a light rifle to his shoulder.

He was Tom Sneyd, the taxi driver.

Ohls grunted and charged the gray car. He fired twice more into the door, then dodged down behind the hood. More explosions occurred behind the car. I kicked the wounded man's gun out of his way, slid past him and sneaked a look over the gas tank. But the man behind had had too many angles to figure.

He was a big man in a brown suit and he made a clatter running hard for the lip of the hill between the two bungalows. Ohls' gun roared. The man whirled and snapped a shot without stopping. Ohls was in the open now. I saw his hat jerk off his head. I saw him stand squarely on well-spread feet, steady his pistol as if he was on the police range.

But the big man was already sagging. My bullet had drilled through his neck. Ohls fired at him very carefully and he fell and the sixth and last slug from his gun caught the man in the chest and twisted him around. The side of his head slapped the curb with a sickening crunch.

We walked towards him from opposite ends of the car. Ohls leaned down, heaved the man over on his back. His face in death had a loose, amiable expression, in spite of the blood all over his neck. Ohls began to go through his pockets.

I looked back to see what the other one was doing. He wasn't doing anything but sitting on the running board holding his right arm against his side and grimacing with pain.

Tom Sneyd scrambled up the bank and came towards us.

Ohls said: "It's a guy named Poke Andrews. I've seen him around the poolrooms." He stood up and brushed off his knee. He had some odds and ends in his left hand. "Yeah, Poke Andrews. Gun work by the day, hour or week. I guess there was a livin' in it—for a while."

"It's not the guy that sapped me," I said. "But it's the guy I was looking at when I got sapped. And if the redhead was giving out any truth at all this morning, it's likely the guy that shot Lou Harger."

Ohls nodded, went over and got his hat. There was a hole in the brim. "I wouldn't be surprised at all," he said, putting his hat on calmly.

Tom Sneyd stood in front of us with his little rifle held rigidly across his chest. He was hatless and coatless, and had sneakers on his feet. His eyes were bright and mad, and he was beginning to shake.

"I knew I'd get them babies!" he crowed. "I knew I'd fix them lousy bastards!" Then he stopped talking and his face began to change color. It got green. He leaned down slowly, dropped his rifle, put both his hands on his bent knees.

Ohls said: "You better go lay down somewhere, buddy. If I'm any judge of color, you're goin' to shoot your cookies."

10

TOM SNEYD was lying on his back on a day bed in the front room of his little bungalow. There was a wet towel across his forehead. A little girl with honey-colored hair was sitting beside him, holding his hand. A young woman with hair a couple of shades darker than the little girl's sat in the corner and looked at Tom Sneyd with tired ecstasy.

It was very hot when we came in. All the windows were shut and all the blinds down. Ohls opened a couple of front windows and sat down beside them, looked out towards the gray car. The dark Mexican was anchored to its steering wheel by his good wrist.

"It was what they said about my little girl," Tom Sneyd said from under the towel. "That's what sent me screwy. They said they'd come back and get her, if I didn't play with them."

Ohls said: "Okey, Tom. Let's have it from the start." He put one of his little cigars in his mouth, looked at Tom Sneyd doubtfully, and didn't light it.

I sat in a very hard Windsor chair and looked down at the cheap, new carpet.

"I was readin' a mag, waiting for time to eat and go to work," Tom Sneyd said carefully. "The little girl opened the door. They come in with guns on us, got us all in here and shut the windows. They pulled down all the blinds but one and the Mex sat by that and kept looking out. He never said a word. The big guy sat on the bed here and made me tell him all about last night—twice. Then he said I was to forget I'd met anybody or come into town with anybody. The rest was okey."

Ohls nodded and said: "What time did you first see this man here?"

"I didn't notice," Tom Sneyd said. "Say eleven-thirty, quarter of twelve. I checked in to the office at one-fifteen, right after I got my hack at the Carillon. It took us a good hour to make town from the beach. We was in the drugstore talkin' say fifteen minutes, maybe longer."

"That figures back to around midnight when you met him," Ohls said.

Tom Sneyd shook his head and the towel fell down over his face. He pushed it back up again.

"Well, no," Tom Sneyd said. "The guy in the drugstore told me he closed up at twelve. He wasn't closing up when we left."

Ohls turned his head and looked at me without expression. He looked back at Tom Sneyd. "Tell us the rest about the two gunnies," he said.

"The big guy said most likely I wouldn't have to talk to anybody about it. If I did and talked right, they'd be back with some dough. If I talked wrong, they'd be back for my little girl."

"Go on," Ohls said. "They're full of crap."

"They went away. When I saw them go on up the street I got screwy. Renfrew is just a pocket—one of them graft jobs. It goes on around the hill half a mile, then stops. There's no way to get off it. So they had to come back this way . . . I got my twenty-two, which is all the gun I have, and hid in the bushes. I got the tire with the second shot. I guess they thought it was a blowout. I missed with the next and that put 'em wise. They got guns loose. I got the Mex then, and the big guy ducked behind the car . . . That's all there was to it. Then you come along."

Ohls flexed his thick, hard fingers and smiled grimly at the girl in the corner. "Who lives in the next house, Tom?"

"A man named Grandy, a motorman on the interurban. He lives all alone. He's at work now."

"I didn't guess he was home," Ohls grinned. He got up and went over and patted the little girl on the head. "You'll have to come down and make a statement, Tom."

"Sure." Tom Sneyd's voice was tired, listless. "I guess I lose my job, too, for rentin' out the hack last night."

"I ain't so sure about that," Ohls said softly. "Not if your boss likes guys with a few guts to run his hacks."

He patted the little girl on the head again, went towards the door and opened it. I nodded at Tom Sneyd and followed Ohls out of the house. Ohls said quietly: "He don't know about the kill yet. No need to spring it in front of the kid."

We went over to the gray car. We had got some sacks out of the basement and spread them over the late Andrews, weighted them down with stones. Ohls glanced that way and said absently: "I got to get to where there's a phone pretty quick."

He leaned on the door of the car and looked in at the Mexican. The Mexican sat with his head back and his eyes half-closed and a drawn expression on his brown face. His left wrist was shackled to the spider of the wheel.

"What's your name?" Ohls snapped at him.

"Luis Cadena," the Mexican said it in a soft voice without opening his eyes any wider.

"Which one of you heels scratched the guy at West Cimarron last night?"

"No understand, señor," the Mexican said purringly.

"Don't go dumb on me, spig," Ohls said dispassionately. "It gets me sore." He leaned on the window and rolled his little cigar around in his mouth.

The Mexican looked faintly amused and at the same time very tired. The blood on his right hand had dried black.

Ohls said: "Andrews scratched the guy in a taxi at West Cimarron. There was a girl along. We got the girl. You have a lousy chance to prove you weren't in on it."

Light flickered and died behind the Mexican's half-open eyes. He smiled with a glint of small white teeth.

Ohls said: "What did he do with the gun?"

"No understand, señor."

Ohls said: "He's tough. When they get tough it scares me."

He walked away from the car and scuffed some loose dirt from the sidewalk beside the sacks that draped the dead man. His toe gradually uncovered the contractor's stencil in the cement. He read it out loud: "Dorr Paving and Construction Company, San Angelo. It's a wonder the fat louse wouldn't stay in his own racket."

I stood beside Ohls and looked down the hill between the two houses. Sudden flashes of light darted from the windshields of cars going along the boulevard that fringed Gray Lake, far below.

Ohls said: "Well?"

I said: "The killers knew about the taxi—maybe—and the girlfriend reached town with the swag. So it wasn't Canales' job. Canales isn't the boy to let anybody play around with twenty-two grand of his money. The redhead was in on the kill, and it was done for a reason."

Ohls grinned. "Sure. It was done so you could be framed for it."

I said: "It's a shame how little account some folks take of human life—or twenty-two grand. Harger was knocked off so I could be framed and the dough was passed to me to make the frame tighter."

"Maybe they thought you'd highball," Ohls grunted. "That would sew you up right."

I rolled a cigarette around in my fingers. "That would have been a little too dumb, even for me. What do we do now? Wait till the moon comes up so we can sing—or go down the hill and tell some more little white lies?"

Ohls spat on one of Poke Andrews' sacks. He said gruffly: "This is county land here. I could take all this mess over to the sub-station at Solano and keep it hush-hush for a while. The hack driver would be tickled to death to keep it under the hat. And I've gone far enough so I'd like to get the Mex in the goldfish room with me personal."

"I'd like it that way too," I said. "I guess you can't hold it down there for long, but you might hold it down long enough for me to see a fat boy about a cat."

11

IT WAS late afternoon when I got back to the hotel. The clerk handed me a slip which read: "Please phone F.D. as soon as possible."

I went upstairs and drank some liquor that was in the bottom of a bottle. Then I phoned down for another pint, scraped my chin, changed clothes and looked up Frank Dorr's number in the book. He lived in a beautiful old house on Greenview Park Crescent.

I made myself a tall smooth one with a tinkle and sat down in an easy chair with the phone at my elbow. I got a maid first. Then I got a man who spoke Mister Dorr's name as though he thought it might blow up in his mouth. After him I got a voice with a lot of silk in it. Then I got a long silence and at the end of the silence I got Frank Dorr himself. He sounded glad to hear from me.

He said: "I've been thinking about our talk this morning, and I have a better idea. Drop out and see me. . . . And you might bring that money along. You just have time to get it out of the bank."

I said: "Yeah. The safe-deposit closes at six. But it's not your money."

I heard him chuckle. "Don't be foolish. It's all marked, and I wouldn't want to have to accuse you of stealing it."

I thought that over, and didn't believe it—about the currency being marked. I took a drink out of my glass and said: "I *might* be willing to turn it over to the party I got it from—in your presence."

He said: "Well—I told you that party left town. But I'll see what I can do. No tricks, please."

I said of course no tricks, and hung up. I finished my drink, called Von Ballin of the *Telegram*. He said the sheriff's people didn't seem to have any ideas about Lou Harger—or give a damn. He was a little sore that I still wouldn't let him use my story. I could tell from the way he talked that he hadn't got the doings over near Gray Lake.

I called Ohls, couldn't reach him.

I mixed myself another drink, swallowed half of it and began to feel it too much. I put my hat on, changed my mind about

the other half of my drink, went down to my car. The early
evening traffic was thick with householders riding home to dinner.
I wasn't sure whether two cars tailed me or just one. At any rate
nobody tried to catch up and throw a pineapple in my lap.

The house was a square two-storied place of old red brick, with
beautiful grounds and a red brick wall with a white stone coping
around them. A shiny black limousine was parked under the porte-
cochère at the side. I followed a red-flagged walk up over two
terraces, and a pale wisp of a man in a cutaway coat let me into
a wide, silent hall with dark old furniture and a glimpse of garden
at the end. He led me along that and along another hall at right
angles and ushered me softly into a paneled study that was dimly
lit against the gathering dusk. He went away, leaving me alone.

The end of the room was mostly open french windows, through
which a brass-colored sky showed behind a line of quiet trees. In
front of the trees a sprinkler swung slowly on a patch of velvety
lawn that was already dark. There were large dim oils on the
walls, a huge black desk with books across one end, a lot of deep
lounging chairs, a heavy soft rug that went from wall to wall.
There was a faint smell of good cigars and beyond that somewhere
a smell of garden flowers and moist earth. The door opened and
a youngish man in nose-glasses came in, gave me a slight formal
nod, looked around vaguely, and said that Mr. Dorr would be
there in a moment. He went out again, and I lit a cigarette.

In a little while the door opened again and Beasley came in,
walked past me with a grin and sat down just inside the windows.
Then Dorr came in and behind him Miss Glenn.

Dorr had his black cat in his arms and two lovely red scratches,
shiny with collodion, down his right cheek. Miss Glenn had on
the same clothes I had seen on her in the morning. She looked
dark and drawn and spiritless, and she went past me as though
she had never seen me before.

Dorr squeezed himself into the high-backed chair behind the
desk and put the cat down in front of him. The cat strolled over
to one corner of the desk and began to lick its chest with a long,
sweeping, businesslike motion.

Dorr said: "Well, well. Here we are," and chuckled pleasantly.

The man in the cutaway came in with a tray of cocktails, passed
them around, put the tray with the shaker down on a low table
beside Miss Glenn. He went out again, closing the door as if he
was afraid he might crack it.

We all drank and looked very solemn.

I said: "We're all here but two. I guess we have a quorum."

Dorr said: "What's that?" sharply and put his head to one side.

I said: "Lou Harger's in the morgue and Canales is dodging cops. Otherwise we're all here. All the interested parties."

Miss Glenn made an abrupt movement, then relaxed suddenly and picked at the arm of her chair.

Dorr took two swallows of his cocktail, put the glass aside and folded his small neat hands on the desk. His face looked a little sinister.

"The money," he said coldly. "I'll take charge of it now."

I said: "Not now or any other time. I didn't bring it."

Dorr stared at me and his face got a little red. I looked at Beasley. Beasley had a cigarette in his mouth and his hands in his pockets and the back of his head against the back of his chair. He looked half asleep.

Dorr said softly, meditatively: "Holding out, huh?"

"Yes," I said grimly. "While I have it I'm fairly safe. You overplayed your hand when you let me get my paws on it. I'd be a fool not to hold what advantage it gives me."

Dorr said: "Safe?" with a gently sinister intonation.

I laughed. "Not safe from a frame," I said. "But the last one didn't click so well. . . . Not safe from being gun-walked again. But that's going to be harder next time too. . . . But fairly safe from being shot in the back and having you sue my estate for the dough."

Dorr stroked the cat and looked at me under his eyebrows.

"Let's get a couple of more important things straightened out," I said. "Who takes the rap for Lou Harger?"

"What makes you so sure *you* don't?" Dorr asked nastily.

"My alibi's been polished up. I didn't know how good it was until I knew how close Lou's death could be timed. I'm clear now . . . regardless of who turns in what gun with what fairy tale. . . . And the lads that were sent to scotch my alibi ran into some trouble."

Dorr said: "That so?" without any apparent emotion.

"A thug named Andrews and a Mexican calling himself Luis Cadena. I daresay you've heard of them."

"I don't know such people," Dorr said sharply.

"Then it won't upset you to hear Andrews got very dead, and the law has Cadena."

"Certainly not," Dorr said. "They were from Canales. Canales had Harger killed."

I said: "So that's your new idea. I think it's lousy."

I leaned over and slipped my empty glass under my chair. Miss Glenn turned her head towards me and spoke very gravely, as if it was very important to the future of the race for me to believe what she said: "Of course—*of course* Canales had Lou killed. . . . At least, the men he sent after us killed Lou."

I nodded politely. "What for? A packet of money they didn't get? They wouldn't have killed him. They'd have brought him in, brought both of you in. You arranged for that kill, and the taxi stunt was to sidetrack me, not to fool Canales' boys."

She put her hand out quickly. Her eyes were shimmering. I went ahead.

"I wasn't very bright, but I didn't figure on anything so flossy. Who the hell would? Canales had no motive to gun Lou, unless it got back the money he had been gypped out of. Supposing he could know that quick he *had* been gypped."

Dorr was licking his lips and quivering his chins and looking from one of us to the other with his small tight eyes. Miss Glenn said drearily: "Lou knew all about the play. He planned it with the croupier, Pina. Pina wanted some getaway money, wanted to move on to Havana. Of course Canales would have got wise, but not too soon, if I hadn't got noisy and tough. *I* got Lou killed—but not the way you mean."

I dropped an inch of ash off a cigarette I had forgotten all about. "All right," I said grimly. "Canales takes the rap. . . . And I suppose you two chiselers think that's all I care about. . . . Where was Lou going to be when Canales was *supposed* to find out he'd been gypped?"

"He was going to be gone," Miss Glenn said tonelessly. "A damn long way off. And I was going to be gone with him."

I said: "Nerts! You seem to forget *I* know *why* Lou was killed."

Beasley sat up in his chair and moved his right hand rather delicately towards his left shoulder. "This wise guy bother you, chief?"

Dorr said: "Not yet. Let him rant."

I moved so that I faced a little more towards Beasley. The sky had gone dark outside and the sprinkler had been turned off. A damp feeling came slowly into the room. Dorr opened a cedarwood box and put a long brown cigar in his mouth, bit the end off with a dry snap of his false teeth. There was the harsh noise of a match striking, then the slow, rather labored puffing of his breath in the cigar.

He said slowly, through a cloud of smoke: "Let's forget all this and make a deal about that money . . . Manny Tinnen hung himself in his cell this afternoon."

Miss Glenn stood up suddenly, pushing her arms straight down at her sides. Then she sank slowly down into the chair again, sat motionless. I said: "Did he have any help?" Then I made a sudden, sharp movement—and stopped.

Beasley jerked a swift glance at me, but I wasn't looking at Beasley. There was a shadow outside one of the windows—a lighter shadow than the dark lawn and darker trees. There was a hollow, bitter, coughing plop; a thin spray of whitish smoke in the window.

Beasley jerked, rose halfway to his feet, then fell on his face with one arm doubled under him.

Canales stepped through the windows, past Beasley's body, came three steps further, and stood silent, with a long, black, small-calibered gun in his hand, the larger tube of a silencer flaring from the end of it.

"Be very still," he said. "I am a fair shot—even with this elephant gun."

His face was so white that it was almost luminous. His dark eyes were all smoke-gray iris, without pupils.

"Sound carries well at night, out of open windows," he said tonelessly.

Dorr put both his hands down on the desk and began to pat it. The black cat put its body very low, drifted down over the end of the desk and went under a chair. Miss Glenn turned her head towards Canales very slowly, as if some kind of mechanism moved it.

Canales said: "Perhaps you have a buzzer on that desk. If the door of the room opens, I shoot. It will give me a lot of pleasure to see blood come out of your fat neck."

I moved the fingers of my right hand two inches on the arm of my chair. The silenced gun swayed towards me and I stopped moving my fingers. Canales smiled very briefly under his angular mustache.

"You are a smart dick," he said. "I thought I had you right. But there are things about you I like."

I didn't say anything. Canales looked back at Dorr. He said very precisely: "I have been bled by your organization for a long time. But this is something else again. Last night I was cheated out of some money. But this is trivial too. I am wanted for the murder of this Harger. A man named Cadena has been made to confess that I hired him. . . . That is just a little too much fix."

Dorr swayed gently over his desk, put his elbows down hard on it, held his face in his small hands and began to shake. His cigar was smoking on the floor.

Canales said: "I would like to get my money back, and I would like to get clear of this rap—but most of all I would like you to say something—so I can shoot you with your mouth open and see blood come out of it."

Beasley's body stirred on the carpet. His hands groped a little. Dorr's eyes were agony trying not to look at him. Canales was rapt and blind in his act by this time. I moved my fingers a little more on the arm of my chair. But I had a long way to go.

Canales said: "Pina has talked to me. I saw to that. You killed Harger. Because he was a secret witness against Manny Tinnen. The D.A. kept the secret, and the dick here kept it. But Harger could not keep it himself. He told his broad—and the broad told you. . . . So the killing was arranged, in a way to throw suspicion with a motive on me. First on this dick, and if that wouldn't hold, on me."

There was silence. I wanted to say something, but I couldn't get anything out. I didn't think anybody but Canales would ever again say anything.

Canales said: "You fixed Pina to let Harger and his girl win my money. It was not hard—because I don't play my wheels crooked."

Dorr had stopped shaking. His face lifted, stone-white, and turned towards Canales, slowly, like the face of a man about to have an epileptic fit. Beasley was up on one elbow. His eyes were almost shut but a gun was laboring upwards in his hand.

Canales leaned forward and began to smile. His trigger finger whitened at the exact moment Beasley's gun began to pulse and roar.

Canales arched his back until his body was a rigid curve. He fell stiffly forward, hit the edge of the desk and slid along it to the floor, without lifting his hands.

Beasley dropped his gun and fell down on his face again. His body got soft and his fingers moved fitfully, then were still.

I got motion into my legs, stood up and went to kick Canales' gun under the desk—senselessly. Doing this I saw that Canales had fired at least once, because Frank Dorr had no right eye.

He sat still and quiet with his chin on his chest and a nice touch of melancholy on the good side of his face.

The door of the room came open and the secretary with the nose-glasses slid in pop-eyed. He staggered back against the door, closing it again. I could hear his rapid breathing across the room.

He gasped: "Is—is anything wrong?"

I thought that very funny, even then. Then I realized that he might be short-sighted and from where he stood Frank Dorr looked natural enough. The rest of it could have been just routine to Dorr's help.

I said: "Yes—but we'll take care of it. Stay out of here."

He said: "Yes, sir," and went out again. That surprised me so much that my mouth fell open. I went down the room and bent over the gray-haired Beasley. He was unconscious, but had a fair pulse. He was bleeding from the side, slowly.

Miss Glenn was standing up and looked almost as dopy as Canales had looked. She was talking to me quickly, in a brittle, very distinct voice: "I didn't know Lou was to be killed, but I couldn't have done anything about it anyway. They burned me with a branding iron—just for a sample of what I'd get. Look!"

I looked. She tore her dress down in front and there was a hideous burn on her chest almost between her two breasts.

I said: "Okey, sister. That's nasty medicine. But we've got to have some law here now and an ambulance for Beasley."

I pushed past her towards the telephone, shook her hand off my arm when she grabbed at me. She went on talking to my back in a thin, desperate voice.

"I thought they'd just hold Lou out of the way until after the trial. But they dragged him out of the cab and shot him without a word. Then the little one drove the taxi into town and the big one brought me up into the hills to a shack. Dorr was there. He told me how you had to be framed. He promised me the money, if I went through with it, and torture till I died, if I let them down."

It occurred to me that I was turning my back too much to people. I swung around, got the telephone in my hands, still on the hook, and put my gun down on the desk.

"Listen! Give me a break," she said wildly. "Dorr framed it all with Pina, the croupier. Pina was one of the gang that got Shannon where they could fix him. I didn't—"

I said: "Sure—that's all right. Take it easy."

The room, the whole house seemed very still, as if a lot of people were hunched outside the door, listening.

"It wasn't a bad idea," I said, as if I had all the time in the world. "Lou was just a white chip to Frank Dorr. The play he figured put us both out as witnesses. But it was too elaborate, took in too many people. That sort always blows up in your face."

"Lou was getting out of the state," she said, clutching at her dress. "He was scared. He thought the roulette trick was some kind of a pay-off to him."

I said: "Yeah," lifted the phone and asked for police headquarters.

The room door came open again then and the secretary barged in with a gun. A uniformed chauffeur was behind him with another gun.

I said very loudly into the phone: "This is Frank Dorr's house. There's been a killing. . . ."

The secretary and the chauffeur dodged out again. I heard running in the hall. I clicked the phone, called the *Telegram* office and got Von Ballin. When I got through giving him the flash Miss Glenn was gone out of the window into the dark garden.

I didn't go after her. I didn't mind very much if she got away.

I tried to get Ohls, but they said he was still down at Solano. And by that time the night was full of sirens.

I had a little trouble, but not too much. Fenweather pulled too much weight. Not all of the story came out, but enough so that the City Hall boys in the two-hundred-dollar suits had their left elbows in front of their faces for some time.

Pina was picked up in Salt Lake City. He broke and implicated four others of Manny Tinnen's gang. Two of them were killed resisting arrest, the other two got life without parole.

Miss Glenn made a clean getaway and was never heard of again. I think that's about all, except that I had to turn the twenty-two grand over to the Public Administrator. He allowed me two hundred dollars fee and nine dollars and twenty cents mileage. Sometimes I wonder what he did with the rest of it.

LESLIE FORD
Death Stops at a Tourist Camp

TERRY ACHESON closed the door of the tiny white cabin, almost concealed under its gorgeous burden of crimson rambler, and leaned against it, eyeing the girl opposite her with a lifted brow.

"The trouble with you, my pet," she said softly, "is that you're scared—utterly and literally pea green."

The girl opposite her had curly yellow hair and odd-colored eyes, rather greener than gray but grayer than green, and she wore a white suede cloth polo shirt, high at the neck, and a very smart white felt hat. She had one hand behind her and the other stuffed into the pocket of her blue flannel skirt. In fact, she was exactly like the girl leaning against the door, her slim brown and white feet planted firmly on the grass rug on the floor—except that her hair was not so golden and her polo shirt not so white and her full lips not so red. The mirrors in the cabins of the Shady Bridge Tourist Camp—forty-eight miles from Richmond—were both mildewed and slightly undulating. So that Terry Acheson, regarding herself in one of them, did look decidedly pea green.

However, she *was* scared. Furthermore, she was willing, now that it was too late to do anything about it, to admit it. She had been so sure she could make Richmond and a proper hotel before dark . . . and she could have, if she hadn't had a flat just after leaving Bristol. And she had promised her father she wouldn't drive after dark. Not that anything could have happened to her in an hour and a quarter, but she *had* promised. Furthermore, it had been darker than she had counted on when she asked the service station attendant at the crossroads about the road, and there was a detour through miles of back lanes.

53

"If I was you, Miss," he had said, "I'd stop at Mis' Dixon's place just up the way. They're mighty nice folks, and it's clean."

Terry had been doubtful. It was a toss-up which her father would dislike most—her traveling deserted roads in the dark, or putting up at a tourist camp that he—and she—knew nothing about.

"It'll be all right, Miss. A sixteen cylinder Cadillac's just gone there."

The man grinned. Terry laughed.

"If it's good enough for sixteen cylinders, it's good enough for eight—is that it? Maybe you're right. Good night."

It wasn't the sixteen cylinders that had made up her mind for her. It was a dark road, a no doubt quite imaginary rattle somewhere in the bowels of her gray sports roadster, and the large "AAA" on the sign at the side of the road. That at least identified it. She had driven in across a shaded bridge through a line of old pollarded cedars, and here she was, the sole if temporary proprietress of a little rose-covered cabin, with a sign hanging over the door that said "Florida" in white letters. "The lady in 'Florida,' " the colored boy who brought her bag in had called her. Standing there in front of the door she felt more like a babe in Timbuktu. It was astonishing how silent it was all around her. Silent, and dark, in spite of the racket the frogs were kicking up and the thousands of fireflies glowing in the shrubs.

Terry tossed her hat on the dresser, tousled her mop of bright curly hair and looked at her watch. It was quarter of ten. Everybody else was in bed, so the goodlooking young man who showed her where to park her car had told her. The young man, in fact, had reassured her more than the "AAA" sign—his grin, to be exact, and a pair of pleasant brown eyes, which was about all she'd seen of him. But he was gone now, and the frogs' dismal dirge didn't make it any more cheerful.

She hung up her blue flannel jacket and tiptoed across to the narrow bed. Tiptoed because the cabin was propped up from the ground, and her heels pounding on the floor sounded like a battalion of army mules crossing the steppes—if they came in battalions, Terry thought. She was suddenly aware that she had only the vaguest notion what steppes were, or how a mule would really sound on one.

She sat down on the edge of the bed and looked around. It *was* clean, and it was amusingly furnished, with a painted dresser and chairs and a lamp with a chintz shade. The sign on the door—"Gentlemen will not, ladies must not throw ashes on the floor"—seemed fair enough, to anyone with a knowledge of the world. The young man with the cheerful grin had probably put that there. On the other side was a narrow door leading to a private shower and lavatory, and there were two small windows, both of them open, with chintz blinds drawn up at the bottom by cords secured on a hook at the side. At least nobody could look in, and that was something. Still Terry did not undress.

Finally she took a shoe off and dropped it firmly with a crash. "You're not going to be a complete fool," she said severely. "It's too late to back out *now!*"

She took off the other shoe and dropped it, and reached for her bag.

"Oh, Lord!" she groaned. She had left it in the car, on the back of the seat. If it was gone, she'd probably have to wash dishes for her night's lodging. That was what they always did in the comic strips, anyway, and there were always immense piles of dishes.

She thrust her shoes back on her feet and rushed to the door. A firefly lighted on her bare arm. She caught it and watched it glow an instant in her hands before she let its little lantern move slowly off into the night. "Lucky they don't make as much noise as frogs," she thought, stepping down out of "Florida" and peering around to get her bearings.

Little white cabins stretched in a row under the maple trees on both sides. "Iowa" was next to her on one side, "New York" on the other. Across the lawn was a corral of parked cars with a light burning over the entrance. She closed her door and ran across, wishing a little that the young man would appear. Not that she couldn't find her car alone.

It was very dark, and dismally quiet barring the frogs. Terry stumbled a little on the uneven turf, and decided that if she walked, and didn't try to run, she wouldn't be so nervy. There was a theory somebody had that you didn't run from bears because you were afraid, you were afraid because you ran. Or something of the sort. She glanced behind her. That was probably a mistake too. You didn't glance behind you because you were afraid of bears, you were afraid of bears because you glanced behind you. A good bear would be rather reassuring, she thought; because the thing she suddenly saw, or thought she saw, under the tree did not look like a bear at all.

At first she thought the light there was a firefly. With so many moving lights it didn't look too solid. But when it dissolved in a shower of fallen sparks against the trunk of the tree, she knew someone was there, and furthermore that he had put out his cigarette so she would not notice him. She tried not to run or let her heart pound against her ribs as she gained the white painted arch and peered around in the dark trying to find her car. There was a flashlight on the back seat too. It would be a relief to have that.

The light on a pole over the parking space shone dimly in the night, but it was enough to show up the shiny surface of the enormous car parked alongside of hers. They were parked quite close together, so that she had to step on the running board and put her hand on the door to get her own door unlocked and open. It occurred to her for an instant that her bag would really be safer there than inside the cabin; but she took it and the flashlight, climbed out and closed the door. Then she stopped, her breath coming in quick gusts. For something inside the big car had moved.

For a moment Terry Acheson's heart pounded madly. She was standing on the running board of the big car—had to, to get out, because the fenders of the two were too close together for her to squeeze through. Her first idea was to run. Then she had an irresistible impulse to look in the dark window. She was probably wrong. It was extraordinary how much oftener she was wrong than right. She lifted the flashlight and turned its beam through the broad window. Then she gasped and lowered it instantly. The car was empty.

Terry stood there for a moment paralyzed. Then she shook herself impatiently. "You're crazy!" she said. "Why shouldn't it be empty?"

She dashed back across the dark lawn as fast as she could go, burst into her cabin door, slammed it behind her and turned the key. Then she turned around . . . and stopped short in her tracks, staring about her.

She could not have been away five minutes at the longest; but her things were entirely gone.

Terry Acheson looked panic-stricken from the narrow bed with its turned-down yellow cover to the chintz blinds drawn up from the bottom, the chintz lamp shade, the grass rug, the painted dresser and chairs, the narrow door leading to the shower. She put her cold hands to her burning forehead, crept across and stared into the mirror, clinging to the dresser, wondering if she had gone out of her mind. Then she crept back to the door, unlocked it and looked outside. It was very dark. She searched among the fireflies for one that was solider than the rest, but whoever was out there had not lighted another cigarette. She stepped out and turned the flashlight up on the sign over the door, and breathed a great sigh of relief.

This cabin was "New York." Of course they all looked just the same, she thought. She ran to the next cabin. The door stood open an inch, and through the crack she could see her coat on the hanger. Suddenly as she stood there she felt a quick inexplicable wave of terror, as if something was just behind her in the night. The hand she instinctively stretched out to the door was paralyzed with fear. She whirled about, back against the white wall, and flashed the beam of her light around the grounds. There was nothing there, only the maple trees and the other cabins.

She was about to lower the flash when something caught her eye. At the foot of the nearest maple, between the big roots, something—a tiny spot—glittered brightly, and beside it rose a thin thread of smoke from a short tube of gray ash. Terry stared at it a moment, then edged open the door with her shoulder, backed into the cabin, closed the door quickly and bolted it. Then she turned around to survey things inside; and her lips parted in dismay.

She had left her traveling bag closed at the foot of her bed. It was closed now, but it was at the head of the bed; and her hat, which she had left mashed in in front of the mirror, was still there, but it was carefully smoothed out.

She stared at them incredulously for a moment, then tiptoed to the small door leading to the shower and pushed it open. There was nothing there. She bent down and looked under the bed. There was nothing there either, not even a fluff of dust.

Terry sat down on the edge of the bed. Someone had been in there while she had been out. That was clear. Unless, of course, she *had* left the bag at the head of the bed. She shook her head slowly. It wouldn't do. It might have been all right except for the hat. She had never been known to push out the folds of a felt hat when she took it off—as her mother had pointed out to her for practically seventeen years, assuming she had begun at two, which was reasonable enough.

"Well, my pet," she said—aloud, because it was a little reassuring to hear somebody talking—"you might as well plan to sit up all night."

If anything did happen to her, she had left tracks enough, anyway. The flat, and the boy at the station. Unless—and a cold shiver went down her already clammy back—it was a plot and the boy was in on it. But that was pretty absurd. People didn't just run into plots, not actually. Terry took off her skirt and put on her dressing gown. Then she got under the covers. For a moment she lay there with the light on, and turned it off. There was no use being a fool. Nevertheless she held her flash tightly in her hand.

"I'll stay awake anyway," she said to herself, and went instantly to sleep.

Suddenly a heavy thud brought her sharply to. She sat bolt upright, her breath strangling in her throat, listening with every nerve. There was nothing—no sound. Nothing but the croaking frogs and the damp strange smell of night. Then she remembered and felt in sudden alarm for the flashlight. It was gone. She reached across to the little square table for the lamp, and turned it on. It was almost half past two. Terry rubbed her eyes. She had been asleep for over three hours.

She glanced at the door. It was still bolted, the shades were still drawn. Her blue bag was still on the table, her bag and hat in their places. The flashlight was beside her shoes on the floor under the bed. Terry took a deep breath and smiled. That was what had waked her—the light dropping out of her hand and rolling off onto the floor. She looked at her watch again. If she stayed awake another half hour, she could go to sleep in peace. She never minded the dark after three. It was morning then, and, so far in Terry Acheson's life, no morning had ever come that had not miraculously put to flight whatever tiny cloud had apparently floated across it the day before.

She woke up again with a start. Somebody was knocking on her door.

"Good morning!" a voice said. "It's five o'clock."

Terry turned over with a groan and yawned sleepily. "Oh, dear!" she said. "Thanks!"

She yawned again. It was very early, but it was just as well, probably, to be up and on her way. She should—she realized a little distressed—have telegraphed her father the night before. Still, if it was five now, she could be in Richmond well in time to call him while he was at breakfast in the garden. So Terry Acheson jumped out of bed, happily unconscious of the terrible and impossible thing that was shortly to happen.

Julius Jones put her ham and eggs and toast down on the table under the mimosa tree and filled her cup from the old silver pot.

"I'm starving," Terry said. She sniffed the red country ham and rich fragrant coffee.

Julius Jones grinned virtually from ear to ear.

"Ah could eat a mule's eah frah'd in grease," he said fervently. "People git up too eah'ly in this yere business fer me. Ah ain' nevah had time t' finish mah breakfas' yet, since Ah been yere."

"You'd better go and finish it now," Terry smiled. "I don't want anything else. This is awfully good. I've got my bag right there."

"Ah'll put it in youah cah, Miss. Hadn' Ah bettah see if you done lef' anythin'?"

Terry waved a hand airily. She could long remember doing that. "Don't bother. I looked around."

She gave him half a dollar. Julius beamed. He picked up her bag, brought the car out of the parking corral into the drive and put the bag in the rumble seat. Then Terry saw him heading towards the cabins and realized with a sigh that he was going to have a look anyway. What was it about her, she wondered, that made porters and maids, waiters and waitresses, friends and parents, always assume she was leaving something behind? She usually was, of course, but anyway. . . . Terry raised her coffee cup and put it to her lips.

Then a sudden scream that had in it all the terror of the trackless jungle and the primitive soul rent the still morning air. Terry put her cup down hastily and looked around.

Julius Jones was flying out of her cabin as if all the fiends of hell were at his heels. The young man with the grin and the pleasant eyes came running out of the big brick house beyond the rock garden. He caught the darky by the shoulder.

"What the hell's the matter with you?" he said curtly.

Julius Jones pointed a trembling finger first at Terry, then at the cabin, tore himself loose and ran on. Young Mr. Jeff Dixon stared after him a moment, stared at Terry and ran across the turf to the cabin. Terry stared too. She got up hastily. It was obviously impossible that she could have left anything in the cabin, but whatever it was it couldn't have been as terrifying as all that. As she ran across the grass she saw a white-haired woman come hurrying over the lawn, wiping her hands on a pink checked apron. Terry got a brief impression of a sweet care-worn face, startled and anxious.

Jeff Dixon had stepped into the cabin and was backing out when Terry came up. He turned round abruptly. The brown eyes that looked into hers were anything but pleasant, and there was no grin on his definitely attractive but not particularly handsome face.

Terry stopped short, staring at him, astonished. He was staring at her, his eyes hard flat discs, his jaw white-ribbed and tight, his lips a thin steely line. The contempt and loathing in his face stung her like a lash across the eyes. She drew back, bewildered and a little frightened without knowing why; and she would not have been Terry Acheson if she had not been angry too.

Then she pushed past him and looked through the door.

Lying huddled in a disgusting heap on the floor under the edge of the bed was a large man. He was very inert, and staring white-faced at him, Terry knew he was dead before she saw the thin dark line of dried blood that smeared the floor under his gray coat.

She turned slowly around to the young man.

"That's why you wanted to sneak out early, is it?" he demanded through tense white lips.

The blank astonishment and fright on Terry Acheson's face turned slowly to sickening desperate horror.

"What . . . what are you talking about?"

The words came only in a hoarse, awed whisper.

Jeff Dixon looked at her with icy fury, tinged with a perverse sort of admiration for her acting.

Anyone not versed in the deceitful ways of woman in general would have been taken in at once by the wide slate gray eyes with greenish lights in them, and the white drained cheeks and sharply brilliant mouth whose brilliance had no relation to the pale trembling lips under it. But Jeff Dixon knew women. He still writhed when he remembered a pair of blue eyes much more innocently blue than these, looking up at him and saying, "But, *Jeff,* you couldn't expect me to marry a boy whose mother runs a *tourist camp!* I always thought it was one of those old Colonial estates with lots of antiques in the attic, and it was just *money* you didn't have."

It flashed into his mind now. Terry saw his white face flush suddenly and his hazel eyes kindle.

"I'm talking about the dead body you were trying to sneak off and leave on us," he said angrily.

She stared at him in horrified bewilderment.

"You . . . you're crazy!"

"Yes? That's the cabin you were in, isn't it? And there's a dead man's body in it, isn't there?"

Terry stared at him still, speechless. It was a simple and unanswerable statement of the whole business. Unanswerable, that is, until Dr. Harp came in. For as far as Terry knew—and she ought to if anyone did—it was actually and literally true.

And Jeff Dixon thought suddenly of his mother, coming across the lawn from the big house now, anxious-eyed, her white hair shining in the sun . . . and about the tough job she'd had to make the Shady Bridge Tourist Camp a paying proposition. First there had been the business of the Roanoke bank teller, then this. It would wreck the whole works. You couldn't have fugitive embezzlers and then murder in a tourist camp and expect people to go on stopping at it. Not the right sort of people.

The little hum and buzz of excited talk had risen slowly, and then drawn nearer, and Terry, looking helplessly about her, saw the people coming, from the big brick house and out of the little cabins up and down the row, crowding around now with curious avid eyes in a little semi-circle about the two of them still standing in front of the cabin that Terry had slept in.

Jeff Dixon spoke curtly. "Won't you all go back to your cabins? There's been a . . . an accident here. Your breakfast is ready when you want it."

Terry looked in a daze from one to another of the strange faces closing in around her, people in bathrobes and slippers. Blurred hostile faces were agog with curiosity. Questions pelted her numb brain like tiny pellets of hail. "What's happened?" "What's she done?" "Did he say *murdered?*" Later she tried to remember how many faces there were, but they remained indistinct and cloudy.

All except two: the motherly gentle face of Mrs. Dixon and the hard white face of her son.

A booming confident voice rose above the buzz and hum.

"What's up, young fellow?"

A large man in a striped wool dressing gown and lavender pajamas, with iron gray hair and an outthrust jaw, elbowed his way to the front of the circle and started towards the door of the cabin.

Jeff Dixon stepped in front of him.

"Sorry, Mr. Baylor. You can't go in there."

Mr. Baylor stopped and looked at him with amused tolerance.

"I guess you know who you're talking to, young man."

Jeff nodded.

"Sorry. Nobody goes in there till the police get here—not even J. P. Morgan."

The color flushed up the back of the big man's neck into the rim of iron gray hair around his sleek bald head. His large red and yellow-striped shoulders stiffened and the look of amused tolerance left his face abruptly. Terry Acheson, looking blankly from one to the other, heard a distinct snicker in the circle round her. She saw a little round woman with silver-rimmed spectacles and her front hair done up in curling kids suddenly flush and put her hand over her mouth, and draw her voluminous gray wool wrapper with lavender ribbon bows closer around her . . . as if whoever had made such a disrespectful noise certainly was not her.

Mr. Baylor seemed more annoyed by the snicker than by the set jaw and firmly planted anatomy in front of him. He glared angrily.

Jeff Dixon spoke patiently. "This girl was getting ready to leave when the boy looked in the cabin and saw a dead man there. That's all there is to it so far. The state police usually drops in here about now, or we'll phone. Now please go back, will you?"

Terry did not see any of the people actually move, but suddenly the space between them and her was much larger. Only the big man held his ground.

"I think the young fellow's being a bit high-handed, Miss . . .?"

Terry whispered her name automatically, but no sound came. Her vocal cords seemed done for. The big man waited a second.

"My name's Baylor," he said. "Howard Baylor. If there's anything I can do, little lady. . . ."

Mr. Baylor hesitated, a natural caution asserting itself.

"That *is* your cabin?"

Terry nodded, helplessly.

"Yes," she whispered. "I . . . I can't understand it."

Her voice came back to her a little, and with it the quick realization of how preposterous her story must sound.

"I did sleep there, and then I came out this morning . . . and I've been sitting right out here all the time. It . . . it's just *mad!*"

Baylor looked up at the green board with the white "Florida" on it, and back at Terry. Doubt seeped into his shrewd light eyes.

A woman's voice spoke up suddenly from the outskirts of the circle.

"You keep out of this, Howard, and let the police handle it."

Terry looked around at her. There was something in the sharp hostility of the woman's voice that for the first time made her realize that this was not merely embarrassing. She was actually in danger.

"You come along. We'll get out of here before this is spread over the front page of every paper in the country."

Terry looked at her, hardly understanding. Mrs. Baylor was fifty, fat, with a sagging heavy face under a tousled permanent. Her hair was black with that shiny hard blackness that does not need the whitish edge along the part to show it is dyed.

Mr. Baylor eased back into the crowd a little uncertainly.

"Sorry!" Jeff Dixon said. "Nobody can leave this place until the police get here. That goes for everybody."

Mrs. Baylor's eyes snapped. "You come along, Howard! Don't you pay any attention to that impertinent young fool. He's probably in on it himself!"

Another voice, drawling and rather bored, rose from the outside of the circle beside Mrs. Baylor.

"Oh, he's probably right, you know, Mother."

Terry's eyes rested for an instant on a young man in a neat white flannel dressing gown, his hair combed and himself perfectly composed.

"You keep your mouth shut," Mr. Baylor said curtly. "Your mother doesn't need your advice."

"That's all right, Harold." Mrs. Baylor nodded sympathetically to her son.

"If you'll all go and get dressed, you'll probably get away quicker," Jeff Dixon said patiently. "I'm sorry about it, but there's nothing else we can do. Somebody has been killed here. We've got to wait for the police."

As the little circle broke up Mrs. Dixon came up to them.

"There's a man dead in 'Florida,' " Jeff said quietly. "Where she stayed last night."

Mrs. Dixon gazed incredulously at Terry and back at her son. "This girl?" she said. "Who is the man?"

Jeff looked at Terry and waited.

"Well?" he demanded coldly. "Who is it?"

Terry gulped.

"I . . . I don't know!" she blurted out. Then she caught herself quickly. She mustn't let herself get hysterical.

"How should I know?" she added more calmly.

"Good God, he's under your bed!"

For an instant their eyes met and held, the anger rising in each of them like storm signals thrown suddenly against a threatening sky.

"I can't help that!" Terry said hotly. Her eyes blazed green venom. "I tell you I never saw the man before in my life!"

"Yes? Queer, isn't it?"

Mrs. Dixon put her hand urgently on his arm. "Don't, Jeff," she said. "There must be some mistake. This child . . . that's too dreadful!"

"I'll say it is. Hello, there's Carter."

A motorcycle streaked around the bend and across the bridge and came to a stop in a cloud of dust, blocking the middle of the road. Jeff Dixon went forward to meet the state policeman. Terry saw him nod back at her as they talked. She saw the policeman staring at her—a man of thirty-five or so with dark hair and a rugged sunburned face. They walked across the grass to the cabin. Jeff pushed open the door.

The policeman said "Jeez!" and stared back at the girl in the white high-throated polo shirt and blue skirt standing trim and erect by the table under the mimosa tree. He turned around and went in the cabin. The hand protruding stiffly from under the bed seemed to beckon like a ghastly relic. Carter reached in and lifted the sheet hanging down over the dead stary-eyed face. He let it fall quickly, straightened up, pushed back his cap and wiped his forehead with the back of his hand.

"Don't touch anything," he said. "The C.A.'s on his way. Who's the dame?"

Jeff shook his head.

"She got in after nine, alone, and slept here. Then she tried to get away first thing this morning. Left a call for five. It burns me up. Mother's had a rotten time trying to make this damn' place go, and just when things are picking up this has to happen. Why the hell couldn't she leave the boyfriend somewhere else?"

Carter nodded. He knew the Dixons, and the job Mrs. Dixon had had after her husband died to send Jeff to college.

"Who is the guy?"

"That's the crazy thing about it. I never saw him before. I mean he's not one of the bunch that stayed here last night."

Carter looked at him, puzzled. He raised the sheet again and took a closer look at the dead man.

"Sure he didn't come in with her, or the other folks?"

Jeff shook his head. Carter left the cabin and walked across the grass to where Terry Acheson was looking out towards the road.

"Look here, sister."

Terry Acheson was willful and headstrong as a wild colt. She could also be eminently levelheaded and cool when she had to be. Moreover, this was not her first encounter with a state policeman, though it was the first where anything worse than seventy miles an hour was involved. She turned calmly around, and met Carter's glance. And then a gleam of recognition came into both their faces.

"Hello!" Carter said. "It's you, is it? Thought you were going to Richmond to see your dying aunt?"

Terry flushed brick red.

"I guess it was your dying uncle, wasn't it?"

Terry's heart sank. It just went to show. You ought never tell a fib . . . not unless it was utterly shockproof.

She tried to steady the voice that seemed suddenly very shaky. "I'm sorry."

"Yeah, I'll bet. Well, come across. What's your name?"

Terry looked at him, and past him to the hard resentful eyes of Jeff Dixon. Something inside her went cold as ice. For the first time in her life she was staring into hostile unbelieving faces. She raised her hand slowly and pushed back the shiny mass of short curls from her forehead.

"I think I'd better phone my father," she said. It was a bewildered far-away little voice that she hardly recognized as hers.

"Yeah," said Carter. "I guess he's dying too. Listen, sister—no

more tricks. See? You answer questions. When there's phoning
to do, we'll do it. Get it?"

Terry saw Mrs. Dixon's troubled glance at her son. She clenched
her even white teeth firmly. This was getting impossible. After all,
she thought desperately, the whole thing was absurd—terrifyingly
absurd.

"What's your name, sister?"

Terry's eyes suddenly shot out green sparks.

"I'm not your sister, officer."

"You sure ain't."

He grinned at the others. It lined them up against her, some
way.

"And what's more, I'm not going to answer any of your absurd
questions till my father gets here."

"O.K., sister. You can just go and cool off in one of them
cabins till the C.A. gets here. How's that?"

"That's swell!" Terry said hotly.

Carter looked a little taken aback.

"Look here," he said. "All I got to do is take your license
number and phone Headquarters, and I'll have your life history
in five minutes."

"Then do it, and shut up about it!"

The hot tears stung her eyelids. She kept her lips pressed tightly
together to keep them from trembling visibly.

"O.K., sister. I'll just do that. You keep an eye on her, Jeff.
And no tricks—see?"

Terry watched him cross the yard towards the house. She felt
suddenly like a red circus balloon with all the air let out of it.
She bit her lips impatiently. She ought to have given him her
name. She was acting like an idiot, they were acting in the most
obvious and reasonable way possible. There *was* a dead man under
the bed, and she *had* slept in the cabin. They couldn't be expected
just to know offhand that she had nothing to do with it. She was
simply acting like a spoiled child.

Terry choked back a little sob and sat down abruptly. The idea
that she, Terry Acheson, could get mixed up in anything of the
sort was so preposterous that she couldn't actually grasp it. Yet
it was true. And nobody even knew she was Terry Acheson. Maybe
if she'd told them, they wouldn't have acted the way they had.

She glanced back at the house. The state policeman was doing
a double-quick back towards them.

Jeff Dixon looked at him, and back at Terry.

"I'll phone your father for you, if you'd like," he said suddenly.

"You needn't bother, thanks!" Terry snapped, and could have bitten her tongue off for doing it.

Jeff flushed.

"O.K. I was just trying to help you out."

He moved off and leaned against the big sycamore tree. Terry looked up at Carter. His face was lighted with triumph.

"No wonder you didn't want to give your name," he said. "Thought you could pull something, didn't you? Listen, sister, you can't get away with that stuff around here."

He looked over at Jeff.

"Her old man's Judge Acheson. Will the C.A. eat that up! They're friendly like two rattlesnakes. Boy, is this going to be good!"

A hot angry flush darkened Jeff Dixon's face. He had a sudden impulse to crack Carter on the jaw. After all, she was only a kid. He looked around at her. She was sitting at the table, staring straight ahead, her face white as her polo shirt. The poor little devil, Jeff thought. He took a step towards her. She looked up, startled; her wideset eyes turned a sudden hostile cat green. Jeff remembered the other girl. He shrugged and turned back to the state policeman. Carter was writing in his notebook.

At first Terry hardly noticed the chubby bright-faced little man in the rumpled white linen suit who was coming hurriedly across the lawn from the big house. Then she noticed him chiefly because his round face with its round gold-rimmed spectacles with thread wrapped around the nosepiece was so comically distressed . . . and because of the way Mrs. Dixon's anxious face smoothed out when she caught sight of him coming, stumping a little rheumatically towards them.

He patted Mrs. Dixon affectionately on the shoulder and listened silently, with pursed lips, to her account of what had happened.

"You must help her, Doctor," Mrs. Dixon entreated, with such an air of quiet confidence that for an instant Terry breathed again.

The little man smiled at Mrs. Dixon and patted her shoulder again. He looked silently at the cabins, at the big house, at the parking corral, at the trees behind the cabins. He looked searchingly and for a very long time at Terry. Then he struck the ground violently with his goldheaded cane.

"Oh, nonsense!" he said. He said it with so much conviction

that the state policeman looked up from his writing a little nettled.

"All right, Professor," he said. "Have a look for yourself. Don't go inside, though."

The professor nodded. Terry watched him stump off with his cane, open the cabin door and stand there a moment peering in. He pulled out a crumpled blue handkerchief and mopped his bald, glistening forehead. Then he came back to them hurriedly.

"But surely!" he said to Carter. Then he turned abruptly towards Terry. "This child? Why, it's . . . it's nonsense!"

Carter shrugged. The little man calmly pulled up the hickory chair by the table, propped his gold-headed cane carefully against it, sat down across from Terry and looked at her earnestly. "My dear," he said, "this is all silly. I hope you'll let me help you."

He fished in his inside coat pocket, brought out a card, rather the worse for wear, and handed it to Terry. She took it automatically. It read:

"Porteus Alexander Harp, A.M., Ph.D., D.Sc."

And, in the lower left-hand corner:

"Professor of Geology, Saginaw College, Saginaw, Mich."

Afterwards it seemed quite incredible to Terry Acheson that anyone so amazing should have walked into her life so informally and with such momentous consequences.

Dr. Harp smiled expectantly at her, peering quite shrewdly over his round spectacles, and Terry managed a smile in return.

Dr. Harp nodded very approvingly. "That's the ticket," he said. "Now, my child. Mrs. Dixon says you deny any knowledge of this . . . affair."

Terry nodded, helplessly.

Dr. Harp nodded. "I thought so," he said. "Now, in that case, my dear, and in my opinion, the thing to do is to put into action what we call the scientific method."

Dr. Harp paused, and looked at her for an instant with a sort of owlish intentness.

"I take it you really didn't stab this man . . . not even in a fit of temporary insanity, or in self-defense?"

Terry stared at him.

"I suggest that," Dr. Harp went on hastily, "because I'm told they are the best defenses a handsome young woman can offer."

"I . . ." Terry said. Her brain whirled. Then she pulled herself together with a great effort. "Listen, Dr. Harp," she said, as firmly as she could. "You don't understand. *I didn't do it. Please* believe me! *I didn't!*"

Dr. Harp nodded serenely.

"One of the features of the scientific method," he said, "is the necessity of having one's premises correct. Because if we proceed from inaccurate premises, why, then our conclusions are bound to be inaccurate. I think we may now get on?"

Terry glanced covertly at Mrs. Dixon and Jeff. Their attitude—even Jeff's—seemed to be indicating, in some odd matter-of-fact way, that everything would be all right now that Dr. Harp was there. Nevertheless Terry found herself wondering if she wouldn't prefer the commonwealth attorney after all.

Dr. Harp nodded to himself.

"Very well," he said. "Roman numeral one: You didn't kill the man in the gray suit."

He pulled a folded and worn envelope out of his waistcoat pocket and made a note.

"Roman numeral two: You did sleep in the cabin last night.—Correct?"

Terry nodded.

"Very well. Roman numeral three: You did not see a dead man in a gray suit under your bed. Correct?"

"Correct," Terry said. After all, it couldn't possibly make things worse.

"In that case, and in my opinion," said Dr. Harp, "there could have been no dead man there when you left the cabin."

He raised his hand quickly. "However. Roman numeral four: There *is* a dead man there. Capital letter A: he has been there for some time, because the blood on the floor around him is dry. Capital letter B: he has not been there for a great period of time, because he does not yet appear to be in rigor mortis. And Capital letter C: there is only one entrance through which a body can (1) enter, or (2) be introduced, into the cabin.

"Therefore—Arabic numeral 1 under Capital letter C—the body was not introduced through that entrance—namely the front and in fact only door—*after* 'X' left the cabin (that's you, my dear), for the simple reason that there were witnesses watching that entrance all the time. That's you again. Correct?"

Terry drew a deep breath.

"Yes," she said. "That's correct."

She knew it was, and yet at the same time it couldn't be.

"Then, where were we?"

Dr. Harp adjusted his spectacles and wiped the point of his fountain pen on the tuft of grayish-black hair behind his right ear. He looked down at his notes. Then he looked at Terry with a troubled frown.

"But . . ." he said, "in that case, and according to the scientific method, you must have killed the man in the gray suit."

"But I didn't!" Terry said.

"I know. And that shows us that something's wrong. But not the method. Depend on it, my dear; the scientific method can't be wrong. It follows simple logic."

He bent over his envelope and went back over the outline he had made, shaking his head, pursing and unpursing his lips very much, Terry thought, like a goldfish at the top of a bowl.

A sudden burst of speed in the road behind them made Terry turn in time to see a large car preceded by a motorcycle cross the bridge and pull up in the drive. As it stopped she recognized the commonwealth attorney in it. With him were half a dozen men. She vaguely recognized the type from having seen them around the courthouse when she drove down afternoons to get her father.

She watched steadily as the commonwealth attorney got out of the car. Mrs. Dixon and Jeff Dixon met him; and behind them was Dr. Harp, shaking hands with him too. Terry felt suddenly very small and alone. If only her father would come!

The Honorable Milton Bassford, Commonwealth Attorney for Bedford County, Virginia, strode across the grounds towards the cabin without so much as a glance her way. Mrs. Dixon smiled at her and went over to where Mrs. Baylor was sitting, like outraged patience on a monument, upright in the back of her big car. Jeff and Dr. Harp were following the commonwealth attorney. Terry shuddered. For the first time she felt a sense of grim tragedy waiting behind the gay white-painted rose-covered little façade. For the first time she found herself fighting against the vague terror seeping into her heart. She moistened her lips. They would never believe her either. It was like a sane person trying to get out of an insane hospital by protesting his sanity. Even Dr. Harp was not sure. She saw it, some way, in the shrewd lines around his eyes.

Terry opened her bag and took out her vanity. It came to her as a little shock that the face gazing back at her in the tiny square mirror was still her own, and still the same. She patted her nose with the puff and looked up quickly, hearing someone coming.

"Oh," she said. "It's you, is it?"

Jeff Dixon flushed angrily.

"Yes," he said. "It is. And how in God's name you can sit there and powder your nose, when they're up there taking pictures of that fellow, and hunting for fingerprints, I don't see."

Terry closed her vanity and put it back in her bag, swallowing down the aching anxiety that kept swelling in her throat.

"What do you expect me to do?" she inquired, with an elaborate nonchalance that anyone but Jeff Dixon would have seen through instantly. "Sit here and wring my hands? I'm not going to. If they'd let me go and phone my father. . . ."

"He's been phoned. He had to go to Knoxville. They're trying to locate him."

"Oh," said Terry. She was silent a moment. It was very dismal. "Who . . . who phoned?"

"I did, if you want to know."

"Oh! After what I said. . . ."

Terry was silent again. "Thanks . . . so much!" she said.

"You don't have to thank me. I just did it because I thought it would be less of a shock to him than if the police did it."

Jeff's voice was very cold, and Terry bit her lip. She felt the hot color rising in her cheeks.

"That's awfully big of you!" she snapped. "I suppose you told him I'd killed a man in my cabin."

"Naturally!"

Terry's eyes shot green venom. "I think you're—"

"Hush up," Jeff said quietly. "Here comes the inquisition. You keep your shirt on, or Bassford'll have you in the jug in five minutes."

He moved aside as the commonwealth attorney came up across the lawn.

"How do you do, Miss Acheson," he said. "I don't think we've ever met, but I know your father."

The Honorable Milton Bassford's hand was cold and slightly damp. Terry looked at him steadily, seeing a pair of shrewd hard eyes and a hawklike beak over a long grooved predatory upper lip. His chin was cleft too, and gave a curiously sardonic look to his thin wide mouth. His eyes flattened themselves against her face for a long appraising moment.

"Sit down," he said. "Sit down, Professor."

Dr. Harp drew his chair a little closer to Terry's. It was a simple act, but it ranged him definitely on her side, and she was grateful to him.

"Carter's phoning your father. He should have let you do it. Makes an awkward situation. We don't have situations like this often, so it's hardly surprising he didn't know what to do."

Terry flushed.

"I believe my father has been called," she said coolly.

Bassford's eyes narrowed. He looked at her again in cold appraisal.

"Who is the dead man, Miss Acheson?"

"I don't know, Mr. Bassford."

Terry drew a deep breath, clenched her two fists tightly, and tried to be as calmly composed as she could.

"All I know about it is this. I came here last night because I was later than I thought, and I didn't like driving on to Richmond after dark when the road is mostly detour. I stopped here and asked them to call me at five. I was leaving when the colored boy went back to my cabin to see if I'd left anything, and found—"

"Found you had," said Bassford drily.

Terry recovered quickly.

"Apparently. I've never seen the man before, I don't know where he came from or how he got there."

Bassford still stared coldly at her.

"I can tell you how he got there," he said. "He was stabbed in the back and shoved under the bed, quite dead, at least five hours ago. You were in there from half past nine last night till five this morning. The surgeon says he's been in there since approximately one o'clock."

He leaned back in the hickory chair and regarded her steadily.

"My advice to you, Miss Acheson, is to come forward with a straight story. It'll be easier for you—and your family—in the long run. You can't hope to hush this up. The President of the United States couldn't hush murder up. You can depend on me to do all I can to make it easy for you. I think your father will tell you I'm a square shooter. I have no interest in convictions for the sake of convictions. My record speaks for itself."

Terry felt the slight pressure of Dr. Harp's foot on her own. She glanced over at him involuntarily. His face was as sober and as shiny as a crockery owl's.

"Who is the man, Miss Acheson?"

"I don't know, Mr. Bassford. I've never seen him before."

Bassford's lips tightened.

"Listen, Miss Acheson," he drawled. "The facts are perfectly clear here, and incontrovertible. You would seem to have a mistaken idea about . . . the powers of the courts."

Terry flushed again.

"If you mean my father, Mr. Bassford, you're wrong," she said steadily. "I'm telling you the absolute truth."

Dr. Harp shook his head quickly and tapped her arm with his chubby forefinger. "No one knows more than a small fraction of *relative* truth, my dear," he said mildly.

The commonwealth attorney gave him a sidelong glance.

"If that man was in the cabin when I left it this morning, I didn't see him," Terry said. "He wasn't there last night, because . . . well, I looked under the bed before I got in it."

Dr. Harp nodded.

"I doubt if you could convince a jury otherwise," he said.

Bassford cut off a small portion of dark tobacco and introduced it surreptitiously into his mouth.

"Suppose you let me take care of that end of it, Professor," he said. He nodded to his stenographer.

"Tell us your version, Miss Acheson."

So Terry repeated the story that nobody believed: about going out to the car to get her bag, coming back, going to sleep with most of her clothes on, and waking up when her flashlight fell.

At that point she stopped suddenly.

"I turned on the light and picked it up . . . and if anybody had been under the bed, I'd have seen him."

"You certainly should have."

Bassford's voice was heavy with irony.

"But I didn't!" Terry snapped. It seemed strange to her even then that one moment she could be so completely terrified by the events closing so ruthlessly in on her, and the next so annoyed and waspish at the incredible, invincible stupidity of the people around her.

Jeff Dixon, standing fifty feet off, by the corral where the cars

were parked, suddenly kicked a small stone out of his path with
quite useless violence.

Carter looked at him and grinned suddenly.

"Pretty, isn't she?" he said.

"Is she?"

Jeff's manner clearly indicated surprise and indifference, as if
he had not noticed the fact and would not have been interested
if he had.

"I don't care if she's pretty or not. I don't like the way they're
hounding her there. After all, she's a girl, she's alone—"

"Hell, she got in it herself, didn't she?"

Carter moved closer and lowered his voice.

"Let Milt handle it," he said. "You keep your shirt on. This
is a break for him, and he's good. This is the biggest thing he's
had since the Farmer's Bank robbery in Roanoke. And did he get
them! The whole caboodle except the president."

Jeff nodded.

"You're telling me," he said bitterly. "He got everything except
the president and a hundred and ten thousand dollars of the
depositors' money—and nine thousand of it belonged to us. Anyway, what gripes me is what if that kid really didn't kill him,
after all?"

Carter stared. Then he winked broadly.

"Listen. If she didn't do it, and old Milt can prove she didn't,
that'll be the best thing he's ever pulled for himself. 'Commonwealth Attorney Proves Old Enemy's Daughter Innocent of Murder
Charge.' Boy, that's telling 'em."

Jeff looked back at the girl in the white polo shirt still at the
table with the commonwealth attorney, and shook his head. He
looked back at the car corral where two plain-clothes men were
working through the parked cars.

"The weapon?" he said.

Carter nodded. "And anything else. They didn't find anything
in his pockets but a watch and a big bulge where his wallet was.
I guess they figure it's around somewhere. Look, Bassford's giving
you the high sign."

Jeff crossed the grass to the little group under the sycamore
tree. Terry Acheson apparently did not even see him.

The commonwealth attorney indicated a chair.

"Sit down, Dixon. You've changed the name of this place since
I was here last. You called it the Haunted Bridge Camp, three
years ago."

Jeff nodded. "We changed it—for two reasons. The name scared people. They used to leave the lights burning all night. And second, you gave us so darn much publicity catching the last of that Roanoke bank gang in the end cabin there that we couldn't handle the crowds."

Bassford smiled drily.

"Sorry if that hurt you," he said. "How many people are here now?"

"Thirteen altogether. Dr. Harp stays in the house. He's practically one of the family."

The chubby little man in the crumpled linen suit blinked behind his gold spectacles.

"I come every vacation," he explained. "I . . . I study geologic formations."

He cleared his throat, glanced sideways at Jeff and reddened. Jeff grinned. His mother could hardly be regarded as a geologic formation, but for the last year or so the little professor had spent much more time holding her yarn, watering her petunias and taking her to movies in the village than he had in the limestone cavern up the hill looking at stalactites and stalagmites. And once or twice he had come on them, Dr. Harp looking wistful and a little hurt and his mother shaking her head very kindly.

"Virginia is rich in natural wonders," Bassford said gravely.

Dr. Harp nodded. "I'm preparing a paper for the National Geological Survey," he said. "I've frequently told Mrs. Dixon—"

The commonwealth attorney cut him off with a suave wave of the hand. "The dead man was not one of the thirteen?"

"No. I've got a list of the people who came in, from noon yesterday, or were here already."

Jeff handed Bassford a typed sheet.

Mr. and Mrs. Howard Baylor, Harold Baylor
NEW YORK CITY

Mr. and Mrs. Glenn Lyons
BALTIMORE, MD.

Miss Ella Green, Miss Lucy Cowie, Miss Viola Sayre
DETROIT, MICH.

Mr. and Mrs. James Perkins
SAN FRANCISCO, CAL.

"And a man and woman with a New Jersey license, who didn't give their names. And Miss Acheson."

"Who didn't give hers."

"I didn't ask for it."

"You do ordinarily ask people's names?"

"Not when they take the cabins. We do if they're in the house. I happen to know the Lyonses, by the way. They've stopped here two or three times a year for some time, on their way to Florida and back."

Bassford nodded. He jerked his head at one of his men standing by him. "Get 'em all over," he said. He settled back on the rear legs of his chair and regarded Terry through narrowed calculating lids. Terry returned the glance steadily, wondering whether her face was turning a guilty red or whether she only felt that it was.

It was a great relief when Bassford turned his head sharply towards Dr. Harp. The rotund little man was bouncing about in his chair, both hands clasped over the head of his stick, and staring down at his notes on the envelope on the table in front of him with an expression of extreme delight.

"Eureka!" Dr. Harp cried.

He picked up the envelope and waved it excitedly in the air.

Bassford lowered his chair and stared at him.

"Eureka *what?*" he demanded.

Dr. Harp looked about as if a little surprised at himself, and settled back into his chair with some dignity.

"Eureka," he said calmly, "means simply that I've found it. In other words, Mr. Bassford, the scientific method has been entirely vindicated. I was discussing it with Miss Acheson prior to your arrival. You see, the scientific method is quite infallible."

Bassford stared again, and smiled very drily.

"I suppose you mean she didn't kill the man?" he drawled.

Dr. Harp nodded serenely.

"Precisely so," he said.

Terry Acheson stared at him, gray eyes widening, lips parted, hardly daring to believe, really, that the absurd kindly little man could have figured something out that would make them all see how ridiculous it was.

She glanced anxiously back at Bassford. He was nodding an ironic thanks to Dr. Harp, with an amused contempt that was hardly concealed.

"Then perhaps you wouldn't mind explaining, Professor, how the man's body got in the cabin—if Miss Acheson did not see it there? When she slept in the cabin and has been sitting out here ever since she left it? And when you can't get a body in there any way except through the front door?"

"That," said Dr. Harp, "is elementary."

He got to his feet, patted Terry reassuringly on the shoulder and bowed to the commonwealth attorney.

"If you'll excuse me," he said, "I shall verify my conclusion by a simple observation. The application of the scientific method to the problem—assuming of course that Miss Acheson did not kill the man—shows plainly that there is only one possible way in which the body could have been introduced—under all the circumstances—into the cabin. I shall make sure that that is so."

Bassford raised his hand. Dr. Harp turned back to the table.

"Just a minute, Professor. Just as a matter of routine, you didn't happen to recognize the body yourself, did you?"

Dr. Harp put his stick under his arm and blinked a little like an owl whose sense of honor had been seriously impugned.

"Certainly not," he said. "Furthermore, I should like to give you my itinerary of yesterday afternoon and evening. I investigated the cavern at the end of the cow pasture after my siesta until five o'clock. I returned, and helped Mrs. Dixon in the flower garden until dinner. I dined, and accompanied Mrs. Dixon to prayer meeting, and returned at nine o'clock. I then went to my room and read until half past ten, when I retired. I was waked this morning by a commotion out here, and came down as soon as I could get my clothes on."

"You weren't out of your room between nine last night and six thirty this morning?"

"No, sir."

Dr. Harp bowed again. "With your permission. . . ."

"Sure, go ahead."

Mr. Bassford grinned a little, looked at Terry and shook his head. Dr. Harp stumped off across the grass. Then he stopped, turned suddenly and came back.

"Mr. Commonwealth Attorney," he said, "I wish to amend my last statement, with your permission—and your indulgence, Miss Acheson. Ah . . . as a matter of fact I *did* leave my room, at about quarter to ten."

The commonwealth attorney looked up, surprised and alert.

"I went across the hall to get a glass of water—begging your pardon, Miss Acheson—for my plates. I . . . I have, as you see, artificial teeth."

He bared his lips over a white even pair of teeth, and then beamed at Terry.

"They're very satisfactory. I thought I should tell you. As I frequently explain to my students, the scientific approach is useless unless one has all the data."

Mr. Bassford nodded soberly. "Thanks, Professor. That sure takes a load off my mind."

Dr. Harp beamed again and stumped off towards the cabins. The commonwealth attorney shook his head. "That man's cuckoo," he said pleasantly to Terry. "My Lord, he's coming back again."

Dr. Harp had paused and turned a second time and was trudging back towards them. As he came up he drew his chair over by Terry and sat down very soberly.

"It occurs to me, my dear," he said calmly, "that possibly I should be of more service to you right here. I shouldn't want them to . . . to put anything over on you, as my students say, in the absence of counsel, as it were. If that's satisfactory to Mr. Bassford."

"Sure," the commonwealth attorney drawled amiably. "But what about the scientific method?"

"That," said Dr. Harp gently, "will keep. Not being dependent upon time or personality for its effect."

Bassford grinned. Terry glanced anxiously at the little man. It was obvious that something else had occurred to him.

Mr. Bassford's eyes ran blandly around the little circle of faces in front of him.

"I'm sorry about this, folks," he said. "I want you to be on your way as soon as possible. But I've got to keep you awhile. A man was murdered here last night, in this young lady's cabin. It looks pretty bad, on the face of it, but it's an axiom of the law that a person is innocent until he's proved guilty. In Virginia that's more than an axiom—it's an actuality. Now I'm going to ask you folks to see if any of you can identify the body that's over there. I'm going to tell you that so far we have not found the weapon that killed him. My men are going through the baggage of every person here."

Mr. Howard Baylor spoke up in the murmur of protest that went around.

"You're not going to ask these ladies to identify the body?"

"I'm afraid so, Mr. Baylor."

Baylor flushed hotly. Bassford shook his head. "I'm certainly sorry about it, sir," he said suavely. "But inasmuch as this young lady is suspected of the murder I could hardly excuse any of the older women here . . . much as I should like to."

And Terry Acheson sat listening to them. Two quite inconsistent thoughts kept persistently shoving themselves up in her consciousness. The first was that it was all preposterously theatrical, utterly and completely impossible and unreal. The second was that granted somehow that it really was real, it was all so perfectly American. They were so perfectly a cross-section of all the country. Mr. Howard Baylor: prosperous, aggressive, slightly pompous, perfectly confident of himself, and not too intelligent. Mrs. Baylor: obviously pulled up by the bootstraps and a snob . . . in contrast to Mrs. Dixon, who was "reduced," but a lady to her fingertips and always would be, no matter where she was or how poor she was. Hal Baylor: groomed, glossy, bored, a little amused in a veiled faintly contemptuous way by all of them, including his parents. The young couple named Smith, the man pale and quiet and quite overborne by the buxom dark-haired deep-bosomed girl with him, wearing a shiny new wedding ring and much too much lipstick . . . and both of them obviously frightened.

The three women standing next to Mrs. Smith were certainly vacationing schoolteachers if Terry had ever seen one. Miss Cowie was plump, bright-eyed and coy, Miss Sayre was thin, and tight-lipped, with pale darting eyes that fastened accusingly on Terry now and then, apparently just as a matter of habit, and Miss Ella Green was large, slow and patient. They all wore hand-knitted sports clothes that had the curiously detached air that sports clothes have on people who obviously do not do sports.

There were two other couples, and they would be the Lyonses and the Perkinses, of Baltimore and San Francisco. The Lyonses were completely at ease and at home. Mrs. Lyons had on a sports outfit too, but it had obviously cost a great deal more than the yarn and needles that had knitted it. She was smart, professionally smart with a professionally brisk and determined air, and perfectly got up, as if she had had her cosmetics matched before she bought them and was an expert at applying them. Mrs. Lyons was very quiet, but gave the impression that she was not missing any tricks. Her husband was lean and dark, with dark hair and graying temples, a hard mouth, hard eyes and hard hands. Terry tried to decide whether it was his too fancy shoes she didn't like, or the ready easy smile. It was like a frankfurter you got at a roadside stand, she thought—shiny and succulent when you looked at it, and cold and rather unpleasant when you bit into it.

And then there were the Perkinses. Terry could see that they did not think much of Mr. Lyons either. He was a big simple man with horn-rimmed glasses and an honest face, and he stood beside the round little woman, also with horn-rimmed glasses, with a protective bulldog air . . . as, Terry thought, he had no doubt been doing for fifty years.

Twelve of them. And Terry Acheson was the thirteenth. And one of them had, somehow, in some way, got a man into her cabin and killed him there.

The commonwealth attorney was going up towards her cabin and everybody was following him. Dr. Harp touched her arm, and she went too. Except that it wasn't Terry that was going. It was somebody else in her skin, while she, the real Terry Acheson, looked on, helpless to free herself from the strange hostile net that held her fast, as in a terrible dream.

She stopped on the narrow path edged with white-washed bricks and bordered with spice pinks. Bassford was at the door of the cabin, the people were approaching the door one by one as Carter told them off.

"You stay here, my dear," Dr. Harp whispered. The next instant she saw him standing alongside the commonwealth attorney quite as if he were a special deputy, and she was by the door of the cabin next to hers, alone. It was odd, the way they all kept away from her . . . all except one of the commonwealth attorney's men who did not get more than ten feet from her at any time.

She sat down on the white doorstep of "Iowa" to wait, and looked up quickly, vaguely aware that someone was looking at her. It was Harold Baylor, and when he caught her eye he moved easily away from his mother and sat down on the step beside her.

"Neat mess," he said pleasantly. "How'd you get mixed up in it?"

"I'm not sure yet," Terry said.

"Serves us right, I guess—stopping at a dump like this. Smoke?"

He held out a thin gold case. Terry shook her head.

"Wonder how long they'll make us stick around?"

He flicked his match into the flower border.

Terry shook her head again.

"You oughtn't to be talking to me. Mr. Bassford will think we're accomplices."

Hal Baylor grinned. "That's O.K. by me, lady," he said. "Who's your friend?"

"Who?"

"The thundercloud guy."

He nodded towards Jeff Dixon.

"He's no friend of mine," Terry said hotly. "He thinks I killed that man."

Baylor yawned. "Probably did it himself."

A sharp voice rose: *"Harold!"*

In front of Terry's cabin Mrs. Baylor was staring at them.

"Guess it's my turn to take a peek," Harold said. "So long— I'll be seeing you."

He sauntered off, and Terry saw him go into the cabin, and come out. Then Dr. Harp came hurrying towards her.

"It's your turn, my dear. I've told them again I don't know who it is. It's just a formality, my dear."

Inside the cabin Bassford was sitting on a chair by the bed, his face almost even with hers as she looked in. He raised the chintz spread and the sheet without taking his eyes off hers.

Terry shook her head slowly. Then she looked again, and felt the blood drain out of her face with a sudden sickening rush.

"So you do recognize him, Miss Acheson."

Bassford's voice was as silky as the slither of a snake through dried corn.

"I . . ."

Terry tried to speak, but at first the words would not come.

"I . . . yes, I do. He was—"

There was a sudden loud shout from outside: *"Hey, Chief!"*

Terry looked behind her through the open door in time to see one of the men who had been searching the cars slam the door of her gray coupé and come running towards them, holding a small object in his hand. She stood watching him with cold fear congealing in her breast.

The man came on into the cabin.

"It's his wallet, Chief. Stuck up on the sun shield over the wheel."

He handed a black leather billfold to the commonwealth attorney.

"I'd have missed it, but the old lady keeps her pocketbook up there, is how I happened to spot it."

Bassford open the billfold, looking steadily at Terry. He took out a motor registration card of the District of Columbia issued to Ernest L. Rose, 1868 K Street N. W., a driver's license in the same name, and four fifty dollar bills. He counted the bills slowly, put them back and put the billfold in his pocket. His face was a cynical mask. Terry gazed at him with dawning horror.

"Who is this fellow, Miss Acheson?" he asked softly. His hand waved at the inert mass under the sheet.

"I . . . I don't know," Terry whispered. "I saw him yesterday . . . at a hot dog stand where I stopped. He was getting gas. I . . . I didn't recognize him before."

Bassford looked steadily at her. He was a little puzzled. It looked cut and dried. But he was not a fool. It almost looked a little too much cut and dried. "If this was my own daughter," he was thinking, "I might think there was something cockeyed." Furthermore, it wouldn't do to make a mistake. Not with Judge Acheson on his way, or even with the pompous little professor standing there in the doorway watching every move he made.

Then the commonwealth attorney shook his head impatiently.

"Find that weapon, Carter," he said through shut teeth.

He stared coldly at Terry.

"What did you kill him for, Miss Acheson? A girl in your position doesn't need two hundred dollars. What did you do it with? Where is the weapon?"

Terry shook her head dumbly.

"I . . . I didn't—"

"Did he come into your cabin?"

Dr. Harp leaned forward quickly. "That's self-defense, my dear," he whispered.

Terry shook her head.

Bassford looked at the little man with a sardonic flicker in his eyes.

"Thought you had it all figured out, Professor."

Dr. Harp hesitated.

"So I have," he said slowly. *"If* she didn't do it. It's entirely dependent on the truth of the premise. The scientific method merely explains how the body got into the cabin, granting Miss Acheson's innocence."

He turned a troubled owlish glance on Terry and back to the commonwealth attorney.

"And I must say, Mr. Bassford, that it involves a very curious business. Very curious indeed."

Bassford nodded sardonically. He turned as Carter stuck his head in the door.

"Say, Chief, the lady over there ain't going to stick around. She says they're leaving. How about it?"

"Who?"

"In the big car."

"Oh, hell, let 'em go."

"Just a moment!" said Dr. Harp earnestly. "Just a moment! *If* my conclusion is correct, they really shouldn't be allowed to go, Mr. Attorney!"

Bassford looked at him curiously. "You still think she didn't do it?"

"I still think," said Dr. Harp, "—in fact I *know*—that the presence of the body here does not necessitate that conclusion."

The commonwealth attorney wiped his forehead. He gave the impression of a strong man struggling to overcome extraordinary provocation.

"Spring it, Professor," he said softly.

Dr. Harp paused to collect his thoughts.

"It's perfectly simple, if you follow the scientific method," he said. "One of three things has *got* to be true. It's the simplest logic. One: Miss Acheson killed this man in the cabin—I hope you'll pardon me, my dear—or outside and dragged him in. It's immaterial. Or Two: he isn't dead in the cabin. Of course that really won't wash. Or Three: He *is* dead in the cabin—*but Miss Acheson did not stay in the cabin.*"

"Which she did," said Bassford blandly.

"No!" said Dr. Harp. "That's just the point. *She didn't!"*

The commonwealth attorney made a sound between a groan and a snarl.

"Hell, Carter, Tell 'em they can go."

"No, no!" Dr. Harp cried. "I'm not joking! I really mean it!"

"Good God, man, she says herself she stayed in the cabin!"

Dr. Harp nodded very placidly.

"I know," he said. "I know. But *she must be wrong.* She *must,* logically!"

He hurried on as Bassford—and Terry—stared at him.

"What I mean is this—that if she stayed there, she *must* have killed him. But if she didn't kill him, then she couldn't *possibly* have stayed there. Don't you see?"

The commonwealth attorney nodded with heavy irony.

"I see," he said. "The answer is that she killed him."

Dr. Harp shook his head patiently.

"You don't see," he said calmly. "But I'll show you."

He turned to Terry, standing there white and bewildered and feeling very much like a bone between two dogs.

"My dear," he said gently. "You left your cabin last night, after you'd got settled in it."

Terry nodded. It seemed to her that if in all her life she had utterly not understood anything, this was the time.

"Precisely," said Dr. Harp. "That is essential to the theory."

Terry saw the exchange of glances between Bassford and the state policeman in the door. If Dr. Harp saw it he gave no sign.

"And now, my dear. Please attend most carefully, because it's very important to you. Did you, or did you not, leave your door open when you went out?"

"I always close doors—quietly," Terry said. "It's the only thing they ever really taught me."

"Precisely," Dr. Harp said. "However, I trust they taught you one other thing. Now, my dear: when you came back, *you came to the wrong cabin.*"

He looked expectantly at Terry, and as she nodded dumbly he looked triumphantly at the commonwealth attorney and the state policeman, and rubbed his hands with the greatest satisfaction.

"Yes," Terry said. "I did. But I . . . I don't know how you know it?"

Bassford stared at the little man. The sardonic manner had disappeared.

"I don't know what difference it makes, Professor," he drawled, "but just how *did* you know it?"

Dr. Harp chuckled.

"I didn't *know* it," he said. "I assumed it. It was demanded by the scientific method—and the scientific method is infallible. So it *had* to be. Now then, my dear. To get on. We will show you what difference it makes. My dear, just tell the commonwealth attorney how you knew you were in the wrong cabin."

It was Terry's turn to stare. "Because it was empty," she said.

Dr. Harp nodded. "The things you had left in it—I mean if it had been your cabin—were not there."

"Yes."

"Precisely. And then you went outside. . . ."

He nodded encouragingly to Terry to go on, and looked to see if the commonwealth attorney was following.

"I went outside and saw I'd got into 'New York' instead of 'Florida.' They all looked exactly alike."

"Precisely. And therefore, my dear, you immediately went on to the right, to your own cabin. To 'Florida.' "

Terry nodded.

"Where the body of Ernest L. Rose was found the next morning," said Mr. Bassford silkily.

Dr. Harp chuckled again.

"That," he said, "if you will pardon a vulgar expression, is what *you* think. Now, my dear. The probability is that I can tell you one more thing you did last night, *if* you were taught in your youth to keep your eyes open—as well as to close doors quietly."

He paused a moment, and continued very deliberately, with the air of a conjurer drawing a giraffe out of an opera hat, and with his round face fairly beaming with personal satisfaction at their obvious bewilderment.

"When you got to your cabin, you found of course that your things were there. *But they were not the way you had left them!*"

He looked expectantly at Terry again, and as the expression on her face, stary-eyed and incredulous, showed him he was right, he chuckled a third time.

"Why . . . why, yes!" Terry said. "My bag was at the head of the bed instead of the foot, and my hat was all smoothed out, and I—"

"And you don't smooth hats out," said Dr. Harp, nodding. "Well, it's all very clear, then. Come outside, Mr. Commonwealth Attorney. I shall demonstrate."

He led the way out into the neatly bordered path, followed by Terry and Mr. Bassford, turned about and looked up at the three rose-covered cabins in front of him: "New York" to the left, "Florida," and "Iowa" to the right.

"Now then," said Dr. Harp. He stumped briskly to the cabin to the right, reached up on tiptoe and with a pair of chubby hands unhooked the little green sign on which "Iowa" was printed in neat white letters. He then stumped briskly down the path to

the left, unhooked the "New York" sign and put "Iowa" there;
came back directly in front of them, substituted "New York" for
the "Florida" on the cabin in which the dead man's body lay,
and put the "Florida" sign on the cabin to the right. He then
came beaming back, turned and surveyed the three cabins. They
were now "Iowa," "New York," and "Florida."

"You see," he said, "it was all quite simple . . . to the scientific
mind and once the scientific method was applied—and realizing
that this child couldn't possibly have killed anybody. It was purely
a matter of—ah—ratiocination. When Miss Acheson admitted
returning to the wrong cabin, it was elementary. And this is what
happened. She did not return to the wrong cabin. Her sense of
direction was perfectly adequate. But in her absence the name of
the cabin had been changed—as I have indicated—and her things
removed. The cabins are practically identical, inside as well as
out, so the subterfuge went unnoticed."

Terry and the commonwealth attorney spoke at the same moment.

"But why—"

"For the simple and nefarious purpose," Dr. Harp interrupted,
"of making it appear that you, my dear, had murdered the man
ostensibly under your bed. The late Mr. Rose. And that it was
definitely plotted to that end is of course further shown by the
fact that the man's wallet was in your car."

He rubbed his hands and looked around, his face shining with
triumph.

"But why *me!*" said Terry.

Dr. Harp blinked and turned a troubled face to her.

"Why?" he repeated. "My dear, I shouldn't know *why*. That is
the commonwealth attorney's field, not mine. The scientific method
can only prove or disprove premises. It can't, so to speak, invent
them."

He turned to Bassford. The commonwealth attorney was staring
at the changed signs over the cabin doors, and nodding his head
slowly.

"I get you, Professor," he said. "Your idea is that Miss Acheson
after going to what she thought was the wrong cabin, then went
on to the right and spent the night in the cabin labeled 'Florida,'
which really was 'Iowa.' So she never was in the cabin with the
body."

Dr. Harp looked a little surprised, as if so obvious a thing really ought not to have to be put into words.

"Oh, certainly," he said. "The signs, of course, were changed back after she'd got in. She might have noticed, as she came out in the morning. However, as you see, she didn't."

Bassford strode abruptly to the cabin to the right that was labeled "Florida" now that Dr. Harp had changed the signs, and opened the door. Terry and Dr. Harp, following, peered in under his arms. And Terry gave a little gasp.

"What is it, my dear?" said Dr. Harp.

"That's my hair brush on the dresser!" Terry said quickly. "I always leave something!"

The commonwealth attorney strode into the cabin and picked it up. On the silver back was engraved in neat letters "Terry Mason Acheson." He stared down at it. Hanging from its stiff white bristles were a dozen short curly golden hairs.

Bassford nodded curtly. "I guess the scientific method wins, Professor," he said. He went to the door. "Carter! Tell the Baylors they'll stay here till I tell 'em to go—and they'll *like* it!"

As far as Terry could see the only people who still regarded her with suspicion were the three schoolteachers, and she put that down to the professional point of view that persecutors always have . . . Terry never having been near the top of a class in her life. Mrs. Baylor in particular was most cordial. Her air towards Terry was very much like that of one hothouse artichoke to another that had suddenly found themselves in a basket of turnips.

"My dear, my son thinks you're perfectly charming," she said. "You must have your lunch with us. What *is* your father, the judge, going to say to you, you impulsive child!"

But there was nothing of the snob about Terry Acheson.

"He'll probably say I was lucky to pick out a family like the Dixons to start a criminal career with," she said coolly. "I think Mrs. Dixon's swell."

Mr. Bassford also was most cordial, in his way, and when Dr. Harp busied himself in a continued application of the scientific method, Terry, in view ostensibly of the very important part she had so far played, was privileged to sit in on the professor's logical statement of the issues yet to be developed, as well as in the public meeting that followed.

With the definite abandonment of the easy and obvious solution that Terry had murdered the dead man whose body was in the cabin that she should have slept in, and the continued failure to find the weapon with which the murder was committed, Dr. Harp's investigation was, as he complained, painfully shy of premises. Shorn of his Roman numerals and Arabic numeral subdivisions, the items that he jotted down on the back of a second envelope even more creased and soiled than the first were as follows:

"Why was the young lady"—Terry saw his pen pause perceptibly before he brought himself to write it—" 'framed'?" It was also carefully enclosed in quotation marks.

"Why did the Baylors stop here?"

"Why are the Smiths so upset?"

"Is there any connection between the dead man and Mr. and Mrs. Glenn Lyons of Baltimore, who stop here two or three days on their way to and from Florida every year . . . and have already been here twice this year?"

And when the rather unexpected information came out in the general meeting later, presided over by the commonwealth attorney, that the little round woman in horn-rimmed spectacles, Mrs. Perkins, whose husband was a retired mail carrier with a pension of $102 a month and two married sons, had seen the dead man at the dog races in Hialeah distributing betting forecasts—Mr. Perkins having decided that it was better to admit they had seen the man before than to conceal information from the law—and further that she had frequently seen Harold Baylor there, Terry watched Dr. Harp's pen scribble:

"Why does Baylor's mother look frightened?"

"Why does Baylor Senior ditto?"

But when the greatest surprise of the morning came Dr. Harp wrote nothing at all. He simply sat looking very troubled and perplexed, as if the scientific method were no longer of any use.

The first definite information connecting the dead man with the Shady Bridge Tourist Camp—outside of the mere fact that his body had been found in it—came when Mrs. Dixon whispered to her son and to the state policeman. Then she caught the commonwealth attorney's eye.

"Was the man's name Rose? Ernest Rose?"

"Yes, ma'am." Bassford shot her a surprised and questioning glance.

"Then he is probably the man who came here in December and wanted to see the place. I didn't connect him, before. He said he was thinking of buying a place here, and I told him to come back . . . sometime."

She turned to Jeff, who was looking at her strangely.

"I didn't tell you, Jeff. You see, I thought I might sell the place, so you could get into some kind of business, and not be tied down to . . . to this place."

She looked away quickly. Jeff's face flushed darkly.

"Did you see him again, ma'am?" Bassford said quickly.

Mrs. Dixon shook her head.

"But I got a letter from him last week from Palm Beach, some big hotel there, saying he would be up some time the last of the month, and he would be in a position to talk business."

"You did?" said Bassford. "Where's the letter? Have you still got it?"

Mrs. Dixon nodded. "Run and get it, dear. It's in my secretary, in the upper left-hand drawer."

Terry watched the swift clean stride that took Jeff Dixon out of sight behind the crêpe myrtle hedge, and looked back, catching Harold Baylor's eye. He seemed rather more amused than alarmed at Mrs. Perkins's having seen him at the dog track, but Terry had thought there was a first little flicker of alarm in his eyes.

"I tried to sell the place after my husband died," Mrs. Dixon said. "It was so much to keep up and pay taxes on. No one wanted it then. And here within a week two people turn up, both wanting to 'take it off my hands.' "

She smiled.

"Just when I'd got it breaking even, at least."

Dr. Harp was looking at her very intently.

"This man Rose, and who else?" Bassford asked.

"A Mr. Henson from Richmond. He's coming down again tomorrow."

Bassford nodded to his stenographer, who made a note.

"How much were they offering?"

"Mr. Rose said five thousand dollars. Mr. Henson four thousand five hundred dollars cash. There's over two hundred acres left, but the land isn't good and the house needs a lot done to it to make it modern."

Jeff Dixon came quickly through the crêpe myrtle hedge as Dr. Harp was muttering "Modern! Nonsense!"

"You must have put it somewhere else, Mother," he said. "It's not in your desk."

Mrs. Dixon was puzzled. "Are you sure?"

"I've been all through it."

Mrs. Dixon got up.

"I'm sure it's there," she said. But when she came back again she was more puzzled than before.

"I know I put it there, because I was going to show it to Mr. Henson when he came tomorrow. I put it away very carefully."

Terry looked, puzzled, from one face to another. Most faces were as puzzled as her own, but the commonwealth attorney's was serious and intent. So was Dr. Harp's.

Bassford looked slowly around the circle, his mouth tightening and sardonic. "All right," he said. "Which one of you got away with that letter? Hand it over!"

No one moved. He turned to Mrs. Dixon. "When did you put it there?"

"Last week. But . . . I saw it there yesterday afternoon."

"How many of these people were in that room since then?"

Mrs. Dixon hesitated.

"There's been a murder here, ma'am," Bassford said curtly. "Nobody who'd kill that fellow would stop at stealing a letter."

"The desk is in the back parlor," Mrs. Dixon said hesitantly. "My son and I have been in there, and the house servants, Julius and the cook, Charity. Then in the afternoon Mr. and Mrs. Lyons came, and the Baylors."

She made a simple gesture of apology as she mentioned the names, as if wanting them to know that she would rather not have had to do so.

"In fact everybody here was in the house except Miss Acheson. You see, we serve dinner in the dining room, and breakfast, unless people want it outside. Most people don't. But of course my desk isn't in the dining room, and Mr. and Mrs. Perkins and Mr. and Mrs. Smith I'm quite sure didn't go in the parlors at all."

"The rest of 'em did?"

"Well, yes. You see many people have the idea that if you take in tourists it's quite all right for them to inspect everything. Of course we're pleased when they like our things."

"Did you see any of 'em near the desk?"

Mrs. Dixon flushed a little.

"Mrs. Baylor and the three ladies."

She smiled at the schoolteachers.

"Mrs. Baylor was kind enough to offer me fifty dollars for the desk . . . which I've refused seven hundred for."

Mrs. Dixon smiled again faintly. "It's hard to get people to understand that you don't want to sell your old things. You did open the drawer, didn't you, Mrs. Baylor?"

Mrs. Baylor was annoyed.

"Just to see if there was a secret panel," she said tartly.

"Of course. I quite understood that."

Mr. Bassford did not.

"Did you see the letter, Mrs. Baylor?" he asked blandly.

"There were papers in there. I didn't look at them."

Bassford nodded. "And how about you, ladies?"

The Misses Green, Cowie and Sayre denied indignantly doing more than poking about, also after secret drawers.

"As a matter of fact," Mr. Lyons said, "Mrs. Dixon mentioned to me that she was thinking about selling the place."

Terry turned to look at him, lean and dark under his heavy coat of Florida tan. He wore a fraternal emblem on his watch chain and a ring with a smooth red stone in it on his little finger. Mrs. Lyons by his side was curiously like him, dark-eyed and dark-haired, well got up, with a hail-fellow air that ought to have made her the life of an ordinary gathering. All she had said so far that Terry had heard was "It certainly looks funny to me, Al."

Dr. Harp was scribbling again on his envelope. Terry read:

"Why in Heaven's name should Mr. Rose wish to buy this place?"

"Why should Mr. Henson?"

"Why should anyone steal Mr. Rose's letter?"

"Mr. and Mrs. Lyons have been stopping three and four times a year for the past three years," Mrs. Dixon was saying. "We think of them as old friends. I hadn't mentioned selling the place to anybody but Dr. Harp"—Mrs. Dixon colored faintly—"and when Mr. Lyons said something about coming down for a week in July I told him I was thinking of selling."

Terry looked around again. It was all too puzzling for her, but she could see from the faces of the commonwealth attorney and Dr. Harp that it meant something.

Bassford nodded slowly.

"I'll have to ask you people to stay on the place," he said shortly. "Carter has orders not to let any car out of here till I say so. You just make yourselves at home."

He turned to Mrs. Dixon.

"I'll have a look inside, ma'am."

Terry looked at Jeff Dixon. He was watching the rest of them move off. Just as his eyes met hers and brightened, Harold Baylor touched her elbow.

"How about having a look at the natural wonders the professor tells about, lady?"

He pointed up to the sloping pasture behind the field of young corn.

"We've got lots of time on our hands."

Terry looked back at Jeff. But he turned and was following his mother and the commonwealth attorney towards the house.

Why she should allow a churlish, ill-mannered, not particularly good-looking young man who ran a tourist camp to get on her nerves, Terry Acheson could not tell. She smiled brightly at Hal Baylor.

"Elegant! When do we start?"

It was after lunch when they started. It was too late to go before, in the first place, and in the second Dr. Harp, commandeered by Mrs. Baylor, had agreed to give, and did give, an impromptu lecture on the stalactites and stalagmites that had been forming through thousands of years in the small cavern above the cow pasture.

"I shall be very happy to conduct a party up there later," Dr. Harp said, "because, in my opinion, while there is nothing in the Dixon cavern to compare with the great caverns across the ridge, it is most interesting geologically. You see the Dixons' place here was regarded for many years as haunted, because of the tiny wraith that floated over the hill above the pasture. Actually the wraith was caused by the cold air coming from the sink hole. You see, air in the caverns remains at about fifty-five degrees Fahrenheit winter and summer, condensing in the warm air when it comes out, in some atmospheres. That one of those so-called apparitions appeared and was seen at the time of the death of Mr. Dixon's father gave rise to the haunted legend. As a matter of fact few colored persons would think of venturing near the cavern, and no native whites are interested except children. That is why I find this spot of unusual interest."

Terry and Harold Baylor wandered away and watched the tadpoles swimming in the clear little pool under the bridge. Mrs. Baylor watched them out of the corner of her eye, a bright interested smile fixed on Dr. Harp's beaming face. As for Dr. Harp, when he talked about stalactites and stalagmites he forgot about everything except the cavern above the cow pasture.

At lunch Terry and Hal Baylor ate at a small table under the mimosa tree. That is how they saw Milton Bassford leave. It is also one reason why they did not see that the newspaper-wrapped parcel under his arm contained a bayonet that Jeff Dixon's grand-father had carried at First and Second Manassas and a long thin-bladed knife that had shaved slices of old country ham in the Dixon kitchen for two generations. Neither did they know that a crumpled half-charred letterhead of the Miami Biltmore had been retrieved from under the white-washed garbage box at the gate of the car corral, and was carefully tucked away in the commonwealth attorney's coat pocket.

Terry watched him go with a sharp pang of apprehension.

"What's the matter?"

Hal Baylor lighted a cigarette and watched her through the smoke.

Terry shrugged. "I don't know. I'm just afraid, somehow. It seems so ghastly, knowing there's somebody here that could do anything like that. It seemed a little . . . safer, when he was here."

Baylor grinned. "You didn't think so when he was busy pinning it on you."

Terry's slim body quivered involuntarily. All that seemed pretty remote and unreal, even though it had been not more than four hours before.

"Who do you think did it?" she whispered.

Hal Baylor shrugged his immaculately tailored white linen shoulders and yawned.

"Your guess is as good as mine. And listen, lady—I don't care. We could stay here the rest of the year and it'd be O.K. with me . . . as long as you were here."

"Thanks," Terry said coolly. "It doesn't make any difference to you that somebody here's going to be hanged in a month or so?"

"Oh, rot. That bird won't find anything he doesn't know already.

He'll end by pinning it on the nigger. That's what they do down here."

The words were hardly out of Baylor's mouth when he felt a stinging slap on the side of his face. He stared stupidly at the girl standing up beside him, her green eyes blazing, her cheeks crimson fire.

"Don't you dare say such a thing!" Terry cried hotly.

"Why, you damned little spitfire!"

Hal Baylor sprang to his feet, his cheek smarting red, his dark eyes smoldering. For an instant they glared at each other across the small littered table. Then he laughed suddenly.

"Sorry—I apologize! I forgot you're a native too. Damn it, I forgot your father's a judge. Don't go! You and I are the only civilized people around here. Sit down, please!"

"Then no more cracks about natives," said Terry dangerously, the quick green anger slowly dying in the cool gray of her eyes.

"I promise. Hope to die and all the rest of it."

The smile in Baylor's eyes was all surface, but Terry was too angry to see that.

"Your mother's probably looking for you anyway," she added curtly.

Baylor grinned. "That makes us even. Sit down—or let's hunt the wraith and the natural wonders before the rest of them."

Terry hesitated. Baylor tucked her arm in his. "Atta girl!" he said. She started to take it away when she saw Jeff Dixon coming from the house along the pink bordered path, and saw that he was watching them.

When they got beyond the row of cabins she drew her arm away. They walked up the narrow cart trail winding in and out between the gray limestone boulders beyond the corn patch. A hundred feet above them was the cow pasture fence and a grove of hickory trees. Standing nonchalantly in front of the gate, his elbows on the top rail and one foot resting on the lowest, was Jeff Dixon. Terry looked at him as they came up, and glanced quickly back at the house. He must have run through the field to get there so quickly.

Baylor stared offensively. "Well, well," he said. "Fancy meeting the farmer boy here, of all places."

The quick anger flared in Terry's eyes. Jeff smiled cheerfully. Furthermore he made no move to get out of their way. Terry's anger shifted instantly. On the whole, she decided, young Mr.

Dixon was being by far the more offensive of the two.

"Will you open the gate, or will you get away so we can do it?" she demanded icily.

Jeff Dixon grinned. He brought his right hand down and extracted a cigarette from his shirt pocket. He put the cigarette between his lips.

"What's the idea, farmer boy?"

Baylor took a step forward and flicked his own cigarette into the plowed field.

Jeff held a lighter to his cigarette and snapped it shut.

"The idea, friends," he said calmly, "is that the little lady with the yellow locks is staying with the folks."

"Yes? You've got your wires crossed. Miss Acheson is going for a walk with me—through that gate."

Jeff shook his head.

"Oh, no. She's going back to the house and stay there—until her father comes to take care of her."

Terry's eyes went a bright green. "Don't be a *complete* fool!" she snapped.

Jeff looked at her.

"I'd rather be a fool than have another corpse to plow under," he said calmly. "You see, young lady—or you would see if you had anything under the yellow topknot—there's been a murder in these parts. If you're the chap that did it, then our city friend isn't safe with you. And if you didn't do it, why then, my child, you aren't safe with . . . anybody."

"Are you implying that I. . . ."

Jeff cut Baylor short with a bland wave of the hand.

"I imply nothing. I'm telling you, in words of one syllable, city guy—if you don't already know it—that somebody around here tried his darndest to pin a swell crime right on Miss Acheson's left cheek . . . and he must have had a reason for doing it. Now it may have been you—I don't know. But I know that whoever it was isn't going to get another crack at the little lady. Not while she's on our hands. It gives the joint a bad name. So trot back, children."

He regarded them with maddening complacency, and Terry's eyes snapped.

Hal Baylor took a step forward. He was an inch or so shorter than Jeff, but heavily built under the crisp whiteness of his linens. Jeff brought his foot off the lower rail to the ground.

"Look here, Dixon," Baylor said curtly. "Miss Acheson and I are going up the hill. And we're going through that gate. Now!"

Jeff shook his head.

"You can go through the gate, Baylor, or you can go under it, or any darn way you want to. Miss Acheson is going back to the house—if the farmer boy has to carry her."

He grinned again.

Terry could not remember having been so angry for at least a month. She walked up to him, her voice as silky as a water moccasin in the lily pads, her eyes sharp emerald needles.

"Will you get out of the way and mind your own business?"

"That's exactly what I'm doing, little one."

He looked down at her with infuriating calm.

"You see, it doesn't make any difference to me whether anything happens to you. I'm not sure it wouldn't be darn good for you if they'd hang you to teach you a lesson. But as long as you're here, you're doing as you're told. Now scoot back to the house before I pack you back."

"Don't you dare speak to me that way!" Terry cried. She stamped her foot. "We're going up there and you can't stop us!"

He grinned again.

"I'll give a swell imitation."

Terry stood there helplessly. Hal Baylor stepped forward.

"One side, farmer," he said easily. One hand shoved Jeff Dixon off, the other reached for the wooden bolt on the gate.

Then Terry caught her breath. Jeff took one step towards him. Baylor swung round and brought up his hands. Jeff's left shoulder swung in, and in front of it a trained flashing left, straight and hard and on the mark. Hal Baylor's head jerked violently back; he staggered away from the gate, lost his balance and sat down abruptly.

"Oh!" Terry said.

She stood breathless, looking down at him. Baylor got up slowly, breathing heavily, killing rage in his dark eyes. He lost his head, rushing wildly, arms swinging, at the cool lean figure by the gate. Terry saw the flashing left again, almost quicker than her eye could follow, and heard the sharp "Smack!" as Baylor slumped into the fence and to the ground. He lay quite still.

Terry took a quick step towards him, then whirled around.

"You *bully!*" she cried.

Then a strong pair of arms went round her waist and lifted her off the ground, and before she quite realized what was happening,

Terry Acheson, kicking and hitting out, was being carried like a sack of meal from the miller's down the crooked trail. She could hear her own breath coming in hard violent sobs as she fought. Then suddenly he put her down, the hot angry futile tears stinging her cheeks. He grinned cheerfully at her and picked up her hat.

"There now. Run along and comb your hair."

"I won't!" Terry cried passionately.

"All right. I'll carry you the rest of the way then. You see, I'm not going to have you hurt."

Jeff's voice was suddenly deeply earnest.

"I don't think I'd like to have you hurt. And there's a murderer around here . . . beautiful!"

He took a step towards her. But Terry dodged and ran like a gold-tipped streak of lightning down the trail and past the row of white cabins.

Jeff stood for an instant looking after her. Then he turned and looked up the trail to the fence. Hal Baylor was getting unsteadily to his feet. Jeff watched him for a moment and went on down the trail.

The Commonwealth Attorney for Bedford County patted his high moist forehead and ran two fingers around the inside of his wilted collar. It was hot and damp and long after his supper hour, and the information neatly tabulated in the sheaf of papers in front of him seemed to him to make the wood of mystery that surrounded the Shady Bridge Tourist Camp shadier than ever.

He went through the sheaf a final time to ponder once more over the information that his office had been able so far to collect about the thirteen people concerned in the murder of the man in "Florida."

Mr. Bassford now knew the reason—or one reason—for the Baylors staying at a tourist camp instead of a Richmond hotel. It was not because of Mrs. Baylor's interest in antiques.

He knew that the murdered man Rose had served two short sentences for high-class confidence games, one in Baltimore and one in Chicago, and that between sentences he had lived alternately at the best hotels in Atlantic City, Palm Beach and Miami and in the dives that cluster around racing centers.

His car, a green 1929 sedan, had been found half a mile below the Shady Bridge Tourist Camp a little off the road. The dead man's baggage consisted of half a dozen new shirts, a tan worsted summer suit, and a pack of stationery from seven of the leading hotels on the eastern seaboard.

The proprietor of the service station and hot dog stand at which Terry Acheson had seen the man had given the information that his wallet had contained, the day of his death, a thick bundle of hundred dollar notes clipped together with an ordinary wire clip. He had shown them accidentally when paying for ten gallons of gas and a quart of oil, and when the station proprietor had asked if he was a mint had explained that he had made a killing at the Hialeah races.

Whoever had killed him, Mr. Bassford reflected, had got away with so much money, apparently, that he could well afford to leave the four fifty dollar bills as a blind.

He shook his head and picked up the sheet marked "Howard Baylor." He wondered if Mrs. Baylor knew that her husband was completely and entirely washed up, and that even the sixteen-cylinder car was liable to be taken up some minutes after it came out of the Holland Tunnel. Would Baylor murder a man for . . .? Bassford shook his head again. For how much? that was the question.

The Perkinses there seemed to be no question about. He had carried mail for thirty years in San Francisco, had a small but adequate pension, what with slight expenses, and with Mrs. Perkins was spending his retirement in traveling.

The Lyonses. Lived in the Bostwick House, Cathedral Street, Baltimore. The landlady knew nothing about them except that Mr. Lyons was in business somewhere and his wife was a buyer in a cloak and suit house on Charles Street. His business took him around a good deal, and Mrs. Lyons went with him twice a year between seasons.

Young Baylor. Mr. Bassford hesitated. If he played the races he might be desperate.

The Smiths. Mr. Bassford smiled a little. Their name was Mr. and Mrs. Burton Forrest. They had been married in Elkton two days before and were terrified that their parents would find it out. Mrs. Forrest had run away from Miss Belt's school in Arden, Pa.

And finally the commonwealth attorney picked up a telegram that was dated from Saginaw, Michigan, and signed "Registrar, Saginaw College." It read: "Glad to know whereabouts of Professor Porteus A. Harp. Please notify am forwarding his last two salary checks today."

Mr. Bassford shook his head wearily and put a paper weight on his sheaf of reports. He was wondering what the scientific method would be able to make out of them.

Terry said good night to Dr. Harp and bent forward, giving Mrs. Dixon a sudden impulsive kiss.

"You've been *awfully* sweet to me!" she said, her eyes suspiciously bright. She turned and ran upstairs quickly.

"She's got a blind spot in her left eye," she heard Jeff say cheerfully, and realized how silly it was for her to try to ignore anybody who was so objectionable as to refuse to be ignored.

All things being equal, she would have stayed in the cabin rather than accept anything from him or his family. But things weren't equal, and she had been more relieved than she cared to admit when both Dr. Harp and Mrs. Dixon had flatly refused to hear of her staying out in the cabin.

"Not that you wouldn't be perfectly safe, my dear," Dr. Harp had said. "With one of Bassford's men in the next cabin snoring hard enough to wake the dead. But nevertheless, and in my opinion, you'd better be inside. Don't you agree, ma'am?"

Mrs. Dixon did agree, and Terry had pretended she didn't even see Jeff, much less hear him say that personally he thought she ought to be chained to the bedpost.

She closed the door behind her. The sight of the high four-poster with the sheet turned down and the old-fashioned counterpane neatly folded on the old chest at the foot made her realize that she was so tired she could drop. She glanced at herself in the long gilt mirror over the carved mantel and pushed back her hair. Last night and this morning with its awful burden seemed a thousand years away. She was glad her father hadn't got back and that they hadn't been able yet to get in touch with him, now that everything was over. She took off her clothes, put on her pajamas, crawled into bed, and was asleep almost before she turned off the light.

Suddenly she sat bolt upright in the bed, wide awake, staring in the pitch dark, her heart pounding in her throat, her hands shaking with terror. She tried to listen, to focus her senses on the thing that had waked her, but the silence and her own beating heart deafened her ears. She tried to control herself, knowing with some instinct as old as the race that no noise had waked her, that it was something deeper than noise, some primitive urge of self-preservation. Her heart was quiet now, and her hands still, every taut nerve obedient. Outside the leaves murmured rustling in the cool air. The light over the car corral trickled dimly through the trees. Terry closed her eyes, listening, shutting out everything, trying to pick out of the silence of the night sounds that were too soft to hear.

After a long time she drew her feet up and let them slip over the side of the high bed, seeking the familiar ridges of the rag carpet. She went over in her mind the layout of the house. Jeff's room was behind hers, Mrs. Dixon's and Dr. Harp's across the wide hall, divided by the narrow stairs leading to the third floor where Julius Jones slept. She put on her dressing gown, crept noiselessly across the floor to her bag and felt among the soft folds of her clothes for her flashlight. She put it in her pocket and listened. There was still no sound.

She crept back to the bed and slipped across to the window, knelt down there, peering out into the yard. Two cabins only were dimly visible, "Arizona" on the end, where the Lyonses were, and "Idaho" with the Smiths. Her eyes, gradually accustoming themselves to the night, made out a shadow moving, and she waited, her cold hands steadying her body in the angle of the window frame. The shadow moved, so slowly that Terry thought it was a trick of the dim night. Then she knew it wasn't.

It was the door of Al Lyon's cabin opening; and after a moment someone slipped out, so quickly that Terry lost him almost before she was sure who it was. She waited again, looking past the cabins, until she saw the dark shadow, almost invisible, slipping stealthily up the hill towards the hickory grove.

Terry stared a moment, wondering where he was going. It was the way she and Hal Baylor had gone that afternoon. Then she crept across the floor, felt for her sneakers and put them on. She tiptoed towards the door, put her hand on the brass knob and turned it quietly, tugging gently. The door did not move. Terry swallowed with vexation and tugged again, harder. Then she let go the knob. Someone had locked her in. For an instant she stood there seething with anger, trying to think whether in all her life she had ever hated anyone as much as she hated Jeff Dixon that moment. She couldn't think of a soul.

"He's got no right to treat me like this!" she whispered.

Something inside her, protesting violently, choked the faint small voice of reason that tried to tell her she was a fool to leave that room.

"I'll just show him!" Terry said stubbornly.

She crept back across the room to the door at right angles to the side window. It would lead into Jeff's room. Terry knew that, because most old Virginia houses are built that way. She held up her flash. Her heart gave a little leap of joy when she saw the white painted bolt. If only there wasn't another on the other side. She put the flash in her pocket again and pulled gently at the bolt. It slipped back easily. Terry smiled to herself in the dark. She'd just show him. She put her hand on the brass knob and turned it, hearing the dull click of the old lock bolts slipping out of place.

The black margin grew as the white door opened. Terry's heart beat quickly as she listened. If she could get through without waking him up! She took a step forward, then another, caught her foot sharply against something, and drew back, waiting there in the dark, suddenly angrier than ever at him for making her be such an idiot.

Then she realized that he hadn't. As she listened there was no sound, and she realized that there was no one in that room—no one but herself. She put her hand in her pocket, took out the flash and waited, listening. Then the yellow ball of light fell squarely on the big bed faintly outlined against the pale light of the window overlooking the kitchen. Terry did not need to hold it there. She knew already from the utter silence of the room that it was empty, and one instant was enough to show her that it had not been slept in.

Terry stood there in the dark, feeling suddenly strange and a little frightened. Somewhere in the silent dark recesses of the house a grandfather clock struck two. A smaller clock chimed, the two thin pelts of sound beating sharply in the sonorous wake of the big clock.

Terry Acheson did not move, for suddenly, with a clarity that made the events of the previous day so plain that she couldn't imagine why she hadn't seen them before, the whole thing dawned on her. She caught her breath sharply, and the green eyes snapped in the dark of the silent room and she could feel her cheeks flushing with hot anger. It was a plant . . . and who was it that could have done it most easily? It was Jeff Dixon who knew she was in "Florida." He would know the simple trick about changing the name boards. He was the last person up. He'd know she was going to be the first out in the morning. He even had an obvious motive for killing the man whose body had been left in her cabin. He didn't want his mother to sell the place. He had found out about it by taking the letter out of the secretary in the back parlor. And why didn't he want to sell it?

Terry thought suddenly of the caverns. She didn't understand, but no doubt that was it. That was why. And it was also why he wouldn't let her and Hal Baylor go up there that afternoon, and why he was no doubt out there himself now.

The shadowy figure of Al Lyons slipping along the path beyond the cabins came back to her. Terry hesitated, and made up her mind.

Later, when she tried to explain it to herself, she couldn't remember what it really was that had made her slip back to her room, roll up the legs of her pajamas, put on a skirt and a sweater and creep back through Jeff's door into the hall and on down the steps . . . instead of doing the ordinarily intelligent thing of either going back to bed and minding her own business, or going across the hall and waking up the man who by the simple use of the scientific method had kept her out of the hands of the grand jury.

But she did. The garden door was unlocked. She closed it softly behind her and crept along the garden path until she came to the shadowy stand of young corn beyond the kitchen orchard. She ran along quickly, shaking the loose soil out of her sneakers like a puppy shaking the water off his feet. There was no other sound that she could hear, and she herself ran lightly. At the end of the long dark row she stopped and peered out. The slope of the hill rose in front of her beyond the cow pasture fence, bare except for the few piles of boulders and the clump of hickory trees along past the gate.

Terry stepped out a little, looking up the slope and beyond it to the dark blue banner of the sky swarming with golden fireflies. She was not afraid, because the only things that really frightened her were cramped cooped-up places full of shadows that she couldn't see. That murder, as grim and cold-blooded as ever stalked the plains, was stalking the Dixon pasture now seemed too strange and remote an idea to disturb her. After all she knew Jeff Dixon—even if she didn't like him—and she knew Al Lyons, even if she had just met him. He knew a lot about horses and dogs. So did Terry. It couldn't be possible that. . . .

Terry shook her head. Nevertheless when she left the shadow
of the trees she went quietly, staying behind the fence, making
the way towards the hickory grove, not a little like a kitten stalking
a deadly spider. The gate was open, propped open a foot or so
with a boulder. Terry slipped through it and stopped suddenly.
Someone was running down the hill.

For one galvanized instant Terry stood rooted to the spot. Then
with an instinct as old as the hill above her she sprang into the
hickory grove and crouched down in the shadows. She knew
without thinking about it that fear was in those flying steps and
that danger was closer to her than it had ever been before. She
held her breath. The steps came nearer. She could hear the labored
breathing of a man as he came out of the shadow of the grove,
nearer and nearer. Terry's hands gripping the tree before her were
numb. Her eyes, glued to the gate, dilated with sudden terror. It
was not Al Lyons there, nor Jeff Dixon; it was someone shorter,
heavy-set. She rose noiselessly to her feet as he went down the
path, going slowly now, transformed instantly from a man fleeing
in terror to one creeping stealthily into hiding.

Terry gripped the tree trunk as a terrible thought came to her.
"Jeff!" she breathed.

In an instant she was out of the shadow of the grove, flying
like the wind up the crooked trail, her heart sick with dread for
the man she hated worse than anyone she had ever known. Her
senses were sharpened with fear not so much because of the look
that she had sensed on Hal Baylor's face as he came dashing
down the trail as the sudden crafty stealth that changed him once
he was safely through the gate, and sent him suddenly creeping
catlike along the corn back to the cabin at the end of the row.
There was something in it so guilty and cunning that it made her
heart sick with fear.

She came up the path towards the clump of scrub oak beyond
a narrow circle of heaped-up rock. It was halfway up the slope,
not a hundred yards from the grove of hickories. Terry peered
ahead of her, afraid for some reason she could not express to
light her flash. She gripped it in her hand and ran on to the pile
of rocks. Then she stopped.

"*Jeff!*" she cried.

Ahead of her, sprawled on his face on the ground, his body
strangely and grotesquely huddled, he lay, quite motionless.

Terry sprang forward, knelt down, pulled the body over, and

recoiled with a sharp horrified cry, staring down in the dark at her hands, sick with loathing. They were wet and warm with something that she knew must be blood. Slowly she wiped them off on the grass beside her, fumbling with nerveless fingers for her flash. She pressed the switch and stared at the body in front of her. It was not Jeff. It was Al Lyons. His eyes were open, staring back at her, but the stare was glazed and expressionless.

Terry backed away. Lyons's body fell back, face down in the soil.

Terry did not hear anyone come up behind her. She was still alone in the night with this thing, until she felt a hand on her shoulder. She looked up slowly. Jeff was looking down at her, incredibly unbelieving.

Terry stared dumbly at him.

"I was afraid it was you!" she whispered.

"Me?"

She nodded, unconscious of the horrified question in the face he bent to hers as he lifted her to her feet. She stood looking down at the dead man. Then doubt and terror seeped gradually into her own face. She turned back to him.

"*Jeff!* You didn't . . . not *you!*"

"*Me?*"

He held her round firm chin up towards him, gazing down into her eyes.

"Didn't *you?*"

Terry shrank back. "Oh, *no!* I *found* him, like this . . . I came out because . . . because you locked me in!"

For a moment—it seemed years to Terry—Jeff Dixon stood there silent, looking down the hill with grim abstracted eyes. Then he turned back to her.

"Look, Terry."

His voice was hard, but there was something in it that Terry had not heard there before.

"I want you to tell me something . . . just because I've got to know it. It won't make any difference, Terry. I'll do anything you want me to. But I've got to know. Did you . . . Oh, hell, I know you didn't. You couldn't!"

Terry shook her head and stretched her hand out timidly until her fingertips brushed his cheek.

"Jeff! *We* didn't do this! It was Harold Baylor—I saw him running down the hill."

She said it in a strange hushed little voice. Jeff looked at her for a moment. "I saw him," he said. Then he shook his head. His hand moved to Terry's and took the round black cylinder gently out of it. She let him have it, and watched him turn the yellow beam slowly over the bloody wound under Al Lyons's shoulder blade.

"Stabbed from behind," he said. He swung the ball of light past the body to where Terry had wiped her hands on the grass, and beyond that to the pile of broken rocks above them. He held it there a moment, and Terry suddenly knew where they were.

"Is that the sink hole?" she whispered.

Jeff nodded. The white circle of the flash in his hand held steadily on one spot, and Terry felt his body tense sharply. She followed as he strode across the inert heap towards the rocks, and looked down where the beam was focused on a single dark red splotch glistening on the smooth gray surface of the stone.

"It's blood!" she whispered.

He nodded again. Before she knew what he was doing he stepped over the low barrier down onto the first step of the sink hole. The cold air came up around them like an icy blanket. Jeff turned back to her.

"Go down to the house," he said curtly. "You'll be all right there. You go back to your room and go to bed."

She drew back involuntarily, bewildered and suddenly angry. He went on down into the cavern. She could see the beam of light faintly for an instant, then it had disappeared.

Terry stood there an instant, stunned, helpless and furious. Then she looked back at the dead man. Something glinted under his shoulder. She went back to him, bent down and picked it up. It was his flashlight. Terry wondered suddenly if Al Lyons had planned to go down into the cavern too.

In another instant she had stepped over the stone barrier and was shivering as she slipped down the narrow mouth of the cavern through the tiny corridor. Her flash revealed a small low room with short rudimentary stalactites hanging from the grayish-white ceiling, and stalagmites no bigger than goblin garden stools on the floor. Terry peered around. It was not the first cavern she had been in; she had been in most of the celebrated ones in the state.

But this was small and unknown and unlighted, and it was a different matter.

She turned off her lamp and tried to see Jeff's light through the narrow openings that must lead on into the heart of the hill. Then she lighted it again. There were two openings, one to the left and one directly ahead. She took the one ahead and crept forward, scraping her head against the wet nubbly ceiling as she went, treading carefully to keep from slipping on the steep incline as the opening lengthened into a narrow corridor before it came out into a large room. For a moment Terry forgot the crimson splotch on the stone outside, and stood waving her light up at the lovely white cascade of limestone veils that hung down from the ceiling of the room, her light playing over it like a golden ball on the snow.

Suddenly she felt a sharp pang of loneliness.

"Jeff!" she called softly.

There was no sound but the echo of her own voice, no light but the yellow shaft she turned anxiously now from one dark glistening pillar to another.

Then in the overwhelming silence she heard a footstep, and turned around, not knowing which way to go to find it. There was no one in the room.

"Jeff!" she called. A far hollow note came back: *"Jeff!"*

Terry let the flashlight out, and blinked, listening, in the solid unrelieved black that surrounded her. There was no sound.

She took a deep breath and shook her head.

"Do you realize, my pet, that you've already probably lost yourself in a labyrinth, and that Mr. Lyons's flashlight will probably run out before you get out?" she said softly. "You'll also probably fall in a hole and break your leg, or hit a stalactite and knock yourself out. I should go back immediately if I were you."

She breathed deeply again and decided for once to take her own advice.

She flashed the light on and went back up the narrow incline. Or it looked like the narrow incline; but in a dozen steps she was going down instead of up, and at the next step her feet suddenly shot out from under her and she was crashing down a steep slope. She clutched the light frantically. Then she stopped as suddenly as she had begun, on the hard wet floor of a lower cave.

Terry closed her eyes, her heart a cold lump in her throat, her body bruised and aching. She pressed the switch on the light. The room, as far as she could see, was precisely like the one above, and she turned the light off. It was already, or she had imagined it, fainter than at first. Terry shook her head. "Thank God I didn't lose it, anyway," she whispered. Her voice was sharp and sibilant in the dark.

She lay there a moment, listening, wondering what to do next, and held her breath, sharply. Someone was there, in the room, near her. She could hear a breath as sharply sibilant as her own. It kept on when hers was still . . . at slow uneven intervals, like someone old or out of breath. Terry suddenly pressed the button on the flash. The light leaped out as she swept it round, bringing into being a room wide and deep and heavily pillared, filled with broken lengths of stone and stalagmites. She raised the light above her. From the ceiling the stone growths hung down like misshapen dwarfed forms, unfriendly, terrifying. Her light moved round. She could no longer hear the heavy breathing.

Then the beam of light jerked and faltered, and Terry Acheson gave a low gasp of horror. Then she steadied the beam, exerting all the power of her soul. Hanging from one of the misshapen stone growths, not ten feet from her, was the body of a man. It was fully clothed, and above the collar a sightless, oddly blackened face stared down at her. It was old and very lifeless.

"Jeff! Jeff!"

Terry shrieked, covering her face with her hands.

The empty echo came back: *"Jeff! Jeff!"*

The sharp sibilant breath behind her loosened again, and a man moved, watching the terror-frozen girl with shrewd cold eyes.

Terry's breath came in hard dry sobs. "Jeff!" she whispered, so pitifully low that there was no echo.

It seemed an hour to Terry before she was able to pull herself together and get to her knees. Her ankle ached poisonously. She kept the flashlight off, because she feared far worse than the dark and the foul thing hanging there, dangling, dripping, blackened, that the battery would run out and leave her still more helpless than she already was.

Then again came the breathing. In the horror of that grotesquely dreadful sight above her she had forgotten that. But nothing living could be so terrible as the dead.

She gripped the light and moistened her lips.

"Who . . . who is it?" she said. But no sound came from her

throat. She tried to swallow, to speak again. "Who is it?" Her voice came. There was no answer.

Terry moved a little again, put her hand up over her head and got slowly to her feet. Then there was more than the breathing, there was the sound of someone treading behind her; and she whirled about, shooting the fading beam of yellow light out into the horrible darkness. Her arm came hard into a slender hanging shaft, there was a sharp crack and the crash of falling stone. Terry swept the beam desperately from right to left as the crash echoed back from the walls, so loud and reverberating that Jeff Dixon in the chambers above stopped, trying to fix the source of it. But no one was in sight of the boring shaft of light.

Then Terry turned the beam down to the ground at her feet to make certain that she did not go down another slide, and suddenly held it there motionless. A little mound of rock had fallen apart at the impact of the stone she had knocked off the ceiling, and lying there in the middle of it she saw a sodden bulging leather bag. She hesitated a moment and bent forward to pick it up. Just as she did so Mr. Al Lyons's flashlight burned silently and irrevocably out; and as she stood there in the pitch black, heart pounding like mad, a voice just behind her in the dark spoke softly.

"How unfortunate, my dear, after I so carefully locked you in!"

For a lightning instant Terry Acheson's heart rose in a great burst of relief . . . and as suddenly it turned as cold as if dead icy fingers had closed over it. The kindly familiar voice was still gentle, but under it was a steely serpent smoothness as cold and inhuman as the pillars of stone that peopled the unendurable darkness of the cavern. She stood motionless. Death must be like this . . . or was it all a ghastly nightmare, and the darkness around her that made shafts of red light shoot through her aching eyeballs just something she had dreamed?

"And fancy your finding—so accidentally—what I've been hunting for . . . let me see—for three years now. Dear, dear. I'm afraid it shows that while the scientific method will eventually triumph, accident often permits us a short cut."

Terry pushed the damp curls off her burning forehead with slow-motion fingers of ice.

"Dr. . . . Dr. Harp?"

It couldn't be! Oh, it couldn't be! But his voice went on.

"I notice, my dear, that you saw the other cave dweller."

A broad white beam of light shot directly on the shrunken gibbeted figure, pendant motionless from the cavern ceiling. Terry shuddered violently and tried to speak. The question that she could not have asked was answered before her mouth was opened.

"No, no. For that I am not responsible. I assure you, my dear. I simply guessed what had happened when he was never found."

"Who is it?"

Terry's voice was quiet; something that had no relation to her tight frozen throat, as if it was just a thought that took shape in the air.

"Who?" Dr. Harp repeated gently. "Why, who indeed but Mr.— Dear, dear, I've forgotten his name.—Gage. Mr. Gage, my dear. He was president of the Farmer's Bank in Roanoke. And there, my dear"—the white ball of light surrounded the sodden leather bag in its nest of shattered limestone—"is undoubtedly one hundred and ten thousand dollars. In cash, my dear. There is also a ticket to the Argentine Republic."

Dr. Harp's quiet chuckle struck into Terry's groping brain like an icicle.

"You see the advantages of the scientific method, my child. The papers were full of it. The robbery of the bank, the disappearance of the president, the apprehending of the teller at the Haunted Bridge Tourist Camp, the energetic efforts of the splendid commonwealth attorney. But no money—no president—trail cold. Now my profession, my dear, has led me through this country many times, and I postulated the simple premise that if the bank president, who undoubtedly had the money, were not above ground, then he must be below. And in a country full of caverns, why not? And obviously not a public cavern—therefore a private. What could be simpler?"

"You . . . you found him?"

"I found him, my dear. I found him my second visit. Let me see. The robbery was in November. I came here on Christmas vacation, and again in Easter, and I found him Easter Day. No one but myself ever came here . . . and I found him. As you see, he had hanged himself by his belt. Because he was a lost man, my dear. In his lefthand coat pocket he has a Richmond newspaper, with his picture, a reproduction of his fingerprints, an account of the teller's confession, and even an account of the ticket to the Argentine taken under an assumed name. I'm afraid he naturally saw it was all quite hopeless . . . and so, like Judas, he went and hanged himself. And there he is . . . and there he will be, forever and forever."

The great white beam played again on the motionless black figure; and as Dr. Harp went on, Terry Acheson could sense that he was shaking his head regretfully.

"What a stalactite he will make in a thousand years, my dear! 'The Hanging Bank President'!"

Dr. Harp made a strange little clucking sound with his tongue against his teeth.

"But I'm really distressed about you, my dear. You see . . . I have no compunction about taking this money. Teaching is a very unsatisfactory profession financially, and robbery is equally so morally. So I have concluded that in a combination of the two the moral disadvantage of robbery will be offset by the moral prestige of teaching, while financially the disadvantage of teaching will be compensated for by the advantages of robbery. I don't know if you follow me, my dear. But that's the value of logic. Women and laymen are silenced by it. It sounds so well."

Terry Acheson sat down on a rock by the leather bag. Her knees seemed to have disappeared. But her brain had stopped whirling, and she was thinking, desperately and clearly. If anything would help, it was to keep him talking.

"Mr. Lyons?" she asked calmly.

"Oh, Lyons," said Dr. Harp. "Mr. Lyons, my dear, in a way had precisely the same idea in mind. So did Mr. Rose, who I believe must have had some connection with the bank gang— because Mr. Rose was quite incapable of doing even the rudimentary thinking of Mr. Bassford. Mr. Lyons is employed by a bonding company that had to pay out a good deal of money. He's been coming here quite as long as I have, my dear. But it was quite accidental—which my coming was not—and Mr. Lyons furthermore made the mistake—until just this evening—of making perfunctory investigations, and those above ground. He did offer me a fee—a mere bag of shells, as my students say—if I came on anything of interest in my researches. Dear, dear, what nitwits men of action think pedagogues are! It is true he did become suspicious at the end."

Dr. Harp chuckled again, and Terry took a long sickening breath. The man was mad.

For the second time Dr. Harp answered an unspoken thought.

"No, no," he said patiently. "I'm very sane, my dear. The lives of men like Rose and Lyons mean nothing to me. You wouldn't hesitate to kill a spider. But to the scientific mind most spiders are more admirable than some men. I don't insist on that as a philosophy, however. No doubt it's merely my own rationalization of the unfortunate necessity of getting them out of the way."

Dr. Harp was silent a moment. Somewhere water dripped, softly and monotonously as it had dripped two hundred thousand years to build up the dark stone forest in which they stood.

Terry Acheson's heart suddenly leaped and beat furiously, for somewhere in the black recesses of the room there was a tiny sound, the sound of a soft padded footfall. She breathed deeply and as quietly as she could, and gripped the stone on which she sat to keep her hands from shaking so that Dr. Harp would know.

"The regrettable thing, my dear, and the only one is . . . well, frankly, you. I really don't want to harm you. It's curiously but definitely true that no teacher can harm his charges and remain honorable in his own sight, and after all I have taught you something—I trust—about the scientific method, and it is my own sight that I must walk in all my days. You are possibly my only blunder in all this matter. If the scientific method took cognizance of fate, I could easily regard you as fate here."

Terry breathed slowly in the overpowering blackness. Her ears, keyed to their keenest pitch, could hear the almost silent steps, and they were coming nearer, infinitely slow and cautious. And then a great chill swept down her spine as she realized that Dr. Harp could not hear them.

He went slowly on.

"You see, both Lyons and Rose sought my professional help and Rose, in the vernacular, was attempting to double-cross me. He wrote to me the same time he wrote to Mrs. Dixon—a very charming lady—and I agreed to meet him. By a curious chance, I set the place of our meeting in the cabin called 'Florida,' at two A.M. that night. The cabins of course were never more than a third full, if that. Why Jeff had to put you in 'Florida' when 'Iowa,' 'New York,' 'Maine,' and 'New Jersey' were all vacant is something the scientific method cannot answer.

"However, it was too late to change my plans. When I saw you leave your cabin the light on your hair made it look white. I think very quickly, my dear, as you may have noticed, and I saw my chance. I changed your bags and the signs. I really had no intention of killing Mr. Rose. In fact I had no means of killing

him, if it had not been for a queer accidental happening which
I trust I shall not have to explain to you. I thought that Mr.
Rose—a very stupid man, my dear—could be turned aside. But
he knew too much, and he was suspicious. He informed me, very
foolishly, that he was prepared to buy the whole place, just on a
gamble, and turn everybody out—including, of course, myself. He
showed me twelve thousand dollars that he had in cash. I knew
of course that Mrs. Dixon would sell for much less. I had only
two courses of action—or give up the prospect of a hundred and
ten thousand dollars. And while one of them would have kept
Rose out, and worked out very well for the Dixons, it would have
worked out equally badly for me."

Terry could sense Dr. Harp shaking his head in the silent room.

"The alternative was to rid myself of Rose, and I chose it. I
then 'planted' him, as they say, on the white-haired lady, of course
changing the signs back later on, putting the billfold in your car,
and so on. I figured idly that you might be up and out of the
way before they found him. Or not; it was immaterial. That was
your problem. I figured that it could easily have been baffling to
the surely very low intellects of the local authorities. But then I
saw you in the morning. You were a mere child, and furthermore
your father was a prominent figure. It was quite impossible, both
from the idealistic and the practical side, to have you accused.
So, as you know, I threw my reasoning—and my prior knowledge—on your side. I thought of implicating the Baylors—most
objectionable people—and certainly should have been able to do
it, but things moved too quickly. That was the point, of course,
of taking Mr. Rose's letter from the secretary. However, I had
also learned that such a course could be definitely a boomerang,
as indeed it turned out in your case. So I simply let things work
themselves out. And I dare say they will."

There was no sound in the darkness pressing in on them.

"How?" said Terry.

Dr. Harp did not answer for a moment.

Then he said, "I don't suppose you could see your way clear
to going back to earth . . . we should become a Proserpine and
Pluto in a sense . . . and saying nothing about all this? Could
you, my dear?"

Terry's heart gave a wild lunge. If she promised, she might be
safe. But she hesitated . . . too long.

"No, I see you couldn't," said Dr. Harp. "I didn't think you could. So, you see there are only two courses for me . . . both of them unpalatable. I must either kill you, or leave you here— I notice your light has gone out, and you would be surprised at how involved this cavern is—to die in the dark. Dear, dear. I do wish you'd stayed in your room! I locked you up so carefully . . . assuming that you'd have more modesty than to go through Jeff's room at night."

The name beat through Terry's brain . . . and with it the quick thought that of course Jeff didn't even know that she was in the cavern. He'd think that she had gone back, as he had told her to.

"I'm afraid I've been pretty . . . obstinate," she said.

It was so terrible . . . but still so preposterous, standing there in the dark cavern, the blackness relieved fitfully as the little man switched his light off and on.

"You've made it very difficult," Dr. Harp said earnestly.

Somewhere in the tomblike silence of the caverns the water dripped slowly on, drip, drip, drip. Century after century. The eternal monotony of the drip, drip, drip. It sounded like Poe . . . dismal, unending. It must have been the drip, drip, drip that made the man hanging there, rigid, blackened, not twenty feet from her head, finally lose his nerve. And suddenly all the warm young blood in her veins welled up in a passionate protest. She didn't want to die. Not alone in this inky blackness . . . with that awful thing hanging there. *"No! No!"* her heart cried.

Terry sprang to her feet.

"Oh, *no!*" she sobbed. *"Jeff! Jeff!"*

The beam of Dr. Harp's light fell full and dazzling in her face, and she could hear the little man take a step towards her.

Then, as Terry shrank back into the stone behind her, a second beam shone for an instant in the great room, not ten feet from them, and there was a rush of catlike feet as Jeff Dixon sprang barefooted across the slippery ground between him and Dr. Harp. Terry screamed. Dr. Harp swung around. His gold-headed stick swept into the air too late as Jeff's hands descended on his wrists. The stick and the flashlight dropped from his hands. A broad white beam shot across the floor of the cavern, and Terry, scrambling forward, picked up the light and turned the beam full on the two.

Dr. Harp stood quite still, his breath coming in sharp gusts.

"Ah, well," he said calmly. "The scientific method is useless here."

"Quite," said Jeff.

He brought the little man's wrists together and held them with one hand while he ran the other over his pockets.

"I am not armed," Dr. Harp said.

Then Jeff reached down to Terry and pulled her to her feet.

"All right?" he said.

And Terry said, "Oh, yes!" and held very firmly to his arm.

Together they stared at the chubby little man, and Jeff looked curiously down at the sodden leather bag.

He looked back at Dr. Harp and shook his head.

"You forgot I spent my childhood exploring these caves," he said.

Dr. Harp nodded calmly.

"Do you think I might have my stick, my dear? My bad knee, you know."

He held out his hand, and Terry placed the cane in it, never taking her eyes, still wide and dazed, off his round little face. For an instant Dr. Harp stood, both hands on the gold head of the stick, the under hand fumbling a little. Then suddenly without warning he raised the gold cap to his lips.

Jeff sprang forward.

Dr. Harp shuddered a little. "Too late, my boy," he said coolly. "You see, even in the scientific method one must be prepared for errors, and accept the consequences. Death isn't necessarily the most terrible."

He moved a step, still holding firmly to his stick. His breath came quickly. Fine beads of perspiration stole out on his forehead like myriads of tiny specks bright in the beam of white light.

Dr. Harp swayed a little as they stared helplessly at him.

"Just one thing, Jeff—for you and your mother—to help you both. Don't sell the cave! Mr. Henson's coming tomorrow—today now, I fancy. He consulted me—he's attorney for Pearly Caverns across the ridge. Your next rooms here happen to be some thirty-five feet from them in a direct line."

Perspiration bathed his forehead; the veins at his temples stood out in purple ridges.

"They're worth a hundred thousand to them, Jeff! They're little gems, your rooms. Don't sell! Lease them on a royalty basis. . .

say ten cents a visitor. They . . . . they had a hundred thousand last year. But don't sell!"

His voice grated, harsh and fitful. The chubby body wavered, the breath came in sharp spasms.

"Don't sell!" Dr. Harp gasped again.

He clutched his cane. One trembling hand moved down the shank. He spoke again with a last desperate effort.

"The weapon, Jeff! I must leave it all . . . tidy. The scientific method. . . ."

Dr. Harp's breath rattled horribly in his throat as he reeled forward, tottered, and lurched suddenly to the ground. As he went down the stick sprang from his hands and rolled across the wet stones with a sharp metallic clang. For an instant Jeff and Terry stood staring down. Out of the innocent shank protruded a thin murderous knife, the bright blade red with blood. Dr. Harp's fingers twitched sharply once and were still . . . forever.

The light in Terry's hand wavered tremulously and steadied again as Jeff's arm closed protectingly around her.

LESLIE CHARTERIS
The Saint in Palm Springs

1

"Look," said Freddie Pellman belligerently. "Your name *is* Simon Templar, isn't it?"

"I think so," Simon told him.

"You *are* the feller they call the Saint?"

"So I'm told."

"The Robin Hood of modern crime?"

Simon was tolerant.

"That's a rather fancy way of putting it."

"Okay then." Pellman lurched slightly on his bar stool, and took hold of his highball glass more firmly for support. "You're the man I want. I've got a job for you."

The Saint sighed.

"Thanks. But I wasn't looking for a job. I came to Palm Springs to have fun."

"You'll have plenty of fun. But you've got to take this job."

"I don't want a job," said the Saint. "What is it?"

"I need a bodyguard," said Pellman.

He had a loud harsh voice that made Simon think of a rusty frog. Undoubtedly it derived some of this attractive quality from his consumption of alcohol, which was considerable. Simon didn't need to have seen him drinking to know this. The blemishes of long indulgence had worked deeply into the mottled puffiness of his complexion, the pinkish smeariness of his eyes, and the sagging lines under them. It was even more noticeable because he was not much over thirty, and could once have been quite good-looking in a very conventional way. But things like that frequently happen to spoiled young men whose only material accomplishment

119

in life has been the by no means negligible one of arranging to be born into a family with more millions than most people hope to see thousands.

Simon Templar knew about him, of course—as did practically every member of the newspaper-reading public of the United States, not to mention a number of other countries. In a very different way, Freddie Pellman was just as notorious a public figure as the Saint. He had probably financed the swallowing of more champagne than any other individual in the twentieth century. He had certainly been thrown out of more night clubs, and paid more bills for damage to more hotels, than any other exponent of the art of uproar. And the number of complaisant show girls and models who were indebted to him for such souvenirs of a lovely friendship as mink coats, diamond bracelets, Packards, and other similar trinkets would have made the late King Solomon feel relatively sex-starved.

He traveled with a permanent entourage of three incredibly beautiful young ladies—one blonde, one brunette, and one redhead. That is, the assortment of colorings was permanent. The personnel itself changed at various intervals, as one faithful collaborator after another would retire to a well-earned rest, to be replaced by another of even more dazzling perfections; but the vacancy was always filled by another candidate of similar complexion, so that the harmonious balance of varieties was retained, and any type of pulchritude could always be found at a glance. Freddie blandly referred to them as his secretaries; and there is no doubt that they had given him great assistance with his life work, which had left a memorable trail of scandal in every playground and every capital city in Europe and the Americas.

This was the man who said he wanted a bodyguard; and the Saint looked at him with cynical speculation.

"What's the matter?" he asked coolly. "Is somebody's husband gunning for you?"

"No, I never mess about with married women—they're too much grief." Pellman was delightfully insensitive and uninhibited. "This is serious. Look."

He dragged a crumpled sheet of paper out of his pocket and unfolded it clumsily. Simon took it and looked it over.

It was a piece of plain paper on which a cutting had been pasted. The cutting was from *Life,* and from the heading it appeared to have formed part of a layout reviewing the curtain calls in the careers of certain famous public enemies. This particular picture showed a crumpled figure stretched out on a sidewalk with two policemen standing over it in attitudes faintly reminiscent of big-game hunters posing with their kill, surrounded by the usual crowd of gaping blankfaced spectators. The caption said:

> *A village policeman's gun wrote finis to the career of "Smoke Johnny" Implicato, three times kidnaper and killer, after Freddie Pellman, millionaire playboy, recognized him in a Palm Springs restaurant last Christmas Day and held him in conversation until police arrived.*

Underneath it was penciled in crude capitals:

DID YOU EVER WONDER HOW JOHNNY FELT? WELL YOU'LL SOON FIND OUT. YOU GOT IT COMING MISTER.

A FRIEND OF JOHNNY.

Simon felt the paper, turned it over, and handed it back. "A bit corny," he observed, "but it must be a thrill for you. How did you get it?"

"It was pushed under the front door during the night. I've rented a house here, and that's where it was. Under the front door. The Filipino boy found it in the morning. The door was locked, of course, but the note had been pushed under."

When Freddie Pellman thought that anything he had to say was important, which was often, he was never satisfied to say it once. He said it several times over, trying it out in different phrasings, apparently in the belief that his audience was either deaf or imbecile but might accidentally grasp the point if it were presented often enough from a sufficient variety of angles.

"Have you talked to the police about it?" Simon asked.

"What, in a town like this? I'd just as soon tell the Boy Scouts. In a town like this, the police wouldn't know what to do with a murderer if he walked into the station and gave them a signed confession."

"They got Johnny," Simon pointed out.

"Listen, do you know who got Johnny? I got Johnny. Who recognized him? I did. I'd been reading one of those true detective magazines in a barber shop, and there was a story about him in it. In one of those true detective magazines. I recognized him from the picture. Did you read what it said in that clipping?"

"Yes," said the Saint; but Freddie was not so easily headed off. He took the paper out of his pocket again.

"You see what it says? *'A village policeman's gun wrote finis to the career. . . .'*"

He read the entire caption aloud, following the lines with his forefinger, with the most careful enunciation and dramatic emphasis, to make sure that the Saint had not been baffled by any of the longer words.

"All right," said the Saint patiently. "So you spotted him and put the finger on him. And now one of his pals is sore about it."

"And that's why I need a bodyguard."

"I can tell you a good agency in Los Angeles. You can call them up, and they'll have a first-class, guaranteed, bonded bodyguard here in three hours, armed to the teeth."

"But I don't want an ordinary agency bodyguard. I want the very best man there is. I want the Saint."

"Thanks," said the Saint. "But I don't want to guard a body."

"Look," said Pellman aggressively, "will you name your own salary? Anything you like. Just name it."

Simon looked around the bar. It was starting to fill up for the cocktail session with the strange assortment of types and costumes which give Palm Springs crowds an unearthly variety that no other resort in America can approach. Everything was represented— cowboys, dudes, tourists, trippers, traveling salesmen, local businessmen, winter residents, Hollywood; men and women of all shapes and sizes and ages, in levis, shorts, business suits, slack suits, sun suits, play suits, Magnin models, riding breeches, tennis outfits, swim suits, and practically nothing. This was vacation and flippancy and fun and irresponsibility for a while; and it was what the Saint had promised himself.

"If I took a job like that," he said, "it'd cost you a thousand dollars a day."

Freddie Pellman blinked at him for a moment with the intense concentration of the alcoholic.

Then he pulled a thick roll of green paper out of his pocket. He fumbled through it, and selected a piece, and pushed it into the Saint's hand. The Saint's blue eyes rested on it with a premonition of doom. Included in its decorative art work was a figure "1" followed by three zeros. Simon counted them.

"That's for today," said Freddie. "You're hired. Let's have a drink."

The Saint sighed.

"I think I will," he said.

2

ONE REASON why there were no gray hairs on the Saint's dark head was that he never wasted any energy on vain regrets. He even had a humorous fatalism about his errors. He had stuck his neck out, and the consequences were strictly at his invitation. He felt that way about his new employment. He had been very sweetly nailed with his own smartness, and the only thing to do was to take it with a grin and see if it might be fun. And it might. After all, murder and mayhem had been mentioned; and to Simon Templar any adventure was always worth at least a glance. It might not be so dull. . . .

"You'll have to move into the house, of course," Pellman said, and they drove to the Mirador Hotel to redeem the Saint's modest luggage, which had already run up a bill of some twenty dollars for the few hours it had occupied a room.

Pellman's house was a new edifice perched on the sheer hills that form the western wall of the town. Palm Springs itself lies on the flat floor of the valley that eases imperceptibly down to the sub-sea level of the Salton Sea; but on the western side it nestles tightly against the sharp surges of broken granite that soar up with precipitous swiftness to the eternal snows of San Jacinto. The private road to it curled precariously up the rugged edges of brown leaping cliffs, and from the jealously stolen lawn in front of the building you could look down and see Palm Springs spread out beneath you like a map, and beyond it the floor of the desert mottled gray-green with greasewood and weeds and cactus and smoke tree, spreading through infinite clear distances across to the last spurs of the San Bernardino mountains and widening southwards towards the broad baking spreads that had once been the bed of a forgotten sea whose tide levels were still graven on the parched rocks that bordered the plain.

The house itself looked more like an artist's conception of an oasis hideaway than any artist would have believed. It was a sprawling bungalow in the California Spanish style that meandered lazily among pools and patios as a man might have dreamed it in an idle hour—a thing of white stucco walls and bright red tile roofs, of deep cool verandas and inconsequential arches, of sheltering palm trees and crazy flagstones, of gay beds of petunias and ramparts of oleanders and white columns dripping with the richness of bougainvillea. It was a place where an illusion had been so skillfully created that with hardly any imagination at all you could feel the gracious tempo of a century that would never come again; where you might see courtly hacendados bowing over slim white hands with the suppleness of velvet and steel, and hear the tinkle of fountains and the shuffle of soft-footed servants, and smell the flowers in the raven hair of laughing señoritas; where at the turn of any corner you might even find a nymph—

Yes, you might always find a nymph, Simon agreed, as they turned a corner by the swimming pool and there was a sudden squeal and he had a lightning glimpse of long golden limbs uncurling and leaping up, and rounded breasts vanishing almost instantaneously through the door of the bath house, so swiftly and fleetingly that he could easily have been convinced that he had dreamed it.

"That's Esther," Freddie explained casually. "She likes taking her clothes off."

Simon remembered the much-publicized peculiarities of the Pellman ménage, and took an even more philosophical attitude towards his new job.

"One of your secretaries?" he murmured.

"That's right," Freddie said blandly. "Come in and meet the others."

The others were in the living room, if such a baronial chamber could be correctly designated by such an ordinary name. From the inside, it looked like a Hollywood studio designer's idea of something between a Cordoban mosque and the main hall of a medieval castle. It had a tiled floor and a domed gold mosaic ceiling, with leopard and tiger skin rugs, Monterey furniture, and fake suits of armor in between.

"This is Miss Starr," Freddie introduced. "Call her Ginny. Mr. Templar."

Ginny had red hair like hot dark gold, and a creamy skin with freckles. You could study all of it except about two square feet which were accidentally concealed by a green lastex swim suit that clung to her soft ripe figure—where it wasn't artistically cut away for better exposures—like emerald paint. She sat at a table by herself, playing solitaire. She looked up and gave the Saint a long disturbing smile, and said: "Hi."

"And this is Lissa O'Neill," Freddie said.

Lissa was the blonde. Her hair was the color of young Indiana corn, and her eyes were as blue as the sky, and there were dew-dipped roses in her cheeks that might easily have grown beside the Shannon. She lay stretched out on a couch with a book propped up on her flat stomach, and she wore an expensively simple white play suit against which her slim legs looked warmly gilded.

Simon glanced at the book. It had the lurid jacket of a Crime Club mystery.

"How is it?" he asked.

"Not bad," she said. "I thought I had it solved in the third chapter, but now I think I'm wrong. What did he say your name was?"

"She's always reading mysteries," Ginny put in. "She's our tame crime expert—Madam Hawkshaw. Every time anyone gets murdered in the papers she knows all about it."

"And why not?" Lissa insisted. "They're usually so stupid, anyone but a detective could see it."

"You must have been reading the right books," said the Saint.

"Did he say 'Templar'?" Lissa asked.

The door opened then, and Esther came in. Simon recognized her by her face, a perfect oval set with warm brown eyes and broken by a red mouth that always seemed to be whispering *"If we were alone. . . ."* A softly waved mane the color of smoked chestnuts framed the face in a dark dreamy cloud. The rest of her was not quite so easily identifiable, for she had wrapped it in a loose blue robe that left a little scope for speculation. Not too much, for the lapels only managed to meet at her waist, and just a little below that the folds shrank away from the impudent obtrusion of a shapely thigh.

"A fine thing," she said. "Walking in on me when I didn't have a stitch on."

"I bet you loved it," Ginny said, cheating a black ten out of the bottom of the pack and slipping it on to a red jack.

"Do we get introduced?" said Esther.

"Meet Miss Swinburne," said Freddie. "Mr. Templar. Now you know everybody. I want you to feel at home. My name's Freddie. We're going to call you Simon. All right?"

"All right," said the Saint.

"Then we're all at home," said Freddie, making his point. "We don't have to have any formality. If any of the girls go for you, that's all right, too. We're all pals together."

"Me first," said Ginny.

"Why you?" objected Esther. "After all, if you'd been there to give him the first preview——"

The Saint took out his cigarette case with as much poise as any man could have called on in the circumstances.

"The line forms on the right," he remarked. "Or you can see my agent. But don't let's be confused about this. I only work here. You ought to tell them, Freddie."

The Filipino boy wheeled in the portable bar, and Pellman threaded his way over to it and began to work.

"The girls know all about that threatening letter. I showed it to them this morning. Didn't I, Lissa? You remember that note I showed you?" Reassured by confirmation, Freddie picked up the cocktail shaker again and said: "Well, Simon Templar is going to take care of us. You know who he is, don't you? The Saint. That's who he is," said Freddie, leaving no room for misunderstanding.

"I thought so," said Lissa, with her cornflower eyes clinging to the Saint's face. "I've seen pictures of you." She put her book down and moved her long legs invitingly to make some room on the couch. "What do you think about that note?"

Simon accepted the invitation. He didn't think she was any less potentially dangerous than the other two, but she was a little more quiet and subtle about it. Besides, she at least had something else to talk about.

"Tell me what you think," he said. "You might have a good point of view."

"I thought it sounded rather like something out of a cheap magazine."

"There you are!" exclaimed Freddie triumphantly, from the middle distance. "Isn't that amazing? Eh, Simon? Listen to this, Ginny. That's what she reads detective stories for. You'll like this. D'you know what Simon said when I showed him that note? What did you say, Simon?"

"I said it sounded a bit corny."

"There!" said Freddie, personally vindicated. "That's the very word he used. He said it was corny. That's what he said as soon as he read it."

"That's what I thought, too," said Esther, "only I didn't like to say so. Probably it's just some crackpot trying to be funny."

"On the other hand," Simon mentioned, "a lot of crackpots have killed people, and plenty of real murders have been pretty corny. And whether you're killed by a crackpot or the most rational person in the world, and whether the performance is corny or not, you end up just as dead."

"Don't a lot of criminals read detective stories?" Lissa asked.

The Saint nodded.

"Most of them. And they get good ideas from them, too. Most writers are pretty clever, in spite of the funny way they look, and when they go in for crime they put in a lot of research and invention that a practicing thug doesn't have the time or the ability to do for himself. But he could pick up a lot of hints from reading the right authors."

"He could learn a lot of mistakes not to make, too."

"Maybe there's something in that," said the Saint. "Perhaps the stupid criminals you were talking about are only the ones who don't read books. Maybe the others get to be so clever that they never get caught, and so you never hear about them at all."

"Brrr," said Ginny. "You're giving me goose pimples. Why don't you just call the cops?"

"Because the Saint's a lot smarter than the cops," said Freddie. "That's what I hired him for. He can run rings round the cops any day. He's been doing it for years. Lissa knows all about him, because she reads things. You tell them about him, Lissa."

He came over with clusters of Manhattans in his hands, poured out in goblets that would have been suitable for fruit punch.

"Let her off," said the Saint hastily. "If she really knows the whole story of my life she might shock somebody. Let's do some serious drinking instead."

"Okay," said Freddie amiably. "You're the boss. You go on being the mystery man. Let's all get stinking."

The fact that they did not all get stinking was certainly no fault of Freddie Pellman's. It could not be denied that he did his generous best to assist his guests to attain that state of ideal ossification. His failure could only be attributed to the superior discretion of the company, and the remarkably high level of resistance which they seemed to have in common.

It was quite a classic performance in its way. Freddie concocted two more Manhattans, built on the same scale as milk shakes. There was then a brief breathing spell while they went to their rooms to change. Then they went to the Doll House for dinner. They had two more normal-sized cocktails before the meal, and champagne with it. After that they had brandy. Then they proceeded to visit all the other bars up and down the main street, working from north to south and back again. They had Zombies at the Luau, Planter's Punches at the Cubana, highballs at the Chi Chi, and more highballs at Bil-Al's. Working back, they freshened up with some beer at Happy's, clamped it down with a Collins at the Del Tahquitz, topped it with Daiquiris at the Royal Palms, and discovered tequila at Claridge's. This brought them back to the Doll House for another bottle of champagne. They were all walking on their own feet and talking intelligibly, if not profoundly. People have received medals for less notable feats. It must be admitted nevertheless that there had been a certain amount of cheating. The girls, undoubtedly educated by past experiences, had contrived to leave a respectable number of drinks unfinished; and Simon Templar, who had also been around, had sundry legerdemains of his own for keeping control of the situation.

Freddie Pellman probably had an advantage over all of them in the insulating effect of past picklings, but Simon had to admit that the man was remarkable. He had been alcoholic when Simon met him, but he seemed to progress very little beyond that stage. Possibly he navigated with a little more difficulty, but he could still stand upright; possibly his speech became a little more slurred, but he could still be understood; certainly he became rather more glassy-eyed, but he could still see what was going on. It was as if there was a definite point beyond which his calloused tissues had no further power to assimilate liquid stimulus: being sodden already, the overflow washed over them without depositing any added exhilaration.

He sat and looked at his glass and said: "There must be some other joints we haven't been to yet."

Then he rolled gently over sideways and lay flat on the floor, snoring.

Ginny gazed down at him estimatingly and said: "That's only

the third time I've seen him pass out. It must be catching up with him."

"Well, now we can relax," said Esther, and moved her chair closer to the Saint.

"I think we'd better get him home," Lissa said.

It seemed like a moderately sound idea, since the head waiter and the proprietor were advancing towards the scene with professional restraint.

Simon helped to hoist Freddie up, and they got him out to the car without waking him. The Saint drove them back to the house, and the lights went up as they stopped at the door. The Filipino boy came out and helped phlegmatically with the disembarkation. He didn't show either surprise or disapproval. Apparently such homecomings were perfectly normal events in his experience.

Between them they carried the sleeper to his room and laid him on the bed.

"Okay," said the boy. "I take care of him now."

He began to work Freddie expertly out of his coat.

"You seem to have the touch," said the Saint. "How long have you been in this job?"

" 'Bout six months. He's all right. You leave him to me, sir. I put him to bed."

"What's your name?"

"Angelo, sir. I take care of him. You want anything, you tell me."

"Thanks," said the Saint, and drifted back to the living room.

He arrived in the course of a desultory argument which suggested that the threat which had been virtually ignored all evening had begun to seem a little less ludicrous with the arrival of bedtime.

"You can move in with me, Ginny," Lissa was saying.

"Nuts," said Ginny. "You'll sit up half the night reading, and I want some sleep."

"For a change," said Esther. "I'll move in with you, Lissa."

"You snore," said Lissa candidly.

"I don't!"

"And where does that leave me?" Ginny protested.

"I expect you'll find company," Esther said sulkily. "You've been working for it hard enough."

Simon coughed discreetly.

"Angelo is in charge," he said, "and I'm going to turn in."

"What, so soon?" pouted Esther. "Let's all have another drink first. I know, let's have a game of strip poker."

"I'm sorry," said the Saint. "I'm not so young as I was this afternoon. I'm going to get some sleep."

"I thought you were supposed to be a bodyguard," said Ginny.

The Saint smiled.

"I am, darling. I guard Freddie's body."

"Freddie's passed out. You ought to keep us company."

"It's all so silly," Lissa said. "I'm not scared. We haven't anything to be afraid of. Even if that note was serious, it's Freddie they're after. Nobody's going to do anything to us."

"How do you know they won't get into the wrong room?" Esther objected.

"You can hang a sign on your door," Simon suggested, "giving them directions. Goodnight, pretty maidens."

He made his exit before there could be any more discussion, and went to his bedroom.

The bedrooms trailed away from the house in a long L-shaped wing. Freddie's room was at the far end of the wing, and his door faced down the broad screened veranda by which the rooms were reached. Simon had the room next to it, from which one of the girls had been moved: their rooms were now strung around the angle of the L towards the main building. There was a communicating door on both sides of his room. He tried the one which should have opened in to Freddie's room, but he found that there was a second door backing closely against it, and that one was locked. He went around by the veranda, and found Angelo preparing to turn out the lights.

"He sleep well now," said the Filipino with a grin. "You no worry."

Freddie was neatly tucked into bed, his clothes carefully folded over a chair. Simon went over and looked at him. He certainly wasn't dead at that point—his snoring was stertorously alive.

The Saint located the other side of the communicating door, and tried the handle. It still wouldn't move, and there was no key in the lock.

"D'you know how to open this, Angelo?" he asked.

The Filipino shook his head.

"Don't know. Is lock?"

"Is lock."

"I never see key. Maybe somewhere."

"Maybe," Simon agreed.

It didn't look like a profitable inquiry to pursue much further, and Simon figured that it probably didn't matter. He still hadn't developed any real conviction of danger overshadowing the house, and at that moment the idea seemed particularly farfetched. He went out of the room, and the Filipino switched off the light.

"Everything already lock up, sir. You no worry. I go to sleep now."

"Happy dreams," said the Saint.

He returned to his own room, and undressed and rolled into bed. He felt in pretty good shape, but he didn't want to start the next day with an unnecessary headache. He was likely to have enough other headaches without that. Aside from the drinking pace and the uninhibited feminine hazards, he felt that a day would come when Freddie Pellman's conversational style would cease to hold him with the same eager fascination that it created at the first encounter. Eventually, he felt, a thousand dollars a day would begin to seem like a relatively small salary for listening to Freddie talk. But that was something that could be faced when the time came. Maybe he would be able to explain it to Freddie and get a raise. . . .

With that he fell asleep. He didn't know how long it lasted, but it was deep and relaxed. And it ended with an electrifying suddenness that was as devastating as the collapse of a tall tower of porcelain. But the sound was actually a little different. It was a shrill shattering scream that brought him wide awake in an instant and had him on his feet while the echo was still ringing in his ears.

3

THERE WAS enough starlight outside for the windows to be rectangles of silver, but inside the room he was only just able to find his dressing gown without groping. His gun was already in his hand, for his fingers had closed on it instinctively where the butt lay just under the edge of the mattress at the natural length of his arm as he lay in bed. He threw the robe on and whipped a knot into the belt, and was on his way to the door within two seconds of waking.

Then the scream came again, louder now that he wasn't hearing it through a haze of sleep, and in a way more deliberate. And it came, he was certain, not from the direction in which he had first automatically placed it, without thinking, but from the opposite quarter—the room on the opposite side of his own.

He stopped in mid-stride, and turned quickly back to the other communicating door. This one was not locked. It was a double door like the one to Freddie's room, but the second handle turned smoothly with his fingers. As he started to open it, the door outlined itself with light: he did the only possible thing, and threw it wide open quickly but without any noise, and stepped swiftly through and to one side, with his gun balanced for instant aiming in any direction.

He didn't see anything to aim at. He didn't see anyone there except Lissa.

She was something to see, if one had the time. She was sitting upright in bed, and she wore a filmy flesh-colored nightgown with white overtones. At least, that was the first impression. After a while, you realized that it was just a filmy white nightgown and the flesh color was Lissa. She had her mouth open, and she looked exactly as if she was going to scream again. Then she didn't look like that any more.

"Hullo," she said, quite calmly. "I thought that'd fetch you."

"Wouldn't there have been a more subtle way of doing it?" Simon asked.

"But there was someone here, really. Look."

Then he saw it—the black wooden hilt of a knife that stood up starkly from the bedding close beside her. The resignation went out of his face again as if it had never been there.

"Where did he go?"

"I don't know—out of one of the doors. If he didn't go into your room, he must have gone out on to the porch or into Ginny's room."

Simon crossed to the other door and stepped out on to the veranda. Lights came on as he did so, and he saw Freddie Pellman swaying in the doorway at the dead end of the L.

"Whassamarrer?" Freddie demanded thickly. "What goes on?"

"We seem to have had a visitor," said the Saint succinctly. "Did anybody come through your room?"

"Anybody come through my room? I dunno. No. I didn't see anybody. Why should anybody come through my room?"

"To kiss you goodnight," said the Saint tersely, and headed in the other direction.

There was no other movement on the veranda. He knocked briefly on the next door down, and opened it and switched on the light. The bed was rumpled but empty, and a shaft of light came through the communicating door. All the bedrooms seemed to have communicating doors, which either had its advantages or it didn't. Simon went on into the next room. The bed in there had the covers pulled high up, and appeared to be occupied by a small quivering hippopotamus. He went up to it and tapped it on the most convenient bulge.

"Come on," he said. "I just saw a mouse crawl in with you."

There was a stifled squeal, and Esther's head and shoulders and a little more jumped into view in the region of the pillow.

"Go away!" she yelped inarticulately. "I haven't done anything—"

Then she recognized him, and stopped abruptly. She took a moment to straighten her dark hair. At the same time the other half of the baby hippopotamus struggled up beside her, revealing that it had a red-gold head and a snub nose.

"Oh, it's you," said Ginny. "Come on in. We'll make room for you."

"Well, make yourselves at home," said Esther. "This just happens to be my room—"

"Little children," said the Saint, with great patience, "I don't want to spoil anybody's fun, but I'm looking for a hairy thug who seems to be rushing around trying to stick knives into people."

They glanced at each other in a moment's silence.

"Wh—who did he stick a knife into?" Ginny asked.

"Nobody. He missed. But he was trying. Did you see him?"

She shook her head.

"Nobody's been in here," said Esther, "except Ginny. I heard a frightful scream, and I jumped up and put the light on, and the next minute Ginny came rushing in and got into my bed."

"It was Lissa," said Ginny. "I'm sure it was. The scream sounded like it was right next door. So I ran in here. But I didn't see anyone." She swallowed, and her eyes grew big. "Is Lissa—?"

"No," said the Saint bluntly. "Lissa's as well as you are. And so is Freddie. But somebody's been up to mischief tonight, and we're looking for him. Now will you please get out of bed and pull yourselves together, because we're going to search the house."

"I can't," said Esther. "I haven't got anything on."

"Don't let it bother you," said the Saint tiredly. "If a burglar sees you he'll probably swoon on the spot, and then the rest of us will jump on him and tie him up."

He took a cigarette from a package beside the bed, and went on his way. It seemed as if he had wasted a lot of time, but actually it had scarcely been a minute. Out on the veranda he saw that the door of Lissa's room was open, and through it he heard Freddie Pellman's obstructed croak repetitiously imploring her to tell him what had happened. As he went on towards the junction of the main building, lights went on in the living room and a small mob of chattering figures burst out and almost swarmed over him as he opened the door into the arched alcove that the bedroom wing took off from. Simon spread out his arms and collected them in a sheaf.

"Were you going somewhere, boys?"

There were three of them, in various interesting costumes. Reading from left to right, they were: Angelo, in red, green, and purple striped pajamas, another Filipino in a pair of very natty bright blue trousers, and a large gentleman in a white nightshirt with spiked moustaches and a vandyke.

Angelo said: "We hear some lady scream, so we come to see what's the matter."

Simon looked at him shrewdly.

"How long have you worked for Mr. Pellman?"

"About six months, sir."

"And you never heard any screaming before?"

The boy looked at him sheepishly, without answering.

The stout gentleman in the nightshirt said with some dignity: "Ziss wass not ordinairy screaming. Ziss wass quite deefairent. It sounds like somebody iss in trobble. So we sink about ze note zat Meestair Pellman receive, and we come to help."

"Who are you?" said the Saint.

"I am Louis, sir. I am ze chef."

"*Enfin, quand nous aurons pris notre assassin, vous aurez le plaisir de nous servir ses rognons, légèrement grillés.*"

The man stared at him blankly for a second or two, and finally said: "I'm sorry, sir, I don't ondairstand."

"You don't speak French?"

"No, sir."

"Then what are you doing with that accent?"

"I am Italian, sir, but I lairn this accent because she iss good business."

Simon gave up for the time being.

"Well, let's get on with this and search the house. You didn't see any strangers on your way here?"

"No, sir," Angelo answered. "Did anyone get hurt?"

"No, but we seem to have had a visitor."

"I no understand," the Filipino insisted. "Everything lock up, sir. I see to it myself."

"Then somebody opened something," said the Saint curtly. "Go and look."

He went on his own way to the front door. It was locked and bolted. He opened it and went outside.

Although there seemed to have been a large variety of action and dialogue since Lissa's scream had awakened him, it had clicked through at such a speed that the elapsed time was actually surprisingly short. As he stood outside and gave his eyes a moment to adjust themselves to the darkness he tried to estimate how long it had been. Not long enough, he was sure, for anyone to travel very far. . . . And then the night cleared from his eyes, and he could see almost as well as a cat could have seen there. He went to the edge of the terrace in front of the house, and looked down. He could see the private road which was the only vehicular approach to the place dropping and winding away to his left like a gray ribbon carelessly thrown down the mountainside, and there was no car or moving shadow on it. Most of the street plan at the foot of the hill was as clearly visible also as if he had been looking down on it from an airplane, but he could see nothing human or mechanical moving there either. And even with all his delays, it hardly seemed possible that anything or anyone could have traveled far enough to be out of sight by that time—at least without making a noise that he would have heard on his way through the house.

There were, of course, other ways than the road. The steep slopes both upwards and downwards could have been negotiated by an agile man. Simon walked very quietly around the building and the gardens, scanning every surface that he could see. Certainly no one climbing up or down could have covered a great distance: on the other hand, if the climber had gone only a little way and stopped moving he would have been very hard to pick out of the ragged patchwork of lights and shadows that the starlight made out of tumbles of broken rock and clumps of cactus and incenso and greasewood. By the same token, a man on foot would be impossibly dangerous game to hunt at night: he only had to keep still, whereas the hunter had to move, and thereby give his quarry the first timed deliberate shot at him.

The Saint could be reckless enough, but he had no suicidal inclinations. He stood motionless for several minutes in different bays of shadow, scanning the slopes with the unblinking patience of a headhunter. But nothing moved, and presently he went back in by the front door and found Angelo.

"Well?" he said.

"I no find anything, sir. Everything all lock up. You come see yourself."

Simon made the circuit with him. Where there were glass doors they were all metal framed, with sturdy locking handles and bolts in addition. All the windows were screened, and the screen frames fastened on the inside. None of them showed a sign of having been forced or tampered with in any way; and the Saint was a good enough burglar in his own right to know that doors and casements of that type could not have been fastened from outside without leaving a sign that any such thing had been done— particularly by a man who was trying to depart from the premises in a great hurry.

His tour ended back in Lissa's room, where the rest of the house party was now gathered. He paused in the doorway.

"All right, Angelo," he said. "You can go back to your beauty sleep. . . . Oh, yes, you could bring me a drink first."

"I've got one for you already," Freddie called out.

Simon went on in.

"That's fine." He stood by the portable bar, which had already been set up for business, and watched Freddie manipulating a bottle. It was a feat which Freddie could apparently perform in any condition short of complete unconsciousness. All things considered, he had really staged quite a comeback. Of course, he had had some sleep. The Saint looked at his watch, and saw that it was a few minutes after four. He said: "I think it's so nice to get up early and catch the best part of the morning, don't you?"

"Did you find out anything?" Freddie demanded.

"Not a thing," said the Saint. "But that might add up to quite something."

He took the highball that Freddie handed him, and strolled

over to the windows. They were the only ones in the house he had not yet examined. But they were exactly like the others—the screens latched and intact.

Lissa still sat up in the bed, the covers huddled up under her chin, staring now and again at the knife driven into the mattress, as if it were a snake that somebody was trying to frighten her with and she wasn't going to be frightened. Simon turned back and sat down beside her. He also looked at the knife.

"It looks like a kitchen knife," he remarked.

"I wouldn't let anyone touch it," she said, "on account of fingerprints."

Simon nodded and smiled, and took a handkerchief from the pocket of his robe. Using the cloth for insulation, he pulled the knife out and held it delicately while he inspected it. It was a kitchen knife—a cheap piece of steel with a riveted wooden handle, but sharp and pointed enough to have done all the lethal work of the most expensive blade.

"Probably there aren't any prints on it," he said, "but it doesn't cost anything to try. Even most amateurs have heard about fingerprints these days, and they all wear gloves. Still, we'll see if we have any luck."

He wrapped the knife carefully in the handkerchief and laid it on a Carter Dickson mystery on the bedside table.

"You're going to get tired of telling the story," he said, "but I haven't heard it yet. Would you like to tell me what happened?"

"I don't really know," she said. "I'd been asleep. And then suddenly for no reason at all I woke up. At least I thought I woke up, but maybe I didn't, anyway it was just like a nightmare. But I just knew there was somebody in my room, and I went cold all over, it was just as if a lot of spiders were crawling all over me, and I didn't feel as if I could move or scream or anything, and I just lay there hardly breathing and my heart was thumping away till I thought it would burst."

"Does that always happen when somebody comes into your room?" Ginny asked interestedly.

"Shut up," said the Saint.

"I was trying to listen," Lissa said, "to see if I couldn't hear something, I mean if he was really moving or if I'd just woken up with the frights and imagined it, and my ears were humming so that it didn't seem as if I could hear anything. But I did hear him. I could hear him breathing."

"Was that when you screamed?"

"No. Well, I don't know. It all happened at once. But suddenly I knew he was awful close, right beside the bed, and then I knew I was wide awake and it wasn't just a bad dream, and then I screamed the first time and tried to wriggle out of bed on the other side from where he was, to get away from him, and he actually touched my shoulder, and then there was a sort of thump right beside me—that must have been the knife—and then he ran away and I heard him rush through one of the doors, and I lay there and screamed again because I thought that would bring you or somebody, and besides if I made enough noise it would help to scare him and make him so busy trying to get away that he wouldn't wait to have another try at me."

"So you never actually saw him at all?"

She shook her head.

"I had the shades drawn, so it was quite dark. I couldn't see anything. That's what made it more like a nightmare. It was like being blind."

"But when he opened one of these doors to rush out—there might have been a little dim light on the other side—"

"Well, I could just barely see something, but it was so quick, it was just a blurred shadow and then he was gone. I don't think I've even got the vaguest idea how big he was."

"But you call him 'he'," said the Saint easily, "so you saw that much, anyway."

She stared at him with big round blue eyes.

"I didn't," she said blankly. "No, I didn't. I just naturally thought it was 'he.' Of course it was 'he.' It had to be." She swallowed, and added almost pleadingly: "didn't it?"

"I don't know," said the Saint, flatly and dispassionately.

"Now wait a minute," said Freddie Pellman, breaking one of the longest periods of plain listening that Simon had yet known him to maintain. "What is this?"

The Saint took a cigarette from a package on the bedside table and lighted it with care and deliberation. He knew that their eyes were all riveted on him now, but he figured that a few seconds' suspense would do them no harm.

"I've walked around outside," he said, "and I didn't see anyone making a getaway. That wasn't conclusive, of course, but it was an interesting start. Since then I've been through the whole house. I've checked every door and window in the place. Angelo did it

first, but I did it again to make sure. Nothing's been touched.
There isn't an opening anywhere where even a cat could have got
in and got out again. And I looked in all the closets and under
the beds too, and I didn't find any strangers hiding around."

"But somebody was here!" Freddie protested. "There's the knife.
You can see it with your own eyes. That proves that Lissa wasn't
dreaming."

Simon nodded, and his blue eyes were crisp and sardonic.

"Sure it does," he agreed conversationally. "So it's a comfort
to know that we don't have to pick a prospective murderer out
of a hundred and thirty million people outside. We know that
this is strictly a family affair, and you're going to be killed by
somebody who's living here now."

4

IT WAS nearly nine o'clock when the Saint woke up again, and
the sun, which had been bleaching the sky before he got back to
bed, was slicing brilliantly through the venetian blinds. He felt a
lot better than he had expected to. In fact, he decided, after a
few minutes of lazy rolling and stretching, he felt surprisingly
good. He got up, sluiced himself under a cold shower, brushed
his hair, pulled on a pair of swimming trunks and a bathrobe,
and went out in search of breakfast.

Through the french windows of the living room he saw Ginny
sitting alone at the long table in the patio beside the barbecue.
He went out and stood over her.

"Hullo," she said.

"Hullo," he agreed. "You don't mind if I join you?"

"Not a bit," she said. "Why should I?"

"We could step right into a Van Druten play," he observed.

She looked at him rather vaguely. He sat down, and in a moment
Angelo was at his elbow, immaculate and impassive now in a
white jacket and a black bow tie.

"Yes, sir?"

"Tomato juice," said the Saint. "With Worcester sauce. Scrambled eggs, and ham. And coffee."

"Yes, sir."

The Filipino departed; and Simon lighted a cigarette and slipped the robe off his shoulders.

"Isn't this early for you to be up?"

"I didn't sleep so well." She pouted. "Esther does snore. You'll find out."

Before the party broke up for the second time, there had been some complex but uninhibited arguments about how the rest of the night should be organized with a view to mutual protection, which Simon did not want revived at that hour.

"I'll have to thank her," he said tactfully. "She's saved me from having to eat breakfast alone. Maybe she'll do it for us again."

"You could wake me up yourself just as well," said Ginny.

The Saint kept his face noncommittal and tried again.

"Aren't you eating?"

She was playing with a glass of orange juice as if it were a medicine that she didn't want to take.

"I don't know. I sort of don't have any appetite."

"Why?"

"Well . . . you *are* sure that it was someone in the house last night, aren't you?"

"Quite sure."

"I mean—one of us. Or the servants, or somebody."

"Yes."

"So why couldn't we just as well be poisoned?"

He thought for a moment, and chuckled.

"Poison isn't so easy. In the first place, you have to buy it. And there are problems about that. Then, you have to put it in something. And there aren't so many people handling food that you can do that just like blowing out a match. It's an awfully dangerous way of killing people. I think probably more poisoners get caught than any other kind of murderer. And any smart killer knows it."

"How do you know this one is smart?"

"It follows. You don't send warnings to your victims unless you think you're pretty smart—you have to be quite an egotist and a show-off to get that far—and anyone who thinks he's really smart usually has at least enough smartness to be able to kid himself. Besides, nobody threatened to kill you."

"Nobody threatened to kill Lissa."

"Nobody did kill her."

"But they tried."

"I don't think we know that they were trying for Lissa."

"Then if they were so halfway smart, how did they get in the wrong room?"

"They might have thought Freddie would be with her."

"Yeah?" she scoffed. "If they knew anything, they'd know he'd be in his own room. He doesn't visit. He has visitors."

Simon felt that he was at some disadvantage. He said with a grin: "You can tie me up, Ginny, but that doesn't alter anything. Freddie is the guy that the beef is about. The intended murderer has very kindly told us the motive. And that automatically establishes that there's no motive for killing anyone else. I'll admit that the attack on Lissa last night is pretty confusing, and I just haven't got any theories about it yet that I'd want to bet on; but I still know damn well that nobody except Freddie is going to be in much danger unless they accidentally find out who the murderer is, and, personally, I'm not going to starve myself until that happens."

He proved it by taking a healthy sip from the glass of tomato juice which Angelo set in front of him, and a couple of minutes later he was carving into his ham and eggs with healthy enthusiasm.

The girl watched him moodily.

"Anyway," she said, "I never can eat anything much for breakfast. I have to watch my figure."

"It looks very nice to me," he said, and was able to say it without the slightest effort.

"Yes, but it has to stay that way. There's always competition."

Simon could appreciate that. He was curious. He had been very casual all the time about the whole organization and mechanics of the ménage, as casual as Pellman himself, but there just wasn't any way to stop wondering about the details of a set-up like that. The Saint put it in the scientific category of post-graduate education. Or he was trying to.

He said, leading her on with a touch so light and apparently disinterested that it could have been broken with a breath: "It must be quite a life."

"It is."

"If I hadn't seen it myself, I wouldn't have believed it was really possible."

"Why not?"

"It's just something out of this world."

"Sheiks and sultans do it."

"I know," he said delicately. "But their women are brought up differently. They're brought up to look forward to a place in a harem as a perfectly normal life. American girls aren't."

One of her eyebrows went up a little in a tired way.

"They are where I came from. And probably most everywhere else, if you only knew. Nearly every man is a wandering wolf at heart, and if he's got enough money there isn't much to stop him. Nearly every woman knows it. Only they don't admit it. So what? You wouldn't think there was anything freakish about it if Freddie kept us all in different apartments and visited around. What's the difference if he keeps us all together?"

The Saint shrugged.

"Nothing much," he conceded. "Except, I suppose, a certain amount of conventional illusion."

"Phooey," she said. "What can you do with an illusion?"

He couldn't think of an answer to that.

"Well," he said, "it might save a certain amount of domestic strife."

"Oh, sure," she said. "We bicker and squabble a bit."

"I've heard you."

"But it doesn't often get too serious."

"That's the point. That's what fascinates me, in a way. Why doesn't anybody ever break the rules? Why doesn't anybody try to ride the others off and marry him, for instance?"

She laughed shortly.

"That's two questions. But I'll tell you. Nobody goes too far because they wouldn't be here if they did. Or they'd only do it once. And then—out. No guy wants to live in the middle of a mountain feud; and after all, Freddie's the meal ticket. He's got a right to have some peace for his money. So everybody behaves pretty well. As for marrying him—that's funny."

"Guys have been married before."

"Not Freddie Pellmans. He can't afford to."

"One thing that we obviously have in common," said the Saint, "is a sense of humor."

She shook her head.

"I'm not kidding. Didn't you know about him?"

"No. I didn't know about him."

"There's a will," she said. "All his money is in a trust fund. He just gets the income. I guess Papa Pellman knew Freddie pretty well, and so he didn't trust him. He sewed everything up tight.

Freddie never will be able to touch most of the capital, but he gets two or three million to play with when he's thirty-five. On one condition. He mustn't marry before that. I guess Papa knew all about girls like me. If Freddie marries before he's thirty-five, he doesn't get another penny. Ever. Income or anything. It all goes to a fund to feed stray cats or something like that."

"So." The Saint poured himself some coffee. "I suppose Papa thought that Freddie would have attained a certain amount of discretion by that time. How long does that keep him safe for, by the way?"

"As a matter of fact," she said, "it's only a few more months."

"Well, cheer up," he said. "If you can last that long you may still have a chance."

"Maybe by that time I wouldn't want it," she said, with her disturbing eyes dwelling on him.

Simon lighted a cigarette and looked up across the patio as a door opened and Lissa and Esther came out. Lissa carried a book, with her forefinger marking a place: she put it down open on the table beside her, as if she was ready to go back to it at any moment. She looked very gay and fresh in a play suit that matched her eyes.

"Have you and Ginny solved it yet?" she asked.

"I'm afraid not," said the Saint. "As a matter of fact, we were mostly talking about other things."

"I'll take two guesses," said Esther.

"Why two?" snapped Ginny. "I thought there was only one thing you could think of."

The arrival of Angelo for their orders fortunately stopped that train of thought. And then, almost as soon as the Filipino had disappeared again and the cast were settling themselves and digging their toes in for another jump, Freddie Pellman made his entrance.

Like the Saint, he wore swimming trunks and a perfunctory terry-cloth robe. But the exposed portions of him were not built to stand the comparison. He had pale blotchy skin and the flesh under it looked spongy, as if it had softened up with inward fermentation. Which was not improbable. But he seemed totally unconscious of it. He was very definitely himself, even if he was nothing else.

"How do you feel?" Simon asked unnecessarily.

"Lousy," said Freddie Pellman, no less unnecessarily. He sank into a chair and squinted blearily over the table. Ginny still had some orange juice in her glass. Freddie drank it, and made a face. He said: "Simon, you should have let the murderer go on with the job. If he'd killed me last night, I'd have felt a lot better this morning."

"Would you have left me a thousand dollars a day in your will?" Simon inquired.

Freddie started to shake his head. The movement hurt him too much, so he clutched his skull in both hands to stop it.

"Look," he said. "Before I die and you have to bury me, who *is* behind all this?"

"I don't know," said the Saint patiently. "I'm only a bodyguard of sorts. I didn't sell myself to you as a detective."

"But you must have some idea."

"No more than I had last night."

A general quietness came down again, casting a definite shadow as if a cloud had slid over the sun. Even Freddie Pellman became still, holding his head carefully in the hands braced on either side of his jawbones.

"Last night," he said soggily, "you told us you were sure it was someone inside the house. Isn't that what he said, Esther? He said it was someone who was here already."

"That's right," said the Saint. "And it still goes."

"Then it could only be one of us—Esther or Lissa or Ginny."

"Or me. Or the servants."

"My God!" Freddie sat up. "It isn't even going to be safe to eat!"

The Saint smiled slightly.

"I think it is. Ginny and I were talking about that. But I've eaten. . . . Let's take it another way. You put the finger on Johnny Implicato last Christmas. That's nearly a year ago. So anybody who wanted to sneak in to get revenge for him must have sneaked in since then. Let's start by washing out anybody you've known more than a year. How about the servants?"

"I hired them all when I came here this season."

"I was afraid of that. However. What about anybody else?"

"I only met you yesterday."

"That's quite true," said the Saint calmly. "Let's include me. Now what about the girls?"

The three girls looked at each other and at Freddie and at the Saint. There was an awkward silence. Nobody seemed to want to speak first; until Freddie scratched his head painfully and said: "I think I've known you longer than anyone, Esther, haven't I?"

"Since last New Year's Eve," she said. "At the Dunes. You remember. Somebody had dared me to do a strip tease—"

"—never dreaming you'd take them up on it," said Ginny.

"All right," said the Saint. "Where did you come in?"

"In a phone booth in Miami," said Ginny. "In February. Freddie was passed out inside, and I had to make a phone call. So I lugged him out. Then he woke up, so we made a night of it."

"What about you, Lissa?"

"I was just reading a book in a drugstore in New York last May. Freddie came in for some Bromo-Seltzer, and we just got talking."

"In other words," said the Saint, "any one of you could have been a girlfriend of Johnny's, and promoted yourselves in here after he was killed."

Nobody said anything.

"Okay," Freddie said at last. "Well, we've got fingerprints, haven't we? How about the fingerprints on that knife."

"We can find out if there are any," said the Saint.

He took it out of the pocket of his robe, where he had kept it with him still wrapped in his handkerchief. He unwrapped it very carefully, without touching any of the surfaces, and laid it on the table. But he didn't look at it particularly. He was much more interested in watching the other faces that looked at it.

"Aren't you going to save it for the police?" asked Lissa.

"Not till I've finished with it," said the Saint. "I can make all the tests they'd use, and maybe I know one or two that they haven't heard of yet. I'll show you now, if you like."

Angelo made his impassive appearance with two glasses of orange juice for Lissa and Esther, and a third effervescent glass for Freddie. He stood stoically by while Freddie drained it with a shudder.

"Anything else, Mr. Pellman?"

"Yes," Freddie said firmly. "Bring me a brandy and ginger ale. And some waffles."

"Yes, sir," said the Filipino; and paused, in the most natural and expressionless way, to gather up three or four plates, a couple of empty glasses, and, rather apologetically, as if he had no idea how it could have arrived there, the kitchen knife that lay in front of the Saint with everyone staring at it.

5

AND THAT, Simon reflected, was as smooth and timely a bit of business as he had ever seen. He sat loose-limbed on his horse and went on enjoying it even when the impact was more than two hours old.

It had a superb simplicity of perfection which appealed to his sardonic sense of humor. It was magnificent because it was so completely incalculable. You couldn't argue with it or estimate it. There was absolutely no percentage in claiming, as Freddie Pellman had done, in a loud voice and at great length, that Angelo had done it on purpose. There wasn't a thing that could be proved one way or the other. Nobody had told Angelo anything. Nobody had asked Angelo to leave the knife alone, or spoken to him about fingerprints. So he had simply seen it on the table, and figured that it had arrived there through some crude mistake, and he had discreetly picked it up to take it away. The fact that by the time it had been rescued from him, with all the attendant panic and excitement, any fingerprints that might have been on the handle would have been completely obscured or without significance, was purely a sad coincidence. And that was the literal and ineluctable truth. Angelo could have been as guilty as hell or as innocent as a newborn babe: the possibilities were exactly that, and if Sherlock Holmes had been resurrected to take part in the argument his guess would have been worth no more than anyone else's.

So the Saint hooked one knee over the saddle horn and admired the pluperfect uselessness of the whole thing, while he lighted a cigarette and let his horse pick its own serpentine trail up the rocky slope towards Andreas Canyon.

The ride had been Freddie's idea. After two more brandies and ginger ale, an aspirin, and a waffle, Freddie Pellman had proclaimed that he wasn't going to be scared into a cellar by any goddam gangster's friends. He had hired the best goddam bodyguard in the world, and so he ought to be able to do just what he wanted. And he wanted to ride. So they were going to ride.

"Not me," Lissa had said. "I'd rather have a gangster than a horse, any day. I'd rather lie out by the pool and read."

"All right," Freddie said sourly. "You lie by the pool and read. That makes four of us, and that's just right. We'll take lunch and make a day of it. You can stay home and read."

So there were four of them riding up towards the cleft where the gray-green tops of tall palm trees painted the desert sign of water. Simon was in the lead, because he had known the trail years before and it came back to him as if he had only ridden it yesterday. Freddie was close behind him. Suddenly they broke over the top of the ridge, and easing out on to the dirt road that had been constructed since the Saint was last there to make the canyon more accessible to pioneers in gasoline-powered armchairs. But bordering the creek beyond the road stood the same tall palms, skirted with the dry drooped fronds of many years, but with their heads still rising proudly green and the same stream racing and gurgling around their roots. To the Saint they were still ageless beauty, unchanged, a visual awakening that flashed him back with none of the clumsy encumbrances of time machines to other more leisured days and other people who had ridden the same trail with him; and he reined his horse and thought about them, and in particular about one straight slim girl whom he had taken there for one stolen hour, and they had never said a word that was not casual and unimportant, and they had never met again, and yet they had given all their minds into each other's hands, and he was utterly sure that if she ever came there again she would remember, exactly as he was remembering. . . . So that it was like the shock of a cold plunge when Freddie Pellman spurred up beside him on the road and said noisily: "Well, how's the mystery coming along?"

The Saint sighed inaudibly and tightened up, and said: "What mystery?"

"Oh, go on," Freddie insisted boisterously. "You know what I'm talking about. The mystery."

"So I gathered," said the Saint. "But I'm not so psychic after a night like last night. And if you want to know, I'm just where I was last night. I just wish you were more careful about hiring servants."

"They had good references."

"So had everybody else who ever took that way in. But what else do you know about them?"

"What else do I know about them?" Freddie echoed, for the sake of greater clarity. "Nothing much. Except that Angelo is the best houseboy and valet I ever had. The other Filipino—Al, he calls himself—is a pal of his. Angelo brought him."

"You didn't ask if they'd ever worked for Smoke Johnny?"

"No." Freddie was surprised. "Why should I?"

"He could have been nice to them," said the Saint. "And Filipinos can be fanatically loyal. Still, that threatening letter seems a little bit literate for Angelo. I don't know. Another way of looking at it is that Johnny's friends could have hired them for the job. . . . And then, did you know that your chef was an Italian?"

"I never thought about it. He's an Italian, is he? Louis? That's interesting." Freddie looked anything but interested. "But what's that got to do with it?"

"So was Implicato," said the Saint. "He might have had some Italian friends. Some Italians do."

"Oh," said Freddie.

They turned over the bridge across the stream, and there was a flurry of hoofs behind them as Ginny caught up at a gallop. She rode well, and she knew it, and she wanted everyone else to know. She reined her pony up to a rearing sliding stop, and patted its damp neck.

"What are you two being so exclusive about?" she demanded.

"Just talking," said the Saint. "How are you doing?"

"Fine." She was fretting her pony with hands and heels, making it step nervously, showing off. "Esther isn't so happy, though. Her horse is a bit frisky for her."

"Don't worry about me," Esther said, coming up. "I'm doing all right. I'm awful hot, though."

"Fancy that," said Ginny.

"Never mind," said the Saint tactfully. "We'll call a halt soon and have lunch."

They were walking down towards a grove of great palms that rose like columns in the nave of a natural cathedral, their rich tufted heads arching over to meet above a cloister of deep whispering shade. They were the same palms that Simon had paused under once before, years ago; only now there were picnic tables at their feet, and at some of them a few hardy families who had driven out there in their automobiles were already grouped in strident fecundity, enjoying the unspoiled beauties of Nature from the midst of an enthusiastic litter of baskets, boxes, tin cans, and paper bags.

"Is this where you meant we could have lunch?" Freddie asked rather limply.

"No. I thought we'd ride on over to Murray Canyon—if they

haven't built a road in there since I saw it last, there's a place there that I think we still might have to ourselves."

He led them down through the trees, and out on a narrow trail that clung for a while to the edge of a steep shoulder of hill. Then they were out on an open rise at the edge of the desert, and the Saint set his horse to an easy canter, threading his way unerringly along a trail that was nothing but a faint crinkling in the hard earth where other horses had followed it before.

It seemed strange to be out riding like that, so casually and inconsequentially, when only a few hours before there had been very tangible evidence that a threat of death to one of them had not been made idly. Yet perhaps they were safer out there than they would have been anywhere else. The Saint's eyes had never stopped wandering over the changing panoramas, behind as well as ahead; and although he knew how deceptive the apparently open desert could be, and how even a man on horseback, standing well above the tallest clump of scrub, could vanish altogether in a hundred yards, he was sure that no prospective sniper had come within sharpshooting range of them. Yet. . . .

He stopped his horse abruptly, after a time, as the broad flat that they had been riding over ended suddenly at the brink of a sharp cliff. At the foot of the bluff, another long column of tall silent palms bordered a rustling stream. He lighted a cigarette, and wondered cynically how many of the spoiled playboys and playgirls who used Palm Springs for their wilder weekends, and saw nothing but the smooth hotels and the Racquet Club, ever realized that the name was not just a name, and that there really were Palm Springs, sparkling and crystal clear, racing down out of the overshadowing mountains to make hidden nests of beauty before they washed out into the extinction of the barren plain. . . .

Freddie Pellman reined in beside him, looked the landscape over, and said, tolerantly, as if it were a production that had been offered for his approval: "This is pretty good. Is this where we eat?"

"If everybody can take it," said the Saint, "there's a pool further up that I'd like to look at again."

"I can take it," said Freddie, comprehensively settling the matter.

Simon put his horse down the steep zigzag, and stopped at the bottom to let it drink from the stream. Freddie drew up beside him again—he rode well enough, having probably been raised to it in the normal course of a millionaire's son's upbringing—and said, still laboring with the same subject: "Do you really think one of the girls could be in on it?"

"Of course," said the Saint calmly. "Gangsters have girlfriends. Girlfriends do things like that."

"But I've known all of them for some time at least."

"That may be part of the act. A smart girl wouldn't want to make it too obvious—meet you one day, and bump you off the next. Besides, she may have a nice streak of ham in her. Most women have. Maybe she thinks it would be cute to keep you in suspense for a while. Maybe she wants to make an anniversary of it, and pay off for Johnny this Christmas."

Freddie swallowed.

"That's going to make some things—a bit difficult."

"That's your problem," Simon said cheerfully.

Freddie sat his saddle unhappily and watched Ginny and Esther coming down the grade. Ginny came down it in a spectacular avalanche, like a mountain cavalry display, and swept off her Stetson to ruffle her hair back with a bored air while her pony dipped its nose thirstily in the water a few yards downstream. Esther, steering her horse down quietly, joined her a little later.

"But this is *Wunn*derful!" Ginny called out, looking at the Saint. "How do you find all these marvelous places?" Without waiting for an answer, she turned to Esther and said in a solicitous undertone which was perfectly pitched to carry just far enough: "How are you feeling, darling? I hope you aren't getting too miserable."

Simon was naturally glancing towards them. He wasn't looking for anything in particular, and as far as he was concerned Esther was only one of the gang, but in those transient circumstances he felt sorry for her. So for that one moment he had the privilege of seeing one woman open her soul in utter stark sincerity to another woman. And what one woman said to another, clearly, carefully, deliberately, quietly, with serious premeditation and the intensest earnestness, was: "You bitch."

"Let's keep a-goin'," said the Saint hastily, in a flippant drawl, and lifted his reins to set his horse at the shallow bank on the other side of the stream.

He led them west towards the mountains with a quicker sureness now, as the sense of the trail came back to him. In a little while it was a track that only an Indian could have seen at all, but it seemed as if he could have found it at the dead of night. There was even a place where weeds and spindly clawed scrub had grown so tall and dense since he had last been there that anyone else would have sworn that there was no trail at all; but he set his horse boldly at the living wall and smashed easily through into a channel that could hardly have been trodden since he last opened it . . . so that presently they found the creek again at a sharp bend, and he led them over two deep fords through swift-running water, and they came out at last in a wide hollow ringed with palms where hundreds of spring floods had built a broad open sandbank and gouged out a deep sheltered pool beside it.

"This is lunch," said the Saint, and swung out of the saddle to moor his bridle to a fallen palm log where his horse could rest in the shade.

They spread out the contents of their saddlebags on the sandbank and ate cold chicken, celery, radishes, and hard-boiled eggs. There had been some difficulty when they set out over convincing Freddie Pellman that it would have been impractical as well as strictly illegal to take bottles of champagne on to the reservation, but the water in the brook was sweet and ice-cold.

Esther drank it from her cupped hands, and sat back on her heels and gazed meditatively at the pool.

"It's awful hot," she said, suggestively.

"Go on," Ginny said to Simon. "Dare her to take her clothes off and get in. That's what she's waiting for."

"I'll go in if you will," Esther said sullenly.

"Nuts," said Ginny. "I can have a good time without that."

She was leaning against the Saint's shoulder for a backrest, and she gave a little snuggling wriggle as she spoke which made her meaning completely clear.

Freddie Pellman locked his arms around his knees and scowled. It had been rather obvious for some time that all the current competition was being aimed at the Saint, even though Simon had done nothing to try and encourage it; and Freddie was not feeling so generous about it as he had when he first invited the girls to take Simon into the family.

"All right," Freddie said gracelessly. "I dare you."

Esther looked as if a load had been taken off her mind.

She pulled off her boots and socks. She stood up, with a slight faraway smile, and unbuttoned her shirt and took it off. She took off her frontier pants. That left her in a wisp of sheer close-fitting scantiness. She took that off, too.

She certainly had a beautiful body.

She turned and walked into the pool, and lowered herself into it until the water lapped her chin. It covered her as well as a sheet of glass. She rolled, and swam lazily up to the far end, and as the water shallowed she rose out again and strolled on up into the low cascade where the stream tumbled around the next curve. She waded on up through the falls, under the palms, the sunlight through the leaves making glancing patterns on her skin, and disappeared around the bend, very leisurely. It was quite an exit.

The rustle of the water seemed very loud suddenly, as if anyone would have had to shout to be heard over it. So that it was surprising when Ginny's voice sounded perfectly easy and normal.

"Well, folks," she said, "don't run away now, because there'll be another super-colossal floor show in just a short while." She nestled against the Saint again and said: "Hullo."

"Hullo," said the Saint restrainedly.

Freddie Pellman got to his feet.

"Well," he said huffily, "I know you won't miss me, so I think I'll take a walk."

He stalked off up the stream the way Esther had gone, stumbling and balancing awkwardly on his high-heeled boots over the slippery rounded boulders.

They watched him until he was out of sight also.

"Alone at last," said Ginny emotionally.

The Saint reached for a cigarette.

"Don't you ever worry about getting complicated?" he asked.

"I worry about not getting kissed," she said.

She looked up at him from under her long sweeping lashes, with bright impudent eyes and red lips tantalizingly parted. The Saint had been trying conscientiously not to look for trouble, but he was not made out of ice cream and bubble gum. He was making good progress against no resistance when the crash of a shot rattled down the canyon over the chattering of the water and brought him to his feet as if he had actually felt the bullet.

6

HE RAN up the side of the brook, fighting his way through clawing scrub and stumbling over boulders and loose gravel. Beyond the bend, the stream rose in a long twisting stairway of shallow cataracts posted with the same shapely palms that grew throughout its length. A couple of steps further up he found Freddie.

Freddie was not dead. He was standing up. He stood and looked at the Saint in a rather foolish way, with his mouth open.

"Come on," said the Saint encouragingly. "Give."

Freddie pointed stupidly to the rock behind him. There was a bright silver scar on it where a bullet had scraped off a layer of lead on the rough surface before it riccoed off into nowhere.

"It only just missed me," Freddie said.

"Where were you standing?"

"Just here."

Simon looked at the scar again. There was no way of reading from it the caliber or make of gun. The bullet itself might have come to rest anywhere within half a mile. He tried a rough sight from the mark on the rock, but within the most conservative limits it covered an area of at least two thousand square yards on the other slope of the canyon.

The Saint's spine tingled. It was a little like the helplessness of his trip around the house the night before—looking up at that raw muddle of shrubs and rocks, knowing that a dozen sharp-shooters could lie hidden there, with no risk of being discovered before they had fired the one shot that might be all that was necessary. . . .

"Maybe we should go home, Freddie," he said.

"Now wait." Freddie was going to be obstinate and valiant after he had found company. "If there's someone up there——"

"He could drop you before we were six steps closer to him," said the Saint tersely. "You hired me as a bodyguard, not a pallbearer. Let's move."

Something else moved, upwards and a little to his left. His reflexes had tautened instinctively before he recognized the flash of movement as only a shifting of bare brown flesh.

From a precarious flat ledge of rock five or six yards up the slope, Esther called down: "What goes on?"

"We're going home," Simon called back.

"Wait for me."

She started to scramble down off the ledge. Suddenly she seemed much more undressed than she had before. He turned abruptly.

"Come along, then."

He went back, around the bend, past the pool, past Ginny, to where they had left the horses, hearing Freddie's footsteps behind him but not looking back. There were no more shots, but he worked quickly checking the saddles and tightening the cinches. The place was still just as picturesque and enchanting, but as an ambush it had the kind of topography where he felt that the defending team was at a great disadvantage.

"What's the hurry?" Ginny complained, coming up beside him; and he locked the buckle he was hauling on and gave the leather a couple of rapid loops through the three-quarter rig slots.

"You heard the shot, didn't you?"

"Yes."

"It just missed Freddie. So we're moving before they try again."

"Something's always happening," said Ginny resentfully, as if she had been shot at herself.

"Life is like that," said the Saint, untying her horse and handing the reins to her.

As he turned to the next horse Esther came up. She was fully dressed again, except that her shirt was only half buttoned; and she looked smug and sulky at the same time.

"Did you hear what happened, Ginny?" she said. "There was a man hiding up in the hills, and he took a shot at Freddie. And if he was where Simon thought he was, he must have seen me sunbathing without anything on."

"Tell Freddie that's what made him miss," Ginny suggested. "It might be worth some new silver foxes to you."

A dumb look came into Esther's beautifully sculptured face. She gazed foggily out at the landscape as the Saint cinched her saddle and thrust the reins into her limp hands.

She said: "Simon."

"Yes?"

"Didn't you say something last night about—about being sure it was someone in the house?"

"I did."

"Then . . . then just now—you were with Ginny, so she couldn't have done anything. And Lissa isn't here. But you know I couldn't— you know I couldn't have hidden a gun anywhere, don't you?"

"I don't know you well enough," said the Saint.

But it was another confusion that twisted around in his mind all the way home. It was true that he himself was an alibi for Ginny—unless she had planted one of those colossally elaborate remote-control gun-firing devices beloved of mystery writers. And Esther couldn't have concealed a gun, or anything else, in her costume—unless she had previously planted it somewhere up the stream. But both those theories would have required them to know in advance where they were going, and the Saint had chosen the place himself. . . . It was true he had mentioned it before they started, but mentioning it and finding it were different matters. He would have sworn that not more than a handful of people besides himself had ever discovered it, and he remembered sections of the trail that had seemed to be completely overgrown since they had last been trodden. Of course, with all his watchfulness, they might have been followed. A good hunter might have stayed out of sight and circled over the hills—he could have done it himself. . . .

Yet in all those speculations there was something that didn't connect, something that didn't make sense. If the theoretical sniper in the hills had been good enough to get there at all, for instance, why hadn't he been good enough to try a second shot before they got away? He could surely have had at least one more try, from a different angle, with no more risk than the first. . . . It was like the abortive attack on Lissa—it made sense, but not absolute sense. And to the Saint's delicately tuned reception that was a more nagging obstacle than no sense at all. . . .

They got back to the stables, and Freddie said: "I need a drink. Let's beat up the Tennis Club before we go home."

For once, the Saint was not altogether out of sympathy with the exigencies of Freddie's thirst.

They drove out to the club, and sat on the balcony terrace looking down over the beautifully terraced gardens, the palm-shaded oval pool and the artificial brook where imported trout lurked under spreading willows and politely awaited the attention of pampered anglers. The rest of them sipped Daiquiris, while Freddie restored himself with three double brandies in quick succession. And then, sauntering over from the tennis courts with a racquet in her hand, Lissa O'Neill herself came up to them. She looked as cool and dainty as she always seemed to look, in one of those abbreviated sun suits that she always seemed to wear which some clairvoyant designer must have invented exclusively for her slim waist and for long tapered legs like hers, in pastel shades that would set off her clear golden skin. But it seemed as if all of them drew back behind a common barrier that made them look at her in the same way, not in admiration, but guardedly, waiting for what she would say.

She said: "Fancy meeting you here."

"Fancy meeting you," said the Saint. "Did you get bored with your book?"

"I finished it, so I thought I'd get some exercise. But the pro has been all booked up for *hours.*"

It was as if all of them had the same question on their lips, but only the Saint could handle his voice easily enough to say, quite lazily: "Hours?"

"Well, it must have been two hours or more. Anyway, I asked for a lesson as soon as I got here, and he was all booked up. He said he'd fit me in if anybody canceled, but I've been waiting around for ages and nobody's given me a chance. . . ."

A part of the Saint's mind felt quite detached and independent of him, like an adding machine clicking over in a different room. The machine tapped out: She should have known that the pro would be booked up. And of course he'd say that he'd be glad to fit her in if he had a cancellation. And the odds are about eight to one that he wouldn't have a cancellation. So she could make him and several other people believe that she'd been waiting all the time. She could always find a chance to slip out of the entrance when there was no one in the office for a moment—she might even arrange to clear the way without much difficulty. She only had to get out. Coming back, she could say she just went to get something from her car. No one would think about it. And if there had been a cancelation, and the pro had been looking for her—well, she'd been in the johnny, or the showers, or at the bottom of the pool. He just hadn't found her. She'd been there all the time. A very passable casual alibi, with only a trivial percentage of risk.

But she isn't dressed to have done what must have been done.

She could have changed.

She couldn't have done it anyway.

Why not? She looks athletic. There are good muscles under that soft golden skin. She might have been sniping revenooers in the mountains of Kentucky since she was five years old, for all you know. What makes you so sure what she could do and couldn't do?

Well, what were Angelo and his pal, and Louis the Italian chef, doing at the same time? You can't rule them out.

Any good reader would rule them out. The mysterious murderer just doesn't turn out to be the cook or the butler any more. That was worked to death twenty years ago.

So of course no cook or butler in real life would ever dream of murdering anyone any more, because they'd know it was just too corny.

"What's the matter with you all?" Lissa asked. "Wasn't the ride any good?"

"It was fine," said the Saint. "Except when your last night's boyfriend started shooting at Freddie."

Then they all began to talk at once.

It was Freddie, of course, who finally got the floor. He did it principally by saying the same things louder and oftener than anyone else. When the competition had been crushed he told the story again, challenging different people to substantiate his statements one by one. He was thus able to leave a definite impression that he had been walking up the canyon when somebody shot at him.

Simon signaled a waiter for another round of drinks and put himself into a self-preservative trance until the peak of the verbal flood had passed. He wondered whether he should ask Freddie for another thousand dollars. He felt that he was definitely earning his salary as he went along.

". . . Then that proves it must be one of the servants," Lissa said. "So if we can find out which of them went out this afternoon——"

"Why does it prove that?" Simon inquired.

"Well, it couldn't have been Ginny, because she was talking to you. It couldn't have been me——"

"Couldn't it?"

She looked at him blankly. But her brain worked. He could almost see it. She might have been reading everything that had been traced through his mind a few minutes ago, line by line.

"It couldn't have been *me*," Esther insisted plaintively. "I didn't have a stitch on. Where could I have hidden a gun?"

Ginny gazed at her speculatively.

"It'll be interesting to see how the servants can account for their time," Simon said hastily. "But I'm not going to get optimistic too quickly. I don't think anything about this business is very dumb and straightforward. It's quite the opposite. Somebody is being so frantically cunning that he must be practically tying himself—or herself—in a knot. So if it is one of the servants, I bet he has an alibi too."

"I still think you ought to tell the police," Ginny said.

The drinks arrived. Simon lighted a cigarette and waited until the waiter had gone away again.

"What for?" he asked. "There was a guy in Lissa's room last night. Nobody saw him. He didn't leave any muddy footprints or any of that stuff. He used one of our own kitchen knives. If there ever were any fingerprints on it, they've been ruined. So—nothing. . . . This afternoon somebody shot at Freddie. Nobody saw him. He didn't leave his gun, and nobody could ever find the bullet. So nothing again. What are the police going to do? They aren't magicians. . . . However, that's up to you, Freddie."

"They could ask people questions," Esther said hopefully.

"So can we. We've been asking each other questions all the time. If anybody's lying, they aren't going to stop lying just because a guy with a badge is listening. What are they going to do—torture everybody and see what they get?"

"They'd put a man on guard, or something," said Ginny.

"So what? Our friend has waited quite a while already. I'm sure he could wait some more. He could wait longer than any police department is going to detail a private cop to nursemaid Freddie. So the scare blows over, and everybody settles down, and sometime later, maybe somewhere else, Freddie gets it. Well, personally I'd rather take our chance now while we're all warmed up."

"That's right," Freddie gave his verdict. "If we scare whoever it is off with the police, they'll only come back another time when we aren't watching for them. I'd rather let them get on with it while we're ready for them."

He looked rather proud of himself for having produced this penetrating reasoning all on his own.

And then his mind appeared to wander, and his eyes changed their focus.

"Hey," he said in an awed voice. "Look at that, will you?"

They looked, as he pointed. "The babe down by the pool. In the sarong effect. Boy, is that a chassis! Look at her!"

She was, Simon admitted, something to look at. The three girls with them seemed to admit the same thing by their rather strained and intent silence. Simon could feel an almost tangible heaviness thicken into the air.

Then Ginny sighed, as if relief had reached her rather late.

"A blonde," she said. "Well, Lissa, it's nice to have known you."

Freddie didn't even seem to hear it. He picked up his glass, still staring raptly at the vision. He put the glass to his lips.

It barely touched, and he stiffened. He took it away and stared at it frozenly. Then he pushed it across the table towards the Saint.

"Smell that," he said.

Simon put it to his nostrils. The hackneyed odor of bitter almonds was as strong and unmistakable as any mystery story fan could have desired.

"It does smell like prussic acid," he said, with commendable mildness. He put the glass down and drew on his cigarette again, regarding the exhibit moodily. He was quite sure now that he was going to collect his day's wages without much more delay. And probably the next day's pay in advance, as well. At that, he thought that the job was poorly paid for what it was. He could see nothing in it at all to make him happy. But being a philosopher, he had to cast around for one little ray of sunshine. Being persistent, he found it. "So anyway," he said, "at least we don't have to bother about the servants any more."

7

IT WAS a pretty slender consolation, he reflected, even after they had returned to the house and he had perfunctorily questioned the servants, only to have them jointly and severally corroborate each other's statements that none of them had left the place that afternoon.

After which, they had all firmly but respectfully announced that they were not used to being under suspicion, that they did not feel comfortable in a household where people were frequently getting stabbed at, shot at, and poisoned at; that in any case they would prefer a less exacting job with more regular hours; that they had already packed their bags; and that they would like to catch the evening bus back to Los Angeles, if Mr. Pellman would kindly pay them up to date.

Freddie had obliged them with a good deal of nonchalance, being apparently not unaccustomed to the transience of domestic help.

After which the Saint went to his room, stripped off his riding clothes, took a shower, wrapped himself in bathrobe, and lay down on the bed with a cigarette to contemplate the extreme sterility of the whole problem.

"This ought to learn you," he told himself, "to just say NO when you don't want to do anything, instead of making smart cracks about a thousand dollars a day."

The servants weren't ruled out, of course. There could be more than one person involved, taking turns to do things so that each would have an alibi in turn.

But one of the girls had to be involved. Only one of them could have poisoned Freddie's drink at the Tennis Club. And any one of them could have done it. The table had been small enough, and everybody's attention had been very potently concentrated on the sarong siren. A bottle small enough to be completely hidden in the hand, tipped over his glass in a casual gesture—and the trick was done.

But why do it then, when the range of possible suspects was so sharply limited?

Why do any of the other things that had happened?

He was still mired in the exasperating paradoxes of partial sense, which was so many times worse than utter nonsense. Utter non-sense was like a code: there was a key to be found somewhere which would make it clear and coherent in an instant, and there was only one exact key that would do it. You knew that you had it or you hadn't. The trouble with partial sense was that while you were straightening out the twisted parts you never knew whether you were distorting the straight ones. . . .

And somewhere beyond that point he heard the handle of his door turning, very softly.

His hand slid into the pocket of his robe where his gun was, but that was the only move he made. He lay perfectly still and relaxed, breathing at the shallow even rate of a sleeper, his eyes closed to all but a slit through which he could watch the door as it opened.

Esther came in.

She stood in the doorway hesitantly for a few seconds, looking at him, and the light behind her showed every line of her breathtaking body through the white crepe negligee she was wearing. Then she closed the door softly behind her and came a little closer. He could see both her hands, and they were empty.

He opened his eyes.

"Hullo," she said.

"Hullo." He stretched himself a little.

"I hope I didn't wake you up."

"I was just dozing."

"I ran out of cigarettes," she said, "and I wondered if you had one."

"I think so."

It was terrific dialogue.

He reached over to the bedside table, and offered her the package that lay there. She came up beside him to take it. Without rising, he struck a match. She sat down beside him to get the light. The negligee was cut down to her waist in front, and it opened more when she leaned forward to the flame.

"Thanks." She blew out a deep inhalation of smoke. She could have made an exit with that, but she didn't. She studied him with her dark dreamy eyes and said: "I suppose you were thinking."

"A bit."

"Have you any ideas yet?"

"Lots of them. Too many."

"Why too many?"

"They contradict each other. Which means I'm not getting anywhere."

"So you still don't know who's doing all these things?"

"No."

"But you know it isn't any of us."

"No, I don't."

"Why do you keep saying that? Ginny was with you all the time this afternoon, and I couldn't have had a gun on me, and Lissa couldn't have followed us and been at the Tennis Club, too."

"Therefore there must be a catch in it somewhere, and that's what I'm trying to find."

"I'm afraid I'm not very clever," Esther confessed.

He didn't argue with her.

She said at last: "Do you think I did it?"

"I've been trying very conscientiously to figure out how you could have."

"But I haven't done anything."

"Everybody else has said that, too."

She gazed at him steadily, and her lovely warm mouth richened with pouting.

"I don't think you really like me, Simon."

"I adore you," he said politely.

"No, you don't. I've tried to get on with you. Haven't I?"

"You certainly have."

"I'm not awfully clever, but I try to be nice. Really. I'm not a cat like Ginny, or all brainy and snooty like Lissa. I haven't any background, and I know it. I've had a hell of a life. If I told you about it, you'd be amazed."

"Would I? I love being amazed."

"There you go again. You see?"

"I'm sorry. I shouldn't kid you."

"Oh, it's all right. I haven't got much to be serious about. I've got a pretty face and a beautiful body. I know I've got a beautiful body. So I just have to use that."

"And you use it very nicely, too."

"You're still making fun of me. But it's about all I've got, so I have to use it. Why shouldn't I?"

"God knows," said the Saint. "I didn't say you shouldn't."

She studied him again for a while.

"You've got a beautiful body, too. All lean and muscular. But you've got brains as well. I'm sorry. I just like you an awful lot."

"Thank you," he said quietly.

She smoked her cigarette for a few moments.

He lighted a cigarette himself. He felt uncomfortable and at a loss. As she sat there, and with everything else in the world put aside, she was something that no man with a proper supply of hormones could have been cold to. But everything else in the world couldn't be put aside quite like that. . . .

"You know," she said, "this is the hell of a life."

"It must be," he agreed.

"I've been watching it. I can think a little bit. You saw what happened this afternoon. I mean——"

"The blonde at the Tennis Club?"

"Yes. . . . Well, it just happened that she was a blonde. She could just as well have been a brunette."

"And then—Esther starts packing."

"That's what it amounts to."

"But it's been fun while it lasted; and maybe you take something with you."

"Oh, yes. But that isn't everything. Not the way I mean. I mean. . . ."

"What do you mean?"

She fiddled with a seam in her negligee for a long time.

"I mean . . . I know you aren't an angel, but you're not just like Freddie. I think you'd always be sincere with people. You're sort of different, somehow. I know I haven't got anything much, except being beautiful, but—that's something, isn't it? And I do really like you so much. I'd—I'd do anything. . . . If I could only stay with you and have you like me a little."

She was very beautiful, too beautiful, and her eyes were big and aching and afraid.

Simon stared at the opposite wall. He would have given his day's thousand dollars to be anywhere the hell out of there.

He didn't have to.

Freddie Pellman's hysterical yell sheared suddenly through the silent house with an electrifying urgency that brought the Saint out of bed and up on to his feet as if he had been snatched up on wires. His instinctive movement seemed to coincide exactly with the dull slam of a muffled shot that gave more horror to the moment. He leapt towards the communicating door, and remembered as he reached it that while he had meant to get it unlocked that morning the episode of the obliterated fingerprints had put it out of his mind. Simultaneously, as he turned to the outer door, he realized that the sound of a door slamming could have been exactly the same, and he cursed his own unguardedness as he catapulted out on to the screened veranda.

One glance up and down was enough to show that there was no other person in sight, and he made that survey without even a check in his winged dash to Freddie's room.

His automatic was out in his hand when he flung the door open, to look across the room at Freddie Pellman, in black trousers and unbuttoned soft dress shirt, stretched out on the davenport, staring with a hideous grimace of terror at the rattlesnake that was coiled on his legs, its flat triangular head drawn back and poised to strike.

Behind him, the Saint heard Esther stifle a faint scream; and then the detonation of his gun blotted out every other sound.

As if it had been photographed in slow motion, Simon saw the snake's shattered head splatter away from its body, while the rest of it kicked and whipped away in series of reflex convulsions that spilled it still writhing spasmodically on to the floor.

Freddie pulled himself shakily up to his feet.

"Good God," he said, and repeated it. "Good God—and it was real! Another second, and it'd have had me!"

"What happened?" Esther was asking shrilly.

"I don't know. I was starting to get dressed—you see?—I'd got my pants and shirt on, and I sat down and had a drink, and I must have fallen asleep. And then that thing landed on my lap!"

Simon dropped the gun back into his pocket.

"Landed?" he said.

"Yes—just as if somebody had thrown it. Somebody must have thrown it. I felt it hit. That was what woke me up. I saw what it was, and of course I let out a yell, and then the door slammed, and I looked round too late to see who it was. But I didn't care who it was, then. All I could see was that Goddamn snake leering at me. I almost thought I was seeing things again. But I knew I couldn't be. I wouldn't have felt it like that. I was just taking a nap, and somebody came in and threw it on top of me!"

"How long ago was this?"

"Just now! You don't think I lay there for an hour necking with a snake, do you? As soon as it fell on me I woke up, and as soon as I woke up I saw it, and of course I let out a yell at once. You heard me yell, didn't you, Esther? And right after that the door banged. Did you hear that?"

"Yes, I heard it," said the Saint.

But he was thinking of something else. And for that once at least, even though she had admitted that she was not so bright, he knew that Esther was all the way there with him. He could feel her mind there with him, even without turning to find her eyes fastened on his face, even before she spoke.

"But that *proves* it, Simon! You must see that, don't you? I couldn't possibly have done it, could I?"

"Why, where were you?" Freddie demanded.

She drew herself up defiantly and faced him.

"I was in Simon's room."

Freddie stood hunched and stiff and staring at them. And yet the Saint realized that it wasn't any positive crystalizing of expression that made him look ugly. It was actually the reverse. His puffy face was simply blank and relaxed. And on that sludgy foundation, the crinkles of unremitting feverish bonhomie, the lines and bunchings of laborious domineering enthusiasm, drained of their vital nervous activation, were left like a mass of soft sloppy scars in which the whole synopsis of his life was hieroglyphed.

"What is it now?" Lissa's voice asked abruptly.

It was a voice that set out to be sharp and matter-of-fact, and failed by an infinitesimal quantity that only such ceaselessly critical ears as the Saint's would catch.

She stood in the doorway, with Ginny a little behind her.

Freddie looked up at her sidelong from under his lowered brows.

"Go away," he said coldly. "Get out."

And then, almost without a pause or a transition, that short-lived quality in his voice was only an uncertain memory.

"Run along," he said. "Run along and finish dressing. Simon and I want to have a little talk. Nothing's the matter. We just had a little scare, but it's all taken care of. I'll tell you presently. Now be nice children and go away and don't make a fuss. You too, Esther."

Reluctantly, hesitantly, his harem melted away.

Simon strolled leisurely across to a side table and lighted himself a cigarette as Freddie closed the door. He genuinely wasn't perturbed, and he couldn't look as if he was.

"Well," Freddie said finally, "how does it look now?"

His voice was surprisingly negative, and the Saint had to make a lightning adjustment to respond to it.

He said: "It makes you look like quite a bad risk. So do you mind if I collect for today and tomorrow? Two G, Freddie. It'd be sort of comforting."

Freddie went to the dressing-table, peeled a couple of bills out of a litter of green paper and small change, and came back with them. Simon glanced at them with satisfaction. They had the right number of zeros after the 1.

"I don't blame you," said Freddie. "If that snake had bitten me——"

"You wouldn't have died," said the Saint calmly. "Unless you've got a very bad heart, or something like that. That's the silly part of it. There are doctors within phone call, there's sure to be plenty of serum in town, and there's a guy like me on the premises who's bound to know the first aid. You'd have been rather sick, but you'd have lived through it. So why should the murderer go through an awkward routine with a snake when he had you cold and could've shot you or slit your throat and made sure of it? . . . This whole plot has been full of silly things, and they're only just starting to add up and make sense."

"They are?"

"Yes, I think so."

"I wish I could see it."

Simon sat on the arm of a chair and thought for a minute, blowing smoke-rings.

"Maybe I can make you see it," he said.

"Go ahead."

"Our suspects were limited to six people the first night, when we proved it was someone in the house. Now, through various events, every one of them has an alibi. That would make you think of a partnership. But none of the servants could have poisoned your drink this afternoon, and it wasn't done by the waiter or the bartender—they've both been at the club for years, and you could bet your shirt on them. Therefore somebody at the table must have been at least part of the partnership, or the whole works if there never was a partnership at all. But everyone at the table has still been alibied, somewhere in the story."

Freddie's brow was creased with the strain of following the argument.

"Suppose two of the girls were in partnership?"

"I thought of that. It's possible, but absolutely not probable. I doubt very much whether any two women could collaborate on a proposition like this, but I'm damned sure that no two of these girls could."

"Then where does that get you?"

"We have to look at the alibis again. And one of them has to be a phony."

The corrugations deepened on Freddie's forehead. Simon watched him silently. It was like watching wheels go round. And then a strange expression came into Freddie's face. He looked at the Saint with wide eyes.

"My God!" he said. "You mean—Lissa. . . ."

Simon didn't move.

"Yes," Freddie muttered. "Lissa. Ginny's got a perfect alibi. She couldn't have shot at me. You were with her yourself. Esther might have done it if she'd hidden a gun there before. But she was in your room when somebody threw that snake at me. She couldn't have faked that. And the servants have all gone. . . . The only alibi Lissa has got is that she was the first one to be attacked. But we've only got her word for it. She could have staged that so easily." His face was flushed with the excitement that was starting to obstruct his voice. "And all that criminology of hers . . . of course . . . she's the one who's always reading these mysteries—she'd think of melodramatic stuff like that snake— she'd have the sort of mind. . . ."

"I owe you an apology, Freddie," said the Saint, with the utmost candor. "I didn't think you had all that brain."

8

HE WAS alone in the house. Freddie Pellman had taken the girls off to the Coral Room for dinner, and Simon's stall was that he had to wait for a long-distance phone call. He would join them as soon as the call had come through.

"You'll have the place to yourself," Freddie had said when he suggested the arrangement, still glowing from his recent accolade. "You can search all you want. You're bound to find *something*. And then we'll have her."

Simon finished glancing through a copy of *Life,* and strolled out on the front terrace. Everything on the hillside was very still. He lighted a cigarette, and gazed out over the thin spread of sparkling lights that was Palm Springs at night. Down below, on the road that led east from the foot of the drive, a rapidly dwindling speck of red might have been the tail light of Freddie's car.

The Saint went back into the living room after a little while and poured himself a long lasting drink of Peter Dawson. He carried it with him as he worked methodically through Esther's and Ginny's rooms.

He wasn't expecting to find anything in either of them, and he didn't. But it was a gesture that he felt should be made.

So after that he came to Lissa's room.

He worked unhurriedly through the closet and the chest of drawers, finding nothing but the articles of clothing and personal trinkets that he had found in the other rooms. After that he sat down at the dresser. The center drawer contained only the laboratory of creams, lotions, powders, paints, and perfumes without which even a modern goddess believes that she has shed her divinity. The top right-hand drawer contained an assortment of handkerchiefs, scarves, ribbons, clips, and pins. It was in the next drawer down that he found what he had been waiting to find.

It was quite a simple discovery, lying under a soft pink froth of miscellaneous underwear. It consisted of a .32 automatic pistol, a small blue pharmacist's bottle labeled *"Prussic Acid*—POISON," and an old issue of *Life*. He didn't really need to open the magazine to know what there would be inside, but he did it. He found the mutilated page, and knew from the other pictures in the layout that the picture which had headed the letter that Freddie had shown him at their first meeting would fit exactly into the space that had been scissored out of the copy in front of him.

He laid the evidence out on the dresser top and considered it while he kindled another cigarette.

Probably any other man would have felt that the search ended there; but the Saint was not any other man. And the strange clairvoyant conviction grew in his mind that that was where the search really began.

He went on with it more quickly, with even more assurance, although he had less idea than before what he was looking for. He only had that intuitive certainty that there should be something—something that would tie the last loose ends of the tangle together and make complete sense of it. And he did find it, after quite a short while.

It was only a shabby envelope tucked into the back of a folding photo frame that contained a nicely glamorized portrait of Freddie. Inside the envelope were a savings bank pass book that showed a total of nearly five thousand dollars, and a folded slip of paper. It was when he unfolded the slip of paper that he knew that the search was actually over and all the questions answered, for he had in his hands a certificate of marriage issued in Yuma ten months before. . . .

"Are you having fun?" Lissa asked.

She had been as quiet as a cat, for he hadn't heard her come in, and she was right behind him. And yet he wasn't surprised.

His mind was filling with a great calm and quietness as all the conflict of contradictions settled down and he knew that the last act had been reached.

He turned quite slowly, and even the small shining gun in her hand, aimed squarely at his chest, didn't surprise or disturb him.

"How did you know?" he drawled.

"I'm not so dumb. I should have seen it before I went out if I'd been really smart."

"You should." He felt very detached and unrealistically balanced. "How did you get back, by the way?"

"I just took the car."

"I see."

He turned and stood up to face her, being careful not to make any abrupt movement, and keeping his hands raised a little; but she still backed away a quick step.

"Don't come any closer," she said sharply.

He was just over an arm's length from her then. He measured it accurately with his eye. And he was still utterly cool and removed from it all. The new stress that was building up in him was different from anything before. He knew now, beyond speculation, that murder was only a few seconds away, and it was one murder that he particularly wanted to prevent. But every one of his senses and reflexes would have to be sharper and surer than they had ever been before to see it coming and to forestall it. . . . Every nerve in his body felt like a violin string that had been tuned to within an eyelash weight of breaking. . . .

And when it came, the warning was a sound so slight that at any other time he might never have heard it—so faint and indeterminate that he was never absolutely sure what it actually was, if it was the rustle of a sleeve or a mere slither of skin against metal or nothing but an unconsciously tightened breath.

It was enough that he heard it, and that it exploded him into action too fast for the eye to follow—too fast even for his own deliberate mental processes to trace. But in one fantastic flow of movement it seemed that his left hand plunged at the gun that Lissa was holding, twisted it aside as it went off, and wrenched it out of her hand and threw her wide and stumbling while another shot from elsewhere chimed into the tight pile-up of sound effects; while at the same time, quite independently, his right hand leapt to his armpit holster in a lightning draw that brought his own gun out to bark a deeper note that practically merged with the other two. . . . And that was just about all there was to it.

The Saint clipped his own gun back in its holster, and dropped Lissa's automatic into his side pocket. It had all been so fast that he hadn't even had time to get a hair of his head disarranged.

"I'm afraid you don't have a very nice husband," he said.

He stepped to the communicating door and dragged the drooping figure of Freddie Pellman the rest of the way into the room and pushed it into a chair.

9

"HE'LL LIVE, if you want him," said the Saint casually. "I only broke his arm."

He picked up the revolver that Freddie had dropped, spilled the shells out, and laid it with the other exhibits on the dresser while Freddie clutched at his reddening sleeve and whimpered. It seemed as if the whole thing took so little time that Lissa was still recovering her balance when he turned and looked at her again.

"The only trouble was," he said, "that you married him too soon. Or didn't you know about the will then?"

She stared at him, white-faced, without speaking.

"Was he drunk when you did it?" Simon asked.

After a while she said: "Yes."

"One of those parties?"

"Yes. We were both pretty high. But I didn't know he was that high."

"Of course not. And you didn't realize that he wouldn't mind framing you into a coffin to keep his gay playboy integrity."

She looked at the collection of exhibits on her dresser, at Freddie, and at the Saint. She didn't seem to be able to get everything coordinated quickly. Simon himself showed her the marriage certificate again.

"This is what I wasn't supposed to find," he said. "In fact, I don't think Freddie even imagined you'd have it around. But it made quite a difference. How much were you going to shake him down for, Lissa?"

"I only asked him for two hundred thousand," she said. "I'd never have said anything. I just didn't want to be like some of the others—thrown out on my ear to be a tramp for the rest of my life."

"But you wanted too much," said the Saint. "Or he just didn't trust you, and he thought you'd always be coming back for more. Anyhow, he figured this would be a better way to pay off."

His cigarette hadn't even gone out. He picked it up and brightened it in a long peaceful draw that expressed all the final settling down of his mind.

"The mistake that all of us made," he said, "was not figuring Freddie for a moderately clever guy. Because he was a bore, we figured he was moderately stupid. Which is a rather dangerous mistake. A bore isn't necessarily stupid. He doesn't necessarily overrate his own intelligence. He just underrates everyone else. That makes him tedious, but it doesn't make him dumb. Freddie isn't dumb. He just sounds dumb because he's talking down to how dumb he thinks the rest of us are. As a matter of fact, he's quite a lively lad. He put a lot of gray matter into this little scheme. As soon as he heard that I'd arrived in town, he had the inspiration that he'd been waiting for. And he didn't waste a day in getting it started. He wrote himself the famous threatening letter at once—it was quite a coincidence, of course, that there was that last Christmas party to hang it on, but if there hadn't been that he'd certainly have thought of something else almost as good. He only had to establish that he was being menaced, and get me into the house to protect him. Then he had to put you in the middle of the first situation, in a set-up that would look swell in the beginning but would get shakier and shakier as things went on. That wasn't difficult either."

The only sound when he paused was Freddie Pellman's heavy sobbing breathing.

"After that, he improvised. He only had to stage a series of incidents that would give everyone else in turn an absolutely ironclad alibi that would satisfy me. It wasn't hard to do—it was just a matter of being ready with a few props to take advantage of the opportunities that were bound to arise. Perhaps he was a bit lucky in having so many chances in such a short space of time, but I don't know. He couldn't go wrong, anyway. Everything had to work in for him, once the primary idea was planted. Even an accident like Angelo picking up the knife was just a break for him—there weren't any fingerprints on it, of course, and it just helped the mystery a little. . . . And this evening he was able to

finish up in style with the snake routine. It wasn't exactly his
fault that the routine fitted in just as well with another pattern
that was gradually penetrating into my poor benighted brain. That's
just one of the natural troubles with trying to create artificial
mysteries—when you're too busy towing around a lot of red
herrings, you don't realize that you may be getting a fishy smell
on your own fingers. . . . That was what Freddie did. He was
being very clever about letting it work out that your alibi was the
only flimsy one; but he forgot that when I had to start questioning
alibis it might occur to me that there was one other person whose
alibis were flimsier still. And that was him."

Simon drew on his cigarette again.

"Funnily enough, I was just leading up to telling him that when
he made his first major mistake. You see, I had an idea what was
going on, but I was going nuts trying to figure out *why*. There
didn't seem to be any point to the whole performance, except as
a terrific and ponderous practical joke. And I couldn't see Freddie
with that sort of humor. So I was just going to come out flatly
and face him with it and see what happened. It's a shock technique
that works pretty well sometimes. And then he took all the wind
out of my sails by insisting on helping me to see how it all pointed
to you. That's what I mean about him underrating other people's
intelligence. He was just a little too anxious to make quite sure
that I hadn't missed any of the points that I was supposed to get.
But it had just the opposite effect, because I happened to know
that your alibi must have been genuine. So then I knew that the
whole plot didn't point *to* you—it was pointed *at* you. And when
Freddie went a little further and helped me to think of the idea
of staying behind tonight and searching your room, I began to
guess that the climax would be something like this. I suppose he
got hold of you privately and told you he'd started to get suspicious
of what I was up to—maybe I was planning to plant some evidence
and frame one of you?"

"Yes."

"So he suggested that the two of you sneak off and see if you
could catch me at it?"

She nodded.

"Then," said the Saint, "you peeked in through the window
and saw me with the exhibits on the dressing table, and he said
'What did I tell you?' . . . And then he said something like: 'Let's
really get the goods on him now. You take this gun and walk in

on him and keep him talking. If he thinks you're alone he'll probably say enough to hang himself. I'll be listening, and I'll be a witness to everything he says.' Something like that?"

"Something like that," she said huskily.

"And then the stage was all set. He only had to wait a minute or two, and shoot you. I was supposed to have suspected you already. I'd found a lot of incriminating evidence in your room. And then you'd walked in on me with a gun. . . . While of course his story would have been that he was suspicious when you sneaked off, that he followed you home, and found you holding me up, and you were just about to give me the works when he popped his pistol and saved my life. Everyone would have said that 'of course' you must have been Smoke Johnny's moll at some time, and nobody would ever have been likely to find the record of that marriage in Yuma unless they were looking for it—and why should they look for it? So you were out of the way, and he was in the clear, and I'd personally be his best, solid, hundred-percent witness that it was justifiable homicide. It would have made one of the neatest jobs that I ever heard of—if it had worked. Only it didn't work. Because just as I knew you had a good alibi all the time, I knew that all this junk in your drawer had been planted there, and so I knew that I still had something else to look for— the real motive for all these things that were going on. Maybe I was lucky to find it so quickly. But even so, from the moment when you walked in, something exciting was waiting to happen. . . . Well, it all worked out all right—or don't you think so, Freddie?"

"You've got to get me a doctor," Freddie said hoarsely.

"Do I have all the right answers?" Simon asked relentlessly.

Freddie Pellman moaned and clutched his arm tighter and raised a wild haggard face.

"You've got to get me a doctor," he pleaded in a rising shout. "Get me a doctor!"

"Tell us first," insisted the Saint soothingly. "Do we know all the answers?"

Pellman tossed his head, and suddenly everything seemed to disintegrate inside him.

"Yes!" he almost screamed. "Yes, damn you! I was going to fix that little bitch. I'll do it again if I ever have the chance. And you, too! . . . Now get me a doctor. Get me a doctor, d'you hear? D'you want me to bleed to death?"

The Saint drew a long deep breath, and put out the stub of his cigarette. He took a pack from his pocket and lighted another. And with that symbolic action he had put one more episode behind him, and the life of adventure went on.

"I don't really know," he said carelessly. "I don't think there'd be any great injustice done if we let you die. Or we might keep you alive and continue with the shakedown. It's really up to Lissa."

He glanced at the girl again curiously.

She was staring at Freddie in a way that Simon hoped no woman would ever look at him, and she seemed to have to make an effort to bring herself back to the immediate present. And even then she seemed to be a little behind.

She said: "I just don't get one thing. How did you know all that stuff had been planted in my drawer? And why were you so sure that my flimsy alibi was good?"

He smiled.

"That was the easiest thing of all. Aren't you the detective-story fan? You might have gotten good ideas from some of your mysteries, but you could hardly have picked up such bad ones. At least you'd know better than to keep a lot of unnecessary incriminating evidence tucked away where anyone with a little spare time could find it. And you'd never have had the nerve to pull an alibi like that first attack on yourself if it was a phony, because you'd have known that anyone else who'd ever read a mystery too would have spotted it for a phony all the time. About the only thing wrong with Freddie is that he had bright ideas, but he didn't read the right books."

"For Christ's sake," Freddie implored shrilly, "aren't you going to get me a doctor?"

"What would they do in a Saint story?" Lissa asked.

Simon Templar sighed.

"I imagine they'd let him call his own doctor, and tell the old story about how he was a cleaning a gun and he didn't know it was loaded. And I suppose we'd go back to the Coral Room and look for Ginny and Esther, because they must be getting hungry, and I know I still am. And I expect Freddie would still pay off in the end, if we all helped him to build up a good story. . . ."

Lissa tucked her arm under his.

"But what are the rest of us going to do tonight?"

"The Hays Office angle on that bothers the hell out of me," said the Saint.

PHILIP WYLIE
Puzzle in Snow

THE WIND blew harder and Tony looked out of the window with a feeling of apprehension. It was not a natural emotion to him. He watched battalions of snow charge at the chrome-steel gargoyle mounted outside his skyscraper apartment. The metal animal bit back at the storm—and the battalions whirled on. It was uncanny, Tony thought. Uncanny, because, less than a week ago, he had been wearing a pith helmet to protect himself from drenching sunshine in South America.

A door opened and he spun around. There was a fire burning in the grate and the opening at the door drove ashes from the hearth.

It was Tony's Filipino boy. He said, "Good evening, Mr. Andrews."

Tony nodded. He had had Pedro for three years—ever since the senior partner in his firm, David Cole, had come to him and said, "I want you to take my Filipino off my hands. He's a fine fellow and a superb cook, as you very well know, but I can't seem to get along with him. We've had two or three furious battles."

Pedro walked to the fire and held out his hands. His brown skin was tinged with blue and he was shivering. Snow still clung to his overcoat.

Tony wondered whether the fact that David Cole had fought with the Filipino boy explained in part why he and Cole had argued so feverishly that afternoon. Maybe Cole was at bottom an irascible and an unreasonable man.

Pedro took a newspaper from his coat pocket. "Your name in

177

my paper three times." He walked across the room and Tony mechanically accepted the tabloid. "Page seven, page eighteen, page twenty-six. Marked in blue pencil."

Tony read. First, Cavalier's column. "Tony Andrews, popular bachelor-at-large, brought the third prettiest girl in New York to the fights last night. . . ."

On page eighteen there was a picture of the Squadron M Polo Team, which, according to the caption, was to "defend its laurels on January 14th." Tony squinted at his likeness—as does every man of thirty-eight—to see if he had lost anything in the last ten years. He saw there a broad-shouldered, level-eyed man, with a lot of curly hair. Then he turned to the third mention of his name, which had been ringed in pencil by Pedro. It was a dignified financial advertisement: "Cole, Boyd & Andrews—Bonds."

That wasn't what he had been expecting; he looked farther, and finally said to Pedro, "I'm mentioned four times. I made a speech at the Advertising Association today." He began to read aloud, with irony in his voice: " 'Anthony Andrews, just returned from South America, stressed again his well-known thesis that a majority of the best brains in America go into business. "Business creates the wealth which gives the scientist his laboratory and the musician his concert hall," he said.' " Tony threw the newspaper into a chair. "That's what I said, Pedro. Businessmen are brainy. And I haven't got brains enough to run my own business!"

The doorbell rang.

Pedro answered it. Leslie Boyd was welcomed into the apartment by another puff of ashes and the scream of wind through the teeth of the gargoyle. The remaining partner in the firm of Cole, Boyd & Andrews was diminutive, electrical, and debonair. He was five feet two and he weighed less than one hundred pounds. His eyes were dancing and gray-green; his smile was quick and human. He was one of those rare undersized men who are obviously neither a martinet nor a self-adjudged Napoleon. His suit was eloquently tailored; an emerald glittered in his tie and two more on his fingers. He had a passion for emeralds, and in his safe-deposit box was a world-famous collection of them.

The ashes from the hearth settled on the carpet. The wind stopped moaning and the snow fell evenly. Pedro went for highballs. Leslie Boyd quit smiling when he sat down. "I came over here, Tony, in spite of this blizzard—"

"—to tell me," Tony interrupted, "that I'm a fool to keep on fighting with Dave Cole."

Pedro brought the drinks and Tony dismissed him for the night. Les waited till the Filipino was gone and then shook his head. "Not exactly. You've been to South America. You know the situation. I'm ready to admit that it's quite possible that Señor Alavo's mines don't warrant the issue. I'm perfectly willing to admit that if we sell ten million dollars' worth of bonds to our customers and they go blooey, it won't help our reputation as a firm. But you know Dave's temperament! You've had hundreds of fights with him! He likes to be unreasonable for a while and then have the pleasure of giving in and making everybody feel that he is doing a favor. If you had just shut up this afternoon instead of storming all over the office like a frustrated gangster, he would have come around all right."

Tony's nod was a calm agreement. "I know it. Dave's just a little bit old-womanish. But, after all, I'd been on the grounds and I knew what I was talking about and he didn't. Les, I've half a notion to resign. More than half."

Boyd smiled again—unhappily. "Damn it, Tony, you know perfectly well that you'll cool off. Dave's an older brother to you. We three guys have been through a lot together and I'm not going to see you and Dave raising hell with each other. If I can't persuade you to let Dave have his head—even if it means we do have to take and sell a bunch of bum bonds—I'm going over to Dave's house and go to work on him. I think Dave would come to his senses if you let him alone, but if you fight with him he'll stand you off all winter. How about it? Tell him tomorrow morning that you made up your mind that the final decision is up to him. Tell him—"

Tony shook his head. He was as stubborn as Dave, he thought. But he was right. He knew he was right. "I'm sorry, Les, but I've decided to make an issue out of this. Either old Dave quits acting like a czar or I leave the firm."

Les sighed, and lighted a cigarette. "The two best friends I have in the world are you and Dave, and I'm prepared to go to any lengths to keep you two birds from acting like bulldogs. I *have* prepared, in fact." He stood up. "But I guess I'm starting from the wrong end, hunh?" His eyes twinkled. "I'll go down and talk to Dave, if I have to hire a snowplow to get there."

Tony didn't say anything.

Les paused at the door. "No hard feelings?"

Tony shook his head. "None. I'm awfully sorry, Les. I hate to hurt you, but I still insist that I have to maintain my attitude."

Boyd chuckled. "O.K., Tony. I'll go down and see Dave. Good night."

"Good night." Tony could hear Les whistling as he waited for the elevator.

But Tony's mood had not been shaken. He sat down in front of the fire and for a long time he did not move.

When the telephone rang he swept back his right arm to take it up. "Hello?"

"Hello." It was Les's voice and he sounded excited.

"Listen, Tony! You've got to get right down to Dave's apartment!"

"What's the matter?"

"Somebody's murdered him!"

"Be right there!"

Tony slammed down the telephone and started for his hat and coat. He put them on and grabbed his doorknob, and only then halted. Perhaps he should call the police—or Jack Raymond— the firm's lawyer. But Les would have done that. The thing to do was to get there, and get there fast. . . .

David Cole lived on the top floor of a converted house on West Ninth Street. He had occupied it for twenty-two years. Mrs. Bunnell, his only servant, had been in his employ since he had fired Pedro. It was her custom to arrive at seven in the morning, prepare his breakfast, serve it, clean his apartment, and leave.

Tony paid the cab, bounded through the driving snow up the six brownstone steps to the vestibule, and rang Dave's bell.

The door latch didn't click.

He rang again.

There was still no answering click. Impatiently he hunted for his key ring. Dave had given both Les and himself duplicate keys to the apartment. Tony let himself in, went up four flights of stairs and knocked on Dave's door.

There was a dark stairway behind him that led to the roof, which Dave used in the summer. The hall was wallpapered with a ship design. There was a crimson carpet on the floor, a refectory table, a couple of antique Spanish chairs, and a sizzling radiator. The hall was hot. Tony noticed those things because he waited a long time after his knock. He was surprised that Les hadn't clicked the door downstairs, or answered his pounding. Presently he unlocked the door with his own key and walked in. He closed the door behind him.

Dave was lying on his face on the floor between two divans with his arms stretched out toward the grate, where a cannel coal fire was glowing. The hilt of a knife stuck up between his shoulder blades. He was wearing dinner clothes. Half a dozen lamps were lighted, but the room was big and the ceiling was so high it looked shadowy. On a table behind one of the two facing center divans were a number of objects that had evidently been recently put there: three or four fishing rods, several boxes of spools of heavy line, two 9/0 reels, and a .45 automatic.

Tony saw all that in one long look. Then he raised his voice: "Les!"

There wasn't any answer. He took off his hat and started to take off his gloves, and changed his mind without exactly deciding why. He crossed the living room, walked down a carpeted hall, opened a door, and turned on a light. The twin beds in Dave's guestroom were covered, the closets were empty.

In Dave's own room the lights were burning and the bureau drawers pulled open. There was a copy of the *Wall Street Post* on the bed and a round spot in the pillow where Dave had lain while reading it. A gray suit with a blue stripe which Dave had worn in the office that day was hanging from one of the bureau drawers with a note pinned on it. Tony walked over and read the note: "Mrs. B—Let's change cleaners. I'm tired of smelling like a benzine refinery." On top of the bureau was a plush-covered case in which were half a dozen sets of studs and cuff buttons worth, Tony thought, after looking them over, a couple of thousand dollars. Beside the case in a clip were five $100 bills, three $20's, two $10's, a $5, and eight $1's, as well as 93 cents in change. He looked into the bathroom. The tub was empty, but there were damp towels and puddles on the floor. Dave always bathed like a grampus.

The kitchen was in Mrs. Bunnell's perfect condition—nothing out of place.

Tony went back to the living room and picked up the telephone. It was a hand phone and the wire was cut at the bottom of the mouthpiece. He decided to go out and get the police. He turned the knob of the front door and pushed, but something was blocking

it and it wouldn't open. He put his shoulder against it and pushed
as hard as he could. Those two Spanish chairs had been quietly
jammed between the door and the staircase while he was investigating the rear of the apartment.

He turned around fast, and in the mirror above the fireplace
he saw that his face was ghastly white. The kitchen door had two
locks on it, one a bolt driven by a key—but the key wasn't there.

He went back to the living room and looked at Dave's .45. It
was loaded and it hadn't been used. He put it in his pocket.
Underneath the .45 was a copy of the *New York Register* open
to a page that had a seven-column advertisement for Wharton
Bros., and a one-column news story. One of the subheads contained
his own name: "A. G. Andrews says best brains are in business."
Penciled on the front page was, "Boyd—14-B."

Tony stared at the newspaper article about brains. He was
trapped with the murdered body of his best friend, with whom
on that very afternoon he had had a quarrel so furious that they
had almost come to blows—and in the presence of half a dozen
other people. He needed brains. More, he thought, than he possessed.

He took out a cigarette. Before he snapped open his lighter he
slowly drew a deep breath. There was perfume in the air, heavy
but very faint. He could not identify it with a person. He knew
only that he had smelled it before. So he postponed lighting his
cigarette. The woman would have been sitting on the divan, talking
to Dave. He walked to the back of one of the divans and sniffed,
but the perfume wasn't any stronger there. Then, after clenching
one of his gloved hands tightly, he tried the opposite divan. He
sniffed along the top right up to the place where it was soaked
with blood—blood that blotted the back and the seat and the
carpet between the divan and the place where Dave lay. Right
beside the stain the scent of the perfume was stronger, but Tony
couldn't recognize it.

He sat down across from the bloody upholstery, and then he
did light his cigarette. Dave was lying with his hands stretched
out and palms flat. The position reminded Tony of something.
He had seen Dave lying like that before. He remembered. Dave
was fifty-one but had kept himself in perfect physical shape—so
perfect, in fact, that once or twice, when his age was mentioned,
he had done a suspension press to show that there was still youth
and vitality in his muscles. To do a suspension press one must

lie face down on the floor, extend one's arms as far forward as possible, and, by pressing down with both palms, bow up one's entire body from hands to toes. Not very many people are able to do it.

Somebody had stabbed Dave, and he had tried to stand up and had fallen on his face, but he had made one last blind, terrific effort to get to his feet by pressing down with his outstretched palms. Then he had died.

There were ashes on Tony's cigarette and he got up and tapped them carefully into the coal grate. Then he sat down again, and he saw a little bit of white material almost concealed by the cushions on the opposite divan. He stepped over Dave's body and pulled out a woman's handkerchief with the initials L. R. on it. He smelled it—but the perfume in the room, the perfume on the upholstery, was not Loretta's. He put the handkerchief on the fire and watched it burn, and mixed up its ashes in the coals with the poker. For the third time he sat down.

He was deathly frightened. Where was Les Boyd? What woman had been in there besides Loretta? If Boyd had gone out to get the police, why weren't they there? And where was the person who had blocked the door? Who was he?

That was fear—but suddenly his fear turned to sheer horror. He was staring at the handle of the knife in Dave's back.

It was the handle of an ordinary hunting knife, a brown, thick handle that gave a good grip. He had one exactly like it. Of course, he thought rapidly, hundreds of other people had such knives. Thousands. Only—only, his knife was a little different. The point was broken. He had broken it trying to kill a moray that he had hauled part way up over the stern of a fishing boat in Florida. He had missed his first stab, deeply nicking the point of his knife against a bronze cleat.

His horror was due to a certainty that the knife in Dave's back was his own.

If so, who could identify it? Pedro. . . . He had to look at that knife. He knelt beside Dave's body, hesitated a moment, and then seized the hilt. It pulled out easily. The point was broken. His knife. He looked at the fire—and the knife. It wouldn't burn. He didn't dare pocket it. Opening the window and throwing it into the street might be more dangerous than useful, because that sort of thing someone might witness. The best thing to do was to put the knife back. He could prove—But he didn't have an alibi. He had gone out for supper alone and had been alone all the evening. The waiter would remember that he had dined at Boland's, but not when or for how long. His heart was banging steadily. Somebody had picked up his knife in his apartment so that he would be convicted of Dave's murder.

He held the knife up to the fire to make sure it was his and, as he did so, the front door behind him slowly opened. He didn't hear it. Carefully he thrust the blade in the wound just as it had been. Then he felt cold air on his back, and as he sprang to his feet he whipped out Dave's automatic.

A girl stood there. A girl with silver-blonde hair and gray eyes. There was snow on her hat and shoulders.

Her name was Wanda Jones. She was Tony's secretary.

His fear faded and in its place came a sort of embarrassment. The girl also seemed embarrassed. She was thinking, perhaps, not that David Cole was dead, but that her employer would wonder why she was visiting his partner at night and without his knowledge.

"You'd better come in and close the door," Tony said.

She did so, not looking toward the fireplace. "Who did it?"

"I don't know." On an impulse he looked into the hall. The two heavy Spanish chairs were in their places, where they had been when he had entered, so he closed the door again.

She took off her coat. "Maybe you'd better tell me about it."

At that time, he did not realize how much the presence of Wanda Jones relieved his mind. For three years her graciousness and capability had made his office more human and more effective and a more desirable place to work. She was diplomatic and dependable and discreet. In three years he had gleaned only a hazy idea of her origin and her way of life. But he was glad she was there, and he told her exactly what had happened, from the moment of Les's telephone call to the opening of the hall door.

Then he said to her, "How did you get in?"

"I had keys. Mr. Cole gave them to me this afternoon."

He looked at the girl with sudden jealousy. "Would you rather I didn't ask you any more questions about yourself and Dave?"

Miss Jones smiled. "I think it would be better if you asked me a lot more. Better still if I told you just what happened. And may I smoke a cigarette?"

He offered his opened case. They sat down. The back of a divan screened Cole's body.

"At five this afternoon you left Mr. Cole's office after telling him flatly that you were against taking over Señor Alavo's bond issue."

" 'Flatly' is a mild word for it."

"Immediately afterward Señora Alavo called up and told Mr. Cole that she was going to call on him this evening at nine— presumably to use her charm to help sell the bonds. Mr. Cole argued in favor of them with you, but after you had gone he began to waver. He didn't seem to relish the idea of entertaining Señora Alavo—"

Tony nodded. "Latin, damn' good-looking, and probably scared old Dave to death."

"—so he asked me if I would appear at nine thirty sharp, apparently to take some important dictation. His own secretary had gone. He gave me keys to the downstairs door and this one, and told me he was sure that if I came in that way, and Señora Alavo were still here, she'd leave."

"No doubt," Tony said dryly.

That explained the perfume. He had connected the heavy aroma with the wife of their South American client the instant Miss Jones had mentioned her name. She had been there. Loretta Raymond had been there. Les Boyd had been there. Possibly Miss Jones had been there earlier in the evening, and was lying. Her story was pretty thin and pretty absurd, but he wanted to believe it, and it had one element in its favor: David Cole was terrified of women, particularly of attractive women, and the South American banker's wife was young and dazzling and very shrewd.

"We'll go downstairs," he said, "and take a cab to the police station."

She put out her cigarette. "You're on the spot, Mr. Andrews," she said. "Does anybody know you're here?"

He shook his head.

"Did Mr. Boyd call you from here?"

"I assumed that he did, but there's no reason for that assumption—is there?"

"No," she answered.

He picked up the ash tray in which she had ground out her cigarette and walked across the room and tossed the stub on the fire, while she continued to talk: "If the police know you were here and that your own knife killed Mr. Cole—it'll be difficult for you. They are bound to find out about the argument you and he had this afternoon. I think that you and I ought to go to the movies."

"What!"

She went on calmly: "That'll give both of us an alibi for the evening. On the way we can call Mr. Boyd. Of course, he may make all this precaution unnecessary. Have you seen any pictures lately?"

"I went to the opening of 'The Arab.' "

"Swell!" the girl said. "I've seen it, too, so we'll only have to go to the theater long enough to buy tickets and lose ourselves inside."

He shook his head. "If you think that I'm going to pretend that I haven't been here tonight—you're mistaken."

"Then why did you keep your gloves on?"

He stared at her. Her face was disarming. Was she kidding him? Was she part of somebody's scheme to enmesh him in the death of his partner? Or was she trying to help him out of appalling jeopardy? He didn't know, but he did know that he was going to take a chance on Miss Jones. He made only one more brief compromise: "Why do you think it's so necessary for me to keep out of this?"

The girl's voice was bitter: "Do you know anything about the police, Mr. Andrews? Because I do. Plenty. You'll have trouble enough if they identify that knife. But if they knew you had been here, you'd be in jail tonight without bail."

"I still think we ought to call them."

"The police," she answered, "are cruel and stupid."

Tony put Dave's automatic back on the table. They went out and closed the door. They saw nobody in the halls. Out on the street, the storm was raging and the night seemed to be colder still. . . .

While they were walking down the stairs the front window of David Cole's apartment was opened from the outside by two men who were standing on a little iron balcony. The icy dementia of the night boiled into the warm living room, and it was followed by the feet of the two men. Their uniforms were covered with snow. They were stiff from bending over in the shadow and listening through the crack they had made at the bottom of the window. They had reached their peculiar post of observation just as Tony took the knife from Cole's back. One of them was young and the other was old.

"So we're stupid?" said the former.

The older man grinned without amusement. "That's what she said, Lieutenant."

"Let's get to work. . . ."

Miss Jones jumped out of a taxicab and into a cigar store and dialed Leslie Boyd's apartment in the Brail Hotel, but there was no answer to her call so she went back to the cab. It dropped them at 48th Street and Broadway. Tony bought two tickets to "The Arab" and they went in. They watched the picture for twenty minutes and left the theater by a side exit.

The girl went into a drugstore, and came back, reporting that she had tried Boyd but that there was still no answer.

After that Tony took charge. "We're going to see Raymond." Raymond was the firm's lawyer.

Miss Jones said, "That's right."

Raymond lived on East 61st Street in a private house. He opened the door. His greeting was genial and he led them into a big room elaborately furnished. "Sit down, old man. I can guess what's brought you here. Dave still wants to sell that bond issue and Les is on the fence as usual. All right. I am on your side."

He was a big man, with cheerful gray eyes.

Tony had an idea. "Where were you earlier this evening?"

"Where but here? Home alone. Loretta's out, but she'll be back after the theater." He chuckled. "She told me that you asked her last night if you could be my son-in-law." His eyes were mischievous. "I warned her that she could never reform you but I gave my permission. I think she's going to accept you, my boy. She's a fine girl, Tony, but if you marry her you'll have to hit her over the head with a beer bottle every week or so."

For some reason Tony looked at Miss Jones. She was quite pale.

"I called you up about nine thirty tonight," Tony said, "and there was no answer."

It was a lie. He wanted to see how Jack Raymond would take it—and Raymond looked utterly baffled. "But that can't be! I was right here, and nobody called."

Tony nodded. "That's right, Jack. I was just checking up on you. . . . Listen, Jack. Dave is lying up in his apartment with my knife through his back."

Raymond took a cigar from the humidor. He had trouble lighting it. He said, "You didn't? . . ."

Tony shook his head. "No, Jack, I didn't." He told his story. All of it—the precise truth.

When Tony finished, Jack picked up the telephone and called Les Boyd. There was still no answer. He turned from the instrument. "When do you think they'll find Dave's body?"

Tony's lips were compressed. "Mrs. Bunnell. In the morning."

"I suggest we go over to Les's place and wait for him."

"All right," Tony said.

In the hall, as they put on their coats, Jack Raymond expressed a feeling Tony had kept back: "Old Dave! That guy was just like my brother."

Tony swallowed hard. Like an older brother, he thought. Dave Cole had picked him from a long list of customers' men and made him a partner and taught him the business. Tony was richer and wiser and happier because of Dave—and somebody had murdered Dave. They'd find that murderer! Sometimes the three men fought furiously over policy—as they had that afternoon— but it was only superficial fury. It never ended in malice.

Tony's steady gray eyes met Jack Raymond's. "Yeah. Dave was like a brother to all of us. Come on."

"I'll take the subway home," Miss Jones said. "You've got your alibi as well established as it can be. If you decide not to use it, though, let me know."

It was 11:15. As they started down the front steps of Raymond's house a limousine stopped in the deepening snow and the chauffeur helped Loretta Raymond out of the car. Jack Raymond told his daughter that they were on a business errand and would be back in a little while.

Loretta whispered in Tony's ear, "I decided *yes.*" He had a glimpse of her swift-line profile and her stormy red hair. He caught her hand and squeezed it.

With Jack, then, he walked to a subway entrance. They said good night to Miss Jones.

It was only a half-dozen blocks to the Brail Hotel. Tony walked across the lobby to the desk and asked for Mr. Boyd.

"He left town, sir," the clerk said.

Tony was stunned. Jack realized the necessity of showing no

emotion at that instant and said to the clerk, with apparent calm, "At what time did he leave?"

"Well over an hour ago."

"I'm Mr. Andrews," Tony cut in; "his partner."

"Yes, Mr. Andrews, I recognized you."

"Did Mr. Boyd say where he was going?"

"No, sir. He simply called up and asked that his bags be sent to him."

"He was packed, then?"

The clerk nodded. "Yes, sir. Our instructions were to put the bags in Lower 6—" The clerk rummaged through a stack of memorandums—"Lower 6 in Car 176 on the ten o'clock for Montreal."

"Was Mr. Boyd aboard the train when your boy delivered the bags?"

"No, sir."

"I think we'd better go up to Boyd's room," Jack said.

The clerk gave them a key.

Leslie Boyd's apartment was in the mild disorder that results from hasty packing.

Tony sat down heavily. "I guess that's the answer, Jack. Les did it. Used my knife. Called me over there and shut me in when I arrived. Probably intended to keep me in there long enough so that I'd leave plenty of fingerprints, and then took the chairs away. I guess I don't need my alibi—such as it is. It's a mess, isn't it?" Drearily he walked toward the door.

"Going home?" Jack asked.

"I thought I'd go over and talk to Loretta first. Who knows but when I get home the cops may be there waiting to carry me off to jail."

The lawyer put his arm around Tony. "You won't have to worry about that! Even if they identify that knife, I know at least five hundred ways of keeping people out of jail."

They thanked the clerk for letting them into Les Boyd's apartment. They went out into the night.

Loretta was waiting for them in the drawing room.

Jack Raymond glanced at his daughter and said, "You won't mind if I excuse myself? I am speaking with what is popularly called elaborate sarcasm. I'll be upstairs if she throws anything, Tony."

Tony looked at the girl who had said she would become his

wife—firelight on her red hair and bright little points of flame in her eyes. Her father's amused kidding about her temper and her behavior was not altogether unfounded. Tony was fond of her. She was exciting. For four or five years he had often been in her company, and a casual habit of saying, "You and I really ought to get married, Loretta," had eventually made him decide that he would ask her to marry him and tame her a little bit, and perhaps himself in the process, and raise sons and daughters who would be just as unmanageable and dramatic in the smart set of 1959.

He had stood looking at her for a long time.

"Would you like a drink?" she said.

"No. What were you doing down at Dave's apartment tonight?"

The minute fires in her eyes burned higher. "You think *I* was in Dave's apartment this evening? Were you there, Charlie?"

"Peeking through a keyhole," Tony answered placidly.

Loretta looked toward the ceiling in a mockery of dismay. She said, "Alas! Then you know all! For years I have been madly in love with Dave. Tomorrow we are going to fly together to the ends of the earth! I chose him rather than you because he is richer than you are, and my poor father's gambling in the market has reduced us to poverty!" She struck a caricatured posture of despair.

Tony did not smile. "Dave was murdered tonight with my hunting knife and I found your handkerchief in the divan. I burned it."

Loretta turned to stone. Finally she said, "Thanks."

Tony walked over to her and took her by the arms. "Well?"

Her eyes met his directly. "What I said is sort of true, Tony." Her voice was a miserable whisper. "When I was eighteen I was infatuated with Dave. I wrote him a lot of letters. You asked me to marry you yesterday, so I thought I'd better ask him if he kept the letters."

"You're a fool." He chucked her lightly under the chin. He kissed her.

Loretta drew a long breath. "Dave said he had destroyed the letters as fast as I wrote them. I left his place about eight o'clock, Tony, because I had to go to the theater. He was alone and alive."

By and by he went into the hall and got his coat. The storm was still raging. He beat snow from his shoulders as he went up in the elevator to his lofty apartment. Pedro was there—looking frightened. Lieutenant Doyle and Sergeant McCluskey were also there. They didn't tell him that, crouched in the storm, they had watched him in Dave Cole's apartment. They described briefly the circumstances in which they had discovered the body.

Tony leaned against the mantel and smoked and looked at the men. They had ruddy, bartender-like faces and eyes that did not look either innocent or intelligent.

The lieutenant finished his description of the finding of the body.

Tony said, "That's horrible, Officer."

McCluskey turned toward his superior. "He don't seem very surprised."

The lieutenant nodded. "What about it? McCluskey's right."

Tony answered quietly, "I'm not an hysterical woman, you know."

"This is a very poor time for you to get fresh, Mr. Andrews."

Tony scrutinized his cigarette. "Perhaps I feel a great deal more grieved by Dave's death than either of you would understand. Perhaps I don't care to share that grief with strangers."

Not his face, but the back of Doyle's neck, became red. "The ritz, eh? Mind condescending to tell us what you did tonight? From seven o'clock on."

Tony said, "I had dinner alone at Boland's. It was Pedro's day off. I came back here and read a book about South America. Right behind you on the table, Lieutenant. Mr. Boyd—my other partner—dropped in for a while." He explained briefly the uncompleted South American bond negotiations. "I had an appointment to take my secretary to see a motion picture that we had discussed this morning—"

"Very interesting," said the lieutenant. "What's her name?"

"Wanda Jones," Tony replied steadily, "2334 Clansdale Avenue, Woodmere. We went to the picture, and then I called on my attorney. I have just come back."

Lieutenant Doyle reached into an inside pocket and took out Tony's knife. "That's all we want to know, Mr. Andrews. Between eight and nine you killed your partner with this knife. It's yours, isn't it? Your Filipino identified it."

Pedro overrode his terror enough to speak for the first time: "I said I thought it looked like one you have. It's gone."

Tony took his knife. "I had one like this with a nick in the point. If mine's gone, I dare say this is mine."

Doyle turned to his aide. "Put the bracelets on him, McCluskey."

Tony didn't move, but there was authority in his voice: "Keep

the bracelets in your pocket, McCluskey. Do you boys want to
be demoted for false arrest? And how about the suit I'd slap down
on you? And where's the warrant? . . . Look here. That knife
has been in my house all winter and I've entertained hundreds
of people. It might have been gone for months. It was in a drawer
with a lot of junk. Dave might have taken it himself, because he
was planning a fishing trip and came over here to borrow some
of my tackle. If my knife killed him it doesn't mean anything.
But think this over: Leslie Boyd, the other partner in our firm,
went to see Dave this evening. He told me he was on his way
there when he called this evening. Mr. Raymond, our lawyer, and
I went over to Boyd's hotel tonight. About ten o'clock this evening
Boyd had his bags put in Lower 6 in Car 176 on the train for
Montreal. Why don't you boys stop Boyd before he gets out of
the country?"

The policemen hesitated.

"Now get the hell out of here," Tony said.

Lieutenant Doyle meditated laboriously. Finally he asked the
name of Boyd's hotel, telephoned, and checked up on Tony's
story. He stood. McCluskey stood. "We'll let you alone for the
present, Mr. Andrews. I hope it won't disturb you none to have
somebody tailing you."

"None," said Tony.

In the morning with his pre-shower cup of coffee Tony read
the story on page 1. He thought that police headquarters had
given out an unusual amount of information and that the reporters
had done a particularly accurate job. He did not know about the
two men who had watched him through the window. He did not
know that the police were smugly playing cat-and-mouse with
him. The story told him two new things: first, that the medical
examiner had set the time of Dave's death between seven and
nine of the previous evening; second, that the police were concentrating on finding Leslie Boyd.

"Mr. Boyd," the newspaper story went on, "had informed no
one of his intention to leave New York, but at about 9:30 he
telephoned to the clerk at the Brail Hotel and ordered that his
bags be placed in Lower 6 in Car 176 on the Montreal train. His
bags were found to be packed and ready and were taken by a
bellboy, Perry Wheaton, to the train. Wheaton reports that Mr.
Boyd was not yet aboard and that he left the bags as he had been

instructed to do. Conductor J. B. Carley, reached by the police at Rouses Point, on the Canadian border, states that Mr. Boyd was aboard the train and that he took up his ticket. Mr. Boyd had already retired when he reached Car 176. The train was held at Rouses Point, where it was found that Boyd was no longer in his berth and his baggage was gone. The train had stopped at Albany, but the porter is positive that Mr. Boyd did not get off at that point. However, the blizzard which raged last night delayed and frequently halted the express, so that it is conceivable that Mr. Boyd could have descended at any of a dozen points along the way. A state-wide search for him has been instituted."

When Tony left his apartment to go to the office it was still snowing, and he hopped into a heated taxicab. When his cab started, another one left the hack stand in its wake. Tony looked out his rear window and made a face at the plain-clothes man who was following him.

His office was in a state of chaos which became a stiff silence when he entered. He lifted his voice: "Listen, everybody. I know how you all feel today. Many of you have known Dave Cole and Les Boyd even longer than I, but I don't think any of you will miss Dave more than I do. I want all of you to go on with your work as well as you can. It will be difficult but it's the best solace. Until—" He halted. The simple dignity with which he had spoken of the senior partner was marred when he spoke about the third member of the firm: "Until Mr. Boyd—returns—I shall assume responsibility for all transactions. Marvin, I want to talk to you and Fletcher and Graham. You can all come in together now."

He felt bleak and alone as he walked past his silent employees. Then he entered his office and saw Wanda. He smiled at her and shut the door. "I used our alibi—though I guess we didn't need it."

She nodded. She looked as if she hadn't slept. "Yes. The police phoned me late last night."

She left the office when Fletcher entered with Graham and Marvin. For two hours the four men discussed the affairs of the firm.

When the men had gone out Tony rang for Miss Jones, and she came in with her book. He had left his desk and was looking out of the window.

"Yes, Mr. Andrews?"

He still stood with his back to her. "I want to ask you some questions."

"All right."

"What do you know about the police that made you say last night they were stupid?"

Her answer came in a slow monotone: "My father was head of the bond department in a bank in the West. It doesn't matter where. It doesn't matter what his name was. Somebody underneath him embezzled a lot of money. Police investigators blamed him. Some of the evidence did point toward him, more or less, but he was innocent. It was in 1931—you remember how things were—"

Tony nodded.

"Father was also interested in politics. He—was against the administration in our city. He—" her voice dropped—"signed a confession."

"Good Lord!" Tony turned around. The girl was sitting limply in her chair.

"They beat it out of him. He was sent up for five years. He died there."

"But couldn't somebody—?"

"Somebody could have, but nobody did. I tried. I went to newspapers. I wrote letters. I talked. The courts took everything away from us, but I kept on—even after he was dead. Then one night a couple of men came around and told me that I'd better not stay in—in that city—any more." She was silent.

"So you came here with a different name?"

Her eyes looked into him and through him and beyond him. "I knew a lot about the bond business. I decided to get a job somewhere and stick at it until I had a chance to lay my hands on a large sum of money. Then I was going to use that money to get the men who killed my father—the judge, the president of the bank, the policemen who beat him—everybody."

"Get them?" Tony echoed.

The girl smiled a little. "Oh—for days I thought that. Weeks. I didn't care what I did. Then—I got just such a job—working for you. I found out that there were some decent men in business, and of course I got over the idea I had for revenge, and of course I fell in love with you—" She added that last remarkable statement in the same monotone she had used to express the story of her tragedy.

Tony walked across the room and sat down on a corner of his desk facing her. "You did that too, did you? When?"

She cast down her eyes and spoke almost in a whisper: "When? In the first month or week or minute. The time doesn't matter. The whole thing doesn't matter. I fell in love with you, and it gave me something to think about besides—Father. I imagined you knew all about it. My being in love, that is."

Tony nodded slowly. "I suppose I did. I never thought about it consciously, though, not once in my life." He pondered for a moment. "You're telling me this now because I'm engaged to Loretta?"

She nodded wretchedly. "Yes."

He didn't know what his own feelings were. The girl just sat there with her face averted. If she had even looked at him or tucked in a curl of her silver-blond hair—it would have changed his feeling. That would have meant that her avowed emotion was not too deep to interfere with the conscious little businesses of being feminine. But Wanda did nothing. She let him see her— drawn, sleepless, miserable, and utterly without hope.

Presently she said, "I've succeeded in adding more weight to the burden you already carry. I think I would rather have died than have told you—what I just did."

"Taking a woman seriously," Tony replied after some time, "is not my habit. It's apt to drive you crazy. That's why I was certain to marry Loretta, or somebody like her. She'd be the first person to maintain that it was a mistake to take her with too much seriousness. In the office, I try to look at people as people, and not as men and women. Again—that's why I wouldn't let myself think of you as anything but a secretary."

"I understand all those things."

"Sure, you do. Now."

She stood up, went to the door, opened it, looked back, and smiled slightly. His smile in response was just as slight.

He was still standing looking at the door through which the girl had gone when his annunciator buzzed. "Señor and Señora Alavo would like to see you if you can spare the time, Mr. Andrews."

"Send them in."

The South American was tall and olive-tinged. He bought his clothes in England. His wife also was tall. She had long black hair heaped voluptuously at the back of the neck. Her clothes came from Paris. One could imagine the Alavos fitting in any setting so long as it was extravagant, but the Alavos, as they entered Tony's office, did not look urbane.

Tony said, "Sit down. Cigarette, Señora? Cigar, Alavo?"

He held a match. Both of them were trembling.

"Naturally," said the South American, "I did not murder your partner, Mr. Cole."

"Hunh!" Tony made no sense of that.

"Mr. Cole favored your acceptance of my bonds." He hesitated. "You were against the proposition."

Tony had been looking at Señora Alavo, his attention drawn to her by the mnemonic scent of the perfume she wore. It brought into his memory a picture of the divan with a blood-soaked back.

Tony moved his eyes from her to the banker. "Nobody has accused you of having anything to do with this tragedy."

"The police have been most polite." Alavo paused. "I assume that there is no further hope for my enterprise?"

Tony shook his head. "I was frank before, Alavo. I went down to South America and looked over the property and the reports. Your bank seemed sound—although there were plenty of rumors that it wasn't. I don't doubt that the ore in those mountains is worth a hundred times the sum you are trying to raise, but it's going to be expensive to get it out, and the market isn't stable."

Alavo nodded. "Your firm is the only one left to which I could go." He smiled briefly, ruefully. "My one hope of success was that Mr. Cole would override your veto." He shrugged. "Since I am now without a champion I will say to you, confidentially, that to return to my country without success will unquestionably mean the ruin of my bank as well as the mining corporation. My wife knew all these things. That's why she went, without my knowledge, to plead with Mr. Cole."

The woman stood up dramatically and cried out, "He was alive when I left him! I swear it!"

Alavo shouted, "Isabella! Be silent!" At that instant he was not a suave banker but a Latin husband giving orders to his Latin wife.

She sat down.

"This procedure"—Alavo was furious—"is, naturally, intolerable to me. I do not know what method my wife used in an attempt to persuade your partner!—"

The woman began to cry.

Tony felt angry. "Look here, Alavo. If you came in here to show me how furious you were, or to punish your wife, you can get out right now. I'd like to ask your wife some questions and I'd rather you didn't go on making a fool of yourself."

Alavo was on his feet, white and trembling. "If you said that to me in South America, young man—"

"It isn't South America, Alavo, and you can go back to your chair and sit down—or get out." He said that because the banker was slowly tiptoeing toward him in a delirium of rage. "Have you told the police?" Tony asked.

"Naturally not." The mention of police brought Alavo back to his senses. He sat down.

Tony turned his attention to the woman. "Just what did you do, Señora?"

She answered dully, without glancing at her husband, "He— went to a dinner. He told me he would be back late. I was to dine in my room. I decided to see Mr. Cole myself. It was my intention to call on you also and on Mr. Boyd. I was afraid"— she shuddered—"of ruin. I telephoned Mr. Cole late in the afternoon to tell him I was coming to see him. I went to his apartment. He was very kindly. He said he had no intention of giving up his position on our bond issue. He said that he expected to convince Mr. Boyd and override your veto. I couldn't have been there more than fifteen minutes."

"Where did you sit?" Tony asked.

Her dark eyes met his with surprise, but she had herself in hand. "I sat at the end of the divan on which he was stabbed."

Alavo shouted, "How do you know which divan he was stabbed on?"

She shrank from her husband but she answered steadily, "There have been diagrams of that room in the morning newspapers. Naturally, I realized Mr. Cole had been stabbed in the middle of the very divan on which I had been sitting."

Her statement checked with Tony's own observation. No doubt she perfumed her hair. "What time was it?"

"I left my room at the hotel at a quarter past eight last night."

"Say from a quarter of nine till nine, then?"

"I should think so. It was about nine thirty when I returned. My husband was in my room waiting for me. He had deliberately lied to me about being out all the evening. He is jealous. He knew that I was acquainted with many people in New York."

Ashamed and bitter, she pulled up one of her sleeves, and Tony saw on her wrist four ugly purple bruises.

That revelation again drove Alavo into a quivering insanity.

Tony looked at him coldly and said, "You're an awful nice fellow, Alavo. You didn't by any chance follow your wife down to Dave's apartment, and go up there after she'd left and pick up my knife from that mess of fishing tackle and stab him?"

"He followed me, yes," the woman said.

Alavo slapped his wife on the mouth. The blow was fierce. She didn't cry out or faint, but merely covered her mouth with her hand. The South American stood up then and said through his clenched teeth, "Come, Isabella."

Rage of that sort is contagious. Tony didn't entertain even so minute a thought as that Alavo was a skunk. His brain merely stopped working. Nobody could sock a woman in his office. Alavo was standing in front of him and Tony got up fast, bringing a haymaker with him. It knocked the banker backward. He collapsed in a chair—out cold.

Wanda Jones entered the room with a sheaf of letters in her hand.

Señora Alavo slowly shook her head and said, in a low, crazed tone, "But he didn't do it, Mr. Andrews. He was back in the hotel before I returned—and when I left Mr. Cole, the knife—and all that fishing tackle—were not—on the table." She wiped her mouth with a handkerchief, because it was bleeding. Tony turned toward his secretary. "Take Señora Alavo to the washroom." The two women went out.

He stood over the unconscious South American, thinking. A month ago, when Alavo had first come up from South America, and before Tony had made his flying trip to investigate Alavo's property, there had been a cocktail party at Tony's apartment. Cole and Boyd and Alavo, his wife, and the usual crowd. Suppose Alavo had picked up the knife at that time? Picked it up, because it had a nick in it and could be identified? Alavo was desperate. He might even have thought that a murder would be necessary to save his cause. In that case, Tony thought, it would have been himself or Boyd, rather than Cole, whom Alavo would have killed.

He walked over to his desk and picked up his thermos carafe. He poured icy water on Alavo's face. As he was doing that Lieutenant Doyle in plain clothes walked through the door from the outer office and said, "What's going on here?"

Tony replied grimly, "Señor Alavo is out cold."

"You didn't kill him, did you?"

Tony glared. "I knocked him out. What the devil are you doing here?"

Doyle bent over the South American. His eyes were still closed but he was moving. "I just wanted to talk things over with you."

Señor Alavo looked up into the policeman's face and then at Tony. He scrambled to his feet. "I've been framed! I didn't go into Cole's apartment! I sat outside in my car!"

The lieutenant said, "We've checked on you. We had your driver down at the station for two hours this morning. And unless he's a better liar than most dagoes, you didn't go into Cole's apartment."

Things began to happen very rapidly. Wanda came in with Mrs. Alavo. Already frightened, she sank in terror on a chair when she saw the policeman.

Tony tried to explain: "The Alavos came down to tell me that Mrs. Alavo had gone to Dave's apartment last night. They had a family row and he socked her, so I socked him."

Doyle smiled mirthlessly at Tony. "You knew I was outside, and when this alibi fell in your lap you put it on ice with a good, hard right. You think awfully fast, Mr. Andrews. It just happens that we think a little faster down at headquarters. This time I've got a warrant."

"What warrant?" Tony said.

"The warrant for your arrest for the murder of David Cole. Mr. Boyd called us last night. We didn't just go busting into Cole's apartment. McCluskey and I got into the one below and climbed up to the balcony above and looked in the window. We watched you in the living room." He turned to Miss Jones. "You, too, Miss Jones—and we'll take you along as a material witness. You see, we got there just before you arrived on the scene."

Wanda drew in a shivering breath.

Alavo walked over to his wife and took her arm. "We may leave?"

Doyle nodded. "I'll be up at your hotel to talk to you later on this afternoon."

Tony was looking at this lieutenant. His mind ran like a speeded-up motion picture. They had seen him in Dave's living room, wearing gloves. They had seen him pull out the knife. They had heard all his conversation with Wanda. No doubt they thought that, having been surprised by his secretary, he had smoothly lied out of his predicament.

Doyle's next words revealed the accuracy of that guess: "You've gotten yourself in a lot of trouble by falling for your boss, Miss *Redmond.*"

The girl sat down. "So you found that out . . . already."

"It was a cinch! Come on, Andrews. Come on, Miss Redmond. Apparently you take after your father."

The cruelty of that remark sent so violent an emotion through Tony that he would have knocked out the lieutenant as he stood there, if Wanda hadn't grabbed his arm. Doyle didn't waste any more time. He pulled out his gun; he handcuffed Tony; he directed them to walk through the outer office. Into the consternation caused by his appearance, Tony bawled one order: "We're being falsely arrested!—Get Raymond, somebody! . . ."

"It's a pretty tough spot," Raymond said. His ordinarily affable face was furrowed with anxiety. "Why in hell didn't you look out the front window?"

Tony grunted. He shifted his weight on the laced steel straps that formed the bed in his cell in the Tombs. "Who in hell would look for people hanging on the front of a building in a blizzard?"

Raymond nodded. "All right. All right. Didn't they see you go to the door and try to get out in order to call the police?"

"They got there later than that." Tony shook his head like a prize fighter trying to clear away the effect of too many blows. "I'd like to know what those fellows think I killed Dave for! Of course, I had a row with him. And a violent one. We've had dozens. Miss Abbott, Dave's secretary, told the cops I called Dave a 'wall-eyed baboon' and a 'chiseling screwball'! But those aren't terms you address to a man you're thinking of murdering."

The lawyer leaned forward, gripped Tony's shoulder, and shook him gently. "You haven't got a good lawyer for nothing, Tony. In the first place, they'll never be able to pin it on you while Boyd is missing. In the second place, when they do find Boyd they'll probably find their answer. Moreover, I may be able to change the charge against you and bail you out. I may be able to get a habeas corpus. The commissioner is an old friend of mine and so is the district attorney. There are a dozen ways out of this."

Tony nodded more calmly. "What about Miss Jones?"

"They were still talking to her when I came over here."

"Bail her out," Tony said.

Raymond looked thoughtfully at his friend. "Sure. I thought you'd want that."

He started toward the door. Tony caught his arm. "I'll tell you one thing you might try right now. If Les actually did kill Dave it might have been about money. Nobody knew just how Les stood, or what he spent. You might get a couple of certified public accountants to check over all our books—just as a . . . well. . . ."

Jack nodded slowly. "All right, Tony. Good. I'll put them on immediately."

They had arrested Tony on Thursday morning. On Friday he was still in jail. The police inspector came to see him and talked to him for several hours.

On Saturday the commissioner came. Tony knew him slightly, but acquaintanceship did not make their interview a friendly one. Tony went over his story once again, but wrathfully. He swore with fervor that as soon as his name was cleared he would sue every officer in New York. The commissioner was at first sympathetic but finally cold and withdrawn. He did not let Tony see that he was pretty thoroughly convinced his prisoner was the wrong man.

On Saturday Jack Raymond called for the third time. He repeated that accountants, working through the night, had found no trace of theft or embezzlement from the firm. All his schemes for liberating Tony had collapsed. He agreed to move his office temporarily into Tony's on Monday to take charge of the neglected affairs of Cole, Boyd & Andrews.

By Sunday afternoon Tony was in a state of high jitters. When a guard came by and said that Miss Raymond wanted to see him, he welcomed Loretta feverishly. She kissed him. She talked such voluble mush that the guard sheepishly walked out of earshot. Then she told Tony that her father was still working desperately, that she believed him innocent, that she wanted to marry him the minute he got out, and that he shouldn't take it so hard. "You know," she said, "you're just wearing yourself out foolishly. Everybody's convinced that your story is true. The police seem to wish they hadn't been so hasty about arresting you. Father even seems to think it's a little bit funny that you were put in the cooler. You know you were awfully stuck-up and sure of yourself, Tony. This will be a good lesson to you."

Such statements might have angered another man than Tony, but, oddly enough, they served to calm him. For three days he had been acting like a trapped tiger—pacing his cell, refusing his food, and doing very little thinking.

When Loretta had kissed him again and departed, Tony walked to the barred window of his cell and glared at the bitter blue sky. So Jack was laughing at his distress? Jack was right. He had been behaving like a school kid. It was time to quit.

After a long period of quiet thinking, Tony walked to the door of his cell and called the guard. He handed him a ten-dollar bill. "I want you to see if you can get hold of Miss Wanda Jones— that is, Miss Redmond—and have her come here as soon as possible." He gave the guard Wanda's telephone number in Woodmere.

It wasn't quite regular, but ten dollars was ten dollars and the guard knew where he could reach a colleague who was off duty and could telephone.

Tony didn't have to receive visitors in the steel-barred room with the little wickets for talking, as did the other prisoners. It was a privilege his prominence allowed him. When they brought Wanda to his cell it was almost dark. Her cheeks were very red but that was due to the cold. Her smile was wan.

The policeman stood outside for this interview, acting upon orders he had received the minute Tony's new visitor announced her name.

Wanda sat down and said, "I wanted terribly to see you, Mr. Andrews, but I was afraid that my coming here would only make things worse for you."

Tony nodded and glanced at the listening policeman. "I'm glad you decided to come." He said that to cover the bribe to the guard, and for a moment she almost gave the guard away by saying that she had been summoned. But in another moment she understood.

Her reply was composed: "I thought that there might be things you would want done in the office tomorrow."

She had a mind, Tony thought, that was fast and brilliant. He said, "Quite right. There are a lot of things that you've got to take care of for me and others you've got to explain to Jack Raymond. He's going to take over at the office until I get out."

He watched the policeman as he ticked off twenty or more business details, details that included the names of all his partners, sums of money, cities, corporations, bond prices, and other data. In the midst of his recitation he included the statement he had summoned Wanda to hear. He had just said, "You will find in David Cole's desk, no doubt, the complete mineralogical reports on A. T. B. and J." "A. T. B. and J." meant nothing to Wanda, so that she was doubly alert to what he said next: "In Mr. Boyd's armoire the residuary habiliments will give me an index of the direction he intended to take in that line."

Wanda's eyes flickered for a second. What Tony had conveyed was that the clothes remaining in Leslie's Boyd's room at the hotel would, by revealing what he had packed in his two suitcases, show more or less where he had intended to go on the fatal night. Wanda said, "I'll check that up."

The policeman had not noticed anything unusual. The use of such words as "residuary" and "index" had a financial sound. It was, he reported to his superior later, simply a business conversation.

On the following day Tony waited impatiently for Wanda. He was filled with a new hope, because now he was doing something to help himself. He had discovered what he thought might be a new line of investigation. He had discovered it by thinking about Les Boyd. It was not like the debonair, gay little man to run out on danger unless he had an impressive reason for doing so. There might have been such a reason. Nobody could tell how much Les had known about the murder, and he might have been following the killer of David Cole or tracking down a clue to his murder. He had started on the train to Montreal, apparently, but nobody could prove how long he had stayed on that train. Certainly he had no business in Canada so far as Tony knew. Quite possibly he had used the Canadian train as a blind to make some other journey.

Nobody had actually seen him on the train. He had presented his tickets from a curtained berth and he might easily have left the train near New York, come back into town, and taken another. Thus, he could have traveled South, or flown South. That was why Tony wanted to know what clothes were left in his hotel apartment. If Les had been intending to go to Montreal he would have provided himself with garments for a cold climate. But if he had been going South his two suitcases would have contained a different set of garments.

Wanda came during her lunch hour. She looked excited, so Tony knew that his idea had brought some sort of result. They had expected to be forced to use the same deceptive methods by which he had asked her to make the search, but the guard allowed them privacy.

Wanda broke her recitation of business facts the moment the guard was out of earshot: "I didn't dare go to the hotel to ask about the clothes, of course. But I know a newspaper reporter quite well. He got a copy of the complete list of the contents of Mr. Boyd's apartment which the police made the day after the murder. Mr. Andrews! He didn't take any winter clothes at all! But a lot of his summer things that I can remember were missing— that light greenish suit and that powder-blue sport coat and all his flannel trousers. And they didn't find his Panama hat in his room." Her voice was low, almost a whisper. "Do you think he could have faked being on that Montreal train and come back and started for—South America?"

"I think we'd better let that matter drop for a moment and see what we can do with the Bigelow issue." Tony replied.

The guard was returning.

That was Tuesday. . . . A whole week passed.

The days went slowly for Tony, but not so slowly as those that had preceded, because he was now constantly expectant of news from Leslie Boyd. He felt certain that somewhere Boyd was working with his brilliant energy to resolve the crime.

Then Tony received a shock.

On the eleventh day of his incarceration the police commissioner himself appeared at the door of Tony's cell and was let in. He looked, Tony thought, unsure of himself and almost embarrassed. He said, "I've got news for you."

Tony waited.

"We've found Boyd."

Tony jumped up. "And? . . ."

"I came down here to express the department's chagrin, personally."

Tony had been right. Good old Les.

"He killed himself yesterday."

Tony sat down again, his face blank, his feelings numb. "Killed himself?"

"A farmer found Boyd's body this morning. It was lying just outside David Cole's summer house at Elkhorn Lake in the Adirondacks."

"But!—" Tony closed his mouth.

The commissioner's eyes showed amusement. "You were going to tell me that Les Boyd was all packed up to go South, weren't you? That was a mighty clever piece of work you did with Miss Jones, or Redmond, or whatever her name is. We wouldn't have known about it if we hadn't kept good track of the girl. We heard her talking to her reporter friend and checked up on Boyd's clothes ourselves—"

Tony shrugged. "All right," he said quietly. "I'm a bum detective. Suppose you tell me just exactly what happened."

"Boyd blew a hole through himself with a shotgun some time last night. A big hole. He fell in the snow, and his body was frozen when the farmer found it. The farmer decided to look around the Cole place when he saw a light in the basement was burning. Boyd had been hiding up there for several days, evidently. They found lots of empty cans and a bed and blankets where he had slept, as well as one other thing that I'll tell you about later."

Tony shook his head. "You can't tell me that Les Boyd killed Dave Cole and then went up to Cole's place in the Adirondacks and committed suicide. It doesn't make sense. He wasn't that kind of a guy."

The police commissioner's face expressed a combination of pity and disdain for so credulous a person as Tony. "If you'd had as much to do with murder as I have you'd know that a man can look like one thing all his life and be another. Besides, Boyd was plainly a pretty dizzy figure. A rich bachelor—love affairs—that collection of emeralds—an early life of busting around the world in all kinds of adventures and scrapes. No, Andrews. It doesn't do any good to deny facts. Boyd decided to kill Cole. He got hold of your knife so that you'd be implicated and clear his trail. He went over to Cole's house and did the job. Then he called you up and locked you in. Being locked in that apartment with a dead body was supposed to get your wind up, throw you into a panic, make you leave fingerprints, or yell for help. Before help came he removed the chairs so nobody would believe you had been locked in.

The police commissioner cleared his throat. "After Boyd called you, and just before you arrived at the apartment—maybe when you were being announced by ringing that bell—Boyd called us, so that there would be policemen on the scene to catch you. Then he went out—maybe down the fire escape from the window in the top-floor hall—and ordered his bags sent down to the station. It was a dandy trap for you! Now, look at his getaway. He has his bags put on a Montreal train. But his bags are full of summer clothes. That's where he was too slick. He figured that we would find out he was packed for the South, and therefore that we would look for him in the South. It just happens that we weren't bright enough to do that. He actually goes North, but he messes up that trail, too. Do you get it?"

Tony nodded slowly, the completeness of the police commissioner's diagnosis overcoming his feelings. "Sure, I get it. He actually went up to the Adirondack camp but he left what looked like a slip, to lead the trail South."

The commissioner shook his head. "He did better than that. He didn't dare stay on that train. He might be nailed by a fluke if anybody saw him. But nobody did—really. His berth was made and his bags were in it. He handed out the ticket through the curtains when the train started. He wanted to disappear, and that was easy, because he had never appeared, really. If he had, we would have found his bags. But he could have opened his window and tossed them into the Harlem River. He could have hopped off the train without them anywhere above 125th Street, by opening the doors, letting himself out, and slamming them after him. There was a blizzard that night, remember, and the train was going along by fits and starts. He could have come back into the New York station by subway and taken another train going north, or he could have picked up an automobile and driven. What he did is not important. The fact is that he left the train to break the trail. We were supposed to think he was going north on that train. Then we were supposed to find out about his bags being packed with summer clothes and start looking for him in the South.

"Just how and when he actually went to Cole's summer place doesn't matter at all. That's the dope. But he lost his nerve, and after he had done what he intended to do he blew a big hole through his backbone with a load of buckshot."

Tony swallowed. "Just what did he intend to do? Why did he go to the house on Elkhorn Lake? Why did he kill Dave?"

"We won't ever know all of that," the commissioner answered. "Boyd went up to Elkhorn Lake to destroy the evidence of his motive for the murder. He used the fireplace to burn a sheaf of papers. We found what was left unburned because it was held together by one of those heavy metal clips. Thirty-seven pages written in pen and ink on the stationery of the Oregon Central Lumber & Douglas Fir Corporation. The rest of it was ashes. And those ashes are the secret of why Boyd killed David Cole. Cole had something on him, a signed confession maybe, something that Boyd had written out and Cole kept. So Boyd killed Cole and went up to the house in the Adirondacks where the document was kept, and found it and destroyed it. Then he lost his nerve and shot himself."

The police commissioner stood up. "I guess that's about all, Andrews. I certainly apologize for the days you've spent here. You can hardly blame us for arresting you after what Doyle and McCluskey saw. I suppose you could bring a suit for false arrest. But I wish you wouldn't do it. In the first place, you might not win the suit. In the second place, you're in a spot now where if you ever need a favor from the police department you will only have to take up your telephone."

"I wasn't thinking of suing," Tony answered absentmindedly.

The police commissioner sagged for an instant with relief and then clasped Tony's hand. "Fine! Fine! Splendid! Any time we can be of service to you—" He walked toward the door of the cell and out. The door was not closed behind him. Tony looked at it without seeing it and then heard the commissioner's booming voice: "Come on, old man! You've done your time! Don't tell me you're stir-daffy."

Tony grinned and walked out of his cell. He wasn't stir-daffy. He was thinking—thinking furiously and purposefully. The newspapers would print the story and the public would accept it. Leslie Boyd had murdered David Cole and implicated Tony Andrews, and made a getaway and finally killed himself, after destroying some sort of confession which David Cole had in his possession. It was about that "confession" that Tony was thinking. More than a year ago Tony, himself, had gone out to Oregon to look over a property. A lumber property. Sitting in an office in Portland, Oregon, Tony had written by hand a report of that property to David Cole. He had written it on the stationery of the Oregon Central Lumber & Douglas Fir Corporation. He had fastened the report together with a heavy metal paper clip. He had sent the report to Cole by air mail. He had numbered the pages in the report, and there had been exactly thirty-seven.

Thus, the document burned beyond reclaim, the document that was supposed to contain the motive for the murder of Cole by Les Boyd, was not a confession at all. It was a business report. Les Boyd would not have taken the trouble to burn it for any sensible reason whatever. It had probably been carried to Cole's summer place in a brief case by Cole himself and filed away, to be forgotten.

He went outdoors. The midday sun was shining and its light was unbearably blinding. He hailed a cab and gave the address of his apartment. All the way uptown he was thinking hard. Why did Boyd burn that report? He had not used the paper to start a log fire, for then even the portion of it held by the clip would have been consumed. There wasn't anything in that report which concerned Les in any way.

Pedro heard Tony's key in the door and opened it and smiled.

"I want a tub full of hot water," Tony said, as he took off his coat. "And bath salts, a shower, and hot coffee, and toast that doesn't bend when you pick it up by one corner. Call up my secretary and tell her to come up here with the mail and anything else that's important. I won't go down to the office until tomorrow."

Tony reached the stage where soap, water, washcloths, back brushes, and nail brushes have done their appointed tasks and a man merely takes his ease beneath the restful patter of a warm spray. He gave sudden voice while in this position: "Holy mackerel!"

A simple and rather obvious explanation of the burned papers had occurred to him. Its implications were appalling. Suppose somebody else had burned that report to make it look as if Les Boyd's motive for killing Cole was to be forever unknown. Tony had imagined that Les was on the trail of Cole's murderer. But suppose it was the other way around: Suppose the murderer had trailed Les! Killed Les—put the shotgun in Les's hands, and burned the papers in a conspicuous place so that Les's suicide would seem motivated! Suppose Les had been murdered to cover up the murder of Cole, to accomplish just what it had accomplished in the mind of the police commissioner.

Such a set of circumstances would have closed the case—had, in fact, closed it.

Tony was sure that he was right. Les Boyd had been murdered

by the same man who had murdered Cole. He gasped under a sudden deluge of cold water, toweled himself furiously, and went into his bedroom. As he began to put on his clothes Pedro knocked on his door. "Miss Jones is outside."

He finished his dressing quickly. The girl was sitting on a divan by the fireplace, and when he came out she stood up. "I'm terribly glad—"

Tony grinned. "Me, too. Are you all ready to do some work?"

She opened her briefcase. "You bet I am! And I hope you are. Smithson is wild to see you; Williams is down in the office talking to Mr. Fletcher right now—" She stopped because Tony was paying no attention to her. He had picked up a newspaper that she had been carrying. On the first page were headlines:

LESLIE BOYD COMMITS SUICIDE
WAS MURDERER OF DAVID COLE
Andrews Released

Tony glanced through the story. He tossed the paper back on the divan. "Look Wanda. I didn't mean business. I meant work on this—" He pointed at the paper. "It wasn't a confession that Les Boyd burned, and he didn't burn it."

He told her rapidly about his assumptions, finishing with the words, "Whoever was up there was also the person in Dave's apartment the night we were there. The murderer. What I want to do—"

She interrupted him excitedly: "Is to check everybody's alibi for last night and the day before! Alavo's and mine and—" She broke off. "But that wouldn't do any good, necessarily, would it?"

"I hadn't thought of it," Tony answered rapidly. "My idea was for you and me to go over everything that happened the night of Dave's murder. To see if we could remember anything that would throw some new light on this. But why not check the alibis? Why wouldn't the easiest thing be to find who was out of town yesterday, when Les was shot?"

Wanda looked frightened. "I was just thinking—"

"Thinking what?"

"Thinking that the paper said Mr. Boyd's body was frozen. Frozen solid. And I was wondering if that didn't mean he could have been dead for days. If a person is frozen, can even a medical man be sure how long he's been dead?"

Tony stared at his secretary. "You mean Boyd might have been lying up there for days?"

"It's just as possible. Why don't you call up a doctor and ask him? Because if it was done a week ago, for example, it would be pretty hard to check anybody's alibi."

Tony picked up the phone and called his own doctor. He explained swiftly that his question must be regarded as an inviolable confidence. The doctor's reply confirmed Wanda's suggestion: "I presume you are talking about Boyd, Tony, but we will skip that. It crossed my mind when I read the papers this noon. How did the country doctor up in the Adirondacks know the length of time Boyd had lain there if he was frozen? Unless he had something like a recent cover of snow to go by, he couldn't possibly know. That is the answer. In a solidly frozen human body no deterioration takes place whatever and I'd defy any medical man to say whether a given individual had been in that condition for hours or weeks."

Tony said, "Thanks," and hung up. He turned to Wanda. "You were right."

"We'd better tell the police."

He shook his head. "Not yet, we won't. Look here, Wanda. You and I know more about this than anybody else alive. I've got a terrific feeling that—"

Her blond head nodded. "I know! You feel that you can almost see who did it!"

"And I want to think a little more about it—about the night Dave was killed. Just what happened. When did it happen? Whose story fails to check with what we know? Wanda!" His voice raised. "We ought to go back to Dave's apartment. We ought to go over the whole evening. Have Dave's things been moved?"

She shook her head. "The police sealed up the apartment just as it was."

Tony again picked up the telephone, and he called the police commissioner. "About that favor you promised me," he said.

The commissioner's voice was hearty: "Anything from a low license number to getting your nephew out of jail."

"I want to go into Cole's apartment with my secretary, and I don't want Doyle and McCluskey peering in the window."

There was a pause. "If you've got something on this, Andrews, maybe you better tell me."

"If I get something, I will tell you."

* * *

By the time a man from headquarters arrived at Tony's apartment with the keys, the afternoon was nearly worn away. The two men and the girl drove down to West Ninth Street. The policeman opened the front door of the house and they filed upstairs. On the door of the apartment itself there was a sign and a padlock. Again keys turned, and the door swung open. The policeman said, "Anything else?"

Tony thanked him. He went down the stairs.

They stood together in Dave's living room and Wanda said, "Don't you think we had better turn on the lights first?"

He nodded. "All the ones that were on that night."

When floor and table lamps drove back the dusk, they could see the stain on the divan and on the floor, dark brown now, and the ashes of the fire that had been burning in Cole's grate. In the bedroom the same suit with the same note pinned on it was still hanging on the bureau drawer. When they were satisfied that they had switched on the proper lights, they returned to the living room.

"Now," Tony said, "you watch me. I've knocked on the door." He walked toward it. "And now I come in." He halted. He said parenthetically, "It must have been about nine o'clock. The door wasn't answered. I unlocked it and walked in. Dave was lying there." Tony acted out what he was saying. "Lying there just as if he had been doing one of his suspension presses—with a knife in his back. . . . Let me see. I called Les." He called—once. "Les!"

He shrugged. "All right. No answer. I walked to the guestroom." Wanda followed him as he went down the dark hall and switched on the guestroom lights. "I took a squint into the closets here and moved on to Dave's room. I read the note to Mrs. Bunnell about the cleaners and I counted the dough on the bureau. Five or six hundred dollars. All right. Next I looked into the bathroom." He did so. "There were a couple of sloppy towels on the floor and a lot of water. Dave always bathed like a sea lion.

"Then the kitchen. There wasn't anything out of order in it." He turned on the kitchen light and they gazed at that room. "So far so good. Let me think. I walked back into the living room to call the police."

He stepped aside and Wanda went ahead. His voice trailed her. "Now. I picked up the telephone. The wire's cut—see? I decided to go out and find the police. Wait a minute. I hadn't taken off my gloves. One of the first thoughts that crossed my mind was not to leave any fingerprints while I was investigating. When I went to the door it wouldn't open. So! Let's see if those chairs will jam the door!"

They went into the hall and Tony put one of the Spanish chairs face down on the hall carpet. It fitted tightly between the door and the newel post of the stairs that led to the roof. "Now you do it and I'll go inside and try to push."

They made the experiment and Tony was unable to open the door. Wanda picked up the chair and put it back in its place. Tony came out. "That's what did it, all right," he said. He glanced around the hall—at the ship wallpaper, the crimson carpet, the table, and the sizzling radiator. He smiled a little at Wanda. "Kind of scary, isn't it?"

Her eyes met his brightly. "It's the weirdest thing I ever did in my life. The feeling that you almost know exactly what happened is terribly intense, though."

He did not reply to that. "When I found I couldn't get out this door I tried the kitchen door. Come on." They went through the house. "It was double-locked. Then back into the living room. I was absolutely positive that Dave's murderer was still in the building, on account of the barricaded door, of course. When I came back from trying the kitchen door—right now, that is—I saw Dave's .45 on the table—here—loaded but not used. I stuck it in my pocket because I thought I might need it any minute. Then I saw that the *Register* was opened at a story about me, and I knew it had been left there by Les. At least, it had his name and apartment number on it. The next thing I noticed was Señora Alavo's perfume, and I sniffed along this divan."

He repeated his actions of the fatal night. "I knew the perfume was familiar but I couldn't remember whose it was. I sat down and tried to think."

Wanda was standing opposite the divan where Tony sat, her face earnest with concentration.

Tony went on: "It was while I was sitting here that it occurred to me that Dave looked as if he had been doing that suspension press. I smoked a cigarette and chucked my ashes in the grate so nobody would look for my brand of cigarettes. I saw Loretta's handkerchief in the other divan, and I burned it. Then I realized the knife in Dave's back was just like my own. I felt compelled to look at this one. So I did. It was just about this time that

McCluskey and Doyle reached the balcony by the front window and began to watch."

He got down on one knee over the spot where Dave had been lying. "It was my knife, but discovering that wasn't any comfort. If I hadn't thought I was still locked in, I might have walked out with it—perhaps. But while I knelt here I felt cold air on my back—"

"And I came in," Wanda said.

Tony stood up. "You will never know how relieved I was to see you. When I felt that cold air I thought my last day had arrived."

For a moment they looked at each other, smiling. And then suddenly Tony started. "Cold air! Was it cold in the hall? Do you remember?"

She frowned, and finally nodded. "It was quite cold. The bottom hall was warm but it got colder as I went up the stairs. That fits with what the police said. The murderer got away by opening the hall window and going down the fire escape."

Tony was shaking his head. "Even on a night like that, opening and shutting a window wouldn't let in enough cold air to chill a couple of halls. It was hotter than Tophet." He stalked across the room and opened the front door of the apartment. "Hotter than blazes out here when I came up. The radiator was steaming away just as it is now. Look!" He rushed down the hall to a window. Outside was the iron fire escape. He opened the window, ducked his head, climbed out on the fire escape, and came back into the hall, shutting the window behind him. A little eddy of cold air had blown through the window, but when they walked back to Dave's door it was still warm in the hall.

Wanda looked back toward the fire escape. "But if the cold air didn't come from that window—" Suddenly and in horror she drew her breath. She had noticed the direction of Tony's eyes. He was looking up the staircase to the roof.

"I don't think the papers ever made any report of an investigation of that roof."

He started slowly up the stairs. When his head and shoulders came in contact with the trap door to the roof he unhooked it and pushed hard. It lifted. He climbed up the rest of the stairs and held his hand for Wanda.

The pink glow of the streets was reflected back dimly on the winter-swept roof. Iron benches, chairs, tables, flower urns, and flower boxes were barely visible. Snow was heaped over shapeless lumps. Tony stood there for a moment, and then walked over to the wall around the edge of the roof and looked down. "It would be a cinch to drop from here to the fire escape," he said slowly.

Tony's gaze rested on the formless lumps of snow which marked the positions of summer furniture. "Are you thinking the same thing I am?" he asked.

Her voice was choked: "I'm thinking that Leslie Boyd could have been murdered that night and carried up here—"

Tony took her hand. "Carried up here," he repeated rapidly. "The snow would have covered him in a few minutes! His body would have looked like another one of those flower boxes. And he'd have frozen, Wanda! It was bitter cold!"

"Then what?" she whispered.

"The murderer," Tony replied, "has had eleven nights to come back here and get that frozen body and drive it up to David Cole's house in the Adirondacks! Listen, Wanda! It could have stayed here frozen till now, even, as far as that goes. It's been cold right along. If Les came into Dave's apartment and found him dead, and the murderer was hiding there and killed Les, too, he could easily have brought him up here. Brought him here and then taken him miles away—" His voice sank. "Thawed out the body and used the shotgun—to erase a stab wound just like the one in Dave's back! Then he could have left the body to freeze again."

"But why didn't the police look up here?" Wanda asked.

"They probably did come up and take a look around. Late that night, or the morning after the murder. If we're right, Les's body was here then. But whoever brought it here could have covered it, and his own tracks, and the gale that night would have blown all the surfaces smooth in ten minutes. The cops came up here and saw nothing, which is understandable. Anyhow, they were sure they had their man. They'd seen me with that knife in my hand—through the front window. They weren't looking for anything else. If they'd been a little more thorough"—he glanced around the roof—"they might have found—"

"Let's go down," she whispered.

Tony murmured, "It would have been as simple as that!"

He helped her on the staircase again and closed the trapdoor. Once more they were standing in front of Cole's apartment.

"The hall's cold now, isn't it?" she said. And she shuddered from head to foot.

He nodded and opened the door to Dave's apartment again. "I'm sure of it now, Wanda. Les Boyd wouldn't have burned that report of mine for any reason in the world. So somebody else did. Les wouldn't have killed himself. Somebody did that to transfer guilt for the murder of Cole—which that person had already committed. Les wasn't out hunting for the murderer for the past eleven days. He was lying dead, and his body was kept just as it was for all that time because it was frozen. He was lying up here on the roof for a while and then in the Adirondacks. It would have been a cinch to get Les's body down that fire escape from the roof and into an automobile. Anybody who saw the thing would have thought Les was a drunk."

Wanda said uncomfortably, "I guess you've got something to tell the commissioner now."

Tony's head moved negatively. "An idea, and nothing to back it up. If my idea is right, and two murders were done in this room that night, there should have been signs of two murders. Up there on the roof I assumed that Les was stabbed, but he might have been struck over the head, for example." Tony's eyes moved toward the divan. "If the murderer had heard Les coming up the stairs and jumped behind that seat—if Les had come in and telephoned me and the police, and sat down opposite Dave to wait for me. . . ."

Thoughtfully he walked to the spot where he had found David Cole lying face down with outstretched arms. He looked at that spot. He gazed from there along the stained carpet to the larger stain on the back of the divan. "I don't suppose it ever occurred to the police to do blood tests," he said slowly.

Half understanding him, she murmured, "What do you mean?"

"Suppose the blood here on the divan was Les's blood?"

"But? . . ."

In a low tone, acting as he talked, Tony explained: "Let's assume that I am the murderer. I kid Dave into showing me he can still do a suspension press. I stab him. That's easy. While I am still kneeling I hear somebody come up the stairs, or perhaps ring the bell. I have just used the knife, so I snatch it and jump behind the divan. Les comes in, sees Dave, walks over to the phone, and calls. Then he seats himself on the divan to wait."

"But," interrupted Wanda, "how did Mr. Boyd get into the

apartment? The murderer wouldn't have opened the door for him."

"Les kept a set of keys to Dave's place. Dave gave me a set, too. He wanted us to feel we could drop in and use his place any time. Les must have rung the bell and got no answer, and decided to come in and wait till Dave came home."

"Yes, I see."

Tony crouched behind the sofa. He pointed at the stain on its back. "Les has made his phone calls and is sitting right here and I am directly behind him with the knife in my hand. I know that a third person as well as the police will be on the scene in a few minutes. I've got to get away before they come, but if Les sees me, it is all over for me. I realize that he is going to sit there and wait. All I have to do is reach over the top of this thing to kill him. You can't hang any harder for two murders than for one, but as I crouch here it dawns on me that if I can make it look as if one man had killed the other and then committed suicide I can forever divert suspicion from myself. And now look, Wanda. I stab Les." Tony made a gesture so realistically that the girl winced. "That makes the stain. I move Les over to where Dave is lying. It's simple, isn't it? Everyone will assume that Dave was stabbed in the divan and fell forward on the floor, leaving a trail of blood. It'll look like one murder only. I have already decided how and where I can hide Les's body for a long time. On the roof in the snow. I put the knife back in Dave's body and I pick up Boyd—and the rest we know."

Wanda frowned. "There's one thing, though. Why did the murderer barricade you in with those chairs? We've thought all along it was to put the crime off on you. But if he had already set the scene to make Mr. Boyd look like the murderer, why did he want to incriminate you, too?"

Tony considered. "Oh, gosh! I suppose we'll never know the truth of all this." He leaned against a chair despondently.

"Maybe it was this way," Wanda said slowly. "You arrived long before the police. Suppose the murderer was just carrying Mr. Boyd up the stairs to the roof when he heard you coming. He wouldn't have time to get out through the trapdoor—it's heavy and awkward and he was—he was carrying something." She stopped short, looking very white.

"Of course," Tony carried on her suggestion, excitedly. "So he hid on the stairs to the roof until I had gone into Dave's apartment and then barred the door with the chairs to keep me from coming out and catching him before he had finished. After he had Les on the roof and covered him with snow, he came back and took the chairs away."

Wanda asked for a cigarette. Her hand trembled. "And how about the other phone call—to the hotel?"

Tony glanced at her quickly. "Other phone call? That's right! Les called his hotel and ordered his bags sent to that Montreal train! That doesn't make very good sense—unless—unless—it was the murderer who called the hotel. We can ask the hotel clerk if he definitely recognized the voice. And that's important! Because if it was the murderer who called, then the murderer knew that Les had *packed his bags!*"

Their eyes met. "That's right," she answered slowly. "If the murderer telephoned the hotel, he probably got on the train himself for a little while, and handed out the tickets and disposed of the bags, and got off the train as soon as possible."

Tony said, "Let's go up and talk to the hotel clerk."

"At least," she said, "what the commissioner believes simply couldn't have happened—on account of that burned report. And what we are imagining certainly *could* have happened—if the man who killed Dave was very clever." They began to turn out the lights in the apartment. Tony called sharply, "Why a 'man'?"

There was blankness in her voice: "A woman?"

"If we are right—why not? Cole was killed while he was lying face down on the floor. A woman could have done it. Les was stabbed in the back when he didn't know there was another person in the apartment. A woman could have done that. And as for carrying Les Boyd's body up the stairs to the roof—Les didn't even weigh a hundred pounds. You could have done it. And you have a husky voice. You might have been able to make the hotel clerk think you were a man!"

The clerk at the Brail Hotel who had taken the order that sent Les Boyd's two suitcases to the railroad station gave them grounds for a reasonable doubt. "I don't remember the voice much. It's noisy in the lobby. It was just a voice—but I'll tell you. Mr. Boyd always used to say, 'This is Boyd—14-B.' Now, some people say, 'This is Mr. Norman K. Jones,' or others say, 'This is Mrs. Wilson, of Apartment So-and-so.' Whoever spoke that night said, 'This is Boyd—14-B,' so I naturally assumed it was Boyd."

Tony and Wanda went out into the street. "It's half past seven," he said. "Will you have supper?"

"Yes."

There was a long silence between them as they rode in a taxicab, a silence that was broken finally when he murmured, "A man or a woman—somebody who was well enough acquainted with Dave to know he could be kidded into doing that suspension press. Somebody who knew Les so well that he or she could telephone exactly the way Les did—someone who knew about Dave's summer place."

He chuckled mirthlessly. "That means you—"

"I didn't get on the Montreal train, and you know it. I was with you."

"You made two telephone calls that night, though. Before and after the few minutes we spent at the movies. One could have been to get Les's bags sent to the train and the other could have been to have somebody take care of the train ride itself. You could have done it if you had had an accomplice. For that matter, so could I if I had had somebody to take care of that train ride. But, for that matter—" He hesitated a moment and went on: "—so could Pedro. He had some kind of grudge against Cole. He could have left the house that evening when Les came in to talk to me, because I didn't see him again until morning, and in the eleven days I was in jail he could easily have transported the body to the Adirondacks."

"I don't think Pedro would have done such a—"

"Neither do I," Tony replied. The cab stopped in front of a restaurant. "But I'm just trying to show you that, if we are right about what happened, it still could have conceivably been done by not only you or me or Pedro, but by Loretta, or Jack—he was home alone that night, and she said she was at the theater— or by either one of the Alavos, or by any one of an unknown number of absolute strangers."

The doorman pushed open the restaurant door. "If we do know how, we still don't know who." She stood beside him as he checked his coat and a headwaiter walked smilingly toward them. "So I haven't got anything at all to tell the commissioner yet, and I don't think we will ever find out which person knew that Boyd was going South and could use that knowledge about the luggage, because obviously disclosing that would give away the person who did know it." Tony was following her among upturned faces, talking to Wanda's back. "In consequence of which dilemma I think I'll try a little notion I've got on all the possible suspects. It is a good notion but I'll probably find myself back in the Tombs for slander or whatever it is." They sat down.

"What's your idea?" she asked.

He shook his head at her. "I won't tell you unless it works. Now. Let's forget all about it. Let's have the best dinner obtainable, and afterward I'm going to send you home." He looked at the menu. "How about oysters?"

She wanted to ask questions, but she saw that he was determined not to talk any more about the deaths of his partners. She was glad, in a way. She hoped that he would talk to her about himself and herself. He did. . . .

Wanda was waiting in his office at 9:30 when he appeared. He was excited. He clapped his hands together when he came through the door. He had a black eye. Wanda stared at the black eye.

"Part of my idea," he said in reply to her unasked question. "We can cross Señor Alavo off our list, Wanda. Furthermore, he evened up things for that sock in the jaw I gave him." She waited for him to say more but he did not, so she handed him the mail. He glanced through it and picked out a single letter. "I want to talk this over with Jack Raymond. Tell him to come in. I persuaded Jack to take a Turkish bath with me last night, by the way."

Her eyes were suddenly alarmed and he shook his head. "We only talked about business. However, I'm going to leave the inner-office communicator open and I want you to listen at the other end." Her face was white and questioning. He shrugged. "Maybe I am just going to get another black eye."

She went out.

Jack entered, sat down, and smiled.

Tony got out of his chair and half sat on his desk. "You killed Dave with my knife, Jack," he said crisply. "Then you killed Les. You carried him up that dark stairway and hid with him while I came up. You blocked the door with a chair while you got him out on the roof. Then you went home. You didn't have time to take the short ride on the Montreal train, so you persuaded somebody else to do it. Your butler? Or Loretta? It doesn't matter. In one of the last eleven nights you took a trip with the body up to the Adirondacks and you made a murder look like a suicide

by burning a sheaf of papers and using a shotgun to destroy a
stab wound."

Jack sat still. Tony's first words had erased his smile, but now
it was on his face again, changed somewhat. "Just why did I do
all these things, Tony?"

Tony hunched himself up on his desk. "Loretta said that you
were broke. That you gambled. She said that she was trying to
marry Dave, or me, to save the family from ruin. I thought she
was kidding. She wasn't. You handle enough of this firm's prop-
erties to embezzle a good deal of money, a good deal without
being caught, but if you've taken any—maybe you've put it back
now. I haven't looked into the records. Dave probably had. You
killed him to keep him from telling us."

Jack's smile was still unabashed. "You've thought up a very
fancy nightmare, Tony. You certainly don't intend to make such
a charge seriously?"

"I intend to."

Then Jack stopped smiling. "I suppose you can prove it?"

Tony reached in his pocket. Jack's hand slid quickly toward his
own pocket, but Tony produced no weapon. He dropped two
small objects on his desk. "Here's a button from the suit you
were wearing that night and a little black notebook from your
vest pocket. I haven't had time to dry the notebook out, you may
notice. It fell into the snow on the roof of Dave Cole's house.
The button was on the staircase to the roof. Funny you haven't
missed—the notebook."

For an instant Jack's eyes stared. "I could have sworn I had it
yesterday—" He reached into his hip pocket then and pulled out
a revolver. His voice was low and splitting in its intensity. "Hand
over the button and the notebook. Then come along with me."

"Where?"

"While Loretta and I pack." He pointed the gun steadily. "We'll
tie you up and put you in a closet, where they'll find you in a
day or so." Jack was smiling once again, and his third smile was
an expression Tony had never seen—a deadly expression. "I don't
need to tell you that I'll use this if I have to—do I?" He put the
gun in his pocket, still keeping it pointed at Tony. "It was clever
work to figure that out, Tony. I did it. And I helped myself to
the firm's funds. Dave only found out through a fluke."

"Tell me one thing," said Tony quietly. "Where was Les going that night? Why were his bags packed for a Southern trip? And how did you know they were packed?"

"He told me. He was determined to stop this quarrel between you and Dave at any cost—even the cost of a trip to South America to check on your findings about the bond issue. He didn't tell you or Dave because he was afraid you'd try to stop him. But he had his bags packed, ready to leave that night, if you two couldn't patch things up. . . . That was one thing you couldn't find out, for all your detective work. And you've made one mistake. You should have had some witnesses to this little scene."

Very delicately Tony tapped the top of his inner-office communicator. "I have." He leaned down a little. "Wanda! Bring everybody in here."

For a second Jack was silent and motionless. Then he said, "I wish you'd do everything you can for Loretta. Keep her out of it. She didn't know why she carried out my orders for her about the Montreal train until the next day."

Tony said, "All right, Jack."

Then the door opened. Wanda was there, with Fletcher and Alavo behind her. . . . The shot made surprisingly little noise, because Jack had pressed the muzzle of his gun close to his body. . . .

Tony and Wanda sat in another taxicab riding toward the police commissioner's office. "He'll be furious." She referred to the commissioner. "Why didn't you tell him that you had found the button and the notebook?"

He turned toward her. "Because I hadn't. The button was from one of my own suits. It was just an ordinary black one—and I snitched the notebook out of his vest yesterday evening at the Turkish bath."

They rode a little longer. There was relief on their faces. Presently she looked up at him with a shadowy smile. "You're terribly clever, aren't you? I guess the best brains do go into business. The first time you dictated that speech I thought it was kind of funny, but now—"

Tony shook his head, and his grin appeared. "If I had brains I would have had the firm's books secretly audited ten days ago." He took her hand and patted it. "If I had brains I would have figured Loretta out sooner for what she is. If I had any brains whatever I would have paid more attention to a gray-eyed, silver-

blond girl about twenty-five years old named Miss Jones. I mean—
Miss Redmond."

"You've been calling her Wanda for the last day."

"Have I? Good for me! Maybe I have some sense, after all!"

The policeman who was chaperoning them to their final interview with the commissioner felt that his office was being imposed
upon somewhat. He looked out the window with evident fascination at a lamppost, a pile of paving stones, and a municipal
ashcan.

ERLE STANLEY GARDNER
The Case of the Crimson Kiss

Preoccupied with problems of her own happiness, Fay Allison failed to see the surge of bitter hatred in Anita's eyes. So Fay, wrapped in the mental warmth of romantic thoughts, went babbling on to her roommate, her tongue loosened by the cocktail which Anita had prepared before their makeshift dinner.

"I'd known I loved him for a long time," she said, "but honestly, Anita, it never occurred to me that Dane was the marrying kind. He'd had that one unfortunate affair, and he'd always seemed so detached and objective about everything. Of course, underneath all that reserve he's romantic and tender. . . . Anita, I'm so lucky, I can hardly believe it's true."

Anita Bonsal, having pushed her dinner dishes to one side, toyed with the stem of her empty cocktail glass. Her eyes were pinpricks of black hatred which she was afraid to let Fay Allison see. "You've fixed a date?" she asked.

"Just as soon as Aunt Louise can get here. I want her to be with me. I—and, of course, I'll want you, too."

"When will Aunt Louise get here?"

"Tomorrow or next day, I think. I haven't heard definitely."

"You've written her?"

"Yes. She'll probably take the night plane. I mailed her my extra keys so she can come right on in whenever she gets here, even if we aren't home."

Anita Bonsal was silent, but Fay Allison wanted to talk. "You know how Dane is. He's always been sort of impersonal. He took you out at first as much as he did me, and then he began to specialize on me. Of course, you're so popular, you didn't mind.

225

It's different with me. Anita, I was afraid to acknowledge even to myself how deeply I felt, because I thought it might lead to heartache."

"All my congratulations, dear."

"Don't you think it will work out, Anita? You don't seem terribly enthusiastic."

"Of course it will work out. It's just that I'm a selfish devil and it's going to make a lot of difference in my personal life—the apartment and all that. Come on; let's get the dishes done. I'm going out tonight and I suppose you'll be having company."

"No, Dane's not coming over. He's going through a ceremony at his bachelor's club—one of those silly things that men belong to. He has to pay a forfeit or something, and there's a lot of horseplay. I'm so excited I'm just walking on air."

"Well," Anita said, "I go away for a three-day weekend and a lot seems to happen around here. I'll have to start looking for another roommate. This apartment is too big for me to carry by myself."

"You won't have any trouble. Just pick the person you want. How about one of the girls at the office?"

Anita shook her head, tight-lipped.

"Well, of course, I'll pay until the fifteenth and then—"

"Don't worry about that," Anita said lightly. "I'm something of a lone wolf at heart. I don't get along too well with most women, but I'll find someone. It'll take a little time for me to look around. Most of the girls in the office are pretty silly."

They did the dishes and straightened up the apartment, Fay Allison talking excitedly, laughing with light-hearted merriment, Anita Bonsal moving with the swift, silent efficiency of one who is skillful with her hands.

As soon as the dishes had been finished and put away, Anita slipped into a long black evening dress and put on her fur coat. She smiled at Fay and said, "You'd better take some of the sleeping pills tonight, dear. You're all wound up."

Fay said, somewhat wistfully, "I am afraid I talked you to death, Anita. I wanted someone to listen while I built air castles. I—I'll read a book. I'll be waiting up when you get back."

"Don't," Anita said. "It'll be late."

Fay said wistfully, "You're always so mysterious about things, Anita. I really know very little about your friends. Don't you ever want to get married and have a home of your own?"

"Not me. I'm too fond of having my own way, and I like life as it is," Anita said, and slipped out through the door.

She walked down the corridor to the elevator, pressed the button, and when the cage came up to the sixth floor, stepped in, pressed the button for the lobby, waited until the elevator was halfway down, then pressed the *Stop* button, then the button for the seventh floor.

The elevator rattled slowly upward and came to a stop.

Anita calmly opened her purse, took out a key, walked down the long corridor, glanced swiftly back toward the elevator, then fitted the key to Apartment 702, and opened the door.

Carver L. Clements looked up from his newspaper and removed the cigar from his mouth. He regarded Anita Bonsal with eyes that showed his approval, but he kept his voice detached as he said, "It took you long enough to get here."

"I had to throw a little wool in the eyes of my roommate, and listen to her prattle of happiness. She's marrying Dane Grover."

Carver Clements put down the newspaper. "The hell she is!"

"It seems he went overboard in a burst of romance, and his attentions became serious and honorable," Anita said bitterly. "Fay has written her aunt, Louise Marlow, and as soon as she gets here they'll be married."

Carver Clements looked at the tall brunette. He said, "I had it figured out that you were in love with Dane Grover, yourself."

"So that's been the trouble with you lately!"

"Weren't you?"

"Heavens, no!"

"You know, my love," Clements went on, "I'd hate to lose you now."

Anger flared in her eyes. "Don't think you own me!"

"Let's call it a lease," he said.

"It's a tenancy-at-will," she flared. "And kindly get up when I come into the room. After all, you might show some manners."

Clements arose from the chair. He was a spidery man with long arms and legs, a thick, short body, a head almost bald, but he spent a small fortune on clothes that were skillfully cut to conceal the chunkiness of his body. He smiled, and said, "My little spitfire! But I like you for it. Remember, Anita, I'm playing for keeps. As soon as I can get my divorce straightened out."

"You and your divorce!" she interrupted. "You've been pulling that line—"

"It isn't a line. There are some very intricate property problems. They can't be handled abruptly. You know that."

She said, "I know that I'm tired of all this pretense. If you're playing for keeps, make me a property settlement."

"And have my wife's lawyers drag me into court for another examination of my assets after they start tracing the checks? Don't be silly."

His eyes were somber in their steady appraisal. "I like you, Anita. I can do a lot for you. I like that fire that you have. But I want it in your heart and not in your tongue. My car's in the parking lot. You go on down and wait. I'll be down in five minutes."

She said, "Why don't you take me out as though you weren't ashamed of me?"

"And give my wife the opportunity she's looking for? Then you *would* have the fat in the fire. The property settlement will be signed within five or six weeks. After that I'll be free to live my own life in my own way. Until then—until then, my darling, we have to be discreet in our indiscretions."

She started to say something, checked herself, and stalked out of the apartment.

Carver Clements's automobile was a big, luxurious sedan equipped with every convenience; but it was cold sitting there, waiting.

After ten minutes, which seemed twenty, Anita grew impatient. She flung open the car door, went to the entrance of the apartment house, and angrily pressed the button of 702.

When there was no answer, she knew that Clements must be on his way down, so she walked back out. But Clements didn't appear.

Anita used her key to enter the apartment house. The elevator was on the ground floor. She made no attempt at concealment this time, but pressed the button for the seventh floor, left the elevator, strode down the corridor, stabbed her key into the metal lock of Clements's apartment, and entered the room.

Carver L. Clements, dressed for the street, was lying sprawled on the floor.

A highball glass lay on its side, two feet from his body. It had apparently fallen from his hand, spilling its contents as it rolled along the carpet. Clements's face was a peculiar hue, and there was a sharp, bitter odor which seemed intensified as she bent toward his froth-flecked lips. Since Anita had last seen him, he had quite evidently had a caller. The print of half-parted lips flared in gaudy crimson from the front of his bald head.

With the expertness she had learned from a course in first-aid, Anita pressed her finger against the wrist, searching for a pulse. There was none.

Quite evidently, Carver L. Clements, wealthy playboy, yachtsman, broker, gambler for high stakes, was dead.

In a panic, Anita Bonsal looked through the apartment. There were all too many signs of her occupancy—nightgowns, lingerie, shoes, stockings, hats, even toothbrushes and her favorite toothpaste.

Anita Bonsal turned back toward the door and quietly left the apartment. She paused in the hallway, making certain there was no one in the corridor. This time she didn't take the elevator, but walked down the fire stairs, and returned to her own apartment. . . .

Fay Allison had been listening to the radio. She jumped up as Anita entered.

"Oh, Anita, I'm so glad! I thought you wouldn't be in until real late. What happened? It hasn't been a half-hour."

"I developed a beastly headache," Anita said. "My escort was a trifle intoxicated, so I slapped his face and came home. I'd like to sit up and have you tell me about your plans, but I do have a headache, and you must get a good night's sleep tonight. You'll need to be looking your best tomorrow."

Fay laughed. "I don't want to waste time sleeping. Not when I'm so happy."

"Nevertheless," Anita said firmly, "we're going to get to bed early. Let's put on pajamas and have some hot chocolate. Then we'll sit in front of the electric heater and talk for just exactly twenty minutes."

"Oh, I'm so glad you came back!" Fay said.

"I'll fix the drink," Anita told her. "I'm going to make your chocolate sweet tonight. You can start worrying about your figure tomorrow."

She went to the kitchen, opened her purse, took a bottle of barbiturate tablets, emptied a good half of the pills into a cup, carefully ground them up into powder, and added hot water until they were dissolved.

When she returned to the living room, carrying the two steaming cups of chocolate frothy with melted marshmallows floating on top, Fay Allison was in her pajamas.

Anita Bonsal raised her cup. "Here's to happiness, darling."

After they had finished the first cup of chocolate, Anita talked Fay into another cup, then let Fay discuss her plans until drowsiness made the words thick, the sentences detached.

"Anita, I'm *so* sleepy all of a sudden. I guess it's the reaction from having been so keyed up. I . . . darling, it's all right if I. . . . You don't care if I. . . ."

"Not at all, dear," Anita said, and helped Fay into bed, tucking her in carefully. Then she gave the situation careful consideration.

The fact that Carver Clements maintained a secret apartment in that building was known only to a few of Clements's cronies. These people knew of Carver Clements's domestic difficulties and knew why he maintained this apartment. Fortunately, however, they had never seen Anita. That was a big thing in her favor. Anita was quite certain Clements's death hadn't been due to a heart attack. It had been some quick-acting, deadly poison. The police would search for the murderer.

It wouldn't do for Anita merely to remove her things from that apartment, and, besides, that wouldn't be artistic enough. Anita had been in love with Dane Grover. If it hadn't been for that dismal entanglement with Carver Clements. . . . However, that was all past now, and Fay Allison, with her big blue eyes, her sweet, trusting disposition, had turned Dane Grover from a disillusioned cynic into an ardent suitor.

Well, it was a world where the smart ones got by. Anita had washed the dishes. Fay Allison had dried them. Her fingerprints would be on glasses and on dishes. The management of the apartment house very considerately furnished dishes identical in pattern, so it needed only a little careful work on her part. The police would find Fay Allison's nightgowns in Carver Clements's secret apartment. They would find glasses that had Fay's fingerprints on them. And when they went to question Fay Allison, they would find she had taken an overdose of sleeping pills.

Anita would furnish the testimony that would make it all check into a composite, sordid pattern. A girl who had been the mistress of a rich playboy, then had met a younger and more attractive man who had offered her marriage. She had gone to Carver Clements and wanted to check out, but with Carver Clements one didn't simply check out. So Fay had slipped the fatal poison into his drink, and then had realized she was trapped when Anita returned home unexpectedly and there had been no chance for Fay to make a surreptitious removal of her wearing apparel from the upstairs apartment. Anita would let the police do the figuring. Anita would be horrified, simply stunned, but, of course, co-operative.

Anita Bonsal deliberately waited three hours until things began to quiet down in the apartment house, then she took a suitcase and quietly went to work, moving with the smooth efficiency of a woman who has been accustomed to thinking out every detail.

When she had finished, she carefully polished the key to Apartment 702 so as to remove any possible fingerprints, and dropped it in Fay Allison's purse. She ground up all but six of the remaining sleeping tablets and mixed the powder with the chocolate which was left in the canister.

After Anita put on pajamas she took the remaining six tablets, washed off the label with hot water, and tossed the empty bottle out of the back window of the apartment. Then she snuggled down into her own twin bed and switched off the lights.

The maid was due to come at eight the next morning to clean up the apartment. She would find two still figures, one dead, one drugged.

Two of the tablets constituted the heaviest prescribed dose. The six tablets Anita had taken began to worry her. Perhaps she had really taken too many. She wondered if she could call a drug store and find out if—A moment later she was asleep. . . .

Louise Marlow, tired from the long airplane ride, paid off the taxicab in front of the apartment house.

The cab driver helped her with her bags to the entrance door. Louise Marlow inserted the key which Fay Allison had sent her, smiled her thanks to the driver, and picked up her bags.

Sixty-five years old, white-headed, steely-eyed, square of shoulder and broad of beam, she had a salty philosophy of her own. Her love was big enough to encompass those who were dear to her with a protecting umbrella. Her hatred was bitter enough to goad her enemies into confused retreat.

With casual disregard for the fact that it was now one o'clock in the morning, she marched down the corridor to the elevator, banged her bags into the cage, and punched the button for the sixth floor.

The elevator moved slowly upward, then shuddered to a stop. The door slid slowly open and Aunt Louise, picking up her bags, walked down the half-darkened corridor.

At length she found the apartment she wanted, inserted her key, opened the door, and groped for a light switch. She clicked it on, and called, "It's me, Fay!"

There was no answer.

Aunt Louise dragged her bags in, pushed the door shut, called out cheerfully, "Don't shoot," and then added by way of explanation, "I picked up a cancellation on an earlier plane, Fay."

The continued silence bothered her. She moved over to the bedroom.

"Wake up, Fay. It's your Aunt Louise!"

She turned on the bedroom light, smiled down at the two sleepers, said, "Well, if you're going to sleep right through everything, I'll make up a bed on the davenport and say hello to you in the morning."

Then something in the color of Fay Allison's face caused the keen eyes to become hard with concentration.

Aunt Louise went over and shook Fay Allison, then turned to Anita Bonsal and started shaking her.

The motion finally brought Anita back to semiconsciousness from drugged slumber. "Who is it?" she asked thickly.

"I'm Fay Allison's Aunt Louise. I got here ahead of time. What's happened?"

Anita Bonsal knew in a drowsy manner that this was a complicating circumstance that she had not foreseen, and despite the numbing effect of the drug on her senses, managed to make the excuse which was to be her first waking alibi.

"Something happened," she said thickly. "The chocolate. . . . We drank chocolate and it felt like . . . I can't remember . . . can't remember . . . I want to go to sleep."

She let her head swing over on a limp neck and became a dead weight in Louise Marlow's arms.

Aunt Louise put her back on the bed, snatched up a telephone directory, and thumbed through the pages until she found the name *Perry Mason, Attorney.*

There was a night number: Westfield 6–5943.

Louise Marlow dialed the number.

The night operator on duty at the switchboard of the Drake Detective Agency, picked up the receiver and said, "Night number of Mr. Perry Mason. Who is this talking, please?"

"This is Louise Marlow talking. I haven't met Perry Mason but I know his secretary, Della Street. I want you to get in touch with her and tell her that I'm at Keystone 9–7600. I'm in a mess and I want her to call me back here just as quick as she can. . . . Yes, that's right! You tell her it's Louise Marlow talking and she'll get busy. I think I may need Mr. Mason before I get done; but I want to talk with Della right now."

Louise Marlow hung up and waited.

Within less than a minute she heard the phone ring, and Della Street's voice came over the line as Aunt Louise picked up the receiver.

"Why, Louise Marlow, whatever are *you* doing in town?"

"I came in to attend the wedding of my niece, Fay Allison," Aunt Louise said. "Now, listen, Della. I'm at Fay's apartment. She's been drugged and I can't wake her up. Her roommate, Anita Bonsal, has also been drugged. Someone's tried to poison them!

"I want to get a doctor who's good, and who can keep his mouth shut. Fay's getting married tomorrow. Someone's tried to kill her, and I propose to find out what's behind it. If anything should get into the newspapers about this, I'll wring someone's neck. I'm at the Mandrake Arms, Apartment 604. Rush a doctor up here, and then you'd better get hold of Perry Mason and—"

Della Street said, "I'll send a good doctor up right away, Mrs. Marlow. You sit tight. I'm getting busy."

When Aunt Louise answered the buzzer, Della Street said, "Mrs. Marlow, this is Perry Mason. This is 'Aunt Louise,' Chief. She's an old friend from my home town."

Louise Marlow gave the famous lawyer her hand and a smile. She kissed Della, said, "You haven't changed a bit, Della. Come on in."

"What does the doctor say?" Mason asked.

"He's working like a house afire. Anita is conscious. Fay is going to pull through, all right. Another hour and it would have been too late."

"What happened?" Mason asked.

"Someone dumped sleeping medicine in the powdered chocolate, or else in the sugar."

"Any suspicions?" Mason asked.

She said, "Fay was marrying Dane Grover. I gather from her

letters he's a wealthy but shy young man who had one bad experience with a girl years ago and had turned bitter and disillusioned, or thought he had.

"I got here around one o'clock, I guess. Fay had sent me the keys. As soon as I switched on the light and looked at Fay's face I knew that something was wrong. I tried to wake her up and couldn't. I finally shook some sense into Anita. She said the chocolate did it. Then I called Della. That's all I know about it."

"The cups they drank the chocolate from?" Mason asked. "Where are they?"

"On the kitchen sink—unwashed."

"We may need them for evidence," Mason said.

"Evidence, my eye!" Louise Marlow snorted. "I don't want the police in on this. You can imagine what'll happen if some sob sister spills a lot of printer's ink about a bride-to-be trying to kill herself."

"Let's take a look around," Mason said.

The lawyer moved about the apartment. He paused as he came to street coats thrown over the back of a chair, then again as he looked at the two purses.

"Which one is Fay Allison's?" he asked.

"Heavens, I don't know. We'll have to find out," Aunt Louise said.

Mason said, "I'll let you two take the lead. Go through them carefully. See if you can find anything that would indicate whether anyone might have been in the apartment shortly before they started drinking the chocolate. Perhaps there's a letter that will give us a clue, or a note."

The doctor, emerging from the bedroom, said, "I want to boil some water for a hypo."

"How are they coming?" Mason asked, as Mrs. Marlow went to the kitchen.

"The brunette is all right," the doctor said, "and I think the blonde will be soon."

"When can I question them?"

The doctor shook his head. "I wouldn't advise it. They are groggy, and there's some evidence that the brunette is rambling and contradictory in her statements. Give her another hour and you can get some facts."

The doctor, after boiling water for his hypo, went back to the bedroom.

Della Street moved over to Mason's side and said in a low voice, "Here's something I don't understand, Chief. Notice the keys to the apartment house are stamped with the numbers of the apartments. Both girls have keys to this apartment in their purses. Fay Allison also has a key stamped 702. What would she be doing with the key to another apartment?"

Mason's eyes narrowed for a moment in speculation. "What does Aunt Louise say?"

"She doesn't know."

"Anything else to give a clue?"

"Not the slightest thing anywhere."

Mason said, "Okay, I'm going to take a look at 702. You'd better come along, Della."

Mason made excuses to Louise Marlow: "We want to look around on the outside," he said. "We'll be back in a few minutes."

He and Della took the elevator to the seventh floor, walked down to Apartment 702, and Mason pushed the bell button.

They could hear the sound of the buzzer in the apartment, but there was no sound of motion inside.

Mason said, "It's a chance we shouldn't take, but I'm going to take a peek, just for luck."

He fitted the key to the door, clicked back the lock, and gently opened the door.

The blazing light from the living room streamed through the open door, showed the body lying on the floor, the drinking glass which had rolled from the dead fingers.

The door from an apartment across the hall jerked open. A young woman with disheveled hair, a bathrobe around her, said angrily, "After you've pressed a buzzer for five minutes at this time of the night you should have sense enough to—"

"We have," Mason interrupted, pulling Della Street into the apartment and kicking the door shut behind them.

Della Street, clinging to Mason's arm, saw the sprawled figure on the floor, the crimson lipstick on the forehead, looked at the overturned chair by the table, the glass which had rolled along the carpet, spilling part of its contents, at the other empty glass standing on the table.

"Careful, Della, we mustn't touch anything."

"Who is he?"

"Apparently he's People's Exhibit A. Do you suppose the nosy dame in the opposite apartment is out of the hall by this time?

We'll have to take a chance anyway." He wrapped his hand with his handkerchief, turned the knob on the inside of the door, and pulled it silently open.

The door of the apartment across the hall was closed.

Mason warned Della Street to silence with a gesture. They tiptoed out into the corridor, pulling the door closed behind them.

As the door clicked shut, the elevator came to a stop at the seventh floor. Three men and a woman came hurrying down the corridor.

Mason's voice was low, reassuring: "Perfectly casual, Della. Just friends departing from a late card game."

They caught the curious glances of the four people, and moved slightly to one side until the quartet had passed.

"Well," Della Street said, "they'll certainly know us if they ever see us again. The way that woman looked me over!"

"I know," Mason said, "but we'll hope that—oh—oh! They're going to 702!"

The four paused in front of the door. One of the men pressed the buzzer button.

Almost immediately the door of the opposite apartment jerked open. The woman with the bathrobe shrilled, "I'm suffering from insomnia. I've been trying to sleep, and this—" She broke off as she saw the strangers.

The man who had been pressing the button grinned and said in a booming voice, "We're sorry, ma'am. I only just gave him one short buzz."

"Well, the other people who went in just before you made enough commotion."

"Other people in here?" the man asked. He hesitated a moment, then went on, "Well, we won't bother him if he's got company."

Mason pushed Della Street into the elevator and pulled the door shut.

"What in the world do we do now?" Della Street asked.

"Now," Mason said, his voice sharp-edged with disappointment, "we ring police headquarters and report a possible homicide. It's the only thing we can do."

There was a phone booth in the lobby. Mason dropped a nickel, dialed police headquarters, and reported that he had found a corpse in Apartment 702 under circumstances indicating probable suicide.

While Mason was in the phone booth, the four people came

out of the elevator. There was a distinct aroma of alcohol as they pushed their way toward the door. The woman, catching sight of Della Street standing beside the phone booth, favored her with a feminine appraisal which swept from head to foot.

Mason called Louise Marlow in Apartment 604. "I think you'd better have the doctor take his patients to a sanitarium where they can have complete quiet," he said.

"He seems to think they're doing all right here."

"I distrust doctors who *seem* to think," Mason said. "I would suggest a sanitarium immediately."

Louise Marlow was silent for a full three seconds.

"I think the patients should have *complete quiet,*" Mason said.

"Damn it," Louise Marlow sputtered. "When you said it the first time I missed it. The second time I got it. You don't have to let your needle get stuck on the record! I was just trying to figure it out."

Mason heard her slam down the phone at the other end of the line.

Mason grinned, hung up the phone, put the key to 702 in an envelope, addressed the envelope to his office, stamped it, and dropped it in the mailbox by the elevator.

Outside, the four persons in the car were having something of an argument. Apparently there was some sharp difference of opinion as to what action was to be taken next, but as a siren sounded they reached a sudden unanimity of decision. They were starting the car as the police radio car pulled in to the curb. The siren blasted a peremptory summons.

One of the radio officers walked over to the other car, took possession of the ignition keys, and ushered the four people up to the door of the apartment house.

Mason hurried across the lobby to open the locked door.

The officer said, "I'm looking for a man who reported a body."

"That's right, I did. My name's Mason. The body's in 702."

"A body!" the woman screamed.

"Shut up," the radio officer said.

"But we know the—Why, we told you we'd been visiting in 702—We—"

"Yeah, you said you'd been visiting a friend in 702, name of Carver Clements. How was he when you left him?"

There was an awkward silence; then the woman said, "We really didn't get in. We just went to the door. The woman across the way said he had company, so we left."

"Said he had company?"

"That's right. But I think the company had left. It was these two here."

"We'll go take a look," the officer said. "Come on."

Lieutenant Tragg, head of the Homicide Squad, finished his examination of the apartment and said wearily to Mason, "I presume by this time you've thought up a good story to explain how it all happened."

Mason said, "As a matter of fact, I don't know this man from Adam. I had never seen him alive."

"I know," Tragg said sarcastically; "you wanted him as a witness to an automobile accident and just happened to drop around in the wee, small hours of the morning.

"But," Tragg went on, "strange as it may seem, Mason, I'm interested to know how you got in. The woman who has the apartment across the corridor says you stood there and rang the buzzer for as long as two minutes. Then she heard the sound of a clicking bolt just as she opened her door to give you a piece of her mind."

Mason nodded gravely. "I had a key."

"A key! The hell you did! Let's take a look at it."

"I'm sorry; I don't have it now."

"Well, now," Tragg said, "isn't that interesting! And where did you get the key, Mason?"

Mason said, "The key came into my possession in a peculiar manner. I found it."

"Phooey! That key you have is the dead man's key. When we searched the body we found that stuff on the table there. There's no key to this apartment on him."

Mason sparred for time, said, "And did you notice that despite the fact there's a jar of ice cubes on the table, a bottle of whiskey, and a siphon of soda, the fatal drink didn't have any ice in it?"

"How do you know?" Tragg asked.

"Because when this glass fell from his hand and the contents spilled over the floor, it left a single small spot of moisture. If there had been ice cubes in the glass they'd have rolled out for some distance and then melted, leaving spots of moisture."

"I see," Tragg said sarcastically, "and then, having decided to commit suicide, the guy kissed himself on the forehead and—"

He broke off as one of the detectives, walking down the hallway, said, "We've traced that cleaning mark, Lieutenant."

The man handed Tragg a folded slip of paper.

Tragg unfolded the paper. "Well, I'll be—"

Mason met Tragg's searching eyes with calm steadiness.

"And I suppose," Tragg said, "you're going to be surprised at this one: Miss Fay Allison, Apartment 604, in this same building, is the person who owns the coat that was in the closet. Her mark from the dry cleaner is on it. I think, Mr. Mason, we'll have a little talk with Fay Allison, and just to see that you don't make any false moves until we get there, we'll take you right along with us. Perhaps you already know the way."

As Tragg started toward the elevator, a smartly dressed woman in the late thirties or early forties stepped out of the elevator and walked down the corridor, looking at the numbers over the doors.

Tragg stepped forward. "Looking for something?"

She started to sweep past him.

Tragg pulled back his coat, showed her his badge.

"I'm looking for Apartment 702," she said.

"Whom are you looking for?"

"Mr. Carver Clements, if it's any of your business."

"I think it is," Tragg said. "Who are you and how do you happen to be here?"

She said, "I am Mrs. Carver L. Clements, and I'm here because I was informed over the telephone that my husband was secretly maintaining an apartment here."

"And what," Tragg asked, "did you intend to do?"

"I intend to show him that he isn't getting away with anything," she said. "You may as well accompany me. I feel certain that—"

Tragg said, "702 is down the corridor, at the corner on the right. I just came from there. Your husband was killed some time between seven and nine o'clock tonight."

Dark brown eyes grew wide with surprise. "You—you're sure?"

Tragg said, "Someone slipped him a little cyanide in his whiskey and soda. I don't suppose you'd know anything about that?"

She said slowly, "If my husband is dead—I can't believe it. He hated me too much to die. He was trying to force me to make a property settlement, and in order to make me properly submissive, he'd put me through a softening-up process, a period during which I didn't have money enough even to dress decently."

"In other words," Tragg said, "you hated his guts."

She clamped her lips together. "I didn't say that!"

Tragg grinned and said, "Come along with us. We're going down to an apartment on the sixth floor. After that I'm going to take your fingerprints and see if they match up with those on the glass which contained the poison."

Louise Marlow answered the buzzer. She glanced at Tragg, then at Mrs. Clements.

Mason, raising his hat, said with the grave politeness of a stranger, "We're sorry to bother you at this hour, but—"

"*I'll* do the talking," Tragg said.

The formality of Mason's manner was not lost on Aunt Louise. She said, as though she had never seen him before, "Well, this is a strange time—"

Tragg pushed his way forward. "Does Fay Allison live here?"

"That's right," Louise Marlow beamed at him. "She and another girl, Anita Bonsal, share the apartment. They aren't here now, though."

"Where are they?" Tragg asked.

She shook her head. "I'm sure I couldn't tell you."

"And who are you?"

"I'm Louise Marlow, Fay's aunt."

"You're living with them?"

"Heavens, no. I just came up tonight to be here for—for a visit with Fay."

"You said, I believe, that they are not here now?"

"That's right."

Tragg said, "Let's cut out the shadow-boxing and get down to brass tacks, Mrs. Marlow. I want to see both of those girls."

"I'm sorry, but the girls are both sick. They're in the hospital. It's just a case of food poisoning. Only—"

"What's the doctor's name?"

"Now, you listen to me," Louise Marlow said. "I tell you, these girls are too sick to be bothered and—"

Lieutenant Tragg said, "Carver L. Clements, who has an apartment on the floor above here, is dead. It looks like murder. Fay Allison had evidently been living up there in the apartment with him and—"

"What are you talking about!" Louise Marlow exclaimed indignantly. "Why, I—"

"Take it easy," Tragg said. "Her clothes were up there. There's a cleaner's mark that has been traced to her."

"Clothes!" Louise Marlow snorted. "Why, it's probably some junk she gave away somewhere, or—"

"I'm coming to that," Lieutenant Tragg said patiently. "I don't want to do anyone an injustice. I want to play it on the up-and-up. Now, then, there are fingerprints in that apartment, the fingerprints of a woman on a drinking glass, on the handle of a toothbrush, on a tube of toothpaste. I'm not going to get tough unless I have to, but I want to get hold of Fay Allison long enough to take a set of fingerprints. You try holding out on me, and see what the newspapers have to say tomorrow."

Louise Marlow reached an instant decision. "You'll find her at the Crestview Sanitarium," she said, "and if you want to make a little money, I'll give you odds of a hundred to one that—"

"I'm not a betting man," Tragg said wearily. "I've been in this game too long."

He turned to one of the detectives and said, "Keep Perry Mason and his charming secretary under surveillance and away from a telephone until I get a chance at those fingerprints. Okay, boy's, let's go."

Paul Drake, head of the Drake Detective Agency, pulled a sheaf of notes from his pocket as he settled down in the big clients' chair in Mason's office.

"It's a mess, Perry," he said.

"Let's have it," Mason said.

Drake said, "Fay Allison and Dane Grover were going to get married today. Last night Fay and Anita Bonsal, who shares the apartment with her, settled down for a nice, gabby little hen party. They made chocolate. Fay had two cups; Anita had one. Fay evidently got about twice the dose of barbiturate that Anita did. Both girls passed out.

"Next thing Anita knew, Louise Marlow, Fay's aunt, was trying to wake her up. Fay Allison didn't recover consciousness until after she was in the sanitarium.

"Anyhow, Tragg went out and took Fay Allison's fingerprints. They check absolutely with those on the glass. What the police call the murder glass is the one that slipped from Carver Clements's fingers and rolled around the floor. It had been carefully wiped clean of all fingerprints. Police can't even find one of Clements's prints on it. The other glass on the table had Fay's prints. The closet was filled with her clothes. She was living there with him. It's a fine mess.

"Dane Grover is standing by her, but I personally don't think he can stand the gaff much longer. When a man's engaged to a girl and the newspapers scream the details of her affair with a wealthy playboy all over the front pages, you can't expect the man to appear exactly nonchalant. The aunt, Louise Marlow, tells me he's being faced with terrific pressure to repudiate the girl, to break the engagement and take a trip.

"The girls insist it's all part of some sinister over-all plan to frame them, that they were drugged, and all that, but how could anyone have planned it that way? For instance, how could anyone have known they were going to take the chocolate in time to—?"

"The chocolate was drugged?" Mason asked.

Drake nodded. "They'd used up most of the chocolate, but the small amount left in the package is pretty well doped with barbiturate.

"The police theory," Drake went on, "is that Fay Allison had been playing house with Carver Clements. She wanted to get married. Clements wouldn't let her go. She slipped him a little poison. She intended to return and get her things out of the apartment when it got late enough so she wouldn't meet someone in the corridor if she came walking out of 702 with her arms full of clothes. Anita, who had gone out, unexpectedly returned, and that left Fay Allison trapped. She couldn't go up and get her things out of the apartment upstairs without disturbing Anita. So she tried to drug Anita and something went wrong."

"That's a hell of a theory," Mason said.

"Try and get one that fits the case any better," Drake told him. "One thing is certain—Fay Allison was living up there in that Apartment 702. As far as Dane Grover is concerned, that's the thing that will make him throw everything overboard. He's a sensitive chap, from a good family. He doesn't like having his picture in the papers. Neither does his family."

"What about Clements?"

"Successful businessman, broker, speculator. Also a wife who was trying to hook him for a bigger property settlement than Clements wanted to pay. Clements had a big apartment where he lived officially. This place was a playhouse. Only a few people knew he had it. His wife would have given a lot of money to have found out about it."

"What's the wife doing now?"

"Sitting pretty. They don't know yet whether Clements left a will, but she has her community property rights, and Clements's books will be open for inspection now. He'd been juggling things around pretty much, and now a lot of stuff is going to come out—safe-deposit boxes and things of that sort."

"How about the four people who met us in the hall?"

"I have all the stuff on them here," Drake said. "The men were Richard P. Nolin, a sort of partner in some of Clements's business; Manley L. Ogden, an income tax specialist; Don B. Ralston, who acted as dummy for Clements in some business transactions; and Vera Payson, who is someone's girlfriend, but I'm darned if I can find out whose.

"Anyhow, those people knew of the hideout apartment and would go up there occasionally for a poker game. Last night, as soon as the dame across the hall said Clements had company, they knew what that meant, and went away. That's the story. The newspapers are lapping it up. Dane Grover isn't going to stay put much longer. You can't blame him. All he has is Fay Allison's tearful denial. Louise Marlow says we have to do something fast."

Mason said, "Tragg thinks I had Carver Clements's key."

"Where *did* you get it?"

Mason shook his head.

"Well," Drake said, "Carver Clements didn't have a key."

Mason nodded. "That is the only break we have in the case, Paul. We know Clements's key is missing. No one else does, because Tragg won't believe me when I tell him Clements hadn't given me his key."

Drake said, "It won't take Tragg long to figure the answer to that one. If Clements didn't give you the key, only one other person could have given it to you."

Mason said, "We won't speculate too much on that, Paul."

"I gathered we wouldn't," Drake said dryly. "Remember this, Perry, you're representing a girl who's going to be faced with a murder rap. You may be able to beat that rap. It's circumstantial evidence. But, in doing it, you'll have to think out some explanation that will satisfy an embarrassed lover who's being pitied by his friends and ridiculed by the public."

Mason nodded. "We'll push things to a quick hearing in the

magistrate's court on a preliminary examination. In the meantime, Paul, find out everything you can about Carver Clements's background. Pay particular attention to Clements's wife. If she had known about that apartment—"

Drake shook his head dubiously. "I'll give it a once-over, Perry, but if she'd even known about that apartment, that would have been all she needed. If she could have raided that apartment with a photographer and had the deadwood on Carver Clements, she'd have boosted her property settlement another hundred grand and walked out smiling. She wouldn't have needed to use any poison."

Mason's strong, capable fingers were drumming gently on the edge of the desk. "There has to be *some* explanation, Paul."

Drake heaved himself wearily to his feet. "That's right," he said without enthusiasm, "and Tragg thinks he has it."

Della Street, her eyes sparkling, entered Mason's private office and said, "He's here, Chief."

"Who's here?" Mason asked.

She laughed. "Don't be like that. As far as this office is concerned, there is only one *he.*"

"Dane Grover?"

"That's right."

"What sort?"

"Tall, sensitive-looking. Wavy, dark brown hair, romantic eyes. He's crushed, of course. You can see he's dying ten thousand deaths every time he meets one of his friends. Gertie, at the switchboard, can't take her eyes off of him."

Mason grinned, and said, "Let's get him in, then, before Gertie either breaks up a romance or dies of unrequited love."

Della Street went out, returned after a few moments, ushering Dane Grover into the office.

Mason shook hands, invited Grover to a seat. Grover glanced dubiously at Della Street. Mason smiled. "She's my right hand, Grover. She takes notes for me, and keeps her thoughts to herself."

Grover said, "I suppose I'm unduly sensitive, but I can't stand it when people patronize me or pity me."

Mason nodded.

"I've had them do both ever since the paper came out this morning."

Again, Mason's answer was merely a nod.

"But," Grover went on, "I want you to know that I'll stick."

Mason thought that over for a moment, then held Grover's eyes. "For how long?"

"All the way."

"No matter what the evidence shows?"

Grover said, "The evidence shows the woman I love was living with Carver Clements as his mistress. The evidence simply can't be right. I love her, and I'm going to stick. I want you to tell her that, and I want you to know that. What you're going to have to do will take money. I'm here to see that you have what money you need—all you want, in fact."

"That's fine," Mason said. "Primarily, what I need is a little moral support. I want to be able to tell Fay Allison that you're sticking, and I want some facts."

"What facts?"

"How long have you been going with Fay Allison?"

"A matter of three or four months. Before then I was—well, sort of squiring both of the girls around."

"You mean Anita Bonsal?"

"Yes. I met Anita first. I went with her for a while. Then I went with both. Then I began to gravitate toward Fay Allison. I thought I was just making dates. Actually, I was falling in love."

"And Anita?"

"She's like a sister to both of us. She's been simply grand in this whole thing. She's promised me that she'll do everything she can."

"Could Fay Allison have been living with Carver Clements?"

"She had the physical opportunity, if that's what you mean."

"You didn't see her every night?"

"No."

"What does Anita say?"

"Anita says the charge is ridiculous."

"Do you know of any place where Fay Allison could have had access to cyanide of potassium?"

"That's what I wanted to tell you about, Mr. Mason. Out at my place the gardener uses it. I don't know just what for, but—well, out there the other day, when he was showing Fay around the place—"

"Yes, yes," Mason said impatiently, as Grover paused; "go on."

"Well, I know the gardener told her to be very careful not to touch that sack because it contained cyanide. I remember she asked him a few questions about what he used it for, but I wasn't paying much attention. It's the basis of some sort of spray."

"Has your gardener read the papers?"

Grover nodded.

"Can you trust him?"

"Yes. He's very loyal to all our family. He's been with us for twenty years."

"What's his name?"

"Barney Sheff. My mother—well, rehabilitated him."

"He'd been in trouble? In the pen?"

"That's right. He had a chance to get parole if he could get a job. Mother gave him the job."

"I'm wondering if you have fully explored the possibilities of orchid growing."

"We're not interested in orchid growing. We can buy them and—"

"I wonder," Mason said in exactly the same tone, "if you have fully investigated the possibilities of growing orchids."

"You mean—Oh, you mean we should send Barney Sheff to—"

"Fully investigate the possibilities of growing orchids," Mason said again.

Dane Grover studied Mason silently for a few seconds. Then abruptly he rose from the chair, extended his hand, and said, "I wanted you to understand, Mr. Mason, that I'm going to stick. I brought you some money. I thought you might need it." He carelessly tossed an envelope on the table. And with that he turned and marched out of the office.

Mason reached for the envelope Grover had tossed on his desk. It was well filled with hundred-dollar bills.

Della Street came over to take the money. "When I get so interested in a man," she said, "that I neglect to count the money, you know I'm becoming incurably romantic. How much, Chief?"

"Plenty," Mason said.

Della Street was counting it when the unlisted telephone on her desk rang. She picked up the receiver, and heard Drake's voice on the line. "Hi, Paul," she said.

"Hi, Della. Perry there?"

"Yes."

"Okay," Drake said wearily, "I'm making a progress report. Tell him Lieutenant Tragg nabbed the Grover gardener, a chap by the name of Sheff. They're holding him as a material witness, seem to be all worked up about what they've discovered. Can't find out what it is."

Della Street sat motionless at the desk, holding the receiver.

"Hello, hello," Drake said; "are you there?"

"I'm here," Della said. "I'll tell him." She hung up the phone.

It was after nine o'clock that night when Della Street, signing the register in the elevator, was whisked up to the floor where Perry Mason had his offices. She started to look in on Paul Drake, then changed her mind and kept on walking down the long, dark corridor, the rapid tempo of her heels echoing back at her from the night silence of the hallway.

She rounded the elbow in the corridor, and saw that lights were on in Mason's office.

The lawyer was pacing the floor, thumbs pushed in the armholes of his vest, head shoved forward, wrapped in such concentration that he did not even notice the opening of the door.

The desk was littered with photographs. There were numerous sheets of the flimsy which Paul Drake used in making reports.

Della stood quietly in the doorway, watching the tall, lean-waisted man pacing back and forth. Granite-hard of face, the seething action of his restless mind demanded a physical outlet, and this restless pacing was just an unconscious reflex.

After almost a minute Della Street said, "Hello, Chief. Can I help?"

Mason looked up at her with a start. "What are you doing here?"

"I came up to see if there was anything I could do to help. Had any dinner?" she asked.

He glanced at his wrist watch, said, "Not yet."

"What time is it?" Della Street asked.

He had to look at his wrist watch again in order to tell her. "Nine forty."

She laughed. "I knew you didn't even look the first time you went through the motions. Come on, Chief; you've got to go get something to eat. The case will still be here when you get back."

"How do we know it will?" Mason said. "I've been talking with Louise Marlow on the phone. She's been in touch with Dane Grover and she knows Dane Grover's mother. Dane Grover says he'll stick. How does *he* know what he'll do? He's never faced a situation like this. His friends, his relatives, are turning the knife in the wound with their sympathy. How can he tell whether he'll stick?"

"Just the same," Della Street insisted, "I think he will. It's through situations such as this that character is created."

"You're just talking to keep your courage up," Mason said. "The guy's undergoing the tortures of the damned. He can't help but be influenced by the evidence. The woman he loves on the night before the wedding trying to free herself from the man who gave her money and a certain measure of security."

"Chief, you simply *have* to eat."

Mason walked over to the desk. "Look at 'em," he said; "photographs! And Drake had the devil's own time obtaining them. They're copies of the police photographs—the body on the floor, glass on the table, an overturned chair, a newspaper half open by a reading chair—an apartment as drab as the sordid affair for which it was used. And somewhere in those photographs I've got to find the clue that will establish the innocence of a woman, not only innocence of murder, but of the crime of betraying the man she loved."

Mason leaned over the desk, picked up the magnifying glass which was on his blotter, and started once more examining the pictures. "Hang it, Della," he said, "I think the thing's here somewhere. That glass on the table, a little whiskey and soda in the bottom, Fay Allison's fingerprints all over it. Then there's the brazen touch of that crimson kiss on the forehead."

"Indicating a woman was with him just before he died?"

"Not necessarily. That lipstick is a perfect imprint of a pair of lips. There was no lipstick on his lips, just there on the forehead. A shrewd man could well have smeared lipstick on his lips, pressed them against Clements's forehead after the poison had taken effect, and so directed suspicion away from himself. This could easily have happened if the man had known some woman was in the habit of visiting Clements in that apartment.

"It's a clue that so obviously indicates a woman that I find myself getting suspicious of it. If there were only something to give me a starting point. If only we had more time."

Della Street walked over to the desk. She said, "Stop it. Come and get something to eat. Let's talk it over."

"Haven't you had dinner?"

She smiled, and shook her head. "I knew you'd be working, and that if someone didn't rescue you, you'd be pacing the floor until two or three o'clock in the morning. What's Paul Drake found out?"

She picked up the sheets of flimsy, placed them together, and anchored everything in place with a paperweight. "Come on, Chief."

But he didn't really answer her question until after he had relaxed in one of the booths in their favorite restaurant. He pushed back the plates containing the wreckage of a thick steak, and poured more coffee, then said, "Drake hasn't found out much— just background."

"What, for instance?"

Mason said wearily, "It's the same old seven and six. The wife, Marline Austin Clements, apparently was swept off her feet by the sheer power of Carver Clements's determination to get her. She overlooked the fact that after he had her safely listed as one of his legal chattels, he used that same acquisitive, aggressive tenacity of purpose to get other things he wanted. Marline was left pretty much alone."

"And so?" Della asked.

"And so," Mason said, "in the course of time, Carver Clements turned to other interests. Hang it, Della, we have one thing to work on, only one thing—the fact that Clements had no key on his body.

"You remember the four people who met us in the corridor. They had to get in that apartment house some way. Remember the outer door was locked. Any of the tenants could release the latch by pressing the button of an electric release. But if the tenant of some apartment didn't press the release button, it was necessary to have a key in order to get in.

"Now, then, those four people got in. How? Regardless of what they say now, one of them must have had a key."

"The missing key?" Della asked.

"That's what we have to find out."

"What story did they give the police?"

"I don't know. The police have them sewed up tight. I've got to get one of them on the stand and cross-examine him. Then we'll at least have something to go on."

"So we have to try for an immediate hearing and then go it blind?"

"That's about the size of it."

"Was that key in Fay Allison's purse Clements's missing key?"

"It could have been. If so, either Fay was playing house or the key was planted. In that case, when was it planted, how, and by whom? I'm inclined to think Clements's key must have been on his body at the time he was murdered. It wasn't there when the police arrived. That's the one really significant clue we have to work on."

Della Street shook her head. "It's too deep for me, but I guess you're going to have to wade into it."

Mason lit a cigarette. "Ordinarily I'd spar for time, but in this case I'm afraid time is our enemy, Della. We're going to have to walk into court with all the assurance in the world and pull a very large rabbit out of a very small hat."

She smiled. "Where do we get the rabbit?"

"Back in the office," he said, "studying those photographs, looking for a clue, and—" Suddenly he snapped to attention.

"What is it, Chief?"

"I was just thinking. The glass on the table in 702—there was a little whiskey and soda in the bottom of it, just a spoonful or two."

"Well?" she asked.

"What happens when you drink whiskey and soda, Della?"

"Why—you always leave a little. It sticks to the side of the glass and then gradually settles back."

Mason shook his head. His eyes were glowing now. "You leave ice cubes in the glass," he said, "and then after a while they melt and leave an inch or so of water."

She matched his excitement. "Then there was no ice in the woman's glass?"

"And none in Carver Clements's. Yet there was a jar of ice cubes on the table. Come on, Della; we're going back and *really* study those photographs!"

Judge Randolph Jordan ascended the bench and rapped court to order.

"People versus Fay Allison."

"Ready for the defendant," Mason said.

"Ready for the Prosecution," Stewart Linn announced.

Linn, one of the best of the trial deputies in the district attorney's office, was a steely-eyed individual who had the legal knowledge of an encyclopedia, and the cold-blooded mercilessness of a steel trap.

Linn was under no illusions as to the resourcefulness of his adversary, and he had all the caution of a boxer approaching a heavyweight champion.

"Call Dr. Charles Keene," he said.

Dr. Keene came forward, qualified himself as a physician and surgeon who had had great experience in medical necropsies, particularly in cases of homicide.

"On the tenth of this month did you have occasion to examine a body in Apartment 702 at the Mandrake Arms?"

"I did."

"What time was it?"

"It was about two o'clock in the morning."

"What did you find?"

"I found the body of a man of approximately fifty-two years of age, fairly well fleshed, quite bald, but otherwise very well preserved for a man of his age. The body was lying on the floor, head toward the door, feet toward the interior of the apartment, the left arm doubled up and lying under him, the right arm flung out, the left side of the face resting on the carpet. The man had been dead for several hours. I fix the time of death as having taken place during a period between seven o'clock and nine o'clock that evening. I cannot place the time of death any closer than that, but I will swear that it took place within those time limits."

"And did you determine the cause of death?"

"Not at that time. I did later."

"What was the cause of death?"

"Poisoning caused by the ingestion of cyanide of potassium."

"Did you notice anything about the physical appearance of the man's body?"

"There was a red smear on the upper part of the forehead, apparently caused by lips that had been heavily coated with lipstick and then pressed against the skin in a somewhat puckered condition. It was as though some woman had administered a last kiss."

"Cross-examine," Linn announced.

"No questions," Mason said.

"Call Benjamin Harlan," Linn said.

Benjamin Harlan, a huge, lumbering giant of a man, promptly proceeded to qualify himself as a fingerprint and identification expert of some twenty years' experience.

Stewart Linn, by skillful, adroit questions, led him through an account of his activities on the date in question. Harlan found no latent fingerprints on the glass which the Prosecution referred to as the "murder glass," indicating this glass had been wiped clean of prints, but there were prints on the glass on the table which the Prosecution referred to as the "decoy glass," on the toothbrush, on the tube of toothpaste, and on various other articles. These latent fingerprints had coincided with the fingerprints taken from the hands of Fay Allison, the defendant.

Harlan also identified a whole series of photographs taken by the police showing the position of the body when it was discovered, the furnishings in the apartment, the table, the overturned chair, the so-called murder glass, which had rolled along the floor, the so-called decoy glass on the table, which bore unmistakably the fresh fingerprints of Fay Allison, the bottle of whiskey, the bottle of soda water, the jar containing ice cubes.

"Cross-examine," Linn said triumphantly.

Mason said, "You have had some twenty years' experience as a fingerprint expert, Mr. Harlan?"

"Yes, sir."

"Now, you have heard Dr. Keene's testimony about the lipstick on the forehead of the dead man?"

"Yes, sir."

"And that lipstick, I believe, shows in this photograph which I now hand you?"

"Yes, sir; not only that, but I have a close-up of that lipstick stain which I, myself, took. I have an enlargement of that negative, in case you're interested."

"I'm very much interested," Mason said. "Will you produce the enlargement, please?"

Harlan produced the photograph from his briefcase, showing a section of the forehead of the dead man, with the stain of lips outlined clearly and in microscopic detail.

"What is the scale of this photograph?" Mason asked.

"Life size," Harlan said. "I have a standard of distances by which I can take photographs to a scale of exactly life size."

"Thank you," Mason said. "I'd like to have this photograph received in evidence."

"No objection," Linn said.

"And it is, is it not, a matter of fact that the little lines shown in this photograph are fully as distinctive as the ridges and whorls of a fingerprint?"

"Just what do you mean?"

"Isn't it a fact well known to identification experts that the little wrinkles which form in a person's lips are fully as individual as the lines of a fingerprint?"

"It's not a 'well-known' fact."

"But it *is* a fact?"

"Yes, sir, it is."

"So that by measuring the distance between the little lines which are shown on this photograph, indicating the pucker lines of the skin, it would be fully as possible to identify the lips which made this lipstick print as it would be to identify a person who had left a fingerprint upon the scalp of the dead man."

"Yes, sir."

"Now, you have testified to having made imprints of the defendant's fingers and compared those with the fingerprints found on the glass."

"Yes, sir."

"Have you made any attempt to take an imprint of her lips and compare that print with the print of the lipstick on the decedent?"

"No, sir," Harlan said, shifting his position uneasily.

"Why not?"

"Well, in the first place, Mr. Mason, the fact that the pucker lines of lips are so highly individualized is not a generally known fact."

"But *you* knew it."

"Yes, sir."

"And the more skilled experts in your profession know it?"

"Yes, sir."

"Why didn't you do it, then?"

Harlan glanced somewhat helplessly at Stewart Linn.

"Oh, if the Court please," Linn said, promptly taking his cue from that glance, "this hardly seems to be cross-examination. The inquiry is wandering far afield. I will object to the question on the ground that it's incompetent, irrelevant, immaterial, and not proper cross-examination."

"Overruled," Judge Jordan snapped. "Answer the question!"

Harlan cleared his throat. "Well," he said, "I just never thought of it."

"Think of it now," Mason said. "Go ahead and take the imprint right now and right here. . . . Put on plenty of lipstick, Miss

Allison. Let's see how your lips compare with those on the dead man's forehead."

"Oh, if the Court please," Linn said wearily, "this hardly seems to be cross-examination. If Mr. Mason wants to make Harlan his own witness and call for this test as a part of the defendant's case, that will be one thing; but this certainly isn't cross-examination."

"It may be cross-examination of Harlan's qualifications as an expert," Judge Jordan ruled.

"Oh, if the Court please! Isn't that stretching a technicality rather far?"

"Your objection was highly technical," Judge Jordan snapped. "It is overruled, and my ruling will stand. Take the impression, Mr. Harlan."

Fay Allison, with trembling hand, daubed lipstick heavily on her mouth. Then, using the make-up mirror in her purse, smoothed off the lipstick with the tip of her little finger.

"Go ahead," Mason said to Harlan; "check on her lips."

Harlan, taking a piece of white paper from his brief-case, moved down to where the defendant was sitting beside Perry Mason and pressed the paper against her lips. He removed the paper and examined the imprint.

"Go ahead," Mason said to Harlan; "make your comparison and announce the results to the Court."

Harlan said, "Of course, I have not the facilities here for making a microscopic comparison, but I can tell from even a superficial examination of the lip lines that these lips did not make that print."

"Thank you," Mason said. "That's all."

Judge Jordan was interested. "These lines appear in the lips only when the lips are puckered, as in giving a kiss?"

"No, Your Honor, they are in the lips all the time, as an examination will show, but when the lips are puckered, the lines are intensified."

"And these lip markings are different with each individual?"

"Yes, Your Honor."

"So that you are now prepared to state to the Court that despite the fingerprints of the defendant on the glass and other objects, her lips definitely could not have left the imprint on the dead man's forehead?"

"Yes, Your Honor."

"That's all," Judge Jordan said.

"Of course," Linn pointed out, "the fact that the defendant did not leave that kiss imprint on the man's forehead doesn't necessarily mean a thing, Your Honor. In fact, he may have met his death *because* the defendant found that lipstick on his forehead. The evidence of the fingerprints is quite conclusive that the defendant was in that apartment."

"The Court understands the evidence. Proceed with your case," Judge Jordan said.

"Furthermore," Linn went on angrily, "I will now show the Court that there was every possibility the print of that lipstick could have been deliberately planted by none other than the attorney for the defendant and his charming and very efficient secretary. I will proceed to prove that by calling Don B. Ralston to the stand."

Ralston came forward and took the stand, his manner that of a man who wishes he were many miles away.

"Your name is Don B. Ralston? You reside at 2935 Creelmore Avenue in this city?"

"Yes, sir."

"And you knew Carver L. Clements in his lifetime?"

"Yes."

"In a business way?"

"Yes, sir."

"Now, on the night—or, rather, early in the morning—of the 10th of this month, did you have occasion to go to Carver Clements's apartment, being Apartment Number 702 in the Mandrake Arms Apartments in this city?"

"I did, yes, sir."

"What time was it?"

"Around—well, it was between one and two in the morning— I would say around one-thirty."

"Were you alone?"

"No, sir."

"Who was with you?"

"Richard P. Nolin, who is a business associate—or was a business associate—of Mr. Clements; Manley L. Ogden, who handled some of Mr. Clements's income tax work; and a Miss Vera Payson, a friend of—well, a friend of all of us."

"What happened when you went to that apartment?"

"Well, we left the elevator on the seventh floor, and as we were walking down the corridor, I noticed two people coming down the corridor toward us."

"Now, when you say 'down the corridor,' do you mean from the direction of Apartment 702?"

"That's right, yes, sir."

"And who were these people?"

"Mr. Perry Mason and his secretary, Miss Street."

"And did you actually enter the apartment of Carver Clements?"

"I did not."

"Why not?"

"When I got to the door of Apartment 702, I pushed the doorbell and heard the sound of the buzzer on the inside of the apartment. Almost instantly the door of an apartment across the hall opened, and a woman complained that she had been unable to sleep because of people ringing the buzzer of that apartment, and stated, in effect, that other people were in there with Mr. Clements. So we left immediately."

"Now, then, Your Honor," Stewart Linn said, "I propose to show that the two people referred to by the person living in the apartment across the hallway were none other than Mr. Mason and Miss Street, who had actually entered that apartment and were in there with the dead man and the evidence for an undetermined length of time."

"Go ahead and show it," Judge Jordan said.

"Just a moment," Mason said. "Before you do that, I want to cross-examine this witness."

"Cross-examine him, then."

"When you arrived at the Mandrake Arms, Mr. Ralston, the door to the street was locked, was it not?"

"Yes, sir."

"What did you do?"

"We went up to the seventh floor and—"

"I understand that, but how did you get in? How did you get past the entrance door? You had a key, didn't you?"

"No, sir."

"Then how *did* you get in?"

"Why *you* let us in."

"*I* did?"

"Yes."

"Understand," Mason said, "I am not now referring to the time you came up from the street in the custody of the radio officer.

I am now referring to the time when you *first* entered that apartment house on the morning of the tenth of this month."

"Yes, sir. I understand. You let us in."

"What makes you say that?"

"Well, because you and your secretary were in Carver Clements's apartment, and—"

"You, yourself, don't *know* we were in there, do you?"

"Well, I surmise it. We met you just after you had left the apartment. You were hurrying down the hall toward the elevator."

Mason said, "I don't want your surmises. You don't even know I had been in that apartment. I want you to tell us how you got past the locked street door."

"We pressed the button of Carver Clements's apartment, and you—or, at any rate, someone—answered by pressing the button which released the electric door catch on the outer door. As soon as we heard the buzzing sound, which indicated the lock was released, we pushed the door open and went in."

"Let's not have any misunderstanding about this," Mason said. "Who was it pushed the button of Carver Clements's apartment?"

"I did."

"I'm talking now about the button in front of the outer door of the apartment."

"Yes, sir."

"And having pressed that button, you waited until the buzzer announced the door was being opened?"

"Yes, sir."

"How long?"

"Not over a second or two."

Mason said to the witness, "One more question: Did you go right up after you entered the house?"

"We—no, sir, not *right* away. We stopped for a few moments there in the lobby to talk about the type of poker we wanted to play. Miss Payson had lost money on one of these wild poker games where the dealer has the opportunity of calling any kind of game he wants, some of them having the one-eyed Jacks wild, and things of that sort."

"How long were you talking?"

"Oh, a couple of minutes."

"And then went right up?"

"Yes."

"Where was the elevator?"

"The elevator was on one of the upper floors. I remember we pressed the button and it took a little while to come down to where we were."

"That's all," Mason said.

Della Street's fingers dug into his arm. "Aren't you going to ask him about the key?" she whispered.

"Not yet," Mason said, a light of triumph in his eyes. "I know what happened now, Della. Give us the breaks, and we've got this case in the bag. First, make him prove we were in that apartment."

Linn said, "I will now call Miss Shirley Tanner to the stand."

The young woman who advanced to the stand was very different from the disheveled and nervous individual who had been so angry at the time Mason and Della Street had pressed the button of Apartment 702.

"Your name is Shirley Tanner, and you reside in Apartment 701 of the Mandrake Arms Apartments?"

"Yes, sir."

"And have for how long?"

She smiled, and said, "Not very long. I put in three weeks apartment hunting and finally secured a sublease on Apartment 701 on the afternoon of the eighth. I moved in on the ninth, which explains why I was tired almost to the point of hysterics."

"You had difficulty sleeping?"

"Yes."

"And on the morning of the tenth did you have any experiences which annoyed you—experiences in connection with the ringing of the buzzer in the apartment next door?"

"I most certainly did, yes, sir."

"Tell us exactly what happened."

"I had been taking sleeping medicine from time to time, but for some reason or other this night I was so nervous the sleeping medicine didn't do me any good. I had been unpacking, and my nerves were all keyed up. I was physically and mentally exhausted but I was too tired to sleep.

"Well, I was trying to sleep, and I think I had just got to sleep when I was awakened by a continual sounding of the buzzer in the apartment across the hall. It was a low, persistent noise which became very irritating in my nervous state."

"Go on," Linn said. "What did you do?"

"I finally got up and put on a robe and went to the door and flung it open. I was terribly angry at the very idea of people making so much noise at that hour of the morning. You see, those apartments aren't too sound-proof and there is a ventilating system over the doors of the apartments. The one over the door of 702 was apparently open and I had left mine open for night-time ventilation. And then I was angry at myself for getting so upset over the noise. I knew it would prevent me from sleeping at all, which is why I lay still for what seemed an interminable time before I opened the door."

Linn smiled. "And you say you *flung* open the door?"

"Yes, sir."

"What did you find?"

"Two people across the hall."

"Did you recognize them?"

"I didn't know them at the time, but I know them now."

"Who were they?"

She pointed a dramatic finger at Perry Mason. "Mr. Perry Mason, the lawyer for the defendant, and the young woman, I believe his secretary, who is sitting there beside him—not the defendant, but the woman on the other side."

"Miss Della Street," Mason said with a bow.

"Thank you," she said.

"And," Linn went on, "what did you see those people do?"

She said, "I saw them enter the apartment."

"Did you see how they entered the apartment—I mean, how did they get the door open?"

"They must have used a key. Mr. Mason was just pushing the door open and I—"

"No surmises, please," Linn broke in. "Did you actually see Mr. Mason using a key?"

"Well, I heard him."

"What do you mean?"

"As I was opening my door I heard metal rasping against metal, the way a key does when it scrapes against a lock. And then, when I had my door all the way open, I saw Mr. Mason pushing his way into 702."

"But you only know he must have had a key because you heard the sound of metal rubbing against metal?"

"Yes, and the click of the lock."

"Did you say anything to Mr. Mason and Miss Street?"

"I most certainly did, and then I slammed the door and went

back and tried to sleep. But I was so mad by that time I couldn't keep my eyes closed."

"What happened after that?"

"After that, when I was trying to sleep—I would say just a few seconds after that—I heard that buzzer again. This time I was good and mad."

"And what did you do?"

"I swung open the door and started to give these people a piece of my mind."

"People?" Linn asked promptingly.

"There were four people standing there. The Mr. Ralston, who has just testified, two other men, and a woman. They were standing there at the doorway, jabbing away at the button, and I told them this was a sweet time to be calling on someone and making a racket, and that anyway the gentleman already had company, so if he didn't answer his door, it was because he didn't want to."

"Did you at that time see Mr. Mason and Miss Street walking down the corridor?"

"No. I did not. I had my door open only far enough to show me the door of Apartment 702 across the way."

"Thank you," Linn said. "Now, you distinctly saw Mr. Mason and Miss Street enter that apartment?"

"Yes."

"And close the door behind them?"

"Yes."

"Cross-examine!" Linn said triumphantly.

Mason, taking a notebook from his pocket, walked up to stand beside Shirley Tanner. "Miss Tanner," he said, "are you certain that you heard me rub metal against the keyhole of that door?"

"Certain," she said.

"My back was toward you?"

"It was when I first opened my door, yes. I saw your face, however, just after you went in the door. You turned around and looked at me over your shoulder."

"Oh, we'll stipulate," Linn said, with an exaggerated note of weariness in his voice, "that the witness couldn't see through Mr. Mason's back. Perhaps learned counsel was carrying the key in his teeth."

"Thank you," Mason said, turning toward Linn. Then, suddenly stepping forward, he clapped his notebook against Shirley Tanner's face.

The witness screamed and jumped back.

Linn was on his feet. "What are you trying to do?" he shouted.

Judge Jordan pounded with his gavel. "Mr. Mason!" he repri-manded. "That is contempt of court!"

Mason said, "Please let me explain, Your Honor. The Prose-cution took the lip-prints of my client. I feel that I am entitled to take the lip-prints of this witness. I will cheerfully admit to being in contempt of court, in the event I am wrong, but I would like to extend this imprint of Shirley Tanner's lips to Mr. Benjamin Harlan, the identification expert, and ask him whether or not the print made by these lips is not the same as that of the lipstick kiss which was found on the dead forehead of Carver L. Clements."

There was a tense, dramatic silence in the courtroom.

Mason stepped forward and handed the notebook to Benjamin Harlan.

From the witness stand came a shrill scream of terror. Shirley Tanner tried to get to her feet. Her eyes were wide and terrified, her face was the color of putty.

She couldn't make it. Her knees buckled. She tried to catch herself, then fell to the floor. . . .

It was when order was restored in the courtroom that Perry Mason exploded his second bombshell.

"Your Honor," he said, "either Fay Allison is innocent or she is guilty. If she is innocent, someone framed the evidence which would discredit her. And if someone did frame that evidence, there is only one person who could have had access to the defendant's apartment, one person who could have transported glasses, toothbrushes, and toothpaste containing Fay Allison's fin-gerprints, one person who could have transported clothes bearing the unmistakable stamp of ownership of the defendant in this case. . . . Your Honor, I request that Anita Bonsal be called to the stand."

There was a moment's silence.

Anita Bonsal, there in the courtroom, felt suddenly as though she had been stripped stark naked by one swift gesture. One moment, she had been sitting there, attempting to keep pace with the swift rush of developments. The next moment, everyone in the courtroom was seeking her out with staring, prying eyes.

In her sudden surge of panic, Anita did the worst thing she could possibly have done: She ran.

They were after her then, a throng of humanity, motivated only by the mass instinct to pursue that which ran for cover.

Anita dashed to the stairs, went scrambling down them, found herself in another hallway in the Hall of Justice. She dashed the length of that hallway, frantically trying to find the stairs. She could not find them.

An elevator offered her welcome haven.

Anita fairly flung herself into the cage.

"What's the hurry?" the attendant asked.

Shreds of reason were beginning to return to Anita's fear-racked mind. "They're calling my case," she said. "Let me off at—"

"I know," the man said, smiling. "Third floor. Domestic Relations Court."

He slid the cage to a smooth stop at the third floor. "Out to the left," he said. "Department Twelve."

Anita's mind was beginning to work now. She smiled at the elevator attendant, walked rapidly to the left, pushed open a door, and entered the partially filled courtroom. She marched down the center aisle and calmly seated herself in the middle seat in a row of benches.

She was now wrapped in anonymity. Only her breathlessness and the pounding of her pulses gave indication that she was the quarry for which the crowd was now searching.

Then slowly the triumphant smile faded from her face. The realization of the effect of what she had done stabbed her consciousness. She had admitted her guilt. She could flee now to the farthest corners of the earth, but her guilt would always follow her.

Perry Mason had shown that she had not killed Carver Clements, but he had also shown that she had done something which in the minds of all men would be even worse. She had betrayed her friend. She had tried to ruin Fay Allison's reputation. She had attempted the murder of her own roommate by giving her an overdose of sleeping tablets.

How much would Mason have been able to prove? She had no way of knowing. But there was no need for him to prove anything now. Her flight had given Mason all the proof he needed.

She must disappear, and that would not be easy. By evening her photograph would be emblazoned upon the pages of every newspaper in the city. . . .

* * *

Back in the courtroom, almost deserted now except for the county officials who were crowding around Shirley Tanner, Mason was asking questions in a low voice.

There was no more stamina left in Shirley Tanner than in a wet dishrag. She heard her own voice answering the persistent drone of Mason's searching questions.

"You knew that Clements had this apartment in 702? . . . You deliberately made such a high offer that you were able to sublease Apartment 701? . . . You were suspicious of Clements and wanted to spy on him?"

"Yes," Shirley said, and her voice was all but inaudible, although it was obvious that the court reporter, standing beside her, was taking down in his notebook all she said.

"You were furious when you realized that Carver Clements had *another* mistress and that all his talk to you about waiting until he could get his divorce was merely bait which you had grabbed?"

Again she said, "Yes." There was no strength in her any more to think up lies.

"You made the mistake of loving him," Mason said. "It wasn't his money you were after, and you administered the poison. How did you do it, Shirley?"

She said, "I'd poisoned the drink I held in my hand. I knew it made Carver furious when I drank, because whiskey makes me lose control of myself, and he never knew what I was going to do when I was drunk.

"I rang his bell, holding that glass in my hand. I leered at him tipsily when he opened the door, and walked on in. I said, 'Hello, Carver darling. Meet your next-door neighbor,' and I raised the glass to my lips.

"He acted just as I knew he would. He was furious. He said, 'You little devil, what're you doing here? I've told you I'll do the drinking for both of us.' He snatched the glass from me and drained it."

"What happened?" Mason asked.

"For a moment, nothing," she said. "He went back to the chair and sat down. I leaned over him and pressed that kiss on his head. It was a goodbye kiss. He looked at me, frowned; then suddenly he jumped to his feet and tried to run to the door, but he staggered and fell face forward."

"And what did you do?"

"I took the key to his apartment from his pocket so I could

get back in to fix things the way I wanted and get possession of the glass, but I was afraid to be there while he was—dying."

Mason nodded. "You went back to your own apartment, and then, after you had waited a few minutes and thought it was safe to go back, you couldn't, because Anita Bonsal was at the door?"

She nodded, and said, "She had a key. She went in. I supposed, of course, she'd call the police and that they'd come at any time. I didn't dare to go in there then. Finally, I decided the police weren't coming, after all. It was past midnight then."

"So then you went back in there? You were in there when Don Ralston rang the bell. You—"

"Yes," she said. "I went back into that apartment. By that time I had put on a bathrobe and pajamas and ruffled my hair all up. If anyone had said anything to me, if I had been caught, I had a story all prepared to tell them, that I had heard the door open and someone run down the corridor, that I had opened my door and found the door of 702 ajar, and I had just that minute looked in to see what had happened."

"All right," Mason said; "that was your story. What did you do?"

"I went in and wiped all my fingerprints off that glass on the floor. Then the buzzer sounded from the street."

"What did you do?"

She said, "I saw someone had fixed up the evidence just the way I had been going to fix it up. A bottle of whiskey on the table, a bottle of soda, a jar of ice cubes."

"So what did you do?"

She said, "I was rattled, I guess, so I just automatically pushed the button which released the downstairs door catch. Then I ducked back into my own apartment, and hadn't any more than got in when I heard the elevator stop at the seventh floor. I couldn't understand that, because I knew these people couldn't possibly have had time enough to get up to the seventh floor in the elevator. I waited, listening, and heard you two come down the corridor. As soon as the buzzer sounded in the other apartment, I opened the door to chase you away, but you were actually entering the apartment, so I had to make a quick excuse, that the sound of the buzzer had wakened me. Then I jerked the door shut. When the four people came up, I thought you were still in the apartment, and I had to see what was happening."

"How long had you known him?" Mason asked.

She said sadly, "I loved him. I was the one that he wanted to marry when he left his wife. I don't know how long this other romance had been going on. I became suspicious, and one time when I had an opportunity to go through his pockets, I found a key stamped, 'Mandrake Arms Apartment, Number 702.' Then I thought I knew, but I wanted to be sure. I found out who had Apartment 701 and made a proposition for a sublease that couldn't be turned down.

"I waited and watched. This brunette walked down the corridor and used *her* key to open the apartment. I slipped out into the corridor and listened at the door. I heard him give her the same old line he'd given me so many times, and I hated him. I killed him—and I was caught."

Mason turned to Stewart Linn and said, "There you are, young man. There's your murderess, but you'll probably never be able to get a jury to think it's anything more than manslaughter."

A much chastened Linn said, "Would you mind telling me how you figured this out, Mr. Mason?"

Mason said, "Clements's key was missing. Obviously he must have had it when he entered the apartment. Therefore, the murderer must have taken it from his pocket. Why? So he or she could come back. And if what Don Ralston said was true, *someone* must have been in the apartment when he rang the bell from the street, someone who let him in by pressing the buzzer.

"What happened to that someone? I must have been walking down the corridor within a matter of seconds after Ralston had pressed the button on the street door. Yet I saw no one leaving the apartment. *Obviously, then, the person who pressed the buzzer must have had a place to take refuge in a nearby apartment!*

"Having learned that a young, attractive woman had only that day taken a lease on the apartment opposite, the answer became so obvious it ceased to be a mystery."

Stewart Linn nodded thoughtfully. "It all fits in," he said.

Mason picked up his briefcase, smiled to Della Street. "Come on, Della," he said. "Let's get Fay Allison and—"

He stopped as he saw Fay Allison's face. "What happened to *your* lipstick?" he asked.

And then his eyes moved over to take in Dane Grover, who was standing by her, his face smeared diagonally across the mouth with a huge, red smear of lipstick.

Fay Allison had neglected to remove the thick coating of lipstick which she had put on when Mason had asked Benjamin Harlan, the identification expert, to take an imprint of her lips. Now, the heavy mark where her mouth had been pressed against the mouth of Dane Grover gave a note of incongruity to the entire proceedings.

On the lower floors a mob of eagerly curious spectators were baying like hounds upon the track of Anita Bonsal. In the courtroom the long, efficient arm of the law was gathering Shirley Tanner into its grasp, and there, amidst the machinery of tragedy, the romance of Fay Allison and Dane Grover picked up where it had left off. . . .

It was the gavel of Judge Randolph Jordan that brought them back to the grim realities of justice.

"The Court," announced Judge Jordan, "will dismiss the case against Fay Allison. The Court will order Shirley Tanner into custody, and the Court will suggest to the Prosecutor that a complaint be issued for Anita Bonsal, upon such charge as may seem expedient to the office of the District Attorney. And the Court does hereby extend its most sincere apologies to the defendant, Fay Allison. And the Court, personally, wishes to congratulate Mr. Perry Mason upon his brilliant handling of this matter."

There was a moment during which Judge Jordan's stern eyes rested upon the lipstick-smeared countenance of Dane Grover. A faint smile twitched at the corners of His Honor's mouth.

The gavel banged once more.

"The Court," announced Judge Randolph Jordan, "is adjourned."

CORNELL WOOLRICH
The Room with Something Wrong

THEY THOUGHT it was the Depression the first time it happened. The guy had checked in one night in the black March of '33, in the middle of the memorable bank holiday. He was well dressed and respectable looking. He had baggage with him, plenty of it, so he wasn't asked to pay in advance. Everyone was short of ready cash that week. Besides, he'd asked for the weekly rate.

He signed the register *James Hopper, Schenectady,* and Dennison, eyeing the red vacancy tags in the pigeonholes, pulled out the one in 913 at random and gave him that. Not the vacancy tag, the room. The guest went up, okayed the room, and George the bellhop was sent up with his bags. George came down and reported a dime without resentment; it was '33, after all.

Striker had sized him up, of course. That was part of his duties, and the house detective found nothing either for him or against him. Striker had been with the St. Anselm two years at that time. He'd had his salary cut in '31, and then again in '32, but so had everyone else on the staff. He didn't look much like a house dick, which was why he was good for the job. He was a tall, lean, casual-moving guy, without that annoying habit most hotel dicks have of staring people out of countenance. He used finesse about it; got the same results, but with sort of a blank, idle expression as though he were thinking of something else. He also lacked the usual paunch, in spite of his sedentary life, and never wore a hard hat. He had a little radio in his top-floor cubbyhole and a stack of vintage "fantastics," pulp magazines dealing with super-science and the supernatural, and that seemed to be all he asked of life.

The newcomer who had signed as Hopper came down again in

about half an hour and asked Dennison if there were any good movies nearby. The clerk recommended one and the guest went to it. This was about eight P.M. He came back at eleven, picked up his key, and went up to his room. Dennison and Striker both heard him whistling lightly under his breath as he stepped into the elevator. Nothing on his mind but a good night's rest, apparently.

Striker turned in himself at twelve. He was subject to call twenty-four hours a day. There was no one to relieve him. The St. Anselm was on the downgrade, and had stopped having an assistant house dick about a year before.

He was still awake, reading in bed, about an hour later when the deskman rang him. "Better get down here quick, Strike! Nine-thirteen's just fallen out!" The clerk's voice was taut, frightened.

Striker threw on coat and pants over his pajamas and got down as fast as the creaky old-fashioned elevator would let him. He went out to the street, around to the side under the 13-line.

Hopper was lying there dead, the torn leg of his pajamas rippling in the bitter March night wind. There wasn't anyone else around at that hour except the night porter, the policeman he'd called, and who had called his precinct house in turn, and a taxi driver or two. Maxon, the midnight-to-morning clerk (Dennison went off at eleven-thirty), had to remain at his post for obvious reasons. They were just standing there waiting for the morgue ambulance; there wasn't anything they could do.

Bob, the night porter, was saying: "I thought it was a pillow someone drap out the window. I come up the basement way, see a thick white thing lying there, flappin' in th' wind. I go over, fix to kick it with my foot—" He broke off. "Golly, man!"

One of the drivers said, "I seen him comin' down." No one disputed the point, but he insisted, "No kidding, I seen him coming down! I was just cruisin' past, one block over, and I look this way, and I see—whisht *ungh*—like a pancake!"

The other cab driver, who hadn't seen him coming down, said: "I seen you head down this way, so I thought you spotted a fare, and I chased after you."

They got into a wrangle above the distorted form. "Yeah you're always chiselin' in on my hails. Follyn' me around. Can't ye get none o' your own?"

Striker crossed the street, teeth chattering, and turned and looked up the face of the building. Half the French window of 913 was open, and the room was lit up. All the rest of the line was dark, from the top floor down.

He crossed back to where the little group stood shivering and stamping their feet miserably. "He sure picked a night for it!" winced the cop. The cab driver opened his mouth a couple of seconds ahead of saying something, which was his speed, and the cop turned on him irritably. "Yeah, we know! You seen him coming down. Go home, will ya!"

Striker went in, rode up, and used his passkey on 913. The light was on, as he had ascertained from the street. He stood there in the doorway and looked around. Each of the 13s, in the St. Anselm, was a small room with private bath. There was an opening on each of the four sides of these rooms: the tall, narrow, old-fashioned room door leading in from the hall; in the wall to the left of that, the door to the bath, of identical proportions; in the wall to the right of the hall door, a door giving into the clothes closet, again of similar measurements. These three panels were in the style of the 'Nineties, not your squat modern aperture. Directly opposite the room door was a pair of French windows looking out onto the street. Each of them matched the door measurements. Dark blue roller-shades covered the glass on the inside.

But Striker wasn't thinking about all that particularly, just then. He was interested only in what the condition of the room could

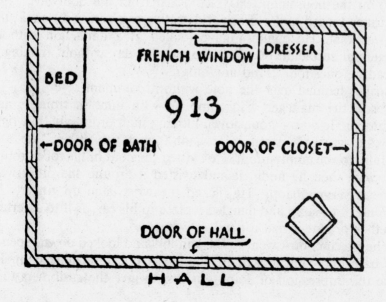

tell him: whether it had been suicide or an accident. The only thing disturbed in the room was the bed, but that was not violently disturbed as by a struggle, simply normally disarranged, as by someone sleeping. Striker, for some reason or other, tested the sheets with the back of his hand for a minute. They were still warm from recent occupancy. Hopper's trousers were neatly folded across the seat of a chair. His shirt and underclothes were draped over the back of it. His shoes stood under it, toe to toe and heel to heel. He was evidently a very neat person.

He had unpacked. He must have intended to occupy the room for the full week he had bargained for. In the closet, when Striker opened it, were his hat, overcoat, jacket and vest, the latter three on separate hangers. The dresser drawers held his shirts and other linen. On top of the dresser was a white-gold wristwatch, a handful of change, and two folded squares of paper. One was a glossy handbill from the show the guest had evidently attended only two hours ago. *Saturday through Tuesday—the laugh riot, funniest, most tuneful picture of the year, "Hips Hips Hooray!" Also "Popeye the Sailor."* Nothing in that to depress anyone.

The other was a note on hotel stationery—*Hotel Management: Sorry to do this here, but I had to do it somewhere.*

It was unsigned. So it was suicide after all. One of the two window halves, the one to the right, stood inward to the room. The one he had gone through.

"You the houseman?" a voice asked from the doorway.

Striker turned and a precinct detective came in. You could tell he was that. He couldn't have looked at a dandelion without congenital suspicion or asked the time of day without making it a leading question. "Find anything?"

Striker handed over the note without comment.

Perry, the manager, had come up with him, in trousers and bathrobe. He was a stout, jovial-looking man ordinarily, but right now he was only stout. "He hadn't paid yet, either," he said ruefully to the empty room. He twisted the cord of his robe around one way, then he undid it and twisted it around the other way. He was very unhappy. He picked the wristwatch up gingerly by the end of its strap and dangled it close to his ear, as if to ascertain whether or not it had a good movement.

The precinct dick went to the window and looked down, opened the bath door and looked in, the closet door and looked in. He gave the impression of doing this just to give the customers their money's worth; in other words, as far as he was concerned, the note had clinched the case.

"It's the old suey, all right," he said and, bending over at the dresser, read aloud what he was jotting down. "James Hopper, Skun-Skunnect—"

Striker objected peevishly. "Why did he go to bed first, then get up and go do it? They don't usually do that. He took the room for a week, too."

The precinct man raised his voice, to show he was a police detective talking to a mere hotel dick, someone who in his estimation wasn't a detective at all. "I don't care if he took it for six months! He left this note and hit the sidewalk, didn't he? Whaddaya trying to do, make it into something it ain't?"

The manager said, "Ssh! if you don't mind," and eased the door to, to keep other guests from overhearing. He sided with the precinct man, the wish being father to the thought. If there's one thing that a hotel man likes less than a suicide, it's a murder. "I don't think there's any doubt of it."

The police dick stooped to reasoning with Striker. "You were the first one up here. Was there anything wrong with the door? Was it forced open or anything?"

Striker had to admit it had been properly shut; the late occupant's key lay on the dresser where it belonged, at that very moment.

The police dick spread his hands, as if to say: "There you are, what more do you want?"

He took a last look around, decided the room had nothing more to tell him. Nor could Striker argue with him on this point. The room had nothing more to tell anyone. The dick gathered up Hopper's watch, change and identification papers, to turn them over to the police property-clerk, until they were claimed by his nearest of kin. His baggage was left in there temporarily; the room was darkened and locked up once more.

Riding down to the lobby, the dick rubbed it in a little. "Here's how those things go," he said patronizingly. "No one got in there or went near him, so it wasn't murder. He left a note, so it wasn't an accident. The word they got for this is suicide. Now y'got it?"

Striker held his palm up and fluttered it slightly. "Teacher, can I leave the room?" he murmured poignantly.

The stout manager, Perry, had a distrait, slightly anticipatory expression on his moon face now; in his mind it was the next day, he had already sold the room to someone else, and had the two dollars in the till. Heaven, to him, was a houseful of full rooms.

The body had already been removed from the street outside. Somewhere, across a coffee counter, a cab driver was saying: "I seen him coming down."

The city dick took his departure from the hotel, with the magnanimous assurance: "It's the depresh. They're poppin' off like popcorn all over the country this week. *I* ain't been able to cash my pay check since Monday."

Perry returned to his own quarters, with the typical managerial admonition, to Maxon and Striker, "Soft pedal, now, you two. Don't let this get around the house." He yawned with a sound like air brakes, going up in the elevator. You could still hear it echoing down the shaft after his feet had gone up out of sight.

"Just the same," Striker said finally, unasked, to the night clerk, "I don't care what that know-it-all says, Hopper didn't have suicide on his mind when he checked in here at seven thirty. He saw a show that was full of laughs, and even came home whistling one of the tunes from it. We both heard him. He unpacked all his shirts and things into the bureau drawers. He intended staying. He went to bed first; I felt the covers, they were warm. Then he popped up all of a sudden and took this standing broad jump."

"Maybe he had a bad dream," Maxon suggested facetiously. His was a hard-boiled racket. He yawned, muscularly magnetized by his boss' recent gape, and opened a big ledger. "Some of 'em put on a fake front until the last minute—whistle, go to a show, too proud to take the world into their confidence, and then— bang—they've crumpled. How do you or I know what was on his mind?"

And on that note it ended. As Maxon said, there was no accounting for human nature. Striker caught the sleepiness from the other two, widened his jaws terrifyingly, brought them together again with a click. And yet somehow, to him, this suicide hadn't run true to form.

He went back up to his own room again with a vague feeling of dissatisfaction, that wasn't strong enough to do anything about, and yet that he couldn't altogether throw off. Like the feeling you get when you're working out a crossword puzzle and one of the words fills up the space satisfactorily, but doesn't seem to have the required meaning called for in the solution.

The St. Anselm went back to sleep again, the small part of it that had been awake. The case was closed.

People came and went from 913 and the incident faded into the limbo of half-forgotten things. Then in the early fall of '34 the room came to specific attention again.

A young fellow in his early twenties, a college type, arrived in a roadster with just enough baggage for overnight. No reservation or anything. He signed in as Allan Hastings, Princeton, New Jersey. He didn't have to ask the desk if there were any shows. He knew his own way around. They were kind of full up that weekend. The only red vacancy tag in any of the pigeonholes was 913. Dennison gave him that—had no choice.

The guest admitted he'd been turned away from two hotels already. They all had the S.R.O. sign out. "It's the Big Game, I guess," he said.

"What Big Game?" Striker was incautious enough to ask.

"Where've you been all your life?" he grinned. But not offensively.

Some football game or other, the house dick supposed. Personally a crackling good super-science story still had the edge on twenty-two huskies squabbling over a pig's inflated hide, as far as he was concerned.

Hastings came back from the game still sober. Or if he'd had a drink it didn't show. "We lost," he said casually at the desk on his way up, but it didn't seem to depress him any. His phone, the operator reported later, rang six times in the next quarter of an hour, all feminine voices. He was apparently getting booked up solid for the rest of the weekend.

Two girls and a fellow, in evening clothes, called for him about nine. Striker saw them sitting waiting for him in the lobby, chirping and laughing their heads off. He came down in about five minutes, all rigged up for the merry-merry, even down to a white carnation in his lapel.

Striker watched them go, half wistfully. "That's the life," he said to the man behind the desk.

"May as well enjoy it while you can," said Dennison philosophically. "Here today and gone tomorrow."

Hastings hadn't come back yet by the time Striker went up and turned in. Not that Striker was thinking about him particularly, but he just hadn't seen him. He read a swell story about mermaids kidnaping a deep-sea diver, and dropped off to sleep.

The call came through to his room at about four-thirty in the morning. It took him a minute or two to come out of the deep sleep he'd been in.

"Hurry it up, will you, Strike?" Maxon was whining impatiently. "The young guy in nine-thirteen has taken a flier out his window."

Striker hung up, thinking blurredly, "Where've I heard that before—nine-thirteen?" Then he remembered—last year, from the very same room.

He filled the hollow of his hand with cold water from the washstand, dashed it into his eyes, shrugged into some clothing, and ran down the fire stairs at one side of the elevator shaft. That was quicker than waiting for the venerable mechanism to crawl up for him, then limp down again.

Maxon, who was a reformed drunk, gave him a look eloquent of disgust as Striker chased by the desk. "I'm getting off the wagon again if this keeps up—then I'll have some fun out of all these bum jolts."

There was more of a crowd this time. The weather was milder and there were more night owls in the vicinity to collect around him and gape morbidly. The kid had fallen farther out into the street than Hopper—he didn't weigh as much, maybe. He was lying there face down in the shape of a St. Andrew's cross. He hadn't undressed yet, either. Only his shoes and dinner jacket had been taken off. One strap of his black suspenders had torn off, due to the bodily contortion of the descent or from the impact itself. The white of his shirt was pretty badly changed by now, except the sleeves. He'd had a good-looking face; that was all gone too. They were turning him over as Striker came up.

The same cop was there. He was saying to a man who had been on his way home to read the after-midnight edition of the coming morning's newspaper: "Lemme have your paper, Mac, will you?"

The man demurred, "I ain't read it myself yet. I just now bought it."

The cop said, "You can buy another. We can't leave him lying like this."

The thing that had been Hastings was in pretty bad shape. The cop spread the paper, separating the sheets, and made a long paper-covered mound. The stain even came through that a little, more like gasoline than anything else. Came though a headline that said something about the King of Yugoslavia being assassinated at Marseilles.

Striker thought, with a touch of mysticism, "Half a world away from each other this afternoon; now they're both together—somewhere—maybe."

The same precinct dick showed up in answer to the routine notification that had been phoned in. His greeting to Striker was as to the dirt under his feet. "You still on the face of the earth?"

"Should I have asked your permission?" answered the hotel man drily.

Eddie Courlander—that, it seemed, was the police dick's tag—squatted down, looked under the pall of newspapers, shifted around, looked under from the other side.

"Peek-a-boo!" somebody in the small crowd said irreverently.

Courlander looked up threateningly. "Who said that? Gawan, get outa here, wise guys! If it happened to one of youse, you wouldn't feel so funny."

Somebody's night-bound coupé tried to get through, honked imperiously for clearance, not knowing what the obstruction was. The cop went up to it, said; "Get back! Take the next street over. There's a guy fell out of a window here."

The coupé drew over to the curb instead, and its occupants got out and joined the onlookers. One was a girl carrying a nightclub favor, a long stick topped with paper streamers. She squealed, *"Ooou, ooou-ooou,"* in a way you couldn't tell if she was delighted or horrified.

Courlander straightened, nodded toward Striker. "What room'd he have? C'mon in."

He didn't remember that it was the same one. Striker could tell that by the startled way he said, "Oh, yeah, that's right too!" when he mentioned the coincidence to him.

Perry and the night porter were waiting outside the room door. "I wouldn't go in until you got here," the manager whispered virtuously to the cop. "I know you people don't like anything touched." Striker, however, had a hunch there was a little superstitious fear at the back of this as well, like a kid shying away from a dark room.

"You're thinking of murder cases," remarked Courlander contemptuously. "Open 'er up."

The light was on again, like the previous time. But there was a great difference in the condition of the room. Young Hastings obviously hadn't had Hopper's personal neatness. Or else he'd been slightly lit up when he came in. The daytime clothes he'd discarded after coming back from the game were still strewn around, some on chairs, some on the floor. The St. Anselm didn't employ maids to straighten the rooms after five in the evening. His patent-leathers lay yards apart as though they had been kicked off into the air and left lying where they had come down. His bat-wing tie was a black snake across the carpet. There was a depression and creases on the counterpane on top of the bed, but it hadn't been turned down. He had therefore lain down on the bed, but not in it.

On the dresser top stood a glittering little pouch, obviously a woman's evening bag. Also his carnation, in a glass of water. Under that was the note. Possibly one of the shortest suicide notes on record. Three words. *What's the use?*

Courlander read it, nodded, showed it to them. "Well," he said, "that tells the story."

He shrugged.

In the silence that followed the remark, the phone rang sharply, unexpectedly. They all jolted a little, even Courlander. Although there was no body in the room and never had been, it was a dead man's room. There was something macabre to the peal, like a desecration. The police dick halted Striker and the manager with a gesture.

"May be somebody for him," he said, and went over and took it. He said, "Hello?" in a wary, noncommittal voice. Then he changed to his own voice, said: "Oh. Have you told her yet? Well, send her up here. I'd like to talk to her."

He hung up, explained: "Girl he was out with tonight is down at the desk, came back to get her bag. He must have been carrying it for her. It has her latchkey in it and she couldn't get into her own home."

Perry turned almost unconsciously and looked into the dresser mirror to see if he needed a shave. Then he fastidiously narrowed the neck opening of his dressing gown and smoothed the hair around the back of his head, which was the only place he had any.

The dick shoved Hastings' discarded clothes out of sight on the closet floor. This was definitely not a murder case, so there was no reason to shock the person he was about to question, by the presence of the clothes.

There was a short tense wait while she was coming up on the slow-motion elevator. Coming up to see someone that wasn't there at all. Striker said rebukingly, "This is giving it to her awful sudden, if she was at all fond of the guy."

Courlander unwittingly gave an insight into his own character when he said callously, "These girls nowadays can take it better than we can—don't worry."

The elevator panel ticked open, and then she came into the square of light thrown across the hall by the open doorway. She was a very pretty girl of about twenty-one or -two, tall and slim, with dark red hair, in a long white satin evening gown. Her eyes were wide with startled inquiry, at the sight of the three of them, but not frightened yet. Striker had seen her once before, when she was waiting for Hastings in the lobby earlier that evening. The other man of the original quartette had come up with her, no doubt for propriety's sake, and was standing behind her. They had evidently seen the second girl home before coming back here. And the side street where he had fallen was around the corner from the main entrance to the hotel.

She crossed the threshold, asked anxiously, "Is Allan— Is Mr. Hastings ill or something? The deskman said there's been a little trouble up here."

Courlander said gently, "Yes, there has." But he couldn't make anything sound gentle. The closest he could get to it was a sort of passive truculence.

She looked around. She was starting to get frightened now. She said, "What's happened to him? Where is he?" Then she saw the right half of the window standing open. Striker, who was closest to it, raised his arm and pushed it slowly closed. Then he just looked at her.

She understood, and whimpered across her shoulder, "Oh, Marty!" and the man behind her put an arm around her shoulder to support her.

They sat down. She didn't cry much—just sat with her head bent looking over at the floor. Her escort stood behind her chair, hands on her shoulders, bucking her up.

Courlander gave her a minute or two to pull herself together, then he started questioning. He asked them who they were. She gave her name. The man with her was her brother; he was Hastings' classmate at Princeton.

He asked if Hastings had had much to drink.

"He had a few drinks," she admitted, "but he wasn't drunk. Mart and I had the same number he did, and we're not drunk." They obviously weren't.

"Do you know of any reason, either one of you, why he should have done this?"

The thing had swamped them with its inexplicability, it was easy to see that. They just shook their heads dazedly.

"Financial trouble?"

The girl's brother just laughed—mirthlessly. "He had a banking business to inherit, some day—if he'd lived."

"Ill health? Did he study too hard, maybe?"

He laughed again, dismally. "He was captain of the hockey team, he was on the baseball team, he was the bright hope of the swimming team. Why should he worry about studying? Star athletes are never allowed to flunk."

"Love affair?" the tactless flatfoot blundered on.

The brother flinched at that. This time it was the girl who answered. She raised her head in wounded pride, thrust out her left hand.

"He asked me to marry him tonight. He gave me this ring. That was the reason for the party. Am I so hard to take?"

The police dick got red. She stood up without waiting to ask whether she could go or not. "Take me home, Mart," she said in a muffled voice. "I've got some back crying to catch up on."

Striker called the brother back again for a minute, while she went on alone toward the elevator; shoved the note before him. "Was that his handwriting?"

He pored over it. "I can't tell, just on the strength of those three words. I've never seen enough of it to know it very well. The only thing I'd know for sure would be his signature—he had a cockeyed way of ending it with a little pretzel twist—and that isn't on there." Over his shoulder, as he turned to go once more, he added: "That was a favorite catchword of his, though. 'What's the use?' I've often heard him use it. I guess it's him all right."

"We can check it by the register," Striker suggested after they'd gone.

The dick gave him a scathing look. "Is it your idea somebody else wrote his suicide note for him? That's what I'd call service!"

"Is it your idea he committed suicide the same night he got engaged to a production number like you just saw?"

"Is it your idea he didn't?"

"Ye-es," said Striker with heavy emphasis, "but I can't back it up."

"You bet you can't!"

The register showed a variation between the two specimens of handwriting, but not more than could be ascribed to the tension and nervous excitement of a man about to end his life. There wasn't enough to the note for a good handwriting expert to have got his teeth into with any degree of certainty.

"How long had he been in when it happened?" Striker asked Maxon.

"Not more than half an hour. Bob took him up a little before four."

"How'd he act? Down in the mouth, blue?"

"Blue nothing, he was tappin' out steps there on the mosaic, waitin' for the car to take him up."

Bob, the night man-of-all-work, put in his two cents' worth without being asked: "On the way up he said to me, 'Think this thing'll last till we get up there? I'd hate to have it drop me now. I got engaged tonight.'"

Striker flashed the police dick a triumphant look. The latter just stood by with the air of one indulging a precocious child. "Now ya through, little boy?" he demanded. "Why don't you quit trying to make noise like a homicide dick and stick to your own little racket?

"It's a suicide, see?" continued the police dick pugnaciously, as though by raising his voice he was deciding the argument. "I've cased the room, and I don't care if he stood on his head or did somersaults before he rode up." He waved a little black pocket-notebook under Striker's nose. "Here's my report, and if it don't suit you, why don't you take it up with the Mayor?"

Striker said in a humble, placating voice: "Mind if I ask you something personal?"

"What?" said the precinct man sourly.

"Are you a married man?"

"Sure I'm married. What's that to—?"

"Think hard. The night you became engaged, the night you first proposed to your wife, did you feel like taking your own life afterwards?"

The police dick went "Arrrr!" disgustedly, flung around on his heel, and stalked out, giving the revolving door an exasperated twirl that kept it going long after he was gone.

"They get sore, when you've got 'em pinned down," Striker remarked wryly.

Perry remonstrated impatiently, "Why are you always trying to make it out worse than it is? Isn't it bad enough without looking for trouble?"

"If there's something phony about his death, isn't it worse if it goes undetected than if it's brought to light?"

Perry said, pointedly thumbing the still-turning door, *"That* was the police we just had with us."

"We were practically alone," muttered his disgruntled operative.

And so they couldn't blame it on the Depression this time. That was starting to clear up now. And besides, Allan Hastings had come from well-to-do people. They couldn't blame it on love either. Perry half-heartedly tried to suggest he hadn't loved the girl he was engaged to, had had somebody else under his skin maybe, so he'd taken this way to get out of it."

"That's a woman's reason, not a man's," Striker said disgustedly. "Men don't kill themselves for love; they go out and get tanked, and hop a train for some place else, instead!" The others both nodded, probing deep within their personal memories. So that wouldn't wash either.

In the end there wasn't anything they could blame it on but the room itself. "That room's jinxed," Maxon drawled slurringly. "That's two in a row we've had in there. I think it's the thirteen on it. You oughta change the number to nine-twelve and a half or nine-fourteen and a half or something, boss."

That was how the legend first got started.

Perry immediately jumped on him full-weight. "Now listen, I won't have any of that nonsense! There's nothing wrong with that room! First thing you know the whole hotel'll have a bad name, and then where are we? It's just a coincidence, I tell you, just a coincidence!"

Dennison sold the room the very second day after to a middle-aged couple on a visit to the city to see the sights. Striker and Maxon sort of held their breaths, without admitting it to each other. Striker even got up out of bed once or twice that first night and took a prowl past the door of nine-thirteen, stopping to listen carefully. All he could hear was a sonorous baritone snore and a silvery soprano one, in peaceful counterpoint.

The hayseed couple left three days later, perfectly unharmed and vowing they'd never enjoyed themselves as much in their lives.

"Looks like the spirits are lying low," commented the deskman, shoving the red vacancy tag back into the pigeonhole.

"No," said Striker, "looks like it only happens to singles. When there's two in the room nothing ever happens."

"You never heard of anyone committing suicide in the presence of a second party, did you?" the clerk pointed out not unreasonably. "That's one thing they gotta have privacy for."

Maybe it had been, as Perry insisted, just a gruesome coincidence. "But if it happens a third time," Striker vowed to himself, "I'm going to get to the bottom of it if I gotta pull the whole place down brick by brick!"

The Legend, meanwhile, had blazed up, high and furious, with the employees; even the slowest-moving among them had a way of hurrying past Room 913 with sidelong glances and fetish mutterings when any duty called them to that particular hallway after dark. Perry raised hell about it, but he was up against the supernatural now; he and his threats of discharge didn't stack up at all against that. The penalty for repeating the rumor to a guest was instant dismissal if detected by the management. *If.*

Then just when the legend was languishing from lack of any further substantiation to feed upon, and was about to die down altogether, the room came through a third time!

The calendar read Friday, July 12th, 1935, and the thermometers all read 90-plus. He came in mopping his face like everyone else, but with a sort of professional good humor about him that no one else could muster just then. That was one thing that tipped Striker off he was a salesman. Another was the two bulky sample cases he was hauling with him until the bellboy took them over. A third was his ability to crack a joke when most people felt like eggs in a frying pan waiting to be turned over.

"Just rent me a bath without a room," he told Dennison. "I'll sleep in the tub all night with the cold water running over me."

"I can give you a nice inside room on the fourth." There were enough vacancies at the moment to offer a choice, these being the dog days.

The newcomer held up his hand, palm outward. "No thanks, not this kind of weather. I'm willing to pay the difference."

"Well, I've got an outside on the sixth, and a couple on the ninth."

"The higher the better. More chance to get a little circulation into the air."

There were two on the ninth, 13 and 19. Dennison's hand paused before 13, strayed on past it to 19, hesitated, came back again. After all, the room had to be sold. This was business, not a kid's goblin story. Even Striker could see that. And it was nine months now since—There'd been singles in the room since then, too. And they'd lived to check out again.

He gave him 913. But after the man had gone up, he couldn't refrain from remarking to Striker: "Keep your fingers crossed. That's the one with the jinx on it." As though Striker didn't know that! "I'm going to do a little more than that," he promised himself privately.

He swung the register around toward him so he could read it. *Amos J. Dillberry, City,* was inscribed on it. Meaning this was the salesman's headquarters when he was not on the road, probably. Striker shifted it back again.

He saw the salesman in the hotel dining room at mealtime that evening. He came in freshly showered and laundered, and had a wisecrack for his waiter. That was the salesman in him. The heat certainly hadn't affected his appetite any, the way he stoked.

"If anything happens," thought Striker with gloomy foreboding, "that dick Courlander should show up later and try to tell me this guy was depressed or affected by the heat! He should just try!"

In the early part of the evening the salesman hung around the lobby a while, trying to drum up conversation with this and that sweltering fellow guest. Striker was in there too, watching him covertly. For once he was not a hotel dick sizing somebody up hostilely, he was a hotel dick sizing somebody up protectively. Not finding anyone particularly receptive, Dillberry went out into the street about ten, in quest of a soulmate.

Striker stood up as soon as he'd gone, and took the opportunity of going up to 913 and inspecting it thoroughly. He went over every square inch of it; got down on his hands and knees and explored all along the baseboards of the walls; examined the electric outlets; held matches to such slight fissures as there were between the tiles in the bathroom; rolled back one half of the carpet at a time and inspected the floorboards thoroughly; even got up on a chair and fiddled with the ceiling light fixture, to see if there was anything tricky about it. He couldn't find a thing wrong. He tested the windows exhaustively, working them back and forth until the hinges threatened to come off. There wasn't anything defective or balky about them, and on a scorching night like this the inmate was bound to leave them wide open and let it go at that, not fiddle around with them in any way during the middle of the night. There wasn't enough breeze, even this high up, to swing a cobweb.

He locked the room behind him, went downstairs again with a helpless dissatisfied feeling of having done everything that was humanly possible—and yet not having done anything at all, really. What was there he could do?

Dillberry reappeared a few minutes before twelve, with a package cradled in his arm that was unmistakably for refreshment purposes up in his room, and a conspiratorial expression on his face that told Striker's experienced eyes what was coming next. The salesman obviously wasn't the solitary drinker type.

Striker saw her drift in about ten minutes later, with the air of a lady on her way to do a little constructive drinking. He couldn't place her on the guest list, and she skipped the desk entirely—so he bracketed her with Dillberry. He did exactly nothing about it—turned his head away as though he hadn't noticed her.

Maxon, who had just come on in time to get a load of this, looked at Striker in surprise. "Aren't you going to do anything about that?" he murmured. "She's not one of our regulars."

"I know what I'm doing," Striker assured him softly. "She don't know it, but she's subbing for night watchman up there. As long as he's not alone, nothing can happen to him."

"Oh, is that the angle? Using her for a chest protector, eh? But that just postpones the showdown—don't solve it. If you keep using a spare to ward it off, how you gonna know what it is?"

"That," Striker had to admit, "is just the rub. But I hate like the devil to find out at the expense of still another life."

But the precaution was frustrated before he had time to see whether it would work or not. The car came down almost immediately afterwards, and the blonde was still on it, looking extremely annoyed and quenching her unsatisfied thirst by chewing gum with a sound like castanets. Beside her stood Manager Perry, pious determination transforming his face.

"Good night," he said, politely ushering her off the car.

"Y'couldda at least let me have one quick one, neat, you big overstuffed blimp!" quoth the departing lady indignantly. "After I helped him pick out the brand!"

Perry came over to the desk and rebuked his houseman: "Where are your eyes, Striker? How did you let that come about? I happened to spot her out in the hall waiting to be let in. You want to be on your toes, man."

"Sorry, chief," said Striker.

"So it looks like he takes his own chances," murmured Maxon, when the manager had gone up again.

"Then I'm elected, personally," sighed Striker. "Maybe it's just as well. Even if something had happened with her up there, she didn't look like she had brains enough to be able to tell what it was afterwards."

In the car, on the way to his own room, he said, "Stop at nine a minute—and wait for me." This was about a quarter to one.

He listened outside 13. He heard a page rustle, knew the salesman wasn't asleep, so he knocked softly. Dillberry opened the door.

"Excuse me for disturbing you. I'm the hotel detective."

"I've been quarantined once tonight already," said the salesman, but his characteristic good humor got the better of him even now. "You can come in and look if you want to, but I know when I'm licked."

"No, it isn't about that." Striker wondered how to put it. In loyalty to his employer he couldn't very well frighten the man out of the place. "I just wanted to warn you to please be careful of those windows. The guard-rail outside them's pretty low, and—"

"No danger," the salesman chuckled. "I'm not subject to dizzy spells and I don't walk in my sleep."

Striker didn't smile back. "Just bear in mind what I said, though, will you?"

Dillberry was still chortling good-naturedly. "If he *did* lose his balance during the night and go out," thought Striker impatiently, "it would be like him still to keep on sniggering all the way down."

"What are you worried they'll do—creep up on me and bite me?" kidded the salesman.

"Maybe that's a little closer to the truth than you realize," Striker said to himself mordantly. Looking at the black, nightfilled aperture across the lighted room from them, he visualized it for the first time as a hungry, predatory maw, with an evil active intelligence of its own, swallowing the living beings that lingered too long within its reach, sucking them through to destruction, like a diabolic vacuum cleaner. It looked like an upright, open black coffin there, against the cream-painted walls; all it needed was a silver handle at each end. Or like a symbolic Egyptian doorway to the land of the dead, with its severe proportions and pitch-black core and the hot, lazy air coming through it from the nether world.

He was beginning to hate it with a personal hate, because it baffled him, it had him licked, had him helpless, and it struck without warning—an unfair adversary.

Dillberry giggled, "You got a look on your face like you tasted poison! I got a bottle here hasn't been opened yet. How about rinsing it out?"

"No, thanks," said Striker, turning away. "And it's none of my business, I know, but just look out for those windows if you've got a little something under your belt later."

"No fear," the salesman called after him. "It's no fun drinking alone. Too hot for that, anyway."

Striker went on up to his own room and turned in. The night air had a heavy, stagnant expectancy to it, as if it were just waiting for something to happen. Probably the heat, and yet he could hardly breathe, the air was so leaden with menace and sinister tension.

He couldn't put his mind to the "fantastic" magazine he'd taken to bed with him—he flung it across the room finally. "You'd think I knew, ahead of time!" he told himself scoffingly. And yet deny it as he might, he did have a feeling that tonight was going to be one of those times. Heat jangling his nerves, probably. He put out his light—even the weak bulb gave too much warmth for comfort—and lay there in the dark, chain-smoking cigarettes until his tongue prickled.

An hour ticked off, like drops of molten lead. He heard the hour of three strike faintly somewhere in the distance, finally. He lay there, tossing and turning, his mind going around and around the problem. What *could* it have been but two suicides, by coincidence both from the one room? There had been no violence, no signs of anyone having got in from the outside.

He couldn't get the infernal room off his mind; it was driving him nutty. He sat up abruptly, decided to go down there and take soundings. Anything was better than lying there. He put on shirt and pants, groped his way to the door without bothering with the light—it was too hot for lights—opened the door and started down the hall. He left the door cracked open behind him, to save himself the trouble of having to work a key on it when he got back.

He'd already rounded the turn of the hall and was at the fire door giving onto the emergency stairs, when he heard a faint trill somewhere behind him. The ding-a-ling of a telephone bell. Could that be his? If it was— He tensed at the implication. It kept on sounding; it must be his, or it would have been answered by now.

He turned and ran back, shoved the door wide open. It was. It burst into full-bodied volume, almost seemed to explode in his face. He found the instrument in the dark, rasped, "Hello?"

"Strike?" There was fear in Maxon's voice now. "It's—it's happened again."

Striker drew in his breath, and that was cold too, in all the heat of the stuffy room. "Nine-thirteen?" he said hoarsely.

"Nine-thirteen!"

He hung up without another word. His feet beat a pulsing tattoo, racing down the hall. This time he went straight to the room, not down to the street. He'd seen too often what "they" looked like, down below, after they'd grounded. This time he wanted to see what that hell box, that four-walled coffin, that murder crate of a room looked like. Right after. Not five minutes or even two, but right after—as fast as it was humanly possible to get there. But maybe five minutes had passed, already; must have, by the time it was discovered, and he was summoned, and he got back and answered his phone. Why hadn't he stirred his stumps a few minutes sooner? He'd have been just in time, not only to prevent, but to see what it was—if there was anything to see.

He got down to the ninth, heat or no heat, in thirty seconds flat, and over to the side of the building the room was on. The door was yawning wide open, and the room light was out. "Caught you, have I?" flashed grimly through his mind. He rounded the jamb like a shot, poked the light switch on, stood crouched, ready to fling himself—

Nothing. No living thing, no disturbance.

No note either, this time. He didn't miss any bets. He looked into the closet, the bath, even got down and peered under the bed. He peered cautiously down from the lethal window embrasure, careful where he put his hands, careful where he put his weight.

He couldn't see the street, because the window was too high up, but he could hear voices down there plainly in the still, warm air.

He went back to the hall and stood there listening. But it was too late to expect to hear anything, and he knew it. The way he'd come galloping down like a war horse would have drowned out any sounds of surreptitious departure there might have been. And somehow, he couldn't help feeling there hadn't been any, anyway. The evil was implicit in this room itself—didn't come from outside, open door to the contrary.

He left the room just the way he'd found it, went below finally. Maxon straightened up from concealing something under the desk, drew the back of his hand recklessly across his mouth. "Bring on your heebie-jeebies," he said defiantly. "See if I care—now!"

Striker didn't blame him too much at that. He felt pretty shaken himself.

Perry came down one car-trip behind him. "I never heard of anything like it!" he was seething. "What kind of a merry-go-round is this anyway?"

Eddie Courlander had been sent over for the third time. Happened to be the only one on hand, maybe. The whole thing was just a monotonous repetition of the first two times, but too grisly—to Striker, anyway—to be amusing.

"This is getting to be a commutation trip for me," the police dick announced with macabre humor, stalking in. "The desk lieutenant only has to say, 'Suicide at a hotel,' and I say right away, 'The St. Anselm,' before he can tell me."

"Only it isn't," said Striker coldly. "There was no note."

"Are you going to start that again?" growled the city dick.

"It's the same room again, in case you're interested. Third time in a little over two years. Now, don't you think that's rubbing it in a little heavy?"

Courlander didn't answer, as though he *was* inclined to think that, but—if it meant siding with Striker—hated to have to admit it.

Even Perry's professional bias for suicide—if the alternative had to be murder, the *bête-noir* of hotel men—wavered in the face of this triple assault. "It does look kind of spooky," he faltered, polishing the center of his bald head. "All the rooms below, on that line, have those same floor-length windows, and it's never taken place in any of the others."

"Well, we're going to do it up brown this time and get to the bottom of it!" Courlander promised.

They got off at the ninth. "Found the door open like this, too," Striker pointed out. "I stopped off here on my way down."

Courlander just glanced at him, but still wouldn't commit himself. He went into the room, stopped dead center and stood there looking around, the other two just behind him. Then he went over to the bed, fumbled a little with the covers. Suddenly he spaded his hand under an edge of the pillow, drew it back again.

"I thought you said there was no note?" he said over his shoulder to Striker.

"You not only thought. I did say that."

"You still do, huh?" He shoved a piece of stationery at him. "What does this look like—a collar button?"

It was as laconic as the first two. *I'm going to hell, where it's cool!* Unsigned.

"That wasn't in here when I looked the place over the first time," Striker insisted with slow emphasis. "That was planted in here between then and now!"

Courlander flung his head disgustedly. "It's white, isn't it? The bedclothes are white too, ain't they? Why don't you admit you missed it?"

"Because I know I didn't! I had my face inches away from that bed, bending down looking under it."

"Aw, you came in half-asleep and couldn't even see straight, probably!"

"I've been awake all night, wider awake than you are right now!"

"And as for your open door—" Courlander jeered. He bent down, ran his thumbnail under the panel close in to the jamb, jerked something out. He stood up exhibiting a wedge made of a folded-over paper match-cover. "He did that himself, to try to get a little circulation into the air in here."

Striker contented himself with murmuring, "Funny no one else's door was left open." But to himself he thought, ruefully, "It's trying its best to look natural all along the line, like the other times; which only proves it isn't."

The city dick answered, "Not funny at all. A woman alone in a room wouldn't leave her door open for obvious reasons; and a couple in a room wouldn't, because the wife would be nervous or modest about it. But why shouldn't a guy rooming by himself do it, once his light was out, and if he didn't have anything of value in here with him? That's why his was the only door open like that. The heat drove him wacky; and when he couldn't get any relief no matter what he did—"

"The heat did nothing of the kind. I spoke to him at twelve and he was cheerful as a robin."

"Yeah, but a guy's resistance gets worn down, it frays, and then suddenly it snaps." Courlander chuckled scornfully. "It's as plain as day before your eyes."

"Well," drawled Striker, "if this is your idea of getting to the bottom of a thing, baby, you're easily pleased! I'll admit it's a little more work to keep digging, than just to write down 'suicide' in your report and let it go at that," he added stingingly.

"I don't want any of your insinuations!" Courlander said hotly. "Trying to call me lazy, huh? All right," he said with the air of doing a big favor, "I'll play ball with you. We'll make the rounds giving off noises like a detective, if that's your idea."

"You'll empty my house for me," Perry whined.

"Your man here seems to think I'm laying down on the job." Courlander stalked out, hitched his head at them to follow.

"You've never played the numbers, have you?" Striker suggested stolidly. "No number ever comes up three times in a row. That's what they call the law of averages. Three suicides from one room doesn't conform to the law of averages. And when a thing don't conform to that law, it's phony."

"You forgot your lantern slides, perfessor," sneered the police dick. He went next door and knuckled 915, first gently, then resoundingly.

The door opened and a man stuck a sleep-puffed face out at them. He said, "Whad-dye want? It takes me half the night to work up a little sleep and then I gotta have it busted on me!" He wasn't just faking being asleep—it was the real article; anyone could see that. The light hurt his eyes; he kept blinking.

"Sorry, pal," Courlander overrode him with a businesslike air, "but we gotta ask a few questions. Can we come in and look around?"

"No, ya can't! My wife's in bed!"

"Have her put something over her, then, 'cause we're comin'!"

"I'm leaving the first thing in the morning!" the man threatened angrily. "You can't come into my room like this, without a search warrant!" He thrust himself belligerently into the door opening.

"Just what have you got to hide, Mr. Morris?" suggested Striker mildly.

The remark had an almost magical effect on him. He blinked, digested the implication a moment, then abruptly swept the door wide open, stepped out of the way.

A woman was sitting up in bed struggling into a wrapper.

Courlander studied the wall a minute. "Did you hear any noise of any kind from the next room before you fell asleep?"

The man shook his head, said: "No."

"About how long ago did you fall asleep?"

"About an hour ago," said the man sulkily.

Courlander turned to the manager. "Go back in there a minute, will you, and knock on the wall with your fist from that side. Hit it good."

The four of them listened in silence; not a sound came through. Perry returned, blowing his breath on his stinging knuckles.

"That's all," Courlander said to the occupants. "Sorry to bother you." He and Striker went out again. Perry lingered a moment to try to smoothe their ruffled plumage.

They went down to the other side of the death chamber and tried 911. "This witch," said Perry, joining them, "has got ears like a dictaphone. If there was anything to hear, she heard it all right! I don't care whether you disturb her or not. I've been trying to get rid of her for years."

She was hatchet-faced, beady-eyed, and had a cap with a draw string tied closely about her head. She seemed rather gratified at finding herself an object of attention, even in the middle of the night, as though she couldn't get anyone to listen to her most of the time.

"Asleep?" she said almost boastfully. "I should say not! I haven't closed my eyes all night." And then, overriding Courlander's attempt at getting in a question, she went on: "Mr. Perry, I know it's late, but as long as you're here, I want to show you something!" She drew back into the center of the room, crooked her finger at him ominously. "You just come here!"

The three men advanced alertly and jockeyed into positions from which they could see.

She swooped down, flung back a corner of the rug, and straightened up again, pointing dramatically. A thin film of dust marked the triangle of flooring that had just been bared. "What do you think of that?" she said accusingly. "Those maids of yours, instead of sweeping the dust *out* of the room, sweep it under the rug."

The manager threw his hands up over his head, turned, and went out. "The building could be burning," he fumed, "and if we both landed in the same fireman's net, she'd still roll over and complain to me about the service!"

Striker lingered behind just long enough to ask her: "You say you've been awake all night. Did you hear anything from the room next door, nine-thirteen, during the past half-hour or so?"

"Why, no. Not a sound. Is there something wrong in there?" The avid way she asked it was proof enough of her good faith. He got out before she could start questioning him.

Courlander grinned, "I can find a better explanation even than the heat for him jumping, now," he remarked facetiously. "He musta seen *that* next door to him and got scared to death."

"That would be beautifully simple, wouldn't it?" Striker said cuttingly. "Let's give it one more spin," he suggested. "No one on either side of the room heard anything. Let's try the room directly underneath—eight-thirteen. The closet and bath arrangement makes for soundproof side-partitions, but the ceilings are pretty thin here."

Courlander gave the manager an amused look, as if to say, "Humor him!"

Perry, however, rolled his eyes in dismay. "Good heavens, are you trying to turn my house upside-down, Striker? Those are the Youngs, our star guests, and you know it!"

"D'you want to wait until it happens a fourth time?" Striker warned him. "It'll bring on a panic if it does."

They went down to the hallway below, stopped before 813. "These people are very wealthy," whispered the manager apprehensively. "They could afford much better quarters. I've considered myself lucky that they've stayed with us. Please be tactful. I don't want to lose them." He tapped apologetically, with just two fingernails.

Courlander sniffed and said, "What's that I smell?"

"Incense," breathed the manager. "*Sh!* Don't you talk out of turn now."

There was a rustling sound behind the door, then it opened and a young Chinese in a silk robe stood looking out at them. Striker knew him, through staff gossip and his own observation, to be not only thoroughly Americanized in both speech and manner but an American by birth as well. He was Chinese only by descent. He was a lawyer and made huge sums looking after the interests of the Chinese businessmen down on Pell and Mott Streets—a considerable part of which he lost again betting on the wrong horses, a pursuit he was no luckier at than his average fellow citizen. He was married to a radio singer. He wore horn-rimmed glasses.

"Hi!" he said briskly. "The Vigilantes! What's up, Perry?"

"I'm so sorry to annoy you like this," the manager began to whine.

"Skip it," said Young pleasantly. "Who could sleep on a night like this? We've been taking turns fanning each other in here. Come on in."

Even Striker had never been in the room before; the Youngs were quality folk, not to be intruded upon by a mere hotel detective. A doll-like creature was curled up on a sofa languidly fanning herself, and a scowling Pekinese nestled in her lap. The woman wore green silk pajamas. Striker took note of a tank containing tropical fish, also a lacquered Buddha on a table with a stick of sandalwood burning before it.

Striker and Courlander let Perry put the question, since being tactful was more in his line. "Have you people been disturbed by any sounds coming from over you?"

"Not a blessed thing," Mrs. Young averred. "Have we, babe? Only that false-alarm mutter of thunder that didn't live up to its promise. But that came from outside, of course."

"Thunder?" said Striker, puzzled. "What thunder? How long ago?"

"Oh, it wasn't a sharp clap," Young explained affably. " 'Way off in the distance, low and rolling. You could hardly hear it at all. There was a flicker of sheet-lightning at the same time—that's how we knew what it was."

"But wait a minute," Striker said discontentedly. "I was lying awake in my room, and I didn't hear any thunder, at any time tonight."

"There he goes again," Courlander slurred out of the corner of his mouth to Perry.

"But your room's located in a different part of the building," Perry interposed diplomatically. "It looks out on a shaft, and that might have muffled the sound."

"Thunder is thunder. You can hear it down in a cellar, when there is any to hear," Striker insisted.

The Chinese couple good-naturedly refused to take offense. "Well, it was very low, just a faint rolling. We probably wouldn't have noticed it ourselves, only at the same time there was this far-off gleam of lightning, and it seemed to stir up a temporary breeze out there, like when a storm's due to break. I must admit we didn't feel any current of air here inside the room, but we both saw a newspaper or rag of some kind go sailing down past the window just then."

"No, that wasn't a—" Striker stopped short, drew in his breath, as he understood what it was they must have seen.

Perry was frantically signaling him to shut up and get outside. Striker hung back long enough to ask one more question. "Did your dog bark or anything, about the time this—'promise of a storm' came up?"

"No, Shan's very well behaved," Mrs. Young said fondly.

"He whined, though," her husband remembered. "We thought it was the heat."

Striker narrowed his eyes speculatively. "Was it right at that same time?"

"Just about."

Perry and Courlander were both hitching their heads at him to come out, before he spilled the beans. When he had joined them finally, the city dick flared up: "What'd you mean by asking that last one? You trying to dig up spooks, maybe?—hinting that their dog could sense something? All it was is, the dog knew more than they did. It knew that wasn't a newspaper flicked down past their window. That's why it whined!"

Striker growled stubbornly. "There hasn't been any thunder or any lightning at any time tonight—I know what I'm saying! I was lying awake in my room, as awake as they were!"

Courlander eyed the manager maliciously. "Just like there wasn't any farewell note, until I dug it out from under the pillow."

Striker said challengingly, "You find me *one other person*, in this building or outside of it, that saw and heard that 'thunder and lightning' the same as they did, and we'll call it quits!"

"Fair enough. I'll take you up on that!" Courlander snapped. "It ought to be easy enough to prove to you that that wasn't a private preview run off in heaven for the special benefit of the Chinese couple."

"And when people pay two hundred a month, they don't lie," said Perry quaintly.

"We'll take that projecting wing that sticks out at right angles," said the dick. "It ought to have been twice as clear and loud out there as down on the eighth. Or am I stacking the cards?"

"You're not exactly dealing from a warm deck," Striker said. "If it was heard below, it could be heard out in the wing, and still have something to do with what went on in 913. Why not pick somebody who was out on the streets at the time and ask him? There's your real test."

"Take it or leave it. I'm not running around on the street this hour of the night, asking people 'Did you hear a growl of thunder thirty minutes ago?' I'd land in Bellevue in no time!"

"This is the bachelor wing," Perry explained as they rounded the turn of the hall. "All men. Even so, they're entitled to a night's rest as well as anyone else. Must you disturb *everyone* in the house?"

"Not my idea," Courlander rubbed it in. "That note is still enough for me. I'm giving this guy all the rope he needs, that's all."

They stopped outside 909. "Peter the Hermit," said Perry disgustedly. "Aw, don't wake him. He won't be any help. He's nutty. He'll start telling you all about his gold mines up in Canada."

But Courlander had already knocked. "He's not too nutty to know thunder and lightning when he hears it, is he?"

Bedsprings creaked, there was a slither of bare feet, and the door opened.

He was about sixty, with a mane of snow-white hair that fell down to his shoulders, and a long white beard. He had mild blue eyes, with something trusting and childlike about them. You only had to look at them to understand how easy it must have been for the confidence men, or whoever it was, to have swindled him into buying those worthless shafts sunk into the ground up in the backwoods of Ontario.

Striker knew the story well; everyone in the hotel did. But others laughed, while Striker sort of understood—put two and two together. The man wasn't crazy, he was just disappointed in life. The long hair and the beard, Striker suspected, were not due to eccentricity but probably to stubbornness; he'd taken a vow never to cut his hair or shave until those mines paid off. And the fact that he hugged his room day and night, never left it except just once a month to buy a stock of canned goods, was understandable too. He'd been "stung" once, so now he was leery of strangers, avoided people for fear of being "stung" again. And then ridicule probably had something to do with it too. The way that fool Courlander was all but laughing in his face right now, trying to cover it with his hand before his mouth, was characteristic.

The guest was down on the register as Atkinson, but no one ever called him anything but Peter the Hermit. At irregular intervals he left the hotel to go "prospecting" up to his mine pits, see if there were any signs of ore. Then he'd come back again disappointed, but without having given up hope, to retire again for another six or eight months. He kept the same room while he was away, paying for it just as though he were in it.

"Can we come in, Pops?" the city dick asked, when he'd managed to straighten his face sufficiently.

"Not if you're going to try to sell me any more gold mines."

"Naw, we just want a weather report. You been asleep or awake?"

"I been awake all night, practickly."

"Good. Now tell me just one thing. Did you hear any thunder at all, see anything like heat-lightning flicker outside your window, little while back?"

"Heat-lightning don't go with thunder. You never have the two together," rebuked the patriarch.

"All right, all right," said Courlander wearily. "Any kind of lightning, plain or fancy, and any kind of thunder?"

"Sure did. Just once, though. Tiny speck of thunder and tiny mite of lightning, no more'n a flash in the pan. Stars were all out and around too. Darnedest thing I ever saw!"

Courlander gave the hotel dick a look that should have withered him. But Striker jumped in without waiting. "About this flicker of lightning. Which direction did it seem to come from? Are you sure it came from above and not"—he pointed meaningly downward—"from *below* your window?"

This time it was the Hermit who gave him the withering look. "Did you ever hear of lightning coming from below, son? Next thing you'll be trying to tell me rain falls up from the ground!" He went over to the open window, beckoned. "I'll show you right about where it panned out. I was standing here looking out at the time, just happened to catch it." He pointed in a northeasterly direction. "There. See that tall building up over thattaway? It come from over behind there—miles away, o' course—but from that part of the sky."

Courlander, having won his point, cut the interview short. "Much obliged, Pops. That's all."

They withdrew just as the hermit was getting into his stride. He rested a finger alongside his nose, trying to hold their attention, said confidentially: "I'm going to be a rich man one of these days, you wait'n see. Those mines o' mine are going to turn into a bonanza." But they closed the door on him.

Riding down in the car, Courlander snarled at Striker: "Now, eat your words. You said if we found one other person heard and saw that thunder and sheet-lightning—"

"I know what I said," Striker answered dejectedly. "Funny— private thunder and lightning that some hear and others don't."

Courlander swelled with satisfaction. He took out his notebook, flourished it. "Well, here goes, ready or not! You can work yourself up into a lather about it by yourself from now on. I'm not wasting any more of the city's time—or my own—on anything as self-evident as this!"

"Self-evidence, like beauty," Striker reminded him, "is in the eye of the beholder. It's there for some, and not for others."

Courlander stopped by the desk, roughing out his report. Striker, meanwhile, was comparing the note with Dillberry's signature in the book. "Why, this scrawl isn't anything like his John Hancock in the ledger!" he exclaimed.

"You expect a guy gone out of his mind with the heat to sit down and write a nice copybook hand?" scoffed the police dick. "It was in his room, wasn't it?"

This brought up their former bone of contention. "Not the first time I looked."

"I only have your word for that."

"Are you calling me a liar?" flared Striker.

"No, but I think what's biting you is, you got a suppressed desire to be a detective."

"I think," said Striker with deadly irony, "you have too."

"Why, you—!"

Perry hurriedly got between them. "For heaven's sake," he pleaded wearily, "isn't it hot enough and messy enough, without having a fist fight over it?"

Courlander turned and stamped out into the suffocating before-dawn murk. Perry leaned over the desk, holding his head in both hands. "That room's a jinx," he groaned, "a hoodoo."

"There's nothing the matter with the room—there can't possibly be," Striker pointed out. "That would be against nature and all natural laws. That room is just plaster and bricks and wooden boards, and they can't hurt anyone—in themselves. Whatever's behind this is some human agency, and I'm going to get to the bottom of it if I gotta sleep in there myself!" He waited a minute, let the idea sink in, take hold of him, then he straightened, snapped his fingers decisively. "That's the next step on the program! I'll be the guinea pig, the white mouse! That's the only way we can ever hope to clear it up."

Perry gave him a bleak look, as though such foolhardiness would have been totally foreign to his own nature, and he couldn't understand anyone being willing to take such an eerie risk.

"Because I've got a hunch," Striker went on grimly. "It's not over yet. It's going to happen again and yet again, if we don't hurry up and find out what it is."

Now that the official investigation was closed, and there was no outsider present to spread rumors that could give his hotel a bad name, Perry seemed willing enough to agree with Striker that it wasn't normal and natural. Or else the advanced hour of the night was working suggestively on his nerves. "B-but haven't you any idea at all, just as a starting point," he quavered, "as to what it could be—if it is anything? Isn't it better to have some kind of a theory? At least know what to look for, not just shut yourself up in there blindfolded?"

"I could have several, but I can't believe in them myself. It could be extramural hypnosis—that means through the walls, you know. Or it could be fumes that lower the vitality, depress, and bring on suicide mania—such as small quantities of monoxide will do. But this is summertime and there's certainly no heat in the pipes. No, there's only one way to get an idea, and that's to try it out on myself. I'm going to sleep in that room myself tomorrow night, to get the *feel* of it. Have I your okay?"

Perry just wiped his brow, in anticipatory horror. "Go ahead if you've got the nerve," he said limply. "You wouldn't catch me doing it!"

Striker smiled glumly. "I'm curious—that way."

Striker made arrangements as inconspicuously as possible the next day, since there was no telling at which point anonymity ended and hostile observation set in, whether up in the room itself or down at the registration desk, or somewhere midway between the two. He tried to cover all the externals by which occupancy of the room could be detected without at the same time revealing his identity. Dennison, the day clerk, was left out of it entirely. Outside of Perry himself, he took only Maxon into his confidence. No one else, not even the cleaning help. He waited until the night clerk came on duty at eleven-thirty before he made the final arrangements, so that there was no possibility of fore-knowledge.

"When you're sure no one's looking—and not until then," he coached the night clerk, "I want you to take the red vacancy tag out of the pigeonhole. And sign a phony entry in the register— John Brown, anything at all. We can erase it in the morning. That's in case the leak is down here at this end. I know the book is kept turned facing you, but there *is* a slight possibility someone could read it upside-down while stopping by here for their key. One other important thing: I may come up against something that's too much for me, whether it's physical or narcotic or magnetic. Keep your eye on that telephone switchboard in case I need help in a hurry. If nine-thirteen flashes, don't wait to answer. I mayn't be able to give a message. Just get up there in a hurry."

"That's gonna do you a lot of good," Maxon objected fearfully. "By the time anyone could get up there to the ninth on that squirrel-cage, it would be all over! Why don't you plant Bob or someone out of sight around the turn of the hall?"

"I can't. The hall may be watched. If it's anything external, and not just atmospheric or telepathic, it comes through the hall. It's got to. That's the only way it can get in. This has got to look *right,* wide open, unsuspecting, or whatever it is won't strike. No, the switchboard'll be my only means of communication. I'm packing a Little Friend with me, anyway, so I won't be exactly helpless up there. Now remember, 'Mr. John Brown' checked in here unseen by the human eye sometime during the evening. Whatever it is, it can't be watching the desk *all* the time, twenty-four hours a day. And for Pete's sake, don't take any nips tonight. Lock the bottle up in the safe. My life is in your hands. Don't drop it!"

"Good luck and here's hoping," said Maxon sepulchrally, as though he never expected to see Striker alive again.

Striker drifted back into the lounge and lolled conspicuously in his usual vantage-point until twelve struck and Bob began to put the primary lights out. Then he strolled into the hotel drug store and drank two cups of scalding black coffee. Not that he was particularly afraid of not being able to keep awake, tonight of all nights, but there was nothing like making sure. There might be some soporific or sedative substance to overcome, though how it could be administered he failed to see.

He came into the lobby again and went around to the elevator bank, without so much as a wink to Maxon. He gave a carefully studied yawn, tapped his fingers over his mouth. A moment later there was a whiff of some exotic scent behind him and the Youngs had come in, presumably from Mrs. Young's broadcasting station. She was wearing an embroidered silk shawl and holding the Peke in her arm.

Young said, "Hi, fella." She bowed slightly. The car door opened.

Young said, "Oh, just a minute—my key," and stepped over to the desk.

Striker's eyes followed him relentlessly. The register was turned facing Maxon's way. The Chinese lawyer glanced down at it, curved his head around slightly as if to read it right side up, then took his key, came back again. They rode up together. The Peke started to whine. Mrs. Young fondled it, crooned: "*Sh,* Shan, be a good boy." She explained to Striker, "It always makes him uneasy to ride up in an elevator."

The couple got off at the eighth. She bowed again. Young said, "G'night." Striker, of course, had no idea of getting off at any but his usual floor, the top, even though he was alone in the car. He said in a low voice to Bob: "Does that dog whine other times when you ride it up?"

"No, sir," the elevator man answered. "It nevah seem' to mind until tonight. Mus' be getting ritzy."

Striker just filed that detail away: it was such a tiny little thing.

He let himself into his little hole-in-the-wall room. He pulled down the shade, even though there was just a blank wall across the shaft from his window. There was a roof ledge farther up. He took his gun out of his valise and packed it in his back pocket. That was all he was taking with him; no "fantastics" tonight. The fantasy was in real life, not on the printed page.

He took off his coat and necktie and hung them over the back of a chair. He took the pillow off his bed and forced it down under the bedclothes so that it made a longish mound. He'd brought a newspaper up with him. He opened this to double-page width and leaned it up against the head of the bed, as though someone were sitting up behind it reading it. It sagged a little, so he took a pin and fastened it to the woodwork. He turned on the shaded reading lamp at his bedside, turned out the room light, so that there was just a diffused glow. Then he edged up to the window sidewise and raised the shade again, but not all the way, just enough to give a view of the lower part of the bed if anyone were looking down from above—from the cornice, for instance. He always had his reading lamp going the first hour or two after he retired other nights. Tonight it was going to burn all night. This was the only feature of the arrangement Perry would have disapproved of, electricity bills being what they were.

That took care of things up here. He edged his door open, made sure the hallway was deserted, and sidled out in vest, trousers, and carrying the .38. He'd done everything humanly possible to make the thing foolproof, but it occurred to him, as he made his way noiselessly to the emergency staircase, that there was one thing all these precautions would be sterile against, if it was involved in any way, and that was mind reading. The thought itself was enough to send a shudder up his spine, make him want to give up before he'd even gone any further, so he resolutely put it from him. Personally he'd never been much of a believer in that sort of thing, so it wasn't hard for him to discount it. But disbelief in a thing is not always a guarantee that it does not exist or exert influence, and he would have been the first to admit that.

The safety stairs were cement and not carpeted like the hallways, but even so he managed to move down them with a minimum of sound once his senses had done all they could to assure him the whole shaft was empty of life from its top to its bottom.

He eased the hinged fire door on the ninth open a fraction of an inch, and reconnoitered the hall in both directions; forward through the slit before him, rearward through the seam between the hinges. This was the most important part of the undertaking. Everything depended on this step. It was vital to get into that room unseen. Even if he did not know what he was up against, there was no sense letting what he was up against know who he was.

He stood there for a long time like that, without moving, almost without breathing, narrowly studying each and every one of the inscrutably closed doors up and down the hall. Finally he broke for it.

He had his passkey ready before he left the shelter of the fire door. He stabbed it into the lock of 913, turned it, and opened the door with no more than two deft, quick, almost soundless movements. He had to work fast, to get in out of the open. He got behind the door once he was through, got the key out, closed the door—and left the room dark. The whole maneuver, he felt reasonably sure, could not have been accomplished more subtly by anything except a ghost or wraith.

He took a long deep breath behind the closed door and relaxed— a little. Leaving the room dark around him didn't make for very much peace of mind—there was always the thought that *It* might already be in here with him—but he was determined not to show his face even to the blank walls.

He was now, therefore, Mr. John Brown, Room 913, for the rest of the night, unsuspectingly waiting to be—whatever it was had happened to Hopper, Hastings, Dillberry. He had a slight edge on them because he had a gun in his pocket, but try to shoot a noxious vapor (for instance) with a .38 bullet!

First he made sure of the telephone, his one lifeline to the outside world. He carefully explored the wire in the dark, inch by inch from the base of the instrument down to the box against the wall, to make sure the wire wasn't cut or rendered useless in any way. Then he opened the closet door and examined the inside of that, by sense of touch alone. Nothing in there but a row of empty hangers. Then he cased the bath, still without the aid of light; tried the water faucets, the drains, even the medicine chest. Next he devoted his attention to the bed itself, explored the mattress and the springs, even got down and swept an arm back and forth under it, like an old maid about to retire for the night. The other furniture also got a health examination. He tested the rug with his foot for unevennesses. Finally there remained the window, that mouthway to doom. He didn't go close to it. He stayed well back within the gloom of the room, even though there was nothing, not even a rooftop or water tank, opposite, from which the interior of this room could be seen; the buildings all around were much lower. It couldn't tell him anything; it seemed to be just a window embrasure. If it was more than that, it was one up on him.

Finally he took out his gun, slipped the safety off, laid it down beside the phone on the nightstand. Then he lay back on the bed, shoes and all, crossed his ankles, folded his hands under his head, and lay staring up at the pool of blackness over him that was the ceiling. He couldn't hear a thing, after that, except the whisper of his breathing, and he had to listen close to get even that.

The minutes pulled themselves out into a quarter hour, a half, a whole one, like sticky taffy. All sorts of horrid possibilities occurred to him, lying there in the dark, and made his skin crawl. He remembered the Conan Doyle story, "The Speckled Band," in which a deadly snake had been lowered through a transom night after night in an effort to get it to bite the sleeper. That wouldn't fit this case. He'd come upon the scene too quickly each time. You couldn't juggle a deadly snake—had to take your time handling it. None of his three predecessors had been heard to scream, nor had their broken bodies shown anything but the impact of the fall itself. None of the discoloration or rigidity of snake venom. He'd looked at the bodies at the morgue.

But it was not as much consolation as it should have been, in the dark. He wished he'd been a little braver—one of these absolutely fearless guys. It didn't occur to him that he was being quite brave enough already for one guy, coming up here like this. He'd stretched himself out in here without any certainty he'd ever get up again alive.

He practiced reaching for the phone and his gun, until he knew just where they both were by heart. They were close enough. He didn't even have to unlimber his elbow. He lit a cigarette, but shielded the match carefully, with his whole body turned toward the wall, so it wouldn't light up his face too much. John Brown could smoke in bed just as well as House Dick Striker.

He kept his eyes on the window more than anything else, almost as if he expected it to sprout a pair of long octopus arms that would reach out, grab him, and toss him through to destruction.

He asked himself fearfully: "Am I holding it off by lying here awake like this waiting for it? Can it *tell* whether I'm awake or asleep? Is it on to me, whatever it is?" He couldn't help wincing at the implication of the supernatural this argued. A guy could go batty thinking things like that. Still, it couldn't be denied that the condition of the bed, each time before this, proved that the victims had been asleep and not awake just before it happened.

He thought, "I can pretend I'm asleep, at least, even if I don't actually go to sleep." Nothing must be overlooked in this battle of wits, no matter how inane, how childish it seemed at first sight.

He crushed his cigarette out, gave a stage yawn, meant to be heard if it couldn't be seen, threshed around a little like a man settling himself down for the night, counted ten, and then started to stage-manage his breathing, pumping it slower and heavier, like a real sleeper's. But under it all he was as alive as a third rail and his heart was ticking away under his ribs like a taximeter.

It was harder to lie waiting for it this way than it had been the other, just normally awake. The strain was almost unbearable. He wanted to leap up, swing out wildly around him in the dark, and yell: "Come on, you! Come on and get it over with!"

Suddenly he tensed more than he was already, if that was possible, and missed a breath. Missed two—forgot all about timing them. Something—what was it?—something was in the air; his nose was warning him, twitching, crinkling, almost like a retriever's. Sweet, foreign, subtle, something that didn't belong. He took a deep sniff, held it, while he tried to test the thing, analyze it, differentiate it, like a chemist without apparatus.

Then he got it. If he hadn't been so worked up in the first place, he would have got it even sooner. Sandalwood. Sandalwood incense. That meant the Chinese couple, the Youngs, the apartment below. They'd been burning it last night when he was in there, a stick of it in front of that joss of theirs. But how could it get up here? And how could it be harmful, if they were right in the same room with it and it didn't do anything to them?

How did he know they were in the same room with it? A fantastic picture flashed before his mind of the two of them down there right now, wearing gauze masks of filters over their faces, like operating surgeons. Aw, that was ridiculous! They'd been in the room a full five minutes with the stuff—he and Perry and Courlander—without masks, and nothing had happened to them.

But he wasn't forgetting how Young's head had swung around a little to scan the reversed register when they came in tonight—nor how their dog had whined, like it had whined when Dillberry's body fell past their window, when—Bob had said—it never whined at other times.

He sat up, pulled off his shoes, and started to move noiselessly around, sniffing like a bloodhound, trying to find out just how and where that odor was getting into the room. It must be at some particular point more than another. It wasn't just *soaking* up through the floor. Maybe it was nothing, then again maybe it was something. It didn't seem to be doing anything to him so far. He could breathe all right, he could think all right. But there was always the possibility that it was simply a sort of smoke-screen or carrier, used to conceal or transport some other gas that was to follow. The sugar-coating for the poison!

He sniffed at the radiator, at the bathroom drains, at the closet door, and in each of the four corners of the room. It was faint, almost unnoticeable in all those places. Then he stopped before the open window. It was much stronger here; it was coming in here!

He edged warily forward, leaned out a little above the low guard-rail, but careful not to shift his balance out of normal, for this very posture of curiosity might be the crux of the whole thing, the incense a decoy to get them to lean out the window. Sure, it was coming out of their open window, traveling up the face of the building, and—some of it—drifting in through his. That was fairly natural, on a warm, still night like this, without much circulation to the air.

Nothing happened. The window didn't suddenly fold up and throw him or tilt him forward, the guard-rail didn't suddenly collapse before him and pull him after it by sheer optical illusion (for he wasn't touching it in any way). He waited a little longer, tested it a little longer. No other result. It was, then, incense and nothing more.

He went back into the room again, stretched out on the bed once more, conscious for the first time of cold moisture on his brow, which he now wiped off. The aroma became less noticeable presently, as though the stick had burned down. Then finally it was gone. And he was just the way he'd been before.

"So it wasn't that," he dismissed it, and reasoned, "It's because they're Chinese that I was so ready to suspect them. They always seem sinister to the Occidental mind."

There was nothing else after that, just darkness and waiting. Then presently there was a gray line around the window enclosure, and next he could see his hands when he held them out before his face, and then the night bloomed into day and the death watch was over.

He didn't come down to the lobby for another hour, until the sun was up and there was not the slimmest possibility of anything happening any more—this time. He came out of the elevator looking haggard, and yet almost disappointed at the same time.

Maxon eyed him as though he'd never expected to see him again. "Anything?" he asked, unnecessarily.

"Nothing," Striker answered.

Maxon turned without another word, went back to the safe, brought a bottle out to him.

"Yeah, I could use some of that," was all the dick said.

"So I guess this shows," Maxon suggested hopefully, "that there's nothing to it after all. I mean about the room being—"

Striker took his time about answering. "It shows," he said finally, "that whoever it is, is smarter than we gave 'em credit for. Knew enough not to tip their mitts. Nothing happened because Someone knew I was in there, knew who I was, and knew *why* I was in there. And *that* shows it's somebody in this hotel who's at the bottom of it."

"You mean you're not through yet?"

"Through yet? I haven't even begun!"

"Well, what're you going to do next?"

"I'm going to catch up on a night's sleep, first off," Striker let him know. "And after that, I'm going to do a little clerical work. Then when that's through, I'm going to keep my own counsel. No offense, but"—he tapped himself on the forehead—"only this little fellow in here is going to be in on it, not you nor the manager nor anyone else."

He started his "clerical work" that very evening. Took the old ledgers for March, 1933, and October, 1934, out of the safe, and copied out the full roster of guests from the current one (July, 1935). Then he took the two bulky volumes and the list of present guests up to his room with him and went to work.

First he canceled out all the names on the current list that didn't appear on either of the former two rosters. That left him with exactly four guests who were residing in the building now and who also had been in it at the time of one of the first two "suicides." The four were Mr. and Mrs. Young, Atkinson (Peter the Hermit), and Miss Flobelle Heilbron (the cantankerous vixen in 911). Then he canceled those of the above that didn't appear on *both* of the former lists. There was only one name left uncanceled now. There was only one guest who had been in occupancy during *each and every one* of the three times that a "suicide" had taken place in 913. Atkinson and Miss Heilbron had been living in the hotel in March, 1933. The Youngs and

Miss Heilbron had been living in the building in October, 1934. Atkinson (who must have been away the time before on one of his nomadic "prospecting trips"), the Youngs, and Miss Heilbron were all here now. The one name that recurred triply was Miss Flobelle Heilbron.

So much for his "clerical work." Now came a little research work.

She didn't hug her room quite as continuously and tenaciously as Peter the Hermit, but she never strayed very far from it nor stayed away very long at a time—was constantly popping in and out a dozen times a day to feed a cat she kept.

He had a word with Perry the following morning, and soon after lunch the manager, who received complimentary passes to a number of movie theaters in the vicinity, in return for giving them advertising space about his premises, presented her with a matinee pass for that afternoon. She was delighted at this unaccustomed mark of attention, and fell for it like a ton of bricks.

Striker saw her start out at two, and that gave him two full hours. He made a bee-line up there and passkeyed himself in. The cat was out in the middle of the room nibbling at a plate of liver which she'd thoughtfully left behind for it. He started going over the place. He didn't need two hours. He hit it within ten minutes after he'd come into the room, in one of her bureau drawers, all swathed up in intimate wearing apparel, as though she didn't want anyone to know she had it.

It was well worn, as though it had been used plenty—kept by her at nights and studied for years. It was entitled *Mesmerism, Self-Taught; How to Impose Your Will on Others.*

But something even more of a giveaway happened while he was standing there holding it in his hand. The cat raised its head from the saucer of liver, looked up at the book, evidently recognized it, and whisked under the bed, ears flat.

"So she's been practicing on you, has she?" Striker murmured. "And you don't like it. Well, I don't either. I wonder who else she's been trying it on?"

He opened the book and thumbed through it. One chapter heading, appropriately enough, was "Experiments at a Distance." He narrowed his eyes, read a few words. "In cases where the subject is out of sight, behind a door or on the other side of a wall, it is better to begin with simple commands, easily transferable. 1—Open the door. 2—Turn around," etc.

Well, "jump out of the window" was a simple enough command. Beautifully simple—and final. Was it possible that old crackpot was capable of—? She was domineering enough to be good at it, heaven knows. Perry'd wanted her out of the building years ago, but she was still in it today. Striker had never believed in such balderdash, but suppose—through some fluke or other—it had worked out with ghastly effect in just this one case?

He summoned the chambermaid and questioned her. She was a lumpy, work-worn old woman, and had as little use for the guest in question as anyone else, so she wasn't inclined to be reticent. "Boss me?" she answered, "Man, she sure do!"

"I don't mean boss you out loud. Did she ever try to get you to do her bidding without, uh, talking?"

She eyed him shrewdly, nodded. "Sure nuff. All the time. How you fine out about it?" She cackled uproariously. "She dippy, Mr. Striker, suh. I *mean!* She stand still like this, look at me *hard,* like this." She placed one hand flat across her forehead as if she had a headache. "So nothing happen', I just mine my business. Then she say: 'Whuffo you don't do what I just tole you?' I say, 'You ain't tole me nothing yet.' She say, 'Ain't you got my message? My sum-conscious done tole you, "Clean up good underneath that chair." '

"I say, 'Yo sum-conscious better talk a little louder, den, cause I ain't heard a thing—and I got good ears!' "

He looked at her thoughtfully. "Did you ever *feel* anything when she tried that stunt? Feel like doing the things she wanted?"

"Yeah man!" she vigorously asserted. "But not what she wanted! I feel like busting dis yere mop-handle on her haid, dass what I feel!"

He went ahead investigating after he'd dismissed her, but nothing else turned up. He was far from satisfied with what he'd got on Miss Heilbron, incriminating as the book was. It didn't *prove* anything. It wasn't strong enough evidence to base an accusation on.

He cased the Youngs' apartment that same evening, while they were at the wife's broadcasting studio. This, over Perry's almost apoplectic protests. And there, as if to confuse the issue still further, he turned up something that was at least as suspicious in its way as the mesmerism handbook. It was a terrifying grotesque mask of a demon, presumably a prop from the Chinese theater down on Doyer Street. It was hanging at the back of the clothes closet,

along with an embroidered Chinese ceremonial robe. It was limned
in some kind of luminous or phosphorescent paint that made it
visible in the gloom in all its bestiality and horror. He nearly
jumped out of his shoes himself at first sight of it. And that only
went to show what conceivable effect it could have seeming to
swim through the darkness in the middle of the night, for instance,
toward the bed of a sleeper in the room above. That the victim
would jump out of the window in frenzy would be distinctly
possible.

Against this could be stacked the absolute lack of motive, the
conclusive proof (two out of three times) that no one had been
in the room with the victim, and the equally conclusive proof
that the Youngs hadn't been in the building at all the first time,
mask or no mask. In itself, of course, the object had as much
right to be in their apartment as the mesmerism book had in
Miss Heilbron's room. The wife was in theatrical business, liable
to be interested in stage curios of that kind.

Boiled down, it amounted to this: that the Youngs were still
very much in the running.

It was a good deal harder to gain access to Peter the Hermit's
room without tipping his hand, since the eccentric lived up to his
nickname to the fullest. However, he finally managed to work it
two days later, with the help of Peter, the hotel exterminator, and
a paperful of red ants. He emptied the contents of the latter outside
the doorsill, then Perry and the exterminator forced their way in
on the pretext of combating the invasion. It took all of Perry's
cajolery and persuasiveness to draw the Hermit out of his habitat
for even half an hour, but a professed eagerness to hear all about
his "gold mines" finally turned the trick, and the old man was
led around the turn of the hall. Striker jumped in as soon as the
coast was clear and got busy.

It was certainly fuller of unaccountable things than either of
the other two had been, but on the other hand there was nothing
as glaringly suspicious as the mask or the hypnotism book. Pyr-
amids of hoarded canned goods stacked in the closet, and quantities
of tools and utensils used in mining operations; sieves, pans, short-
handled picks, a hooded miner's lamp with a reflector, three fishing
rods and an assortment of hooks ranging from the smallest to big
triple-toothed monsters, plenty of tackle, hip boots, a shotgun, a
pair of scales (for assaying the gold that he had never found),
little sacks of worthless ore, a mallet for breaking up the ore

specimens, and the pair of heavy knapsacks that he took with him each time he set out on his heartbreaking expeditions. It all seemed legitimate enough. Striker wasn't enough of a mining expert to know for sure. But he was enough of a detective to know there wasn't anything there that could in itself cause the death of anyone two rooms over and at right angles to this.

He had, of necessity, to be rather hasty about it, for the old man could be heard regaling Perry with the story of his mines just out of sight around the turn of the hall the whole time Striker was in there. He cleared out just as the exterminator finally got through killing the last of the "planted" ants.

To sum up: Flobelle Heilbron still had the edge on the other two as chief suspect, both because of the mesmerism handbook and because of her occupancy record. The Chinese couple came next, because of the possibilities inherent in that mask, as well as the penetrative powers of their incense and the whining of their dog. Peter the Hermit ran the others a poor third. Had it not been for his personal eccentricity and the location of his room, Striker would have eliminated him altogether.

On the other hand, he had turned up no real proof yet, and the motive remained as unfathomable as ever. In short, he was really no further than before he'd started. He had tried to solve it circumstantially, by deduction, and that hadn't worked. He had tried to solve it first hand, by personal observation, and that hadn't worked. Only one possible way remained, to try to solve it at *second hand,* through the eyes of the next potential victim, who would at the same time be a material witness—if he survived. To do this it was necessary to anticipate it, *time* it, try to see if it had some sort of spacing or rhythm to it or was just hit-or-miss, in order to know more or less when to expect it to recur. The only way to do this was to take the three dates he had and average them.

Striker took the early part of that evening off. He didn't ask permission for it, just walked out without saying anything to anyone about it. He was determined not to take anyone into his confidence this time.

He hadn't been off the premises a night since he'd first been hired by the hotel, and this wasn't a night off. This was strictly business. He had seventy-five dollars with him that he'd taken out of his hard-earned savings at the bank that afternoon. He didn't go where the lights were bright. He went down to the Bowery.

He strolled around a while looking into various barrooms and "smoke houses" from the outside. Finally he saw something in one that seemed to suit his purpose, went in and ordered two beers.

"Two?" said the barman in surprise. "You mean one after the other?"

"I mean two right together at one time," Striker told him.

He carried them over to the table at the rear, at which he noticed a man slumped with his head in his arms. He wasn't asleep or in a drunken stupor. Striker had already seen him push a despairing hand through his hair once.

He sat down opposite the motionless figure, clinked the glasses together to attract the man's attention. The derelict slowly raised his head.

"This is for you," Striker said, pushing one toward him.

The man just nodded dazedly, as though incapable of thanks any more. Gratitude had rusted on him from lack of use.

"What're your prospects?" Striker asked him bluntly.

"None. Nowhere to go. Not a cent to my name. I've only got one friend left, and I was figgerin' on looking him up 'long about midnight. If I don't tonight, maybe I will tomorrow night. I surely will one of these nights, soon. His name is the East River."

"I've got a proposition for you. Want to hear it?"

"You're the boss."

"How would you like to have a good suit, a clean shirt on your back for a change? How would you like to sleep in a comfortable bed tonight? In a three dollar room, all to yourself, in a good hotel uptown?"

"Mister," said the man in a choked voice, "if I could do that once again, just once again, I wouldn't care if it was my last night on earth! What's the catch?"

"What you just said. It's liable to be." He talked for a while, told the man what there was to know, the little that he himself knew. "It's not certain, you understand. Maybe nothing'll happen at all. The odds are about fifty-fifty. If nothing does happen, you keep the clothes, the dough, and I'll even dig up a porter's job for you. You'll be that much ahead. Now I've given it to you straight from the shoulder. I'm not concealing anything from you, you know what to expect."

The man wet his lips reflectively. "Fifty-fifty—that's not so bad.

Those are good enough odds. I used to be a gambler when I was young. And it can't hurt more than the river filling up your lungs. I'm weary of dragging out my days. What've I got to lose? Mister, you're on." He held out an unclean hand hesitantly. "I don't suppose you'd want to—"

Striker shook it as he stood up. "I never refuse to shake hands with a brave man. Come on, we've got a lot to do. We've got to find a barber shop, a men's clothing store if there are any still open, a luggage shop, and a restaurant."

An hour and a half later a taxi stopped on the corner diagonally opposite the St. Anselm, with Striker and a spruce, well-dressed individual seated in it side by side. On the floor at their feet were two shiny, brand-new valises, containing their linings and nothing else.

"Now there it is over there, on the other side," Striker said. "I'm going to get out here, and you go over in the cab and get out by yourself at the entrance. Count out what's left of the money I gave you."

His companion did so laboriously. "Forty-nine dollars and fifty cents."

"Don't spend another penny of it, get me? I've already paid the cabfare and tip. See that you carry your own bags in, so they don't notice how light they are. Remember, what's left is all yours if—"

"Yeah, I know," said the other man unabashedly. "If I'm alive in the morning."

"Got your instructions straight?"

"I want an outside room. I want a ninth floor outside room. No other floor will do. I want a ninth floor outside room with a bath."

"That'll get you the right one by elimination. I happen to know it's vacant. You won't have to pay in advance. The two bags and the outfit'll take care of that. Tell him to sign Harry Kramer for you—that what you said your name was? Now this is your last chance to back out. You can still welsh on me if you want—I won't do anything to you."

"No," the man said doggedly. "This way I've got a chance at a job tomorrow. The other way I'll be back on the beach. I'm glad somebody finally found some use for me."

Striker averted his head, grasped the other's scrawny shoulder encouragingly. "Good luck, brother—and God forgive me for doing this, if I don't see you again." He swung out of the cab, opened a newspaper in front of his face, and narrowly watched over the top of it until the thin but well-dressed figure had alighted and carried the two bags up the steps and into a doorway from which he might never emerge alive.

He sauntered up to the desk a few minutes later himself, from the other direction, the coffee shop entrance. Maxon was still blotting the ink on the signature.

Striker read, *Harry Kramer, New York City—913.*

He went up to his room at his usual time, but only to get out his gun. Then he came down to the lobby again. Maxon was the only one in sight. Striker stepped in behind the desk, made his way back to the telephone switchboard, which was screened from sight by the tiers of mailboxes. He sat down before the switchboard and shot his cuffs, like a wireless operator on a ship at sea waiting for an SOS. The St. Anselm didn't employ a night operator. The desk clerk attended to the calls himself after twelve.

"What's the idea?" Maxon wanted to know.

Striker wasn't confiding in anyone this time. "Can't sleep," he said noncommittally. "Why should you object if I give you a hand down here?"

Kramer was to knock the receiver off the hook at the first sign of danger, or even anything that he didn't understand or like the looks of. There was no other way to work it than this, roundabout as it was. Striker was convinced that if he lurked about the ninth floor corridor within sight or earshot of the room, he would simply be banishing the danger, postponing it. He didn't want that. He wanted to know what it was. If he waited in his own room he would be even more cut off. The danger signal would have to be relayed up to him from down here. The last three times had shown him how ineffective that was.

A desultory call or two came through the first hour he was at the board, mostly requests for morning calls. He meticulously jotted them down for the day operator. Nothing from 913.

About two o'clock Maxon finally started to catch on. "You going to work it all night?"

"Yeh," said Striker shortly. "Don't talk to me. Don't let on I'm behind here at all."

At two thirty-five there were footsteps in the lobby, a peculiar sobbing sound like an automobile tire deflating, and a whiff of sandalwood traveled back to Striker after the car had gone up. He called Maxon guardedly back to him.

"The Youngs?"

"Yeah, they just came in."

"Was that their dog whining?"

"Yeah. I guess it hadda see another dog about a man."

Maybe a dead man, thought Striker morosely. He raised the plug toward the socket of 913. He ought to call Kramer, make sure he stayed awake. That would be as big a giveaway as pussy-footing around the hall up there, though. He let the plug drop back again.

About three o'clock more footsteps sounded. Heavy ones stamping in from the street. A man's voice sounded hoarsely. "Hey, desk! One of your people just tumbled out, around on the side of the building!"

The switchboard stool went over with a crack, something blurred streaked across the lobby, and the elevator darted crazily upward. Striker nearly snapped the control lever out of its socket, the way he bore down on it. The car had never traveled so fast before, but he swore horribly all the way up. Too late again!

The door was closed. He needled his passkey at the lock, shouldered the door in. The light was on, the room was empty. The window was wide open, the guy was gone. The fifty-fifty odds had paid off—the wrong way.

Striker's face was twisted balefully. He got out his gun. But there was only empty space around him.

He was standing there like that, bitter, defeated, granite-eyed, the gun uselessly in his hand, when Perry and Courlander came. It would be Courlander again, too!

"Is he dead?" Striker asked grimly.

"That street ain't quilted," was the dick's dry answer. He eyed the gun scornfully. "What're you doing? Holding the fort against the Indians, sonny boy?"

"I suggest instead of standing there throwing bouquets," Striker said, "you phone your precinct house and have a dragnet thrown around this building." He reached for the phone. Courlander's arm quickly shot out and barred him. "Not so fast. What would I be doing that for?"

"Because this is murder!"

"Where've I heard that before?" He went over for the inevitable note. "What's this?" He read it aloud. *"Can't take it any more."*

"So you're still going to trip over those things!"

"And you're still going to try to hurdle it?"

"It's a fake like all the others were. I knew that all along. I couldn't prove it until now. This time I can! Finally."

"Yeah? How!"

"Because the guy couldn't write! Couldn't even write his own name! He even had to have the clerk sign the register for him downstairs. And if that isn't proof there's been somebody else in this room, have a look at that." He pointed to the money Kramer had left neatly piled on the dresser top. "Count that! Four-fifty. Four singles and a four-bit piece. He had forty-nine dollars and fifty cents on him when he came into this room, and he didn't leave the room. He's down there in his underwear now. Here's all his outer clothing up here. What became of that forty-five bucks?"

Courlander looked at him. "How do you know so much about it? How do you know he couldn't write, and just what dough he had?"

"Because I planted him up here myself!" Striker ground out exasperatedly. "It was a setup! I picked him up, outfitted him, staked him, and brought him in here. He ran away to sea at twelve, never even learned his alphabet. I tested him and found out he was telling the truth. He couldn't write a word, not even his own name! Now do you understand? Are you gonna stand here all night or are you going to do something about it?"

Courlander snatched up the phone, called his precinct house. "Courlander. Send over a detail, quick! St. Anselm. That suicide reported from here has the earmarks of a murder."

"Earmarks!" scoffed Striker. "It's murder from head to foot, with a capital *M!*" He took the phone in turn. "Pardon me if I try to lock the stable door after the nag's been stolen. . . . H'lo, Maxon? Anyone left the building since this broke, anyone at all? Sure of that? Well, see that no one does. Call in that cop that's looking after the body. Lock up the secondary exit through the coffee shop. No one's to leave, no one at all, understand?" He threw the phone back at Courlander. "Confirm that for me, will you? Cops don't take orders from me. We've got them! They're still in the building some place! There's no way to get down from the roof. It's seven stories higher than any of the others around it."

But Courlander wasn't taking to cooperation very easily. "All this is based on your say-so that the guy couldn't write and had a certain amount of money on him when he came up here. So far so good. But something a little more definite than that better turn up. Did you mark the bills you gave him?"

"No, I didn't," Striker had to admit. "I wasn't figuring on robbery being the motive. I still don't think it's the primary one, I think it's only incidental. I don't think there is any consistent motive. I think we're up against a maniac."

"If they weren't marked, how do you expect us to trace them? Everyone in this place must have a good deal more than just forty-five dollars to their name! If you did plant somebody, why didn't you back him up, why didn't you look after him right? How did you expect to be able to help him if you stayed all the way downstairs, nine floors below?"

"I couldn't very well hang around outside the room. That would've been tipping my hand. I warned him, put him on his guard. He was to knock the phone over. That's all he had to do. Whatever it was, was too quick even for that."

Two members of the Homicide Squad appeared. "What's all the fuss and feathers? Where're the earmarks you spoke of, Courlander? The body's slated for an autopsy, but the examiner already says it don't look like anything but just the fall killed him."

"The house dick here," Courlander said, "insists the guy couldn't write and is short forty-five bucks. He planted him up here because he has an idea those other three cases—the ones I covered, you know—were murder."

They started to question Striker rigorously as though he himself were the culprit. "What gave you the idea it would happen tonight?"

"I didn't know it would happen tonight. I took a stab at it, that's all. I figured it was about due somewhere around now."

"Was the door open or locked when you got up here?"

"Locked."

"Where was the key?"

"Where it is now—over there on the dresser."

"Was the room disturbed in any way?"

"No, it was just like it is now."

They took a deep breath in unison, a breath that meant they were being very patient with an outsider. "Then what makes you think somebody beside himself was in here at the time?"

"Because that note is in here, and he couldn't write! Because there's forty-five dollars—"

"One thing at a time. Can you prove he couldn't write?"

"He proved it to *me!*"

"Yes, but can you prove it to *us?*"

Striker caught a tuft of his own hair in his fist, dragged at it, let it go again. "No, because he's gone now."

The other one leaned forward, dangerously casual. "You say you warned him what to expect, and yet he was willing to go ahead and chance it, just for the sake of a meal, a suit of clothes, a bed. How do you explain that?"

"He was at the end of his rope. He was about ready to quit anyway."

Striker saw what was coming.

"Oh, he was? How do you know?"

"Because he told me so. He said he was—thinking of the river."

"Before you explained your proposition or after?"

"Before," Striker had to admit.

They blew out their breaths scornfully, eyed one another as though this man's stupidity was unbelievable. "He brings a guy up from the beach," one said to the other, "that's already told him *beforehand* he's got doing the Dutch on his mind, and then when the guy goes ahead and does it, he tries to make out he's been murdered."

Striker knocked his chair over, stood up in exasperation. "But can't you get it through your concrete domes? What was driving him to it? The simplest reason in the world! *Lack of shelter, lack of food, lack of comfort.* Suddenly he's given all that at one time. Is it reasonable to suppose he'll cut his own enjoyment of it short, put an end to it halfway through the night? Tomorrow night, yes, after he's out of here, back where he was again, after the letdown has set in. But not tonight."

"Very pretty, but it don't mean a thing. The swell surroundings only brought it on quicker. He wanted to die in comfort, in style, while he was about it. That's been known to happen too, don't forget. About his not being able to write, sorry, but"—they flirted the sheet of notepaper before his eyes—"this evidence shows he *was* able to write. He must have put one over on you. You probably tipped your mitt in giving him your writing test. He caught on you were looking for someone who couldn't write, so he played 'possum. About the money—well, it musta gone out

the window with him even if he *was* just in his underwear, and
somebody down there snitched it before the cop came along. No
evidence. The investigation's closed as far as we're concerned."
They sauntered out into the hall.

"Damn it," Striker yelled after them, "you can't walk out of
here! You're turning your backs on a murder!"

"We *are* walking out," came back from the hallway. "Put that
in your pipe and smoke it!" The elevator door clicked mockingly
shut.

Courlander said almost pityingly, "It looks like tonight wasn't
your lucky night."

"It isn't yours either!" Striker bellowed. He swung his fist in a
barrel-house right, connected with the city dick's lower jaw, and
sent him volplaning back on his shoulders against the carpet.

Perry's moonface and bald head were white as an ostrich egg
with long-nursed resentment. "Get out of here! You're fired! Bring
bums into my house so they can commit suicide on the premises,
will you? You're through!"

"Fired?" Striker gave him a smouldering look that made Perry
draw hastily back out of range. "I'm quitting, is what you mean!
I wouldn't even finish the night out in a murder nest like this!"
He stalked past the manager, clenched hands in pockets, and went
up to his room to pack his belongings.

His chief problem was to avoid recognition by any of the staff,
when he returned there nearly a year later. To achieve this after
all the years he'd worked in the hotel, he checked in swiftly and
inconspicuously. The mustache he had been growing for the past
eight months and which now had attained full maturity, effectively
changed the lower part of his face. The horn-rimmed glasses, with
plain inserts instead of ground lenses, did as much for the upper
part, provided his hat brim was tipped down far enough. If he
stood around, of course, and let them stare, eventual recognition
was a certainty, but he didn't. He put on a little added weight
from the long months of idleness in the furnished room. He hadn't
worked in the interval. He could no doubt have got another berth,
but he considered that he was still on a job—even though he was
no longer drawing pay for it—and he meant to see it through.

A lesser problem was to get the room itself. If he couldn't get
it at once, he fully intended taking another for a day or two until
he could, but this of course would add greatly to the risk of

recognition. As far as he could tell, however, it was available right now. He'd walked through the side street bordering the hotel three nights in a row, after dark, and each time that particular window had been unlighted. The red tag would quickly tell him whether he was right or not.

Other than that, his choice of this one particular night for putting the long-premeditated move into effect was wholly arbitrary. The interval since the last time it had happened roughly approximated the previous intervals, and that was all he had to go by. One night, along about now, was as good as another.

He paid his bill at the rooming house and set out on foot, carrying just one bag with him. His radio and the rest of his belongings he left behind in the landlady's charge, to be called for later. It was about nine o'clock now. He wanted to get in before Maxon's shift. He'd been more intimate with Maxon than the other clerks, had practically no chance of getting past Maxon unidentified.

He stopped in at a hardware store on his way and bought two articles: a long section of stout hempen rope and a small sharp fruit, or kitchen, knife with a wooden handle. He inserted both objects in the bag with his clothing, right there in the shop, then set out once more. He bent his hat brim a little lower over his eyes as he neared the familiar hotel entrance, that was all. He went up the steps and inside unhesitatingly. One of the boys whom he knew by sight ducked for his bag without giving any sign of recognition. That was a good omen. He moved swiftly to the desk without looking around or giving anyone a chance to study him at leisure. There was a totally new man on now in Dennison's place, someone who didn't know him at all. That was the second good omen. And red was peering from the pigeonhole of 913.

His eye quickly traced a vertical axis through it. Not another one in a straight up-and-down line with it. It was easy to work it if you were familiar with the building layout, and who should be more familiar than he?

He said, "I want a single on the side street, where the traffic isn't so heavy." He got it the first shot out of the box!

He paid for it, signed *A. C. Sherman, New York,* and quickly stepped into the waiting car, with his head slightly lowered but not enough so to be conspicuously furtive.

A minute later the gantlet had been successfully run. He gave the boy a dime, closed the door, and had gained his objective undetected. Nothing had been changed in it. It was the same as when he'd slept in it that first time, nearly two years ago now. It was hard to realize, looking around at it, that it had seen four men go to their deaths. He couldn't help wondering, "Will I be the fifth?" That didn't frighten him any. It just made him toughen up inside and promise, "Not without a lotta trouble, buddy, not without a lotta trouble!"

He unpacked his few belongings and put them away as casually as though he were what he seemed to be, an unsuspecting newcomer who had just checked into a hotel. The coiled rope he hid under the mattress of the bed for the time being; the fruit knife and his gun under the pillows.

He killed the next two hours, until the deadline was due; undressed, took a bath, then hung around in his pajamas reading a paper he'd brought up with him.

At twelve he made his final preparations. He put the room light out first of all. Then in the dark he removed the whole bedding, mattress and all, transferred it to the floor, laying bare the framework and bolted-down coils of the bed. He looped the rope around the bed's midsection from side to side, weaving it inextricably in and out of the coils. Then he knotted a free length to a degree that defied undoing, splicing the end for a counter-knot.

He coiled it three times around his own middle, again knotting it to a point of Houdini-like bafflement. In between there was a slack of a good eight or ten feet. More than enough, considering the ease with which the bed could be pulled about on its little rubber-tired casters, to give him a radius of action equal to the inside limits of the room. Should pursuit through the doorway become necessary, that was what the knife was for. He laid it on the nightstand, alongside his gun.

Then he replaced the bedding, concealing the rope fastened beneath it. He carefully kicked the loose length, escaping at one side, out of sight under the bed. He climbed in, covered up.

The spiny roughness and constriction of his improvised safety-belt bothered him a good deal at first, but he soon found that by lying still and not changing position too often, he could accustom himself to it, even forget about it.

An hour passed, growing more and more blurred as it neared its end. He didn't try to stay awake, in fact encouraged sleep, feeling that the rope would automatically give him more than a fighting chance, and that to remain awake and watchful might in

some imponderable way ward off the very thing he was trying to
come to grips with.

At the very last he was dimly conscious, through already som-
nolent faculties, of a vague sweetness in the air, lulling him even
further. Sandalwood incense. "So they're still here," he thought
indistinctly. But the thought wasn't sufficient to rouse him to
alertness; he wouldn't let it. His eyelids started to close of their
own weight. He let them stay down.

Only once, after that, did his senses come to the surface. The
scratchy roughness of the rope as he turned in his sleep. "Rope,"
he thought dimly, and placing what it was, dropped off into
oblivion again.

The second awakening came hard. He fought against it stubbornly, but it slowly won out, dragging him against his will. It
was twofold. Not dangerous or threatening, but mentally painful,
like anything that pulls you out of deep sleep. Excruciatingly
painful. He wanted to be let alone. Every nerve cried out for
continued sleep, and these two spearheads—noise and glare—
continued prodding at him, tormenting him.

Then suddenly they'd won out. *Thump!*—one last cruelly jolting
impact of sound, and he'd opened his eyes. The glare now attacked
him in turn; it was like needles boring into the pupils of his
defenseless, blurred eyes. He tried to shield them from it with one
protective hand, and it still found them out. He struggled dazedly
upright in the bed. The noise had subsided, was gone, after that
last successful bang. But the light—it beat into his brain.

It came pulsing from beyond the foot of the bed, so that meant
it was coming through the open bathroom door. The bed was
along the side wall, and the bathroom door should be just beyond
its foot. He must have forgotten to put the light out in there.
What a brilliance! He could see the light through the partly open
door, swinging there on its loose, exposed electric-cord. That is
to say, he could see the pulsing gleam and dazzle of it, but he
couldn't get it into focus; it was like a sunburst. It was torture,
it was burning his sleepy eyeballs out. Have to get up and snap
it out. How'd that ever happen anyway? Maybe the switch was
defective, current was escaping through it even after it had been
turned off, and he was sure he had turned it off.

He struggled out of bed and groped toward it. The room around
him was just a blur, his senses swimming with the combination

of pitch-blackness and almost solar brilliance they were being subjected to. But it was the bathroom door that was beyond the foot of the bed, that was one thing he was sure of, even in his sleep-fogged condition.

He reached the threshold, groped upward for the switch that was located above the bulb itself. To look upward at it was like staring a blast furnace in the face without dark glasses. It had seemed to be dangling there just past the half-open door, so accessible. And now it seemed to elude him, swing back a little out of reach. Or maybe it was just that his fumbling fingers had knocked the loose cord into that strange, evasive motion.

He went after it, like a moth after a flame. Took a step across the threshold, still straining upward after it, eyes as useless as though he were standing directly in a lighthouse beam.

Suddenly the doorsill seemed to rear. Instead of being just a flat strip of wood, partitioning the floor of one room from the other, it struck him sharply, stunningly, way up the legs, just under the kneecaps. He tripped, overbalanced, plunged forward. The rest was hallucination, catastrophe, destruction.

The light vanished as though it had wings. The fall didn't break; no tiled flooring came up to stop it. The room had suddenly melted into disembodied night. No walls, no floor, nothing at all. Cool air of out-of-doors was rushing upward into the vacuum where the bathroom apparently had been. His whole body was turning completely over, and then over again, and he was going down, down, down. He only had time for one despairing thought as he fell at a sickening speed: "I'm *outside* the building!"

Then there was a wrench that seemed to tear his insides out and snap his head off at his neck. The hurtling fall jarred short, and there was a sickening, swaying motion on an even keel. He was turning slowly like something on a spit, clawing helplessly at the nothingness around him. In the cylindrical blackness that kept wheeling about him he could make out the gray of the building wall, recurring now on this side, now on that, as he swiveled. He tried to get a grip on the wall with his fingertips, to steady himself, gain a fulcrum! Its sandpapery roughness held no indentation to which he could attach himself even by one wildly searching thumb.

He was hanging there between floors at the end of the rope which had saved his life. There was no other way but to try to climb back along its length, until he could regain that treacherous guard rail up there over his head. It could be done, it had to be.

Fortunately the rope's grip around his waist was automatic. He was being held without having to exert himself, could use all his strength to lift himself hand over hand. That shouldn't be impossible. It was his only chance, at any rate.

The tall oblong of window overhead through which he had just been catapulted bloomed yellow. The room lights had been put on. Someone was in there. Someone had arrived to help him. He arched his back, straining to look up into that terrifying vista of night sky overhead—but that now held the warm friendly yellow patch that meant his salvation.

"Grab that rope up there!" he bellowed hoarsely. "Pull me in! I'm hanging out here! Hurry! There isn't much time!"

Hands showed over the guard-rail. He could see them plainly, tinted yellow by the light behind them. Busy hands, helping hands, answering his plea, pulling him back to the safety of solid ground.

No, wait! Something flashed in them, flashed again. Sawing back and forth, slicing, biting into the rope that held him, just past the guard-rail. He could feel the vibration around his middle, carried down to him like the hum along a wire. Death-dealing hands, completing what had been started, sending him to his doom. With his own knife, that he'd left up there beside the bed!

The rope began to fritter. A little severed outer strand came twining loosely down the main column of it toward him, like a snake. Those hands, back and forth, like a demon fiddler drawing his bow across a single tautened violin string in hurried, frenzied funeral march that spelled Striker's doom!

"Help!" he shouted in a choked voice, and the empty night sky around seemed to give it mockingly back to him.

A face appeared above the hands and knife, a grinning derisive face peering down into the gloom. Vast mane of snow-white hair and long white beard. It was Peter the Hermit.

So now he knew at last—too late. Too late.

The face vanished again, but the hands, the knife, were busier than ever. There was a microscopic dip, a *give,* as another strand parted, forerunner of the hurtling, whistling drop to come, the hurtling drop that meant the painful, bone-crushing end of him.

He burst into a flurry of helpless, agonized motion, flailing out with arms and legs—at what, toward what? Like a tortured fly caught on a pin, from which he could never hope to escape.

Glass shattered somewhere around him; one foot seemed to puncture the solid stone wall, go all the way through it. A red-hot wire stroked across his instep and he jerked convulsively.

There was a second preliminary dip, and a wolf howl of joy from above. He was conscious of more yellow light, this time from below, not above. A horrified voice that was trying not to lose its self-control sounded just beneath him somewhere. "Grab this! Don't lose your head now! Grab hold of this and don't let go whatever happens!"

Wood, the wood of a chair back, nudged into him, held out into the open by its legs. He caught at it spasmodically with both hands, riveted them to it in a grip like rigor mortis. At the same time somebody seemed to be trying to pull his shoe off his foot, that one foot that had gone in through the wall and seemed to be cut off from the rest of him.

There was a nauseating plunging sensation that stopped as soon as it began. His back went over until he felt like he was breaking in two, then the chair back held, steadied, reversed, started slowly to draw him with it. The severed rope came hissing down on top of him. From above there was a shrill cackle, from closer at hand a woman's scream of pity and terror. Yellow closed around him, swallowed him completely, took him in to itself.

He was stretched out on the floor, a good solid floor—and it was over. He was still holding the chair in that viselike grip. Young, the Chinese lawyer, was still hanging onto it by the legs, face a pasty gray. Bob, the night porter, was still holding onto his one ankle, and blood was coming through the sock. Mrs. Young, in a sort of chain arrangement, was hugging the porter around the waist. There was broken glass around him on the floor, and a big pool of water with tropical fish floundering in it from the overturned tank. A dog was whining heartbreakingly somewhere in the room. Other than that, there was complete silence.

None of them could talk for a minute or two. Mrs. Young sat squarely down on the floor, hid her face in her hands, and had brief but high-powered hysterics. Striker rolled over and planted his lips devoutly to the dusty carpet, before he even took a stab at getting to his shaky and undependable feet.

"What the hell happened to *you?*" heaved the lawyer finally, mopping his forehead. "Flying around out there like a bat! You scared the daylights out of me."

"Come on up to the floor above and get all the details," Striker invited. He guided himself shakily out of the room, stiff-arming himself against the door frame as he went. His legs still felt like rubber, threatening to betray him.

The door of 913 stood open. In the hallway outside it he motioned them cautiously back. "I left my gun in there, and he's got a knife with him too, so take it easy." But he strode into the lighted opening as though a couple of little items like that weren't stopping him after what he'd just been through and nearly didn't survive.

Then he stopped dead. There wasn't anyone at all in the room— any more.

The bed, with the severed section of rope still wound securely around it, was upturned against the window opening, effectively blocking it. The entire bedding, mattress and all, had slid off it, down into the street below. It was easy to see what had happened. The weight of his body, dangling out there, had drawn it first out into line with the opening (and it moved so easily on those rubber-tired casters!), then tipped it over on its side. The mattress and all the encumbering clothes had spilled off it and gone out of their own weight, entangling, blinding, and carrying with them, like a linen avalanche, whatever and whoever stood in their way. It was a fitting finish for an ingenious, heartless murderer.

The criminal caught neatly in his own trap.

"He was too anxious to cut that rope and watch me fall at the same time," Striker said grimly. "He leaned too far out. A feather pillow was enough to push him over the sill!"

He sauntered over to the dresser, picked up a sheet of paper, smiled a little—not gaily. "My 'suicide note'!" He looked at Young. "Funny sensation, reading your own farewell note. I bet not many experience it! Let's see what I'm supposed to have said to myself. *I'm at the end of my rope.* Queer, how he hit the nail on the head that time! He made them short, always. So there wouldn't be enough to them to give the handwriting away. He never signed them, either. Because he didn't know their names. He didn't even know what they looked like."

Courlander's voice sounded outside, talking it over with someone as he came toward the room. ". . . mattress and all! But instead of him landing on it, which might have saved his life, *it* landed on *him.* Didn't do him a bit of good! He's gone forever."

Striker, leaning against the dresser, wasn't recognized at first.

"Say, wait a minute, where have I seen *you* before?" the city

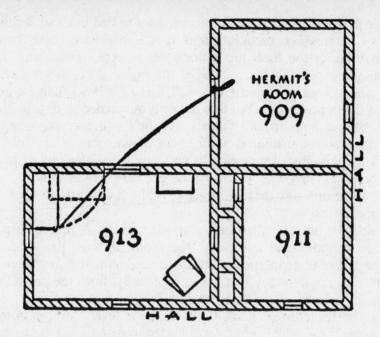

dick growled finally, after he'd given a preliminary look around the disordered room.

"What a detective you turned out to be!" grunted the shaken Striker rudely.

"Oh, it's you, is it? Do you haunt the place? What do you know about this?"

"A damn sight more than you!" was the uncomplimentary retort. "Sit down and learn some of it—or are you still afraid to face the real facts?"

Courlander sank back into a chair mechanically, mouth agape, staring at Striker.

"I'm not going to *tell* you about it," Striker went on. "I'm going to demonstrate. That's always the quickest way with kindergarten-age intelligences!" He caught at the overturned bed, righted it, rolled it almost effortlessly back into its original position against the side wall, *foot facing directly toward the bathroom door.*

"Notice that slight vibration, that humming the rubber-tired casters make across the floorboards? That's the 'distant thunder' the Youngs heard that night. I'll show you the lightning in just a minute. I'm going over there to his room now. Before I go, just let me point out one thing: the sleeper goes to bed in an unfamiliar room, and his last recollection is of the bathroom door being down there at the foot, the windows over here on this side. He wakes up dazedly in the middle of the night, starts to get out of bed, and comes up against the wall first of all. So then he gets out at the opposite side; but this has only succeeded in disorienting him, balling him up still further. All he's still sure of, now, is that the bathroom door is somewhere down there *at the foot of the bed!* Now just watch closely and you'll see the rest of it in pantomime. I'm going to show you just how it was done."

He went out and they sat tensely, without a word, all eyes on the open window.

Suddenly they all jolted nervously, in unison. A jumbo, triple-toothed fishhook had come into the room, through the window, on the end of three interlocked rods—a single line running through them from hook to reel. It came in diagonally, from the projecting wing. It inclined of its own extreme length, in a gentle arc that swept the triple-threat hook down to floor level. Almost immediately, as the unseen "fisherman" started to withdraw it, it snagged the lower right-hand foot of the bed. It would have been hard for it not to, with its three barbs pointing out in as many directions at once. The bed started to move slowly around after it, on those cushioned casters. There was not enough vibration or rapidity to the maneuver to disturb a heavy sleeper. The open window was now at the foot of the bed, where the bathroom had been before the change.

The tension of the line was relaxed. The rod jockeyed a little until the hook had been dislodged from the bed's "ankle." The liberated rod was swiftly but carefully withdrawn, as unobtrusively as it had appeared a moment before.

There was a short wait, horrible to endure. Then a new object appeared before the window opening—flashing refracting light, so that it was hard to identify for a minute even though the room lights were on in this case and the subjects were fully awake. It was a lighted miner's lamp with an unusually high-powered reflector behind it. In addition to this, a black object of some kind, an old sweater or miner's shirt, was hooded around it so that it was almost invisible from the street or the windows on the floor below—all its rays beat inward to the room. It was suspended from the same trio of interlocked rods.

It swayed there motionless for a minute, a devil's beacon, an invitation to destruction. Then it nudged inward, knocked repeatedly against the edge of the window frame, as though to deliberately awaken whoever was within. Then the light coyly retreated a little farther out into the open, but very imperceptibly, as if trying to snare something into pursuit. Then the light suddenly whisked up and was gone, drawn up through space.

With unbelievable swiftness, far quicker than anybody could have come up from the street, the closed door flew back at the touch of Striker's passkey, he darted in, tossed the "suicide note" he was holding onto the dresser, then swiveled the bed back into its original position in the room, scooped up imaginary money.

He stepped out of character and spread his hands conclusively. "See? Horribly simple and—simply horrible."

The tension broke. Mrs. Young buried her face against her husband's chest.

"He was an expert fisherman. Must have done a lot of it up around those mines of his," Striker added. "Probably never failed to hook that bed first cast off the reel. This passkey, that let him in here at will, must have been mislaid years ago and he got hold of it in some way. He brooded and brooded over the way he'd been swindled; this was his way of getting even with the world, squaring things. Or maybe he actually thought these various people in here were spies who came to learn the location of his mines. I don't know, I'm no psychiatrist. The money was just secondary, the icing to his cake. It helped him pay for his room here, staked him to the supplies he took along on his 'prospecting' trips.

"A few things threw me off for a long time. He was away at the time young Hastings fell out. The only possible explanation is that that, alone of the four, was a genuine suicide. By a freak coincidence it occurred in the very room the Hermit had been using for his murders. And this in spite of the fact that Hastings had less reason than any of the others; he had just become engaged. I know it's hard to swallow, but we'll have to. I owe you an apology on that one suicide, Courlander."

"And I owe you an apology on the other three, and to show you I'm no bad loser, I'm willing to make it in front of the whole Homicide Squad of New York."

Young asked curiously, "Have you any idea of just where those mines of his that caused all the trouble are located? Ontario, isn't it? Because down at the station tonight a Press Radio news flash came through that oil had been discovered in some abandoned gold-mine pits up there, a gusher worth all kinds of money, and they're running around like mad trying to find out in whom the title to them is vested. I bet it's the same ones!"

Striker nodded sadly. "I wouldn't be surprised. That would be just like one of life's bum little jokes."

JOHN D. MacDONALD
Murder for Money

LONG AGO he had given up trying to estimate what he would find in any house merely by looking at the outside of it. The interior of each house had a special flavor. It was not so much the result of the degree of tidiness, or lack of it, but rather the result of the emotional climate that had permeated the house. Anger, bitterness, despair—all left their subtle stains on even the most immaculate fabrics.

Darrigan parked the rented car by the curb and, for a long moment, looked at the house, at the iron fence, at the cypress shade. He sensed dignity, restraint, quietness. Yet he knew that the interior could destroy these impressions. He was in the habit of telling himself that his record of successful investigations was the result of the application of unemotional logic—yet his logic was often the result of sensing, somehow, the final answer and then retracing the careful steps to arrive once more at that same answer.

After a time, as the September sun of west-coast Florida began to turn the rented sedan into an oven, Darrigan pushed open the door, patted his pocket to be sure his notebook was in place, and walked toward the front door of the white house. There were two cars in the driveway, both of them with local licenses, both of them Cadillacs. It was perceptibly cooler under the trees that lined the walk.

Beyond the screen door the hallway was dim. A heavy woman came in answer to his second ring, staring at him with frank curiosity.

"I'd like to speak to Mrs. Davisson, please. Here's my card."

The woman opened the screen just enough for the card to be passed through, saying, with Midwest nasality, "Well, she's resting right now. . . . Oh, you're from the insurance?"

"Yes, I flew down from Hartford."

"Please come in and wait and I'll see if she's awake, Mr. Darrigan. I'm just a neighbor. I'm Mrs. Hoke. The poor dear has been so terribly upset."

"Yes, of course," Darrigan murmured, stepping into the hall. Mrs. Hoke walked heavily away. Darrigan could hear the mumble of other voices, a faint, slightly incongruous laugh. From the hall he could see into a living room, two steps lower than the hall itself. It was furnished in cool colors, with Florida furniture of cane and pale fabrics.

Mrs. Hoke came back and said reassuringly, "She was awake, Mr. Darrigan. She said you should wait in the study and she'll be out in a few minutes. The door is right back here. This is such a dreadful thing, not knowing what has happened to him. It's hard on her, the poor dear thing."

The study was not done in Florida fashion. Darrigan guessed that the furniture had been shipped down from the North. A walnut desk, a bit ornate, leather couch and chairs, two walls of books.

Mrs. Hoke stood in the doorway. "Now don't you upset her, you hear?" she said with elephantine coyness.

"I'll try not to."

Mrs. Hoke went away. This was Davisson's room, obviously. His books. A great number of technical works on the textile industry. Popularized texts for the layman in other fields. Astronomy, philosophy, physics. Quite a few biographies. Very little fiction. A man, then, with a serious turn of mind, dedicated to self-improvement, perhaps a bit humorless. And certainly very tidy.

Darrigan turned quickly as he heard the step in the hallway. She was a tall young woman, light on her feet. Her sunback dress was emerald green. Late twenties, he judged, or possibly very early thirties. Brown hair, sun-bleached on top. Quite a bit of tan. A fresh face, wide across the cheekbones, heavy-lipped, slightly Bergman in impact. The mouth faintly touched with strain.

"Mr. Darrigan?" He liked the voice. Low, controlled, poised.

"How do you do, Mrs. Davisson. Sorry to bother you like this."

"That's all right. I wasn't able to sleep. Won't you sit down, please?"

"If you don't mind, I'll sit at the desk, Mrs. Davisson. I'll have to make some notes."

She sat on the leather couch. He offered her a cigarette. "No, thank you, I've been smoking so much I have a sore throat. Mr. Darrigan, isn't this a bit . . . previous for the insurance company to send someone down here? I mean, as far as we know, he isn't—"

"We wouldn't do this in the case of a normal policyholder, Mrs. Davisson, but your husband carries policies with us totaling over nine hundred thousand dollars."

"Really! I knew Temple had quite a bit, but I didn't know it was that much!"

He showed her his best smile and said, "It makes it awkward for me, Mrs. Davisson, for them to send me out like some sort of bird of prey. You have presented no claim to the company, and you are perfectly within your rights to tell me to be on my merry way."

She answered his smile. "I wouldn't want to do that, Mr. Darrigan. But I don't quite understand why you're here."

"You could call me a sort of investigator. My actual title is Chief Adjuster for Guardsman Life and Casualty. I sincerely hope that we'll find a reasonable explanation for your husband's disappearance. He disappeared Thursday, didn't he?"

"He didn't come home Thursday night. I reported it to the police early Friday morning. And this is—"

"Tuesday."

He opened his notebook, took his time looking over the pages. It was a device, to give him a chance to gauge the degree of tension. She sat quite still, her hands resting in her lap, unmoving.

He leaned back. "It may sound presumptuous, Mrs. Davisson, but I intend to see if I can find out what happened to your husband. I've had reasonable success in such cases in the past. I'll cooperate with the local police officials, of course. I hope you won't mind answering questions that may duplicate what the police have already asked you."

"I won't mind. The important thing is . . . to find out. This not knowing is. . . ." Her voice caught a bit. She looked down at her hands.

"According to our records, Mrs. Davisson, his first wife, Anna

Thorn Davisson, was principal beneficiary under his policies until her death in 1978. The death of the beneficiary was reported, but it was not necessary to change the policies at that time as the two children of his first marriage were secondary beneficiaries, sharing equally in the proceeds in case of death. In 1979, probably at the time of his marriage to you, we received instructions to make you the primary beneficiary under all policies, with the secondary beneficiaries, Temple C. Davisson, Junior, and Alicia Jean Davisson, unchanged. I have your name here as Dinah Pell Davisson. That is correct?"

"Yes, it is."

"Could you tell me about your husband? What sort of man is he?"

She gave him a small smile. "What should I say? He is a very kind man. Perhaps slightly autocratic, but kind. He owned a small knitting mill in Utica, New York. He sold it, I believe, in 1972. It was incorporated and he owned the controlling stock interest, and there was some sort of merger with a larger firm, where he received payment in the stock in the larger firm in return for his interest. He sold out because his wife had to live in a warmer climate. She had a serious kidney condition. They came down here to Clearwater and bought this house. Temple was too active to retire. He studied real estate conditions here for a full year and then began to invest money in all sorts of property. He has done very well."

"How did you meet him, Mrs. Davisson?"

"My husband was a sergeant in the Air Force. He was stationed at Drew Field. I followed him here. When he was sent overseas I had no special place to go, and we agreed I should wait for him here. The Davissons advertised for a companion for Mrs. Davisson. I applied and held the job from early 1974 until she died in 1978."

"And your husband?"

"He was killed in a crash landing. When I received the wire, the Davissons were very kind and understanding. At that time my position in the household was more like a daughter receiving an allowance. My own parents died long ago. I have a married sister in Melbourne, Australia. We've never been close."

"What did you do between the time Mrs. Davisson died and you married Temple Davisson?"

"I left here, of course. Mrs. Davisson had money of her own.

She left me five thousand dollars and left the rest to Temple, Junior, and Alicia. Mr. Davisson found me a job in a real estate office in Clearwater. I rented a small apartment. One night Mr. Davisson came to see me at the apartment. He was quite shy. It took him a long time to get to the reason he had come. He told me that he tried to keep the house going, but the people he had hired were undependable. He also said that he was lonely. He asked me to marry him. I told him that I had affection for him, as for a father. He told me that he did not love me that way either, that Anna had been the only woman in his life. Well, Jack had been the only man in my life, and life was pretty empty. The Davissons had filled a place in my life. I missed this house. But he is sixty-one, and that makes almost exactly thirty years' difference in ages. It seemed a bit grotesque. He told me to think it over and give him my answer when I was ready. It occurred to me that his children would resent me, and it also occurred to me that I cared very little what people thought. Four days later I told him I would marry him."

Darrigan realized that he was treading on most dangerous ground. "Has it been a good marriage?"

"Is that a question you're supposed to ask?"

"It sounds impertinent. I know that. But in a disappearance of this sort I must consider suicide. Unhappiness can come from ill health, money difficulties, or emotional difficulties. I should try to rule them out."

"I'll take one of those cigarettes now, Mr. Darrigan," she said. "I can use it."

He lit it for her, went back to the desk chair. She frowned, exhaled a cloud of smoke.

"It has not been a completely happy marriage, Mr. Darrigan."

"Can you explain that?"

"I'd rather not." He pursed his lips, let the silence grow. At last she said, "I suppose I can consider an insurance man to be as ethical as a doctor or a lawyer?"

"Of course."

"For several months it was a marriage in name only. I was content to have it go on being that way. But he is a vigorous man, and after a while I became aware that his attitude had changed and he had begun to . . . want me." She flushed.

"But you had no feeling for him in that way," he said, helping her.

"None. And we'd made no actual agreement, in so many words. But living here with him, I had no ethical basis for refusing him. After that, our marriage became different. He sensed, of course, that I was merely submitting. He began to . . . court me, I suppose you'd call it. Flowers and little things like that. He took off weight and began to dress much more youthfully. He tried to make himself younger, in his speech and in his habits. It was sort of pathetic, the way he tried."

"Would you relate that to . . . his disappearance?"

For a moment her face was twisted in the agony of self reproach. "I don't know."

"I appreciate your frankness. I'll respect it, Mrs. Davisson. How did he act Thursday?"

"The same as always. We had a late breakfast. He had just sold some lots in the Lido section at Sarasota, and he was thinking of putting the money into a Gulf-front tract at Redington Beach. He asked me to go down there with him, but I had an eleven o'clock appointment with the hairdresser. His car was in the garage, so he took my convertible. He said he'd have lunch down that way and be back in the late afternoon. We were going to have some people in for cocktails. Well, the cocktail guests came and Temple didn't show up. I didn't worry. I thought he was delayed. We all went out to dinner and I left a note telling him that he could catch up with us at the Belmonte, on Clearwater Beach.

"After dinner the Deens brought me home. They live down on the next street. I began to get really worried at ten o'clock. I thought of heart attacks and all sorts of things like that. Of accidents and so on. I phoned Morton Plant Hospital and asked if they knew anything. I phoned the police here and at Redington and at St. Petersburg. I fell asleep in a chair at about four o'clock and woke up at seven. That was when I officially reported him missing.

"They found my car parked outside a hotel apartment on Redington Beach, called Aqua Azul. They checked and found out he'd gone into the Aqua Azul cocktail lounge at eight thirty, alone. He had one dry martini and phoned here, but of course I had left by that time and the house was empty. He had another drink and then left. But apparently he didn't get in the car and drive away. That's what I don't understand. And I keep thinking that the Aqua Azul is right on the Gulf."

"Have his children come down?"

"Temple, Junior, wired that he is coming. He's a lieutenant

colonel of ordnance stationed at the Pentagon."

"How old is he?"

"Thirty-six, and Alicia is thirty-three. Temple, Junior, is married, but Alicia isn't. She's with a Boston advertising agency, and when I tried to phone her I found out she's on vacation, taking a motor trip in Canada. She may not even know about it."

"When is the son arriving?"

"Late today, the wire said."

"Were they at the wedding?"

"No. But I know them, of course. I met them before Mrs. Davisson died, many times. And only once since my marriage. There was quite a scene then. They think I'm some sort of dirty little opportunist. When they were down while Mrs. Davisson was alive, they had me firmly established in the servant category. I suppose they were right, but one never thinks of oneself as a servant. I'm afraid Colonel Davisson is going to be difficult."

"Do you think your husband might have had business worries?"

"None. He told me a few months ago, quite proudly, that when he liquidated the knitting-company stock he received five hundred thousand dollars. In 1973 he started to buy land in this area. He said that the land he now owns could be sold off for an estimated million and a half dollars."

"Did he maintain an office?"

"This is his office. Mr. Darrigan, you used the past tense then. I find it disturbing."

"I'm sorry. It wasn't intentional." Yet it had been. He had wanted to see how easily she would slip into the past tense, showing that in her mind she considered him dead.

"Do you know the terms of his current will?"

"He discussed it with me a year ago. It sets up trust funds, one for me and one for each of the children. He insisted that it be set up so that we share equally. And yet, if I get all that insurance, it isn't going to seem very equal, is it? I'm sorry for snapping at you about using the past tense, Mr. Darrigan. I think he's dead."

"Why?"

"I know that amnesia is a very rare thing, genuine amnesia. And Temple had a very sound, stable mind. As I said before, he is kind. He wouldn't go away and leave me to this kind of worry."

"The newspaper picture was poor. Do you have a better one?"

"Quite a good one taken in July. Don't get up. I can get it. It's right in this desk drawer."

She sat lithely on her heels and opened the bottom desk drawer. Her perfume had a pleasant tang. Where her hair was parted he could see the ivory cleanness of her scalp. An attractive woman, with a quality of personal warmth held in reserve. Darrigan decided that the sergeant had been a most fortunate man. And he wondered if Davisson was perceptive enough to measure the true extent of his failure. He remembered an old story of a man held captive at the bottom of a dark, smooth-sided well. Whenever the light was turned on, for a brief interval, he could see that the circular wall was of glass, with exotic fruits banked behind it.

"This one," she said, taking out a 35-millimeter color transparency mounted in paperboard. She slipped it into a green plastic viewer and handed it to him. "You better take it over to the window. Natural light is best."

Darrigan held the viewer up to his eye. A heavy bald man, tanned like a Tahitian, stood smiling into the camera. He stood on a beach in the sunlight, and he wore bathing trunks with a pattern of blue fish on a white background. There was a doggedness about his heavy jaw, a glint of shrewdness in his eyes. His position was faintly strained and Darrigan judged he was holding his belly in, arching his wide chest for the camera. He looked to be no fool.

"May I take this along?" Darrigan asked, turning to her.

"Not for keeps." The childish expression was touching.

"Not for keeps," he said, smiling, meaning his smile for the first time. "Thank you for your courtesy, Mrs. Davisson. I'll be in touch with you. If you want me for any reason, I'm registered at a place called Bon Villa on the beach. The owner will take a message for me."

Darrigan left police headquarters in Clearwater at three o'clock. They had been as cool as he had expected at first, but after he had clearly stated his intentions they had relaxed and informed him of progress to date. They were cooperating with the Pinellas County officials and with the police at Redington.

Temple Davisson had kept his appointment with the man who owned the plot of Gulf-front property that had interested him. The potential vendor was named Myron Drynfells, and Davisson had picked him up at eleven fifteen at the motel he owned at Madeira Beach. Drynfells reported that they had inspected the property but were unable to arrive at a figure acceptable to both

of them. Davisson had driven him back to the Coral Tour Haven,
depositing him there shortly after twelve thirty. Davisson had
intimated that he was going farther down the line to take a look
at some property near St. Petersburg Beach.

There was one unconfirmed report of a man answering Davisson's description seen walking along the shoulder of the highway
up near the Bath Club accompanied by a dark-haired girl, some
time shortly before nine o'clock on Thursday night.

The police had no objection to Darrigan's talking with Dynfells
or making his own attempt to find the elusive dark-haired girl.
They were reluctant to voice any theory that would account for
the disappearance.

Following a map of the area, Darrigan had little difficulty in
finding his way out South Fort Harrison Avenue to the turnoff
to the Belleaire causeway. He drove through the village of Indian
Rocks and down a straight road that paralleled the beach. The
Aqua Azul was not hard to find. It was an ugly four-story building
tinted pale chartreuse with corner balconies overlooking the Gulf.
From the parking area one walked along a crushed-shell path to
tile steps leading down into a pseudo-Mexican courtyard where
shrubbery screened off the highway. The lobby door, of plate glass
with a chrome push bar, opened off the other side of the patio.
The fountain in the center of the patio was rimmed with small
floodlights with blue-glass lenses. Darrigan guessed that the fountain
would be fairly garish once the lights were turned on.

Beyond the glass door the lobby was frigidly air-conditioned. A
brass sign on the blond desk announced that summer rates were
in effect. The lobby walls were rough tan plaster. At the head of
a short wide staircase was a mural of lumpy, coffee-colored, semi-
naked women grinding corn and holding infants.

A black man was slowly sweeping the tile floor of the lobby.
A girl behind the desk was carrying on a monosyllabic phone
conversation. The place had a quietness, a hint of informality,
that suggested it would be more pleasant now than during the
height of the winter tourist season.

The bar lounge opened off the lobby. The west wall was entirely
glass, facing the beach glare. A curtain had been drawn across the
glass. It was sufficiently opaque to cut the glare, subdue the light
in the room. Sand gritted underfoot as Darrigan walked to the
bar. Three lean women in bathing suits sat at one table, complete
with beach bags, tall drinks, and that special porcelainized facial

expression of the middle forties trying, with monied success, to look like middle thirties.

Two heavy men in white suits hunched over a corner table, florid faces eight inches apart, muttering at each other. A young couple sat at the bar. They had a honeymoon flavor about them. Darrigan sat down at the end of the bar, around the corner, and decided on a rum collins. The bartender was brisk, young, dark, and he mixed a good drink.

When he brought the change, Darrigan said, "Say, have they found that guy who wandered away and left his car here the other night?"

"I don't think so, sir," the bartender said with no show of interest.

"Were you on duty the night he came in?"

"Yes, sir."

"Regular customer?"

The bartender didn't answer.

Darrigan quickly leafed through a half dozen possible approaches. He selected one that seemed suited to the bartender's look of quick intelligence and smiled ingratiatingly. "They ought to make all cops take a sort of internship behind a bar. That's where you learn what makes people tick."

The slight wariness faded. "That's no joke."

"Teddy!" one of the three lean women called. "Another round, please."

"Coming right up, Mrs. Jerrold," Teddy said.

Darrigan waited with monumental patience. He had planted a seed, and he wanted to see if it would take root. He stared down at his drink, watching Teddy out of the corner of his eye. After the drinks had been taken to the three women, Teddy drifted slowly back toward Darrigan. Darrigan waited for Teddy to say the first word.

"I think that Davisson will show up."

Darrigan shrugged. "That's hard to say." It put the burden of proof on Teddy.

Teddy became confidential. "Like you said, sir, you see a lot when you're behind a bar. You learn to size them up. Now, you take that Davisson. I don't think he ever came in here before. I didn't make any connection until they showed me the picture. Then I remembered him. In the off season, you get time to size people up. He came in alone. I'd say he'd had a couple already.

Husky old guy. Looked like money. Looked smart, too. That kind, they like service. He came in about eight thirty. A local guy. I could tell. I don't know how. You can always tell them from the tourists. One martini, he wants. Very dry. He gets it very dry. He asks me where he can phone. I told him about the phone in the lobby. He finished half his cocktail, then phoned. When he came back he looked satisfied about the phone call. A little more relaxed. You know what I mean. He sat right on that stool there, and one of the regulars, a Mrs. Kathy Marrick, is sitting alone at that table over there. That Davisson, he turns on the stool and starts giving Mrs. Marrick the eye. Not that you can blame him. She is something to look at. He orders another martini. I figure out the pitch then. That Davisson, he went and called his wife and then he was settling down to an evening of wolfing around. Some of those older guys, they give us more trouble than the college kids. And he had that look, you know what I mean.

"Well, from where he was sitting he couldn't even see first base, not with Mrs. Marrick, and I saw him figure that out for himself. He finished his second drink in a hurry, and away he went. I sort of decided he was going to look around and see where the hunting was a little better."

"And that makes you think he'll turn up?"

"Sure. I think the old guy just lost himself a big weekend, and he'll come crawling out of the woodwork with some crazy amnesia story or something."

"Then how do you figure the car being left here?"

"I think he found somebody with a car of her own. They saw him walking up the line not long after he left here, and he was with a girl, wasn't he? That makes sense to me."

"Where would he have gone to find that other girl?"

"I think he came out of here, and it was just beginning to get dark, and he looked from the parking lot and saw the lights of the Tide Table up the road, and it was just as easy to walk as drive."

Darrigan nodded. "That would make sense. Is it a nice place, that Tide Table?"

"A big bar and bathhouses and a dance floor and carhops to serve greasy hamburgers. It doesn't do this section of the beach much good."

"Was Davisson dressed right for that kind of a place?"

"I don't know. He had on a white mesh shirt with short sleeves
and tan slacks, I think. Maybe he had a coat in his car. He didn't
wear it in here. The rules here say men have to wear coats in
the bar and dining room after November first."

"That Mrs. Marrick wouldn't have met him outside, would
she?"

"Not her. No, sir. She rents one of our cabañas here."

"Did she notice him?"

"I'd say she did. You can't fool Kathy Marrick."

Darrigan knew that Teddy could add nothing more. So Darrigan
switched the conversation to other things. He made himself talk
dully and at length so that when Teddy saw his chance, he eased
away with almost obvious relief. Darrigan had learned to make
himself boring, merely by relating complicated incidents which
had no particular point. It served its purpose. He knew that Teddy
was left with a mild contempt for Darrigan's intellectual resources.
Later, should anyone suggest to Teddy that Darrigan was a uniquely
shrewd investigator, Teddy would hoot with laughter, completely
forgetting that Darrigan, with a minimum of words, had extracted
every bit of information Teddy had possessed.

Darrigan went out to the desk and asked if he might see Mrs.
Marrick. The girl went to the small switchboard and plugged one
of the house phones into Mrs. Marrick's cabaña. After the phone
rang five times a sleepy, soft-fibered voice answered.

He stated his name and his wish to speak with her. She agreed,
sleepily. Following the desk girl's instructions, Darrigan walked
out the beach door of the lobby and down a shell walk to the
last cabaña to the south. A woman in a two-piece white terry-
cloth sun suit lay on an uptilted Barwa chair in the hot sun. Her
hair was wheat and silver, sun-parched. Her figure was rich, and
her tan was coppery. She had the hollowed cheeks of a Dietrich
and a wide, flat mouth.

She opened lazy sea-green eyes when he spoke her name. She
looked at him for a long moment and then said, "Mr. Darrigan,
you cast an unpleasantly black shadow on the sand. Are you one
of the new ones with my husband's law firm? If so, the answer
is still no, in spite of the fact that you're quite pretty."

"I never heard of you until ten minutes ago, Mrs. Marrick."

"That's refreshing, dear. Be a good boy and go in and build us
some drinks. You'll find whatever you want, and I need a fresh
gin and tonic. This glass will do for me. And bring out a pack

of cigarettes from the carton on the bedroom dressing table."

She shut her eyes. Darrigan shrugged and went into the cabaña. It was clean but cluttered. He made himself a rum collins, took the two drinks out, handed her her drink and a pack of cigarettes. She shifted her weight forward and the chair tilted down.

"Now talk, dear," she said.

"Last Friday night at about eight thirty you were alone in the bar and a bald-headed man with a deep tan sat at the bar. He was interested in you."

"Mmm. The missing Mr. Davisson, eh? Let me see now. You can't be a local policeman. They all either look like fullbacks from the University of Florida or skippers of unsuccessful charter boats. Your complexion and clothes are definitely northern. That might make you FBI, but I don't think so somehow. Insurance, Mr. Darrigan?"

He sat on a canvas chair and looked at her with new respect. "Insurance, Mrs. Marrick."

"He's dead, I think."

"His wife thinks so too. Why do you?"

"I was alone. I'm a vain creature, and the older I get the more flattered I am by all little attentions. Your Mr. Davisson was a bit pathetic, my dear. He had a lost look. A . . . hollowness. Do you understand?"

"Not quite."

"A man of that age will either be totally uninterested in casual females or he will have an enormous amount of assurance about him. Mr. Davisson had neither. He looked at me like a little boy staring into the candy shop. I was almost tempted to help the poor dear, but he looked dreadfully dull. I said to myself, Kathy, there is a man who suddenly has decided to be a bit of a rake and does not know just how to go about it."

"Does that make him dead?"

"No, of course. It was something else. Looking into his eyes was like looking into the eyes of a photograph of someone who has recently died. It is a look of death. It cannot be described. It made me feel quite upset."

"How would I write that up in a report?"

"You wouldn't, my dear. You would go out and find out how he died. He was looking for adventure last Friday night. And I believe he found it."

"With a girl with dark hair?"

"Perhaps."

"It isn't much of a starting place, is it?" Darrigan said ruefully.

She finished her drink and tilted her chair back. "I understand that the wife is young."

"Comparatively speaking. Are you French?"

"I was once. You're quick, aren't you? I'm told there's no accent."

"No accent. A turn of phrase here and there. What if the wife is young?"

"Call it my French turn of mind. A lover of the wife could help your Mr. Davisson find . . . his adventure."

"The wife was with a group all evening."

"A very sensible precaution."

He stood up. "Thank you for talking to me."

"You see, you're not as quick as I thought, Mr. Darrigan. I wanted you to keep questioning me in a clever way, and then I should tell you that Mr. Davisson kept watching the door during his two drinks, as though he were expecting that someone had followed him. He was watching, not with worry, but with . . . annoyance."

Darrigan smiled. "I thought you had something else to tell. And it seemed the quickest way to get it out of you, to pretend to go."

She stared at him and then laughed. It was a good laugh, full-throated, rich. "We could be friends, my dear," she said, when she got her breath.

"So far I haven't filled in enough of his day. I know what he did up until very early afternoon. Then there is a gap. He comes into the Aqua Azul bar at eight-thirty. He has had a few drinks. I like the theory of someone following him, meeting him outside. That would account for his leaving his car at the lot."

"What will you do now?"

"See if I can fill in the blanks in his day."

"The blank before he arrived here, and the more important one afterward?"

"Yes."

"I'm well known up and down the Gulf beaches, Mr. Darrigan. Being with me would be protective coloration."

"And besides, you're bored."

"Utterly."

He smiled at her. "Then you'd better get dressed, don't you think?"

He waited outside while she changed. He knew that she would be useful for her knowledge of the area. Yet not sufficiently useful to warrant taking her along had she not been a mature, witty, perceptive woman.

She came out wearing sandals and a severely cut sand-colored linen sun dress, carrying a white purse. The end tendrils of the astonishing hair were damp-curled where they had protruded from her shower cap.

"Darrigan and Marrick," she said. "Investigations to order. This might be fun."

"And it might be dull."

"But we shan't be dull, Mr. Darrigan, shall we. What are you called?"

"Gil, usually."

"Ah, Gil, if this were a properly conceived plot, I would be the one who lured your Mr. Davisson to his death. Now I accompany the investigator to allay suspicion."

"No such luck, Kathy."

"No such luck." They walked along the shell path to the main building of the Aqua Azul. She led the way around the building toward a Cadillac convertible the shade of raspberry sherbet.

"More protective coloration?" Darrigan asked.

She smiled and handed him the keys from her purse. After he shut her door he went around and got behind the wheel. The sun was far enough gone to warrant having the top down. She took a dark bandanna from the glove compartment and tied it around her hair.

"Now how do you go about this, Gil?" she asked.

"I head south and show a picture of Davisson in every bar until we find the one he was in. He could have called his wife earlier. I think he was the sort to remember that a cocktail party was scheduled for that evening. Something kept him from phoning his wife."

"Maybe he didn't want to phone her until it was too late."

"I'll grant that. First I want to talk to a man named Drynfells. For this you better stay in the car."

The Coral Tour Haven was a pink hotel with pink iron flamingos stuck into the lawn and a profusion of whitewashed boulders marking the drive. Drynfells was a sour-looking man with a withered face, garish clothes, and a cheap Cuban cigar.

Darrigan had to follow Drynfells about as they talked. Drynfells ambled around, picking up scraps of cellophane, twigs, burned matches from his yard. He confirmed all that the Clearwater police had told Darrigan.

"You couldn't decide on a price, Mr. Drynfells?"

"I want one hundred and forty-five thousand for that piece. He offered one thirty-six, then one thirty-eight, and finally one forty. He said that was his top offer. I came down two thousand and told him that one forty-three was as low as I'd go."

"Did you quarrel?"

Drynfells gave him a sidelong glance. "We shouted a little. He was a shouter. Lot of men try to bull their way into a deal. He couldn't bulldoze me. No, sir."

They had walked around a corner of the motel. A pretty girl sat on a rubberized mattress at the side of a new wading pool. The ground was raw around the pool, freshly seeded, protected by stakes and string.

"What did you say your name was?" Drynfells asked.

"Darrigan."

"This here is my wife, Mr. Darrigan. Beth, this man is an insurance fellow asking about that Davisson."

Mrs. Drynfells was striking. She had a heavy strain of some Latin blood. Her dark eyes were liquid, expressive.

"He is the wan who is wanting to buy our beach, eh?"

"Yeah. That bald-headed man that the police were asking about," Drynfells said.

Mrs. Drynfells seemed to lose all interest in the situation. She lay back and shut her eyes. She wore a lemon-yellow swimsuit.

Drynfells wandered away and swooped on a scrap of paper, balling it up in his hand with the other debris he had collected.

"You have a nice place here," Darrigan said.

"Just got it open in time for last season. Did pretty good. We got a private beach over there across the highway. Reasonable rates, too."

"I guess things are pretty dead in the off season."

"Right now we only got one unit taken. Those folks came in yesterday. But it ought to pick up again soon."

"How big is that piece of land you want one hundred and forty-five thousand for?"

"It's one hundred and twenty feet of Gulf-front lot, six hundred feet deep, but it isn't for sale any more."

"Why not?"

"Changed my mind about it, Mr. Darrigan. Decided to hold onto it, maybe develop it a little. Nice property."

Darrigan went out to the car. They drove south, stopping at the obvious places. There were unable to pick up the trail of Mr. Davisson. Darrigan bought Kathy Marrick dinner. He drove her back to the Aqua Azul. They took a short walk on the beach and he thanked her, promised to keep in touch with her, and drove the rented sedan back to Clearwater Beach.

It was after eleven and the porch of the Bon Villa was dark. He parked, and as he headed toward his room a familiar voice spoke hesitantly from one of the dark chairs.

"Mr. Darrigan?"

"Oh! Hello, Mrs. Davisson. You startled me. I didn't see you there. Do you want to come in?"

"No, please. Sit down and tell me what you've learned."

He pulled one of the aluminum chairs over close to hers and sat down. A faint sea breeze rattled the palm fronds. Her face was a pale oval, barely visible.

"I didn't learn much, Mrs. Davisson. Not much at all."

"Forgive me for coming here like this. Colonel Davisson arrived. It was as unpleasant as I'd expected. I had to get out of the house."

"It makes a difficult emotional problem for both of you—when the children of the first marriage are older than the second wife."

"I don't really blame him too much, I suppose. It looks bad."

"What did he accuse you of?"

"Driving his father into some crazy act. Maybe I did."

"Don't think that way."

"I keep thinking that if we never find out what happened to Temple, his children will always blame me. I don't especially want to be friends with them, but I do want their . . . respect, I guess you'd say."

"Mrs. Davisson, do you have any male friends your own age?"

"How do you mean that?" she asked hotly.

"Is there any man you've been friendly enough with to cause talk?"

"N-no, I—"

"Who were you thinking of when you hesitated?"

"Brad Sharvis. He's a bit over thirty, and quite nice. It was his real estate agency that Temple sent me to for a job. He has worked with Temple the last few years. He's a bachelor. He has dinner with us quite often. We both like him."

"Could there be talk?"

"There could be, but it would be without basis, Mr. Darrigan," she said coldly.

"I don't care how angry you get at me, Mrs. Davisson, so long as you tell me the truth."

After a long silence she said, "I'm sorry. I believe that you want to help."

"I do."

She stood up. "I feel better now. I think I'll go home."

"Can I take you home?"

"I have my car, thanks."

He watched her go down the walk. Under the streetlight he saw her walking with a good long stride. He saw the headlights, saw her swing around the island in the center of Mandalay and head back for the causeway to Clearwater.

Darrigan went in, showered, and went to bed. He lay in the dark room and smoked a slow cigarette. Somewhere, hidden in the personality or in the habits of one Temple Davisson, was the reason for his death. Darrigan found that he was thinking in terms of death. He smiled in the darkness as he thought of Kathy Marrick. A most pleasant companion. So far in the investigation he had met four women. Of the four only Mrs. Hoke was unattractive.

He snubbed out the cigarette and composd himself for sleep. A case, like a score of other cases. He would leave his brief mark on the participants and go out of their lives. For a moment he felt the ache of self-imposed loneliness. The ache had been there since the day Doris had left him, long ago. He wondered sourly, on the verge of sleep, if it had made him a better investigator.

Brad Sharvis was a florid, freckled, overweight young man with carrot hair, blue eyes, and a salesman's unthinking affability. The small real estate office was clean and bright. A girl was typing a lease agreement for an elderly couple.

Brad took Darrigan back into his small private office. A window air conditioner hummed, chilling the moist September air.

"What sort of man was he, Mr. Sharvis?"

"Was he? Or is he? Shrewd, Mr. Darrigan. Shrewd and honest. And something else. Tough-minded isn't the expression I want."

"Ruthless?"

"That's it exactly. He started moving in on property down here soon after he arrived. You wouldn't know the place if you saw it back then. The last ten years down here would take your breath away."

"He knew what to buy, eh?"

"It took him a year to decide on policy. He had a very simple operating idea. He decided, after his year of looking around, that there was going to be a tremendous pressure for waterfront land. At that time small building lots on Clearwater Beach, on the Gulf front, were going for as little as seventy-five hundred dollars. I remember that the first thing he did was pick up eight lots at that figure. He sold them in 1980 for fifty thousand apiece."

"Where did the ruthlessness come in, Mr. Sharvis?"

"You better call me Brad. That last name makes me feel too dignified."

"Okay, I'm Gil."

"I'll tell you, Gil. Suppose he got his eye on a piece he wanted. He'd go after it. Phone calls, letters, personal visits. He'd hound a man who had no idea of selling until, in some cases, I think they sold out just to get Temple Davisson off their back. And he'd fight for an hour to get forty dollars off the price of a twenty-thousand-dollar piece."

"Did he handle his deals through you?"

"No. He turned himself into a licensed agent and used this office for his deals. He pays toward the office expenses here, and I've been in with him on a few deals."

"Is he stingy?"

"Not a bit. Pretty free with his money, but a tight man in a deal. You know, he's told me a hundred times that everybody likes the look of nice fat batches of bills. He said that there's nothing exactly like counting out fifteen thousand dollars in bills onto a man's desk when the man wants to get seventeen thousand."

Darrigan felt a shiver of excitement run up his back. It was always that way when he found a bit of key information.

"Where did he bank?"

"Bank of Clearwater."

"Do you think he took money with him when he went after the Drynfells plot?"

Sharvis frowned. "I hardly think he'd take that much out there, but I'll wager he took a sizable payment against it."

"Twenty-five thousand?"

"Possibly. Probably more like fifty."

"I could check that at the bank, I suppose."

"I doubt it. He has a safe in his office at his house. A pretty good one, I think. He kept his cash there. He'd replenish the supply in Tampa, picking up a certified check from the Bank of Clearwater whenever he needed more than they could comfortably give him."

"He was anxious to get the Drynfells land?"

"A very nice piece. And with a tentative purchaser all lined up for it. Temple would have unloaded it for one hundred and seventy thousand. He wanted to work fast so that there'd be no chance of his customer getting together with Drynfells. It only went on the market Wednesday, a week ago today."

"Drynfells held it a long time?"

"Several years. He paid fifty thousand for it."

"Would it violate any confidence to tell me who Davisson planned to sell it to?"

"I can't give you the name because I don't know it myself. It's some man who sold a chain of movie houses in Kansas and wants to build a motel down here, that's all I know."

Darrigan walked out into the morning sunlight. The death of Temple Davisson was beginning to emerge from the mists. Sometime after he had left the Coral Tour Haven and before he appeared at the Aqua Azul, he had entangled himself with someone who wanted that cash. Wanted it badly. They had not taken their first opportunity. So they had sought a second choice, had made the most of it.

He parked in the center of town, had a cup of coffee. At such times he felt far away from his immediate environment. Life moved brightly around him and left him in a dark place where he sat and thought. Thought at such a time was not the application of logic but an endless stirring at the edge of the mind, a restless groping for the fleeting impression.

Davisson had been a man whose self-esteem had taken an inadvertent blow at the hands of his young wife. To mend his self-esteem, he had been casting a speculative eye at the random female. And he had been spending the day trying to engineer a deal that would mean a most pleasant profit.

Darrigan and Kathy Marrick had been unable to find the place where Davisson had taken a few drinks before stopping at the Aqua Azul. Darrigan paid for his coffee and went out to the car, spread the road map on the wheel, and studied it. Granted that Davisson was on his way home when he stopped at the Aqua Azul, it limited the area where he could have been. Had he been more than three miles south of the Aqua Azul, he would not logically have headed home on the road that would take him through Indian Rocks and along Belleaire Beach. He would have cut over to Route 19. With a pencil Darrigan made a circle. Temple Davisson had taken his drinks somewhere in that area.

He frowned. He detested legwork, that dullest stepsister of investigation. Sharing it with Mrs. Marrick made it a bit more pleasant, at least. It took him forty-five minutes to drive out to the Aqua Azul. Her raspberry convertible was under shelter in the long carport. He parked in the sun and went in, found her in the lobby chattering with the girl at the desk.

She smiled at him. "It can't be Nero Wolfe. Not enough waistline."

"Buy you a drink?"

"Clever boy. The bar isn't open yet. Come down to the cabaña and make your own and listen to the record of a busy morning."

They went into the cypress-paneled living room of the beach cabaña. She made the drinks.

"We failed to find out where he'd been by looking for him, my dear. So this morning I was up bright and early and went on a hunt for somebody who might have seen the car. A nice baby-blue convertible. They're a dime a dozen around here, but it seemed sensible. Tan men with bald heads are a dime a dozen too. But the combination of tan bald head and baby-blue convertible is not so usual."

"Any time you'd like a job, Kathy."

"Flatterer! Now prepare yourself for the letdown. All I found out was something we already knew. That the baby-blue job was parked at that hideous Coral Tour Haven early in the afternoon."

Darrigan sipped his drink. "Parked there?"

"That's what the man said. He has a painful little store that sells things made out of shells, and sells shells to people who want to make things out of shells. Say that three times fast."

"Why did you stop there?"

"Just to see if anybody could remember the car and man if

they had seen them. He's across the street from that Coral Tour thing."

"I think I'd like to talk to him."

"Let's go, then. He's a foolish little sweetheart with a tic."

The man was small and nervous, and at unexpected intervals his entire face would twitch uncontrollably. "Like I told the lady, mister, I saw the car parked over to Drynfells's. You don't see many cars there. Myron doesn't do so good this time of year."

"And you saw the bald-headed man?"

"Sure. He went in with Drynfells, and then he came out after a while."

"After how long?"

"How would I know? Was I timing him? Maybe twenty minutes."

Darrigan showed him the picture. "This man?"

The little man squinted through the viewer. "Sure."

"You got a good look at him?"

"Just the first time."

"You mean when he went in?"

"No, I mean the first time he was there. The second time it was getting pretty late in the day, and the sun was gone."

"Did he stay long the second time?"

"I don't know. I closed up when he was still there."

"Thanks a lot."

The little man twitched and beamed. "A pleasure, certainly."

They went back out to Darrigan's car. When they got in Kathy said, "I feel a bit stupid, Gil."

"Don't think I suspected that. It came out by accident. One of those things. It happens sometimes. And I should have done some better guessing. I found out this morning that when Temple Davisson wanted a piece of property he didn't give up easily. He went back and tried again."

"And Mr. Drynfells didn't mention it."

"A matter which I find very interesting. I'm dropping you back at the Aqua Azul and then I'm going to tackle Drynfells."

"Who found the little man who sells shells? You are not leaving me out."

"It may turn out to be unpleasant, Kathy."

"So be it. I want to see how much of that tough look of yours is a pose, Mr. Darrigan."

"Let me handle it."

"I shall be a mouse, entirely."

He waited for two cars to go by and made a wide U-turn, then turned right into Drynfells's drive. The couple was out in back. Mrs. Drynfells was basking on her rubberized mattress, her eyes closed. She did not appear to have moved since the previous day. Myron Drynfells was over near the hedge having a bitter argument with a man who obviously belonged with the battered pickup parked in front.

Drynfells was saying, "I just got damn good and tired of waiting for you to come around and finish the job."

The man, a husky youngster in work clothes, flushed with anger, said, "Okay, okay. Just pay me off, then, if that's the way you feel. Fourteen hours' labor plus the bags and the pipe."

Drynfells turned and saw Darrigan and Kathy. "Hello," he said absently. "Be right back." He walked into the back door of the end unit with the husky young man.

Mrs. Drynfells opened her eyes. She looked speculatively at Kathy. "Allo," she said. Darrigan introduced the two women. He had done enough work on jewelry theft to know that the emerald in Mrs. Drynfells's ring was genuine. About three carats, he judged. A beauty.

Drynfells came out across the lawn, scowling. He wore chartreuse slacks and a dark blue seersucker sport shirt with a chartreuse flower pattern.

"Want anything done right," he said, "you got to do it yourself. What's on your mind, Mr. Darrigan?"

"Just checking, Mr. Drynfells. I got the impression from the police that Mr. Davisson merely dropped you off here after you'd looked at the land. I didn't know he'd come in with you."

"He's a persistent guy. I couldn't shake him off, could I, honey?"

"Talking, talking," Mrs. Drynfells said, with sunstruck sleepiness. "Too moch."

"He came in and yakked at me, and then when he left he told me he could find better lots south of here. I told him to go right ahead."

"How long did he stay?"

Drynfells shrugged. "Fifteen minutes, maybe."

"Did he wave big bills at you?"

"Sure. Kid stuff. I had my price and he wouldn't meet it. Waving money in my face wasn't going to change my mind. No, sir."

"And that's the last you saw of him?" Darrigan asked casually.

"That's right."

"Then why was his car parked out in front of here at dusk on Friday?"

"In front of here?" Drynfells said, his eyes opening wide.

"In front of here."

"I don't know what you're talking about, mister. I wasn't even here, then. I was in Clearwater on a business matter."

Mrs. Drynfells sat up and put her hand over her mouth. "Ai, I forget! He did come back. Still talking, talking, I send him away, that talking wan."

Drynfells stomped over to her and glared down at her. "Why did you forget that? Damn it, that might make us look bad."

"I do not theenk."

Drynfells turned to Darrigan with a shrug. "Rattleheaded, that's what she is. Forget her head if it wasn't fastened on."

"I am sorree!"

"I think you better phone the police and tell them, Mr. Drynfells, just in case."

"Think I should?"

"The man is still missing."

Drynfells sighed. "Okay, I better do that."

The Aqua Azul bar was open. Kathy and Darrigan took a corner table, ordered pre-lunch cocktails. "You've gone off somewhere, Gil."

He smiled at her. "I am sorree!"

"What's bothering you?"

"I don't exactly know. Not yet. Excuse me. I want to make a call."

He left her and phoned Hartford from the lobby. He got his assistant on the line. "Robby, I don't know what source to use for this, but find me the names of any men who have sold chains of movie houses in Kansas during the past year."

Robby whistled softly. "Let me see. There ought to be a trade publication that would have that dope. Phone you?"

"I'll call back at five."

"How does it look?"

"It begins to have the smell of murder."

"By the beneficiary, we hope?"

"Nope. No such luck."

"So we'll get a statistic for the actuarial boys. Luck, Gil. I'll rush that dope."

"Thanks, Robby. 'Bye."

He had sandwiches in the bar with Kathy and then gave her her instructions for the afternoon. "Any kind of gossip, rumor, anything at all you can pick up on the Drynfellses. Financial condition. Emotional condition. Do they throw pots? Where did he find the cutie?"

"Cute, like a derringer."

"I think I know what you mean."

"Of course you do, Gil. No woman is going to fool you long, or twice."

"That's what I keep telling myself."

"I hope, wherever your lady fair might be, that she realizes by now what she missed."

"You get too close for comfort sometimes, Kathy."

"Just love to see people wince. All right. This afternoon I shall be the Jack Anderson of Madeira Beach and vicinity. When do I report?"

"When I meet you for cocktails. Sixish?"

On the way back to Clearwater Beach he looked in on Dinah Davisson. There were dark shadows under her eyes. Temple Davisson's daughter had been reached. She was flying south. Mrs. Hoke had brought over a cake. Darrigan told her he had a hunch he'd have some real information by midnight. After he left he wondered why he had put himself out on a limb.

At four-thirty he grew impatient and phoned Robby. A James C. Brock had sold a nine-unit chain in central Kansas in July.

Darrigan thanked him. It seemed like a hopeless task to try to locate Brock in the limited time before he would have to leave for Redington Beach. He phoned Dinah Davisson and told her to see what she could do about finding James Brock. He told her to try all the places he might stop, starting at the most expensive and working her way down the list.

He told her that once she had located Mr. Brock she should sit tight and wait for a phone call from him.

Kathy was waiting at her cabaña. "Do I report right now, sir?"

"Right now, Operative Seventy-three."

"Classification one: financial. Pooie. That Coral Tour thing ran way over estimates. It staggers under a mortgage. And he got a loan on his beach property to help out. The dollie is no help in the financial department. She's of the gimme breed. A Cuban. Miami. Possibly nightclub training. Drynfells's first wife died several centuries ago. The local pitch is that he put that plot of land on the market to get the dough to cover some postdated checks that are floating around waiting to fall on him."

"Nice work, Kathy."

"I'm not through yet. Classification two: Emotional. Pooie again. His little item has him twisted around her pinkie. She throws pots. She raises merry hell. She has tantrums. He does the housekeeping chores. She has a glittering eye for a pair of shoulders, broad shoulders. Myron is very jealous of his lady."

"Any more?"

"Local opinion is that if he sells his land and lasts until the winter season is upon him, he may come out all right, provided he doesn't have to buy his little lady a brace of Mercedeses and minks to keep in good favor. He's not liked too well around here. Not a sociable sort, I'd judge. And naturally the wife doesn't mix too well with the standard-issue wives hereabouts."

"You did very well, Kathy."

"Now what do we do?"

"I buy you drinks. I buy you dinner. Reward for services rendered."

"Then what?"

"Then we ponder."

"We can ponder while we're working over the taste buds, can't we?"

"If you'd like to ponder."

They went up to the bar. Martinis came. Kathy said, "I ponder out loud. Davisson's offer was too low. But he waved his money about. They brooded over that money all day. He came back and waved it about some more. Mrs. Drynfells's acquisitive instincts were aroused. She followed him, met him outside of here, clunked him on the head, pitched him in the Gulf, and went home and hid the money under the bed."

"Nice, but I don't like it."

"Okay. You ponder."

"Like this. Drynfells lied from the beginning. He sold the land to Temple Davisson. They went back. Drynfells took the bundle of cash, possibly a check for the balance. Those twenty minutes inside was when some sort of document was being executed.

Davisson mentions where he's going. In the afternoon Drynfells gets a better offer for the land. He stalls the buyer. He gets hold of Davisson and asks him to come back. Davisson does so. Drynfells wants to cancel the sale. Maybe he offers Davisson a bonus to tear up the document and take his money and check back. Davisson laughs at him. Drynfells asks for just a little bit of time. Davisson says he'll give him a little time. He'll be at the Aqua Azul for twenty minutes. From here he phones his wife. Can't get her. Makes eyes at you. Leaves. Drynfells, steered by his wife's instincts, has dropped her off and gone up the road a bit. She waits by Temple Davisson's car. He comes out. He is susceptible, as Mrs. Drynfells has guessed, to a little night walk with a very pretty young lady. She walks him up the road to where Drynfells is waiting. They bash him, tumble him into the Drynfells car, remove document of sale, dispose of body. That leaves them with the wad of cash, plus the money from the sale to the new customer Drynfells stalled. The weak point was the possibility of Davisson's car being seen at their place. That little scene we witnessed this morning had the flavor of being very well rehearsed."

Kathy snapped her fingers, eyes glowing. "It fits! Every little bit of it fits. They couldn't do it there, when he came back, because that would have left them with the car. He had to be seen someplace else. Here."

"There's one fat flaw, Kathy."

"How could there be?"

Just how do we go about proving it?"

She thought that over. Her face fell. "I see what you mean."

"I don't think that the dark-haired girl he was seen with could be identified as Mrs. Drynfells. Without evidence that the sale was consummated, we lack motive—except, of course, for the possible motive of murder for the money he carried."

Kathy sat with her chin propped on the backs of her fingers, studying him. "I wouldn't care to have you on my trail, Mr. Darrigan."

"How so?"

"You're very impressive, in your quiet little way, hiding behind that mask."

"A mask, yet."

"Of course. And behind it you sit, equipped with extra senses, catching the scent of murder, putting yourself neatly in the murderer's shoes, with all your reasoning based on emotions, not logic."

"I'm very logical. I plod. And I now plod out to the phone and see if logic has borne any fruit."

He went to the lobby and phoned Dinah Davisson.

"I found him, Mr. Darrigan. He's staying at the Kingfisher with his wife."

"Did you talk to him?"

"No. Just to the desk clerk."

"Thanks. You'll hear from me later, Mrs. Davisson."

He phoned the Kingfisher and had Mr. Brock called from the dining room to the phone. "Mr. Brock, my name is Darrigan. Mr. Temple Davisson told me you were interested in a plot of Gulf-front land.

"Has he been found?"

"No, he hasn't. I'm wondering if you're still in the market."

"Sorry, I'm not. I think I'm going to get the piece I want."

"At Redington Beach?"

Brock had a deep voice. "How did you know that?"

"Just a guess, Mr. Brock. Would you mind telling me who you're buying it from?"

"A Mr. Drynfells. He isn't an agent. It's his land."

"He contacted you last Friday, I suppose. In the afternoon?"

"You must have a crystal ball, Mr. Darrigan. Yes, he did. And he came in to see me late Friday night. We inspected the land Sunday. I suppose you even know what I'll be paying for it."

"Probably around one seventy-five."

"That's too close for comfort, Mr. Darrigan."

"Sorry to take you away from your dinner for no good reason. Thanks for being so frank with me."

"Quite all right."

Gilbert Darrigan walked slowly back into the bar. Kathy studied him. "Now you're even more impressive, Gil. Your eyes have gone cold."

"I feel cold. Right down into my bones. I feel this way when I've guessed a bit too accurately." She listened, eyes narrowed, as he told her the conversation.

"Mr. Drynfells had a busy Friday," she said.

"Now we have the matter of proof."

"How do you go about that? Psychological warfare, perhaps?"

"Not with that pair. They're careful. They're too selfish to have very much imagination. I believe we should consider the problem of the body."

She sipped her drink, stared over his head at the far wall. "The dramatic place, of course, would be under the concrete of that new pool, with the dark greedy wife sunbathing beside it, sleepy-eyed and callous."

He reached across the table and put his fingers hard around her wrist. "You are almost beyond price, Kathy. That is exactly where it is."

She looked faintly ill. "No," she said weakly. "I was only—"

"You thought you were inventing. But your subconscious mind knew, as mine did."

It was not too difficult to arrange. The call had to come from Clearwater. They drove there in Kathy's car, and Darrigan, lowering his voice, said to Drynfells over the phone, "I've got my lawyer here and I'd like you to come in right now, Mr. Drynfells. Bring your wife with you. We'll make it business and pleasure both."

"I don't know as I—"

"I have to make some definite arrangement, Mr. Drynfells. If I can't complete the deal with you, I'll have to pick up a different plot."

"But you took an option. Mr. Brock!"

"I can forfeit that, Mr. Drynfells. How soon can I expect you?"

After a long pause Drynfells said, "We'll leave here in twenty minutes."

On the way back out to Madeira Beach, Darrigan drove as fast as he dared. Kathy refused to be dropped off at the Aqua Azul. The Coral Tour Haven was dark, the "No Vacancy" sign lighted.

They walked out to the dark back yard, Kathy carrying the flash, Darrigan carrying the borrowed pickaxe. He found the valve to empty the shallow pool, turned it. He stood by Kathy. She giggled nervously as the water level dropped.

"We'd better not be wrong," she said.

"We're not wrong," Darrigan murmured. The water took an infuriating time to drain out of the pool. He rolled up his pants legs, pulled off shoes and socks, stepped down in when there was a matter of inches left. The cement had set firmly. It took several minutes to break through to the soil underneath. Then, using the pick point as a lever, he broke a piece free. He got his hands on it and turned it over. The flashlight wavered. Only the soil underneath was visible. Again he inserted a curved side of the pick, leaned his weight against it, lifted it up slowly. The flashlight beam focused on the side of a muddy white shoe, a gray sock encasing a heavy ankle. The light went out and Kathy Marrick made a moaning sound, deep in her throat.

Darrigan lowered the broken slab back into position, quite gently. He climbed out of the pool.

"Are you all right?" he asked.

"I . . . think so."

He rolled down his pants legs, pulled socks on over wet feet, shoved his feet into the shoes, laced them neatly and tightly.

"How perfectly dreadful," Kathy said in a low tone.

"It always is. Natural death is enough to give us a sort of superstitious fear. But violent death always seems obscene. An assault against the dignity of every one of us. Now we do some phoning."

They waited, afterwards, in the dark car parked across the road. When the Drynfellses returned home, two heavy men advanced on their car from either side, guns drawn, flashlights steady. There was no fuss. No struggle. Just the sound of heavy voices in the night, and a woman's spiritless weeping.

At the Aqua Azul, Kathy put her hand in his. "I won't see you again," she said. It was statement, not question.

"I don't believe so, Kathy."

"Take care of yourself." The words had a special intonation. She made her real meaning clear: Gil, don't let too many of these things happen to you. Don't go too far away from life and from warmth. Don't go to that far place where you are conscious only of evil and the effects of evil.

"I'll try to," he said.

As he drove away from her, drove down the dark road that paralleled the beaches, he thought of her as another chance lost, as another milepost on a lonely road that ended at some unguessable destination. There was a shifting sourness in his mind, an unease that was familiar. He drove with his eyes steady, his face fashioned into its mask of tough unconcern. Each time, you bled a little. And each time the hard flutter of excitement ended in this sourness. Murder for money. It was seldom anything else. It was seldom particularly clever. It was invariably brutal.

Dinah Davisson's house was brightly lighted. The other houses on the street were dark. He had asked that he be permitted to inform her.

She was in the long pastel living room, a man and a woman with her. She had been crying, but she was undefeated. She carried her head high. Something hardened and tautened within him when he saw the red stripes on her cheek, stripes that only fingers could have made, in anger.

"Mr. Darrigan, this is Miss Davisson and Colonel Davisson."

They were tall people. Temple had his father's hard jaw, shrewd eye. The woman was so much like him that it was almost ludicrous. Both of them were very cool, very formal, slightly patronizing.

"You are from Guardsman Life?" Colonel Davisson asked. "Bit unusual for you to be here, isn't it?"

"Not entirely. I'd like to speak to you alone, Mrs. Davisson."

Anything you wish to say to her can be said in front of us," Alicia Davisson said acidly.

"I'd prefer to speak to her alone," Gil said, quite softly.

"It doesn't matter, Mr. Darrigan," the young widow said.

"The police have found your husband's body," he said bluntly, knowing that bluntness was more merciful than trying to cushion the blow with mealy half-truths.

Dinah closed her lovely eyes, kept them closed for long seconds. Her hand tightened on the arm of the chair and then relaxed. "How—"

"I knew a stupid marriage of this sort would end in some kind of disaster," Alicia said.

The cruelty of that statement took Darrigan's breath for a moment. Shock gave way to anger. The colonel walked to the dark windows, looked out into the night, hands locked behind him, head bowed.

Alicia rapped a cigarette briskly on her thumbnail, lighted it.

"Marriage had nothing to do with it," Darrigan said. "He was murdered for the sake of profit. He was murdered by a thoroughly unpleasant little man with a greedy wife."

"And our young friend here profits nicely," Alicia said.

Dinah stared at her. "How on earth can you say a thing like that when you've just found out? You're his daughter. It doesn't seem—"

"Kindly spare us the violin music," Alicia said.

"I don't want any of the insurance money," Dinah said. "I don't want any part of it. You two can have it. All of it."

The colonel wheeled slowly and stared at her. He wet his lips. "Do you mean that?"

Dinah lifted her chin. "I mean it."

The colonel said ingratiatingly, "You'll have the trust fund, of course, as it states in the will. That certainly will be enough to take care of you."

"I don't know as I want that, either."

"We can discuss that later," the colonel said soothingly. "This is a great shock to all of us. Darrigan, can you draw up some sort of document she can sign where she relinquishes her claim as principal beneficiary?" When he spoke to Darrigan, his voice had a Pentagon crispness.

Darrigan had seen this too many times before. Money had changed the faces of the children. A croupier would recognize that glitter in the eyes, that moistness of mouth. Darrigan looked at Dinah. Her face was proud, unchanged.

"I could, I suppose. But I won't," Darrigan said.

"Don't be impudent. If you can't, a lawyer can."

Darrigan spoke very slowly, very distinctly. "Possibly you don't understand, Colonel. The relationship between insurance company and policyholder is one of trust. A policyholder does not name his principal beneficiary through whim. We have accepted his money over a period of years. We intend to see that his wishes are carried out. The policy options state that his widow will have an excellent income during her lifetime. She does not receive a lump sum, except for a single payment of ten thousand. What she does with the income is her own business, once it is received. She can give it to you, if she wishes."

"I couldn't accept that sort of . . . charity," the colonel said stiffly. "You heard her state her wishes, man! She wants to give up all claims against the policies."

Darrigan allowed himself a smile. "She's only trying to dissociate herself from you two scavengers. She has a certain amount of pride. She is mourning her husband. Maybe you can't understand that."

"Throw him out, Tem," Alicia whispered.

The colonel had turned white. "I shall do exactly that," he said.

Dinah stood up slowly, her face white. "Leave my house," she said.

The colonel turned toward her. "What do—"

"Yes, the two of you. You and your sister. Leave my house at once."

The tension lasted for long seconds. Dinah's eyes didn't waver. Alicia shattered the moment by standing up and saying, in tones of infinite disgust, "Come on, Tem. The only thing to do with that little bitch is start dragging her through the courts."

They left silently, wrapped in dignity like stained cloaks.

Dinah came to Darrigan. She put her face against his chest, her brow hard against the angle of his jaw. The sobs were tiny spasms, tearing her, contorting her.

He cupped the back of her head in his hand, feeling a sense of wonder at the silk texture of her hair, at the tender outline of fragile bone underneath. Something more than forgotten welled up within him, stinging his eyes, husking his voice as he said, "They aren't worth . . . this."

"He . . . was worth . . . more than . . . this," she gasped.

The torment was gone as suddenly as it had come. She stepped back, rubbing at streaming eyes with the backs of her hands, the way a child does.

"I'm sorry," she said. She tried to smile. "You're not a wailing wall."

"Part of my official duties, sometimes."

"Can they turn this into . . . nastiness?"

"They have no basis. He was of sound mind when he made the provisions. They're getting enough. More than enough. Some people can never have enough."

"I'd like to sign it over."

"Your husband had good reasons for setting it up the way he did."

"Perhaps."

"Do you have anyone to help you?" he asked impulsively. He knew at once he had put too much of what he felt in his voice. He tried to cover by saying, "There'll be a lot of arrangements. I mean, it could be considered part of my job."

He detected the faintly startled look in her eyes. Awareness made them awkward. "Thank you very much, Mr. Darrigan. I think Brad will help."

"Can you get that woman over to stay with you tonight?"

"I'll be all right."

He left her and went back to the beach to his room. In the morning he would make whatever official statements were considered necessary. He lay in the darkness and thought of Dinah, of the way she was a promise of warmth, of integrity.

And, being what he was, he began to look for subterfuge in her attitude, for some evidence that her reactions had been part of a clever act. He ended by despising himself for having gone so far that he could instinctively trust no one.

In the morning he phoned the home office. He talked with Palmer, a vice-president. He said, "Mr. Palmer, I'm sending through the necessary reports approving payment of the claim."

"It's a bloody big one," Palmer said disconsolately.

"I know that, sir," Darrigan said. "No way out of it."

"Well, I suppose you'll be checking in then by, say, the day after tomorrow?"

"That should be about right."

Darrigan spent the rest of the day going through motions. He signed the lengthy statement for the police. The Drynfellses were claiming that in the scuffle for the paper, Davisson had fallen and hit his head on a bumper guard. In panic they had hidden the body. It was dubious as to whether premeditation could be proved.

He dictated his report for the company files to a public stenographer, sent it off airmail. He turned the car in, packed his bag. He sat on the edge of his bed for a long time, smoking cigarettes, looking at the far wall.

The thought of heading north gave him a monstrous sense of loss. He argued with himself. Fool, she's just a young, well-heeled widow. All that sort of thing was canceled out when Doris left you. What difference does it make that she should remind you of what you had once thought Doris was?

He looked into the future and saw a long string of hotel rooms, one after the other, like a child's blocks aligned on a dark carpet.

If she doesn't laugh in your face, and if your daydream should turn out to be true, they'll nudge each other and talk about how Gil Darrigan fell into a soft spot.

She'll laugh in your face.

He phoned at quarter of five and caught Palmer. "I'd like to stay down here and do what I can for the beneficiary, Mr. Palmer. A couple of weeks, maybe."

"Isn't that a bit unusual?"

"I have a vacation overdue, if you'd rather I didn't do it on company time."

"Better make it vacation, then."

"Anything you say. Will you put it through for me?"

"Certainly, Gil."

At dusk she came down the hall, looked through the screen at him. She was wearing black.

He felt like a kid trying to make his first date. "I thought I could stay around a few days and . . . help out. I don't want you to think I—"

She swung the door open. "Somehow I knew you wouldn't leave," she said.

He stepped into the house, with a strange feeling of trumpets and banners. She hadn't laughed. And he knew in that moment that during the years ahead, the good years ahead of them, she would always know what was in his heart, even before he would know it. And one day, perhaps within the year, she would turn all that warmth suddenly toward him, and it would be like coming in out of a cold and rainy night.

ROBERT VAN GULIK
The Morning of the Monkey

JUDGE DEE was enjoying the cool summer morning in the open gallery built along the rear of his official residence. He had just finished breakfast inside with his family, and now was having his tea there all alone, as had become his fixed habit during the year he had been serving as magistrate of the lake district Hay-yuan. He had drawn his rattan armchair close to the carved marble balustrade. Slowly stroking his long black beard, he gazed up contentedly at the tall trees and dense undergrowth covering the mountain slope that rose directly in front of the gallery like a protecting wall of cool verdure. From it came the busy twitter of small birds, and the murmur of the cascade farther along. It was a pity, he thought, that these relaxed moments of peaceful enjoyment were so brief. Presently he would have to go to the chancery in the front section of the tribunal compound, and have a look at the official correspondence that had come in.

Suddenly there was the sound of rustling leaves and breaking twigs. Two furry black shapes came rushing through the treetops, swinging from branch to branch by their long, thin arms, and leaving a rain of falling leaves in their wake. The judge looked after the gibbons with a smile. He never tired of admiring their lithe grace as they came speeding past. Shy as they were, the gibbons living on the mountain slope had become accustomed to that solitary figure sitting there every morning. Sometimes one of them would stop for one brief moment and deftly catch the banana Judge Dee threw at him.

Again the leaves rustled. Now another gibbon came into sight. He moved slowly, using only one long arm and his hand-like feet.

He was carrying a small object in his left hand. The gibbon halted in front of the gallery and, perched on a lower branch, darted an inquisitive look at the judge from his round, brown eyes. Now Judge Dee saw what the animal had in his left hand: it was a golden ring with a large, sparkling green stone. He knew that gibbons often snatch small objects that catch their fancy, but also that their interest is short-lived, especially if they find they can't eat what they have picked up. If he couldn't make the gibbon drop the ring then and there, he would throw it away somewhere in the forest, and the owner would never recover it.

Since the judge had no fruit at hand to distract the gibbon's attention from the ring, he quickly took his tinderbox from his sleeve and began to arrange its contents on the tea-table, carefully examining and sniffing at each object. He saw out of the corner of his eye that the gibbon was watching him. Soon he let the ring drop, swung himself down to the lowest branch and remained hanging there by his long, spidery arms, following Judge Dee's every gesture with eager interest. The judge noticed that a few blades of straw were sticking to the gibbon's black fur. He couldn't hold the fickle animal's attention for long. The gibbon called out a friendly "Wak wak!" then swung itself up onto a higher branch, and disappeared among the green leaves.

Judge Dee stepped over the balustrade and down onto the moss-covered boulders that lined the foot of the mountain slope. Soon he had spotted the glittering ring. He picked it up and climbed back onto the gallery. A closer examination proved that it was rather large, evidently a man's ring. It consisted of two intertwined dragons of solid gold, and the emerald was unusually big and of excellent quality. The owner would be glad to get this valuable antique specimen back. Just when he was about to put the ring away in his sleeve, his eye fell on a few rust-brown spots on its inside. Creasing his bushy eyebrows, he brought the ring closer. The stains looked uncommonly like dried blood.

He turned round and clapped his hands. When his old house steward came shuffling out to the gallery, he asked:

"What houses stand on the mountain slope over there, steward?"

"There are none, sir. The slope is much too steep, and covered entirely by the dense forest. There are several villas on top of the ridge, though."

"Yes, I remember having seen those summer villas. Do you happen to know who is living there?"

"Well, sir, the pawnbroker Leng, for instance. And also Wang, the pharmacist."

"Leng I don't know. And Wang, you say? I suppose you mean the owner of the large pharmacy in the marketplace, opposite the Temple of Confucius? A small, dapper fellow, always looking rather worried?"

"Yes indeed, sir. He has good reasons to look worried, too, sir. His business isn't going very well this year, I heard. And his only son is mentally defective. He'll be twenty next year, and still he can neither read nor write. I don't know what is to become of a boy like that. . . ."

Judge Dee nodded absentmindedly. The villas on the ridge were out, for gibbons are too shy to venture into an inhabited area. He could have picked it up, of course, in a quiet corner of a large garden up there. But even then he would have thrown it away long before he had traversed the forest and arrived at the foot of the slope. The gibbon must have found the ring much farther down.

He dismissed the steward and had another look at the ring. The glitter of the emerald seemed to have become dull suddenly, it had become a somber eye that fixed him with a mournful stare. Annoyed at his discomfiture, he quickly put it back into his sleeve. He would issue a public notice describing the ring, and then the owner would soon present himself at the tribunal and that would be the end of it. He went inside, and walked through his residence to his front garden, and from there on to the large central courtyard of the tribunal compound.

It was fairly cool there, for the big buildings surrounding the yard protected it from the morning sun. The headman of the constables was inspecting the equipment of a dozen of his men, lined up in the center of the courtyard. All sprang to attention when they saw the magistrate approaching. Judge Dee was about to walk past them, on to the chancery over on the other side, when a sudden thought made him halt in his steps. He asked the headman:

"Do you know of any inhabited place in the forest on the mountain slope, behind my residence?"

"No, Your Honor, there are no houses, as far as I know. Halfway up there is a hut, though. A small log cabin, formerly used by a woodcutter. It has been standing empty for a long time now." Then he added importantly: "Vagabonds often stay there for the night, sir. That's why I go up there regularly. Just to see that they make no mischief."

This might fit. In a deserted hut, halfway up the slope. . . .

"What do you call regularly?" he asked sharply.

"Well, I mean to say . . . once every five or six weeks, sir. I. . . ."

"I don't call that regularly!" the judge interrupted him curtly. "I expect you to. . . ." He broke off in mid-sentence. This wouldn't do. A vague, uneasy feeling oughtn't to make him lose his temper. It must be the savory sitting heavily on his stomach that had spoiled his pleasant, relaxed mood. He shouldn't take meat with the morning rice. . . . He resumed, in a more friendly manner:

"How far is that hut from here, headman?"

"A quarter of an hour's walk, sir. On the narrow footpath that leads up the slope."

"Right. Call Tao Gan here!"

The headman ran to the chancery. He came back with a gaunt, elderly man, clad in a long robe of faded brown cotton and with a high square cap of black gauze on his head. He had a long, melancholy face with a drooping moustache and a wispy chinbeard, and three long hairs waxed from the wart on his left cheek. When Tao Gan had wished his chief a good morning, Judge Dee took his assistant to the corner of the yard. He showed him the ring and told him how he had got it. "You notice the dried blood sticking to it. Probably the owner cut his hand when taking a walk in the forest. He took the ring off before washing his hand in the brook, and then the gibbon snatched it. Since it is quite a valuable piece, and since we have still an hour before the morning session begins, we'll go up there and have a look. Perhaps the owner is still wandering about searching for his ring. Were there any important letters by the morning courier?"

Tao Gan's long, sallow face fell as he replied:

"There was a brief note from Chiang-pei, from our Sergeant Hoong, sir. He reports that Ma Joong and Chiao Tai haven't yet succeeded in discovering a clue."

Judge Dee frowned. Sergeant Hoong and his two other lieutenants had left for the neighboring district of Chiang-pei two days before, in order to assist Judge Dee's colleague there who was working on a difficult case with ramifications in his own district. "Well," he said with a sigh, "let's go. A brisk walk will do us

good!" He beckoned the headman and told him to accompany
them with two constables.

They left the tribunal compound by the back door, and, a little
way along the narrow mud road, the headman took a footpath
that led up into the forest.

The path rose gradually in a zig-zag pattern but it was still a
stiff climb. They met nobody and the only sound they heard was
the twittering of the birds, high up in the treetops. After about a
quarter of an hour the headman halted and pointed at a cluster
of tall trees farther up.

"There it is, sir!" he announced.

Soon they found themselves in a small clearing surrounded by
high oak trees. In the rear stood a small log cabin with a mossy
thatched roof. The door was closed, the only window shuttered.
In front stood a chopping block made of an old tree trunk; beside
it was a heap of straw. It was still as the grave; the place seemed
completely deserted.

Judge Dee walked through the tall, wet grass and pulled the
door open. In the semi-dark interior he saw a deal table with two
footstools, and against the back wall a bare plank bed. On the
floor in front lay the still figure of a man, clad in a jacket and
trousers of faded blue cloth. His jaw was sagging, his glazed eyes
wide open.

The judge quickly turned around and ordered the headman to
open the shutters. Then he and Tao Gan squatted down by the
side of the prone figure. It was an elderly man, thin but rather
tall. He had a broad, regular face with a grey moustache and a
short, neatly trimmed goatee. The grey hair on top of the head
was a mass of clotted blood. The right hand was folded over the
breast, the left stretched out, close against the side of the body.
Judge Dee tried to lift the arm but found it had stiffened completely. "Must have died late last night!" he muttered.

"What happened to his left hand, sir?" Tao Gan asked.

Four fingers had been cut off just at the last joint, leaving only
blood-covered stumps. Only the thumb was intact.

The judge studied the sunburnt, mutilated hand carefully.

"Do you see that narrow band of white skin around the index,
Tao Gan? Its irregular outline corresponds to that of the intertwined
dragons of the emerald ring. My hunch was right. This is the
owner, and he was murdered." He got up and told the headman,
"Let your men carry the corpse outside!"

While the two constables were dragging the dead man away, Judge Dee and Tao Gan quickly searched the hut. The floor, the table and the two stools were covered by a thick layer of dust, but the plank bed had been cleaned very thoroughly. They did not see a single bloodstain. Pointing at the many confused footprints in the dust on the floor, Tao Gan remarked:

"Evidently a number of people were about here last night. This print here would seem to be left by a small, pointed woman's shoe. And that there by a man's shoe, and a very big one too!"

The judge nodded. He studied the floor a while, then said: "I don't see any traces of the body having been dragged across the floor, so it must have been carried inside. They neatly cleaned the plank bed. Then, instead of putting the body there, they deposited it on the floor! Strange affair! Well, let's have a second look at the corpse."

Outside Judge Dee pointed at the heap of straw and resumed:

"Everything fits, Tao Gan. I noticed a few blades of straw clinging to the gibbon's fur. When the body was being carried to the hut, the ring slipped from the stump of the left index and fell into the straw. When the gibbon passed by here early this morning, his sharp eyes spotted the glittering object among the straw, and he picked it up. It took us a quarter of an hour to come here along the winding path, but as the crow flies it's but a short distance from here to the trees at the foot of the slope, behind my house. It took the gibbon very little time to rush down through the treetops."

Tao Gan stooped and examined the chopping block.

"There are no traces of blood here, sir. And the four cut-off fingers are nowhere to be seen."

"Evidently the man was mutilated and murdered somewhere else," the judge said. "His dead body was carried up here afterwards."

"Then the murderer must have been a hefty fellow, sir. It isn't an easy job to carry a body all the way up here. Unless the murderer had assistance, of course."

"Search him!"

As Tao Gan began to go through the dead man's clothes, Judge Dee carefully examined the head. He thought that the skull must have been bashed in from behind, with a fairly small but heavy instrument, probably an iron hammer. Then he studied the intact right hand. The palm and the inside of the fingers were rather horny, but the nails were fairly long and well kept.

"There's absolutely nothing, sir!" Tao Gan exclaimed as he righted himself. "Not even a handerchief! The murderer must have taken away everything that could have led to the identification of his victim."

"We do have the ring, however," the judge observed. "He had doubtless planned to take that too. When he found it missing, he must have realized that it fell off the mutilated hand somewhere on the way here. He probably searched for it with a lantern, but in vain." He turned to the headman, who was chewing on a toothpick with a bored look, and asked curtly: "Ever seen this man before?"

The headman sprang to attention.

"No, Your Honor. Never!" He cast a questioning look at the two constables. When they shook their heads, he added: "Must be a vagabond from up-country, sir."

"Tell your men to make a stretcher from a couple of thick branches and take the body to the tribunal. Let the clerks and the rest of the court personnel file past it, and see whether any of them knows the man. After you have warned the coroner, go to Mr. Wang's pharmacy in the marketplace, and ask him to come and see me in my office."

While walking downhill Tao Gan asked curiously:

"Do you think that pharmacist knows more about this, sir?"

"Oh no. But it had just occurred to me that the dead body might as well have been carried down as up hill! Therefore I want to ask Wang whether there was a fight among vagabonds or other riffraff on the ridge last night. At the same time I want to ask him who else is living there, beside himself and that pawnbroker Leng. Heaven, my robe is caught!"

As Tao Gan was prying loose the thorny branch, Judge Dee went on: "The dead man's dress points to a laborer or an artisan, but he has the face of an intellectual. And his sunburned and calloused but well-kept hand suggests an educated man of means, who likes to live outdoors. I conclude that he was a man of means from the fact that he possessed that expensive emerald ring."

Tao Gan remained silent the rest of the way. When they had arrived at the mud road, however, he said slowly:

"I don't think that the expensive ring proves that the man was rich, sir. Vagrant crooks are very superstitious as a rule. They will often hang on to a piece of stolen jewelry, just because they believe it brings them good luck."

"Quite. Well, I'll go and change now, for I am wet all over. You'll find me presently, in my private office."

After Judge Dee had taken a bath and changed into his ceremonial robe of green brocade, he had just time for one cup of tea. Then Tao Gan helped him to put the black winged judge's cap on his head, and they went together to the court hall, adjoining Judge Dee's private office. Only a few routine matters came up, so the judge could rap his gavel and close the session after only half an hour. Back in his private office, he seated himself behind his large writing desk, pushed the pile of official documents aside and placed the emerald ring before him. Then he took his folding fan from his sleeve and said, pointing with it at the ring:

"A queer case, Tao Gan! What could those cut-off fingers mean? That the murderer tortured his victim prior to killing him, in order to make him tell something? Or did he cut the fingers off after the murder, because they bore some mark or other that might prove the dead man's identity?"

Tao Gan did not reply at once. He poured a cup of hot tea for the judge, then sat down again on the stool in front of the desk and began, slowly pulling at the three long hairs that sprouted from his left cheek:

"Since the four fingers seem to have been cut off together with one blow, I think your second supposition is right, sir. According to our headman, that deserted hut was often used by vagabonds. Now, many of those vagrant ruffians are organized in regular gangs or secret brotherhoods. Every prospective member must swear an oath of allegiance to the leader of the gang and, as proof of his sincerity and his courage, himself solemnly cut off the tip of his left little finger. If this is indeed a gang murder, then the killers may well have hacked off the four fingers in order to conceal the mutilation of the little finger, and thus destroy an important clue to the background of the crime."

Judge Dee tapped his fan on the desk.

"Excellent reasoning, Tao Gan. Let's start by assuming that you are right. In that case. . . ."

There was a knock on the door. The coroner came in and respectfully greeted the judge. He placed a filled-out official form on the desk and said:

"This is my autopsy report, Your Honor. I have written in all details, except the name, of course. The deceased must have been about fifty years old, and he was apparently in good health. I didn't find either any bodily defects, or larger birthmarks or scars. There were no bruises or other signs of violence. He was killed by one blow on the back of his head, presumably from an iron hammer, small but heavy. Four fingers of the left hand have been chopped off, either directly before or after the murder. He must have been killed late last night."

The coroner scratched his head, then resumed somewhat diffidently:

"I must confess that I am rather puzzled by those missing fingers, sir. I could not make out how exactly they were cut off. The bones of the remaining stumps are not crushed, the flesh along the cuts is not bruised, and the skin shows no ragged ends. The hand must have been spread out on a flat surface, then all four fingers chopped off at the same time by one blow of some heavy, razor-edged cutting tool. If it had been done with a large axe, or a two-handed sword, one would never have obtained that perfectly straight, clean cut. I really don't know what to think!"

Judge Dee glanced through the report. Looking up, he asked the coroner:

"What about his feet?"

"Their condition pointed to a tramp, sir. Callosities in the usual places, and torn toenails. The feet of a man who walks a great deal, often barefooted."

"I see. Did anybody recognize him?"

"No sir. I was present while the personnel of the tribunal filed past the dead body. Nobody had ever seen him before."

"Thank you. You may go."

The headman, who had been waiting in the corridor till the interview was over, now came in and reported that Mr. Wang, the pharmacist, had arrived.

Judge Dee closed his fan. "Show him in!" he ordered the headman.

The pharmacist was a small, dapper man with a slight stoop, very neatly dressed in a robe of black silk and square black cap. He had a pale, rather reserved face, marked by a jet-black moustache and goatee. After he had made his bow, Judge Dee told him affably:

"Do sit down, Mr. Wang! We are not in the tribunal here. I

am sorry to disturb you, but I need some information on the situation up on the ridge. During the daytime you are always in your shop in the marketplace, of course, but I assume that you pass the evening and night in your mountain villa?"

"Yes indeed, Your Honor," Wang replied in a cultured, measured voice. "It's much cooler up there than here in town, this time of year."

"Precisely. I heard that some ruffians created a disturbance up there last night."

"No, everything was quiet last night, sir. It is true that all kinds of tramps and other riffraff are about there. They pass the night in the forest, because they are afraid to enter the city at a late hour when the nightwatch might arrest them. The presence of those scoundrels is the only drawback of that otherwise most desirable neighborhood. Sometimes we hear them shout and quarrel on the road, but all the villas there, including mine, have a high outer wall, so we need not be afraid of attempts at robbery, and we just ignore them."

"I would appreciate it if you would also ask your servants, Mr. Wang. The disturbance may not have taken place on the highway, but behind your house, in the wood."

"I can inform Your Honor now that they haven't seen or heard anything. I was at home the entire evening, and none of us went out. You might ask Mr. Leng, the pawnbroker, sir. He lives next door, and he . . . he keeps rather irregular hours."

"Who else is living there, Mr. Wang?"

"At the moment nobody, sir. There are three more villas, but those belong to wealthy merchants from the capital who come for their summer holiday only. All three are standing empty now."

"I see. Well, thanks very much, Mr. Wang. Would you mind going to the mortuary with the headman? I want you to have a look at the dead body of a vagabond, and let me know whether you have seen him in your neighborhood lately."

After the pharmacist had taken his leave with a low bow, Tao Gan said:

"We must also reckon with the possibility that the man was murdered here in town, sir. In a winehouse or in a low class brothel."

Judge Dee shook his head.

"If that had been the case, Tao Gan, they would have hidden the body under the floor, or thrown it in a dry well. They would never have dared take the risk of conveying it to the mountain slope, for then they would have been obliged to pass close by this tribunal." He took the ring from his sleeve again and handed it to Tao Gan. "When the coroner came in, I was just about to ask you to go down into the town and show this ring around in the small pawnshops there. You can do so now. You needn't worry about the routine of the chancery, Tao Gan! I shall take care of that, this morning."

He dismissed his lieutenant with an encouraging smile, then he began to sort out the official correspondence that had come in that morning. He had the dossiers he needed fetched from the archives, and set to work. He was disturbed only once, when the headman came in to report that Mr. Wang had viewed the body and stated that he did not recognize the dead tramp.

At noon the judge sent for a tray with rice gruel and salted vegetables and ate at his desk, attended upon by one of the chancery clerks. While sipping a cup of strong tea he went over in his mind the case of the murdered vagabond. He slowly shook his head. Although the facts that had come to light thus far pointed to a gang murder, he was still groping for another approach. He had to admit, however, that his doubts rested on flimsy grounds: just his impression that the dead man had not been a tramp, but an educated, intelligent man, and of a strong character. He decided that for the time being he would not communicate his indecision to his lieutenant. Tao Gan had been in his service only ten months, and he was so eager that the judge felt reluctant to discourage him by questioning the validity of his theory about the significance of the missing four fingers. And it would be very wrong to teach him to go by hunches rather than by facts!

With a sigh Judge Dee set his teacup down and pulled a bulky dossier towards him. It contained all the papers relating to the smuggling case in the neighboring district of Chiang-pei. Four days before, the military police had surprised three men who were trying to get two boxes across the river that formed the boundary between the two districts. The men had fled into the woods of Chiang-pei, leaving the boxes behind. They proved to be crammed with small packages containing gold and silver dust, camphor, mercury, and *ginseng*—the costly medicinal root imported from Korea—and all these goods were subject to a heavy road tax. Since the seizure had taken place in Chiang-pei, the case concerned Judge Dee's colleague, the magistrate of that district. But he happened to be short-handed and had requested Judge Dee's assistance. The judge had agreed at once, all the more readily since he suspected that the smugglers had accomplices in his own district. He had sent his trusted old adviser Sergeant Hoong to Chiang-pei, together with his two lieutenants Ma Joong and Chiao Tai. They had established their headquarters in the military guard-post, at the bridge that crossed the boundary river.

The judge took the sketchmap of the region from the file, and studied it intently. Ma Joong and Chiao Tai had scoured the woods with the military police, and interrogated the peasants living in the fields beyond, without discovering a single clue. It was an awkward affair, for the higher authorities always took a grave view of evasion of the road taxes. The Prefect, the direct superior of Judge Dee and his colleague of Chiang-pei, had sent the latter a peremptory note, stating that he expected quick results. He had added that the matter was urgent, for the large amount and the high cost of the contraband proved that it had not been an incidental attempt by local smugglers. They must have a powerful organization behind them that directed the operations. The three smugglers were only important in so far as they could give a lead to the identity of their principal. The metropolitan authorities suspected that a leading financier in the capital was the ringleader. If this master criminal was not tracked down, the smuggling would continue.

Shaking his head the judge poured himself another cup of tea.

Tao Gan came back to the marketplace dog tired and in a very bad temper. In the hot and smelly quarter behind the fishmarket down town, he had visited no less than six pawnshops and made exhaustive enquiries in a number of small gold and silver shops, and also in a few disreputable hostels and dosshouses. Nobody had ever seen an emerald ring with two entwined dragons, nor heard about a gang fight in or outside the city.

He went up the broad stone steps of the Temple of Confucius, crowded with the stalls of street vendors, and sat down on the bamboo stool in front of the stand of an oilcake hawker. Rubbing his sore legs he reflected sadly that he had failed in the first assignment Judge Dee had given him to carry out alone; for up to now he had always worked together with Ma Joong and Chiao Tai. He had lost this rare chance of proving his mettle! "It's true," he told himself, "that I lack the physical strength and experience in detecting of my colleagues, but I know as much as they about the ways and byways of the underworld, if not more! Why . . .?"

"This place is meant for business, not for taking a gratis rest!" the cake vendor told him sourly. "Besides, your long face keeps other customers away!"

Tao Gan have him a dirty look and invested five coppers in a handful of oilcakes. Those would have to do for his luncheon for he was a very parsimonious man. Munching the cakes, he let his eyes rove over the marketplace. He bestowed an envious look upon the beautiful front of Wang's pharmacy over on the other side, lavishly decorated with gold lacquer. The tall greystone building next door looked simple but dignified. Over the barred windows hung a small signboard reading. "Leng's Pawnshop."

"Vagabonds wouldn't patronize such a high-class pawnshop," Tao Gan muttered. "But since I am here anyway, I might as well have a look there too. And Leng has a villa on the ridge. He may have heard or seen something last night." He rose and elbowed his way through the market crowd.

About a dozen neatly dressed customers were standing in front of the high counter that ran across the high, spacious room, talking busily with the clerks. In the rear a large, fat man was sitting at a massive desk, working an enormous abacus with his white, podgy hands. He wore a wide grey robe, and a small black cap. Tao Gan reached into his capacious sleeve and handed to the nearest clerk an impressive red visiting card. It bore in large letters the inscription "Kan Tao, antique gold and silver bought and sold." And in the corner the address: the famous street of jewelers in the capital. This was one of the many faked visiting cards Tao Gan had used during his long career as a professional swindler; upon entering Judge Dee's service he had been unable to bring himself to do away with that choice collection.

When the clerk had shown the card to the fat man, he got up at once and came waddling to the counter. His round, haughty face was creased in a friendly smile when he asked:

"And what can we do for you today, sir?"

"I just want some confidential information, Mr. Leng. A fellow offered me an emerald ring at only one-third of the value. I suspect it has been stolen, and was wondering whether someone might have tried to pawn it here."

So speaking he took the ring from his sleeve and laid it on the counter.

Leng's face fell.

"No," he replied curtly, "never seen it before." Then he snapped at the cross-eyed clerk who was peeping over his shoulder: "None of your business!" To Tai Gan he added: "Very sorry I can't help you, Mr. Kan!" and went back to his desk.

The cross-eyed clerk winked at Tao Gan and pointed with his chin at the door. Tao Gan nodded and went outside. Seeing the red-marble bench in the porch of Wang's pharmacy next door, he sat there to wait.

Through the open window he watched with interest what was going on inside. Two shop assistants were turning pills between wooden disks, another was slicing a thick medicinal root on an iron chopping board by means of the huge cleaver attached to it by a hinge. Two of their colleagues were sorting out dried centipedes and spiders; Tao Gan knew that these substances, pounded in a mortar together with the exuviae of cicadas and then dissolved in warm wine, made an excellent cough medicine.

Suddenly he heard footsteps. The cross-eyed clerk came up to him and sat down by his side.

"That thick-skulled boss of mine didn't recognize you," the clerk said with a self-satisfied smirk, "but I placed you at once! I remember clearly having seen you in the tribunal, sitting at the table of the clerks!"

"Come to the point!" Tao Gan told him crossly.

"The point is that the fat bastard lied, my dear friend! He had seen that ring before. Had it in his hands, at the counter."

"Well, well. He has forgotten all about it, I suppose."

"Not on your life! That ring was brought to us two days ago, by a damned good-looking girl. Just as I was going to ask her whether she wanted to pawn it, the boss comes up and pushes me away. He is always after pretty young women, the old goat! Well, I watched them, but I couldn't hear what they were whispering about. Finally the wench picks up the ring again, and off she went."

"What kind of a woman was she?"

"Not a lady, that I can tell you! Dressed in a patched blue jacket and trousers, like a scullery maid. Holy heaven, if I were rich I wouldn't mind having a maid like that about the house, not a bit! Wasn't she a stunner! Anyway, my boss is a crook, I tell you. He's mixed up in all kinds of shady deals, and he also cheats with his taxes."

"You don't seem very fond of your boss."

"You should know how he's sweating us! And he and that snooty son of his keep their eyes on me and my colleagues all the time, fat chance we have to make any money on the side!" The clerk heaved a deep sigh, then resumed, businesslike: "If the tribunal pays me ten coppers a day, I shall collect evidence on his tax evasion. For the information I gave you just now, twenty-five coppers will do."

Tao Gan rose and patted the other's shoulder.

"Carry on, my boy!" he told him cheerfully. "Then you'll also become a big fat bully in due time, working an enormous abacus." Then he added sternly: "If I need you I'll send for you. Goodbye!"

The disappointed clerk scurried back to the pawn shop. Tao Gan followed him at a more sedate pace. Inside he rapped on the counter with his bony knuckles and peremptorily beckoned the portly pawnbroker. Showing him his identity document bearing the large red stamp of the tribunal, he told him curtly:

"You'll have to come with me to the tribunal, Mr. Leng. His Excellency the magistrate wants to see you. No, there is no need to change. That grey dress of yours is very becoming. Hurry up, I don't have all day!"

They were carried to the tribunal in Leng's luxurious padded palankeen.

Tao Gan told the pawnbroker to wait in the chancery. Leng let himself down heavily on the bench in the anteroom and at once began to fan himself vigorously with a large silk fan. He jumped up when Tao Gan came to fetch him.

"What is it all about, sir?" he asked worriedly.

Tao Gan gave him a pitying look. He was thoroughly enjoying himself.

"Well," he said slowly, "I can't talk about official business, of course. But I'll say this much: I am glad I am not in your shoes, Mr. Leng!"

When the sweating pawnbroker was ushered in by Tao Gan into Judge Dee's office, and he saw the judge sitting behind his desk, he fell onto his knees and began to knock his forehead on the floor.

"You may skip the formalities, Mr. Leng!" Judge Dee told him coldly. "Sit down and listen! It is my duty to warn you that if you don't answer my questions truthfully, I shall have to interrogate you in court. Speak up, where were you last night?"

"Merciful Heaven! So it is just as I feared!" the fat man exclaimed. "It was just that I had had a few drops too much, Excellency! I swear it! When I was closing up, my old friend Chu the goldsmith dropped in and invited me to have a drink in the winehouse on the corner. We had two jugs, sir! At the most! I was still steady on my legs. The old man told you that, I suppose?"

Judge Dee nodded. He didn't have the faintest idea what the excited man was talking about. If Leng had said he was at home the previous night the judge had planned to ask him whether there had been a commotion on the ridge, and then he would have confronted him with his lying about the emerald ring. Now he told him curtly: "I want to hear everything again, from your own mouth!"

"Well, after I had taken leave of my friend Chu, Excellency, I told my palankeen bearers to carry me up to my villa on the ridge. When we were rounding the corner of your tribunal here, a band of young rascals, grown-up guttersnipes, began to jeer at me. As a rule I don't pay any attention to that kind of thing, but . . . well, as I said, I was. . . . Anyway, I got angry and told my bearers to put the palankeen down and teach the scum a lesson. Then suddenly that old vagabond appears. He kicks against my palankeen and starts calling me a dirty tyrant. Well, I mean a man in my position can't take that lying down! I step from my palankeen and I give the old scoundrel a push. Just a push, Excellency. He falls down, and remains lying there on his back."

The pawnbroker produced a large silk handkerchief and rubbed his moist face.

"Did his head bleed?" the judge asked.

"Bleed? Of course not, sir! He fell on to the soft shoulder of the mud road. But I should've had a good look, of course, to see whether he was all right. However, those young hoodlums began to shout again, so I jumped in my palankeen and told the bearers to carry me away. It was only when I was about halfway up the road to the ridge, and when the evening breeze had cooled my head a bit, that I realized that the old tramp might have had a heart attack. So I stepped out and told the bearers that I would walk a bit and that they could go on ahead to the villa. Then I walked downhill, back to the place of the quarrel. But. . . ."

"Why didn't you simply tell your chair-bearers to take you back there?" Judge Dee interrupted.

The pawnbroker looked embarrassed.

"Well, sir, you know what those coolies are nowadays. If that tramp had really fallen ill, I wouldn't want my bearers to know that, you see. Those impudent rascals aren't beyond trying a bit of blackmail. . . . Anyway, when I came to the street corner here, the old tramp was nowhere to be seen. A hawker told me that the old scoundrel had scrambled up again shortly after I had left. He had said some very bad things about me, then he took the road to the ridge, as chipper as can be!"

"I see. What did you do next?"

"I? Oh, I rented a chair, and was carried home. But the incident had upset my stomach, and when I descended in front of my gate, I suddenly became very ill. Fortunately Mr. Wang and his son were just coming back from a walk, and his son carried me inside. Strong as an ox, that boy is. Well, then I went straight to bed." He again mopped his face before he concluded: "I fully realized that I shouldn't have laid hands on that old vagabond, Excellency. And now he has lodged a complaint, of course. Well, I am prepared to pay any indemnity, within reason, of course and. . . ."

Judge Dee had risen.

"Come with me, Mr. Leng," he said evenly. "I want to show you something."

The judge left the office, followed by Tao Gan and the bewildered pawnbroker. In the courtyard the judge told the headman to take them to the mortuary in the gatehouse. He led them to a musty room, bare except for a deal table on trestles, covered with a reed mat. The judge lifted up the end of the mat, and asked:

"Do you know this man, Mr. Leng?"

After one look at the old tramp's face, Leng shouted:

"He is dead! Holy Heaven, I killed him!"

He fell on his knees and wailed: "Mercy, Excellency, have mercy! It was an accident, I swear it! I. . . ."

"You'll be given an opportunity to explain when you are standing trial," Judge Dee told him coldly. "Now we'll go back to my office, for I am not yet through with you, Mr. Leng. Not by a long shot!"

Back in his private office the judge sat down behind his desk and motioned Tao Gan to take the stool in front. Leng was not invited to be seated so he had to remain standing there, under the watchful eye of the headman.

Judge Dee silently studied him for a while, slowly caressing his long sidewhiskers. Then he sat up, took the emerald ring from his sleeve and asked:

"Why did you tell my assistant that you had never seen this ring before?"

Leng stared at the ring with raised eyebrows. He did not seem much disturbed by Judge Dee's sudden question.

"I couldn't have known that this gentleman belonged to the tribunal, could I, sir?" he asked, annoyed. "Otherwise I would have told him, of course. But the ring reminded me of a rather unpleasant experience, and I didn't feel like discussing that with a complete stranger."

"All right. Now tell me who that young woman was."

Leng shrugged his round shoulders.

"I really couldn't tell you, sir! She was dressed rather poorly, and she belonged to a band of vagabonds for the tip of her little finger was missing. But a good-looking wench. Very good-looking, I must say. Well, she puts the ring on the table and asks what it's worth. It's a nice antique piece, as you can see for yourself, sir, worth about six silver pieces. Ten, perhaps, to a collector. So I tell her, 'I can let you have here and now one good shining silver piece if you want to pawn it, and two if you sell it outright.' Business is business, isn't it? Even if your customer happens to be a pretty piece of goods. But does she take my offer? No sir! She snatches the ring from my hands, snaps 'Not for sale!' and off she goes. And that was the last I saw of her."

"I heard a quite different story," Judge Dee said dryly. "Speak up, what were you two whispering about?"

Leng's face turned red.

"So my clerks, those good-for-nothings, have been spying on me again! Well, then you'll understand how awkward it was, sir. I asked her only because I thought that such a good-looking girl from up-country, all alone in this town . . . well, that she might meet the wrong people, and. . . ."

Judge Dee hit his fist on the table.

"Don't stand there twaddling, man! Tell me exactly what you said!"

"Well," Leng replied with a sheepish look, "I proposed that we should meet later in a teahouse near by, and . . . and I patted her hand a bit, just to assure her I meant well, you know. The wench suddenly flew into a rage, said that if I didn't stop bothering

her, she would call her brother who was waiting outside. Then
. . . then she rushed off."

"Quite. Headman, put this man under lock and key. The charge
is manslaughter."

The headman grabbed the protesting pawnbroker and took him
outside.

"Pour me another cup of tea, Tao Gan," Judge Dee said. "A
curious story! And did you notice the discrepancy between Leng's
account of his meeting with the girl and that given by the clerk?"

"I did, sir!" Tao Gan said eagerly. "That wretched clerk said
nothing about their having a quarrel at the counter. According to
him they held a whispered conversation. I think that in fact the
girl accepted Leng's proposal, sir. The quarrel Leng spoke of
occurred afterwards, in the house of assignation. And that is why
Leng murdered the old tramp!"

Judge Dee, who had been slowly sipping his tea, now put his
cup down. Leaning back in his chair, he said:

"Develop your theory further, Tao Gan!"

"Well, this time Leng's philandering led to serious trouble! For
the girl, her brother and the old tramp belonged to one and the
same organized gang; the girl was their call bird. As soon as Leng
had arrived in the house of assignation and began to make up to
the girl, she shouted that he was assaulting her—the old, familiar
trick. Her brother and the old tramp came rushing inside, and
demanded money. Leng succeeded in escaping. When he was on
his way to the ridge, however, the old tramp waylaid him and
tried to make Leng pay up by making a scene in the street. Leng's
bearers were beating up the young hoodlums, so they couldn't
hear what Leng and the old man were quarreling about. Leng
silenced the tramp by knocking him down. What do you think
of that as a theory, sir?"

"Plausible, and in perfect accordance with Leng's character.
Continue!"

"While Leng was being carried up to the ridge he did indeed
become worried. Not about the condition of the old tramp, however, but about the other members of the gang. He was afraid
that when they found the old tramp, they would come after him
to take revenge. When the hawker told Leng that the tramp had
taken the road uphill, Leng followed him. About halfway up he
struck him down from behind, with a sharp piece of rock, or
perhaps the hilt of his dagger."

Tao Gan paused. When the judge nodded encouragingly, he resumed:

"It was comparatively easy for Leng, who is a powerful fellow and perfectly familiar with that area, to carry the dead body to the deserted hut. And Leng also had a good reason for cutting off his victim's fingers, namely to hide the fact that the man was a member of a gang. But as to where and how Leng cut off the fingers, I confess that that is a complete riddle to me, sir."

Judge Dee sat up straight. Stroking his long black beard, he said with a smile:

"You did very well indeed. You have a logical mind, and at the same time strong powers of imagination, a combination that'll go a long way to make you a good investigator! I shall certainly keep your theory in mind. However, its weak point is that it is based entirely on the assumption that the eyewitness account of the clerk regarding the meeting in the pawnshop is absolutely correct. But when I mentioned the discrepancy between the two accounts just now, my intention was to quote it as an example of how little trust can be put in eyewitness accounts. As a matter of fact, it is too early yet to formulate theories, Tao Gan. First we must verify the facts we have, and try to discover additional data."

Noticing Tao Gan's crestfallen look, Judge Dee went on quickly:

"Thanks to your excellent work this afternoon, we now have at our disposal three well-established facts. First, that a beautiful vagabond girl is connected with the ring. Second, that she has a brother; for no matter what really happened, Leng had no earthly reason to invent a brother. And third, that there is a connection between the girl, her brother and the murdered man. Probably they belonged to the same gang, and if so, it probably was a gang from outside this district; for none of our personnel knew the dead man by sight, and Leng thought the girl was from up-country.

"So now your next step is to locate the girl and her brother. That shouldn't be too difficult, for a vagabond girl of such striking beauty will attract attention. As a rule the women who join those gangs are cheap prostitutes."

"I could ask the Chief of the Beggars, sir! He is a clever old scoundrel, and fairly cooperative."

"Yes, that's a good idea. While you are busy in the town, I shall check Leng's story. I shall interrogate that rascally clerk of his, his friend the goldsmith Chu, and his chairbearers. I shall

also order the headman to locate one or more of the young
hoodlums who jeered at Leng, and the hawker who saw the old
man scramble up. Finally I shall ask Mr. Wang whether Leng
was really dead drunk when he came home. All these routine jobs
would be meat and drink to old Hoong, Ma Joong and Chiao
Tai, but since they are away I'll gladly take care of them myself.
This work will help to take my mind off that smuggling case that
is worrying me considerably. Well, set to work, and success!"

The only occupant of the smelly taproom of the Red Carp was
the greybeard who stood behind the high counter. He wore a long,
shabby blue gown, and had a greasy black skull cap on his head.
His long, wrinkled face was adorned by a ragged moustache and
a spiky chinbeard. Staring into the distance he was moodily picking
his broken teeth. His busy time would come late in the night,
when his beggars gathered there in order to pay him his share of
their earnings. The old man looked on silently while Tao Gan
poured himself uninvited a cup of wine from the cracked earthen-
ware pot. Then he quickly grabbed the pot, and put it away under
the counter.
    "You had quite a busy morning, Mr. Tao," he croaked. "Asking
about gang fights, and golden rings."
    Tao Gan nodded. He knew that the greybeard's omnipresent
beggars kept him informed about everything that went on downtown. He put his winecup down and said cheerfully:
    "That's why I got the afternoon off! I was thinking of amusing
myself a bit. Not with a professional, mind you. With a freelance!"
    "Very clever!" the greybeard commented sourly. "So as to turn
her in afterwards for practicing without a licence. Have your fun
gratis, and on top of that a bonus from the tribunal!"
    "What do you take me for? I want a freelance, and from out
of town, because I have to think of my reputation."
    "Why should you, Mr. Tao?" the Chief of the Beggars asked
blandly. "Your reputation being what it is?"
    Tao Gan decided to let the barbed remark pass. He said pen-
sively:
    "Something young, and pretty. But cheap, mind you!"
    "You'll have to prove that you'll appreciate my advice, Mr.
Tao!"
    The greybeard watched Tao Gan as he laboriously counted out
five coppers on the counter, but he made no move to take the

money. With a deep sigh Tao Gan added five more. Now the old man scooped them up with his claw-like hand.

"Go to the Inn of the Blue Clouds," he muttered. "Two streets down, the fourth house on your left. Ask for Seng Kiu. He's her brother, and he concludes the deals, I am told." He gave Tao Gan a thoughtful look, then added with a lopsided grin: "You'll like Seng Kiu, Mr. Tao! A straightforward, open-minded man. And very hospitable. Have a good time, Mr. Tao. You really deserve it!"

Tao Gan thanked him and went out.

He walked as quickly as the irregular cobblestones of the narrow alley would allow, for he did not put it beyond the greybeard to send one of his beggars ahead to the inn to warn Seng Kiu that a minion of the law was on his way.

The Inn of the Blue Clouds was a miserable small place, wedged in between the shops of a fishmonger and a vegetable dealer. In the dimly lit space at the bottom of the narrow staircase a fat man sat dozing in a bamboo chair. Tao Gan poked him hard in his ribs with his thin, bony forefinger and growled:

"I want Seng Kiu!"

"You may have him and keep him! Upstairs, second door! Ask him when he's going to pay the rent!" When Tao Gan was about to ascend, the man, who had taken in his frail stooping figure, called out: "Wait! Have a look at my face!"

Tao Gan saw that his left eye was closed, the cheek swollen and discolored.

"That's Seng Kiu for you!" the man said. "Mean bastard!"

"How many are they?"

"Three. Besides Seng Kiu and his sister there's his friend Chang. Also a mean bastard. There was a fourth, but he has cleared out."

Tao Gan nodded. While climbing the stairs he reflected with a wry smile that he now knew the reason for the greybeard's secret amusement. He would get even with that old rascal, some day!

After he had rapped his knuckles vigorously on the door indicated, a raucous voice called out from inside:

"Tomorrow you'll get your money, you son of a dog!"

Tao Gan pushed the door open and walked inside. On either side of the bare, dingy room stood a plank bed. On the one on the right lay a giant of a man, clad in a patched brown jacket and trousers. He had a broad, bloated face, surrounded by a bristling short beard. His hair was bound up with a dirty rag. On the other bed a long, wiry man lay snoring loudly, his muscular arms folded under his closely cropped head. In front of the window sat a good-looking young woman mending a jacket. She wore only a pair of wide blue trousers, her shapely torso was bare.

"Maybe I could help with the rent, Seng Kiu," Tao Gan said. He pointed with his chin at the girl.

The giant scrambled up. He looked Tao Gan up and down with his small bloodshot eyes, scratching his hairy breast. Tao Gan noticed that the tip of his left little finger was missing. His scrutiny completed, the giant asked gruffly: "How much?"

"Fifty coppers."

Seng Kiu woke up the other by a kick against his leg that was dangling over the foot of the bed.

"This kind old gentleman," he informed him, "wants to lend us fifty coppers, because he likes our faces. The trouble is that I don't like his!"

"Take his money and kick him out!" the girl told her brother. "No need to beat him up, the scarecrow is ugly enough as it is!"

The giant swung round to her.

"None of your business!" he barked. "You shut up and stay shut up! You bungled that affair with Uncle Twan, couldn't even get that emerald ring of his! Useless slut!"

She came to her feet with amazing speed and kicked him hard against his shins. He promptly gave her a blow to her stomach. She folded double, gasping for air. But that was only a trick, for when he came for her, she quickly thrust her head into his midriff. As he stepped back, she pulled a long hairpin from her coiffure and asked venomously:

"Want to get that into your gut, dear brother?"

Tao Gan was thinking how he could get these three to the tribunal. Since they probably weren't very familiar with the city yet, he thought he would manage it.

"I'll settle with you later!" Seng Kiu promised his sister. And to his friend: "Grab the bastard, Chang!"

While Chang was keeping Tao Gan's arms pinned behind his back in an iron grip, Seng Kiu expertly searched him.

"Yes, only fifty coppers!" he said with disgust. "You hold him while I teach him not to disturb our sleep!"

He took a long bamboo stick from the corner and made to hit Tao Gan on his head. But suddenly he half turned and let the end come down on the behind of his sister, who was bending over her jacket again. She jumped aside with a yell of pain. Her brother bellowed with laughter. But then he had to duck, for she threw the heavy iron scissors at his head.

"I don't like interrupting," Tao Gan said dryly, "but there's a deal of five silver pieces I wanted to discuss."

The giant who had been trying to get hold of his sister now let her go. He turned round and asked panting:

"Five silver pieces, you said?"

"It's a very private matter, just between you and me."

Seng Kiu gave a sign to Chang to let Tao Gan go. The thin man drew the tall ruffian into the corner and told him in a low voice:

"I don't care a fig about that sister of yours. It's my boss who sent me!"

Seng Kiu went pale under his tan.

"Does the Baker want five silver pieces? Holy Heaven, has he gone mad? How . . .?"

"I don't know any baker," Tao Gan said crossly. "My boss is a big landowner, a wealthy lecher who pays well for his little amusements. He has got fed up with all those dainty damsels from the Willow Quarter nowadays. Suddenly he wants them buxom and rough-and-ready like. I do the collecting for him. He has heard about your sister, and he has sent me to offer you five silver pieces for having her in the house a couple of days."

Seng Kiu had been listening with growing astonishment. Now he exclaimed:

"Are you crazy? There isn't a woman in the whole wide world who has got something to sell worth that much!" He thought deeply for a while, creasing his low forehead. Suddenly he burst out: "That proposal of yours stinks, brother! I want my sister to keep a whole skin. I am planning to set her up in business, you see? So she gets me a regular income."

Tao Gan shrugged his narrow shoulders.

"All right. There are other vagabond girls on the loose. Give me back my fifty coppers, then I'll say good-bye."

"Hey there, not so fast!" The giant rubbed his face. "Five silver pieces! That means living nicely for at least a year, without doing a stroke of work! Well, it doesn't matter much really whether she's handled a bit roughly, after all. She can stand a lot, and it'll cut her down to size, maybe. All right, it's a deal! But me and Chang are going to see her off. I want to know where and with whom she is staying."

"So that you can blackmail my boss later, eh? Nothing doing!"

"You are lying! You are a buyer for a brothel, you dirty rat!"

"All right, come with me then and see for yourself. But don't blame me if my boss gets angry and has his men beat you up. Pay me twenty coppers, that's my commission."

After protracted haggling, they agreed on ten coppers. Seng Kiu gave Tao Gan his fifty coppers back, and ten extra. The gaunt man put these in his sleeve with a satisfied smile, for now he had recovered the money he had paid the Chief of the Beggars.

"The boss of this fellow wants to stand us a drink," Seng Kiu told Chang and his sister. "Let's go to his place and hear what he has got to say."

They went up town by the main road, but then Tao Gan took them through a maze of narrow alleys to the back of a tall greystone compound. As he opened the small iron door with a key he took from his sleeve, Seng Kiu remarked, impressed:

"Your boss must be rolling in it! Substantial property!"

"Very substantial," Tao Gan agreed. "And this is only the back entrance, mind you. You should see the main gate!" So speaking, he herded them into a long corridor. He carefully relocked the door and said: "Just wait here a moment while I go to inform my boss!"

He disappeared around the corner.

After a while the girl exclaimed:

"I don't like the smell of this place. Could be a trap!"

Then the headman and six armed guards came tramping round the corner. Chang cursed and groped for his knife.

"Please attack us!" the headman told him with a grin, raising his sword. "Then we'll get a bonus for cutting you down!"

"Leave it, Chang!" the giant told his friend disgustedly. "These bastards are professional murderers. They get paid for killing the poor!"

The girl tried to slip past the headman, but he caught her and soon she also was in chains. They were taken to the jail in the adjoining building.

After Tao Gan had run to the guardhouse and told the headman to arrest two vagabonds and their wench who were waiting near the back door, he went straight to the chancery and asked the senior clerk where he could find Judge Dee.

"His Excellency is in his office, Mr. Tao. Since the noon rice he has interrogated a number of people there. Just when he had let them go, young Mr. Leng, the son of the pawnbroker, came and asked to see the judge. He hasn't come out yet."

"What is that youngster doing here? He wasn't on the list of people the judge wanted to interrogate."

"I think he came to find out why his father had been arrested, Mr. Tao. It might interest you to know that, before he went inside, he had been asking the guards at the gate all kinds of questions about the dead body that was found this morning in the hut in the forest. You might tell the judge."

"Thank you, I will. Those guards are not supposed to hand out information, though!"

The old clerk shrugged his shoulders.

"They all know young Mr. Leng, sir. They often go there towards the end of the month to pawn something or other, and young Leng always gives them a square deal. Besides, since the entire personnel has seen the body, it isn't much of a secret any more."

Tao Gan nodded and walked on to Judge Dee's office.

The judge was sitting behind his desk, now wearing a comfortable robe of thin grey cotton, and with a square black cap on his head. In front of the desk stood a well-built young man of about twenty-five, clad in a neat brown robe and wearing a flat black cap. He had a handsome but rather reserved face.

"Take a seat!" Judge Dee told Tao Gan. "This is Mr. Leng's eldest son. He is worried about his father's arrest. I just explained to him that I suspect his father of having taken part in the murder of an old vagrant, and that I shall hear the case at tonight's session of the court. That's all I can say, Mr. Leng. I have to terminate our interview now, for I have urgent matters to discuss with my lieutenant here."

"My father couldn't possibly have committed a murder last night, sir," the youngster said quietly.

Judge Dee raised his eyebrows.

"Why?"

"For the simple reason that my father was dead drunk, sir. I myself opened the door when Mr. Wang brought him in. My father had passed out, and Mr. Wang's son had to carry him inside."

"All right, Mr. Leng. I shall keep this point in mind."

Young Leng made no move to take his leave. He cleared his throat and resumed, rather diffidently this time:

"I think I have seen the murderers, sir."

Judge Dee leaned forward in his chair.

"I want a complete statement about that!" he said sharply.

"Well, sir, it is rumored that the dead body of a tramp was found this morning in a deserted hut in the forest, halfway up the slope. May I ask whether that is correct?" As the judge nodded, he continued: "Last night a bright moon was in the sky and there was a cool evening breeze, so I thought I would take a little walk. I took the footpath behind our house that leads down into the forest. After having passed the second bend, I saw two people some distance ahead of me. I couldn't see them very well, but one seemed very tall, and he was carrying a heavy load on his shoulders. The other was small, and rather slender. Since all kind of riffraff often frequents the forest at night, I decided to call off my walk, and went back home. When I heard the rumor about the dead tramp, it occurred to me that the burden the tall person was carrying might well have been the dead body."

Tao Gan tried to catch Judge Dee's eye, for Leng's description fitted exactly Seng Kiu and his sister. But the judge was looking intently at his visitor. Suddenly he said:

"This means that I can set your father free at once, and arrest you as suspect in his stead! For you have just proved beyond doubt that, whereas your father could not have committed the murder, you yourself had every opportunity!"

The youngster stared dumbfounded at the judge.

"I didn't do it!" he burst out. "I can prove it! I have a witness who. . . ."

"Just as I thought! You weren't alone. A young man like you doesn't go out for a solitary walk in the forest at night. It's only when you have reached a riper age that you discover that enjoyment. Speak up, who was the girl?"

"My mother's chambermaid," the young man replied with a red face. "We can't see much of each other inside the house, of course. So we meet now and then in the hut, down the slope. She can bear out my statement that we went into the forest together, but she can't give more information about the people I saw, because I was walking ahead and she didn't see them." Giving the judge a shy look he added: "We plan to get married, sir. But if my father knew that we. . . ."

"All right. Go to the chancery, and let the senior clerk take down your statement. I shall use it only if absolutely necessary. You may go!"

As the youngster made to take his leave, Tao Gan asked:

"Could that smaller figure you saw have been a girl?"

Young Leng scratched his head.

"Well, I couldn't see them very well, you know. Now that you ask me, however. . . . Yes, it might have been a woman, I think."

As soon as young Leng had gone, Tao Gan began excitedly:

"Everything is clear now, sir! I . . . ."

Judge Dee raised his hand.

"One moment, Tao Gan. We must deal with this complicated case methodically. I shall first tell you the result of my routine check. First, that clerk of Leng's is a disgusting specimen. Close questioning proved that, after he had seen the girl place the ring on the counter, Leng told him to make himself scarce. Other customers came in between them, and later he only saw the girl snatch up the ring and go out. The whispering bit he made up, in order to prove that his boss is a lecher. And as to his boss being guilty of tax evasion, he could only quote vague rumors. I dismissed the fellow with the reminder that there's a law on slander, and sent for the master of the Bankers' Guild. He told me that Mr. Leng is a very wealthy man who likes to do himself well. He is not averse to a bit of double dealing, and one has to look sharp when doing business with him, but he is careful to keep on the right side of the law. He travels a lot, however, passing much of his time in the neighboring district of Chiang-pei; and the guildmaster did not, of course, know anything about his activities there. Second, Leng did indeed have a heavy drinking bout with his friend the goldsmith. Third, the headman has located two of the young hoodlums who jeered at Leng. They said that this was obviously the first time Leng had seen the old tramp, and that no girl was mentioned during their quarrel. Leng did push the old man, but he was on his feet again directly after Leng had been carried off in his chair. He stood there cursing Leng for a blasted tyrant, then he walked off. Finally, those boys made one curious remark. They said that the old man didn't speak like a tramp at all, he used the language of a gentleman. I had planned to ask Mr. Wang whether Mr. Leng was really drunk when he came home, but after what his son told us just now, that doesn't seem necessary any more."

The judge emptied his teacup, then added: "Tell me now how it went down town!"

"I must first tell you, sir, that young Leng questioned the guards thoroughly about the discovery of the body in the hut, prior to seeing you. However, that seems immaterial now, for I have proof that he did not make up the story about the two people he saw in the forest."

Judge Dee nodded.

"I didn't think he was lying. The boy impressed me as very honest. Much better than that father of his!"

"The people he saw must have been a gangster called Seng Kiu, and his sister—a remarkably beautiful young girl. The Chief of the Beggars directed me to the inn where they were staying, together with another plug-ugly called Chang. There was a fourth man, but he had left. I heard Seng Kiu scolding his sister for having spoiled what he called 'the affair of Uncle Twan,' and for having failed to obtain his emerald ring. Evidently that Uncle Twan is our dead tramp. All three are from another district, but they know a gangster boss called the Baker here. I had them locked up in jail, all three of them."

"Excellent!" Judge Dee exclaimed. "How did you get them here so quickly?"

"Oh," Tao Gan replied vaguely, "I told them a story about easy money to be made here, and they came along gladly. As to my theory about Mr. Leng, sir, you were quite right in calling it premature! Leng had nothing to do with the murder. It was pure coincidence that the gangsters crossed his path twice. First when the girl wanted the ring appraised, and the second time when the old tramp took offense at Leng's high-handed way of dealing with the young hoodlums."

The judge made no comment. He pensively tugged at his moustache. Suddenly he said:

"I don't like coincidences, Tao Gan. I admit they do occur, now and then. But I always begin by distrusting them. By the way, you said that Seng Kiu mentioned a gangster boss called the Baker. Before I interrogate him, I want you to ask our headman what he knows about that man."

While Tao Gan was gone, the judge poured himself another cup from the tea basket on his desk. He idly wondered how his lieutenant had managed to get those three gangsters to the tribunal. "He was remarkably vague when I asked him," he told himself with a wry smile. "Probably he has been acting the part of confidence man again—his old trade! Well, as long as it is in a good cause. . . ."

Tao Gan came back.

"The headman knew the Baker quite well by name, sir. But he is not of this town; the scoundrel is a notorious gangster boss in our neighboring district, Chiang-pei. That means that Seng Kiu is from there too."

"And our friend Mr. Leng often stays there," the judge said slowly. "We are getting too many coincidences for my liking, Tao Gan! Well, I shall interrogate those people separately, beginning with Seng Kiu. Tell the headman to take him to the mortuary—without showing him the dead body, of course. I'll go there presently."

When Judge Dee came in he saw the tall figure of Seng Kiu standing between two constables, in front of the table on which the corpse was lying, covered by the reed mat. There hung a sickly smell in the bare room. The judge reflected that it wouldn't do to leave the body there too long, in this hot weather. He folded the mat back and asked Seng Kiu:

"Do you know this man?"

"Holy Heaven, that's him!" Seng shouted.

Judge Dee folded his arms in his wide sleeves. He spoke harshly:

"Yes, that's the dead body of the old man you cruelly did to death."

The gangster burst out in a string of curses. The constable on his right hit him over his head with his heavy club. "Confess!" he barked at him. The blow didn't seem to bother the giant much. He just shook his head, then shouted:

"I didn't kill him! The old fool was still alive and kicking when he left the inn last night!"

"Who was he?"

"A rich fool, called Twan Mou-tsai. Owned a big drugstore, in the capital."

"A rich drug dealer? What was his business with you?"

"He was gone on my sister, the silly old goat! He wanted to join us!"

"Don't try to foist your stupid lies on me, my friend!" Judge Dee said coldly. The constable hit out at Seng Kiu's head again, but he ducked expertly and blurted out:

"It's the truth, I swear it! He was crazy about my sister! Even wanted to pay for being allowed to join us! But my sister, the silly wench, she wouldn't take one copper from him. And look at the trouble the stubborn little strumpet has got us in now! A murder, if you please!"

Judge Dee smoothed down his long beard. The man was an uncouth brute, but his words bore the hallmark of truth. Seng Kiu interpreted his silence as a sign of doubt, and resumed in a whining voice:

"Me and my mate, we have never done anything like murder, noble lord! Maybe we took along a stray chicken or a pig here and there, or borrowed a handful of coppers from a traveler— such things will happen when you have to make your living by the road. But we never killed a man, I tell you. And why should I kill Uncle Twan, of all people? I told you he gave me money, didn't I?"

"Is your sister a prostitute?"

"A what?" Seng Kiu asked suspiciously.

"A streetwalker."

"Oh, that!" Seng scratched his head, then replied cautiously: "Well, to tell you the truth, sir, she is and she isn't, so to speak. If we need money badly, she may take on a fellow, on occasion. But most of the time she only takes youngsters she fancies, and they get it gratis for nothing. Dead capital, that's what she is, sir! Wish she were a regular, then she'd bring in some money at least! If you'd kindly tell me, sir, how to go about getting proper papers for her, those things that say she has the right to walk the streets, and. . . ."

"Only answer my questions!" Judge Dee interrupted him testily. "Speak up, when did you begin working for Leng the pawnbroker?"

"A pawnbroker? Not me, sir! I don't deal with those bloodsuckers! My boss is Lew the Baker, of Chiang-pei. Lives over the winehouse, near the west gate. He *was* our boss, that is. We bought ourselves out, Me, Sis and Chang."

Judge Dee nodded. He knew that, according to the unwritten rules of the underworld, a sworn member of a gang can sever relations with his boss if he pays a certain sum of money, from which his original entrance fee, and his share in the earnings of the gang are deducted. This settling of accounts often gave rise to bitter quarrels.

"Was everything settled to the satisfaction of both parties?" he asked.

"Well, there was a bit of trouble, sir. The Baker tried to rob us, the mean son of a dog! But Uncle Twan, he was a real wizard with figures. He takes a piece of paper, does a bit of reckoning, and proves the Baker is dead wrong. The Baker didn't like that, but there were a couple of other fellows who had been following the argument, and they all said Uncle Twan was right. So the Baker had to let us go."

"I see. Why did you want to leave the Baker's gang?"

"Because the Baker was getting too uppity, and because he was taking on jobs we didn't fancy. Jobs above our station, so to speak. The other day he wanted me and Chang to lend a hand putting two boxes across the boundary. I said no, never. First, if we get caught, we are in for big trouble. Second, the men who did those kind of big jobs for the Baker usually died in accidents afterwards. Accidents will happen, of course. But they happened too often, for my taste."

The judge gave Tao Gan a significant look.

"When you and Chang refused, who took on the job?"

"Ying, Meng and Lau," Seng replied promptly.

"Where are they now?"

Seng passed his thumb across his throat.

"Just accidents, mind you!" he said with a grin. But there was a glint of fear in his small eyes.

"To whom were those two boxes to be delivered?" the judge asked again.

The gangster shrugged his broad shoulders.

"Heaven knows! I overheard the Baker telling Ying something about a richard who has a big store in the marketplace here. I didn't ask, it wasn't my business, the less I knew about it the better. And Uncle Twan said I was dead right."

"Where were you last night?"

"Me? I went with Sis and Chang to the Red Carp, for a bite and a little dice game. Uncle Twan said he'd eat somewhere outside, he didn't fancy dice games. When we came home at midnight, the old man hadn't come back. The poor old geezer got his head bashed in! He shouldn't have gone out alone, in a town he didn't know!"

Judge Dee took the emerald ring from his sleeve.

"Do you know this trinket?" he asked.

"Of course! That was Uncle Twan's ring. Had it from his father. 'Ask him to give it to you!' I told Sis. But she said no. It's hard luck, sir, to be cursed with a sister like her!"

"Take this man back to his cell!" Judge Dee ordered the headman. "Then tell the matron to bring Miss Seng to my office."

While crossing the courtyard, the judge said excitedly to Tao Gan:

"You made a very nice haul! This is the first clue we've got to the smuggling case! I shall send a special messenger to my colleague in Chiang-pei at once, asking him to arrest the Baker. He will tell who his principal is, and to whom the boxes were to be delivered here. I wouldn't be astonished if that man turned out to be our friend Leng the pawnbroker! He is a wealthy man with a large store in the marketplace, and he visits Chiang-pei regularly."

"Do you think that Seng Kiu is really innocent of Twan's murder, sir? That story told by Leng's son seemed to fit him and his sister all right."

"We shall know more about that when we have discovered the truth about that enigmatic Twan Mou-tsai, Tao Gan. I had the impression that Seng Kiu told us all he knew just now. But there must be many things that Seng does not know! We shall see what his sister has to say."

They had entered the chancery. The senior scribe rose hurriedly and came to meet them. Handing the judge a document, he said:

"I happened to overhear Mr. Tao asking our headman about a gangster called Lew the Baker, Your Honor. This routine report about the proceedings in the tribunal of Chiang-pei just came in. It contains a passage concerning that gangster."

Judge Dee quickly glanced the paper through. With an angry exclamation he gave it to Tao Gan.

"Of all the bad luck!" he exclaimed. "Here, read this, Tao Gan! Yesterday morning the Baker was killed in a drunken brawl!"

He walked on to his private office, angrily swinging his sleeves.

When he had sat down behind his desk he gave Tao Gan a somber look and said dejectedly:

"I thought we were about to solve the smuggling case! And now we are back where we started. The three men who could have told us for whom the contraband was destined were murdered by the Baker. Small wonder that Ma Joong and Chiao Tai can't find them! Their bones must be rotting in a dry well, or buried under a tree in the forest! And the Baker, the only man who could have told us who the ringleaders of the smuggling are, he had to get killed!" He angrily tugged at his beard.

Tao Gan slowly wound the three long hairs that grew on his cheek round his thin forefinger. After a while he said:

"Perhaps a thorough interrogation of the Baker's associates in Chiang-pei might. . . ."

"No," Judge Dee said curtly. "The Baker killed off the men who did the dirty work for him. That he took that extreme measure proves that he was under orders from his principal to keep everything connected with the smuggling strictly secret." He took his fan from his sleeve and began to fan himself. After a while he resumed: "Twan's murder must be closely connected with the smuggling case. I have the distinct feeling that if we succeed in solving that crime, we shall have the key to the riddle of the smuggling ring. Come in!"

There had been a knock on the door. Now a tall, rawboned woman, clad in a simple brown robe and with a black piece of cloth wound round her head, entered the office, pushing a slender young girl in front of her.

"This is Miss Seng, Your Honor," the matron reported in a hoarse voice.

Judge Dee gave the girl a sharp look. She stared back at him defiantly with her large, expressive eyes. Her oval, suntanned face was of a striking beauty. She didn't wear any makeup and she did not need it either. Her small petulant mouth was as red as a cherry, the long eyebrows above her finely chiseled nose had a natural graceful curve and the hair that hung in two tresses down to her shoulders was long and glossy. The shabby blue jacket and the patched blue trousers seemed an incongruous attire for such a beauty. She remained standing in front of the desk, her hands stuck in the straw rope round her middle that served as a belt.

After the judge had studied her for a while, he said evenly:

"We are trying to trace the whereabouts of Mr. Twan Mou-tsai. Tell me where and how you met him."

"If you think you'll get anything out of me, Mister Official," she snapped, "you are making the worst mistake of your life!"

The matron stepped forward to slap her face, but the judge raised his hand. He said calmly:

"You are standing before your magistrate, Miss Seng. You have to answer my questions, you know."

"Think I am afraid of the whip? You can beat me as much as you like, I can stand it!"

"You won't be whipped," Tao Gan spoke up by her side. "Quite apart from the matter of Uncle Twan, you are guilty of vagrancy and prostitution without a license. You'll be branded on both your cheeks."

She suddenly grew pale.

"Don't worry!" Tao Gan added affably. "If you put on lots of powder, the marks won't show. Not too much, at least."

The girl stood very still, staring at the judge with scared eyes. Then she shrugged and said:

"Well, I have done nothing wrong. And I don't believe that Uncle Twan said bad things about me. Never! Where I met him? In the capital, about one year ago. I had cut my leg and walked into Twan's store to buy myself a plaster. He happened to be standing at the counter, and struck up a conversation with me, friendly like. It was the first time that such a rich fellow had shown interest in me without at once beginning to talk about you know what, and I liked him for that. I agreed to meet him that night, and so one thing led to another, if you know what I mean. He is an old man, of course, well over fifty, I'd say. But a real gentleman, nicely spoken and always ready to listen to my small talk."

She fell silent, and looked expectantly at the judge.

"How long did the affair last?" he asked.

"A couple of weeks. Then I told Uncle Twan that we'd have to say good-bye, because we would be going on to the next place. He wants to give me a silver piece but I say no, I am not a whore, thank Heaven, though my brother'd love that, the lazy pimp! So that was that. But three weeks later, when we are in Kwang-yeh, Twan suddenly comes walking into our inn. He tells me he wants me to become his second wife, and that he'll give my brother a handsome present, in cash."

She wiped her face with her sleeve, pulled her jacket straight and went on:

"I tell Twan much obliged but I don't want no money, no nothing. I just want my freedom, and I am not dreaming of getting myself shut up within four walls, say m'lady to his first wife, and be after the servants from morning to night. Twan goes off, the poor old fellow is very sad. Me too—for then I have fight with my brother and he beats me black and blue! Well, the next month, when we are in a village up-river, near our home Chiang-pei, old Twan again turns up. He says he has sold his drug business to his partner, for he has decided to join us. My brother says he's welcome provided he pays him a regular salary, for he's nobody's nursemaid for nothing, he says. I tell my brother nothing doing. Twan can come along, I say, and he can sleep with me if and when I feel like it. But I don't want one copper from him. My brother flies into a real rage, he and Chang catch me and pull my trousers down. I'd have got a thorough caning, but Twan came in between. He took my brother aside, and they worked out some kind of arrangement. Well, if Twan wants to pay my brother for teaching him the tricks of the road, that's his business. So Twan joined up with us and he has been with us for nearly a year. Until last night."

"Do you mean to say," Judge Dee asked, "that Mr. Twan, a wealthy merchant accustomed to all the luxuries of the capital, shared your life and roamed about as a common vagabond?"

"Of course he did! He liked it, I tell you. He told me a hundred times that he had never been so happy before. He said he had become fed up with life in the capital. His wives had been all right when they were young, but now they did nothing but nag, and his sons had grown up and kept interfering with his business and always wanted to teach him how he should run the store. He had been very fond of his only daughter, but she had married a merchant down south and he didn't see her any more. Also, he said, he had to attend parties every other night and that had given him a bad stomach. But after he joined us he never had any trouble with his stomach no more, he said. Besides, Chang taught him how to fish, and Uncle Twan took a powerful liking to that. Became quite good at it, too."

The judge observed her for a while, tugging at his moustache. Then he asked:

"I suppose that Mr. Twan visited many business acquaintances in the places you passed through?"

"Not him! He said he was done with all that. He only visited a colleague now and then, to get money."

"Did Mr. Twan carry large amounts of cash on his person?"

"Wrong again! About me he was silly all right, but apart from that Uncle Twan was a mighty slick business man, believe me! Never carried more than a handful of coppers on him. But every time we came to a larger city, he would go to a silver shop, and cash a draft, as he called it. Then he gave the money he received to a colleague of his, to keep for him. A wise measure, my brother being the kind of sneaky rat he is! But Uncle Twan could always get his hands on plenty of money should he need it. And when I say plenty, I mean plenty! When we came here to Han-yuan, he had five gold bars on him. Five gold bars, beg your pardon! I never knew one man could have that much money all to himself! For Heaven's sake don't let my brother see that, I told Twan; he's not a killer, but for that much gold he would gladly murder the whole town! Uncle Twan smiled that little smile of his, and said he knew a safe place for putting it away. And the next day he sure enough had only one string of coppers in his pocket. Can I have a cup of tea?"

Judge Dee gave a sign to the matron. She poured the girl a cup, but her sour face clearly indicated that she disapproved of this infringement of prison rules. The judge did not notice it, for he was looking at Tao Gan. Tao Gan nodded. They were getting on the right track. After the girl had taken a few sips, Judge Dee asked:

"To whom did Mr. Twan give those gold bars?"

She shrugged her shapely shoulders.

"He told me a lot about himself, but never a word about business, and I never asked him. Why should I? On our first day here, he told my brother he had to see a man who had a shop in the marketplace. 'I thought you had never been to Han-yuan before?' my brother asks. 'I haven't,' Uncle Twan says. 'But I have friends!' "

"When did you see Mr. Twan last?"

"Yesterday night, just before dinner. He went out and didn't come back. Had enough of it, I suppose, and went back home to the capital. That's his right, he is a free man, isn't he? But he ought to have known there was no need trying to fool me. He even went out of his way last night to tell me that he was planning to join our gang officially, so to speak, and take the oath! Why not tell me outright that we were through? I'd have missed him a bit, but not too much. A young girl like me can do without an uncle, can't she?"

"Quite. Where did he say he was going?"

"Oh, he said with that same secret smile of his that he was going to have a bite in the house of the friend he had seen our first day here. And I swallowed that!"

Judge Dee put the emerald ring on the table.

"You stated that you never accepted anything from Mr. Twan. Why then did you try to pawn this ring of his?"

"I didn't! I rather liked the thing, so Uncle Twan often let me play around with if for a few days. When we happened to pass a big pawnshop the other day, I walked in to ask what it was worth, just for fun. But that fat pawnbroker tried to make up to me at once, grabbed my sleeve and whispered dirty proposals. So I walked out again." She pushed a stray lock away from her forehead and went on with a half smile: "It sure enough was my unlucky day! As soon as I come out, a tall bully grabs my arm and says I am his sweetheart! Gave me the creeps the way he looked at me with his bulging eyes! But Uncle Twan says at once: 'Hands off, she's my girl!,' and my brother he twists his arm and sends him on his way with a good kick to his behind. All men are the same, I tell you! They think you have just to lift your little finger to a vagabond girl, and hey presto she throws her arms round your neck! No, Uncle Twan was a white crow all right! And if you tell me that he has accused me of something or other, then I'll call you a liar to your face!"

Tao Gan noticed that Judge Dee did not seem to have heard her last words. Staring straight ahead, he was caressing his side-whiskers, his thoughts apparently elsewhere. It struck Tao Gan that the judge seemed rather depressed, and he wondered what had caused this sudden change, for before the interview with Miss Seng he had been keen enough on obtaining more clues to the smuggling case. And the girl had unwittingly supplied them with valuable information. The judge too must have deduced from her rambling account that Twan had joined the gangsters only as a cover for his illegal activities; probably Twan had been the pay-master of the smuggling ring. An excellent cover, too, for who would suspect a tramp roaming the country with a couple of outlaws? And the man Twan had gone to visit in the morning must be one of the agents who distributed the contraband. A house-to-house search of all the shops in the marketplace and a close interrogation of the owners would doubtless bring to light who that agent was. And through him they could find out who the ringleader was . . . the man the central authorities were so eager to discover! Tao Gan cleared his throat several times, but Judge Dee did not seem to notice it. The matron also was astonished at the prolonged silence. She darted a questioning look at Tao Gan, but the thin man could only shake his head.

The girl began to fidget. "Stand still!" the matron snapped at her. Judge Dee looked up, startled from his musings. He pushed his cap back and told Miss Seng quietly:

"Mr. Twan was murdered last night."

"Murdered you say?" the girl burst out. "Uncle Twan murdered? Who did it?"

"I thought you would be able to tell us," the judge replied.

"Where was he found?" she asked tensely.

"In a deserted hut, in the forest. Halfway up the mountain slope."

She hit her small fist on the desk and shouted with sparkling eyes:

"That bastard Lew did it! The Baker sent his men after him, because Uncle Twan had helped us to leave that rotten crowd of his! And Uncle Twan fell into the trap! The bastard, the stinking bastard!"

She buried her face in her hands and burst out in sobs.

Judge Dee waited till she had calmed down a bit. He pointed at her cup and when she had drunk again he asked:

"Did Mr. Twan, when he joined you, also cut off the tip of his left little finger?"

She smiled through her tears.

"He wanted to, but he didn't have the guts! I don't know how many times he tried, him standing with his left hand on a tree trunk and a chopper in his right, and me standing beside him and counting one two three! But he always funked it!"

The judge nodded. He thought for a few moments, then he shook his head, heaved a deep sigh and took his writing brush. He jotted down a brief message on one of his large red visiting cards, put it in an envelope and wrote a few words on the outside. "Call a clerk!" he ordered Tao Gan.

When Tao Gan came back with the senior scribe, the judge gave him the envelope and said: "Let the headman deliver this at once." Then he turned to the girl again, gave her a thoughtful look and asked: "Haven't you got a regular young man somewhere?"

"Yes. He's a boatman in Chiang-pei. He wants to marry me, but I told him to wait a year or two. Then he'll have a boat of his own, and I'll have had the fun I want. We'll travel up and down the canal carrying freight, making enough to keep our ricebowl filled and having a good time into the bargain!" She darted an anxious look at the judge. "Are you really going to have my face branded, like the beanpole there said?"

"No, we won't. But you'll have to do with less freedom, for some time to come. One can have too much even of that, you know!"

He gave a sign to the matron. She took the girl's arm and led her away.

"How she rattled on!" Tao Gan exclaimed. "It was hard to get her started, but then she went on and on without stopping!"

"I let her tell everything in her own way. A strict cross-examination is indicated only when you notice that a person is telling lies. Remember that for a subsequent occasion, Tao Gan." He clapped his hands, and ordered the clerk who answered his summons to bring a hot towel.

"Twan Mou-tsai was a clever scoundrel, sir," Tao Gan resumed. "That girl is no fool, but she never understood that Twan was directing a smuggling ring."

Judge Dee made no comment. He rearranged the papers on his desk and placed the emerald ring in the cleared space, right in front of him. The clerk brought a copper basin of hot scented water. The judge picked a towel from it, and thoroughly rubbed his face and hands. Then he leaned back in his chair and said:

"Open the window, Tao Gan. It's getting stuffy here." He thought for a brief while, then looked up at Tao Gan and resumed: "I don't know whether Twan was clever or not. The picture Miss Seng gave was drawn from life: an elderly man who suddenly begins to doubt the validity of all accepted standards, and wonders what he has been living for, all those years. Many men pass through this stage after they have reached a certain age. For a year or two they are a nuisance to themselves and their housemates, then they usually come round again, and laugh at their own folly. With Twan, however, it was different. He decided to make a clean break, and carried that decision to its logical conclusion, namely the starting of an entirely new life. Whether he would have regretted that decision after a few years must remain an open question. He must have been an interesting man, that Mr. Twan. Eccentric, but certainly of strong character."

The judge fell silent. Tao Gan began to shift impatiently in his chair. He was eager to discuss the next phase of the investigation. He cleared his throat a few times, then asked a bit diffidently:

"Shall we have Chang brought in for questioning now, sir?" Judge Dee looked up.

"Chang? Oh yes, that friend of Seng Kiu, you mean. You can take care of that, Tao Gan, tomorrow. Just the routine questions. He and Seng Kiu are no problem. I was wondering about the girl, really. I don't know what to do about her! The government takes a grave view of vagrancy because it may lead to robbery and other disturbances of the peace. And also of unlicensed prostitution, because that is a form of tax evasion and therefore affects the Treasury. According to the law, she should be flogged and put in prison for two years. But I am convinced that that would turn her into a hardened criminal, who would end up either on the scaffold or in the gutter. That would be a pity, for she certainly has some sterling qualities. We must try to find another solution."

He worriedly shook his head, and resumed:

"As to Seng Kiu and that other rascal, I'll sentence them to one year's compulsory service with the labor corps of our Northern Army. That'll cure them of their lazy habits, and give them an opportunity to show what they are worth. If they do well, they can in due course request to be enlisted as free soldiers. As regards Seng's sister. . . . Yes, that's the solution, of course! I'll assign her as a bondmaid to Mr. Han Yung-han! Han is a very strict, old-fashioned gentleman who keeps his large household in excellent order. If she works there for a year, she'll come to know all the advantages of a more regular life, and in due time make that young boatman of hers a good housewife!"

Tao Gan gave the judge a worried look. He thought he really seemed very tired, his face was pale and the lines beside his mouth had become more marked. It had indeed been a long day. Would the judge consider it presumptuous if he proposed to take charge of the routine check of the shops in the marketplace? Or let him question Leng again? He decided first to ascertain what Judge Dee's own plans were.

"What do you think should be our next step now, sir? I thought. . . ."

"Our next step?" the judge asked raising his tufted eyebrows. "There is no next step. Didn't you see that all our problems are solved? Now we know how and why Twan was murdered, who took his dead body to the hut, everything! Including, of course, who was acting as local agent for the smuggling ring." As Tao

Gan stared at him, dumbfounded, the judge went on impatiently: "Heavens, you have heard all the evidence, haven't you? If I am now winding up with you the side-issues it's only because I have nothing better to do while I am waiting for the central figure of this tragedy to make his appearance."

Tao Gan opened his mouth to speak but Judge Dee went on quickly:

"Yes, it is indeed a tragedy. Often, Tao Gan, the final solution of a complicated case gives me a feeling of satisfaction, the satisfaction of having righted a wrong, and solved a riddle. This, however, is a case that depresses me. Strange, I had a vague foreboding of it when I had this ring here in my hand early this morning, just after I had got it from the gibbon. This ring emanated an atmosphere of human suffering. . . . Suffering is a terrible thing, Tao Gan. Sometimes it dignifies, mostly it degrades. Presently we shall see how it affected the main actor in this drama, and. . . ."

He broke off his sentence and glanced at the door. Footsteps had sounded in the corridor outside. The headman ushered in Mr. Wang.

The pharmacist, small and dapper in his glossy robe of black silk, made a low bow.

"What can this person do for Your Honor?" he asked politely.

Judge Dee pointed at the emerald ring before him and said evenly:

"You may tell me why you didn't take this ring too when you removed the dead man's possessions."

Wang gave a violent start when he saw the ring. But he quickly mastered himself and said indignantly:

"I don't understand this at all, Your Honor! The headman brought me your visiting card with the request to come here to give some information, and. . . ."

"Yes," the judge interrupted him. "Information about the murder of your colleague Twan Mou-tsai!" The pharmacist wanted to speak but Judge Dee raised his hand. "No, listen to me! I know exactly what happened. You badly needed the five gold bars Mr. Twan had entrusted to you, for your plan to smuggle two boxes of valuable contraband from Chiang-pei into Han-yuan had miscarried. The Baker's men whom you had hired bungled it, and the military police seized the costly merchandise you probably hadn't even paid for. Twan's desire to join Miss Seng's gang by taking the formal oath and cutting off the tip of his left little finger gave you an excellent opportunity for murdering that unfortunate man."

The headman moved up close to Wang, but Judge Dee shook his head at him. He continued:

"Twan lacked the courage to cut off the fingertip himself, and you had promised to perform the operation for him last night, in your own house up on the ridge. You had agreed that it would be done with the large chopper used for cutting medicinal roots into thin slices. One end of the heavy, razor-edged knife is attached with a hinge to the cutting board, the handle is on the other end. By means of this precision instrument, which every pharmacist and drug dealer has at hand, the operation could be performed without the risk of cutting off too much or too little, and so quickly and smoothly that the pain would be reduced to a minimum. Twan went to all this trouble because he wanted to prove to the vagabond girl he loved that he intended to stay with her forever."

The judge paused. Wang stared at him with wide, unbelieving eyes.

"Before Twan had even placed his hand in the right position on the cutting board, the large chopper came down and cut off four of his fingers. Then the unfortunate old man was finished off by bashing in his skull with the iron pestle of a drug mortar. Afterwards his dead body was carried from your house downhill to the deserted hut. There it would have been discovered, probably after many weeks, in an advanced state of decay. Moreover, you had taken the precaution of searching the body and removing everything that could have given a clue to the dead man's identity. I would have had the corpse burned as that of an unidentified tramp. But a gibbon of the forest put me on the right track."

"A . . . a gibbon?" Wang stammered.

"Yes, the gibbon who found Twan's emerald ring, which I have here before me. But that is no concern of yours."

Judge Dee fell silent. It was completely quiet in the small office. Wang's face had turned ashen and his lips were twitching. He swallowed a few times before he spoke, in a voice so hoarse that it was hardly audible:

"Yes, I confess that I murdered Twan Mou-tsai. Everything happened exactly as you said. With the exception of your remark about the two boxes of contraband. Those were not my property,

I was acting only as an agent, I was to have redistributed their contents." He sighed and continued in a detached voice: "I have had a number of financial reverses, these last two years, and my creditors were pressing me. The man whom I was most indebted to was a banker, in the capital." He mentioned a name which Judge Dee recognized; the man was a well-known financier, a cousin of the Director of the Treasury. "He wrote me a letter saying that, if I would come to see him, he was willing to talk matters over. I traveled to the capital and he received me most kindly. He said that, if I agreed to collaborate with him on a certain financial scheme of his, he would not only cancel my bonds, but also give me a generous share in the proceeds. Of course I agreed. Then, to my horrified amazement, he went on to explain coolly that he had organized a nationwide smuggling ring!"

Wang passed his hand over his eyes. Shaking his head, he resumed:

"When he mentioned the enormous profits, I weakened. Finally I gave in. I . . . I can't afford to become a poor man. And when I thought of all that money I would receive . . . I should have known better! Instead of canceling my bonds, the cruel devil held on to them, and his idea of rewarding me for my services was to lend me money at an atrocious interest. Soon I was completely in his clutches. When Twan entrusted the five gold bars to me, I thought at once that this was my chance to pay my principal, and become a free man again. I knew that Twan had told nobody that he would come to my house last night, for he didn't want others to know that he lacked the courage to perform the operation himself. He had insisted that I wouldn't even tell my family of his impending visit. I myself let him in, by the back door."

The pharmacist took a silk handkerchief from his sleeve and wiped his moist face. Then he said firmly:

"If Your Honor will kindly let me have a sheet of paper, I shall now write out my formal confession that I willfully murdered Twan Mou-sai."

"I haven't asked you for a formal confession yet, Mr. Wang," Judge Dee said calmly. "There are a few points that have to be clarified. In the first place: why did Mr. Twan want to have such large sums of money always at his disposal?"

"Because he kept hoping that some day that vagabond girl would consent to marry him. He told me that he wanted to be able to pay off her brother at once, and buy a nice country seat somewhere, to start a new life."

"I see. Second: why didn't you tell Twan frankly that you needed his gold because you were in serious financial trouble? Isn't it the old-established custom that members of the same guild always assist each other? And Mr. Twan was a very wealthy man who could well afford to lend you five gold bars."

Wang seemed greatly upset by these questions. His lips moved, but he could not bring out a word. Judge Dee did not pursue the matter further and went on:

"Third, you are a slightly built elderly man. How did you manage to carry the corpse all the way to the hut? It's true that it is downhill, but even so I don't think you could have done it."

Wang had taken hold of himself. Shaking his head disconsolately he answered:

"I can't understand myself how I did it, sir! But I was frantic, obsessed by the idea that I had to hide the body, at once. That gave me the force to drag the corpse to the garden, and from there to the forest. When I came back to the house, I was more dead than alive. . . ." Again he mopped his face. Then he added in a firmer voice: "I fully realize that I have murdered a good man because of his money, sir, and that I shall have to pay for that crime with my life."

Judge Dee sat up straight. Placing his elbows on the desk he leaned forward and told Wang in a gentle voice:

"You didn't realize, however, that if you formally confess to this murder, all your possessions will be confiscated, Mr. Wang. Besides, your son wouldn't inherit in any case, for I shall have to have him certified as of unsound mind."

"What do you mean?" Wang shouted. He bent forward and crashed his fist on the desk. "It isn't true, it's a lie! My son is very sound of mind, I tell you! The boy's mental development is only a bit retarded, and he's only twenty, after all! When he grows older, his mind will doubtless improve. . . . With a little patience, and if one avoids getting him excited, he is perfectly normal!"

He gave the judge an imploring look and went on with a shaking voice:

"He is my only son, sir, and such a nice, obedient boy! I assure you, sir. . . ."

Judge Dee spoke quietly:

"I shall personally see to it that he is given every possible care,

Mr. Wang, during your term in prison. I give you my word for that. But if we don't take adequate measures, your son will cause more accidents. He must be placed in ward, that's the only solution. Two days ago, when he came out of your shop, he happened to see that vagabond girl who was just leaving Leng's pawnshop. She is very beautiful, and in his confused mind your son thought she was his sweetheart. He wanted to take hold of her, but Mr. Twan told him she was *his* sweetheart, and then Miss Seng's brother chased your son away. This occurrence made a deep impression on his poor, deranged mind. Yesterday, when Twan came to visit you, your son must have seen him. Convinced that this was the man who had stolen his sweetheart from him, he killed him. Then you let your son carry the corpse to the hut, you leading the way. For your son that was an easy job, for like many young men of unsound mind, he is exceptionally strong and tall."

Wang nodded dazedly. Deep lines marked his pale, drawn face, his shoulders were sagging. He had suddenly changed from a dapper, efficient merchant into a tired old man.

"So that is why he kept talking about the girl and Twan. . . . I was taken completely unawares last night, for the boy had been in such a good mood, the whole day. . . . In the afternoon I had taken him for a walk in the woods, and he was so happy, watching the gibbons in the trees. . . . He dined with the housemaster, then he went to bed, for he tires easily. . . . I had told the housemaster that I would dine alone, in my library, had him put a cold snack there ready for me. When I was eating there with Twan, I told him about the gold. He said at once that I needn't worry about that, he could easily order more from the capital should he need it, and I could pay him back in installments. "The kind help you shall extend to me presently," he added with a smile, "I shall consider as the interest on the loan!" Twan was like that, sir. A truly remarkable man. He quickly emptied a large beaker of wine, then we went to the small workshop I have in my garden shed, to experiment with new drugs. Twan put his left hand on the cutting board, and closed his eyes. Just when I was adjusting the chopper, someone gave a push against my elbow. 'The bad old man has stolen my girl!' my son cried out behind me. The chopper had clapped down and cut off four fingers of Twan's hand. He fell forward over the table, with a frightened cry. I quickly looked round for a jar of powder, to staunch the bleeding. Suddenly my son grabbed an iron pestle from the table and hit him a terrible blow on the back of his head. . . ."

He gave the judge a forlorn look. Then, grabbing the edge of the desk with both hands, he said:

"The bright moon shining into his bedroom had wakened the boy, and looking out of his window he had seen Twan and me going to the garden shed. The moonlight always brings him into a kind of trance. . . . My boy didn't know what he did, Your Honor! He is so gentle as a rule, he. . . ." His voice trailed off.

"Your son shan't be prosecuted, of course, Mr. Wang. Mentally deficient persons are outside the pale of the law. Mr. Tao here will now take you to his own office next door, and there you will draw up a document describing to the best of your knowledge the organization and activities of the smuggling ring, adding the names and addresses of all other agents known to you. Is Mr. Leng, the pawnbroker, among them, by the way?"

"Oh no, sir! Why should you suspect him? He is my neighbor, and I never. . . ."

"I was told that he regularly visits Chiang-pei, one of the important bases of your smuggling organization."

"Mr. Leng's wife is extremely jealous," Wang remarked dryly. "She doesn't allow him to have other women in the house. Therefore he established a separate household in Chiang-pei."

"Quite. Well, after you have signed and sealed the document I mentioned, Mr. Wang, you will then write a complete account of Mr. Twan's fatal accident. This very night I shall send both documents by special messenger to the capital. I shall add a recommendation for clemency, pointing out that you voluntarily furnished the information that will enable the authorities to break up the smuggling ring. I hope this will result in your prison term being substantially reduced. However that may be, I shall try to arrange that your son is allowed to visit you from time to time in prison. Take Mr. Wang to your room, Tao Gan. Supply him with writing material, and give strict orders that he is not to be disturbed."

When Tao Gan came back, he found Judge Dee standing in front of the open window, his hands behind his back. He was enjoying the cool air that came inside from the small walled-in garden, planted with banana trees. Pointing at the mass of luxuriant green leaves he said:

"Look at those magnificent bunches of bananas, Tao Gan! They have just ripened. Tell the headman to bring a few to my private residence, so that I can give the gibbons some, tomorrow morning."

Tao Gan nodded, his long face creased in a broad smile.

"Allow me to congratulate you, sir, on. . . ."

Judge Dee raised his hand.

"It was thanks to your prompt and efficient action that we could solve this complicated case so quickly, Tao Gan. I apologize for being rather curt with you, just before Mr. Wang came in. The fact is that I was dreading that interview, for I hate nothing more than to see a man go all to pieces in front of me—even if he is a criminal. But Mr. Wang bore himself well. His great love for his son lent him dignity, Tao Gan."

The judge resumed his seat behind the desk.

"I shall write a letter to Sergeant Hoong in Chiang-pei at once, informing him that the smuggling case has been solved, and that he and my other two lieutenants must come back here tomorrow. And you can issue the necessary orders for the release from prison of our friend the pawnbroker. Those hours in jail will have given him an opportunity for reflection, I hope."

He took up his writing-brush, but suddenly he checked himself and resumed:

"Now that I have worked together closely with you alone on a case, Tao Gan, I want to tell you that I shall be very glad to have you on my permanent staff. I have but one piece of advice to give to you for your further career as a criminal investigator. That is that you must never allow yourself to become emotionally involved in the cases you are dealing with. This is most important, Tao Gan, but most difficult to achieve. I ought to know. I have never learned it."

GEORGES SIMENON
Maigret's Christmas

THE ROUTINE never varied. When Maigret went to bed he must have muttered his usual, "Tomorrow morning I shall sleep late." And Madame Maigret, who over the years should have learned to pay no attention to such casual phrases, had taken him at his word this Christmas Day.

It was not quite daylight when he heard her stirring cautiously. He forced himself to breathe regularly and deeply as though he were still asleep. It was like a game. She inched toward the edge of the bed with animal stealth, pausing after each movement to make sure she had not awakened him. He waited anxiously for the inevitable finale, the moment when the bedsprings, relieved of her weight, would rise back into place with a faint sigh.

She picked up her clothing from the chair and turned the knob of the bathroom door so slowly that it seemed to take an eternity. It was not until she had reached the distant fastness of the kitchen that she resumed her normal movements.

Maigret had fallen asleep again. Not deeply, nor for long. Long enough, however, for a confused and disturbing dream. Waking, he could not remember what it was, but he knew it was disturbing because he still felt vaguely uneasy.

The crack between the window drapes, which never quite closed, became a strip of pale, hard daylight. He waited a while longer, lying on his back with his eyes open, savoring the fragrance of fresh coffee. Then he heard the apartment door open and close, and he knew that Madame Maigret was hurrying downstairs to buy him hot *croissants* from the bakery at the corner of the Rue Amelot.

He never ate in the morning. His breakfast consisted of black coffee. But his wife clung to her ritual: on Sundays and holidays he was supposed to lie in bed until midmorning while she went out for *croissants.*

He got up, stepped into his slippers, put on his dressing gown, and drew the curtains. He knew he was doing wrong. His wife would be heartbroken. But while he was willing to make almost any sacrifice to please her, he just could not stay in bed longer than he felt like it.

It was not snowing. It was nonsense, of course, for a man past fifty to be disappointed because there was no snow on Christmas morning; but then middle-aged people never have as much sense as young folks sometimes imagine.

A dirty, turbid sky hung over the rooftops. The Boulevard Richard Lenoir was completely deserted. The words *Fils et Cie., Bonded Warehouses,* on the sign above the porte-cochere across the street, stood out as black as mourning crepe. The *F,* for some strange reason, seemed particularly dismal.

He heard his wife moving about in the kitchen again. She came into the dining room on tiptoe, as though he were still asleep instead of looking out the window. He glanced at his watch on the night table. It was only ten past eight.

The night before the Maigrets had gone to the theater. They would have loved dropping in for a snack at some restaurant, like everyone else on Christmas Eve, but all tables were reserved for *Réveillon* supper. So they had walked home arm in arm, getting in a few minutes before midnight. So they hadn't long to wait before exchanging presents.

He got a pipe, as usual. Her present was an electric coffeepot, the latest model that she had wanted so much, and, not to break with tradition, a dozen finely embroidered handkerchiefs.

Still looking out the window, Maigret absently filled his new pipe. The shutters were still closed on some of the windows across the boulevard. Not many people were up. Here and there a light burned in a window, probably left by children who had leaped out of bed at the crack of dawn to rush for their presents under the Christmas tree.

In the quiet Maigret apartment the morning promised to be a lazy one for just the two of them. Maigret would loiter in his dressing gown until quite late. He would not even shave. He would dawdle in the kitchen, talking to his wife while she put the lunch on the stove. Just the two of them.

He wasn't melancholy exactly, but his dream—which he couldn't remember—had left him jumpy. Or perhaps it wasn't his dream. Perhaps it was Christmas. He had to be extra careful on Christmas Day, careful of his words, the way Madame Maigret had been careful of her movements in getting out of bed. Her nerves, too, were especially sensitive on Christmas.

Oh well, why think of all that? He would just be careful to say nothing untoward. He would be careful not to look out of the window when the neighborhood children began to appear on the sidewalks with their Christmas toys.

All the houses in the street had children. Or almost all. The street would soon echo to the shrill blast of toy horns, the roll of toy drums, and the crack of toy pistols. The little girls were probably already cradling their new dolls.

A few years ago he had proposed more or less at random: "Why don't we take a little trip for Christmas?"

"Where?" she had replied with her infallible common sense.

Where, indeed? Whom would they visit? They had no relatives except her sister, who lived too far away. And why spend Christmas in some second-rate country hotel, or in a hotel in some strange town?

Oh well, he'd feel better after he had his coffee. He was never at his best until he'd drunk his first cup of coffee and lit his first pipe.

Just as he was reaching for the knob, the door opened noiselessly and Madame Maigret appeared carrying a tray. She looked at the empty bed, then turned her disappointed eyes upon her husband. She was on the verge of tears.

"You got up!" She looked as though she had been up for hours herself, every hair in place, a picture of neatness in her crisp clean apron. "And I was so happy about serving your breakfast in bed."

He had tried a hundred times, as subtly as he could, to make her understand that he didn't like eating breakfast in bed. It made him uncomfortable. It made him feel like an invalid or a senile old gaffer. But for Madame Maigret breakfast in bed was the symbol of leisure and luxury, the ideal way to start Sunday or a holiday.

"Don't you want to go back to bed?"

No, he did not. Decidedly not. He hadn't the courage.

"Then come to breakfast in the kitchen. And Merry Christmas."

"Merry Christmas! . . . You're not angry?"

They were in the dining room. He surveyed the silver tray on a corner of the table, the steaming cup of coffee, the golden-brown *croissants*. He put down his pipe and ate a *croissant* to please his wife, but he remained standing, looking out the window.

"It's snowing."

It wasn't real snow. It was a fine white dust sifting down from the sky, but it reminded Maigret that when he was a small boy he used to stick out his tongue to lick up a few of the tiny flakes.

His gaze focused on the entrance to the building across the street, next door to the warehouse. Two women had just come out, bareheaded. One of them, a blonde of about thirty, had thrown a coat over her shoulders without stopping to slip her arms into the sleeves. The other, a brunette, older and thinner, was hugging a shawl.

The blonde seemed to hesitate, ready to turn back. Her slim little companion was insistent and Maigret had the impression that she was pointing up toward his window. The appearance of the concierge in the doorway behind them seemed to tip the scales in favor of the little brunette. The blonde looked back apprehensively, then crossed the street.

"What are you looking at?"

"Nothing . . . two women. . . ."

"What are they doing?"

"I think they're coming here."

The two women had stopped in the middle of the street and were looking up in the direction of the Maigret apartment.

"I hope they're not coming here to bother you on Christmas Day. My housework's not even done." Nobody would have guessed it. There wasn't a speck of dust on any of the polished furniture. "Are you sure they're coming here?"

"We'll soon find out."

To be on the safe side, he went to comb his hair, brush his teeth, and splash a little water on his face. He was still in his room, relighting his pipe, when he heard the doorbell. Madame Maigret was evidently putting up a strong hedgehog defense, for it was some time before she came for him.

"They insist on talking to you," she whispered. "They claim it's very important and they need advice. I know one of them."

"Which one?"

"The skinny little one, Mademoiselle Doncoeur. She lives across the street on the same floor as ours. She's a very nice person and she does embroidery for a firm in the Faubourg Saint Honoré. I sometimes wonder if she isn't in love with you."

"Why?"

"Because she works near the window, and when you leave the house in the morning she sometimes gets up to watch you go down the street."

"How old is she?"

"Forty-five to fifty. Aren't you getting dressed?"

Doesn't a man have the right to lounge in his dressing gown, even if people come to bother him at eight-thirty on Christmas morning? Well, he'd compromise. He'd put his trousers on underneath the robe.

The two women were standing when he walked into the dining room.

"Excuse me, mesdames. . . ."

Perhaps Madame Maigret was right. Mademoiselle Doncoeur did not blush; she paled, smiled, lost her smile, smiled again. She opened her mouth to speak but said nothing.

The blonde, on the other hand, was perfectly composed. She said with a touch of humor, "Coming here wasn't my idea."

"Won't you sit down?"

Maigret noticed that the blonde was wearing a house dress under her coat and that her legs were bare. Mademoiselle Doncoeur was dressed as though for church.

"You perhaps wonder at our boldness in coming to you like this," Mademoiselle Doncoeur said finally, choosing her words carefully. "Like everyone in the neighborhood, we are honored to have such a distinguished neighbor. . . ." She paused, blushed, and stared at the tray. "We're keeping you from your breakfast."

"I've finished. I'm at your service."

"Something happened in our building last night, or rather this morning, which was so unusual that I felt it was our duty to speak to you about it immediately. Madame Martin did not want to disturb you, but I told her—"

"You also live across the street, Madame Martin?"

"Yes, monsieur." Madame Martin was obviously unhappy at being forced to take this step. Mademoiselle Doncoeur, however, was now fully wound up.

"We live on the same floor, just across from your windows."

She blushed again, as if she were making a confession. "Monsieur Martin is often out of town, which is natural enough since he is a traveling salesman. For the past two months their little girl has been in bed, as a result of a silly accident. . . ."

Maigret turned politely to the blonde. "You have a daughter?"

"Well, not a daughter exactly. She's our niece. Her mother died two years ago and she's been living with us ever since. The girl broke her leg on the stairs. She should have been up and about after six weeks, but there were complications."

"Your husband is on the road at present?"

"He should be in Bergerac."

"I'm listening, Mademoiselle Doncoeur."

Madame Maigret had detoured through the bathroom to regain the kitchen. The clatter of pots and pans had resumed. Maigret stared through the window at the leaden sky.

"I got up early this morning as usual," said Mademoiselle Doncoeur, "to go to first Mass."

"And you did go to church?"

"Yes. I stayed there for three Masses. I got home about seven-thirty and made my breakfast. You may have seen the light in my window."

Maigret's gesture indicated that he had not been watching.

"I was in a hurry to take a few goodies to Colette. It's very sad for a child to spend Christmas in bed. Colette is Madame Martin's niece."

"How old is she?"

"Seven. Isn't that right, Madame Martin?"

"She'll be seven in January."

"So at eight o'clock I knocked at the door of their apartment—"

"I wasn't up," the blonde interrupted. "I sometimes sleep rather late."

"As I was saying, I knocked. Madame Martin kept me waiting for a moment while she slipped on her negligee. I had my arms full, and I asked if I could take my presents in to Colette."

Maigret noted that the blonde was making a mental inventory of the apartment, stopping occasionally to dart a sharp, suspicious glance in his direction.

"We opened the door to her room together—"

"The child has a room of her own?"

"Yes. There are two bedrooms in the apartment, a dressing room, a kitchen, and a dining room. But I must tell you—No,

I'm getting ahead of myself. We had just opened the door and, since the room was dark, Madame Martin had switched on the light—"

"Colette was awake?"

"Yes. It was easy to see she'd been awake for some time, waiting. You know how children are on Christmas morning. If she could use her legs, she would certainly have got up long since to see what Father Christmas had brought her. Perhaps another child would have called out. But Colette is already a little lady. She's much older than her age. She thinks a lot."

Now Madame Martin was looking out the window. Maigret tried to guess which apartment was hers. It must be the last one to the right, the one with the two lighted windows.

"I wished her a Merry Christmas," Mademoiselle Doncoeur continued. "I said to her, and these were my exact words, 'Darling, look what Father Christmas left in my apartment for you.'"

Madame Martin was clasping and unclasping her fingers.

"And do you know what she answered me, without even looking to see what I'd brought? They were only trifles, anyhow. She said, 'I saw him.'

" 'Whom did you see?'

" 'Father Christmas.'

" 'When did you see him?' I asked. 'Where?'

" 'Right here, last night. He came to my room.'

"That's exactly what she said, isn't it, Madame Martin? With any other child, we would have smiled. But as I told you, Colette is already a little lady. She doesn't joke. I said, 'How could you see him, since it was dark?'

" 'He had a light.'

" 'You mean he turned on the electricity?'

" 'No. He had a flashlight. Look, Mamma Loraine.'

"I must tell you that the little girl calls Madame Martin 'Mamma,' which is natural enough, since her own mother is dead and Madame Martin has been taking her place."

The monologue had become a confused buzzing in Maigret's ears. He had not drunk his second cup of coffee and his pipe had gone out. He asked without conviction, "Did she really see someone?"

"Yes, Monsieur l'Inspecteur. And that's why I insisted that Madame Martin come to speak to you. Colette did see someone and she proved it to us. With a shy little smile she threw back the bed sheet and showed us a magnificent doll . . . a beautiful big doll she was cuddling and I swear was not in the house yesterday."

"You didn't give your niece a doll, Madame Martin?"

"I was going to give her one, but mine was not nearly as nice. I got it yesterday afternoon at the Galeries, and I was holding it behind me this morning when we came into her room."

"In other words, someone *did* come into your apartment last night?"

"That's not all," said Mademoiselle Doncoeur quickly; she was not to be stopped. "Colette never tells lies. She's not a child who imagines things. And when we questioned her, she said the man was certainly Father Christmas because he wore a white beard and a bright red coat."

"At what time did she wake up?"

"She doesn't know—sometime during the night. She opened her eyes because she thought she saw a light. And there was a light, shining on the floor near the fireplace."

"I can't understand it," sighed Madame Martin. "Unless my husband has some explanation. . . ."

But Mademoiselle Doncoeur was not to be diverted from her story. It was obvious that she was the one who had questioned the child, just as she was the one who had thought of Maigret. She resumed:

"Colette said, 'Father Christmas was squatting on the floor, and he was bending over, as if he were working at something.'"

"She wasn't frightened?"

"No. She just watched him. This morning she told us he was busy making a hole in the floor. She thought he wanted to go through the floor to visit the people downstairs—that's the Delormes, who have a little boy of three—because the chimney was too narrow. The man must have sensed she was watching him, because he got up, came over to the bed, and gave Colette the big doll. Then he put his finger to his lips."

"Did she see him leave?"

"Yes."

"Through the floor?"

"No, by the door."

"Into what room does this door open?"

"Directly into the outside hall. There is another door that opens into the apartment, but the hall door is like a private entrance because the room used to be rented separately."

"Wasn't that door locked?"

"Of course," Madame Martin intervened. "I wouldn't let the child sleep in a room that wasn't locked from the outside."

"Then the door was forced?"

"Probably. I don't know. Mademoiselle Doncoeur immediately suggested we come to see you."

"Did you find the hole in the floor?"

Madame Martin shrugged wearily, but Mademoiselle Doncoeur answered for her.

"Not a hole exactly, but you could see that the floor boards had been moved."

"Tell me, Madame Martin, have you any idea what might have been hidden under the flooring?"

"No, monsieur."

"How long have you lived in this apartment?"

"Since my marriage, five years ago."

"And this room was part of the apartment then?"

"Yes."

"You know who lived there before you?"

"My husband. He's thirty-eight. He was thirty-three when we were married, and he had his own furniture then. He liked to have his own home to come back to when he returned to Paris from the road."

"Do you think he might have wanted to surprise Colette?"

"He is six or seven hundred kilometers from here."

"Where did you say?"

"In Bergerac. His itinerary is planned in advance for he rarely deviates from his schedule."

"For what firm does he travel?"

"He covers the central and southwest territory for Zenith watches. It's an important line, as you probably know. He has a very good job."

"There isn't a finer man on earth!" exclaimed Mademoiselle Doncoeur. She blushed, then, "Except you, Monsieur l'Inspecteur."

"As I understand it then, someone got into your apartment last night disguised as Father Christmas."

"According to the little girl."

"Didn't you hear anything? Is your room far from the little girl's?"

"There's a dining room between us."

"Don't you leave the connecting doors open at night?"

"It isn't necessary. Colette is not afraid, and as a rule she never wakes up. If she wants anything, she has a little bell on her night table."

"Did you go out last night?"

"I did not, Monsieur l'Inspecteur," Madame Martin was annoyed.

"Did you receive visitors?"

"I do not receive visitors while my husband is away."

Maigret glanced at Mademoiselle Doncoeur, whose expression did not change. So Madame Martin was telling the truth.

"Did you go to bed late?"

"I read until midnight. As soon as the radio played 'Minuit, Chrétiens,' I went to bed."

"And you heard nothing unusual?"

"Nothing."

"Have you asked the concierge if she clicked the latch to let in any strangers last night?"

"I asked her," Mademoiselle Doncoeur volunteered. "She says she didn't."

"And you found nothing missing from your apartment this morning, Madame Martin? Nothing disturbed in the dining room?"

"No."

"Who is with the little girl now?"

"No one. She's used to staying alone. I can't be at home all day. I have marketing to do, errands to run. . . ."

"I understand. You told me Colette is an orphan?"

"Her mother is dead."

"So her father is living. Where is he?"

"Her father's name is Paul Martin. He's my husband's brother. As to telling you where he is—" Madame Martin sketched a vague gesture.

"When did you see him last?"

"About a month ago. A little longer. It was around All Saints' Day. He was finishing a novena."

"I beg your pardon?"

"I may as well tell you everything at once," said Madame Martin with a faint smile, "since we seem to be washing our family linen." She glanced reproachfully at Mademoiselle Doncoeur. "My brother-in-law, especially since he lost his wife, is not quite respectable."

"What do you mean exactly?"

"He drinks. He always drank a little, but he never used to get into trouble. He had a good job with a furniture store in the Faubourg Saint Antoine. But since the accident. . . ."

"The accident to his daughter?"

"No, to his wife. He borrowed a car from a friend one Sunday about three years ago and took his wife and little girl to the country. They had lunch at a roadside inn near Mantes la Jolie and he drank too much white wine. He sang most of the way back to Paris—until he ran into something near the Bougival bridge. His wife was killed instantly. He cracked his own skull and it's a miracle he's still alive. Colette escaped without a scratch. Paul hasn't been a man since then. We've practically adopted the little girl. He comes to see her occasionally when he's sober. Then he starts over again. . . ."

"Do you know where he lives?"

Another vague gesture. "Everywhere. We've seen him loitering around the Bastille like a beggar. Sometimes he sells papers in the street. I can speak freely in front of Mademoiselle Doncoeur because unfortunately the whole house knows about him."

"Don't you think he might have dressed up as Father Christmas to call on his daughter?"

"That's what I told Mademoiselle Doncoeur, but she insisted on coming to see you anyhow."

"Because I see no reason for him to take up the flooring," said Mademoiselle Doncoeur acidly.

"Or perhaps your husband returned to Paris unexpectedly. . . ."

"It's certainly something of the sort. I'm not at all disturbed. But Mademoiselle Doncoeur—"

Decidedly Madame Martin had not crossed the boulevard light-heartedly.

"Do you know where your husband might be staying in Bergerac?"

"Yes. At the Hôtel de Bordeaux."

"You hadn't thought of telephoning him?"

"We have no phone. There's only one in the house—the people on the second floor, and they hate to be disturbed."

"Would you object to my calling the Hôtel de Bordeaux?"

Madame Martin started to nod, then hesitated. "He'll think something terrible has happened."

"You can speak to him yourself."

"He's not used to my phoning him on the road."

"You'd rather he not know what's happening?"

"That's not so. I'll talk to him if you like."

Maigret picked up the phone and placed the call. Ten minutes later he was connected with the Hôtel de Bordeaux in Bergerac. He passed the instrument to Madame Martin.

"Hello . . . Monsieur Martin, please . . . Yes, Monsieur Jean Martin . . . It doesn't matter. Wake him up."

She put her hand over the mouthpiece. "He's still asleep. They've gone to call him."

Then she retreated into silence, evidently rehearsing the words she was to speak to her husband.

"Hello? . . . Hello, darling. . . . What? . . . Yes, Merry Christmas! . . . Yes, everything's all right. . . . Colette is fine. . . . No, that's not why I phoned. . . . No, no, no! Nothing's wrong. Please don't worry!" She repeated each word separately! "Please . . . don't . . . worry! I just wanted to tell you about a strange thing that happened last night. Somebody dressed up like Father Christmas and came into Colette's room. . . . No, no! He didn't hurt her. He gave her a big doll. . . . Yes, *doll!* . . . And he did strange things to the floor. He removed two boards which he put back in a hurry. . . . Mademoiselle Doncoeur thought I should report it to the police inspector who lives across the street. I'm there now. . . . You don't understand? Neither do I. . . . You want to talk to him?" She passed the instrument to Maigret. "He wants to speak to you."

A warm masculine voice came over the wire, the voice of an anxious, puzzled man.

"Are you sure my wife and the little girl are all right? . . . It's all so incredible! If it were just the doll, I might suspect my brother. Loraine will tell you about him. Loraine is my wife. Ask her. . . . But he wouldn't have removed the flooring. . . . Do you think I'd better come home? I can get a train for Paris at three this afternoon. . . . What? . . . Thank you so much. It's good to know you'll look after them."

Loraine Martin took back the phone.

"See darling? The inspector says there's no danger. It would be foolish to break your trip now. It might spoil your chances of being transferred permanently to Paris. . . ."

Mademoiselle Doncoeur was watching her closely and there was little tenderness in the spinster's eyes.

". . . I promise to wire you or phone you if there's anything new. . . . She's playing quietly with her new doll. . . . No, I haven't had time yet to give her your present. I'll go right home and do it now."

Madame Martin hung up and declared, "You see." Then, after a pause, "Forgive me for bothering you. It's really not my fault. I'm sure this is all the work of some practical joker . . . unless it's my brother-in-law. When he's been drinking there's no telling what he might do."

"Do you expect to see him today? Don't you think he might want to see his daughter?"

"That depends. If he's been drinking, no. He's very careful never to come around in that condition."

"May I have your permission to come over and talk with Colette a little later?"

"I see no reason why you shouldn't—if you think it worth while. . . ."

"Thank you, Monsieur Maigret!" exclaimed Mademoiselle Doncoeur. Her expression was half grateful, half conspiratorial. "She's such an interesting child! You'll see!"

She backed toward the door.

A few minutes later Maigret watched the two women cross the boulevard. Mademoiselle Doncoeur, close on the heels of Madame Martin, turned to look up at the windows of the Maigret apartment.

Madame Maigret opened the kitchen door, flooding the dining room with the aroma of browning onions. She asked gently:

"Are you happy?"

He pretended not to understand. Luckily he had been too busy to think much about the middle-aged couple who had nobody to make a fuss over this Christmas morning.

It was time for him to shave and call on Colette.

He was just about to lather his face when he decided to make a phone call. He didn't bother with his dressing gown. Clad only in pajamas, he dropped into the easy chair by the window—*his* chair—and watched the smoke curling up from all the chimney pots while his call went through.

The ringing at the other end—in headquarters at the Quai des Orfèvres—had a different sound from all other rings. It evoked for him the long empty corridors, the vacant offices, the operator stuck with holiday duty at the switchboard. . . . Then he heard the operator call Lucas with the words: "The boss wants you."

He felt a little like one of his wife's friends who could imagine no greater joy—which she experienced daily—than lying in bed all morning, with her windows closed and curtains drawn, and telephoning all her friends, one after the other. By the soft glow of her night light she managed to maintain a constant state of just having awakened. "What? Ten o'clock already? How's the weather? Is it raining? Have you been out yet? Have you done all your marketing?" And as she established telephonic connection with the hurly-burly of the workaday world, she would sink more and more voluptuously into the warm softness of her bed.

"That you, Chief?"

Maigret, too, felt a need for contact with the working world. He wanted to ask Lucas who was on duty with him, what they were doing, how the shop looked on this Christmas morning.

"Nothing new? Not too busy?"

"Nothing to speak of. Routine. . . ."

"I'd like you to get me some information. You can probably do this by phone. First of all, I want a list of all convicts released from prison the last two or three months."

"Which prison?"

"All prisons. But don't bother with any who haven't served at least five years. Then check and see if any of them have ever lived on Boulevard Richard Lenoir. Got that?"

"I'm making notes."

Lucas was probably somewhat bewildered, but he would never admit it.

"Another thing. I want you to locate a man named Paul Martin, a drunk, no fixed address, who frequently hangs out around the Place de la Bastille. I don't want him arrested. I don't want him molested. I just want to know where he spent Christmas Eve. The commissariats should help you on this one."

No use trying. Maigret simply could not reproduce the idle mood of his wife's friend. On the contrary, it embarrassed him to be lolling at home in his pajamas, unshaven, phoning from his favorite easy chair, looking out at a scene of complete peace and quiet in which there was no movement except the smoke rising from the chimneys, while at the other end of the line good old Lucas had been on duty since six this morning and was probably already unwrapping his sandwiches.

"That's not quite all, old man. I want you to call Bergerac long distance. There's a traveling salesman by the name of Jean Martin staying at the Hôtel de Bordeaux there. No, Jean. It's his brother. I want to know if Jean Martin got a telegram or a phone call from Paris last night or any time yesterday. And while you're about it, find out where he spent Christmas Eve. I think that's all."

"Shall I call you back?"

"Not right away. I've got to go out for a while. I'll call you when I get home."

"Something happen in your neighborhood?"

"I don't know yet. Maybe."

Madame Maigret came into the bathroom to talk to him while he finished dressing. He did not put on his overcoat. The smoke curling slowly upward from so many chimneys blended with the gray of the sky and conjured up the image of just as many overheated apartments, cramped rooms in which he would not be invited to make himself at home. He refused to be uncomfortable. He would put on his hat to cross the boulevard, and that was all.

The building across the way was very much like the one he lived in—old but clean, a little dreary, particularly on a drab December morning. He didn't stop at the concierge's lodge, but noted that she watched him with some annoyance. Doors opened silently as he climbed the stairs. He heard whispering, the padding of slippered feet.

Mademoiselle Doncoeur, who had doubtless been watching for him, was waiting on the fourth-floor landing. She was both shy and excited, as if keeping a secret tryst with a lover.

"This way, Monsieur Maigret. She went out a little while ago."

He frowned, and she noted the fact.

"I told her that you were coming and that she had better wait for you, but she said she had not done her marketing yesterday and that there was nothing in the house. She said all the stores would be closed if she waited too long. Come in."

She had opened the door into Madame Martin's dining room, a small, rather dark room that was clean and tidy.

"I'm looking after the little girl until she comes back. I told Colette that you were coming to see her, and she is delighted. I've spoken to her about you. She's only afraid you might take back her doll."

"When did Madame Martin decide to go out?"

"As soon as we came back across the street, she started dressing."

"Did she dress completely?"

"I don't understand."

"I mean, I suppose she dresses differently when she goes downtown than when she merely goes shopping in the neighborhood."

"She was quite dressed up. She put on her hat and gloves. And she carried her shopping bag."

Before going to see Colette, Maigret stepped into the kitchen and glanced at the breakfast dishes.

"Did she eat before you came to see me?"

"No. I didn't give her a chance."

"And when she came back?"

"She just made herself a cup of black coffee. I fixed breakfast for Colette while Madame Martin got dressed."

There was a cooler on the ledge of the window looking out on the courtyard. Maigret carefully examined its contents: butter, eggs, vegetables, some cold meat. He found two uncut loaves of fresh bread in the kitchen cupboard. Colette had eaten *croissants* with her hot chocolate.

"How well do you know Madame Martin?"

"We're neighbors, aren't we? And I've seen more of her since Colette has been in bed. She often asks me to keep an eye on the little girl when she goes out."

"Does she go out much?"

"Not very often. Just for her marketing."

Maigret tried to analyze the curious impression he had had on entering the apartment. There was something in the atmosphere that disturbed him, something about the arrangement of the furniture, the special kind of neatness that prevailed, even the smell of the place. As he followed Mademoiselle Doncoeur into the dining room, he thought that he knew what it was.

Madame Martin had told him that her husband had lived in this apartment before their marriage. And even though Madame Martin had lived there for five years, it had remained a bachelor's apartment. He pointed to the two enlarged photographs standing on opposite ends of the mantelpiece.

"Who are they?"

"Monsieur Martin's father and mother."

"Doesn't Madame Martin have photos of her own parents about?"

"I've never heard her speak of them. I suppose she's an orphan."

Even the bedroom was without the feminine touch. He opened

a closet. Next to the neat rows of masculine clothing the woman's clothes were hanging, mostly severely tailored suits and conservative dresses. He did not open the bureau drawers but he was sure that they did not contain the usual trinkets and knickknacks that women collect.

"Mademoiselle Doncoeur!" called a calm little voice.

"Let's talk to Colette," said Maigret.

The child's room was as astere and cold as the others. The little girl lay in a bed too large for her, her face solemn, her eyes questioning but trusting.

"Are you the inspector, monsieur?"

"I'm the inspector, my girl. Don't be afraid."

"I'm not afraid. Hasn't Mamma Loraine come home yet?"

Maigret pursed his lips. The Martins had practically adopted their niece, yet the child said "Mamma Loraine," not just "Mamma."

"Do you believe it was Father Christmas who came to see me last night?" Colette asked Maigret.

"I'm sure it was."

"Mamma Loraine doesn't believe it. She never believes me."

The girl had a dainty, attractive little face, with very bright eyes that stared at Maigret with level persistence. The plaster cast that sheathed one leg all the way to the hip made a thick bulge under the blankets.

Mademoiselle Doncoeur hovered in the doorway, evidently anxious to leave the inspector alone with the girl. She said, "I must run home for a moment to make sure my lunch isn't burning."

Maigret sat down beside the bed, wondering how to go about questioning the girl.

"Do you love Mamma Loraine very much?" he began.

"Yes, monsieur." She replied without hesitation and without enthusiasm.

"And your papa?"

"Which one? Because I have two papas, you know—Papa Paul and Papa Jean."

"Has it been a long time since you saw Papa Paul?"

"I don't remember. Perhaps several weeks. He promised to bring me a toy for Christmas, but he hasn't come yet. He must be sick."

"Is he often sick?"

"Yes, often. When he's sick he doesn't come to see me."

"And your Papa Jean."

"He's away on a trip, but he'll be back for New Year's. Maybe then he'll be appointed to the Paris office and won't have to go away any more. That would make him very happy, and me too."

"Do many of your friends come to see you since you've been in bed?"

"What friends? The girls in school don't know where I live. Or maybe they know but their parents don't let them come alone."

"What about Mamma Loraine's friends? Or your papa's?"

"Nobody comes, ever."

"Ever? Are you sure?"

"Only the man to read the gas meter, or for the electricity. I can hear them, because the door is almost always open. I recognize their voices. Once a man came and I didn't recognize his voice. Or twice."

"How long ago was that?"

"The first time was the day after my accident. I remember because the doctor just left."

"Who was it?"

"I didn't see him. He knocked at the other door. I heard him talking and then Mamma Loraine came and closed my door. They talked for quite a while but I couldn't hear very well. Afterward Mamma Loraine said it was a man who wanted to sell her some insurance. I don't know what that is."

"And he came back?"

"Five or six days ago. It was night and I'd already turned off my light. I wasn't asleep, though. I heard someone knock, and then they talked in low voices like the first time. Mademoiselle Doncoeur sometimes comes over in the evening, but I could tell it wasn't she. I thought they were quarreling and I was frightened. I called out, and Mamma Loraine came in and said it was the man about the insurance again and I should go to sleep."

"Did he stay long?"

"I don't know. I think I fell asleep."

"And you didn't see him either time?"

"No, but I'd recognize his voice."

"Even though he speaks in low tones."

"Yes, that's why. When he speaks low it sounds just like a big bumblebee. I can keep the doll, can't I? Mamma Loraine bought me two boxes of candy and a little sewing kit. She bought me a doll, too, but it wasn't nearly as big as the doll Father Christmas gave me, because she's not rich. She showed it to me this morning before she left, and then she put it back in the box. I have the big one now, so I won't need the little one and Mamma Loraine can take it back to the store."

The apartment was overheated, yet Maigret felt suddenly cold. The building was very much like the one across the street, yet not only did the rooms seem smaller and stuffier, but the whole world seemed smaller and meaner over here.

He bent over the floor near the fireplace. He lifted the loose floor boards but saw nothing but an empty, dusty cavity smelling of dampness. There were scratches on the planks which indicated that they had been forced up with a chisel or some similar instrument.

He examined the outside door and found indications that it had been forced. It was obviously an amateur's work, and, luckily for him, the job had been an easy one.

"Father Christmas wasn't angry when he saw you watching him?"

"No, monsieur. He was busy making a hole in the floor so he could go and see the little boy downstairs."

"Did he speak to you?"

"I think he smiled at me. I'm not sure, though, because of his whiskers. It wasn't very light. But I'm sure he put his fingers to his lips so I wouldn't call anybody, because grownups aren't supposed to see Father Christmas. Did you ever see him?"

"A very long time ago."

"When you were little?"

Maigret heard footsteps in the hallway. The door opened and Madame Martin came in. She was wearing a gray tailored suit and a small beige hat and carried a brown shopping bag. She was visibly cold, for her skin was taut and very white, yet she must have hurried up the stairs, since there were two pink spots on her cheeks and she was out of breath. Unsmiling, she asked Maigret:

"Has she been a good girl?" Then, as she took off her jacket, "I apologize for making you wait. I had so many things to buy, and I was afraid the stores would all be closed later on."

"Did you meet anyone?"

"What do you mean?"

"Nothing. I was wondering if anyone tried to speak to you."

She had had plenty of time to go much farther than the Rue

Amelot or the Rue de Chemin Vert, where most of the neighborhood shops were located. She had even had time to go across
Paris and back by taxi or the Métro.

Mademoiselle Doncoeur returned to ask if there were anything
she could do. Madame Martin was about to say no when Maigret
intervened: "I'd like you to stay with Colette while I step into
the next room."

Mademoiselle Doncoeur understood that he wanted her to keep
the child busy while he questioned the foster mother. Madame
Martin must have understood too, but she gave no indication.

"Please come in. Do you mind if I take off my things?"

Madame Martin put her packages in the kitchen. She took off
her hat and fluffed out her pale blonde hair. When she had closed
the bedroom door, she said, "Mademoiselle Doncoeur is all excited.
This is quite an event, isn't it, for an old maid—particularly an
old maid who cuts out every newspaper article about a certain
police inspector, and who finally has the inspector in her own
house. . . . Do you mind?"

She had taken a cigarette from a silver case, tapped the end,
and snapped a lighter. The gesture somehow prompted Maigret's
next question.

"You're not working, Madame Martin?"

"It would be difficult to hold a job and take care of the house
and the little girl too, even when the child is in school. Besides,
my husband won't allow me to work."

"But you did work before you met him?"

"Naturally. I had to earn a living. Won't you sit down?"

He lowered himself into a rude raffia-bottomed chair. She rested
one thigh against the edge of a table.

"You were a typist?"

"I have been a typist."

"For long?"

"Quite a while."

"You were still a typist when you met Martin? You must forgive
me for asking these personal questions."

"It's your job."

"You were married five years ago. Were you working then? Just
a moment. May I ask your age?"

"I'm thirty-three. I was twenty-eight then, and I was working
for a Monsieur Lorilleux in the Palais Royal arcades."

"As his secretary?"

"Monsieur Lorilleux had a jewelry shop. Or more exactly, he sold souvenirs and old coins. You know those old shops in the Palais Royal. I was salesgirl, bookkeeper, *and* secretary. I took care of the shop when he was away."

"He was married?"

"And father of three children."

"You left him to marry Martin?"

"Not exactly. Jean didn't want me to go on working, but he wasn't making very much money then and I had quite a good job. So I kept it for the first few months."

"And then?"

"Then a strange thing happened. One morning I came to work at nine o'clock as usual, and I found the door locked. I thought Monsieur Lorilleux had overslept, so I waited. . . ."

"Where did he live?"

"Rue Mazarine with his family. At half past nine I began to worry."

"Was he dead?"

"No. I phoned his wife, who said he had left the house at eight o'clock as usual."

"Where did you telephone from?"

"From the glove shop next door. I waited all morning. His wife came down and we went to the commissariat together to report him missing, but the police didn't take it very seriously. They just asked his wife if he'd ever had heart trouble, if he had a mistress—things like that. But he was never seen again, and nobody ever heard from him. Then some Polish people bought out the store and my husband made me stop working."

"How long was this after your marriage?"

"Four months."

"Your husband was already traveling in the southwest?"

"He had the same territory he has now."

"Was he in Paris when your employer disappeared?"

"No, I don't think so."

"Didn't the police examine the premises?"

"Nothing had been touched since the night before. Nothing was missing."

"Do you know what became of Madame Lorilleux?"

"She lived for a while on the money from the sale of the store. Then she bought a little dry-goods shop not far from here, on the Rue du Pas de la Mule. Her children must be grown up now, probably married."

"Do you still see her?"

"I go into her shop once in a while. That's how I know she's in business in the neighborhood. The first time I saw her there I didn't recognize her."

"How long ago was that?"

"I don't know. Six months or so."

"Does she have a telephone?"

"I don't know. Why?"

"What kind of man was Lorilleux?"

"You mean physically?"

"Let's start with the physical."

"He was a big man, taller than you, and broader. He was fat, but flabby, if you know what I mean. And rather sloppy-looking."

"How old?"

"Around fifty. I can't say exactly. He had a little salt-and-pepper mustache, and his clothes were always too big for him."

"You were familiar with his habits?"

"He walked to work every morning. He got down fifteen minutes ahead of me and cleared up the mail before I arrived. He didn't talk much. He was a rather gloomy person. He spent most of the day in the little office behind the shop."

"No romantic adventures?"

"Not that I know of."

"Did he ever try to make love to you?"

"No!" the monosyllable was tartly emphatic.

"But he thought highly of you?"

"I think I was a great help to him."

"Did your husband ever meet him?"

"They never spoke. Jean sometimes came to wait for me outside the shop, but he never came in." A note of impatience, tinged with anger, crept into her voice. "Is that all you want to know?"

"May I point out, Madame Martin, that you are the one who came to get me?"

"Only because a crazy old maid practically dragged me there so she could get a close-up look at you."

"You don't like Mademoiselle Doncoeur?"

"I don't like people who can't mind their own business."

"People like Mademoiselle Doncoeur?"

"You know that we've taken in my brother-in-law's child. Believe

me or not, I've done everything I can for her. I treat her the way
I'd treat my own child. . . ." She paused to light a fresh cigarette,
and Maigret tried unsuccessfuly to picture her as a doting mother.
". . . And now that old maid is always over here, offering to help
me with the child. Every time I start to go out, I find her in the
hallway, smiling sweetly, and saying. 'You mustn't leave Colette
all alone, Madame Martin. Let me go in and keep her company.'
I sometimes wonder if she doesn't go through my drawers when
I'm out."

"You put up with her, nevertheless."

"How can I help it? Colette asks for her, especially since she's
been in bed. And my husband is fond of her, because when he
was a bachelor, she took care of him when he was sick with
pleurisy."

"Have you already returned the doll you bought for Colette's
Christmas?"

She frowned and glanced at the door to the child's bedroom.
"I see you've been questioning the little girl. No, I haven't taken
it back for the very good reason that all the big department stores
are closed today. Would you like to see it?"

She spoke defiantly, expecting him to refuse, but he said nothing.
He examined the cardboard box, noting the price tag. It was a
very cheap doll.

"May I ask where you went this morning?"

"I did my marketing."

"Rue Amelot or Rue de Chemin Vert?"

"Both."

"If I may be indiscreet, what did you buy?"

Furious, she stormed into the kitchen, snatched up her shopping
bag, and dumped it on the dining room table. "Look for yourself!"

There were three cans of sardines, butter, potatoes, some ham,
and a head of lettuce.

She fixed him with a hard, unwavering stare. She was not in
the least nervous. Spiteful, rather.

"Any more questions?"

"Yes. The name of your insurance agent."

"My insurance. . . ." She was obviously puzzled.

"Insurance agent. The one who came to see you."

"I'm sorry. I was at a loss for a moment because you spoke of
my agent as though he were really handling a policy for me. So
Colette told you that, too? Actually, a man did come to see me

twice, trying to sell me a policy. He was one of those door-to-door salesmen, and I thought at first he was selling vacuum cleaners, not life insurance. I had a terrible time getting rid of him."

"Did he stay long?"

"Long enough for me to convince him that I had no desire to take out a policy."

"What company did he represent?"

"He told me but I've forgotten. Something with "Mutual" in it."

"And he came back later?"

"Yes."

"What time does Colette usually go to sleep?"

"I put out her light at seven-thirty, but sometimes she talks to herself in the dark until much later."

"So the second time the insurance man called, it was later than seven-thirty?"

"Possibly." She saw the trap. "I remember now I was washing the dishes."

"And you let him in?"

"He had his foot in the door."

"Did he call on other tenants in the building?"

"I haven't the slightest idea, but I'm sure you will inquire. Must you cross-examine me like a criminal, just because a little girl imagines she saw Santa Claus? If my husband were here—"

"By the way, does your husband carry life insurance?"

"I think so. In fact, I'm sure he does."

Maigret picked up his hat from a chair and started for the door. Madame Martin seemed surprised.

"Is that all?"

"That's all. It seems your brother-in-law promised to come and see his daughter today. If he should come, I would be grateful if you let me know. And now I'd like a few words with Mademoiselle Doncoeur."

There was a convent smell about Mademoiselle Doncoeur's apartment, but there was no dog or cat in sight, no antimacassars on the chairs, no bric-a-brac on the mantelpiece.

"Have you lived in this house long, Mademoiselle Doncoeur?"

"Twenty-five years, Monsieur l'Inspecteur. I'm one of the oldest tenants. I remember when I first moved in you were already living across the street, and you wore long mustaches."

"Who lived in the next apartment before Martin moved in?"

"A public-works engineer. I don't remember his name, but I could look it up for you. He had a wife and daughter. The girl was a deaf-mute. It was very sad. They went to live somewhere in the country."

"Have you been bothered by a door-to-door insurance agent recently?"

"Not recently. There was one who came around two or three years ago."

"You don't like Madame Martin, do you?"

"Why?"

"I asked if you liked Madame Martin."

"Well, if I had a son. . . ."

"Go on."

"If I had a son I don't think I would like Madame Martin for a daughter-in-law. Especially as Monsieur Martin is such a nice man, so kind."

"You think he is unhappy with his wife?"

"I wouldn't say that. I have nothing against her, really. She can't help being the kind of woman she is."

"What kind of woman is she?"

"I couldn't say, exactly. You've seen her. You're a better judge of those things that I am. In a way she's not like a woman at all. I'll wager she never shed a tear in her life. True, she is bringing up the child properly, decently, but she never says a kind word to her. She acts exasperated when I tell Colette a fairy tale. I'm sure she's told the girl there is no Santa Claus. Luckily Colette doesn't believe her."

"The child doesn't like her either, does she?"

"Colette is always obedient. She tries to do what's expected of her. I think she's just as happy to be left alone."

"Is she alone much?"

"Not much. I'm not reproaching Madame Martin. It's hard to explain. She wants to live her own life. She's not interested in others. She doesn't even talk much about herself."

"Have you ever met her brother-in-law—Colette's father?"

"I've seen him on the landing, but I've never spoken to him. He walks with his head down, as if he were ashamed of something. He always looks as if he slept in his clothes. No, I don't think it was he last night, Monsieur Maigret. He's not the type. Unless he was terribly drunk."

On his way out Maigret looked in at the concierge's lodge, a dark cubicle where the light burned all day.

It was noon when he started back across the boulevard. Curtains stirred at the windows of the house behind him. Curtains stirred at his own window, too. Madame Maigret was watching for him so she would know when to put the chicken in the oven. He waved to her. He wanted very much to stick out his tongue and lick up a few of the tiny snowflakes that were drifting down. He could still remember their taste.

"I wonder if that little tyke is happy over there," sighed Madame Maigret as she got up from the table to bring the coffee from the kitchen.

She could see that he wasn't listening. He had pushed back his chair and was stuffing his pipe while staring at the purring stove. For her own satisfaction she added, "I don't see how she could be happy with that woman."

He smiled vaguely, as he always did when he hadn't heard what she said, and continued to stare at the tiny flames licking evenly at the mica windows of the salamander. There were at least ten similar stoves in the house, all purring alike in ten similar dining rooms with wine and cakes on the table, a carafe of cordial waiting on the sideboard, and all the windows pale with the same hard, gray light of a sunless day.

It was perhaps this very familiarity that had been confusing his subconscious since morning. Nine times out of ten his investigations plunged him abruptly into new surroundings, set him at grips with people of a world he barely knew, people of a social level whose habits and manners he had to study from scratch. But in this case, which was not really a case since he had no official assignment, the whole approach was unfamiliar because the background was too familiar. For the first time in his career something professional was happening in his own world, in a building that might just as well be his building.

The Martins could easily have been living on his floor instead of across the street, and it would probably have been Madame Maigret who would look after Colette when her aunt was away. There was an elderly maiden lady living just under him who was a plumper, paler replica of Mademoiselle Doncoeur. The frames of the photographs of Martin's father and mother were exactly the same as those that framed Maigret's father and mother, and the enlargements had probably been made by the same studio.

Was that what was bothering him? He seemed to lack perspective. He was unable to look at people and things from a fresh, new viewpoint.

He had detailed his morning activities during dinner—a pleasant little Christmas dinner that had left him with an overstuffed feeling—and his wife had listened while looking at the windows across the street with an air of embarrassment.

"Is the concierge sure that nobody could have come in from outside?"

"She's not so sure any more. She was entertaining friends until after midnight. And after she had gone to bed, there were considerable comings and goings, which is natural for Christmas Eve."

"Do you think something more is going to happen?"

That was a question that had been plaguing Maigret all morning. First of all, he had to consider that Madame Martin had not come to see him spontaneously, but only on the insistence of Mademoiselle Doncoeur. If she had got up earlier, if she had been the first to see the doll and hear the story of Father Christmas, wouldn't she have kept the secret and ordered the little girl to say nothing?

And later she had taken the first opportunity to go out, even though there was plenty to eat in the house for the day. And she had been so absent-minded that she had bought butter, although there was still a pound in the cooler.

Maigret got up from the table and resettled himself in his chair by the window. He picked up the phone and called the Quai des Orfèvres.

"Lucas?"

"I got what you wanted, Chief. I have a list of all prisoners released for the last four months. There aren't as many as I thought. And none of them has lived on Boulevard Richard Lenoir at any time."

That didn't matter any more now. At first Maigret had thought that a tenant across the street might have hidden money or stolen goods under the floor before he was arrested. His first thought on getting out of jail would be to recover his booty. With the little girl bedridden, however, the room was occupied day and night. Impersonating Father Christmas would not have been a bad idea to get into the room. Had this been the case, however, Madame Martin would not have been so reluctant to call in Maigret. Nor would she have been in so great a hurry to get out of the house afterward on such a flimsy pretext. So Maigret had abandoned that theory.

"You want me to check each prisoner further?"

"Never mind. Any news about Paul Martin?"

"That was easy. He's known in every station house between the Bastille and the Hôtel de Ville, and even on Boulevard Saint Michel."

"What did he do last night?"

"First he went aboard the Salvation Army barge to eat. He's a regular there one day a week and yesterday was his day. They had a special feast for Christmas Eve and he had to stand in line quite a while."

"After that?"

"About eleven o'clock he went to the Latin Quarter and opened doors for motorists in front of a night club. He must have collected enough money in tips to get himself a sinkful, because he was picked up dead drunk near Place Maubert at four in the morning. He was taken to the station house to sleep it off, and was there until eleven this morning. They'd just turned him loose when I phoned, and they promised to bring him to me when they find him again. He still had a few francs in his pocket."

"What about Bergerac?"

"Jean Martin is taking the afternoon train for Paris. He was quite upset by a phone call he got this morning."

"He got only one call?"

"Only one this morning. He got a call last night while he was eating dinner."

"You know who called him?"

"The desk clerk says it was a man's voice, asking for Monsieur Jean Martin. He sent somebody into the dining room for Martin but when Martin got to the phone, the caller had hung up. Seems it spoiled his whole evening. He went out with a bunch of traveling salesmen to some local hot spot where there were pretty girls and whatnot, but after drinking a few glasses of champagne, he couldn't talk about anything except his wife and daughter. The niece he calls his daughter, it seems. He had such a dismal evening that he went home early. Three o'clock. That's all you wanted to know, Chief?"

When Maigret didn't reply, Lucas had to satisfy his curiosity.

"You still phoning from home, Chief? What's happening up your way? Somebody get killed?"

"I still can't say. Right now all I know is that the principles are a seven-year-old girl, a doll, and Father Christmas."

"Ah?"

"One more thing. Try to get me the home address of the manager of Zenith Watches, Avenue de l'Opéra. You ought to be able to raise somebody there, even on Christmas Day. Call me back."

"Soon as I have something."

Madame Maigret had just served him a glass of Alsatian plum brandy that her sister had sent them. He smacked his lips. For a moment he was tempted to forget all about the business of the doll and Father Christmas. It would be much simpler just to take his wife to the movies. . . .

"What color eyes has she?"

It took him a moment to realize that the only person in the case who interested Madame Maigret was the little girl.

"Why, I'm not quite sure. They can't be dark. She has blonde hair."

"So they're blue."

"Maybe they're blue. Very light, in any case. And they are very serious."

"Because she doesn't look at things like a child. Does she laugh?"

"She hasn't much to laugh about."

"A child can always laugh if she feels herself surrounded by people she can trust, people who let her act her age. I don't like that woman."

"You prefer Mademoiselle Doncoeur?"

"She may be an old maid but I'm sure she knows more about children than that Madame Martin. I've seen *her* in the shops. Madame Martin is one of those women who watch the scales, and take their money out of their pocketbooks, coin by coin. She always looks around suspiciously, as though everybody was out to cheat her."

The telephone rang as Madame Maigret was repeating, "I don't like that woman."

It was Lucas calling, with the address of Monsieur Arthur Godefroy, general manager in France for Zenith Watches. He lives in a sumptuous villa at Saint Cloud, and Lucas had discovered that he was at home. He added:

"Paul Martin is here, Chief. When they brought him in, he

started crying. He thought something had happened to his daughter. But he's all right now—except for an awful hangover. What do I do with him?"

"Anyone around who can come up here with him?"

"Torrence just came on duty. I think he could use a little fresh air. He looks as if he had a hard night too. Anything more from me, Chief?"

"Yes. Call Palais Royal station. About five years ago a man named Lorilleux disappeared without a trace. He sold jewelry and old coins in the Palais Royal arcades. Get me all the details you can on his disappearance."

Maigret smiled as he noted that his wife was sitting opposite him with her knitting. He had never before worked on a case in such domestic surroundings.

"Do I call you back?" asked Lucas.

"I don't expect to move an inch from my chair."

A moment later Maigret was talking to Monsieur Godefroy, who had a decided Swiss accent. The Zenith manager thought that something must have happened to Jean Martin, for anyone to be making inquiries about him on Christmas Day.

"Most able . . . most devoted . . . I'm bringing him into Paris to be assistant manager next year. . . . Next week, that is. . . . Why do you ask? Has anything—Be still, you!" He paused to quiet the juvenile hubbub in the background. "You must excuse me. All my family is with me today and—"

"Tell me, Monsieur Godefroy, has anyone called your office these last few days to inquire about Monsieur Martin's current address?"

"Yesterday morning, as a matter of fact. I was very busy with the holiday rush, but he asked to speak to me personally. I forget what name he gave. He said he had an extremely important message for Jean Martin, so I told him how to get in touch with Martin in Bergerac."

"He asked you nothing else?"

"No. He hung up at once. Is anything wrong?"

"I hope not. Thank you very much, monsieur."

The screams of children began again in the background and Maigret said good-by.

"Were you listening?"

"I heard what you said. I didn't hear his answers."

"A man called the office yesterday morning to get Martin's

address. The same man undoubtedly called Bergerac that evening to make sure Martin was still there, and therefore would not be at his Boulevard Richard Lenoir address for Christmas Eve."

"The same man who appeared last night as Father Christmas?"

"More than likely. That seems to clear Paul Martin. He would not have to make two phone calls to find out where his brother was. Madame Martin would have told him."

"You're really getting excited about this case. You're delighted that it came up, aren't you? Confess!" And while Maigret was racking his brain for excuses, she added, "It's quite natural. I'm fascinated too. How much longer do you think the child will have to keep her leg in a cast?"

"I didn't ask."

"I wonder what sort of complications she could have had?"

Maigret looked at her curiously. Unconsciously she had switched his mind onto a new track.

"That's not such a stupid remark you just made."

"What did I say?"

"After all, since she's been in bed for two months, she should be up and around soon, barring really serious complications."

"She'll probably have to walk on crutches at first."

"That's not the point. In a few days then, or a few weeks at most, she will no longer be confined to her room. She'll go for a walk with Madame Martin. And the coast will be clear for anyone to enter the apartment without dressing up like Father Christmas."

Madame Maigret's lips were moving. While listening to her husband, and watching his face, she was counting stitches.

"First of all, the presence of the child forced our man to use trickery. She's been in bed for two months—two months for him to wait. Without complications the flooring could have been taken up several weeks ago. Our man must have had urgent reasons for acting at once, without further delay."

"Monsieur Martin will return to Paris in a few days?"

"Exactly."

"What do you suppose the man found underneath the floor?"

"Did he really find anything? If not, his problem is still as pressing as it was last night. So he will take further action."

"What action?"

"I don't know."

"Look, Maigret, isn't the child in danger? Do you think she's safe with that woman?"

"I could answer that if I knew where Madame Martin went this morning on the pretext of doing her shopping." He picked up the phone again and called Police Judiciaire.

"I'm pestering you again, Lucas. I want you to locate a taxi that picked up a passenger this morning between nine and ten somewhere near Boulevard Richard Lenoir. The fare was a woman in her early thirties, blonde, slim but solidly built. She was wearing a gray suit and a beige hat. She carried a brown shopping bag. I want to know her destination. There couldn't have been so many cabs on the street at that hour."

"Is Paul Martin with you?"

"Not yet."

"He'll be there soon. About that other thing, the Lorilleux matter, the Palais Royal boys are checking their files. You'll have the data in a few minutes."

Jean Martin must be taking his train in Bergerac at this moment. Little Colette was probably taking her nap. Mademoiselle Doncoeur was doubtless sitting behind her window curtain, wondering what Maigret was up to.

People were beginning to come out now, families with their children, the children with their new toys. There were certainly queues in front of the movie houses. . . .

A taxi stopped in front of the house. Footsteps sounded in the stairway. Madame Maigret went to the door. The deep bass voice of Torrence rumbled, "You there, Chief?"

Torrence came in with an ageless man who hugged the walls and looked humbly at the floor. Maigret went to the sideboard and filled two glasses with plum brandy.

"To your health," he said.

The man looked at Maigret with surprised, anxious eyes. He raised a trembling, hesitant hand.

"To your health, Monsieur Martin. I'm sorry to make you come all the way up here, but you won't have far to go now to see your daughter."

"Nothing has happened to her?"

"No, no. When I saw her this morning she was playing with her new doll. You can go, Torrence. Lucas must need you."

Madame Maigret had gone into the bedroom with her knitting. She was sitting on the edge of the bed, counting her stitches.

"Sit down, Monsieur Martin."

The man had touched his lips to the glass and set it down. He looked at it uneasily.

"You have nothing to worry about. Just tell yourself that I know all about you."

"I wanted to visit her this morning," the man sighed. "I swore I would go to bed early so I could wish her a Merry Christmas."

"I know that, too."

"It's always the same. I swear I'll take just one drink, just enough to pick me up. . . ."

"You have only one brother, Monsieur Martin?"

"Yes, Jean. He's six years younger than I am. He and my wife and my daughter were all I had to love in this world."

"You don't love your sister-in-law?"

He shivered. He seemed both startled and embarrassed.

"I have nothing against Loraine."

"You entrusted your child to her, didn't you?"

"Well, yes, that is to say, when my wife died, and I began to slip. . . ."

"I understand. Is your daughter happy?"

"I think so, yes. She never complains."

"Have you ever tried to get back on your feet?"

"Every night I promise myself to turn over a new leaf, but next day I start all over again. I even went to see a doctor. I followed his advice for a few days. But when I went back, he was very busy. He said I ought to be in a special sanatorium."

He reached for his glass, then hesitated. Maigret picked up his own glass and took a swallow to encourage him.

"Did you ever meet a man in your sister-in-law's apartment?"

"No. I think she's above reproach on that score."

"Do you know where your brother first met her?"

"In a little restaurant on the Rue Beaujolais where he used to eat when he was in Paris. It was near the shop where Loraine was working."

"Did they have a long engagement?"

"I can't say. Jean was on the road for two months and when he came back he told me he was getting married."

"Were you his best man?"

"Yes. Loraine has no family in Paris. She's an orphan. So her landlady acted as her witness. Is there something wrong?"

"I don't know yet. A man entered Colette's room last night

dressed as Father Christmas. He gave your girl a doll, and lifted two loose boards from the floor."

"Do you think I'm in fit condition to see her?"

"You can go over in a little while. If you feel like it you can shave here. Do you think your brother would be likely to hide anything under the floor?"

"Jean? Never!"

"Even if he wanted to hide something from his wife?"

"He doesn't hide things from his wife. You don't know him. He's one of those rare humans—a scrupulously honest man. When he comes home from the road, she knows exactly how much money he has left, to the last centime."

"Is she jealous?"

Paul Martin did not reply.

"I advise you to tell me what you know. Remember that your daughter is involved in this."

"I don't think that Loraine is especially jealous. Not of women, at least. Perhaps about money. At least that's what my poor wife always said. She didn't like Loraine."

"Why not?"

"She used to say that Loraine's lips were too thin, that she was too polite, too cold, always on the defensive. My wife always thought that Loraine set her cap for Jean because he had a good job with a future and owned his own furniture."

"Loraine had no money of her own?"

"She never speaks of her family. I understand her father died when she was very young and her mother did housework somewhere in the Glacière quarter. My poor wife used to say, 'Loraine knows what she wants.' "

"Do you think she was Lorilleux's mistress?"

Paul Martin did not reply. Maigret poured him another finger of plum brandy. Martin gave him a grateful look but he did not touch the glass. Perhaps he was thinking that his daughter might notice his breath when he crossed the street later on.

"I'll get you a cup of coffee in a moment. . . . Your wife must have had her own ideas on the subject."

"How did you know? Please note that my wife never spoke disparagingly of people. But with Loraine it was almost pathological. Whenever we were to meet my sister-in-law, I used to beg my wife not to show her antipathy. It's funny that you should bring all that up now, at this time in my life. Do you think I did wrong in letting her take Colette? I sometimes think so. But what else could I have done?"

"You didn't answer my question about Loraine's former employer."

"Oh—yes. My wife always said it was very convenient for Loraine to have married a man who was away from home so much."

"You know where she lived before her marriage?"

"In a street just off Boulevard Sébastopol, on the right as you walk from Rue de Rivoli toward the boulevard. I remember we picked her up there the day of the wedding."

"Rue Pernelle?"

"That's it. The fourth or fifth house on the left side of the street in a quiet rooming house, quite respectable. People who work in the neighborhood live there. I remember there were several little actresses from the Châtelet."

"Would you like to shave, Monsieur Martin?"

"I'm ashamed. Still, since my daughter is just across the street. . . ."

"Come with me."

Maigret took him through the kitchen so he wouldn't have to meet Madame Maigret in the bedroom. He set out the necessary toilet articles, not forgetting a clothes brush.

When he returned to the dining room, Madame Maigret poked her head through the door and whispered, "What's he doing?"

"He's shaving."

Once more Maigret reached for the telephone. He was certainly giving poor Lucas a busy Christmas Day.

"Are you indispensable at the office?"

"Not if Torrence sits in for me. I've got the information you wanted."

"In just a moment. I want you to jump over to Rue Pernelle. There's a rooming house a few doors down from Boulevard Sébastopol. If the proprietor wasn't there five years ago try to dig up someone who lived there then. I want everything you can find out on a certain Loraine—"

"Loraine who?"

"Just a minute, I didn't think of that."

Through the bathroom door he asked Martin for the maiden name of his sister-in-law. A few seconds later he was on the phone again.

"Loraine Boitel," he told Lucas. "The landlady of this rooming house was witness at her marriage to Jean Martin. Loraine Boitel was working for Lorilleux at the time. Try to find out if she was more than a secretary to him, and if he ever came to see her. And work fast. This may be urgent. What have you got on Lorilleux?"

"He was quite a fellow. At home on Rue Mazarine he was a good respectable family man. In his Palais Royal shop he not only sold old coins and souvenirs of Paris, but he had a fine collection of pornographic books and obscene pictures."

"Not unusual for the Palais Royal."

"I don't know what else went on there. There was a big divan covered with red silk rep in the back room, but the investigation was never pushed. Seems there were a lot of important names among his customers."

"What about Loraine Boitel?"

"The report barely mentions her, except that she waited all morning for Lorilleux the day he disappeared. I was on the phone about this when Langlois of the Financial Squad came into my office. The name Lorilleux rang a bell in the back of his mind and he went to check his files. Nothing definite on him, but he'd been making frequent trips to Switzerland and back, and there was a lot of gold smuggling going on at that time. Lorilleux was stopped and searched at the frontier several times, but they never found anything on him."

"Lucas, old man, hurry over to Rue Pernelle. I'm more than ever convinced that this is urgent."

Paul Martin appeared in the doorway, his pale cheeks close-shaven.

"I don't know how to thank you. I'm very embarrassed."

"You'll visit your daughter now, won't you? I don't know how long you usually stay, but today I don't want you to leave until I come for you."

"I can't very well stay all night, can I?"

"Stay all night if necessary. Manage the best you can."

"Is the little girl in danger?"

"I don't know, but your place today is with your daughter."

Paul Martin drank his black coffee avidly, and started for the stairway. The door had just closed after him when Madame Maigret rushed into the dining room.

"You can't let him go to see his daughter empty-handed on Christmas Day!"

"But—" Maigret was about to say that there just didn't happen to be a doll around the house, when his wife thrust a small shiny object into his hands. It was a gold thimble that had been in her sewing basket for years but was never used.

"Give him that. Little girls always like thimbles. Hurry!"

He shouted from the landing. "Monsieur Martin! Just a minute, Monsieur Martin!"

He closed the man's fingers over the thimble. "Don't tell a soul where you got this."

Before re-entering the dining room he stood for a moment on the threshold, grumbling. Then he sighed, "I hope you've finished making me play Father Christmas."

"I'll bet she likes the thimble as well as a doll. It's something grownups use, you know."

They watched the man cross the boulevard. Before going into the house he turned to look up at Maigret's windows, as if seeking encouragement.

"Do you think he'll ever be cured?"

"I doubt it."

"If anything happens to that woman, to Madame Martin."

"Well?"

"Nothing. I was thinking of the little girl. I wonder what would become of her."

Ten minutes passed. Maigret had opened his newspaper and lighted his pipe. His wife had settled down again with her knitting. She was counting stitches when he exhaled a cloud of smoke and murmured, "You haven't even seen her."

Maigret was looking for an old envelope, on the back of which he had jotted down a few notes summing up the day's events. He found it in a drawer into which Madame Maigret always stuffed any papers she found lying around the house.

This was the only investigation, he mused, that he had ever conducted practically in its entirety from his favorite armchair. It was also unusual in that no dramatic stroke of luck had come to his aid. True, luck had been on his side, in that he had been able to muster all his facts by the simplest and most direct means. How many times had he deployed scores of detectives on an all-night search for some minor detail. This might have happened,

for instance, if Monsieur Arthur Godefroy of Zenith had gone
home to Zurich for Christmas, or if he had been out of reach of
a telephone. Or if Monsieur Godefroy had been unaware of the
telephone inquiry regarding the whereabouts of Jean Martin.

When Lucas arrived shortly after four o'clock, his nose red and
his face pinched with the cold, he too could report the same kind
of undramatic luck.

'A thick yellow fog, unusual for Paris, had settled over the city.
Lights shone in all the windows, floating in the murk like ships
at sea or distant beacons. Familiar details had been blotted out
so completely that Maigret half expected to hear the moan of
foghorns.

For some reason, perhaps because of some boyhood memory,
Maigret was pleased to see the weather thicken. He was also
pleased to see Lucas walk into his apartment, take off his overcoat,
sit down, and stretch out his frozen hands toward the fire.

In appearance, Lucas was a reduced-scale model of Maigret—
a head shorter, half as broad in the shoulders, half as stern in
expression although he tried hard. Without conscious imitation
but with conscious admiration Lucas had copied his chief's slightest
gestures, postures, and changes of expression—even to the ceremony of inhaling the fragrance of the plum brandy before touching
his lips to the glass.

The landlady of the rooming house on Rue Pernelle had been
killed in a subway accident two years earlier, Lucas reported.
Luckily the place had been taken over by the former night watchman, who had been in trouble with the police on morals charges.

"So it was easy enough to make him talk," said Lucas, lighting
a pipe much too large for him. "I was surprised that he had the
money to buy the house, but he explained that he was front man
for a big investor who had money in all sorts of enterprises but
didn't like to have his name used."

"What kind of place is it?"

"Looks respectable. Clean enough. Office on the mezzanine.
Rooms by the month, some by the week, and a few on the second
floor by the hour."

"He remembers Loraine?"

"Very well. She lived there more than three years. I got the
impression he didn't like her because she was tightfisted."

"Did Lorilleux come to see her?"

"On my way to Rue Pernelle I picked up a photo of Lorilleux

at the Palais Royal station. The new landlord recognized him right away."

"Lorilleux went to her room often?"

"Two or three times a month. He always had baggage with him, he always arrived around one o'clock in the morning, and always left before six. I checked the timetables. There's a train from Switzerland around midnight and another at six in the morning. He must have told his wife he was taking the six o'clock train."

"Nothing else?"

"Nothing, except that Loraine was stingy with tips, and always cooked her dinner on an alcohol burner, even though the house rules said no cooking in the rooms."

"No other men?"

"No. Very respectable except for Lorilleux. The landlady was witness at her wedding."

Maigret glanced at his wife. He had insisted that she remain in the room when Lucas came. She stuck to her knitting, trying to make believe she was not there.

Torrence was out in the fog, going from garage to garage, checking the trip sheets of taxi fleets. The two men waited serenely, deep in their easy chairs, each holding a glass of plum brandy with the same pose. Maigret felt a pleasant numbness creeping over him.

His Christmas luck held out with the taxis, too. Sometimes it took days to run down a particular taxi driver, particularly when the cab in question did not belong to a fleet. Cruising drivers were the hardest to locate; they sometimes never even read the newspapers. But shortly before five o'clock Torrence called from Saint Ouen.

"I found one of the taxis," he reported.

"One? Was there more than one?"

"Looks that way. This man picked up the woman at the corner of Boulevard Richard Lenoir and Boulevard Voltaire this morning. He drove her to Rue de Maubeuge, opposite the Gare du Nord, where she paid him."

"Did she go into the railway station?"

"No. The driver says she went into a luggage shop that stays open on Sundays and holidays. After that he doesn't know."

"Where's the driver now?"

"Right here in the garage. He just checked in."

"Send him to me, will you? Right away. I don't care how he gets here as long as it's in a hurry. Now I want you to find me the cab that brought her home."

"Sure, Chief, as soon as I get myself a coffee with a stick in it. It's damned cold out here."

Maigret glanced through the window. There was a shadow against Mademoiselle Doncoeur's curtains. He turned to Lucas.

"Look in the phone book for a luggage shop across from the Gare du Nord."

Lucas took only a minute to come up with a number, which Maigret dialed.

"Hello, this is the Police Judiciaire. Shortly before ten this morning a young woman bought something in your shop, probably a suitcase. She was a blonde, wearing a gray suit and beige hat. She carried a brown shopping bag. Do you remember her?"

Perhaps trade was slack on Christmas Day. Or perhaps it was easier to remember customers who shopped on Christmas. In any case, the voice on the phone replied:

"Certainly, I waited on her myself. She said she had to leave suddenly for Cambrai because her sister was ill, and she didn't have time to go home for her bags. She wanted a cheap suitcase, and I sold her a fiber model we have on sale. She paid me and went into the bar next door. I was standing in the doorway and a little later I saw her walking toward the station, carrying the suitcase."

"Are you alone in your shop?"

"I have one clerk on duty."

"Can you leave him alone for half an hour? . . . Fine! Then jump in a taxi and come to this address. I'll pay the fare, of course."

"And the return fare? Shall I have the cab wait?"

"Have him wait, yes."

According to Maigret's notes on the back of the envelope, the first taxi driver arrived at 5:50 P.M. He was somewhat surprised, since he had been summoned by the police, to find himself in a private apartment. He recognized Maigret, however, and made no effort to disguise his curious interest in how the famous inspector lived.

"I want you to climb to the fourth floor of the house just across the street. If the concierge stops you, tell her you're going to see Madame Martin."

"Madame Martin. I get it."

"Go to the door at the end of the hall and ring the bell. If a blonde opens the door and you recognize her, make some excuse— you're on the wrong floor, anything you think of. If somebody else answers, ask to speak to Madame Martin personally."

"And then?"

"Then you come back here and tell me whether or not she is the fare you drove to Rue de Maubeuge this morning."

"I'll be right back, Inspector."

As the door closed, Maigret smiled in spite of himself.

"The first call will make her worry a little. The second, if all goes well, will make her panicky. The third, if Torrence has any luck—"

Torrence, too, was having his run of Christmas luck. The phone rang and he reported:

"I think I've found him, Chief. I dug up a driver who picked up a woman answering your description at the Gare du Nord, only he didn't take her to Boulevard Richard Lenoir. He dropped her at the corner of Boulevard Beaumarchais and the Rue du Chemin Vert."

"Send him to me."

"He's a little squiffed."

"It doesn't matter. Where are you?"

"The Barbès garage."

"Then it won't be much out of your way to stop by the Gare du Nord. Go to the checkroom. Unfortunately it won't be the same man on duty, but try to find out if a small new suitcase was checked between nine-thirty and ten this morning. It's made of fiber and shouldn't be too heavy. Get the number of the check. They won't let you take the suitcase without a warrant, so try to get the name and address of the man on duty this morning."

"What next?"

"Phone me. I'll wait for your second taxi driver. If he's been drinking, better write down my address for him, so he won't get lost."

Madame Maigret was back in the kitchen, preparing the evening meal. She hadn't dared ask whether Lucas would eat with them.

Maigret wondered if Paul Martin were still across the street with his daughter. Had Madame Martin tried to get rid of him?

The bell rang again. Two men stood at the door.

The first driver had come back from Madame Martin's and had

climbed Maigret's stairs behind the luggage dealer.

"Did you recognize her?"

"Sure. She recognized me, too. She turned pale. She ran to close a door behind her, then she asked me what I wanted."

"What did you tell her?"

"That I had the wrong floor. I think maybe she wanted to buy me off, but I didn't give her a chance. But she was watching from the window when I crossed the street. She probably knows I came here."

The luggage dealer was baffled and showed it. He was a middle-aged man, completely bald and equally obsequious. When the driver had gone, Maigret explained what he wanted, and the man objected vociferously.

"One just doesn't do this sort of thing to one's customers," he repeated stubbornly. "One simply does not inform on one's customers, you know."

After a long argument he agreed to call on Madame Martin. To make sure he didn't change his mind, Maigret sent Lucas to follow him.

They returned in less than ten minutes.

"I call your attention to the fact that I have acted under your orders, that I have been compelled—"

"Did you recognize her?"

"Will I be forced to testify under oath?"

"More than likely."

"That would be very bad for my business. People who buy luggage at the last minute are very often people who dislike public mention of their comings and goings."

"You may not have to go to court. Your deposition before the examining magistrate may be sufficient."

"Very well. It was she. She's dressed differently, but I recognized her all right."

"Did she recognize you?"

"She asked immediately who had sent me."

"What did you say?"

"I . . . I don't remember. I was quite upset. I think I said I had rung the wrong bell."

"Did she offer you anything?"

"What do you mean? She didn't even offer me a chair. Luckily. It would have been most unpleasant."

Maigret smiled, somewhat incredulously. He believed that the taxi driver had actually run away from a possible bribe. He wasn't so sure about his prosperous-looking shopkeeper who obviously begrudged his loss of time.

"Thank you for your co-operation."

The luggage dealer departed hastily.

"And now for Number Three, my dear Lucas."

Madame Maigret was beginning to grow nervous. From the kitchen door she made discreet signs to her husband, beckoning him to join her. She whispered, "Are you sure the father is still across the street?"

"Why?"

"I don't know. I can't make out exactly what you're up to, but I've been thinking about the child, and I'm a little afraid. . . ."

Night had long since fallen. The families were all home again. Few windows across the street remained dark. The silhouette of Mademoiselle Doncoeur was still very much in evidence.

While waiting for the second taxi driver Maigret decided to put on his collar and tie. He shouted to Lucas:

"Pour yourself another drop. Aren't you hungry?"

"I'm full of sandwiches, Chief. Only one thing I'd like when we go out: a tall beer, right from the spigot."

The second driver arrived at six twenty. At six-thirty-five he had returned from across the street, a gleam in his eye.

"She looks even better in her negligee than she does in her street clothes," he said thickly. "She made me come in and she asked who sent me. I didn't know what to say, so I told her I was a talent scout for the Folies Bergère. Was she furious! She's a fine hunk of woman, though, and I mean it. Did you get a look at her legs?"

He was in no hurry to leave. Maigret saw him ogling the bottle of plum brandy with envious eyes, and poured him a glass—to speed him on his way.

"What are you going to do next, Chief?" Lucas had rarely seen Maigret proceed with such caution, preparing each step with such care that he seemed to be mounting an attack on some desperate criminal. And yet the enemy was only a woman, a seemingly insignificant little housewife.

"You think she'll still fight back?"

"Fiercely. And what's more, in cold blood."

"What are you waiting for?"

"The phone call from Torrence."

As if on cue, the telephone rang. Torrence, of course.

"The suitcase is here all right. It feels practically empty. As you predicted, they won't give it to me without a warrant. The checkroom attendant who was on duty this morning lives in the suburbs, near La Varenne-Saint Hilaire." A snag at last? Or at least a delay? Maigret frowned. But Torrence continued. "We won't have to go out there, though. When he finishes his day's work here, he plays cornet in a *bal musette* on Rue de Lappe."

"Go get him for me."

"Shall I bring him to your place?"

Maigret hesitated, thinking of Lucas's yearning for a glass of draft beer.

"No, I'll be across the street. Madame Martin's apartment, fourth floor."

He took down his heavy overcoat. He filled his pipe.

"Coming?" he said to Lucas.

Madame Maigret ran after him to ask what time he'd be home for dinner. After a moment of hesitation he smiled.

"The usual time," was his not very reassuring answer.

"Look out for the little girl, will you?"

At ten o'clock that evening the investigation was still blocked. It was unlikely that anyone in the whole building had gone to sleep, except Colette. She had finally dozed off, with her father sitting in the dark by her bedside.

Torrence had arrived at seven-thirty with his part-time musician and checkroom attendant, who declared:

"She's the one. I remember she didn't put the check in her handbag. She slipped it into a big brown shopping bag." And when they took him into the kitchen he added, "That's the bag. Or one exactly like it."

The Martin apartment was very warm. Everyone spoke in low tones, as if they had agreed not to awaken the child. Nobody had eaten. Nobody, apparently, was even hungry. On their way over Maigret and Lucas had each drunk two beers in a little café on Boulevard Voltaire.

After the cornetist had spoken his piece, Maigret took Torrence inside and murmured fresh instructions.

Every corner of the apartment had been searched. Even the photos of Martin's parents had been taken from their frames, to make sure the baggage check had not been secreted between picture and backing. The dishes had been taken from their shelves and piled on the kitchen table. The cooler had been emptied and examined closely. No baggage check.

Madame Martin was still wearing her pale blue negligee. She was chain-smoking cigarettes. What with the smoke from the two men's pipes a thick blue haze swirled about the lamps.

"You are of course free to say nothing and answer no questions. Your husband will arrive at eleven-seventeen. Perhaps you will be more talkative in his presence."

"He doesn't know any more than I do."

"Does he know as much?"

"There's nothing to know. I've told you everything."

She had sat back and denied everything, all along the line. She had conceded only one point. She admitted that Lorilleux had dropped in to see her two or three times at night when she lived on Rue Pernelle. But she insisted there had been nothing between them, nothing personal.

"In other words he came to talk business—at one o'clock in the morning?"

"He used to come to town by a late train, and he didn't like to walk the streets with large sums of money on him. I already told you he might have been smuggling gold, but I had nothing to do with it. You can't arrest me for his activities."

"Did he have large sums of money on him when he disappeared?"

"I don't know. He didn't always take me into his confidence."

"But he did come to see you in your room at night?"

Despite the evidence she clung to her story of the morning's marketing. She denied ever having seen the two taxi drivers, the luggage dealer, or the checkroom attendant.

"If I had really left a package at the Gare du Nord, you would have found the check, wouldn't you?"

She glanced nervously at the clock on the mantel, obviously thinking of her husband's return.

"Admit that the man who came last night found nothing under the floor because you changed the hiding place."

"I know of nothing that was hidden under the floor."

"When you learned of his visit, you decided to move the treasure to the checkroom for safekeeping."

"I haven't been near the Gare du Nord. There must be thousands of blondes in Paris who answer my description."

"I think you know where we'll find the check."

"You're so very clever."

"Sit over here at this table," Maigret produced a fountain pen and a sheet of paper. "Write your name and address."

She hesitated, then obeyed.

"Tonight every letter mailed in this neighborhood will be examined, and I'll wager we will find one addressed in your handwriting, probably to yourself."

He handed the paper to Lucas with an order to get in touch with the postal authorities. Much to his surprise the woman reacted visibly.

"You see, it's a very old trick, Little One." For the first time he called her "Little One," the way he would have done if he were questioning her in his office, Quai des Orfèveres.

They were alone now. Maigret slowly paced the floor, while she remained seated.

"In case you're interested," Maigret said slowly, "the thing that shocks me most about you is not what you have done but the cold-blooded way you have done it. You've been dangling at the end of a slender thread since early this morning, and you still haven't blinked an eye. When your husband comes home, you'll try to play the martyr. And yet you know that sooner or later we'll discover the truth."

"But I've done nothing wrong."

"Then why do you lie?"

She did not reply. She was still far from the breaking point. Her nerves were calm, but her mind was obviously racing at top speed, seeking some avenue of escape.

"I'm not saying anything more," she declared. She sat down and pulled the hem of her negligee over her bare knees.

"Suit yourself," Maigret made himself comfortable in a chair opposite her.

"Are you going to stay here all night?" she asked.

"At least until your husband gets home."

"Are you going to tell him about Monsieur Lorilleux's visits to my room?"

"If necessary."

"You're a cad! Jean knows nothing about all this. He had no part in it."

"Unfortunately he is your husband."

When Lucas came back, they were staring at each other in silence.

"Janvier is taking care of the letter, Chief. I met Torrence downstairs. He says the man is in that little bar, two doors down from your house."

"She sprang up. "What man?"

Maigret didn't move a muscle. "The man who came here last night. You must have expected him to come back, since he didn't find what he was looking for. And he might be in a different frame of mind this time."

She cast a dismayed glance at the clock. The train from Bergerac was due in twenty minutes. Her husband could be home in forty. She asked. "You know who this man is?"

"I can guess. I could go down and confirm my suspicion. I'd say it is Lorilleux and I'd say he is very eager to get back his property."

"It's not his property!"

"Let's say that, rightly or wrongly, he considers it his property. He must be in desperate straits, this man. He came to see you twice without getting what he wanted. He came back a third time disguised as Father Christmas. And he'll come back again. He'll be surprised to find you have company. I'm convinced that he'll be more talkative than you. Despite the general belief, men always speak more freely than women. Do you think he is armed?"

"I don't know."

"I think he is. He is tired of waiting. I don't know what story you've been telling him, but I'm sure he's fed up with it. The gentleman has a vicious face. There's nothing quite as cruel as a weakling with his back up."

"Shut up!"

"Would you like us to go so that you can be alone with him?"

The back of Maigret's envelope contained the following note: "10:38 P.M.—she decides to talk."

It was not a very connected story at first. It came out in bits and pieces, fragments of sentences interlarded with venomous asides, supplemented by Maigret's own guesses, which she either confirmed or amended.

"What do you want to know?"

"Was it money that you left in the checkroom?"

"Bank notes. Almost a million.

"Did the money belong to Lorilleux?"

"No more to him than to me."

"To one of his customers?"

"Yes. A man named Julian Boissy."

"What became of him?"

"He died."

"How?"

"He was killed."

"By whom?"

"By Monsieur Lorrilleux."

"Why?"

"Because I gave him to understand that if he could raise enough money—real money—I might run away with him."

"You were already married?"

"Yes."

"You're not in love with your husband?"

"I despise mediocrity. All my life I've been poor. All my life I've been surrounded by people who have had to scrimp and save, people who have had to sacrifice and count centimes. I've had to scrimp and sacrifice and count centimes myself." She turned savagely on Maigret, as if he had been responsible for all her troubles. "I just didn't want to be poor any more."

"Would you have gone away with Lorilleux?"

"I don't know. Perhaps for a while."

"Long enough to get your hands on his money?"

"I hate you!"

"How was Boissy murdered?"

"Monsieur Boissy was a regular customer of long standing."

"Pornographic literature?"

"He was a lascivious old goat, sure. So are all men. So is Lorilleux. So are you, probably. Boissy was a widower. He lived alone in a hotel room. He was very rich and very stingy. All rich people are stingy."

"That doesn't work both ways, does it? You, for instance, are not rich."

"I would have been rich."

"If Lorilleux had not come back. How did Boissy die?"

"The devaluation of the franc scared him out of his wits. Like everybody else at that time, he wanted gold. Monsieur Lorilleux used to shuttle gold in from Switzerland pretty regularly. And he always demanded payment in advance. One afternoon Monsieur

Boissy came to the shop with a fortune in currency. I wasn't there. I had gone out on an errand."

"You planned it that way?"

"No."

"You had no idea what was going to happen?"

"No. Don't try to put words in my mouth. When I came back, Lorilleux was packing the body into a big box."

"And you blackmailed him?"

"No."

"Then why did he disappear after having given you the money?"

"I frightened him."

"You threatened to go to the police?"

"No. I merely told him that our neighbors in the Palais Royal had been looking at me suspiciously and that I thought he ought to put the money in a safe place for a while. I told him about the loose floor board in my apartment. He thought it would only be for a few days. Two days later he asked me to cross the Belgian frontier with him."

"And you refused?"

"I told him I'd been stopped and questioned by a man who looked like a police inspector. He was terrified. I gave him some of the money and promised to join him in Brussels as soon as it was safe."

"What did he do with the corpse?"

"He put the box in a taxi and drove to a little country house he owned on the banks of the Marne. I suppose he either buried it there or threw it into the river. Nobody ever missed Monsieur Boissy."

"So you sent Lorilleux to Belgium without you. How did you keep him away for five years?"

"I used to write him, general delivery. I told him the police were after him, and that he probably would read nothing about it in the papers because they were setting a trap for him. I told him the police were always coming back to question me. I even sent him to South America."

"He came back two months ago?"

"About. He was at the end of his rope."

"Didn't you send him any money?"

"Not much."

"Why not?"

She did not reply. She looked at the clock.

"Are you going to arrest me? What will be the charge? I didn't kill Boissy. I wasn't there when he was killed. I had nothing to do with disposing of his body."

"Stop worrying about yourself. You kept the money because all your life you wanted money—not to spend, but to keep, to feel secure, to feel rich and free from want."

"That's my business."

"When Lorilleux came back to ask for money, or to ask you to keep your promise and run away with him, you used Colette as a pretext. You tried to scare him into leaving the country again, didn't you?"

"He stayed in Paris, hiding." Her upper lip curled slightly "What an idiot! He could have shouted his name from the housetops and nobody would have noticed."

"The business of Father Christmas wasn't idiotic."

"No? The money wasn't under the floor board any longer. It was right here under his nose, in my sewing basket."

"Your husband will be here in ten or fifteen minutes. Lorilleux across the street probably knows it. He's been in touch with Bergerac by phone, and he can read a timetable. He's surely armed. Do you want to wait here for your two men?"

"Take me away! I'll slip on a dress. . . ."

"The checkroom stub?"

"General delivery, Boulevard Beaumarchais."

She did not close the bedroom door after her. Brazenly she dropped the negligee from her shoulders and sat on the edge of the bed to pull on her stockings. She selected a woolen dress from the closet, tossed toilet articles and lingerie into an overnight bag.

"Let's hurry!"

"Your husband?"

"That fool? Leave him for the birds."

"Colette?"

She shrugged.

Mademoiselle Doncoeur's door opened a crack as they passed. Downstairs on the sidewalk she clung fearfully to the two men, peering into the fog.

"Take her to the Quai des Orfèvres, Lucas. I'm staying here."

She held back. There was no car in sight, and she was obviously frightened by the prospect of walking into the night with only Lucas to protect her. Lucas was not very big.

"Don't be afraid. Lorilleux is not in this vicinity."

"You lied to me! You—you—"

Maigret went back into the house.

The conference with Jean Martin lasted two hours.

When Maigret left the house at one-thirty, the two brothers were in serious conversation. There was a crack of light under Mademoiselle Doncoeur's door, but she did not open the door as he passed.

When he got home, his wife was asleep in a chair in the dining room. His place at table was still set. Madame Maigret awoke with a start.

"You're alone?" When he looked at her with amused surprise, she added, "Didn't you bring the little girl home?"

"Not tonight. She's asleep. You can go for her tomorrow morning."

"Why, then we're going to. . . ."

"No, not permanently. Jean Martin may console himself with some decent girl. Or perhaps his brother will get back on his feet and find a new wife. . . ."

"In other words, she won't be ours?"

"Not in fee simple, no. Only on loan. I thought that would be better than nothing. I thought it would make you happy."

"Why, yes, of course. It will make me very happy. But . . . but. . . ."

She sniffled once and fumbled for her handkerchief. When she couldn't find it, she buried her face in her apron.

STUART PALMER AND CRAIG RICE
Withers and Malone, Brain-Stormers

"THEY'RE AFTER ME!" gasped John J. Malone as he stumbled into Miss Hildegarde Withers' cottage. He set down his tinkling briefcase and sank wearily into her easiest chair.

"Who? The men with the strait jacket?" queried the surprised schoolteacher. She had heard nothing of the handsome, irrepressible little lawyer for more than two years, but now here he was—and obviously beside himself. She sensibly shot the night bolt, then peered out through the venetian blinds, but the side street in Santa Monica-by-the-Sea seemed as quiet as usual. "I don't see anyone," she reassured him. "But it is said that the guilty flee when no man pursueth. . . ."

"Well," protested Malone, who was at the moment trying to regain his breath and also to fend off the overfriendly advances of Talley the standard French poodle, "I may be guilty and I may not—that's for the jury. But somebody did pursueth me most of the way from the airport. I had to jump out of my taxi a couple of blocks from here and do a sprint across lots and through alleys. It was two men in a black sedan, and boding me no good, believe me!"

"But *who?* Surely you must have some idea."

He shrugged. "Anybody! I am *persona non grata* with Harbin Hamilton, deputy D.A. for Cook County. And with Captain von Flanagan, detective bureau of the Chicago police. *And* with Filthy Phil Pappke the bail bondsman, *and* with a wealthy bastrich named Bedford, *and* even with Joe the Angel at the City Hall Bar. To say nothing of Maggie."

"Then it must be bad! You're welcome here, even if I haven't done my breakfast dishes. But go on—tell me what brings you all the way out to California."

"Murder," Malone admitted dismally. "Maybe two murders, and one of 'em my own."

The Withers eyebrows shot up. "I don't quite understand."

"So do I! We've got to prevent a murder, only—" He sighed. "It's a *long* story. Any refreshments in the house?"

"I can offer you some coffee and cookies," she said firmly, and disappeared into the kitchen. Life had been rather dull of late for the retired schoolteacher, but now she was perking up. Whenever she had crossed paths—and sometimes swords—with John J. Malone in the past the adventures had always been memorable. She even had the scars to prove it. In a moment she was plying her unexpected guest with dull refreshments and sharp questions. Malone spiked the coffee from a bottle stashed in his topcoat pocket, and fed the cookies to the eager poodle whenever he thought Hildegarde's back was turned

"I'm really out here looking for a girl," he confessed.

"Quite out of my line," Miss Withers told him. "I'm a Miss, not a Madam. Have you tried breaking a hundred-dollar bill in a hotel bar? I thought that was your sure-fire method of making friends."

"Listen, Hildegarde! I mean one special girl—name of Nancy Jorgens. A lovely, very impetuous and very unpredictable girl, age 24, size 38–24–36. . . ."

"Spare me the vital statistics."

"Nancy is supposed to be out here—somewhere in the Los Angeles area anyway. But it's like looking for a needle in a haystack."

"Which is not such a difficult task, if you have a big enough magnet!" Miss Withers was brightening. "In this case, the magnet being whoever or whatever brought her out here—"

"That would be Paul Bedford." The little lawyer spoke the name as if it had a bad taste. Then he added hopefully, lifting his cup, "Do you mind if I sweeten this?"

"You've already *sweetened* it three times, but who's counting?" The schoolteacher sniffed disapprovingly. "Anyway, get on with your story."

"You'll remember that it's always been my proudest boast that I never lost a client yet? Well, that's been true—up to now."

"An execution? But I thought the murder hadn't happened yet."

Malone shook his head, spilling cigar ashes over his new Finchley suit and flamboyant Countess Mara tie. "I mean lost, literally. Nancy flew the coop yesterday. She's a fugitive from justice and because of her I'm a fugitive, period! You see, it was because of that paternity suit I lost—then the forgery indictment, the conspiracy charges, and—" The little lawyer sighed. "But I'll tell you about it on the way downtown."

"The way downtown *where?*"

"L.A. police headquarters. There's so little time—we've got to have official help. Surely, with your connections—"

"This is not Manhattan—there's no friendly Inspector Oscar Piper out here. I am known downtown at Headquarters, yes— but I'm afraid I'm known as anathema. We can expect no help from that quarter."

"But we've *got* to find Bedford before Nancy finds him! She disappeared yesterday, just after I got her out on bail, taking with her only some summer-weight clothes and a pistol that was a prop in the show she'd been playing in when she got arrested. But there was a note in last Sunday's *Trib* society section saying that Paul Bedford, of the Winnetka Bedfords, had left town to spend a few weeks in the Sunny Southland of California. Nancy must have seen that item. She didn't even phone me to say goodbye—probably afraid I'd try to talk her out of it."

"Does she know where Bedford is?"

"They were pretty close at one time, so maybe she does. But *we* don't."

"Hmmm," mused Miss Withers. "Is Bedford a prominent person?"

"And how. Even before the trial and all that publicity, he was front-page or society-page stuff. Football star in some Ivy League college, also crew and track. Flew a desk in the Pentagon during the war, but got a decoration. And his collection of rare autographs is famous—he has a complete set of the signers of the Declaration of Independence, including a disputed Button Gwinnett that a book got written about. He and his sister Doris inherited over four million bucks when their mother died a few years ago—"

"Enough, Malone. The gilded rich have predictable habits, like migratory wildfowl. He'll almost certainly be in Palm Springs, Santa Barbara, La Jolla, Malibu Beach, or Balboa Island. And never underestimate the power of a long-distance phone call. Who could put through a person-to-person call from Chicago to any of those places? How about Maggie?"

"Maggie takes a dim view of all this. But you could ask her."

Hildegarde proceeded to do just that. "Miss Withers!" finally came Maggie's voice across the miles. "I might have known that you'd get dragged into it! So Malone got as far as your place. Is he—?"

"Medium so. I am about to make some more coffee."

"Good! But try to keep him away from *that woman!*"

The schoolteacher never batted an eye. "Yes, but it's Bedford we've got to locate." She explained her plan, in detail. "And hurry, Maggie!" Hanging up, Miss Withers turned to Malone. "She'll try. But just why does Maggie refer to Nancy Jorgens as 'that woman' and advise me to keep you away from her?"

Malone fidgeted. "Maggie's prejudiced. You see, Nancy came into my office one day about a year ago—and a visitor of loveliness she was. Hair like spun honey, eyes blue as the Lakes of Killarney, a figure that—"

"Skip it. She's an actress, you said?"

"Model, singer, actress—she was just another pretty girl trying to break into show business. But what I was going to say about her figure—when she came into my office, *her slip showed.*"

"I beg your pardon?" And then Miss Withers read between the lines. "Oh!"

Malone nodded. "She was 'in trouble.' Said the man was Paul Bedford, of the canned-beef Bedfords. According to Nancy it was the old, old story, right out of *East Lynne.* She'd appealed to him when she discovered her indelicate condition, but—"

"He just sneered?"

"No, he told her to go see a shady doctor. When she refused to do that, he had her thrown out and the door slammed in her face."

"The skunk! Only I apologize to the entire genus mephitis."

"So I brought suit against Bedford on bastardy charges. I thought sure he'd settle out of court for maybe a cool hundred grand— but no dice. I think that vinegary-Vassary sister of his, Doris, put him up to fighting it. Anyway, they yelled 'legal blackmail,' and got Walt Hamilton to stand for the defense—he's the younger brother of Deputy D.A. Harbin Hamilton, who's been trying to nail my hide to the barn door for years. So my client and I had to go to court. . . ."

"Let me put a little more coffee in your whisky," Miss Withers offered sympathetically.

"Thanks. In court I had a regular field day—at first. I was never more eloquent, if I do say so myself. By the time the case came to trial Nancy had had her baby and got her figure back—she made a very appealing witness. It was an all-male jury, and when I rested our case, with Nancy sitting there in the courtroom with little Johnny in her arms, there wasn't a dry eye in the house."

"I can imagine—" She did a double take. "Little *Johnny?*"

"Yes," sighed Malone. "She named the little tyke after me, out of gratitude. You see, I'd paid the doctor and the hospital—any attorney would have done the same for a client. I'd even found a nice foster home for the kid—with some relatives of Maggie's out in Berwyn."

"Hmm-mm," murmured Miss Withers. "Go on."

"And then the defense pulled a knife on me—right in my back. They produced a parade of witnesses, gentlemen—and I use the word in quotes—who swore on their sacred oath that they had bounced in the—pardon me, I mean swore they had enjoyed the favors of my fair client."

"Oh, no!"

"Oh, yes! Some of them were probably just hired from a casting office—it must have cost Bedford plenty. Anyway, we were snowed under. There was no time and no money to finance an overnight investigation of those lying witnesses. A couple of them had actually had dates with Nancy, and there were notes and autographed photos to prove it. She had accepted trinkets from some of them— nothing big like mink or emeralds—but you know how girls in the profession are."

"I hope," murmured the schoolteacher, "that we're speaking of the *same* profession?"

"Objection!" said the little lawyer, reddening. "Nancy Jorgens isn't—"

"Go on, Malone."

"Well, unfortunately she didn't have any letters of Bedford's written during their brief but flaming affair. That in itself proves she wasn't mercenary!"

"Or that he was too cautious to write any! So you lost the case?"

"Not quite. I got a mistrial—a hung jury. Of course I was going to move for a new trial when either Nancy or I could dig up the costs. But meanwhile she has to eat, and she's supporting the baby, a cute little shaver. So she gets a part in a melodrama some shoestring theater group is putting on, mostly on the strength of her cheesecake publicity at the time of the trial. And she proves she really can act!"

"I have no doubt of it," admitted Miss Withers. "Particularly when she has a sympathetic male audience. How long have you been in love with her, Malone?"

"Me in love? Don't be silly! Anyway, Nancy gets good reviews in the play and the show moves into a downtown Loop theater and everything is going swell—then blooie! She gets herself arrested on the charge of forging Paul Bedford's name to a $25,000 check!"

"Dear, dear!"

" 'Dear-dear' isn't the word for it. It comes as a complete surprise to me. You see, she received the check in the mail, she says—"

"She *says!* "

"—and she rushes jubilantly over to me with it. I endorse it and then Joe the Angel, my old pal who runs the City Hall Bar, puts it through his bank for her. Do we celebrate *that* night!"

"I can imagine. But the check bounces—I mean bounced?"

"Higher than the Wrigley Building. Before I know it, my client is in jail, and I'm up to my ears in trouble. Harbin Hamilton in the D.A.'s office throws the book at Nancy. He's out to get me for conspiracy, accessory before the fact—or at the least disbarred!"

"Was the signature such an obvious forgery, then?"

"No, it was almost perfect. You can see yourself—I've got the enlarged photocopies in my briefcase here, along with the transcript of the preliminary examination. But every single handwriting expert said it was traced—they can tell by the variations in pressure used on the pen or something." Malone rose suddenly, tripped over the poodle, apologized, and then began to stalk up and down. "According to Nancy, the check simply arrived in the mail. The envelope and all the rest of it were typed, including an 'In Release of All Claims' just above where the endorsement would go. Naturally she thought Bedford had had a change of heart, and so did I." Malone was now peering out the window. "Say, that black sedan has gone by twice!"

"Relax, Malone. You're safe here. But this whole thing doesn't make sense! How could anybody in his right mind believe that a girl would forge a check like that, knowing that it would immediately come to light—or just as soon as the man got his bank statement?"

"The D.A.'s office had an answer for that. You see, Paul Bedford was supposed to be going off on a world cruise about that time—according to another of those squibs in the society column; but at the last minute the trip had been canceled because of his sister's health—she probably needed a transfusion of ice water. The authorities thought that *Nancy thought* that he wouldn't find out about the check until she had got the money and disappeared with it!"

"And of course such an idea would never occur to her?"

"Of course not. Unfortunately, however—on the same day I got the check cashed for her—she went to a travel agency and made a reservation to fly to Mexico City. Perfectly innocently, of course."

"Of course. She came into money, so she was going to leave her career—and leave you—"

"I was going along," Malone confessed sheepishly.

"Just for a week or so. I haven't had a real vacation in years and I needed one."

"You needed to have your head examined! But never mind that. I still don't see that the prosecution has much of a case against your client. How could a girl like that prepare an almost perfect forgery?"

"Hamilton didn't say that—he thinks I took care of that angle. You see, I got Harry the Penman acquitted only a few months ago, and others in the profession owe me favors. Not that I'd ever stoop to a thing like that."

"I'm sure you wouldn't. I wish I were as sure about Nancy. Because it all boils down to *cui bono,* Malone. Who stood to benefit? Who stood to pocket the $25,000, except the person to whom the check was made out? Riddle me that!"

"I know," admitted Malone, still eying the window. "Oh-oh, there goes that black sedan again. Hildegarde, we've gotta get out of here! Why oh *why* doesn't Maggie call?"

"Possess your soul in patience, Malone. Be calm—whoops!" The phone had barely started to ring when the schoolteacher pounced on it. "Hello? Yes—yes, this is she! Put her on, and hurry! Hello, Maggie?"

It really was Maggie, being the perfect secretary again. And the plot had worked; Paul Bedford had been located, up at Malibu.

". . . so he's sitting by that phone, waiting for the call to be completed," came Maggie's excited voice. "And I don't dare answer the office phone because I don't have anything to say to him; I don't even dare use it—I'm calling from a phone booth and I'm out of quarters—"

"Bless you!" cried Miss Withers. "Goodbye!"

"Wait!" Maggie screamed. "Tell Malone I just got a tip that Harbin Hamilton is on a plane headed for California, with a bench warrant in his pocket! It's not for the Jorgens girl, it's for—" And just then the operator cut them off.

"Good for Maggie," said Malone. "It's nice to be warned about Hamilton, but it'll all be over before he gets here. So Bedford is at Malibu. No address?"

"Just the phone number—Grove 2-2533. But we'll find it."

"What are we waiting for?" the little lawyer demanded.

"For my hat." She rushed out, and Malone took advantage of the opportunity to replace the empty pint with a full one from his briefcase; there might be snakes at Malibu. The schoolteacher's hat, he decided immediately upon her return, was something that could only have been inspired by a Rorschach ink blot test, but he followed her in silence as she led the way out through the back door. "We'll take Talley with us," Miss Withers decided, as she quietly raised the garage door. "Since we're headed up Snob Hill, the presence of a French poodle may give us a certain *cachet*. . . ."

Malone climbed into the ancient coupé, with some mental reservations. But the schoolteacher eventually got it going, and then they were headed down the alley, bouncing along a short street, then down more alleys, winding and twisting. "Just to throw anybody off," she explained.

"You just about threw *me* off at that last corner!" the little lawyer said through clenched teeth. He hung on tight as she whirled the little coupé onto Wilshire, down the ramp, and onto the Coast Highway heading north. The dog now had his head resting on the back of the seat between them, whining.

"Maybe he wants to drive," Malone suggested. "I wish *somebody* would—you missed that gravel truck by half an inch." They rolled on, at a dizzy fifty miles per hour. Then it was fifty-five, then sixty. "Will you please slow down?" Malone begged.

Every nut and bolt in the venerable chariot was protesting audibly. "I tried slowing down," Miss Withers said. "But it seems that black sedan behind us slows down whenever I do. And then it speeds up when I try to move ahead. Do you suppose—?"

"I do." Malone shook his head sadly. "Probably Phil Pappke's strong-arm boys. I should never have talked him into going bail for Nancy; he isn't known around City Hall as Filthy Phil for nothing."

"But it was Nancy Jorgens who jumped her bail. He should be annoyed at your client, not you."

"Well, I'm afraid that as partial surety for her I put up a building I own, out on the South Side. Unfortunately I won it in a poker game, so the title is cloudy. And it's been condemned anyway. Naturally Pappke got irritated when he found that out, after Nancy skipped town yesterday. In fact, Filthy Phil lived up to his moniker by giving me until midnight either to produce Nancy or the money—*or else.*"

"Midnight tonight?" gasped Miss Withers, passing a line of other cars and neatly getting back to her favorite position—directly over the white line.

"Midnight *last* night," Malone said. "On the other hand, this may not be Phil's henchmen at all. He's only one of many who want my scalp; he'll have to wait in line. Hildegarde, you see beside you a very unhappy man."

"You're not the first to be put behind the eight-ball by a woman," she reminded him. "Well, we're getting into Malibu now."

"Probably too late," the little lawyer moaned. "All we've got to do now is to get rid of that tail, then find out where Paul Bedford is hiding out—"

"Leave it to me," said Miss Withers. Then, ignoring his hopeful suggestion that they could inquire about Bedford at the nearest liquor store, she turned smack-dab into a parking lot just beside a small, squarish building which flew both the American and California flags.

"Hey, that's the sheriff's office!" Malone cried.

"Certainly. You'll notice that this move already takes care of the black sedan—it just went by, and very fast. Now if you'll give me a moment to fix Talley up—luckily he just had a clipping and looks quite silly enough to be anybody's pampered darling. . . ." She put a rhinestone collar around the poodle's neck and affixed a green bow to his topknot. "Presents from Inspector Piper," she explained over her shoulder, as she led the bedizened dog out of the car and into the sheriff's substation.

Behind the rail sat a dough-faced, stolid man in a black uniform, engaged in reading a paperback titled *2,000 Questions from Civil Service Exams*. "Good morning, Sergeant," Miss Withers said brightly, keeping a firm grip on Talley's leash. And then she asked the crucial question.

The officer blinked. "The Bedford house? Why, it's closed up."

"No, it isn't, Griggsy," said a male voice from an inner room. "Bedford and his sister opened it up. They're camping out there—roughing it without even any servants."

"Oh, good!" exclaimed the schoolteacher. "Because I mislaid the address, and I'd hate to go all the way back to the kennels without delivering Miss Doris' dog."

"The number's 12 Loretta Lane," said the other uniformed man, appearing suddenly in a doorway. "You turn in about a mile up the pike, third gate from here, then take the first to the left, then left again at the circle." He smiled a Boy Scout smile. "It's not easy to find—maybe I could ride along?"

He was looking not at her but at the sergeant, who started to frown.

"Thanks, anyway," said Miss Withers hastily. "I'm quite sure I can find it." And she dragged Talley hastily away.

Sergeant Griggs returned to his *2,000 Questions*. Then he looked up. "Hey, didn't I see a flimsy go through on this guy Bedford?"

The other shrugged. "Not that I know of. Except that we were supposed to keep an eye on the place while it was boarded up. But the folks are living there, all right. They phoned in a big order to the Market Basket yesterday—I know because my kid brother delivered it. A raft of canned goods, caviar, champagne, brandy, smoked oysters, Westphalian ham—all sorts of fancy stuff."

"No fancier than that dog. A diamond collar yet!"

"Bud said they wanted a lot of candles and a Coleman stove and all the newspapers, too. Looks like the high-and-mighty Bedfords are planning to rough it for a while. Bud said they hadn't even taken the shutters off the windows except around to the south, on the ocean side."

Griggs was frowning. "That's funny! No servants, no utilities except the phone, calling in their orders. Maybe they don't want it known they're here! And maybe you shouldn't have been so helpful with that old biddy—she might be the finger woman for a mob." He reached for the phone. "Your brother in high school now?"

"Yeah, Bud's a senior."

"I just wanted to ask him if there was any dog food in that order."

While his partner derisively hummed the boomp-de-boomp-boomp theme music of a popular cops-and-robbers TV show, Griggs made the call—he had been bucking for lieutenant for years.

But the damage was already done.

Malone, Miss Withers and Talley had found the rambling rose-pink house at 12 Loretta Lane, perched on the edge of the cliff high above a small private beach and the broad Pacific. It stood shuttered, silent, asleep. Yet, just as they were about to disembark, they heard the muffled but unmistakable sound of a pistol shot within. It was immediately followed by another shot, then by a choked feminine scream.

"Too late!" cried Malone, as they dashed up the sidewalk.

Miss Withers knocked and knocked, and the little lawyer rattled the doorknob, without avail. "Break it down?" she suggested. He rammed it with his shoulder, then shook his head.

"You stay here!" he ordered. "I'll try the back." He ran off, followed by the poodle, who didn't quite understand the game but wanted to get into it.

"Well, I never!" said the schoolteacher, somewhat vexed. She banged on the door again, then tried to peer into one of the shuttered windows. "The dickens with it!" She raced to the back, around the garage wing, and came suddenly into the blazing sunshine and onto a wide, roughstone patio gay with grass and flowering shrubs, outdoor furniture and umbrellas, and an immense but empty swimming pool.

She arrived just in time to see John J. Malone with a naked girl in his arms.

"Excuse *me!*" Miss Withers cried, aghast.

But on second look the girl wasn't quite naked after all; she wore flesh-colored bikini-type halter and shorts. Still, she was what the schoolteacher would have called "a scandal to the jaybirds," and her breathtaking beauty only made it more scandalous.

"Damn it, darling," she was almost screaming, "let me go!" The young woman squirmed like an eel, trying desperately to get away toward the flight of wooden steps that descended down the cliff to the little beach below.

Malone had a good grip; he not only held his prize but he shook her fiercely. "Listen, Nancy! Listen to me! I'm your attorney, remember? He tried to strangle you, and you shot him in self-defense—remember that!"

"Oh, you don't understand! Let me go!"

But Miss Withers understood. Nancy Jorgens had a nasty little pistol in one hand, and it was still smoking. Without hesitation the schoolteacher crept up silently and snatched it away. "There," she said. "Now will somebody please tell me—" But nobody did. Talley had the most to say, barking his head off with happy excitement.

The girl finally went limp in Malone's grasp. "Back inside," he said sternly. "I'm taking over now." And he half carried the curvaceous beauty through the French doors into the house. After a thoughtful moment Miss Withers followed, carefully closing the doors behind her, right in Talley's puzzled face.

From then on things remained nightmarish. They were in an immense living room full of modern chairs and furniture and garnished with Picasso and Modigliani prints and metal mobiles— a room that smelled of perfume, of the sea, and of raw cordite. A thin rigid woman of around forty—obviously Doris Bedford, the sister—was standing near the fireplace. Not doing anything, just standing. A clock ticked away somewhere, and the waves crashed booming on the rocks below.

Paul Bedford, slightly overweight, slightly tanned, slightly dead, lay all akimbo at the farther end of the room near an open window, staring thoughtfully at the ceiling. A vagrant breeze drifted in uninvited and ruffled his curly, thinning hair.

"I didn't—!" screamed Nancy Jorgens, before Malone's hand clamped over her mouth.

"Now what happened here?" the little lawyer demanded, looking accusingly at Doris Bedford.

"Who are you?" she whispered, hardly moving her pale lips. She wasn't looking at the intruders or at the body of her brother— she wasn't looking at anything.

Miss Withers came to life, "Never mind arguing. What matters is whether—is if—" She steeled herself, then moved to bend over Paul Bedford. This sort of thing was not exactly her cup of tea; she preferred her murders at secondhand. A mental problem in applied criminology was one thing, but this. . . .

"My brother is dead," said Doris hollowly. "You needn't bother trying his pulse or putting a mirror to his lips. He's dead, I tell you. And *she* shot him, just as I knew she would!"

"You—you weren't even in the room!" cried Nancy, twisting away from Malone again.

But the little lawyer caught her, and his hand clamped over her mouth. Then he shoved her into a chair so hard that her teeth rattled. "Shut up!" he whispered fiercely. "We *want* her to have been in the room, maybe! I said let me handle this!" He turned to face Doris Bedford. "I am John J. Malone, Miss Jorgens' attorney. Please tell us in your own words exactly what happened."

"Just what I feared would happen, if Paul didn't get far enough away from *her!* She came bursting in here uninvited—she must have swum out around the rocks and trespassed on our beach. That was while my brother and I were waiting for a very important phone call from Chicago to be put through to us. She insisted that she had to talk to Paul alone, so I went out. But naturally I could hear. . . ."

"Then you don't claim to have witnessed the alleged crime?" began Malone in his best courtroom manner.

Miss Withers had had enough. "For heaven's sake!" she cried. "This man may *not* be dead! I don't see a wound or any blood. None of us is a doctor—where's the phone, quick? An ambulance—"

"Never mind the ambulance. Get . . . police . . ." murmured Doris Bedford. And then she crumpled to the floor in a dead faint.

Miss Withers tried to move in two directions at once. She didn't quite make it.

"Wait," snapped Malone. "Maybe all three of us should blow this joint fast—it's only her word against ours. Listen, Hildegarde—"

Hildegarde was listening—to the brief, *sotto voce skrr* of a siren outside, and almost immediately afterward to a hammering on the front door. "I'm not compounding any felonies," she said. "And I'm afraid my running days are over. You both stay put— I'm going to open the door."

"Yes?" she said politely to the man outside, her recent acquaintance of the substation, Sergeant Griggs. His round, perspiring face wore a look of worried deference.

"Excuse me for busting in, but—" he began. Then he recognized her. "Say, what's going on here?" At that inauspicious moment Talley the poodle came bounding through the flowerbeds, darting in past them through the open door, then stopping short at the entrance to the living room. He set up an ear-splitting barking, and by the time his distraught mistress could grab him and shut him up, the fat was in the fire.

"It's murder," she admitted to the officer. "You may as well come in. It's in there."

Griggs got as far as the door, and froze. "Migawd!" he cried, unbelievingly. "It's *wholesale!*"

Miss Withers was helpful. "I think Miss Bedford has only fainted," she said softly. "Her brother seems to be the victim. . . ."

"If there was a victim," Malone spoke up. He was sitting calmly on the arm of Nancy's chair, one hand firmly on her bare shoulder. "My client has absolutely nothing to say at this time." It was not the exact truth—Nancy had "Ouch!" to say, reacting to his warning pinch.

Sergeant Griggs knelt for a moment over what was left of Paul Bedford. "Colder'n Kelsey," he said hollowly. "This is it, folks." Nobody said anything. Nancy Jorgens looked guilty, Malone looked guilty, and Miss Withers suspected that she looked guiltier than either of them.

For the sake of the professional reputations of Mr. John J. Malone and Miss Hildegarde Withers, it might be well to draw the mantle of charity over the next hour. Everything had, as Malone aptly put it, "gone to hell in a handbasket." Paul Bedford was a stiffening corpse. His sister had come out of her faint only long enough to point at Nancy and scream, "She shot him, she shot him twice!" and then had relapsed into a coma.

The police were everywhere, doubled and redoubled. "And three down, vulnerable," Miss Withers whispered to the little lawyer. "Bridge, you know."

"Nobody should burn their bridges until they come to them," he whispered back absently. "I wish you'd shut up and let me think." Typically, the retired schoolteacher had from time to time been making helpful suggestions about the way an on-the-spot murder investigation should be conducted, none of which Sergeant Griggs took in the right spirit. For some reason, the officer seemed inclined to consider Miss Withers as hot a suspect as the other two. That tied Hildegarde's hands, if not her tongue.

Nor was Malone in his best form, either. With a knowledge of women which, like Dr. Watson's, "extended over three continents," he must have had some doubts about his lovely client and the extent to which she had bedazzled him for her own ends. The ground was not firm beneath his immaculate Italian oxfords. Unfortunately, one of the first things the officers had done was to have everybody searched, and his pint bottle of snake-bite remedy had been summarily impounded. That was the last straw. He was in the depths, but he was still trying to think fast.

Nancy Jorgens seemed the coolest of all. She had found a cigarette in a little box on a mosaic table beside her, and she lit it with a steady hand. Miss Withers was beginning to admit to herself a sneaking liking for the young woman. "There is more to that girl than meets the eye," she said to herself. "And at the moment there is certainly a good deal of her *to* meet the eye!" But Nancy seemed magnificently unaware of her seminakedness.

Around the three of them the breakers of the law dashed higher and higher; the house was so full of uniforms that it looked like a St. Patrick's Day parade in Manhattan. There were doctors and coroner's physicians and a police crime-lab squad with cameras and fingerprint powders and tiny vacuum cleaners—and everyone was having a field day.

The three suspects had been herded into the playroom, near a dusty ping-pong table and an ornate but understocked bar, with one of the sheriff's deputies on guard and taking his duties very seriously. "I was just thinking—" began Miss Withers.

"No talking," the officer told her.

"But I was only going to say that it isn't sensible to lock my dog in the kitchen. He can open refrigerators and cupboards!"

"Quiet!" So the three of them just sat there. Doris Bedford had been taken tenderly to her bedroom and was now under the care of a doctor and a nurse; Miss Withers might have considered trying a maidenly swoon herself, but her curiosity had got the better of her. She had to see Malone talk his way out of this one!

After a time Sergeant Griggs stalked in on them, complete with notebook and pen. The case was his baby, and he made that perfectly clear. "This happened in unincorporated county territory," he told them. "So I'm in charge. I'm taking your statements—"

"One at a time, separately," put in Miss Withers. "I believe that's the correct procedure."

"Yes, one at a—be quiet! *You* first." He jabbed at Nancy. "Mac, take the other two away and sit on 'em."

"I object!" spoke up Malone. "I am John J. Malone, Miss Jorgens' attorney-of-record. You will question her in my presence or not at all. Furthermore, if you question me I will give my name and address only. I was not a witness to the alleged crime, arriving on the scene only after whatever happened happened. Anything my client may have said to me is a privileged communication unless the court later decides it is properly part of the *res gestae.* . . ."

"I said *QUIET!*" roared Griggs. He turned on Miss Withers. "Now you, ma'am—"

"This lady is also my client," Malone interposed. "I insist—"

"Nonsense," interrupted the schoolteacher. She took a deep breath. Then, not looking at the little lawyer, she said calmly, "Mr. Malone is mistaken when he says he is my attorney. He is just a friend of mine. I only drove him up here because he was in a hurry to see his client, Miss Jorgens, and thought she might have come here. Just as we arrived we heard two shots. Mr. Malone tried the front door, then told me to watch there while he ran around to the back of the house. I got tired of waiting and followed him, just in time to see him with Miss Jorgens on the patio. We three came inside immediately through the open French doors and found the body—"

"Okay, okay!" said Sergeant Griggs, scribbling. "But not so fast."

"We saw Miss Bedford standing near her brother's body. She said something about the girl's having shot him—"

Malone was so busy giving Hildegarde withering glances that he had momentarily forgotten Nancy, who spoke up with the determined insistence of a balked child. "She wasn't even in the room, I tell you!"

"But you do admit shooting him, don't you?"

"This is absolutely improper!" cried Malone desperately. "You are putting words in her mouth. And if there was any shooting it was solely in self-defense!"

"That would be just dandy," remarked the Sergeant dryly. "Only in self-defense nobody but nobody shoots an unarmed man in the back!" They froze at that. "There wasn't any wound or any

blood on the front of the corpse, or I would have noticed it!"
Griggs added triumphantly.

Nancy cried, "Oh, no, no! I—"

"Miss Jorgens," Malone interrupted, "denies everything!"

Griggs seemed at the point of spontaneous combustion; Miss
Withers fancied she could already see smoke coming out of his
big red ears. But at that moment they were relieved by the sound
of a heavy knocking at the door. The officer who had been called
Mac opened it, listened, then beckoned to his superior. Griggs
hesitated, gave the suspects a warning glance and went reluctantly
out. Mac stayed in the doorway, more interested in what was
going on in the hall than in the room. Malone managed to catch
Hildegarde's eye and whispered reproachfully, "Nice going, Miss
Blabbermouth!"

"I'm afraid I've only just begun," the schoolteacher whispered
back, feeling rather like Benedict Arnold. But she was convinced
that what had to be done had to be done.

Meanwhile, the cause of all this commotion sat perfectly still,
her lovely legs crossed, her pale hair unmussed. Nancy was like
a child who had idly dropped a lighted match in the underbrush
and now was only a mildly interested spectator at the holocaust.
Perhaps she had not chosen the almost invisible bathing suit as
the perfect costume in which to be arrested, but it certainly gave
her a definite edge—with the opposite sex, anyway. If Griggs had
known his business, Miss Withers was thinking, he would have
found a robe or a blanket and made the girl put it on, so he and
the rest of the officers could keep their minds on their work.

But their inquisitor came back, too soon. With him now were
reinforcements in the shape of a number of sober-faced gentlemen
in casual sports attire who were still obviously detectives or officials;
one of them Miss Withers thought she remembered from the
recent McWalters murder affair. He was a man named Dade, who
was supposed to be something important in the D.A.'s office
downtown. He had given her little or no trouble then—but that
time she had been on the other side of the fence. Now he did
not even nod.

In addition there was a pudgy civilian in sober "eastern" clothes,
who wore an expression of unadulterated glee on his pale, slightly
greenish face. "Well, Malone!" said the great Harbin Hamilton.
"It is a pleasure, a great pleasure, to meet you like this!"

The little lawyer was obviously staggered. All he needed right now was the unwelcome sight of the Deputy D.A. of Cook County. "Hello, Harbin," he managed to say. "So you had to fly out and get into the act! You look even unhealthier than usual—rough trip, I hope I hope?"

"It was worth every bit of it, shyster," said Hamilton.

"All right!" cut in Sergeant Griggs, still trying to keep control of his first big murder case. "Never mind the personalities." He walked over and put his thick hand on Nancy's bare shoulder. "Nancy Jorgens, I arrest you on suspicion of murder!"

Nancy took his hand and removed it, as if it had been a damp clam. "Am I supposed to say something?" she asked coolly.

"Play it your own way, sister. The doctor says you missed Bedford both times, and the bullets went out through the open window behind him. But you were the cause of a fatal heart attack, so it's exactly the same as if you'd taken dead aim. We know all about the trouble you had with him back in Chicago—"

"She tried to shake him down with a phony lawsuit, and when that failed she forged his name to a check for $25,000; she's under indictment for that now!" put in Harbin Hamilton helpfully. "And having jumped her bail, she's a fugitive from justice." He took a step toward Nancy. "We know you had a gun with you when you came out here from Chicago. You were aware that Bedford was hiding out with his sister—hiding out from you. You located him at this beach place, you knew you couldn't get in the front way, so you swam around the rocks to the private beach and came up here to have it out with him, then—"

Malone drew a deep breath. "A clever concatenation of pusillanimous, suppositional, hypothetical fabrications. I demand—"

"Shut up," Griggs said. "You have no privileged status here as an attorney. Mr. Hamilton has a bench warrant for you, on several charges of conspiracy. But murder takes precedence." Griggs's hand came down heavily on Malone's padded shoulder. "The charge is accessory after the fact and concealment of evidence—the pistol."

"What pistol? The presence of a weapon here has not been established!" But the little lawyer was standing on the thinnest of legal ground.

Griggs motioned to Miss Withers. "This lady here says she heard two shots, just as you arrived. The room stank of cordite when

I got here. That's enough evidence for me—and we'll find the gun!"

Harbin Hamilton was obviously enjoying every moment. "That seems to settle you, once and for all," he told Malone. "And your girlfriend, too." He nudged Sergeant Griggs. "What'll we do with the Withers woman? She's in on it too, isn't she? I seem to remember her being in cahoots with Malone once before—"

"Listen!" cried Nancy suddenly. "I can't stand any more of this. If I sign a confession will you let these people go? Mr. Malone and Miss Withers haven't done anything!" Her voice throbbed.

Sergeant Griggs was brightening, but Malone cut in. "I will not permit it!"

"I won't either," said Hamilton. "A confession to first degree murder can't be pled anyway. And we don't need a confession."

"That's right," agreed Griggs. He turned to the schoolteacher, who could already hear those iron doors clanging behind her.

"I'll go," Hildegarde said, "but I'll not go quietly! As a matter of fact, there are a number of things I must call to your attention. In my opinion, you're going about this investigation in entirely the wrong way, and—"

Just then Mr. Dade, the sober-faced gentleman from the D.A.'s office, drew the sergeant aside and whispered to him. Griggs listened, looked surprised and nodded. "Thanks for tipping me off, Mr. Dade," he said. Then he turned back to Miss Withers, who had her fingers crossed behind her back. "As for you, ma'am— I hear that you've meddled in police business before, and managed to make an unholy nuisance of yourself. On the other hand, you've helped us this time by making a statement. So if you'll wait while it's typed up—"

"But I'm certainly not going to leave right now!" she broke in. "I'm needed here! I've probably had a great deal more experience in murder cases than any of you, and I'll be happy to advise you!"

"You'll get out now," interrupted the sergeant wildly. "The statement can be signed later. And take that screwy-looking dog with you!"

Miss Withers looked as crestfallen as the traditional old maid in the limerick, who went to a Birth Control Ball. "Well, I *never!*" she huffed. But the party was over. Nancy was led away, belatedly covered with one of Doris Bedford's beach robes. Malone, at Harbin Hamilton's spiteful insistence, went through the ignominious experience of being handcuffed. The schoolteacher found herself being propelled firmly toward the door, but she did manage to flicker a reassuring wink over her shoulder in his general direction. Malone didn't see it, or perhaps he didn't wish to see it.

It just wasn't Miss Withers' day. To add to her troubles, just as she'd feared, Talley had pawed open the refrigerator and made smorgasbord of its contents. Leading him outside, she had to run the gauntlet of the press—evidently the Bedford murder was already front-page news. The photographers flashed cameras at her, and the reporters demanded statements.

"Stand back!" she warned them, holding Talley firmly.

"Does he bite?" one newsman asked.

"No, but he throws up!"

Somehow she made her way back to the little coupé and got it started. Talley, quite unused to lunching on smoked oysters and caviar, climbed slowly onto the back seat and curled up to sleep. Miss Withers felt rather like curling up too. Malone, one of her best friends, had come to her in his greatest hour of need, and now she was abandoning him to the jackals. She alone was free— but free to do what? The case against Nancy, a girl perhaps more sinned against than sinning, was utterly damning—and Malone was in it up to and including his ears.

And to make everything absolutely perfect, Miss Withers had not got ten miles down the coast on the way home before she saw the familiar black sedan tailing her. It hung on, perhaps an eighth of a mile back, as implacable as death and taxes. The schoolteacher's immediate reaction was a rush of righteous wrath to the head—but she remained cool, concocting a plan that was fiendishly simple.

"I think, Talley, we've been pushed around just about enough for one day!" She speeded up, dashing on down the highway until she saw a side road leading inland up one of the narrow canyons. Rashly she turned up it—a winding, two-lane road with looming cliffs on one hand and a dizzy drop-off on the other. The black sedan followed.

She gave a last burst of speed before taking one of the sharpest blind curves, then jammed on the brakes and stopped short, with the little coupé swung across the road.

The big sedan had excellent brakes, but no driver on earth could have seen that improvised roadblock in time. Rubber smoked

and screeched—and then there was a resounding crash. Miss
Withers' ancient Chevy rolled sluggishly over—and then disappeared. Topanga Canyon echoed a few seconds later to another,
a very final crash, from far below. . . .

"Why don't you look where I'm going?" demanded Miss Hildegarde Withers, leaning precariously against the face of the rock
cliff and holding Talley with both hands. "If we hadn't jumped
in the nick of time—"

She addressed the two men in the front seat of the sedan, both
of whom were pale and shaking. "Lady!" cried the driver, a middle-
aged man in a chauffeur's cap. "I didn't—I'm only a hire-drive
car—"

"Well-insured, I hope?" She turned to the other, a bulky young
man in a sports shirt, whose five-o'clock shadow was hours ahead
of schedule. "And you, I suppose, are Filthy Phil Pappke?"

"I'm his brother William, and no cracks! I don't know where
you come in, but you got Phil all wrong. He's a businessman, an
investor like—and he's got a lot of money invested in a tomato
name of Nancy Jorgens because he went her bail and if she isn't
back in Chi by tomorrow, it's forfeit. I was just tagging Malone,
figuring he'd maybe be a lead to the dame."

"The dame is beyond your reach, and so is Malone. They're
arrested."

"Ouch! Those police cars I saw—say, maybe it's okay and she
gets sent back to Chi!"

"Nothing is okay. They'll be held here—for murder." Willie
scowled, and started to mumble something about his brother's not
going to like this. "Be quiet," she told him. "An accident to
Malone isn't going to save your brother his money. Driver, just
how serious is the damage to your car?"

"She'll still run, I guess."

"Then the least you can do is to drive me home!" She climbed
in, the dog in her arms. "Willie, on the way back you and I are
going to have a heart-to-heart talk!"

Willie protested that he had to get to a phone right away and
call his brother, but she told him that he was welcome to use
hers. "Because I want a word with Filthy Phil Pappke myself!"

A little later Willie made his telephone report, which consisted
mostly of listening to staccato sounds over long distance, until
the schoolteacher got tired and took over. "Hello, Mr. Pappke?
This is Miss Withers, the lady whose automobile was demolished

by your shenanigans. Lucky I wasn't killed. What? Well, perhaps it isn't illegal to have somebody shadowed, but it is illegal to annoy a lady, in or out of a car. I intend to see my lawyer at once—that car was a collector's item and it had sentimental—"

"Listen, whoever you are! All I want—" came the protesting voice.

"All you want is to save $25,000! And let me tell you that your only chance in this world is to help me get John J. Malone out of jail, because he can straighten this out if anyone can. The moment his bail is set, you'd better have a man there with the money. What? I don't care how you feel about Malone; the point is that you've got to cooperate with us now—or else! Think about that—and while you're thinking, think about my lawsuit!" She hung up.

"That ain't the way to handle my brother Phil," Willie Pappke told her.

"The only way I would handle either of you is with a pair of ten-foot tongs! Now get out of here, I have work to do." Willie got.

Work to do, indeed? But what work, and where to begin? Malone had brought her a hopeless mess, and now it was a thousand times worse. But give him the benefit of the doubt. Suppose that in spite of his having brought a paternity suit involving a baby named after him and paid for by him, he had acted in good faith. In desperation would he have been a party to forgery, even forgery which might have seemed morally justifiable? Yet Nancy was a breath-taking blonde, and breath-taking blondes were Malone's worst weakness—or one of his worst weaknesses.

As these unpleasant thoughts were bubbling in Miss Withers' mind, she was studying the legal papers in the little lawyer's briefcase—after first putting the one remaining bottle safely away. She read through the trial transcript and the transcript of the forgery prelim. She studied the photo-enlargements of the handwriting on the questioned check. The signature of Paul Bedford looked perfectly good to her, but pinned to it was the verdict of three famous handwriting experts who had all pronounced it queerer than a three-dollar bill.

The forgery and the fact that Paul Bedford had obviously died at Nancy's hand were unarguable. Still—

In the midst of her speculations another call from Chicago came in. It was Maggie, this time in tears. "I just this minute heard!"

she was crying hysterically. "It's on the press tickers. Oh, I *told* you to keep him away from *that woman!*"

"Wild horses couldn't. Be quiet, Maggie. We've got to work fast. At the moment I'm quite ready to clutch at straws. But I'm happy to announce that we now have the cooperation of a very powerful, if somewhat unethical, ally. Yes, Filthy Phil Pappke. What? No matter how, I put the fear of lucre in him. The first thing you've got to do is to find out who the Bedford family doctor was, and arrange to have Mr. Pappke have somebody do a little strong-arm stuff. And stick by a phone. I may think of something else."

Five minutes later Miss Withers was headed downtown in a taxi, her first stop being the Hall of Justice in Los Angeles. That vast grim mausoleum of humanity's hopes and dreams was crowded, but nobody in the place could tell her if Malone had yet been brought in and taken to the jail floors; even if he were there, she couldn't get into the special jail elevator because she was neither his attorney nor his next-of-kin, though she made a stab at pretending to be the latter.

Well, that was that; she would have to proceed solo. On a sudden inspiration she stopped at the Information Desk and struck up a conversation with the elderly officer in charge. "Oh," she said, pointing to a man nearby, "isn't that what's-his-name, the famous handwriting expert who always testifies for the prosecution?"

"No, ma'am," said the officer. "That's just some two-bit lawyer. He doesn't look a bit like J. Edgar Salter. Salter's a thinner man, with a bald head and glasses." She thanked him as she left, with the name and description committed to memory. Mr. Salter had offices on Hill Street, she discovered by looking in a phone book; but she drew a blank on the call—he was in conference and could not be disturbed.

Which daunted the schoolteacher not at all. "I must go round-about, as the Boyg advised Peer Gynt," she said to herself. And without more ado she hurried over to the Public Library, a vast pseudo-Moorish edifice on Fifth. Libraries were usually her last resort; there in the musty stacks was everything anybody in the world would want to know, if he only knew where to look.

She stayed until closing time, then stopped at a late-open bookstore to make one small purchase, and finally took a bus home. It had been a long, long day.

She had barely fed Talley, prepared a peanut butter sandwich and cup of tea for herself, and changed into robe and slippers when the doorbell rang. This, she knew, would be the police, coming to get her statement. Or maybe to arrest her, the way luck was running. She braced herself for the inevitable, and opened the door. "Good heavens!" she cried. "This is where I came in!"

It was John J. Malone, looking the worse for wear. He entered, shoulders sagging, and sank wearily into her easiest chair. "I promised myself," he said slowly, "that next time we met I would bop you one, lady or no lady."

"I was afraid you'd misunderstand. But at least one of us had to be free and up and doing. Don't tell me you broke jail? Or did Filthy Phil actually send someone to put up your bail?"

He shook his head. "Released on my own recognizance," he said. "When they got me downtown, it turned out that several of the big wheels in the D.A.'s office knew me by reputation. And I guess Harbin Hamilton threw his weight around too much; he forgot that this wasn't Cook County. The D.A.'s office let me loose as a professional courtesy—but I'm still in a jam. And there's certain extradition back to Chicago even if I squirm out of this. Meanwhile there's Nancy. I don't know what to do about her!"

"I suppose you pondered over it in every bar on your way here?"

"Only two! I was in the U.C.L.A. Law Library, reading up. But I don't see a single loophole. Nancy may not get the works, but she'll get ten years at least."

"And in spite of everything, you're still in love with her?" John J. Malone nodded dismally as she went on. "Well, then! If you love her you don't have any choice but to believe her!"

"Yes—but we both heard those two shots, and I caught her trying to escape with the gun in her hand. Wish I knew where that gun disappeared to."

"I know, but skip it. What comes next, a grand-jury hearing?"

"Arraignment, two o'clock tomorrow—a formality that will take ten minutes. Nancy and I appear, the judge sets the date for the prelim and the amount of bail—any amount of which will be too much."

"Tomorrow! Oh, dear." The schoolteacher cocked her head. "Look, Malone, I have a wild idea. You know those meetings they have among scientists and researchers when everybody takes turns suggesting the wildest idea that comes into his head? Brain-washing, they call it—"

"Brain-storming," he corrected. "But by all the saints—"

"Let's try it, please! If you'll play I'll even show you where I hid your bottle!" He gave in promptly. "Very well," she began. "We'll release our mental brakes. Let me think. Nancy is completely innocent—it's a frame. Doris forged the check!"

"She wouldn't know how, and she wouldn't dare hire anybody—"

"You're not playing! Say something, no matter how fantastic!"

He sighed. "Doris hated Nancy. She not only forged the check to frame her, she thought that all her brother's money should be hers, so she killed him when he complained about her cooking. Wild enough?"

"Now you're swinging! Doris poisoned him with her cooking!"

"No, she used something that wouldn't show in the autopsy— a huge dose of adrenalin or digitalis. Or maybe *he's* the real murderer, he killed himself out of pure meanness!"

"Maybe Harbin Hamilton forged the check . . . ?"

So it went, for an hour. At last they ran out of not only the improbable but also the impossible.

"It's no earthly use," Malone said dismally. "We're not getting anywhere. You and I both know that Nancy fired the shots that indirectly killed Bedford, and as for the forgery—"

"Stop thinking like the police! What is the unlikeliest possibility of all? There must be one factor in this case that has led everybody astray because we've been tricked into looking at it wrong side up or endways!"

"But we just haven't enough to go on!"

"I'm not so sure. I have a couple of irons in the fire, or where I could possibly start a fire." And she told him all about her afternoon. "If we could only find out a few things about Bedford's medical record—and what books he has in his library."

"So what? The prelim won't be for a week or so, and the trial not for months, and all that time Nancy will be in jail. You couldn't even get in to see this guy Salter, and if you do he'll just back up the other experts." She shook her head firmly, but he went on. "And you've missed the point in trying to sic Maggie onto Filthy Phil. Even if he will cooperate because you have him over a barrel, what's the use of roughing up the Bedford family doctor, and breaking into the Bedford house?"

"Just brain-storming," she admitted. "But I want to know more about certain things than anybody else knows. A shot in the dark will often scare something out of the bushes." Miss Withers yawned.

"Well, I don't know about you, but I'm going to bed and sleep on it. You're welcome to the couch here."

But Malone had promised the boys at the D.A.'s office to check in at a certain downtown hotel, just to make it look good. He departed, not forgetting his bottle. And he was no sooner out the door than Miss Withers was on the long distance phone to Maggie again, with new instructions. "Try to go along on the job yourself," she urged. "Here's what to look for. . . . What? Well, wouldn't you risk it if it will save Malone's neck? . . . There's a dear!"

All of which ended a memorable day. The schoolteacher even omitted her usual hundred strokes with the hairbrush, and crawled wearily into her maidenly couch, murmuring instead of a prayer— "Tomorrow is another day."

And so it was—a day that neither of them was ever likely to forget. They were both too busy in the forenoon to have a conference, except briefly by telephone. The telephone was also hot all the way to Chicago, where Maggie, the world's most devoted secretary, and Filthy Phil Pappke, surprisingly enough the world's most cooperative conspirator, were equally busy. That part of the story neither of them will talk about—at least, not until the statute of limitations runs out.

Both Miss Withers and the little lawyer were in Department 30 of the Hall of Justice, eighth floor, well ahead of time. There were only a few bored attendants in the courtroom. The plaque on the bench read *Herbert Winston, Judge,* but there was no sign yet of His Honor. Malone, very much in his element, plumped his briefcase confidently on the counsel table. Miss Withers took a seat in the front row and prayed.

Policemen, sheriff's deputies—among them Sergeant Griggs, of course—came in leisurely. Then two deputies, looking like lady wrestlers in spite of their trimly feminine uniforms, arrived with Nancy between them. Even the drab jail uniform could not cancel Nancy Jorgens' luscious measurements, but her eyes were haunted. She flicked a wan smile over to Miss Withers as she was led over to wait in the empty jury box, but her eyes were for Malone. He rose eagerly and started toward her.

"No, you don't!" came a harsh voice. Enter Harbin Hamilton,

with several of the D.A.'s staff—one of them Mr. Dade, to whom
the Chicagoan turned excitedly. "I protest against this man's trying
to have a conference with his fellow conspirator!"

Dade smiled, a little stiffly. "Well, Mr. Malone is a member of
the bar, and it's customary—"

"He is here as an *accused*—he has no attorney status!"

"Whether or not he is representing Miss Jorgens, there's nothing
to prevent him from acting as his own attorney, is there?" Dade
walked over and formally shook hands with Malone. They talked
briefly, but in so low a tone that Miss Withers could only hear
something about a "plea" and see Dade shake his head slowly.

More people were coming in; it was evidently close to zero
hour. The hands of the clock showed ten past two, and Miss
Withers found herself trying to hold her breath. She let it go as
she saw Doris Bedford enter, wearing an unbecoming mutation
mink, and seat herself on the aisle. Half a dozen other spectators
also drifted in, by ones and by twos. One of them, a tall, bald,
very lean man in a charcoal gray suit and glasses, seated himself
directly behind Miss Withers. But she barely noticed. Everybody
was springing to attention; cigars and cigarettes vanished, and
Judge Winston, robes and all, appeared and sat down on the
bench. He looked rather like an animated prune.

They were finally under way, for better or for worse. It was all
a blur to Miss Withers, though later she remembered Malone's
air of absolute confidence—it should have won him an Academy
Award nomination.

Court was in session: *The People versus Jorgens and Malone.*

"We intend to plead guilty, Your Honor," Malone started.

Harbin Hamilton stood up from his chair beside Mr. Dade and
objected on the grounds that Malone had no status. The Judge
looked at Dade.

"Mr. Malone, I don't believe you've been admitted to the bar
of this state," Dade said. "Your status is that of co-defendant."

"Prisoners are entitled to counsel," interposed the Court. He
looked slightly annoyed. "For your information, Mr. Malone, the
State of California permits *only* a plea of not guilty in capital
offenses. We are here merely to set the date for the preliminary
hearing and to discuss bail—"

"Yes, Your Honor. But—"

"Nancy Jorgens, are you represented by counsel?" asked the
Judge.

Nancy shook her head. "Not if Mr. Malone isn't—I won't have just anybody! I can be my own attorney too, can't I?"

"It is so noted," said Judge Winston. "Proceed."

Dade said, "As for bail, the law is clear. A defendant charged with an offense punishable by death cannot be admitted to bail when proof of guilt is indicated. It seems to be the case here—"

"Just a moment!" interrupted Malone. "Your Honor, I think that is open to argument. I have a request to make. If my learned colleague has no objection, I'd like to ask for a short recess in your chambers. I believe it may save the state the expense of a long-drawn-out trial."

"Well, I object!" boomed Harbin Hamilton. But one of the D.A.'s men touched his shoulder, and reminded him that he himself had no status. Mr. Dade looked somewhat confused.

"Mine is a reasonable request," Malone pointed out. "I am sure that in a few minutes we can come to an agreement." He looked at Mr. Dade, who frowned, then shrugged.

Judge Winston hesitated. Then he too frowned—Harbin Hamilton was audibly mumbling something about "the most ridiculous travesty of justice. . . ." *Cr-r-rack!* sounded the gavel. "I will have order in the court!" roared the Judge. "Mr. Dade, will you speak on this most unusual request?"

Dade wavered, then a slow smile crept across his face. He had quite evidently had a good deal of Mr. Harbin Hamilton in the past twenty-four hours. "No objection whatever," he said, smiling.

"So ruled," said Judge Winston. "Court will recess until quarter of three." He started to rise, then sat down again. "By the way, gentlemen, there is no need to crowd into my chambers. I suggest you hold the discussion right here, and I'll listen. Clear the court of all but the interested parties."

Everybody looked at everybody else, then everybody looked at Malone, who was out on a long limb and knew it. He gave Nancy a big reassuring smile, then slowly and dramatically came over and held the gate open for Miss Withers, seating her formally in one of the attorneys' chairs at his end of the counsel table. She gave a quick look behind her and saw that Doris Bedford was coming forward, with a strange glint in her eye. But there was someone else—the man in the charcoal gray suit. "That's him!" whispered the schoolteacher to Malone, her excitement smothering her grammar. "But heaven knows if he's on our side or theirs!"

Malone nodded, waiting for the last of the casual spectators to be hustled out of the room by the officers. "May I proceed, Your Honor?"

"Go ahead," said Judge Winston. He took out a pipe and lit it, his face showing a hint of amusement.

"Your Honor, Mr. Dade, gentlemen—ladies and gentlemen, I should say," began Malone. "I asked for this chance, quite aware of the fact that I am sticking my neck out a mile, because I believe wholeheartedly that the sole purpose of any court is to serve the ends of justice. I intend to prove that bail *is* admissible in this case. Miss Jorgens has been charged with having willfully and with premeditation caused the death of Paul Bedford by heart failure while attempting to commit a felony—in this case, the attempt to take his life with a pistol. Is that not the situation, Mr. Dade?"

"You can hardly expect the State to lay bare its case at this time," Dade pointed out. "This is not the prelim."

"Quite right!" Malone set a cigar afire. "I'll just go on and state what I think your case is, and you can correct me if I'm wrong. You will contend, when this case comes to trial, that my client had a grievance against the deceased—"

"I'll say she had!" cut in Hamilton. "This woman committed one crime, maybe two, in Chicago. Bedford had her arrested and charged with forgery; she was indicted and skipped her bail!" At this point Mr. Dade said acidly that he understood all that to be true, and furthermore—

"I'll stipulate, if you like, that Miss Jorgens did bring suit against Paul Bedford, claiming him to be the father of her child." Malone waved his hand. "And I'll stipulate that she did utter a forgery or what appears to be a forgery. But would she have brought that check to me to cash if she had *known* it was a forgery? And would I have cashed it for her if I had even suspected it wasn't legitimate?"

Nancy was staring at Malone with a look in her big beautiful eyes which almost brought tears to Miss Withers'. "I agree," Malone went on, "to stipulate some more of Mr. Dade's case. Nancy Jorgens did borrow a pistol, and she did bring it with her to California—a pistol, remember, that had been one of the props in a play. She was on the trail of Mr. Bedford, who had prudently taken to his heels at the first word of her getting out on bail. She did go to his family's beach house, she did lie in wait for him, she did finally enter and confront him, and she did then and there, in the middle of an argument, fire that pistol twice!"

There was absolute silence in the courtroom. "Now if I were presiding instead of being part of the audience," spoke up Judge Winston, "I'd expect an objection from somebody—maybe from the lady!"

"It's the truth," said Nancy Jorgens very calmly.

"Mr. Malone is making a strong case—for us!" Mr. Dade commented.

"Am I? But I contend that there is absolutely no basis for a murder charge. Unfortunately, the weapon has disappeared. . . ."

"I'm responsible for that," Miss Withers spoke up. "The girl was struggling in Mr. Malone's arms, and I took the gun away from her and threw it into the ocean, where it couldn't do any more harm."

That was a minor bombshell.

Mr. Dade looked hard at Miss Withers, then remarked pointedly that it looked as if he might have some additional charges.

"But that pistol was just a stage prop!" Malone picked up again. "Such guns, for obvious reasons, fire only blanks! It is too bad that Miss Withers, with the best intentions in the world, put it beyond recall—"

"It ain't!" spoke up Sergeant Griggs. "That's what I come downtown to tell somebody. We found the gun this morning at low tide, half buried in the sand. I got it here—and it *is* a phony!"

The sergeant displayed the gun.

"Maybe she didn't know it wasn't a real weapon!" said Harbin Hamilton eagerly.

"I think anyone in show business would know that," Judge Winston suggested quietly. "Mr. Dade, does this change your attitude on the question of possible admission to bail?"

Dade hesitated—and then Harbin Hamilton, who quite evidently believed that an attorney should keep not only an open mind but an open mouth, cut in again. "What if the girl was only trying to scare Bedford—she scared him to death, didn't she? And any death caused during the commission of a felony is homicide— even, I believe, out here in California! And since Nancy Jorgens had been intimate with the man, certainly she must have known he had a weak heart!" He turned to Doris Bedford, bowing. "You knew it, didn't you, Miss Bedford?"

"Yes," said Doris. "Of course. But why are you wasting all this time? She killed my brother, and I object to this incredibly asinine attempt to get her free! I tell you one and all, I'm going to use every resource in my power to see that this case isn't glossed over."

Mr. Dade held up his hand. "The State of California has even more resources than you, Miss Bedford. We are merely trying to get to the facts."

"Of course she knew Paul had a weak heart!" Doris snapped back. "I tell you, she wanted him out of the way so he couldn't be the complaining witness against her at the forgery trial—"

"Thank you," said Dade, shaking his head at her. "But we'd better get on—I'm afraid we are trying the patience of the court. Mr. Malone, I don't see your purpose in all this. We are not now involved with whatever happened back in Chicago. Your eloquence hasn't changed my mind so far as Miss Jorgens is concerned. We still refuse to admit her to bail. As for you—I admit that all we had against you was concealment of the gun, and now we have somebody else confessing to that. We'll consider admitting you to bail, or perhaps dropping the accessory charge entirely."

Malone, the schoolteacher realized, had now got himself *out* of trouble—but he had got Nancy and herself *in* even deeper. However, the little lawyer wasn't finished. "Mr. Dade," he said slowly, "I want you to reconsider your charges against my client. She meant only to throw a scare into Bedford—as a matter of fact, she had some wild hope of getting him to write out a statement clearing her of all charges. And when he just laughed at her, she let go with the blank cartridges. Is that *murder?*"

"She knew it would probably kill him!" Hamilton interrupted again.

"No! Because Paul Bedford *himself* didn't know he had a bum heart! I have here a telegram from J. Willoughby Howe, the Bedford family doctor, in which he states that at Doris Bedford's insistence the bad news was kept from her brother, an ex-athlete who knew all about athlete's heart and therefore might worry himself to death over it." Malone tossed a yellow piece of paper to Dade. "We are prepared to bring Dr. Howe into court at the trial—"

"Dr. Howe would never say that!" shouted Doris wildly. "He gave me his solemn promise. . . ." Then she bit her lip.

"I think perhaps the doctor yielded to *persuasion*," said Miss Withers, at the moment forgiving Filthy Phil all his trespasses. She had been silent longer than was her custom, but it still wasn't quite her time to get into the fray. "Why doesn't somebody ask Miss Jorgens herself?"

Nancy stood up. "I never dreamed—I never meant to kill Paul. I'd always hoped that some day he'd acknowledge his son. I once loved him, or thought I did. I'm sorry I caused his death, but I never in the world meant to kill him!"

Malone nodded his approval. "Well, Mr. Dade?"

Dade was in conference with his associates. Harbin Hamilton, who had been obviously left out, rose suddenly. "I see what is happening!" he stormed. "Go ahead and drop your charges here. I'll drag the woman back to Chicago, and the high-and-mighty Mr. Malone with her. She'll get twenty years for the forgery, anyway!" He caught the Judge's eye, and sat down suddenly.

"I'm coming to that forgery," said Malone very softly.

"But we're not talking about that case!" Dade protested. "We're supposed to be just discussing bail, and our time is about up."

"It is," said His Honor. "Gentlemen, I enjoy a break in the routine as much as anybody else, but—will you please conclude, Mr. Malone?"

"Yes, Your Honor. I need only a couple of minutes, most of which I'll turn over to somebody else. This lady beside me is Miss Hildegarde Withers, who has had some experience in criminology—"

"I know," said Mr. Dade with a stiffish smile. "The McWalters case. She committed justifiable mayhem."

"A simpler case than this one," said Miss Withers, bobbing her head. "Anyone in my profession—and I was a teacher in public schools for over thirty years—has to be interested in forgery. We run up against it in examination papers and on report cards. What bothered me from the very beginning about this affair was the fact that every handwriting expert agreed that Paul Bedford's name was forged to that check, yet—"

"And you can't get away from that!" Harbin Hamilton was irrepressible. "Don't forget, nobody had anything to gain from that forgery except Nancy Jorgens, and presumably her accomplice Malone! The forgery and the murder are tied up together!"

"But I never *dreamed* it was a forgery!" Nancy spoke up. "It looked exactly like Paul's signature, and I thought he'd had a change of heart! I couldn't believe he was all bad."

"If she didn't forge it she knows who did," the Chicago D.A. insisted, too loudly. By this time both the Judge and Dade were glaring at him. But he went on. "Ask her, some of you!"

"I believe I still have the floor," said Miss Withers. "You could ask me, but I'm afraid you wouldn't accept my answer. But there is somebody in this room who does know—"

Doris Bedford suddenly rose. "I do *not*—" she blurted out. Then she sat down again, realizing that nobody had been talking about her. Miss Withers was pointing at the man in the charcoal gray suit, who now came up to the counsel table with a big roll of papers. He nodded casually at the Judge, and at Dade.

"I was about to say, when I was interrupted by a lady who doth protest too much," continued Miss Withers, "that there is somebody in this room who knows all about disputed signatures. Most of you have probably heard of J. Edgar Salter, the author of *Handwriting Investigation,* the last word in its field."

"We'll stipulate him as an expert," agreed Mr. Dade, smiling. "But which case are we talking about, will somebody tell me?"

"There's only one!" Malone told him confidently. "You wait and see."

"I've heard of Mr. Salter," said Harbin Hamilton. "And nobody is going to tell me that he doesn't think that check is forged!"

All eyes were on Mr. Salter, who shook his head, then nodded. "Precisely," said Miss Withers. "But just *why* is it a forgery?"

The famous expert spread out his papers on the table, holding them up in turn. "Because," he said, "in these blowups, enlarged one hundred times, it isn't hard to see that the degrees of pressure used on the pen vary greatly. That is never true of a genuine signature."

"Wait!" said Malone. "You mean that you can tell by looking at a photograph of a signature just how hard the writer pressed down?"

"Almost to the ounce of pressure," Salter said. "It all shows up, right here. See this—and this? Why, we can even note the pulse beat!"

"Funny," said the little lawyer, "that the people in the bank who refused the check happened to notice it at all—since it hadn't yet been photographed and enlarged!"

"Unless somebody had phoned them and tipped them off!" Miss Withers said helpfully. But this time Doris Bedford did not rise to the bait; she sat with her lips pressed tight together. The schoolteacher turned back to Salter. "Why not go on, and tell them what I asked you?"

The man was amused. "This is one for the book," he chuckled. "Miss Withers got into my private office on the pretext of asking me to autograph a copy of my book, a lure which no author can resist. Then without warning she sprung a new one on me. I confess I laughed out loud. Then I thought it over and made some experiments with my own signature, and—well, what I found out rather staggered me!"

"Go on!" said the Judge.

"The lady had asked me—would it be possible for a man to *forge his own handwriting?* By that I mean, to write his name so that it would present all the typical signs of having been forged. And, so help me, it is!"

The courtroom was hushed. "Now does this begin to tie up?" Malone whispered to Mr. Dade. Then he turned to the expert. "And is that what happened in this case, in your opinion?"

"Well, it could have, certainly. But—"

"That's enough!" Malone boomed. "It was a fiendish frame! *De mortuis* and all that, but I submit to you that Paul Bedford, intent on getting rid of a girl whom he had wronged and who was a perpetual menace to him, *forged his own name* on a check and mailed it to her so he could have her arrested and sent off to prison! Paul Bedford is the real villain in this case!"

"You can't speak those lies about my brother!" screamed Doris.

Miss Withers decided it was time to leap in. "I happen to know where Bedford picked up his knowledge of handwriting. He collected autographs of the signers of the Declaration of Independence, among them a disputed Button Gwinnett signature that was the subject of a book which is in most public libraries: *The Gwinnett Letter and Other Queers.* Naturally it goes into the forgery question rather thoroughly."

"My brother never went *near* a public library!"

"Perhaps not, Miss Bedford. But since the book was based on something in his own collection, I thought it likely he'd own a copy."

"Well, he didn't!" The thin woman was almost at her wits' end.

"I suggest that you go back home to Winnetka and look on the shelf just under the big window in your brother's study. Third from the north end—a slim red book. I have it on excellent authority, though I'm not at liberty to say whose."

Doris Bedford opened her mouth, gasping like a fish, but no words came. Harbin Hamilton was also silent. The Judge's prune-like face broke into an expression of utter rapture. "I'm going to write my memoirs and get this in," he announced, sighing happily.

But the Assistant District Attorney was shaking his head. "Yes, Your Honor. All very interesting. But all this isn't proof—it isn't even evidence. Mr. Salter only says that it *could* have happened—nobody can differentiate between an actual forgery and a simulated one! I believe he was going on to say that when he was interrupted by our enthusiastic friend here."

Malone shrugged, obviously an archer who had shot all his bolts. "Is that all you have to tell us, Mr. Salter?" he said slowly.

The expert shook his head. "I was just going to call your attention to the signature again," he said. "See here? This—and this—and this are the pulse beats—little jumps. Except that the markings in this case are unusually irregular."

"Irregular!" echoed Malone. "The pulse—that's the heartbeat! Who would be more likely to have an irregular heartbeat than a man who had heart trouble?"

"And what would be more natural than for a man with a cardiac condition to have it show strongly when he was tense and engaged in committing a crime!" added Miss Withers. "Isn't that so, Mr. Salter?"

"Well—" said the expert. "I never heard of diagnosing cardiac trouble by studying handwriting, but—I guess I'll have to run a string of tests and maybe revise my book."

"Your move, Mr. Dade," said Malone. He began whistling "St. James Infirmary" under his breath.

Harbin Hamilton tried once more. "This isn't evidence!"

"And court is not in session," snapped the Judge. "I wish it were, so I could fine you for contempt! Mr. Dade?"

The room was by now in a turmoil, and Malone and Miss Withers were almost dancing a jig. The Assistant District Attorney's face was in something of a turmoil too—a study in mixed emotions. "I—I'll admit that the provocation seems to have been most unusual," he said. "My learned friend here has just about ruined Mr. Hamilton's case back in Chicago, I'd say. But we are faced with the fact that a man was killed—"

"He died accidentally!" Malone pointed out quickly.

"Under the circumstances," continued Dade, "I think we can agree on a lesser charge in this case. Maybe manslaughter. Maybe something. . . ."

"Make it anything at all!" Malone challenged. "Come now, Mr.

Dade. After what Bedford pulled on Nancy Jorgens, do you honestly dare to go before a jury because he dropped dead when she tried to scare him? They wouldn't leave the box, and you know it!"

"And as for me," said His Honor, "I'll guarantee that, no matter what charge is brought, I'll release the prisoner here on her attorney's own recognizance until the trial, if the wheels of justice have to be gummed up with a trial at all!" He beamed paternally at Nancy, whose eyes were shining. The gavel cracked again. "Court is in session!"

Everybody came to attention.

"Your Honor," said Mr. Dade, resignedly but not too unhappily, "in the case of *The People versus Jorgens and Malone* the prosecution drops all charges against the defendants."

There was a buzz through the courtroom. "Release the prisoners," ordered Judge Winston. "Or is there still a charge against them?"

Harbin Hamilton drew himself up to his full height. "No, there isn't!" he roared. "But I'd like five minutes in which to express my opinion of the way court is conducted here, and—"

"You are in contempt," said the Judge gleefully. "One hundred dollars, or ten days!" He smacked his gavel down so hard it broke.

Which made Malone's day almost perfect. It was all over, or almost. Nancy's release would be within the hour; presumably they were sending out for some clothes for her so she wouldn't stop all downtown Los Angeles traffic. Miss Withers and John J. Malone went down the corridor, arm in arm. "You know," he said, "you were wonderful, Hildy—you and your brain-storming!"

"It was you who gave me the idea about the forgery while we were running wild with our crazy guesses, when you said maybe Bedford was the murderer and killed himself! He didn't commit that crime, but he did commit the other!"

"So we wind up with no murder and no murderer." Malone grinned.

"Isn't that all right—in a love story?" She broke off as they ran into Doris Bedford and Harbin Hamilton, waiting for an elevator. It was one of those moments—and then the Chicago D.A. stepped forward and held out his hand, smiling a smile that must have hurt. Another nominee for Academy acting honors, Miss Withers thought.

"No hard feelings, Malone?"

"Believe me, it's a pleasure—" Malone began. But Doris Bedford forced herself between them.

"Don't think *I'm* not going to see my lawyer," she blurted out. "My lawyer can lick your lawyer any day in the week!" snapped Miss Withers, proudly clinging to Malone's arm. "And just to make your day complete, Miss Bedford, may I remind you to notify your bank to honor that check?"

"Wait a minute!" Hamilton protested. "No check written by a deceased person can be honored—"

"Correction," said Malone. "The check was presented to the bank while Bedford was still alive. They've got to pay, or face suit." At that moment the elevator arrived, and Miss Withers and the little lawyer got in, leaving the other two playing Human Statues. "Wait until I tell Nancy this!" gloated Malone.

"I'm not waiting," Hildegarde said firmly. "You two have a right to be alone in your big moment."

"But I'm not good enough for her," Malone said, surprisingly. "Look, Hildegarde—if I do get up nerve enough to propose to her, you gotta be there!"

"It had better be matrimony that you propose," Miss Withers warned him. "And don't think I won't be at the wedding, complete with shotgun!"

ED McBAIN
Death Flight

SQUAK MOUNTAIN was cold at this time of the year. The wind groaned around Davis, and the trees trembled bare limbs, and even at this distance he could hear the low rumble of planes letting down at Boeing and Renton. He found the tree about a half-mile east of the summit. The DC-4 had struck the tree and then continued flying. He looked at the jagged, splintered wood and then his eyes covered the surrounding terrain. Parts of the DC-4 were scattered all over the ridge in a fifteen-hundred-foot radius. He saw the upper portion of the plane's vertical fin, the number-two propeller, and a major portion of the rudder. He examined these very briefly, and then he began walking toward the canyon into which the plane had finally dropped.

Davis turned his head sharply once, thinking he had heard a sound. He stood stock-still, listening, but the only sounds that came to him were the sullen moan of the wind and the muted hum of aircraft in the distant sky.

He continued walking.

When he found the plane, it made him a little sick. The Civil Aeronautics Board report had told him that the plane was demolished by fire. The crash was what had obviously caused the real demolition. But the report had only been typed words. He saw *impact* now, and *causing fire,* and even though the plane had been moved by the investigating board, he could imagine something of what had happened.

It had been in nearly vertical position when it struck the ground, and the engines and cockpit had bedded deep in soft, muddy loam. Wreckage had been scattered like shrapnel from a hand

515

grenade burst, and fire had consumed most of the plane, leaving a ghostlike skeleton that confronted him mutely. He stood watching it for a time, then made his way down to the charred ruins.

The landing gear was fully retracted, as the report had said. The wings flaps were in the twenty-five-degree down position.

He studied these briefly and then climbed up to the cockpit. The plane still stank of scorched skin and blistered paint. When he entered the cockpit, he was faced with complete havoc. It was impossible to obtain a control setting or an instrument reading from the demolished instrument panel. The seats were twisted and tangled. Metal jutted into the cockpit and cabin at grotesque angles. The windshield had shattered into a million jagged shards.

He shook his head and continued looking through the plane, the stench becoming more overpowering. He was silently grateful that he had not been here when the bodies were still in the plane, and he still wondered what he was doing here anyway, even now.

He knew that the report had proved indication of an explosion prior to the crash. There had been no structural failure or malfunctioning of the aircraft itself. The explosion had occurred in the cabin, and the remnants of the bomb had shown it to be a home-made job. He'd learned all this in the past few days, with the co-operation of the CAB. He also knew that the Federal Bureau of Investigation and the Military Police were investigating the accident, and the knowledge had convinced him that this was not a job for him. Yet here he was.

Five people had been killed. Three pilots, the stewardess, and Janet Carruthers, the married daughter of his client, George Ellison. It could not have been a pleasant death.

Davis climbed out of the plane and started toward the ridge. The sun was high on the mountain, and it cast a feeble, pale yellow tint on the white pine and spruce. There was a hard gray winter sky overhead. He walked swiftly, with his head bent against the wind.

When the shots came, they were hard and brittle, shattering the stillness as effectively as twin-mortar explosions.

He dropped to the ground, wriggling sideways toward a high outcropping of quartz. The echo of the shots hung on the air and then the wind carried it toward the canyon and he waited and listened, with his own breathing the loudest sound on the mountain.

I'm out of my league, he thought. *I'm way out of my league.*

I'm just a small-time detective, and this is something big. . . .

The third shot came abruptly. It came from some high-powered rifle, and he heard the sharp *twang* of the bullet when it struck the quartz and ricocheted into the trees.

He pressed his cheek to the ground, and he kept very still, and he could feel the hammering of his heart against the hard earth. His hands trembled and he waited for the next shot.

The next shot never came. He waited for a half-hour, and then he bundled his coat and thrust it up over the rock, hoping to draw fire if the sniper was still with him. He waited for several minutes after that, and then he backed away from the rock on his belly, not venturing to get to his feet until he was well into the trees.

Slowly, he made his way down the mountain.

"You say you want to know more about the accident?" Arthur Porchek said. "I thought it was all covered in the CAB report."

"It was," Davis said. "I'm checking further. I'm trying to find out who set that bomb."

Porchek drew in on his cigarette. He leaned against the wall and the busy hum of radios in Seattle Approach Control was loud around them. "I've only told this story a dozen times already."

"I'd appreciate it if you could tell it once more," Davis said.

"Well," Porchek said heavily, "it was about twenty-thirty-six or so." He paused. "All our time is based on a twenty-four-hour check, like the Army."

"Go ahead."

"The flight had been cleared to maintain seven thousand feet. When they contacted us, we told them to make a standard range approach to Boeing Field and requested that they report leaving each one-thousand-foot level during the descent. That's standard, you know."

"Were you doing all the talking to the plane?" Davis asked.

"Yes."

"All right, what happened?"

"First I gave them the weather."

"And what was that?"

Porchek shrugged, a man weary of repeating information over and over again. "Boeing Field," he said by rote. "Eighteen hundred scattered, twenty-two hundred overcast, eight-miles, wind south-southeast, gusts to thirty, altimeter twenty-nine, twenty-five; Seattle-Tacoma, measured nineteen hundred broken with thirty-one hundred overcast."

"Did the flight acknowledge?"

"Yes, it did. And it reported leaving seven thousand feet at twenty-forty. About two minutes later, it reported being over the outer marker and leaving the six-thousand-foot level."

"Go on." Davis said.

"Well, it didn't report leaving five thousand and then at twenty-forty-five, it reported leaving four thousand feet. I acknowledged that and told them what to do. I said, 'If you're not VFR by the time you reach the range you can shuttle on the northwest course at two thousand feet. It's possible you'll break out in the vicinity of Boeing Field for a south landing.' "

"What's VFR?" Davis asked, once again feeling his inadequacy to cope with the job.

"Visual Flight Rules. You see, it was overcast at twenty-two hundred feet. The flight was on instruments above that. They've got to report to us whether they're on IFR or VFR."

"I see. What happened next?"

"The aircraft reported at twenty-fifty that it was leaving three thousand feet, and I told them they were to contact Boeing Tower on one eighteen, point three for landing instructions. They acknowledged with 'Roger,' and that's the last I heard of them."

"Did you hear the explosion?"

"I heard something, but I figured it for static. Ground witnesses heard it, though."

"But everything was normal and routine before the explosion, is that right?"

Porchek nodded his head emphatically. "Yes, sir. A routine letdown."

"Almost," Davis said. He thanked Porchek for his time, and then left.

He called George Ellison from a pay phone. When the old man came on the line, Davis said, "This is Milt Davis, Mr. Ellison."

Ellison's voice sounded gruff and heavy, even over the phone, "Hello, Davis," he said "How are you doing?"

"I'll be honest with you, Mr. Ellison, I'd like out."

"Why?" He could feel the old man's hackles rising.

"Because the FBI and the MPs are already onto this one. They'll crack it for you, and it'll probably turn out to be some nut with a grudge against the government. Either that, or a plain case of sabotage. This really doesn't call for a private investigation."

"Look, Davis," Ellison said. "I'll decide whether this calls for. . . ."

"All right, you'll decide. I'm just trying to be frank with you. This kind of stuff is way out of my line. I'm used to trailing wayward husbands, or skip tracing, or an occasional bodyguard stint. When you drag in bombed planes, I'm in over my head."

"I heard you were a good man," Ellison said. "You stick with it. I'm satisfied you'll do a good job."

Davis sighed. "Whatever you say," he said. "Incidentally, did you tell anyone you'd hired me?"

"Yes, I did. As a matter of fact. . . ."

"Who'd you tell?"

"Several of my employees. The word got to a local reporter somehow, though, and he came to my home yesterday. I gave him the story. I didn't think it would do any harm."

"Has it reached print yet?"

"Yes," Ellison said. "It was in this morning's paper. A small item. Why?"

"I was shot at today, Mr. Ellison. At the scene of the crash. Three times."

There was a dead silence on the line. Then Ellison said, "I'm sorry, Davis, I should have realized." It was a hard thing for a man like Ellison to say.

"That's all right," Davis assured him. "They missed."

"Do you think—do you think whoever set the bomb shot at you?"

"Possibly. I'm not going to start worrying about it now."

Ellison digested this and then said, "Where are you going now, Davis?"

"To visit your son-in-law, Nicholas Carruthers. I'll call in again."

"Fine, Davis."

Davis hung up, jotting down the cost of the call, and then made reservations on the next plane to Burbank. Nicholas Carruthers was chief pilot of Intercoastal Airways' Burbank Division. The fatal flight had been made in two segments; the first from Burbank to San Francisco, and the second from Frisco to Seattle. The DC–4 was to let down at Boeing, with Seattle-Tacoma designated as an alternate field. It was a simple ferry flight, and the plane was to pick up military personnel in Seattle, in accordance with the company's contract with the Department of National Defense.

Quite curiously, Carruthers had been along on the Burbank-to-Frisco segment of the hop, as company observer. He'd disembarked at Frisco, and his wife, Janet, had boarded the plane there as a non-revenue passenger. She was bound for a cabin up in Washington, or so old man Ellison had told Davis. He'd also said that Janet had been looking forward to the trip for a long time.

When Davis found Captain Nicholas Carruthers in the airport restaurant, he was sitting with a blonde in a black cocktail dress, and he had his arm around her waist. They lifted their martini glasses and clinked them together, the girl laughing. Davis studied the pair from the doorway and reflected that the case was turning into something he knew a little more about.

He hesitated inside the doorway for just a moment and then walked directly to the bar, taking the stool on Carruthers' left. He waited until Carruthers had drained his glass and then he said, "Captain Carruthers?"

Carruthers turned abruptly, a frown distorting his features. He was a man of thirty-eight or so, with prematurely graying temples and sharp gray eyes. He had thin lips and a thin straight nose that divided his face like an immaculate stone wall. He wore civilian clothing.

"Yes," he said curtly.

"Milton Davis. Your father-in-law has hired me to look into the DC–4 accident." Davis showed his identification. "I wonder if I might ask you a few questions?"

Carruthers hesitated, and then glanced at the blonde, apparently realizing the situation was slightly compromising. The blonde leaned over, pressing her breasts against the bar top, looking past Carruthers to Davis.

"Take a walk, Beth," Carruthers said.

The blonde drained her martini glass, pouted, lifted her purse from the bar, and slid off the stool. Davis watched the exaggerated swing of her hips across the room and then said, "I'm sorry if. . . ."

"Ask your questions," Carruthers said.

Davis studied him for a moment. "All right, Captain," he said mildly. "I understand you were aboard the crashed DC–4 on the flight segment from Burbank to San Francisco. Is that right?"

"That's right," Carruthers said. "I was aboard as observer."

"Did you notice anything out of the ordinary on the trip?"

"If you mean did I see anyone with a goddamn bomb, no."

"I didn't—"

"And if you're referring to the false alarm, Mister What-ever-the-Hell-Your-Name-Is, you can just start asking your questions straight. You know all about the false alarm."

Davis felt his fists tighten on the bar top. "You tell me about it again."

"Sure," Carruthers said testily. "Shortly after take-off from Burbank, we observed a fire-warning signal in the cockpit. From number three engine."

"I'm listening," Davis said.

"As it turned out, it was a false warning. When we got to Frisco, the mechanics there checked and found no evidence of a fire having occurred. Mason told the mechanics—"

"Was Mason pilot in command?"

"Yes." A little of Carruthers' anger seemed to be wearing off. "Mason told the mechanics he was satisfied from the inspection that no danger of fire was present. He did not delay the flight."

"Were *you* satisfied with the inspection?" Davis asked.

"It was Mason's command."

"Yes, but your wife boarded the plane in Frisco. Were you satisfied there was no danger of fire?"

"Yes, I was."

"Did your wife seem worried about it?" Davis asked.

"I didn't get a chance to talk to Janet in Frisco," Carruthers said.

Davis was silent for a moment. Then he asked, "How come?"

"I had to take another pilot up almost the moment I arrived."

"I don't understand."

"For a hood test. I had to check him out. I'm chief pilot, you know. That's one of my jobs."

"And there wasn't even enough time to stop and say hello to your wife?"

"No. We were a little ahead of schedule. Janet wasn't there when we landed."

"I see."

"I hung around while the mechanics checked the fire-warning system, and Janet still hadn't arrived. This other pilot was waiting to go up, so I left."

"Then you didn't see your wife at all," Davis said.

"Well, that's not what I meant. I meant I hadn't spoken to her.

As we're taxiing for take-off, I saw her come onto the field."

"Alone?"

"No," Carruthers said. "She was with a man." The announce-
ment did not seem to disturb him.

"Do you know who he was?"

"No. They were rather far from me, and I was in a moving
ship. I recognized Janet's red hair immediately, of course, but I
couldn't make out the man with her. I waved, but I guess she
didn't see me."

"She didn't wave back?"

"No. She went directly to the DC-4. The man helped her
aboard, and then the plane was behind us and I couldn't see any
more."

"What do you mean, helped her aboard?"

"Took her elbow, you know. Helped her up the ladder."

"I see. Was she carrying luggage?"

"A suitcase, yes. She was bound for our cabin, you know."

"Yes," Davis said. "I understand she was on a company pass.
What does that mean exactly, Captain?"

"We ride for a buck and a half," Carruthers said. "Normally,
any pilot applies to his chief pilot for written permission for his
wife to ride and then presents the permission at the ticket window.
He then pays one-fifty for the ticket. Since I'm chief pilot, I simply
got the ticket for Janet when she told me she was going up to
the cabin."

"Mmm," Davis said. "Did you know all the pilots on the ship?"

"I knew one of them. Mason. The other two were new on the
route. That's why I was along as observer."

"Did you know Mason socially?"

"No. Just business."

"And the stewardess?"

"Yes, I knew her. Business, of course."

"Of course," Davis said, remembering the blonde in the cocktail
dress. He stood up and moved his jacket cuff off his wristwatch.
"Well, I've got to catch a plane, Captain. Thanks for your help."

"Not at all," Carruthers said. "When you report in to Dad,
give him my regards, won't you?"

"I'll do that," Davis said. He thanked Carruthers again, and
then went out to catch his return plane.

He bought twenty-five thousand dollars' worth of insurance for
fifty cents from one of the machines in the waiting room, and

then got aboard the plane at about five minutes before take-off. He browsed through the magazine he'd picked up at the newsstand, and when the fat fellow plopped down into the seat beside him, he just glanced up and then turned back to his magazine again. The plane left the ground and began climbing, and Davis looked back through the window and saw the field drop away below him.

"First time flying?" the fellow asked.

Davis looked up from the magazine into a pair of smiling green eyes. The eyes were embedded deep in soft, ruddy flesh. The man owned a nose like the handle of a machete, and a mouth with thick, blubbery lips. He wore an orange sports shirt against which the color of his complexion seemed even more fiery.

"No," Davis said. "I've been off the ground before."

"Always gives me a thrill," the man said. "No matter how many times I do it." He chuckled and added, "An airplane ride is just like a woman. Lots of ups and downs, and not always too smooth—but guaranteed to keep a man up in the air."

Davis smiled politely, and the fat man chuckled a bit more and then thrust a beefy hand at him. "MacGregor," he said. "Charlie or Chuck or just plain Mac, if you like."

Davis took his hand and said, "Milt Davis."

"Glad to know you, Milt," MacGregor said. "You down here on business?"

"Yes," he said briefly.

"Me, too," MacGregor said. "Business mostly." He grinned slyly. " 'Course, what the wife don't know won't hurt her, eh?"

"I'm not married," Davis told him.

"A wonderful institution," MacGregor said. He laughed aloud, and then added, "But who likes being in an institution?"

Davis hoped he hadn't winced. He wondered if he was to be treated to MacGregor's full repertoire of wornout gags before the trip was over. To discourage any further attempts at misdirected wit, he turned back to the magazine as politely as he could, smiling once to let MacGregor know he wasn't being purposely rude.

"Go right ahead," MacGregor said genially. "Don't mind me."

That was easy, Davis thought. *If it lasts.*

He was surprised that it did last. MacGregor stretched out in the seat beside him, closing his eyes. He did not speak again until the plane was ten minutes out of San Francisco.

"Let's walk to the john, eh, Milt?" he said.

Davis lifted his head and smiled. "Thanks, but—"

"This is a .38 here under my overcoat, Milt," MacGregor said softly.

For a second, Davis thought it was another of the fat man's tired jokes. He turned to look at MacGregor's lap. The overcoat was folded over his chunky left arm, and Davis could barely see the blunt muzzle of a pistol poking from beneath the folds.

He lifted his eyebrows a little. "What are you going to do after you shoot me, MacGregor? Vanish into thin air?"

MacGregor smiled. "Now who mentioned anything about shooting, Milt? Eh? Let's go back, shall we, boy?"

Davis rose and moved past MacGregor into the aisle. MacGregor stood up behind him, the coat over his arm, the gun completely hidden now. Together, they began walking toward the rear of the plane, past the food buffet on their right, and past the twin facing seats behind the buffet. An emergency window was set in the cabin wall there, and Davis sighed in relief when he saw that the seats were occupied.

When they reached the men's room, MacGregor flipped open the door and nudged Davis inside. Then he crowded in behind him, putting his wide back to the door. He reached up with one heavy fist, rammed Davis against the sink, and then ran his free hand over Davis' body.

"Well," he said pleasantly. "No gun."

"My name is Davis, not Spade," Davis told him.

MacGregor lifted the .38, pointing it at Davis' throat. "All right, Miltie, now give a listen. I want you to forget all about that crashed DC–4, I want you to forget there are even such things as airplanes, Miltie. Now, I know you're a smart boy, and so I'm not even going to mark you up, Miltie. I could mark you up nice with the sight and butt of this thing." He gestured with the .38 in his hand. "I'm not going to do that. Not now. I'm just telling you, nice-like, to lay off. Just lay off and go back to skip-tracing, Miltie boy, or you're going to get hurt. Next time, I'm not going to be so considerate."

"Look . . ." Davis started.

"So let's not have a next time, Miltie. Let's call it off now. You give your client a ring and tell him you're dropping it, Miltie boy. Have you got that?"

Davis didn't answer.

"Fine," MacGregor said. He reached up suddenly with his left hand, almost as if he were reaching up for a light cord. At the same time, he grasped Davis' shoulder with his right hand and spun him around, bringing the hand with the gun down in a fast motion, flipping it butt-end up.

The walnut stock caught Davis at the base of his skull. He stumbled forward, his hands grasping the sink in front of him. He felt the second blow at the back of his head, and then his hands dropped from the sink, and the aluminum deck of the plane came up to meet him suddenly, all too fast. . . .

Someone said, "He's coming around now," and he idly thought, *Coming around where?*

"How do you feel, Mr. Davis?" a second voice asked.

He looked up at the ring of faces. He did not recognize any of them. "Where am I?" he asked.

"San Francisco," the second voice said. The voice belonged to a tall man with a salt-and-pepper mustache and friendly blue eyes. MacGregor had owned friendly green eyes, Davis remembered.

"We found you in the men's room after all the passengers had disembarked," the voice went on. "You've had a nasty fall, Mr. Davis. Nothing serious, however. I've dressed the cut, and I'm sure there'll be no complications."

"Thank you," Davis said. "I wonder . . . did you say all the passengers have already gone?"

"Why, yes."

"I wonder if I might see the passenger list? There was a fellow aboard I promised to look up, and I'm darned if I haven't forgotten his name."

"I'll ask the stewardess," the man said. "By the way, I'm Doctor Burke."

"How do you do?" Davis said. He reached for a cigarette and lighted it. When the stewardess brought the passenger list, he scanned it hurriedly.

There was no MacGregor listed, Charles or otherwise. This fact did not surprise him greatly. He looked down the list to see if there were any names with the initials C.M., knowing that when a person assumes an alias, he will usually choose a name with the same initials as his real name. There were no C.M.s on the list, either.

"Does that help?" the stewardess asked.

"Oh, yes. Thank you. I'll find him now."

The doctor shook Davis' hand, and then asked if he'd sign a

release stating he had received medical treatment and absolving the airline. Davis felt the back of his head, and then signed the paper.

He walked outside and leaned against the building, puffing idly on his cigarette. The night was a nest of lights. He watched the lights and listened to the hum of aircraft all around him. It wasn't until he had finished his cigarette that he remembered he was in San Francisco.

He dropped the cigarette to the concrete and ground it out beneath his heel. Quite curiously, he found himself ignoring MacGregor's warning. He was a little surprised at himself, but he was also pleased. And more curious, he found himself wishing that he and MacGregor would meet again.

He walked briskly to the cyclone fence that hemmed in the runway area. Quickly, he showed the uniformed guard at the gate his credentials and then asked where he could find the hangars belonging to Intercoastal Airways. The guard pointed them out.

Davis walked through the gate and towards the hangars the guard had indicated, stopping at the first one. Two mechanics in greasy coveralls were leaning against a work bench, chatting idly. One was smoking, and the other tilted a Coke bottle to his lips, draining half of it in one pull. Davis walked over to them.

"I'm looking for the mechanics who serviced the DC–4 that crashed up in Seattle," he said.

They looked at him blankly for a few seconds, and then the one with the Coke bottle asked, "You from the CAB?"

"No," Davis said. "I'm investigating privately."

The mechanic with the bottle was short, with black hair curling over his forehead, and quick brown eyes that silently appraised Davis now. "If you're thinking about that fire warning," he said, "it had nothing to do with the crash. There was a bomb aboard."

"I know," Davis said. "Were you one of the mechanics?"

"I was one of them," he said.

"Good." Davis smiled and said, "I didn't catch your name."

"Jerry," the man said. "Mangione." His black brows pulled together suspiciously. "Who you investigating for?"

"A private client. The father of the girl who was a passenger."

"Oh. Carruthers' wife, huh?"

"Yes. Did you know her?"

"No. I just heard it was his wife. He's chief pilot down Burbank, ain't he?"

"Yes," Davis said.

Mangione paused and studied Davis intently. "What'd you want to know?"

"First, was the fire-warning system okay?"

"Yeah. We checked it out. Just one of those things, you know. False alarm."

"Did you go into the plane?"

"Yeah, sure. I had to check the signal in the cockpit. Why?"

"I'm just asking."

"You don't think *I* put that damn bomb on the plane, do you?"

"Somebody did," Davis said.

"That's for sure. But not me. There were a lot of people on that plane, mister. Any one of 'em could've done it."

"Be a little silly to bring a bomb onto a plane you were going to fly."

"I guess so. But don't drag me into this. I just checked the fire-warning system, that's all."

"Were you around when Mrs. Carruthers boarded the plane?"

"The redhead? Yeah, I was there."

"What'd she look like?"

Mangione shrugged. "A broad, just like any other broad. Red hair."

"Was she pretty?"

"The red hair was the only thing gave her any flash. In fact, I was a little surprised."

"Surprised? What about?"

"That Tony would bother, you know."

"Who? Who would bother?"

"Tony. Tony Radner. He brought her out to the plane."

"What?" Davis said.

"Yeah, Tony. He used to sell tickets inside. He brought her out to the plane and helped her get aboard."

"Are you sure about that? Sure you know who the man with her was?"

Mangione made an exasperated gesture with his hairy hands. "Hell, ain't I been working here for three years? Don't I know Tony when I see him? It was him, all right. He took the broad right to her seat. Listen, it was him, all right. I guess maybe . . . well, I was surprised, anyway."

"Why?"

"Tony's a good-looking guy. And this Mrs. Carruthers, well,

she wasn't much. I'm surprised he went out of his way. But I guess maybe she wasn't feeling so hot. Tony's a gent that way."

"Wasn't feeling so hot?"

"Well, I don't like to talk about anybody's dead, but she looked like she had a snootful to me. Either that, or she was pretty damn sick."

"What makes you say that?"

"Hell, Tony had to help her up the ladder, and he practically carried her to her seat. Yeah, she musta been looped."

"You said Radner used to work here. Has he quit?"

"Yeah, he quit."

"Do you know where I can find him?"

Mangione shrugged. "Maybe you can get his address from the office in the morning. But, mister, I wouldn't bother him right now, if I was you."

"Why not?"

Mangione smiled. "Because he's on his honeymoon," he said.

He slept the night through and when he awoke in the morning, the back of his head hardly hurt at all. He shaved and washed quickly, downed a breakfast of orange juice and coffee, and then went to the San Francisco office of Intercoastal Airways.

Radner, they told him, was no longer with them. But they did have his last address, and they parted with it willingly. He grabbed a cab, and then sat back while the driver fought with the California traffic. When he reached Radner's address, he paid and tipped the cabbie, and listed the expenditure in his book.

The rooming house was not in a good section of the city. It was red brick, with a brown front stoop. There was an old-fashioned bell pull set in the wide, wooden door jamb. He pulled this and heard the sound inside, and then he waited for footsteps. They came sooner than he expected.

The woman who opened the door couldn't have been more than fifty. Her face was still greasy with cold cream, and her hair was tied up in rags. "Yes?"

"I'm looking for Tony Radner," Davis said. "I'm an old friend of his, knew him in the Army. I went out to Intercoastal, but they told me he doesn't work for them any more. I wonder if you know where I can reach him."

The landlady regarded him suspiciously for a moment. "He doesn't live here anymore," she said.

"Darn," Davis said. He shook his head and assumed a false smile. "Isn't that always the way? I came all the way from New York, and now I can't locate him."

"That's too bad," the landlady agreed.

"Did he leave any forwarding address?" Davis asked.

"No. He left because he was getting married."

"Married!" Davis said. "Well, I'll be darned! Old Tony getting married!"

The landlady continued to watch Davis, her small eyes staring fixedly.

"You wouldn't know who he married, would you?"

"Yes," she said guardedly. "I guess I would."

"Who?" he asked.

"Trimble," the landlady said. "A girl named Alice Trimble."

"Alice Trimble," Davis said reflectively. "You wouldn't have her phone number, would you?"

"Come on in," the landlady said, finally accepting Davis at face value. She led him into the foyer of the house, and Davis followed her to the pay phone on the wall.

"They all scribble numbers here," she said. "I keep washing them off, but they keep putting them back again."

"Shame," Davis said sympathetically.

"Hers is up there, too. You just wait a second, and I'll tell you which one." She stepped close to the phone and examined the scribbled numbers on the wall. She stood very close to the wall, moving her head whenever she wanted to move her eyes. She stepped back at last and placed a long white finger on one of the numbers. "This one. This is the one he always called."

Davis jotted down the number hastily, and then said, "Well, gee, thanks a million. You don't know how much I appreciate this."

"I hope you find him," the landlady said. "Nice fellow, Mr. Radner."

"One of the best," Davis said.

He called the number from the first pay phone he found. He listened to the phone ring four times on the other end, and then a voice said, "Hello?"

"Hello," he said, "May I speak to Miss Trimble, please?"

"This is Miss Trimble," the voice said.

"My name is Davis," he said. "I'm an old friend of Tony Radner's. He asked me to look him up if ever I was in town. . . ."

He paused and forced himself to laugh in embarrassment.
"Trouble is, I can't seem to find him. His landlady said you and
Tony. . . ."

"Oh," the girl said. "You must want my sister. This is *Anne*
Trimble."

"Oh," he said. "I'm sorry. I didn't realize. . . ." He paused.
"Is your sister there?"

"No, she doesn't live with me any more. She and Tony got
married."

"Well, now, that's wonderful," Davis said. "Know where I can
find them."

"They're still on their honeymoon."

"Oh, that's too bad." He thought for a few seconds, and then
said, "I've got to catch a plane back tonight. I wonder . . . I
wonder if I might come over and . . . well, you could fill me in
on what Tony's been doing and all. Hate like the devil to go back
without knowing *something* about him."

The girl hesitated, and he could sense her reluctance.

"I promise I'll make it a very short visit. I've still got some
business to attend to here. Besides . . . well, Tony loaned me a
little money once, and I thought . . . well, if you don't mind,
I'd like to leave it with you."

"I . . . I suppose it would be all right," she said.

"Fine. May I have the address?"

She gave it to him, and he told her he'd be up in about an
hour, if that was all right with her. He went to the coffee counter,
ordered coffee and a toasted English, and browsed over them until
it was time to go. He bought a plain white envelope on the way
out, slipped twenty dollars into it, and sealed it. Then he hailed
a cab.

He found the mailbox marked *A. Trimble,* and he realized the
initial sufficed for both Alice and Anne. He walked up two flights,
stopped outside apartment 22, and thumbed the ivory stud in the
door jamb. A series of chimes floated from beyond the door, and
then the peephole flap was thrown back.

"I'm Mr. Davis," he said to the flap. "I called about—"

"Oh, yes," Anne Trimble said. The flap descended, and the
door swung wide.

She was a tall brunette, and her costume emphasized her height.
She was wearing tightly tailored toreador slacks. A starched white
blouse with a wide collar and long sleeves was tucked firmly into

the band of the slacks. A bird in flight, captured in sterling, rested on the blouse just below the left breast pocket.

"Come in," she said, "won't you?" She had green eyes and black eyebrows, and she smiled pleasantly now.

Davis stepped into the cool apartment, and she closed the door behind him.

"I'm sorry if I seemed rude when you called me," she said. "I'm afraid you woke me."

"Then I should be the one to apologize," Davis said.

He followed her into a sunken living room furnished in Swedish modern. She walked to a long, low coffee table and took a cigarette from a box there, offering the box to him first. Davis shook his head and watched her as she lighted the cigarette. Her hair was cut close to her head, ringing her face with ebony wisps. She wore only lipstick, and Davis reflected that this was the first truly beautiful woman he had ever met. Two large, silver hoop earrings hung from her ears. She lifted her head, and the earrings caught the rays of the sun streaming through the blinds.

"Now," she said. "You're a friend of Tony's, are you?"

"Yes," he answered. He reached into his jacket pocket and took out the sealed envelope. "First, let me get this off my mind. Please tell Tony I sincerely appreciate the loan, won't you?"

She took the envelope without comment, dropping it on the coffee table.

This is a very cool one, Davis thought.

"I was really surprised to learn that Tony was married," he said.

"It was a little sudden, yes," she said.

"Oh? Hadn't he known your sister long?"

"Three months, four months."

Davis shook his head. "I still can't get over it. How'd he happen to meet your sister?"

"Like that," Anne said. "How do people meet? A concert, a club, a soda fountain." She shrugged. "You know, people meet."

"Don't you like Tony?" he asked suddenly.

She seemed surprised. "Me? Yes, as a matter of fact, I do. I think he'll be very good for Alice. He has a strong personality, and she needs someone like him. Yes, I like Tony."

"Well, that's good," Davis said.

"When we came to Frisco, you see, Alice was sort of at loose ends. We'd lived in L.A. all our lives, and Alice depended on

Mom a good deal, I suppose. When Mom passed away, and this
job opening came for me . . . well, the change affected her. Moving
and all. It was a good thing Tony came along."

"You live here alone then, just the two of you?"

Anne Trimble smiled and sucked in a deep cloud of smoke.
"Just two little gals from Little Rock," she said.

Davis smiled with her. "L.A., you mean."

"The same thing. We're all alone in the world. Just Alice and
me. Dad died when we were both little girls. Now, of course,
Alice is married. Don't misunderstand me. I'm very happy for
her."

"When were they married?"

"January 6th," she answered. "It's been a long honeymoon."

January 6th, Davis thought. *The day the DC-4 crashed.*

"Where are they now?" he asked.

"Las Vegas."

"Where in Las Vegas?"

Anne Trimble smiled again. "You're not planning on visiting
a pair of honeymooners, are you, Mr. Davis?"

"God, no," he said. "I'm just curious."

"Fact is," Anne said, "I don't know where they're staying. I've
only had a wire from them since they were married. I don't
imagine they're thinking much about me. Not on their honeymoon."

"No, I guess not," Davis said. "I understand Tony left his job.
Is that right?"

"Yes. It didn't pay much, and Tony is really a brilliant person.
He and Alice said they'd look around after the honeymoon and
settle wherever he could get located."

"When did he quit?"

"A few days before they were married, I think. No, wait, it was
on New Year's Eve, that's right. He quit then."

"Then he wasn't selling tickets on the day of. . . ."

Anne looked at him strangely. "The day of what?"

"The day he was married," Davis said quickly.

"No, he wasn't." She continued looking at him, and then asked,
"How do you happen to know Tony, Mr. Davis?"

"Oh, the Army," Davis said. "The last war, you know."

"That's quite a feat," Anne said.

"Huh?" Davis looked up.

"Tony was in the Navy."

Once again, he felt like a damn fool. He cursed the crashed plane, and he cursed George Ellison, and he cursed the stupidity that had led him to take the job in the first place. He sighed deeply.

"Well," he said. "I guess I pulled a bloomer."

Anne Trimble stared at him coldly. "Maybe you'd better get out, Mr. Davis. If that's your name."

"It's my name. Look," he said, "I'm a private eye. I'm investigating the crash for my client. I thought. . . ."

"*What* crash?"

"A DC–4 took a dive in Seattle. My client's daughter was aboard her when she went down. There was also a bomb aboard."

"Is this another one of your stories?"

Davis lifted his right hand. "God's truth, s'help me. I'm trying to find whoever put the bomb aboard."

"And you think Tony did?"

"No, I didn't say that. But I've got to investigate all the possibilities."

Anne suddenly smiled. "Are you new at this business?"

"No, I've been at it a long time now. This case is a little out of my usual line."

"You called yourself a private eye. Do private eyes really call themselves that? I thought that was just for the paperback trade."

"I'm afraid we really do," Davis said. "Private Investigator, shortened to Private I, and then naturally to Private eye."

"It must be exciting."

"Well, I'm afraid it's usually deadly dull." He rose and said, "Thanks very much for your time, Miss Trimble. I'm sorry I got to see you on a ruse, but. . . ."

"You should have just asked. I'm always willing to help the cause of justice." She smiled. "And I think you'd better take this money back."

"Well, thanks again," he said, taking the envelope.

"Not at all," she said. She led him to the door, and shook his hand, and her grip was firm and warm. "Good luck."

The door whispered shut behind him. He stood in the hallway for a few moments, sighed, and then made his way down to the courtyard and the street.

The time has come, he thought, *to replenish the bank account. If Ellison expects me to chase hither and yon, then Ellison should also realize that I'm a poor boy, raised by the side of a railroad*

*car. And if a trip to Vegas is in the offing . . . the time has come
to replenish the bank account.*

He thought no more about it. He hailed a cab for which Ellison
would pay, and headed for the old man's estate.

The butler opened the door and announced, "Mr. Davis, sir,"

Davis smiled at the butler and entered the room. It was full of
plates and pitchers and cups and saucers and mugs and jugs and
platters. For a moment Davis thought he'd wandered into the
pantry by error, but then he saw Ellison seated behind a large
desk.

Ellison did not look old, even though Davis knew he was
somewhere in his seventies. He had led an easy life, and the rich
are expert at conserving their youth. The only signs of age on
Ellison were in his face. It was perhaps a bit too ruddy for good
health, and it reminded him of MacGregor's complexion—but
Ellison was not a fat man. He had steel-gray hair cropped close
to his head. His brows were black, in direct contrast to the hair
on his head, and his eyes were a penetrating pale blue. Davis
wondered from whom Janet had inherited her red hair, then let
the thought drop when Ellison rose and extended his hand.

"Ah, Davis, come in, come in."

Davis walked to the desk, and Ellison took his hand in a tight
grip.

"Hope you don't mind talking in here," he said. "I've got a
new piece of porcelain, and I wanted to mount it."

"Not at all," Davis said.

"Know anything about porcelain?" Ellison asked.

"Not a thing, sir."

"Pity. Volkstedt wouldn't mean anything to you then, would
it?"

"No, sir."

"Or Rudolstadt? It's more generally known as that."

"I'm afraid not, sir," Davis said.

"Here now," Ellison said. "Look at this sauce boat."

Davis looked.

"This dates back to 1783, Davis. Here, look." He turned over
the sauce boat, but he did not let it out of his hands. "See the
crossed hayforks? That's the mark, you know, shows it's genuine
stuff. Funny thing about this. The mark so resembles the Meissen
crossed swords. . . ." He seemed suddenly to remember that he

was not talking to a fellow connoisseur. He put the sauce boat down swiftly but gently. "Have you learned anything yet, Davis?"

"A little, Mr. Ellison. I'm here mainly for money."

Ellison looked up sharply and then began chuckling. "You're a frank man, aren't you?"

"I try to be," Davis said. "When it concerns money."

"How much will you need?"

"A thousand will do it. I'll probably be flying to Vegas and back, and I may have to spread a little money for information while I'm there."

Ellison nodded briefly. "I'll give you a check before you leave. What progress have you made, Davis?"

"Not very much. Do you know a Tony Radner?"

Ellison looked up swiftly. "Why?"

"He put your daughter on the DC–4, sir. Do you know him?"

Ellison's mouth lengthened, and he tightened his fists on the desk top. "Has that son of a bitch got something to do with this?" he asked.

"Do you know him, sir?"

"Of course I do! How do you know he put Janet on that plane?"

"An eyewitness, sir."

"I'll kill that bastard!" Ellison shouted. "If he had anything to do with. . . ."

"How do you know him, Mr. Ellison?"

Ellison's rage subsided for a moment. "Janet was seeing him," he said.

"What do you mean, seeing him?"

"She fancied herself to be in love with him," Ellison said. "He's a no-good, Davis, a plain. . . ."

"You mean she wanted to marry him, rather than Carruthers?"

"No, that's not what I mean. I mean she was seeing Radner. *After* she and Nick were married. She . . . she had the supreme gall to tell me she wanted a divorce from Nick." Ellison clenched his hands and then relaxed them again. "You don't know Nick, Davis. He's a fine boy, one of the best. I feel toward him the way I'd feel toward my own son. I never had any boys, Davis, and Janet wasn't much of a daughter." He paused. "I'm grateful I've still got Nick," he said.

"Your daughter wanted to divorce Carruthers?"

"Yes," Ellison said.

"Did she tell Carruthers?"

"Yes, she did. But I told *her* I'd cut her off without a penny if she did any such damn-fool thing. She changed her mind mighty fast after that. Janet was used to money, Davis. The idea of marrying a ticket seller didn't appeal to her when she knew she'd have to do without it."

"So she broke it off with him?"

"On the spot."

"When was this?"

"About six months ago," Ellison said.

"And she hadn't seen him since?"

"Not that I knew of. Now you tell me he put her on that plane. I don't know what to think."

Davis nodded. "It *is* a little confusing."

"Do you suppose she was going to keep a rendezvous in Washington with Radner?" Ellison shook his head. "Dammit, I wouldn't put it past her."

"I don't think so. At least . . . well, I should think they'd have left together if that were the case."

"Not if she didn't want to be seen. She was traveling on a company pass, you know."

"That seems odd," Davis said. "I mean—"

"You mean, with all my money, why should she travel on a pass?" Ellison smiled. "I like to help Nick out, Davis. I keep him living well; did it when Janet was alive, and still do it. But he's a proud boy, and I've got to be careful with my methods of seeing to his welfare. Getting Janet her ticket was one of the things that kept his pride going."

"I see." Davis washed his hand over his face. "Well, I'll talk to Radner. Did you know he was married now?"

"No, I didn't."

"Yes. On the day of the crash."

"On the day . . . then what on earth was he doing with Janet?"

"That's a good question," Davis said. He paused, and then added, "Can I have that check now?"

It was not until after supper that evening that Nicholas Carruthers showed up. Davis had eaten lightly, and after a hasty cigarette he had begun packing a small bag for the Vegas trip. When the knock sounded on the door to his apartment, he dropped a pair of shorts into the suitcase and called, "Who is it?"

"Me. Carruthers."

"Second," Davis said. He went to the door rapidly, wondering what had occasioned this visit from the pilot. He threw back the night latch, and then unlocked the door.

Carruthers was in uniform this time. He wore a white shirt and black tie, together with the pale blue trousers and jacket of the airline, and a peaked cap.

"Surprised to see you, Carruthers," Davis said. "Come on in."

"Thanks," Carruthers said. He glanced around the simply furnished apartment noncommittally, then stepped inside and took off his cap, keeping it in his hands.

"Something to drink?" Davis asked. "Scotch okay?"

"Please," Carruthers replied.

Davis poured, and when Carruthers had downed the drink, he refilled the glass. "What's on your mind, Carruthers?"

Carruthers looked into the depths of his glass, sipped a bit of the scotch, and then looked up. "Janet," he said.

"What about her?"

"Let it lie. Tell the old man you're dropping it. Let it lie."

"Why?"

"How much is the old man paying you?" Carruthers asked, avoiding Davis' question.

"That's between the old man and myself."

"I'll match it," Carruthers said. "And then some. Just let's drop the whole damn thing."

Davis thought back to the genial Mr. MacGregor. "You remind me of someone else I know," he said.

Carruthers did not seem interested. "Look, Davis, what does this mean to you, anyway? Nothing. You're getting paid for a job. All right, I'm willing to pay you what you would have made. So why are you being difficult?"

"Am I being difficult? I didn't say I *wouldn't* drop it, did I?"

"Will you?"

"It depends. I'd like to know why you want it dropped."

"Let's just say I'd like it better if the whole thing were forgotten."

"A lot of people would like it better that way. Including the person who put that bomb on the plane."

Carruthers opened his eyes wide. "You don't think I did that, do you?"

"You were aboard the plane. You could have."

"Why would I do a thing like that?"

"I can think of several reasons," Davis said.

"Like what?" Carruthers sipped at the bourbon again.

"Maybe you didn't like the idea of Janet playing around with Tony Radner."

Carruthers laughed a short, brittle laugh. "You think that bothered me? That two-bit punk? Don't be ridiculous." He drank some more scotch and then said, "I was used to Janet's excursions. Radner didn't bother me at all."

"You mean there were others?"

"Others? Janet collected them the way the old man collects porcelain. A hobby, you know."

"Did the old man know this?"

"I doubt it. He knew his daughter was a bitch, but I think Radner was the first time it came into the open. He squelched that pretty damn fast, you can bet."

"But you knew about it? And it didn't bother you?"

"Not in the least. I'm no angel myself, Davis. If Janet wanted to roam, fine. If she thought of leaving me, that was another thing."

"That you didn't like," Davis said.

"That I didn't like at all." Carruthers paused. "Look, Davis, I like money. The old man has a lot of it. Janet was my wife, and the old man saw to it that we lived in style. I could have left the airline any time I wanted to, and he'd have set me up for life. Fact is, I like flying, so I stayed on. But I sure as hell wasn't going to let my meal ticket walk out."

"That's not the way I heard it," Davis said.

"What do you mean?"

"Janet's gone, and the old man is still feeding the kitty."

"Sure, but I didn't know it would work that way."

"Didn't you?"

Carruthers swallowed the remainder of his scotch. "I don't get you, Davis."

"Look at it this way, Carruthers. Janet's a handy thing to have around. She comes and goes, and you come and go, and the old man sees to it that you come and go in Cadillacs. A smart man may begin wondering why he needs Janet at all. If he can be subsidized even after she's gone, why not get rid of her? Why not give her a bomb to play with?"

"Why not?" Carruthers asked. "But I didn't."

"That's what they all say," Davis told him. "Right up to the gas chamber."

"You're forgetting that I didn't know what the old man's reactions would be. Still don't know. It's early in the game yet, and he's still crossing my palm, but that may change. Look, Davis, when a man takes out accident insurance, it's not because he hopes he'll get into an accident. The same thing with Janet. I needed her. She was my insurance. As long as she was around, my father-in-law saw to it that I wasn't needing." Carruthers shook his head. "No, Davis, I couldn't take a chance on my insurance lapsing."

"Perhaps not. Why do you want me to drop the case?"

"Because I want a status quo. The memory of Janet is fresh in the old man's mind. I'm coupled with the memory. That means he keeps my Cadillac full of gas. Suppose you crack this damned thing? Suppose you find out who set that bomb? It becomes something that's resolved. There's a conclusion, and the old man can file it away like a piece of rare porcelain. He loses interest— and maybe my Cadillac stops running."

"You know something, Carruthers? I don't think I like you very much."

Carruthers smiled. "Why? Because I'm trying to protect an investment? Because I don't give a damn that Janet is gone? Look, Davis, let's get this thing straight. We hated each other's guts. I stayed with her because I like the old man's money. And she stayed with me because she knew she'd be cut off penniless if she didn't. A very simple arrangement." He paused. "What do you say, Davis?"

"I say get the hell out of here."

"Be sensible, Davis. Look at it. . . ."

"Take a walk, Carruthers. Take a long walk and don't come back."

Carruthers stared at Davis for a long time. He said nothing, and there was no enmity in his eyes. At last he rose and settled his cap on his head.

At the door, he turned and said, "You're not being smart, Davis."

Davis didn't answer him.

Maybe he *wasn't* being smart. Maybe Carruthers was right.

It would have been so much easier to have said no, right from the start. No, Mr. Ellison, I'm sorry. I won't take the case. Sorry.

That would have been the easy way. He had not taken the easy way. The money had appealed to him, yes, and so he'd stepped into something that was really far too big for him, something that still made very little sense to him. A bomb seemed an awfully elaborate way of killing someone, assuming the death of Janet Carruthers was, in fact, the reason for the bomb. It would have been so much easier to have used a knife, or a gun, or a rope, or even poison.

Unless the destruction of the plane was an important factor in the killing.

Did the killer have a grudge against the airline as well?

Carruthers worked for the airline, but he was apparently well satisfied with his job. Liked flying, he'd said. Besides, to hear him tell it, he'd never even considered killing his wife. Sort of killing the goose, you know. She was too valuable to him. She was—what had he alluded to?—insurance, yes, insurance.

Which, in a way, was true. Carruthers had no way of knowing how Ellison would react to his daughter's death. He could just as easily have washed his hands of Carruthers, and a man couldn't take a chance on. . . .

"I'll be goddamned!" Davis said aloud.

He glanced at his watch quickly. It was too late now. He would have to wait until morning.

"I'll be goddamned," he said again.

It would be a long night.

Mr. Schlemmer was a balding man in his early fifties. A pair of rimless glasses perched on his nose, and his blue eyes were genial behind them.

"I can only speak for Aircraft Insurance Association of America, you understand," he said. "Other companies may operate on a different basis, though I think it unlikely."

"I understand," Davis said.

"First, you wanted to know how much insurance can be obtained from our machines at the San Francisco airport." Schlemmer paused. "We sell it at fifty cents for twenty-five thousand dollars' worth. Costs you two quarters in the machine."

"And what's the maximum insurance for any one person?"

"Two hundred thousand," Schlemmer said. "The premium is four dollars."

"Is there anything in your policy that excludes a woman traveling on a company pass?" Davis asked.

"No," Schlemmer said. "Our airline trip policy states 'traveling on ticket or pass.' No, this woman would not be excluded."

"Suppose the plane's accident occurred because of a bomb explosion aboard the plane while it was in flight? Would that invalidate a beneficiary's claim?"

"I should hardly think so. Just a moment, I'll read you the exclusions." He dug into his desk drawer and came out with a policy which he placed on the desk top, leafing through it rapidly. "No," he said. "The exclusions are disease, suicide, war, and of course, we will not insure the pilot or any active member of the crew."

"I see," Davis said. "Can I get down to brass tacks now?"

"By all means, do," Schlemmer said.

"How long does it take to pay?"

"Well, the claim must be filed within twenty days after the occurrence. Upon receipt of the claim, and within fifteen days, we must supply proof-of-loss forms to the claimant. As soon as these are completed and presented to us, we pay. We've paid within hours on some occasions. Sometimes it takes days, and sometimes weeks. It depends on how rapidly the claim is made, the proof of loss submitted—and all that. You understand?"

"Yes," Davis said. He took a deep breath. "A DC-4 crashed near Seattle on January 6th. Was anyone on that plane insured with your company?"

Schlemmer smiled, and a knowing look crossed his face. "I had a suspicion you were driving at that, Mr. Davis. That was the reason for your 'bomb' question, wasn't it?"

"Yes. Was anyone insured?"

"There was only one passenger," Schlemmer said. "We would not, of course, insure the crew."

"The passenger was Janet Carruthers," Davis said. "Was she insured?"

"Yes."

"For how much?"

Schlemmer paused. "Two hundred thousand dollars, Mr. Davis." He wiped his lips and said, "You know how it works, of course. You purchase your insurance from a machine at the airport. An envelope is supplied for the policy, and you mail this directly to your beneficiary or beneficiaries as the case may be, before you board the flight."

"Yes, I've taken insurance," Davis said.

"A simple matter," Schlemmer assured him, "and well worth

the investment. In this case, the beneficiaries have already received a check for two hundred thousand dollars."

"They have?"

"Yes. The claim was made almost instantly, proof of loss filed, the entire works. We paid at once."

"I see," Davis said. "I wonder . . . could you tell me . . . you mentioned suicide in your excluding clause. Was there any thought about Mrs. Carruthers' death being suicide?"

"We considered it," Schlemmer said. "But quite frankly, it seemed a bit absurd. An accident like this one is hardly conceivable as suicide. I mean, a person would have to be seriously unbalanced to take a plane and its crew with her when she chose to kill herself. Mrs. Carruthers' medical history showed no signs of mental instability. In fact, she was in amazingly good health all through her life. No, suicide was out. We paid."

Davis nodded. "Can you tell me who the beneficiaries were?" he asked.

"Certainly," Schlemmer said. "Mr. and Mrs. Anthony Radner."

He asked her to meet him in front of DiAngelo's and they lingered on the wharf a while, watching the small boats before entering the restaurant. When they were seated, Anne Trimble asked, "Have you ever been here before?"

"I followed a delinquent husband as far as the door once," he answered.

"Then it's your first time."

"Yes."

"Mine, too." She rounded her mouth in mock surprise. "Goodness, we're sharing a first."

"That calls for a drink," he said.

She ordered a daiquiri, and he settled for scotch on the rocks, and he sipped his drink slowly, thinking, *I wish I didn't suspect her sister of complicity in murder.*

They made small talk while they ate, and Davis felt he'd known her for a long time, and that made his job even harder. When they were on their coffee, she said, "I'm a silly girl, I know. But not silly enough to believe this is strictly social."

"I'm an honest man," he said. "It isn't."

She laughed. "Well, what is it then?"

"I want to know more about your sister."

"Alice? For heaven's sake, why?" Her brow furrowed, and she

said, "I really should be offended, you know. You take me out and then want to know more about my sister."

"You've no cause for worry," he said very softly. He was not even sure she heard him. She lifted her coffee cup, and her eyes were wide over the brim.

"Will you tell me about her?" he asked.

"Do you think she put the bomb on the plane?"

He was not prepared for the question. He blinked his eyes in confusion.

"Do you?" she repeated. "Remember, you're an honest man."

"Maybe she did," he said.

Anne considered this, and then took another sip of coffee. "What do you want to know?" she asked.

"I want to. . . ."

"Understand, Mr. Davis. . . ."

"Milt," he corrected.

"All right. Understand that I don't go along with you, not at all. Not knowing my sister. But I'll answer any of your questions because that's the only way you'll see she had nothing to do with it."

"That's fair enough," he said.

"All right, Milt. Fire away."

"First, what kind of a girl is she?"

"A simple girl. Shy, often awkward. Honest, Milt, very honest. Innocent. I think Tony Radner is the first man she ever kissed."

"Do you come from a wealthy family, Anne?"

"No."

"How does your sister feel about—"

"About not having a tremendous amount of money?" Anne shrugged. "All right, I suppose. We weren't destitute, even after Dad died. We always got along very nicely, and I don't think she ever yearned for anything. What are you driving at, Milt?"

"Would two hundred thousand dollars seem like a lot of money to Alice?"

"Yes," Anne answered without hesitation. "Two hundred thousand would seem like a lot of money to anyone."

"Is she easily persuaded? Can she be talked into doing things?"

"Perhaps. I know damn well she couldn't be talked into putting a bomb on a plane, though."

"No. But could she be talked into sharing two hundred thousand that was come by through devious means?"

"Why all this concentration on two hundred thousand dollars? Is that an arbitrary sum, or has a bank been robbed in addition to the plane crash?"

"Could she be talked," Davis persisted, "into drugging another woman?"

"No," Anne said firmly.

"Could she be talked into forging another woman's signature on an insurance policy?"

"Alice wouldn't do anything like that. Not in a million years."

"But she married Radner. A man without money, a man without a job. Doesn't that seem like a shaky foundation upon which to build a marriage?"

"Not if the two people are in love."

"Or unless the two people were going to come into a lot of money shortly."

Anne said, "You're making me angry. And just when I was beginning to like you."

"Then please don't be angry. I'm just digging, believe me."

"Well, dig a little more gently, please."

"What does your sister look like?"

"Fairly pretty, I suppose. Well, not really. I suppose she isn't pretty, in fact. I never appraised her looks."

"Do you have a picture of her?"

"Yes, I do."

She put her purse on the table and unclasped it. She pulled out a red leather wallet, unsnapped it, and then removed one of the pictures from the gatefold. "It's not a good shot," she apologized.

The girl was not what Davis would have termed pretty. He was surprised, in fact, that she could be Anne's sister. He studied the black-and-white photograph of a fair-haired girl with a wide forehead, her nose a bit too long, her lips thin. He studied the eyes, but they held the vacuous smile common to all posed snapshots.

"She doesn't look like your sister," he said.

"Don't you think so?"

"No, not at all. You're much prettier."

Anne screwed up her eyebrows and studied Davis seriously. "You have blundered upon my secret, Mr. Davis," she said with mock exaggeration.

"You wear a mask, Miss Trimble," he said, pointing his finger at her like a prosecuting attorney.

"Almost, but not quite. I visit a remarkable magician known as Antoine. He operates a beauty salon and fender-repair shop. He is responsible for the midnight of my hair and the ripe apple of my lips. He made me what I am today, and now you won't love me any more." She brushed away an imaginary tear.

"I'd love you if you were bald and had green lips," he said, hoping his voice sounded light enough.

"Goodness!" she said, and then she laughed suddenly, a rich, full laugh he enjoyed hearing. "I may very well be bald after a few more tinting sessions with Antoine."

"May I keep the picture?" he asked.

"Certainly," she said. "Why?"

"I'm going up to Vegas. I want to find your sister and Radner."

"Then you're serious about all this," she said softly.

"Yes, I am. At least, until I'm convinced otherwise. Anne. . . ."

"Yes?"

"It's just a job. I. . . ."

"I'm not really worried, you understand. I know you're wrong about Alice, and Tony, too. So I won't worry."

"Good," he said. "I hope I *am* wrong."

She lifted one raven brow, and there was no coyness or archness in the motion. "Will you call me when you get back?"

"Yes," he said. "Definitely."

"If I'm out when you call, you can call my next-door neighbor, Freida. She'll take the message." She scribbled the number on a sheet of paper. "You will call, won't you, Milt?"

He covered her hand with his and said, "Try and stop me."

He went to City Hall right after he left her. He checked on marriage certificates issued on January 6th, and he was not surprised to find that one had been issued to Anthony Louis Radner and Alice May Trimble. He left there and went directly to the airport, making a reservation on the next plane for Las Vegas. Then he headed back for his apartment to pick up his bag.

The door was locked, just as he had left it. He put his key into the lock, twisted it, and swung the door wide.

"Close it," MacGregor said.

MacGregor was sitting in the armchair to the left of the door. One hand rested across his wide middle and the other held the familiar .38, and this time it was pointed at Davis' head. Davis closed the door, and MacGregor said, "Better lock it, Miltie."

"You're a bad penny, MacGregor," Davis said, locking the door.

MacGregor chuckled. "Ain't it the truth, Miltie?"

"Why are you back, MacGregor? Three strikes and I'm out, is that it?"

"Three . . ." MacGregor cut himself short, and then grinned broadly. "So you figured the mountain, huh, Miltie?"

"I figured it."

"I wasn't aiming at you, you know. I just wanted to scare you off. You don't scare too easy, Miltie."

"Who's paying you, MacGregor?"

"Now, now," MacGregor said chidingly, waving the gun like an extended forefinger. "That's a secret now, ain't it?" Davis watched the way MacGregor moved the gun, and he wondered if he'd repeat the gesture again. It might be worth remembering, for later.

"So what do we do?" he asked.

"We take a little ride, Miltie."

"Like in the movies, huh? Real melodrama."

MacGregor scratched his head. "Is a pleasant little ride melodrama?"

"Come on, MacGregor, who hired you?" He poised himself on the balls of his feet, ready to jump the moment MacGregor started wagging the gun again. MacGregor's hand did not move.

"Don't let's be silly, Miltie boy," he said.

"Do you know *why* you were hired?"

"I was told to see that you dropped the case. That's enough instructions for me."

"Do you know that two hundred grand is involved? How much are you getting for handling the sloppy end of the stick?"

MacGregor lifted his eyebrows and then nodded his head. "Two hundred grand, huh?"

"Sure. Do you know there's a murder involved, MacGregor? Five murders, if you want to get technical. Do you know what it means to be accessory after?"

"Can it, Davis. I've been in the game longer than you're walking."

"Then you know the score. And you know I can go down to R and I, and identify you from a mug shot. Think about that, MacGregor. It adds up to rock-chopping."

"Maybe you'll never get to see a mug shot."

"Maybe not. But that adds another murder to it. Are they paying you enough for a homicide rap, MacGregor?"

"Little Miltie, we've talked enough."

"Maybe we haven't talked enough yet. Maybe you don't know that the Feds are in on this thing, and that the Army. . . ."

"Oh, come on, Miltie. Come on now, boy. You're reaching."

"Am I? Check around, MacGregor. Find out what happens when sabotage is suspected, especially on a plane headed to pick up military personnel. Find out if the Feds aren't on the scene. And find out what happens when a big-time fools with the government."

"I never done a state pen," MacGregor said, seemingly hurt. "Don't call me a big-time."

"Then why are you juggling a potato as hot as this one? Do you yearn for Quentin, MacGregor? Wise up, friend. You've been conned. The gravy is all on the other end of the line. You're getting all the cold beans, and when it comes time to hang a frame, guess who'll be it? Give a good guess, MacGregor."

MacGregor said seriously, "You're a fast talker."

"What do you say, MacGregor? How do you feel, playing the boob in a big ante deal? How much are you getting?"

"Four G's," MacGregor said. "Plus."

"Plus what?"

MacGregor smiled the age-old smile of a man who has known a woman and is reluctant to admit it. "Just plus," he said.

"All right, keep the dough and forget you were hired. You've already had the 'plus,' and you can keep that as a memory."

"I've only been paid half the dough," MacGregor said.

"When's the rest due?"

"When you drop the case."

"I can't match it, MacGregor, but I'll give you a thou for your trouble. You're getting off easy, believe me. If I don't crack this, the Feds will, and then you'll really be in hot water."

"Yeah," MacGregor said, nodding.

"You'll forget it then?"

"Where's the G-note?"

Davis reached for his wallet on the dresser. "Who hired you, MacGregor?" He looked up, and MacGregor's smile had widened now.

"I'll take it all, Miltie."

"Huh?"

"All of it." MacGregor waved the gun. "Everything in the wallet. Come on."

"You *are* a jackass, aren't you?" Davis said. He fanned out the money in the wallet, and then held it out to MacGregor. MacGregor reached for it, and Davis loosened his grip, and the bills began fluttering towards the floor.

MacGregor grabbed for them with his free hand, turning sideways at the same time, taking the gun off Davis.

It had to be then, and it had to be right, because the talking game was over and MacGregor wasn't buying anything.

Davis leaped, ramming his shoulder against the fat man's chest. MacGregor staggered back, and then swung his arm around just as Davis' fingers clamped on his wrist. He did not fire, and Davis knew he probably didn't want to bring the apartment house down around his ears.

They staggered across the room in a clumsy embrace, like partners at a dance school for beginners. Davis had both hands on MacGregor's gun wrist now, and the fat man swung his arm violently, trying to shake the grip. They didn't speak or curse. MacGregor grunted loudly each time he swung his arm, and Davis' breath was audible as it rushed through his parted lips. He did not loosen his grip. He forced MacGregor across the room, and when the fat man's back was against the wall Davis began methodically smashing the gun hand against the plaster.

"Drop it," he said through clenched teeth. "Drop it."

He hit the wall with MacGregor's hand again, and this time the fingers opened and the gun clattered to the floor. Davis stepped back for just an instant, kicking the gun across the room, and then rushed forward with his fist clenched.

He felt his fist sink into the flesh around MacGregor's middle. The fat man's face went white, and then he buckled over, his arms embracing his stomach. Davis dropped his fist and then brought it up from his shoe-laces, catching MacGregor on the point of his jaw. MacGregor lurched backward, slamming into the wall, knocking a picture to the floor. Davis hit him once more, and MacGregor pitched forward onto his face. He wriggled once, and was still.

Davis stood over him, breathing hard. He waited until he caught his breath, and then he glanced at his watch.

Quickly, he picked up the .38 from where it lay on the floor. He broke it open, checked the load, and then brought it to his suitcase, laying it on top of his shirts.

He snapped the suitcase shut, called the police to tell them he'd

just subdued a burglar in his apartment, and then left to catch
his Las Vegas plane.

He started with the hotels. He started with the biggest ones.

"Mr. and Mrs. Anthony Radner," he said. "Are they registered
here?"

The clerks all looked the same.

"Radner, Radner. The name doesn't sound familiar, but I'll
check, sir."

Then the shifting of the ledger, the turning of pages, the signatures, largely scrawled, and usually illegible.

"No, sir, I'm sorry. No Radner."

"Perhaps you'd recognize the woman, if I showed you her
picture?"

"Well. . . ." The apologetic cough. "Well, we get an awful lot
of guests, sir."

And the fair-haired girl emerging from the wallet. The black
and white, stereotyped photograph of Alice Trimble, and the
explanation, "She's a newlywed—with her husband."

"We get a lot of newlyweds, sir."

The careful scrutiny of the head shot, the tilting of one eyebrow,
the picture held at arm's length, then closer.

"No, I'm sorry. I don't recognize her. Why don't you try . . . ?"

He tried them all, all the hotels, and then all the rooming
houses, and then all the motor courts. They were all very sorry.
They had no Radners registered, and couldn't identify the photograph.

So he started making the rounds then. He lingered at the
machines, feeding quarters into the slots, watching the oranges
and lemons and cherries whirl before his eyes, but never watching
them too closely, always watching the place instead, looking for
the elusive woman named Alice Trimble Radner.

Or he sat at the bars, nursing along endless scotches, his eyes
fastened to the mirrors that commanded the entrance doorways.
He was bored, and he was tired, but he kept watching, and he
began making the rounds again as dusk tinted the sky, and the
lights of the city flicked their siren song on the air.

He picked up the newspaper by chance. He flipped through it
idly, and he almost turned the page, even after he'd read the small
head: FATAL ACCIDENT.

The item was a very small one. It told of a Pontiac convertible

with defective brakes which had crashed through the guard rail
on the highway, killing its occupant instantly. The occupant's
name was Anthony Radner. There was no mention of Alice in
the article.

Little Alice Trimble, Davis thought. *A simple girl. Shy, often
awkward. Honest.*

Murder is a simple thing. All it involves is killing another person
or persons. You can be shy and awkward, and even honest—but
that doesn't mean you can't be a murderer besides. So what is it
that takes a simple girl like Alice Trimble and transforms her into
a murderess?

Figure it this way. Figure a louse named Tony Radner who
sees a way of striking back at the girl who jilted him and coming
into a goodly chunk of dough besides. Figure a lot of secret
conversation, a pile of carefully planned moves. Figure a wedding,
planned to coincide with the day of the plotted murder, so the
murderers can be far away when the bomb they planted explodes.

Radner gets to see Janet Carruthers on some pretext, perhaps
a farewell drink to show there are no hard feelings. This is his
wedding day, and he introduces her to his bride, Alice Trimble.
They share a drink, perhaps, but the drink is loaded and Janet
suddenly feels very woozy. They help her to the airport, and they
stow the bomb in her valise. None of the pilots know Radner.
The only bad piece of luck is the fact that the fire-warning system
is acting up, and a mechanic named Mangione recognizes him.
But that's part of the game.

He helps her aboard and then goes back to his loving wife,
Alice. They hop the next plane for Vegas, and when the bomb
explodes they're far, far away. They get the news from the papers,
file claim, and come into two hundred thousand bucks.

Just like falling off Pier 8.

Except that it begins to get sour about there. Except that maybe
Alice Trimble likes the big time now. Two hundred G's is a nice
little pile. Why share it?

So Tony Radner meets with an accident. If he's not insured,
the two hundred grand is still Alice's. If he is insured, there's
more for her.

The little girl has made her debut. The shy, awkward thing has
emerged.

Portrait of a killer.

Davis went back to the newsstand, bought copies of all the local newspapers and then went back to the hotel.

When he was in his room, he called room service and asked for a tall scotch, easy on the ice. He took off his shoes and threw himself on the bed.

The drink came, and he went back to the bed again.

The easy part was over, of course. The hard part was still ahead. He still had to tell Anne about it, and he'd give his right arm not to have that task ahead of him. Alice Trimble? The police would find her. She'd probably left Vegas the moment Radner piled up the Pontiac. She was an amateur, and it wouldn't be too hard to find her. But telling Anne, that was the difficult thing.

Davis sat upright, took a long swallow of the scotch, and then swung his stockinged feet to the floor. He walked to the pile of newspapers on the dresser, picked them up, and carried them back to the bed.

He thumbed through the first one until he found the item about Radner's accident. It was a small notice, and it was basically the same as the one he'd read. It did add that Alice Trimble was on her honeymoon, and that she had come from San Francisco where she lived with her sister.

He leafed through the second newspaper, scanning the story quickly. Again, basically the same facts. Radner had taken the car for a spin. Alice hadn't gone along because of a headache. The accident had been attributed to faulty brakes, and there was speculation that Alice might have grounds for suit, if she cared to press charges, against the dealer who'd sold them the car.

The third newspaper really did a bang-up job. They treated the accident as a human-interest piece, playing up the newly-wed angle. They gave it the tearful head, "FATE CHEATS BRIDE," and then went on to wring the incident dry. There was also a picture of Alice Trimble leaving the coroner's office. She was raising her hand to cover her face when the picture had been taken. It was a good shot, close up, clear. The caption read: *Tearful Alice Radner, leaving the coroner's office after identifying the body of her husband, Anthony Radner.*

Davis did not notice any tears on Alice Trimble's face.

He looked at the photograph again.

He sat erect and took a long gulp of his scotch, and then he brought the newspaper closer to his face and stared at the picture for a long time.

And he suddenly remembered something important he'd forgotten to ask Anne about her sister. Something damned important. So important he nearly broke his neck getting to the phone.

He asked long distance for Anne's number, and then let the phone ring for fifteen minutes before he gave up. He remembered the alternate number she'd given him then, the one belonging to Freida, the girl next door. He fished the scrap of paper out of his wallet, studying the number in Anne's handwriting, recalling their conversation in the restaurant. He got long distance to work again, and the phone was picked up on the fourth ring.

"Hello?"

"Hello, Freida?"

"Yes?"

"My name is Milt Davis. You don't know me, but Anne said I could leave a message here if. . . ."

"Oh, yes. Anne's told me all about you, Mr. Davis."

"Well, good, good, I just tried to phone her, and there was no answer. I wonder if you know where I can reach her?"

"Why, yes," Freida said. "She's in Las Vegas."

"What!"

"Yes. Her brother-in-law was killed in a car crash there. She. . . ."

"You mean she's here? Now?"

"Well, I suppose so. She caught a plane early this evening. Yes, I'm sure she's there by now. Her sister called, you see. Alice. She called and asked Anne to come right away. Terrible thing, her husband getting killed like. . . ."

"Oh, Christ!" Davis said. He thought for a moment and then asked, "Did she say where I could reach her?"

"Yes. Just a moment."

Freida put the phone down with a clatter, and Davis waited impatiently. By the time she returned, he was ready to start chewing the mouthpiece.

"What's the address?" he asked.

"It's outside of Las Vegas. A rooming house. Alice and Tony were lucky to get such a nice. . . ."

"Please, the address!"

"Well, all right," Freida said, a little miffed. She read off the address and Davis scribbled it quickly. He said goodbye, and hung up immediately. There was no time for checking plane schedules now. No time for finding out which plane Anne had caught out of Frisco, nor for finding out what time it had arrived in Vegas.

There was only time to tuck MacGregor's .38 into the waistband of his trousers and then run like hell down to the street. He caught a cab and reeled off the address, and then sat on the edge of his seat while the lights of Vegas dimmed behind him.

When the cabbie pulled up in front of the clapboard structure, he gave him a fiver and then leaped out of the car. He ran up the front steps and pulled the door pull, listening to steps approaching inside. A white-haired woman opened the door, and Davis said, "Alice Radner. Where?"

"Upstairs, but who . . . ?"

Davis shoved the woman aside and started up the flight of steps, not looking back. There was a door at the top of the stairwell, and he rapped on it loudly. When he received no answer, he shouted, "I know you're in there! Open the goddamn door!"

The door opened instantly, and Davis found himself looking into the bore of a .22.

"Come in," a woman's voice said softly.

"Where is she?" he asked.

"I'm afraid I had to tie her and gag her. She raised a bit of a fuss when she got here."

He stepped into the room, and she closed the door behind him. Anne was lying on the bed, her hands tied behind her, a scarf stuffed in her mouth. He made a move toward her and the voice came from the doorway, cool and crisp.

"Leave her alone."

"Why?" Davis said. "It's all over now, anyway."

She smiled, but there was no mirth in her eyes. "You should have stayed out of it. From the very beginning."

"Everybody's been telling me that," Davis said. "Right from go."

"You should have paid more attention to them, Mr. Davis. All this might have been avoided then."

"All what?"

She did not answer. She opened the door again, and called, "It's all right, Mrs. Mulready. He's a friend of mine." Then she slammed the door and bolted it.

"That takes care of her," she said, the .22 steady in her hand. She was a beautiful woman with a pale complexion and blue eyes set against the ivory of her skin. She stared at Davis solemnly.

"It all seemed out of whack," Davis said, "but I didn't know just where. It all pointed to Tony Radner and Alice Trimble, but

I couldn't conceive of her as a murderess. Sure, I figured Tony led her into it. A woman in love can be talked into anything. But when I learned about Tony's accident here, a new Alice Trimble took shape. Not the gal who was talked into anything, and not the gal who'd do anything for love. This new Alice Trimble was a cold-blooded killer, a murderess who. . . ."

Davis saw Anne's eyes widen. She struggled to speak.

"Anne," he said, "tell me something. Was your sister a redhead?"

Anne nodded dumbly, and he saw the confused look that stabbed her eyes. It was then that he realized he'd unconsciously used the past tense in talking about her sister.

"I'm sorry," he said. "I'm sorry as hell, Anne." He paused and drew a deep breath. "Alice is dead."

It was almost as if he'd struck her. She flinched, and then a strangled cry tried to shove its way past the gag.

"Believe me," he said, "I'm sorry. I. . . ." He wiped his hand across his lips and then said, "I never thought to ask. About her hair, I mean. Hell, I had her picture and that was all I needed to identify her. I'm . . . I'm sorry, Anne."

He saw the tears spring into her eyes, and he went to her in spite of the .22 that was still pointed at him. He ripped the gag from her mouth, and she said, "I don't understand. I . . . what . . . what do you mean?"

"Alice left you on the sixth," he said, "to meet Tony Radner, allegedly to marry him. She didn't know about the trap that had been planned by Tony and Janet Carruthers."

Anne took her eyes from Davis and looked at the .22 in the woman's hand. "Is . . . is that who. . . ."

"Janet Carruthers," Davis said, "who wanted to be free of her husband more than anything else in the world. But not at the expense of cutting herself off without a cent. So she and Tony figured it all out, and they started looking for a redhead who would take the hook. Your sister came along, starry-eyed and innocent, and Radner led her to the chopping block."

Davis paused and turned to the redhead with the gun. "I can fill it in, if you like. A lot of guessing, but I think I'm right."

"Go ahead," Janet said. "Fill it in."

"Sure. Alice met Tony as scheduled on the day they were to be married. He probably suggested a drink in celebration, drugged her, and then took her some place to get her into some of your clothes. He drove her to the airport because your signature was necessary on the insurance policy. You insured Alice, who was now in Janet Carruthers' clothing, with Janet Carruthers' identification in case anything was left of her after the crash, for two hundred thousand dollars. And Janet Carruthers' beneficiaries were Mr. and Mrs. Anthony Radner. You knew that Nick would be on the DC-4, but outside of him, no one else on the plane knew what you looked like. It would be simple to substitute Alice for you. You left the airport, probably to go directly to City Hall to wait for Tony. Tony waited until Nick took a pilot up on a test, and then brought Alice to the plane, dumped her into her seat, with the bomb in her suitcase, and left to meet you. You got married shortly after the DC-4 took off. You used Alice Trimble's name, and most likely the identification—if it was needed—that Tony had taken from her. The switch had been completed, and you were now Mrs. Radner. You flew together to Las Vegas, and as soon as the DC-4 crashed, you made your claim for the two hundred G's."

"You're right except for the drug, Mr. Davis. That would have been overdoing it a bit."

"All right, granted. What'd Tony do, just get her too damned drunk to walk or know what was going on?"

"Exactly. Her wedding day, you know. It wasn't difficult."

Davis heard a sob catch in Anne's throat. He glanced at her briefly and then said to Janet, "Did Tony know he was going to be driving into a pile of rocks?"

Janet smiled. "Poor Tony. No, I'm afraid he didn't know. That part was all my idea. Even down to stripping the brakes. Tony never knew what hit him."

"Neither did all the people on that DC-4. It was a long way to go for a lousy hunk of cash," Davis said. "Was Tony insured, too?"

"Yes," Janet said, "but not for much." She smiled, "Enough, though."

Davis nodded. "One after the other, right down the line. And then you sent for Anne because she was the only living person who could know you were *not* Alice Trimble. And it had to be fast, especially after that picture appeared in the Las Vegas paper."

"Was that how you found out?" she asked.

"Exactly how. The picture was captioned *Alice Radner* but the girl didn't match the one in the photo I had. Then I began thinking about the color of Alice's hair, which I knew was light, and it got clear as a bell." He shook his head sadly. "I still don't know how you hoped to swing it. You obviously sent for Anne because you were afraid someone would recognize you in Frisco. Hell, someone would have recognized you sooner or later, anyway."

"In Mexico?" Janet asked. "Or South America? I doubt it. Two hundred thousand can do a lot outside of this country, Mr. Davis. Plus what I'll get on Tony's death. I'll manage nicely, don't you worry." She smiled pleasantly.

Davis smiled back. "Go ahead," he said. "Shoot. And then try to explain the shots to your landlady."

Janet Carruthers walked to the dresser, keeping the gun on Davis. "I hadn't wanted to do it here," she said, shrugging. "I was going to take Miss Trimble away after everyone was asleep. You're forcing my hand, though." She opened a drawer and came out with a long, narrow cylinder. The cylinder had holes punched into its sides, and Davis knew a silencer when he saw one. He saw Janet fitting the silencer to the end of the .22 and he saw the dull gleam in her eyes and knew it was time to move. He threw back his coat and reached for the .38 in his waistband. The .22 went off with a sharp *pouff,* and he felt the small bullet rip into his shoulder. But he'd squeezed the trigger of the .38 and he saw her arm jerk as his larger bullet tore flesh and bone. Her fingers opened, and the silenced gun fell to the floor.

Her face twisted in pain. She closed her eyes, and he kicked the gun away, and then she began swearing. She kept swearing when he took her good arm and twisted it behind her back.

He heard footsteps rushing up the stairs, and then the landlady shouted. "What is it? *What is it?*"

"Get the police!" he yelled through the closed door. "Get them fast."

"You don't know what you're doing," Janet said. "This will kill my father."

Davis looked over to where Anne sat sobbing on the bed. He wanted to go to her and clasp her into his arms, but there would be time for that later.

"My father . . ." Janet started.

"Your father still has Nick," Davis said, "and his porcelain." His shoulder ached, and the trickle of blood down his jacket front was not pleasant to watch. He paused and lifted his eyes to Janet's. "That's all your father ever had."

BILL PRONZINI
Who's Calling?

1

WEDNESDAY MORNING, late January.

The weather was good, clear and mostly warm, but with a nip in the air that reminded you there was still some icy wind and rain between now and spring. Nearly everybody on the streets was smiling, even the men cleaning up the last of the broken bottles, confetti and other litter from the celebration on Sunday and the victory parade to City Hall on Monday. About the only person who wasn't smiling was me.

The reason everybody was so cheerful was not the weather; it was the same reason there had been a two-day celebration on Sunday and Monday. The Forty-niners had just won the ultimate prize in professional football, the Super Bowl—San Francisco's first-ever national championship in any sport. I had watched the game myself on TV, and done some smiling and mild celebrating of my own when it was over. But I had celebrated alone, inside my Pacific Heights flat, instead of out on the streets where hordes of other people congregated.

I don't like crowds much, particularly the kind of crowd that keeps fueling itself on alcohol. Ninety-nine percent of the people are all right, even in a riotous mass of merrymakers. It's the other 1 percent you have to worry about. That 1 percent is made up of troublemakers and vandals, criminals looking for a chance to pick pockets or loot stores or commit armed robbery, and just plain loonies. Several people had been hurt during the festivities; dozens more had been arrested.

Well, any city of substantial size has its criminal element and its lunatic fringe; San Francisco was no exception. In a sense, the

outlaws kept me in business—not that I was grateful to them for
the privilege. I did not mind the crooks so much; for the most
part they acted in predictable ways, and if you knew what you
were doing, you could deal with them all right. It was the crazies
who bothered me. I didn't often get a job that involved a crazy,
and for that I *was* grateful. But every now and then, such a job
comes along. And sometimes, in spite of my better judgment, I
decide to take it on.

A job involving a crazy had come along this morning. I was
probably going to take it on, too, because I needed the money.
At least I had agreed to go and talk to the man who wanted to
hire me, an attorney named Jud Canale.

And that was why, on this clear and mostly warm Wednesday
morning three days after the Forty-niners had won the Super Bowl,
I wasn't smiling along with everybody else.

The corporate law firm of Tellmark, Graham, Canale and Isaacs
was located in one of the newer high-rise office buildings on
Montgomery Street, in the financial district. It occupied most of
the fifteenth floor, and judging from the reception room the firm
was doing very well, thank you. Oak-paneled walls, matching oak
furniture covered in autumn-colored fabric, rust-brown carpeting
and a decorative young lady behind the reception desk. The lady
had auburn hair to match the motif; I wondered, a little cynically,
if that was why she'd been hired.

Jud Canale's office turned out to be similarly appointed, though
his secretary was a little less decorative and had blond hair; the
room was windowed on two sides, with the other two walls taken
up with shelves of law books. Canale himself looked to be about
my age, early fifties, and he had iron-gray hair and penetrating
gray eyes. The three-piece pinstripe suit he wore, combined with
that gray hair, gave him a dignified appearance. He was standing
behind his somewhat cluttered desk when the secretary showed
me in; beyond him, through the windows, I could see more than
I cared to of the Transamerica Pyramid—a high-rise building that
resembled an ice-cream cone turned upside down, as a local
newspaper columnist had once aptly described it.

Canale came around the desk as I approached, stopped with
his face a few inches from mine and said in grave tones, "Thank
you for coming."

"Not at all, Mr. Canale."

We shook hands. He was still standing close to me—one of those people who had a penchant, conscious or unconscious, for intruding on other people's space—and I could see the worry in his eyes; the skin across his cheekbones had a stretched look. I let go of his hand and backed up a step. My space was my own, and I did not want anyone else occupying it. Nor did I want to stand that close to another man's fear.

Canale nodded toward the nearest of two leather visitors' chairs, waited until I had seated myself, and then went around and plunked himself down in his own chair. He leaned forward with his hands flat on the desk blotter and looked at me as if I were a witness on the stand in court.

"There's been another call," he said.

"When?"

"Last night, late. I called Lynn after I spoke to you, and she admitted it."

"Same sort of thing?"

"Yes. She wouldn't go into details."

"How is she?"

"She says she's all right, but I don't believe her. A thing like this. . . ." He shook his head. "She's only twenty," he said.

"She's not alone today, is she?"

"No. One of her girlfriends is staying with her at her apartment."

I was silent a couple of seconds before I said, "Mr. Canale, are you sure you want to go through with this—hiring me? As I told you on the phone, I don't know that there's much I can do in a case like this. The police department and the telephone company investigate hundreds of complaints about obscene calls every year—"

"I know that—"

"—but even with the man power and facilities at their disposal, they aren't able to catch or even identify more than a handful of the callers. Besides, almost none of these crazies ever molest the women they call up. They're talkers, usually, not doers; according to psychological profiles, most of them are afraid of women. What they do is pick names out of the telephone directory, at random—"

"I know that, too," Canale said; "the police told me the same thing when I contacted them two days ago. But the man who keeps harassing Lynn is not a random caller. I think he knows her, and she knows him. In fact, I'm sure of it." He held up a hand as I started to speak. "I know what I said to you on the phone; I said it was a possibility that ought to be explored, and that was why I wanted to hire a detective. But now I'm convinced that's the case."

"What convinced you?"

"That call to Lynn last night. She had her number changed yesterday afternoon, at my insistence. Her new number is unlisted."

I said slowly, "I see."

"Yes. How could some anonymous crank find out a person's brand-new unlisted telephone number in less than twelve hours?"

"I doubt if one could. Unless he worked for the phone company, or knew someone who did."

"That strikes me as unlikely," Canale said. "No, it's someone Lynn knows well enough to have given her new number to. Or someone who got the number secondhand from one of her friends."

"Do you have any idea who it might be?"

"No."

"What does your daughter say?"

"She refuses to believe it's anyone she knows."

"Did she tell you who she'd given the number to?"

"No. She wouldn't talk about it, at least not to me."

"Why not to you?"

Canale smiled sardonically, without humor. "We haven't been close in the past couple of months," he said. "Ever since she became engaged to a young man named Larry Travers."

"You don't approve of this Travers?"

"No. And of course Lynn rebelled when I made my feelings clear to her."

"Is there any particular reason you don't like him?"

"I don't think he'll be good for her. Besides, she's too young to marry." He made a small suffering sound in his throat. "Father-daughter relationships can be difficult sometimes," he said. "Particularly when the father is the only parent. My wife and I were divorced when Lynn was a year old; neither Lynn nor I has seen her since."

I was not qualified to comment on any of that, never having been either a husband or a father, so I remained silent.

Canale watched me for a moment. "So. Am I correct in assuming you'll investigate the matter for me?"

"Yes, sir," I said. "As long as you understand that there's only a limited chance of success on my part. All I can guarantee you is my time and an honest effort."

"That's all I ask of any man." He leaned back in his chair. "I expect you'll want to talk to Lynn right away."

"Yes."

"Good. I told her when I talked to her that I was hiring a detective, and I gave her your name as the probable man. She'll be expecting you."

He wrote me a retainer check, and I told him I would be in touch as soon as I had anything to report, and he showed me out. The check was for two hundred dollars, my daily rate; I took it out and looked at it again in the elevator on the way down. It made me feel a little more cheerful than I was when I got there.

2

LYNN CANALE lived in one of the apartment buildings in Park-merced, near the San Francisco State College campus where she was a student. She had moved out of her father's house in the Forest Hill district two years ago, when she first entered school; Canale had told me on the phone earlier that she was strong-willed and self-sufficient, and that she had insisted on being on her own, rather than living at home, while she pursued a bachelor's degree in history. He had tried to talk her into moving back home with him when he found out about the calls, but she had refused. Stubbornness and a highly developed sense of pride were two other facets of her personality, Canale had said. I suspected she'd inherited them from him.

She had received the first call two weeks ago. There had been two others the first week, and since then she'd been getting them almost daily. She hadn't told her father about the calls until three days ago and then reluctantly, when he pressed her because she seemed tense and nervous at a family dinner. She hadn't offered any details of what the caller said to her; all she would say was that he made lewd suggestions and that his tone of voice frightened her.

I parked my car on Grijalva Drive, just down the street from

Lynn's building. She lived in 3–C, and she buzzed me in immediately when I identified myself on the intercom above her mailbox in the entrance alcove. When I went upstairs to 3–C I found that she was a slim, graceful girl with the fine-boned face that attracts fashion photographers and portrait painters. She had thick brown hair, worn long and straight, and brownish-gold eyes under long natural lashes; the eyes told me she was as worried as her father, even though she was trying not to show it. She wore white slacks and a dark blue tunic.

The living room she led me into was small and over-furnished, so that it had a cramped feel. The window drapes were open, and the room was brightly lit by sunshine and by a hammered-brass curio lamp. Books and papers were scattered on a writing desk and on an old mohair sofa that looked as though it had come out of somebody's attic.

A little apologetically, she said, "I hope you don't mind the mess. I've been trying to study."

I thought about my flat, with the dirty dishes and the pulp magazines I collect strewn around, the dust-mice under the furniture; her apartment, compared to the home of a slob like me, was immaculate. "Not at all," I said. "Are you alone, Miss Canale? Your father said someone was staying with you."

"Someone is. Connie Evans, a friend from school. But she had a ten o'clock class, and this is the week final exams start for the fall semester."

"Will she be coming back?"

"Yes." She gave me a faintly defiant look. "I don't mind being alone, you know."

I didn't say anything.

"Well," she said. "Sit down, won't you?"

I sat in an armchair opposite the sofa; it was not very comfortable, but it was better than the only other places to sit—a couple of beanbag chairs. Lynn asked me if I wanted some coffee, and I said no, nothing. Then she sat on the sofa, tucked her legs under her and regarded me solemnly.

"I'm not sure this is a good idea," she said.

"What do you mean?"

"My father hiring a detective. I mean, lots of women get obscene telephone calls, don't they?"

"Yes," I said. "But in most cases, the calls don't keep coming as frequently as you've been receiving them."

"I'm not afraid," she said. "He's just a crank."

"Are you certain of that?"

She averted her eyes. "Oh, God, I wish he'd just go away and leave me alone."

"Maybe I can see to it that he does. Will you tell me about the calls?"

"Not what he says, no. I won't repeat that filth."

"Sexual suggestions, that sort of thing?"

"Yes. In great detail. It made my skin crawl, the first time I heard it."

"Has he threatened you at any time?"

"Not in so many words."

"Implied threats?"

"Yes. The things he wanted to do to me . . . well, they involved pain. You know, S and M stuff."

"Yeah," I said. "I know."

"He's an animal. Just . . . an animal."

"Is his voice at all familiar to you?"

"No."

"You're sure you've never heard it in person?"

"I'm sure," Lynn said.

"Is there anything distinctive about it? An accent, a lisp, anything like that?"

"Well, it sounds sort of adolescent . . . you know, high-pitched. And muffled, as if it's coming from a long way off."

"That might mean he's trying to disguise it," I said.

"I know, I've thought of that."

"Because if he didn't, you'd recognize who he was."

She pursed her lips. "My father thinks he's one of my friends. Is that what you think, too?"

"I don't know enough to think anything yet. But you did have your number changed yesterday; and you did get another call last night."

"I can't account for that," she said. "I don't *know* how he got my new number, or why he's doing this to me. All I know is, I want him to *stop*."

I let a few seconds pass in silence; any more reassurances or solicitous comments would only have sounded empty. Or fatherly, which might be worse. When I spoke again I made my voice gentle. "How many people did you give the new number to?"

"Not many," she said. She sounded calm again. "My father. Connie. Larry. Tim Downs—"

"Wait, now. One at a time. Who would Larry be?"

"Larry Travers, my fiancé. We plan to be married in June."

"Congratulations. Have you known him long?"

"We met three months ago. He was going with Connie at the time, but I didn't know her very well then, not until after they broke up and Larry and I started dating. Anyhow, it didn't take long for both of us to know that . . . well, that we were in love."

"Does he also attend S.F. State?"

"No. U.C. He's a phys-ed major."

U.C. was the University of California, across the bay in Berkeley.

"Does he live in the East Bay?" I asked.

"No. Here in the city. On Potrero Hill."

"I'll need the address, if you don't mind."

She told me a number on Missouri Street and I wrote it down in my notebook. "You mentioned someone named Tim Downs," I said then. "Who would he be?"

"A friend of Larry's."

"Also a student at U.C.?"

"No. He's an apprentice plumber. He lives near Larry and he's a sports nut; that's how they became friends. Larry is a sports nut, too."

"Why did you give Downs your unlisted number?"

"Because he's Larry's friend."

"Did he ask you for it?"

"No. He and Larry stopped over last night, on their way to another Super Bowl party; Larry wanted me to go along, but I had studying to do. While they were here I gave Larry the new number, and Tim, too, because he was standing right there."

I asked her where Downs lived and where he worked, and she told me. Then I said, "Is there anyone else you gave the new number to?"

"No."

"Has anyone else been here besides Connie Evans? Anyone who might have seen the number on the phone itself?"

"No, I haven't had any . . . wait, yes I have. Joel Reeves stopped by yesterday while the man from the phone company was here. He only stayed a couple of minutes—Joel, I mean— but he might have noticed the number."

"This Reeves is a friend of yours?"

"Yes. Well, an acquaintance. He's a T.A. in the History Department at State."

"T.A.?"

"Teaching assistant. A graduate student who assists the professors. He lives in this building, up in Five–E."

"Why did he stop by yesterday?"

"He wanted to borrow a book of mine on Victorian poetry. The Victorian era is Joel's primary historical interest."

"Has he ever indicated any romantic interest in you?"

She laughed. "Joel? My God, no. All he cares about is history and old books."

"The serviceman from the telephone company," I said. "Had you ever seen him before yesterday?"

"No, never."

"Do you know anyone who works in the phone company?"

"No. You don't think—"

The door buzzer sounded. Lynn glanced at her wristwatch and said, "That's probably Connie. She said she'd be back after her exam."

It was Connie. "What time is it?" I heard her ask when Lynn let her into the foyer. "My damn watch stopped again."

"Five of one. You don't have another class today, do you?"

"No. I want to catch 'Another World.' " She sounded relieved, as if missing an episode of a TV soap opera would have been a major blow to her. "The exam lasted longer than I expected."

"How do you think you did?"

"Not too bad." The two girls came into the living room, and Connie Evans and I saw each other for the first time. "Oh," she said. "You must be the detective Lynn's dad hired."

"Yes."

Lynn introduced us, and Connie came over and shook my hand somberly. She was about Lynn's age, not as attractive, with dark blond hair cut short, a Cupid's-bow mouth and a somewhat harried expression. Levi's and an S.F. State sweat shirt covered her angular body.

She asked me, "Do you really think you can find out who's making those calls to Lynn?"

"I'm going to try," I said.

"Well, if there's anything I can do to help. . . ."

"I do have a couple of questions."

"Sure. Let me get a Coke first, okay? I'm dying of thirst."

"You and your Coke," Lynn said.

Connie disappeared into the kitchen. I asked Lynn, "Does anyone else beside you have a key to this apartment?"

"No, no one."

"Not even your fiancé?"

Faint color came into her cheeks; in this permissive age, it was nice to see that young girls could still blush. "Of course not," she said. "Larry and I don't have that kind of relationship."

Connie came back drinking from a can of Coca-Cola, walking with her eyes closed and her head tilted back; only young people seemed able to perform that little trick without stumbling into something. When she lowered the can I asked her, "Did you give Lynn's new unlisted number to anyone?"

"No," she said. "Absolutely not."

"Did you mention to anyone that she had a new number?"

"No."

"Did you happen to call her for any reason while you were with someone else?"

"No. I've been here most of the time since—"

And the telephone rang.

The sudden sound of the bell had an effect on all three of us. Lynn bit at her lower lip. I stiffened. Connie had been lifting the can of Coke; she froze with it halfway to her mouth.

The thing rang again. Lynn said, "It's probably Larry. Or my father." She went over to where the telephone sat on a driftwood stand; I followed her. She hesitated, and then, as it rang a third time, she caught up the receiver and said, "Hello?"

She didn't say anything else. Her face went white; a little sound came out of her throat that was half-gasp and half-moan. I plucked the receiver out of her hand. But I did not get to hear anything except a whirring click, then the buzzing of an empty line.

In a hushed voice Connie said, "Was it him?"

Lynn nodded convulsively as I cradled the handset.

"What did he say?" I asked her.

She shook her head; the fear in her eyes made them look enormous.

"Lynn, what did he say?"

"He said. . . ." The words seemed to catch in her throat; it was a few seconds before she could get them out. "He said he's going to kill me."

3

I SPENT another couple of minutes in Lynn's apartment—the only other thing the caller had said was that if he couldn't have her, nobody would—and then left her with Connie Evans. Maybe the threat was meaningless, just another element of verbal abuse; but the bastard might also be crazy enough to mean it. There was just no way of telling yet. But it was my job to treat it as the real thing, and I felt a sense of urgency. The feeling was enhanced by the fact that talking to Jud Canale about the call, and about what protective measures he might want to take, would have to wait; he had told me he would be in court all afternoon.

I took the elevator up to the fifth floor, found apartment 5–E and rapped on the door. Pretty soon a voice said from inside, "Yes?"

"Joel Reeves?"

"Yes. Who are you?"

I told him who I was, and what I did for a living, and that I was investigating the anonymous calls Lynn Canale had been receiving.

Reeves said, "Oh, well, just a second," and the lock snicked free and the door opened on a chain. "I'd like to see some identification, please."

I showed him the photostat of my investigator's license. He studied it pretty good, and when he was finished doing that he studied me for a couple of seconds. Then, satisfied, he took the chain off and let me come in.

"Cautious, aren't you?" I said as he closed and relocked the door.

"We've had burglaries in this building. And I own some valuable books."

He was in his mid-to-late twenties, dumpy, weak-chinned, with sparse black hair and watery green eyes behind Ben Franklin glasses. He had a studious, preoccupied air about him—the kind of kid who would grow into a tweedy, middle-aged stereotype of the college professor. Or so it seemed on the surface, anyway.

His apartment was similar in size and layout to Lynn's, except that the windows faced west, toward Lake Merced and the Harding Park golf course. It was neatly if unimaginatively furnished, with filled bookcases dominating two of the walls in the living room.

When Reeves led me in there, I noticed the titles on a couple of the books. They brought me over to the cases for a closer look.

Nearly all of the books were from or about Victorian England; Lynn had told me Reeves was a budding Victorian scholar. But what she hadn't told me was that one of his particular interests was Victorian erotica. At least two shelves were jammed with such pornographic novels and "confessions" as *My Secret Life, May's Account of Her Introduction to the Art of Love, A Night in a Moorish Harem, Venus in India* and *The Amatory Experiences of a Surgeon;* several bound volumes, dated 1879 and 1880, of an underground sex journal called *The Pearl;* and more than a dozen contemporary references, some scholarly and some designed to titillate.

I turned to face Reeves. "Nice collection of books you've got there," I said.

"Thank you. Some are quite rare."

"The erotica, for instance?"

"Oh, yes. Those bound volumes of *The Pearl* are worth . . . well, they're quite valuable."

"How do you happen to have them?"

"I bought them in London last summer." He gave me a prideful smile. "At auction. I outbid several antiquarian book dealers for them."

"You must be well off financially."

"What? Oh, no—not at all. My father left me a small inheritance when he died seven years ago, enough to put me through school and to finance the London trip and the book purchases."

"Then you must have wanted those volumes of *The Pearl* pretty badly."

"I did," Reeves said. "They don't generally turn up for sale."

I moved away from the bookcase. "Aren't you a little young to be so interested in erotica?"

"Young?" He blinked at me owlishly behind his Ben Franklin glasses. "What does age have to do with a person's interest in history?"

"Is that why you collect sex books—because of historical curiosity?"

"Of course. And for research purposes. The same reasons I collect Victoriana of all types. I'm doing my master's dissertation on popular and underground Victorian literature."

"Uh-huh," I said. But I was thinking that Lynn was an attractive young woman, and Reeves was an unattractive young man whose interest in erotica may or may not have been purely academic. He also seemed to be the obsessive type, judging from what he had told me about those volumes of *The Pearl;* if that type of man wanted a woman and knew he could never have her, and if he was a little unbalanced to begin with, he might take the obscene-phone-call route.

Reeves said, "Has Lynn had more of those calls? Is that why you've been hired?"

"Two more. One last night, one this morning. The last one wasn't obscene; it was threatening."

"Threatening?"

"The man said he was going to kill her."

Reeves looked shocked. "Good Lord!"

"So I'm sure you can understand that I want to find out who he is as soon as possible."

"Yes, certainly. But I don't know how I can help."

"Just answer a few questions for me."

"Of course."

"Lynn said you dropped by her apartment yesterday, while the telephone serviceman was there. Did you happen to notice her new number?"

"No, I didn't."

"But you knew she was having a new phone put in?"

"Well, she didn't say so, but I assumed that was what the serviceman was doing there."

"How long did you stay?"

"Only a minute or so."

"Okay. A few other questions and I'll be on my way. Do you know Lynn's fiancé, Larry Travers?"

"I've met him, yes."

"What's your opinion of him?"

"I don't like the man," he said flatly.

"No? Why not?"

"He's arrogant and self-centered and not very bright. All he ever talks about are sports and how much beer he can drink without gaining weight. Lynn is intelligent and serious about her studies; I don't know how she could have chosen someone like Travers."

"Love is blind sometimes," I said.

He sighed. "Yes. So it is."

"Do you know a friend of Travers' named Tim Downs?"

"No, I don't think so. May I ask why you're so concerned with people Lynn knows? Surely you don't believe the man on the phone is one of her friends?"

"There's a good possibility he might be. The only people she gave her new number to are friends. And she's had those two calls since the new phone was installed yesterday."

"I see." He sighed again. "Poor Lynn. She must be very upset."

"She's bearing up. Connie Evans is staying with her."

"Oh yes, the computer woman."

"Pardon?"

"A computer science major." Reeves made a wry mouth. "I don't like computer science," he said.

"Why is that?"

"It's cold, dehumanizing. Computers, *machines,* are symptomatic of what's wrong with today's world; in fact, they may be at the root of the problem. That's why I prefer the past. It may be imperfect, but I would much rather have lived a century ago than today. And I would much rather live today than a century from now; the probable shape of the future horrifies me."

"Maybe it won't turn out as badly as you think," I said.

"Yes, it will. It certainly will."

I gave him one of my business cards, just in case, and then left him and left the building to pick up my car. The way it looked now, there were only three people on the list of suspects—Reeves, Larry Travers and Tim Downs. But would it stay narrowed down to those three?

I went looking for Travers and Downs, to find out.

4

POTRERO HILL was an older section of the city, built on one of San Francisco's forty-three hills—residential on its upper slopes, industrial down at the base. It had become a fashionable "in" place to live for the young and ambitious among the city's population; there were a lot of old Victorian houses up there, and the young people had begun buying and fixing them up. The appearance and tenor of the neighborhood had improved markedly in recent years.

The address Lynn had given me for Larry Travers was a Stick-style Victorian—one of the tall, vertical row houses that had been the dominant architectural style in the 1880's. It had a false front adorned with a "French" cap, and it had been painted recently in two not very harmonious shades of blue. It also had a *Flat for Rent* sign, with the name of a Mission Street realtor on it, on the garage door under the big, rectangular bay window.

The pair of mailboxes on the porch told me that the building had been divided into two flats and that the upper floor belonged to Travers. I pushed the button alongside his name, listened to the bell ring inside. There was no response. And none when I rang the bell a second time either.

So maybe he was still in school; it was only three-thirty. But that *Flat for Rent* sign had me curious. I poked the bell beside the name on the second mailbox, Rodriguez, and pretty soon a thin, middle-aged woman opened the door to the downstairs flat. The look she gave me was full of annoyance.

"They only put the damn sign up an hour ago," she said.

"Ma'am?"

"The realtors. I told 'em people would start bothering me, even though it says right on the sign 'Do Not Disturb Residents,' and they said oh no, don't worry, that won't happen. Hah. It didn't even take an hour for it to happen." She glared at me. "Don't you read what it says on signs, mister?"

"I'm not here about the flat," I said.

"No? Then what do you want? If you're selling something, we don't want any."

"I'm not selling anything. I'm looking for Larry Travers."

"Oh," the woman said. "Well, I don't know if he's still here or not."

"Still here?"

"I saw him moving some of his stuff out this morning, but I don't know if he took it all. Maybe he'll be back."

"It's the upstairs flat that's for rent, then? Travers' flat?"

"Sure. My husband and me, we been here twenty-five years, and we'll be here another twenty-five if the government don't starve us out or blow us up."

"Do you know where Travers is moving to?"

"I didn't ask him. I don't care where he's going."

"Hasn't he been a good neighbor?"

"Too many loud parties," Mrs. Rodriguez said. "Different girls, booze, noise until all hours. Probably dope, too, for all I know."

"You mean he's brought different girls here himself, or his friends have?"

"Who knows? They came and they went; sometimes they stayed all night. Orgies, that's what he's been having up there, right over my head. I'm a respectable woman, I go to church, I pay taxes, I shouldn't have to listen to orgies in the middle of the night."

"Did you talk to Travers about these wild parties?"

"Sure, I talked to him, my husband and me both. He told us to mind our own business, the young snot. So we called the cops on him, twice, but what good did it do? The cops came and the party stopped, they went away and it started right up again. You'd think the cops could break up an orgy so decent people could get their sleep, wouldn't you?"

"Yes, ma'am."

"Cops," Mrs. Rodriguez said, and shook her head. Then a thought seemed to strike her and she frowned warily. "Say, *you're* not a cop, are you?"

"No, I'm not."

"Good. How come you're looking for Travers?"

"A private matter."

"Huh," she said. "He in some sort of trouble?"

"I don't know. Probably not."

"Well, it wouldn't surprise me if he was. Kids nowadays, they got no respect for nothing, not even the law. If you ask me—"

"Thanks for your help, Mrs. Rodriguez," I said, and left her standing there with her mouth open.

On the way back to my car, I did some wondering about Larry Travers. The fact that he was in the process of moving out of his flat didn't have to mean anything; people move every day for a hundred different reasons. But it seemed odd that Lynn hadn't mentioned it when she gave me his address. Maybe Travers hadn't got around to telling her about the move yet; but that was odd, too, if so. He and Lynn were engaged. Why wouldn't he tell her he was moving?

Mrs. Rodriguez's diatribe about loud parties didn't have to mean anything either. The testimony of a complainer and a busybody wasn't always reliable, and the way she had kept using the word "orgy" made exaggeration another of her faults. Still, there was probably a fair amount of truth in what she'd told me. So was Travers playing around on Lynn Canale or wasn't he?

The one person besides Travers who could give me the answer to that question figured to be Tim Downs. He might still be at work, but I seemed to remember that plumbers quit for the day at three-thirty. I decided to try his home first because it was closer than LeCosta Plumbing and Heating, over on Harrison, where Lynn had told me Downs worked.

I drove up to De Haro. The building Downs lived in was also a Stick-style Victorian, in a somewhat shabbier state of repair, and like the one on Missouri it sat near the top of a steep hill; it would command a nice view of the city from its rear windows. I parked down the block, trudged uphill and climbed onto the porch.

Downs had the main-floor flat, and he didn't have it alone; a second name was written below his on the mailbox card; Pam Scott. Girlfriend, probably. I rang the bell. No answer here either. I was just about to start back down the steps when a dark-green Toyota pulled into the driveway below and a young guy dressed in a soiled work uniform and carrying a lunch pail got out.

He gave me a curious glance and then mounted the stairs, taking his time about it. He was a big kid, mid-twenties, built like a football player. His black hair hung to his shoulders, curling up on the ends, and he wore one of those bushy mustache-and-sideburns combinations that were popular back in the 1890s. Deep-set blue eyes studied me levelly when he reached the porch and stopped a couple of paces away.

"You looking for me?" he asked.

"I am if your name is Tim Downs."

"That's my name. What can I do for you?"

I told him who I was and more or less why I was there; I also showed him my license photostat. Nothing much changed in his blue eyes. He wasn't impressed one way or another. "Who hired you?" he asked. "Lynn's old man?"

"Yes."

"Yeah, that figures. He's the type."

"What type is that?"

"The Establishment type. Always overreacting."

"Why do you think he's overreacting?"

"Lots of women get obscene telephone calls," Downs said. "It's no big deal. San Francisco is full of creeps."

"Lots of women don't have their life threatened," I said.

"Is that straight? The guy threatened Lynn?"

"This morning. He said he was going to kill her."

"Christ. You think he means it?"

"Maybe. There's no way to tell without knowing who he is. You wouldn't have any ideas, would you?"

He shook his head. And then he scowled and said, "Why ask me? I don't know anything about those calls."

"You're a friend of Lynn's, aren't you?"

"So? She's got a lot of friends."

"She had her phone number changed yesterday. Except for her father, you and Larry Travers are the only ones she gave the new number to."

"What the hell?" he said. There was hostility in his voice now, in the set of his voice now, in the set of his mouth. "You think maybe I'm the one who called her up and threatened her?"

"Did I say that? I don't have any ideas about you one way or another; all I'm here for is to ask you some questions. You don't have to answer them if you don't want to."

"What questions?"

"Did you give Lynn's new phone number to anyone?"

"No. Why should I?"

"Are you sure?"

"Sure, I'm sure. I didn't even tell Pam."

"Who's Pam?"

"Pam Scott, the lady I live with."

"Do you know if Travers gave the number to anyone?"

"No. Ask him, why don't you?"

"I stopped by his flat before I came here. He wasn't home."

"Yeah, well, he's been busy lately."

"There's a *Flat for Rent* sign on his building," I said. "The woman who lives below him said he's moving out."

"That's right, he is."

"Where to? Another place here in the city?"

Downs hesitated. "No. He's splitting."

"You mean he's leaving San Francisco?"

"This coming weekend, yeah."

"Where's he going?"

"San Diego."

"Why? He decide to change schools, or what?"

"Not exactly. He dropped out of U.C. at the end of last semester;

he may stay out until the fall, sign up at San Diego State. It all depends."

"On what?"

"On whether this deal he's got going works out."

"What deal?"

Downs hesitated again. Then he shrugged and said, "Him and another guy are taking a boat down to Dago for the guy's old man. Guy he met over in Berkeley. The old man bought the boat when he was up here over Christmas, had it put in for some minor repairs; he owns a bunch of boats down south. Larry figures maybe he can get a regular job with him."

"Does Lynn know about this deal?"

Another shrug. "Maybe Larry didn't tell her yet. Ask him."

"He didn't tell her he'd dropped out of school either, did he? Or that he was leaving San Francisco?"

"So he hasn't told her, so what?"

"He's engaged to marry the girl."

"Yeah, sure," Downs said, and grinned crookedly.

"What does that mean? He isn't going to marry her?"

"Larry's not the marrying type."

"No? Then why the hell did he get engaged to her?"

"Come on, man, why do you think?"

"You tell me."

"You met her, didn't you? She's a nice kid, but a little square; she's got old-fashioned ideas. Getting engaged was the only way Larry could score with her."

Anger clotted my throat; I didn't trust myself to speak for a moment. Some sweet guy, this Larry Travers. A girl like Lynn won't go to bed with him, so he tells her he loves her, promises to marry her and strings her along until he's had enough of her and her body. Then he drops her, shatters her dreams and away he goes without giving her another thought. A bum like that was capable of just about anything. Including a series of obscene and threatening telephone calls, for whatever warped reason of his own.

What I was thinking must have been plain on my face. Downs said, "Hey, man, why get so uptight about it? Lynn'll get over it; they always do. It's no big deal."

"It's a big deal to me, sonny."

His jaw tightened. "Don't call me sonny."

"I'll call you any damn thing I feel like calling you. Where can I find Travers?"

He glared at me without answering. I glared right back at him. He was half my age and in better physical shape, but the way I felt right now, I was ready to beat the crap out of him and Travers both. Maybe he saw that in my face, too; or maybe he just didn't feel like mixing it up with anybody on his front stoop. His eyes shifted away from me, and he muttered something under his breath and started past me to the front door.

I blocked his way. "I asked you a question. Where can I find Travers?"

"How should I know?"

"Where does he hang out when he's not home?"

"I don't have to answer your questions, man—"

"Not mine, maybe. How about the police?"

"You can't put the cops on me. I ain't done anything. . . ."

"I can and I will. I used to be a cop myself; I've still got friends on the force. Now, do you want to tell me where Travers hangs out or don't you?"

He muttered something else under his breath that I didn't catch. Then he said, tight-mouthed and sullen, "Elrod's, on Eighteenth and Connecticut. He's there most days around five."

"He still living in his flat or not?"

"Some nights. Other nights he spends on the boat."

"Where?"

"China Basin. The Basin Boatyard."

"What's the name of the boat?"

"The *Hidalgo*."

"All right," I said. "If you talk to Travers before I do, tell him I'm looking for him. Tell him I think he's one of those creeps San Francisco is full of."

I brushed by Downs and clumped down the stairs. And I didn't look back.

5

ELROD'S WAS a neighborhood tavern that had been outfitted to resemble an English pub—British and Irish beer signs on the walls, a couple of dart boards, a big fireplace with some logs blazing inside. From the look of the twenty or so patrons, it catered to the under-thirty crowd and was probably what passed for a singles bar on Potrero Hill. I was the oldest person in there by at least ten years.

The bartender was a young guy with a bright red beard. I ordered a pint of Bass ale and then asked him if he knew Larry Travers. Sure, he said, but Larry hadn't come in yet today. A great guy, Larry. Drank beer like it was going out of style; drank beer for *breakfast,* once poured some on a bowl of cereal to prove it. A hell of a guy.

Yeah, I thought. A hell of a guy.

A dollar tip got the bartender to agree to point Travers out to me if he showed up. Then I took my ale into a telephone booth at the rear and called Tellmark, Graham, Canale and Isaacs. Jud Canale was back from court and in his office—it was almost five o'clock—and he came on the line immediately.

"A couple of things to report," I said, "neither of them good." I told him about the call to Lynn this morning, the threat against her life. And I told him what I'd found out about Larry Travers. The only thing I didn't tell him was the reason why Travers had pretended to want to marry Lynn; I just said he'd been seeing other women all along and was backing out of the marriage by running off to San Diego. Lynn Canale's sex life was her own business, not her father's.

Canale let me tell it straight through without interrupting. When I was finished he said in a thin, angry voice, "Have you talked to Travers yet?"

"Not yet. I haven't been able to find him. I will, though. I'm calling from a place where he hangs out; he's liable to show up here sooner or later."

"Did you tell Lynn what you found out?"

"No. I didn't think it was my place."

"You're right, it isn't. It's mine. I'll drive over and talk to her right away."

"Whatever you think best, Mr. Canale."

He gave me his home phone number and asked me to call him again as soon as I talked to Travers. Then he rang off, and I went back to the bar and found a place to sit where I could watch the entrance. The place was full now and getting fuller—a more or less even mix of male and female kids in their twenties. I felt out of place among them; I felt old and anachronistic, a product of a different world that they could never really understand, anymore than I could really understand theirs. Several of them gave me curious glances, and the look on one girl's face said that she was wondering if I might be a pervert. It might have been funny in other circumstances. As it was, with Lynn Canale and Larry Travers on my mind, it wasn't funny at all. It was only sad.

Five-thirty came and went. So did a second pint of Bass ale. But Travers didn't come.

He still hadn't shown at six. I gave him another twenty minutes, until the crowd began to thin out for dinner and other activities, and when the bartender came over and shrugged and said, "I guess Larry's not coming in tonight," I decided it was time to call it quits. I paid my tab and went out into the early-evening darkness.

The wasted time had made me irritable, and the ale and the noise and smoky atmosphere of Elrod's had given me a headache. I didn't want food; I didn't want to go home yet. I was still fixated on Travers.

I took my car back to Missouri Street. And there was a light on in the Victorian's upper flat, Travers' flat, and parked in the driveway was a battered old Triumph TR–3. Well, well, I thought. The prodigal returns. But I couldn't find a goddamn parking space anywhere on the block, and I did not want to risk putting the car into somebody else's driveway. It took me a couple of minutes to locate a space a block and a half away.

When I came huffing and puffing up the hill, the upstairs light in Travers' flat had been put out. The sports car was still in the driveway, though, and I could see a guy loading something into its trunk. There was enough light from a nearby street lamp to tell me that he was big, blond and young. He heard me coming, glanced around and then straightened as I approached him.

"Larry Travers?"

"That's right. You're the detective, right?"

I nodded. "Your friend Downs tell you about me?"

"Yes." There was no hostility in his voice, as there had been in Downs's; he was playing it neutral. "I'm sorry you feel the way you do about me, I really am. But you just don't understand how things are."

"I understand how things are, all right," I said. "I also understand that somebody threatened Lynn Canale's life this afternoon. Or don't you care about that?"

"Sure, I care about it."

"How about her? Do you care about her?"

"Why do you think I don't? Because I'm moving to San Diego and I haven't told Lynn yet? That doesn't make me a bad guy; and it doesn't mean I'm trying to run out on her, or that we won't see each other again."

He sounded very earnest, and in the pale light from the street lamp his expression was guileless. He was a handsome kid: athletic build, boyish features, long blond hair and a neat blond mustache. But it was all on the surface. Inside, where it counted, he wasn't handsome at all.

I said, "Where were you at one o'clock this afternoon?"

"Why? Is that when Lynn got the threatening call?"

"Where were you?"

"I didn't make that call, if that's what you think," Travers said. "Lynn is special to me; the last thing in the world I want is to see her hurt. Why don't you go find out who did do it, instead of bothering me?"

I took a step toward him. "Answer my question, Travers. Where were you at one o'clock this afternoon?"

He didn't answer the question. Instead, he slammed the trunk lid, moved away from me to the driver's door and hauled it open. I went after him, but he was quick and agile; by the time I got around there, he was inside and he had the door shut again. He shoved the lock button down as I caught hold of the handle.

"Travers!"

But he wasn't listening. The starter whirred and the engine came to life; he ground gear teeth getting the transmission into reverse. I stepped back out of the way just before he released the clutch and took the Triumph, tires squealing, out into the street. A couple of seconds later, he was rocketing off down the hill. And a couple of seconds after that, he was gone.

There was no point in trying to follow him; my car was too far away. I swallowed my anger and made myself walk slowly down the steep sidewalk. Round one to Travers. But there would be a round two, and that one, by God, would be mine.

When I got to where I had left my car, I debated driving over to China Basin. But that might not be where Travers was headed; and, in any event, you couldn't get into a boatyard at night without a key or somebody letting you in. So I pointed the car in the opposite direction and went home to my flat in Pacific Heights. I had done enough for one day. As long as Lynn was in a safe place, Travers could wait until tomorrow.

I opened myself a beer, took it into the bedroom and dialed Jud Canale's home number. He wasn't in yet; there was a whirring click and I got his recorded voice on his answering machine. I left a brief message outlining my abortive talk with Travers and said I would get in touch again in the morning.

Dinner was leftover pizza and another beer. After which I took a 1935 issue of *Black Mask* off one of the shelves where I keep my collection of mystery and detective pulp magazines, and crawled into bed with it. I got halfway through an Erle Stanley Gardner story about Ed Jenkins, the Phantom Crook, but my head wasn't into it. I kept thinking about Lynn Canale, and about Travers, and about those calls.

I shut the light off finally and waited for my thoughts to wind down and sleep to come. I was still waiting two hours later. . . .

6

JUD CANALE got in touch with me in the morning, while I was having toast and coffee a few minutes past eight. He sounded tired and upset, and one of the reasons turned out to be that Lynn had refused to go home with him last night, or any night to come. She hadn't even spent the entire evening in her apartment; she had gone off with Connie Evans to a Drama Club meeting, because she said she couldn't stand staying cooped up. But she was all right so far. There hadn't been any more anonymous calls during the night, or any other disturbances. Canale had insisted that she phone him first thing this morning, to check in; she had done that a few minutes before he called me.

The second reason he was upset was that Lynn had also refused to accept the truth about Travers. Even if Travers had dropped out of U.C. and given up his apartment, even if he was going to take a boat to San Diego, even if he hadn't told her any of this yet, she was convinced he had his reasons and that he still loved her. She was certain he hadn't been fooling around with other women either. That sort of loyalty and trust was good to see in a young person like Lynn, but in this case it was tragically misplaced. When she did accept the truth, as she would have to sooner or later, it was going to go twice as hard for her. Love, like dreams and old beliefs, dies hard.

"What are you going to do about Travers?" Canale asked. "Talk to him again today?"

"Yes. I'm driving down to China Basin as soon as I finish my breakfast. Chances are he spent the night on the boat; he should still be there, this early."

"And if you can't get anything out of him? What then?"

"I don't know. I'll just have to play it by ear."

"All right. But tell him something for me, will you? Tell him if he ever tries to see Lynn again, I'll kill him."

"Look, Mr. Canale—"

"Tell him," Canale said, and rang off.

I didn't want any more toast and coffee; the conversation with Canale had taken away my appetite. I got my coat, went out and picked up my car, and headed crosstown to Third Street and the waterfront.

China Basin was on the southeast side of the city, at the foot of the Embarcadero and not all that far from Potrero Hill. Back in the 1860s, the long deep-water channel had been the place where the "China Clippers" of the Pacific Mail Steamship Line berthed; that was how it had got its name. Today, incoming and outgoing freighters tied up at the industrial docks there, and there were boatyards and a military shipyard, and a few small waterfront cafés where you could sit at outside tables and watch what was going on in the basin and on the bay beyond.

The Basin Boatyard was on Channel Street, just down from the Banana Terminal where freighters carrying tropical fruit from South America were once unloaded. There was a good deal of activity in the area: trucks coming and going, strings of freight cars maneuvering on the network of rail tracks. Mornings were always the busiest time along the waterfront. Parking was at a premium, but I managed to find a place to wedge my car—and when I neared the open boatyard gates on foot, I noticed a battered

black Triumph TR–3 dwarfed and half-hidden behind a massive
tractor-trailer rig. Travers was here, all right.

I went in through the open gates. The boatyard was fairly large,
cluttered with wooden buildings with corrugated-iron roofs, a rusty-
looking crane, a variety of boats in and out of the water, and a
couple of employees at their jobs. At the far end was a moorage—
a half-dozen slips extending into the basin on either side of a
rickety board float. About half of the slips were occupied.

A beefy guy dressed in paint-stained overalls intercepted me as
I started toward the moorage. "Something I can do for you,
mister?"

"I'm looking for Larry Travers," I said.

"Haven't seen him this morning."

"His car's out front. Maybe he's still sacked in on the *Hidalgo.*"

"You a friend of his?"

"No. I've got business with him."

The guy shrugged. "Been here before?"

"No."

"*Hidalgo's* the sloop-rigged centerboarder in the last slip out."

"Thanks."

I went the rest of the way to the moorage, out onto the board
float. The day was another clear one, not too cold in the sun or
in sheltered places; but out here, with the wind gusting in off the
bay, it was chilly enough to make me shiver inside my light coat.
I bunched the fabric at my throat, hunched my shoulders. Overhead, a seagull cut loose with its screaming laugh, as if mocking
me.

Until I came in sight of the *Hidalgo,* I had no idea what a
"sloop-rigged centerboarder" was. But it wasn't anything exotic—
just a thirty-foot, cruise-type sailboat, the kind with an auxiliary
inboard engine that makes it capable of an extended ocean passage.
It was made out of fiberglass, with aluminum spars, and it had
plenty of deck space and a low, squat cabin that would probably
sleep four below deck.

I caught hold of the aluminum siderail and swung onto the
deck aft. The fore cabin window was uncurtained, so I could see
that the cockpit was empty. I moved around to the companionway
that led below. A lamp burned down there; I could make out
part of two quarter-berths and not much else.

"Travers?" I called, and then identified myself. "I want to talk
to you."

No answer.

I called his name again; the only answer I got this time was another cry from a passing gull. All right, I thought. I went down the companion ladder, into the living quarters below.

There was plenty of space, and all of it seemed to be deserted. On the port side, I saw a good-sized galley complete with sink, icebox, and stove, and ample locker space for food and utensils; to starboard opposite, there was an enclosed toilet and a hanging locker. A galley table set up between the two quarter-berths was littered with the remains of a McDonald's fast-food supper, some empty beer bottles and soft drink cans. And up forward, separated from the rest of the cabin by a bulkhead and curtain, were what figured to be the two remaining berths; I couldn't see in there because the curtain was drawn.

A vague, tingly feeling started up on the back of my neck. It was a sensation I'd had too many times before—a premonitory feeling of wrongness. I stayed where I was for several seconds, but it did not go away.

"Travers?"

Silence.

I took a breath, and my legs worked and carried me over to the forward bulkhead. I was still holding my breath when I swept the curtain aside; then my stomach kicked and the air came out between my teeth in a flat, hissing sound.

Travers hadn't gone anywhere; he would never go anywhere again. He was lying back-sprawled on the rumpled port-side bunk, one leg hanging off to the deck. Just above his right cheekbone was a blackened hole caked with dried blood. The gun that had evidently killed him was a .38 caliber Smith & Wesson automatic; it was in his right hand, with his fingers lax around it.

So it looked as though he'd shot himself—maybe because he was the caller who'd been deviling Lynn Canale and his conscience had got the better of him, maybe for some other reason. It looked like a simple case of suicide.

But I didn't believe it for a minute.

It was a case of murder, and it wasn't simple at all.

I CALLED the Hall of Justice from a phone in the boatyard office. The man I asked for was Lieutenant Eberhardt, probably my best friend on or off the force, but it was his day off; I had to settle for potluck. It worked out all right, though, because one of the two Homicide inspectors who showed up was Jack Logan, whom I also knew.

He listened to my story, more or less sympathetically, and to my speculation that Travers had not died by his own hand: "The kid just wasn't the type to kill himself, Jack; he was too arrogant, too wrapped up in himself. And even if he was the type, he wouldn't have bothered to move out of his flat, make all his plans for the trip to San Diego, if he was going to do the Dutch." But Logan was a methodical cop, and he wasn't making any judgments of his own until he had all the facts. Not the least of which, he said, was a nitrate test on Travers' hand to determine whether or not he had fired the .38 automatic.

Logan had gone back aboard the *Hidalgo* to confer again with the assistant coroner and the lab boys, and I was standing out on the float, when Jud Canale got there. I had called Canale's office right after notifying the police, and he'd said he would come right down. His only reaction to the news of Travers' death had been to say, grimly, that the circumstances being what they were, he wasn't sorry to hear it.

The patrolman standing guard at the shore end of the moorage had been given Canale's name and let him pass. I went ahead to meet Canale halfway; I wanted a few words alone with him before he talked to the inspectors.

"Mr. Canale," I said, "how long did you stay at your daughter's apartment last night?"

He squinted at me. The wind had picked up and it was sharp enough to make his eyes water. "What does that have to do with anything?"

"Just answer the question, please."

"I was there until about six-thirty," he said.

"Then what?"

"I went home."

"You weren't home when I called your house at a quarter to eight."

"I stopped for a couple of drinks on the way; I felt I needed them." He bent toward me, putting his face close to mine, intruding on my space again. "Why do you want to know where I was last night?"

I did not back away from him this time. "The assistant coroner says rigor mortis has already come and gone in Travers' body; he thinks Travers was shot sometime last evening. Before midnight."

"My God, do you think *I* shot him? I thought you told me he'd killed himself."

"I said it looked that way. But it wasn't suicide, Mr. Canale; it was murder."

"How do you know that?"

"I don't know it; I suspect it."

"Why would anyone murder Travers?"

"You've got a pretty good motive, for one," I said. "You told me this morning to tell him that if he ever went near Lynn again, *you'd* kill him."

"I didn't mean that literally. I was angry."

I just looked at him.

"Besides, I said that to you this morning. Why would I do that if I'd already shot Travers last night?"

"Smoke screen, maybe. To make you look innocent."

Canale made a disgusted sound. "This is ridiculous," he said, and gave me his courtroom stare. "I did not kill Larry Travers. I don't suppose that satisfies you, but it happens to be the truth."

"The ones you want to satisfy are the police," I said. "They'll be asking you the same questions pretty soon."

He'd had enough of me for the time being; he sidestepped me and went down to the *Hidalgo.* I watched him stop abaft of the boat and stand there stiff-backed against the wind, and I wondered if he was guilty after all. There was no question that he had a good motive—but then, he wasn't the only one. Somebody else had the same motive, just as strong and maybe stronger.

His daughter, the woman Travers had been about to run out on.

It was a little past noon before Logan gave me permission to leave the boatyard. Canale was still there; I asked him if he wanted me to continue my investigation into the calls, and he said, a little stiffly, that he hadn't decided yet, he wanted to see whether the police turned up anything that might identify Travers as the caller. I told him I would be available if he still wanted me.

I drove downtown to the building on Taylor Street where I have my office. A cup of coffee seemed like a good idea, so I took the office pot into the little side alcove, filled it from the sink there, and brought it back and put it on the hot plate.

While I waited for the water to boil I switched on my answering machine. There had been only one call, but whoever it was had hung up without leaving a message; some people do not care to talk to machines, not that I blame them much. I shut the thing off and started to go through my mail.

Machines. . . .

And then I just sat there. Things had begun to happen inside my head. My mental processes worked that way; if you tossed enough scraps of information, enough impressions and other factors, into my subconscious, sooner or later something would act as a catalyst and they would start to connect up. And pretty soon the answer to whatever case or problem I was working on would emerge.

It took me fifteen minutes and most of a cup of coffee to get the answer to this one. And when I had it, it turned me cold and a little scared. I told myself that I could be wrong, that I might be misinterpreting the facts. But I wasn't wrong, any more than I was wrong about Larry Travers' death being murder and not suicide.

I knew who had shot Travers, and I knew who had made all those phone calls to Lynn Canale.

The proper thing to do was to call the police. But I had no proof; all I had were circumstantial evidence, and supposition, and the burning hunch that I was right. Calling Jack Logan, explaining it all to him, would take time . . . and maybe I didn't have much time. For all I knew—and this was what scared me— I might already be too late.

I hurried out of the office and out of the building, got my car and took it as fast as I dared out Highway 280 and into Parkmerced. In the foyer of Lynn Canale's building, I punched the doorbell button beside her name. But her voice didn't come over the intercom; nobody anwered the bell.

That made me a little panicky. I pushed the button for 5–E, kept my finger on it. Joel Reeves was home, and when I identified myself and told him to let me in, he obeyed without question.

I took the stairs to the third floor, half-running, so that I was winded by the time I got to Lynn's door. I tried the knob; locked.

Then I banged on the door, loudly, and called Lynn's name. All that got me was a woman poking her head out of a door down the hall and demanding to know what I thought I was doing. I told her I was a cop, to save time, and asked her if she'd seen Lynn today; she said she hadn't.

I turned back to 3-C. Breaking the door down was an extreme measure; there did not have to be anything wrong inside. It occurred to me that someone on the premises might have a passkey, a building superintendent, somebody like that. I was just about to ask the woman when the door to the stairwell opened and Joel Reeves appeared.

"I thought this was where you'd gone," he said. "What's going on?"

"Where's Lynn? Have you seen her?"

"A little while ago, yes; downstairs in the lobby. I was just coming back from school and she was on the way out. She seemed very upset—"

"Was she alone?"

"No. Connie Evans was with her."

"Did either of them say where they were going?"

Reeves shook his head. He could see the alarm in my face and he was frowning behind his Ben Franklin glasses. "But Lynn was carrying an overnight case," he said.

"Where does Connie Evans live?"

"Somewhere in the Sunset district, I think. Out near the Great Highway. Why are you so upset? Lynn's safe with Connie, isn't she?"

I ran for the stairwell without answering him. The hell Lynn was safe with Connie; the hell she was.

Connie Evans was both the anonymous caller and the person who had murdered Larry Travers.

8

THE DIRECTORY in a public telephone booth near Lynn's building contained a listing for a C. Evans on Forty-seventh Avenue. That was the only C. Evans in the Sunset district, and the only Evans near the Great Highway. I had to take the chance that it was the right one; the address was only fifteen minutes from Parkmerced.

I barreled my car around the edge of the lake and down Sloat Boulevard past the zoo. Despite the fact that Forty-seventh Avenue was the closest residential street to Ocean Beach, it wasn't a particularly desirable neighborhood in which to live; the weather was foggy a good part of the time, and when the sea wind blew heavily it swept sand across the Great Highway, which paralleled the beach for several miles, and slapped it against the building faces. It was like living in a sandblast zone, some days.

The address for C. Evans was an old-fashioned, shingled cottage tucked back between a two-unit apartment building and a crumbling stucco row house. There was a car parked in front; I pulled up behind it, blocking the row house driveway, and the hell with that. I pushed through a sagging gate, climbed onto a front porch littered with dying plants and rang the bell.

Nothing happened for several seconds. The palms of my hands were sweaty and my stomach was knotted with tension. I reached out to ring the bell again—and the door opened and Connie Evans stood there looking at me.

"Oh," she said in a dull voice, "hello. What do you—"

I hit the door with my shoulder, not lightly; it smacked into her, sent her backpedaling into the middle of the room. I went in and shut the door and glanced around. Living room. And we were the only two people in it.

"Where's Lynn?"

Evans stood rubbing her arm where the door had hit it. Her expression was as dull as her voice had been. Under her eyes were smudges so dark they looked like lampblack smeared on skin that was pale white, almost translucent. There was a zombielike quality about her, as if she had lost some of her grasp on reality.

I moved up close to her. "Answer me. Where's Lynn?"

"In the bedroom."

Two doors led off the living room. One was open and through it I could see part of the kitchen; the other one was closed. I hurried over to the closed one, opened it and went into a short hallway. The bedroom was at the far end, at the rear of the house.

The drapes had been drawn in there and the room was dim; Lynn Canale was a small, still mound under a quilted comforter on the bed. But she stirred when I pulled the comforter down and lifted one of her arms to check her pulse; and the pulse was strong and steady. I let out a relieved breath. Lynn moaned softly as I lowered her arm; she rolled onto her back, but she didn't wake up. Her face appeared puffy, the lips dry and cracked.

I covered her again and returned to the living room. Connie Evans was sitting curled up in an ancient morocco chair, sipping from a can of Coca-Cola. Her eyes were vacant, staring at something only she could see.

I went around in front of the chair. "What did you give Lynn?"

She focused on me. "What?"

"You gave her some kind of drug, didn't you?"

"Oh. Yes. Some sleeping pills."

"How many sleeping pills?"

"Two or three. She was very upset . . . about Larry being dead. She shouldn't have been though; he wasn't worth it." Evans shook her head, as if she were still a little awed by the fact. "He wasn't worth it."

"How did Lynn find out about Travers' death? Did you tell her?"

"No. Her father . . . he called. He said he was coming over to take her home, but she didn't want to see him, she didn't want to go home."

"So you brought her over here."

"She asked if she could stay here tonight. It was her idea. . . ." She drank some more of her Coke. "You know, don't you," she said.

"Yeah," I said, "I know."

"Everything?"

"I think so."

"How did you find out?" she asked, but not as if it mattered much to her.

I didn't answer right away. Most of the tension had drained out of me; Lynn was all right and I did not think Evans was going to give me any trouble. I backed away from her, over to where she had fashioned a work space in one corner of the room; I had noticed it when I first came in. There were a desk and a couple of tables, arranged so that they formed a little ell, and on them was a variety of electronic equipment. A bank of stereo components—tape recorder, phonograph, AM-FM radio, VHS videotape deck, even an oscilloscope. An answering machine hooked up to the telephone. A small cassette recorder. And an Apple home computer with an oversized readout screen.

From there I said, "Yesterday, when Lynn got the threatening call while the three of us were together and I took the phone away from her, I heard the connection being broken. A whirring click. It didn't mean anything to me at the time, but it should have. There's always a click on the line when somebody hangs up, but you only get the whirring when a machine is involved. An answering machine, for example. I called Lynn's father last night; he wasn't home and I got his answering machine and there was the whirring click when it came on. The same thing happened when I checked my office answering machine this afternoon. That was what finally started me thinking and remembering."

I paused, but Evans had nothing to say. She just sat there looking at me, sipping from that damned can of Coke.

"There's another kind of machine that makes a whirring click," I said. "A machine that can deliver messages, not just take them— a cassette recorder like this one here. If you've got the right equipment and some knowledge of electronics, you can tape a message on a cassette, hook up the recorder to the phone and to a home computer, and program the computer to *make* a call whenever you want it to. Isn't that right, Connie?"

"Yes," she said.

"Sure. The computer opens the line at a preset time, 'dials' a programmed number and switches on the recorder so it can play the message you've taped. As soon as the message ends, the computer shuts everything off and breaks the connection . . . with a little whirring click." I tapped the recorder on the table. "What would I hear if I played this cassette? Or did you already erase the tape?"

"No." Another sip. "You know what you'd hear."

"Was yesterday the first time you used a tape to make one of those calls to Lynn?"

"Yes."

"Why? Because she told you her father had hired a private detective who was coming over to see her, and you thought that if you timed a call to come in while you were there, the detective would never suspect the truth? Or was it just that you wanted to see Lynn's face when you told her on the tape you were going to kill her?"

Sip. Sip.

But it didn't really matter. The facts were, she had timed the call for one o'clock, probably before she'd gone to her ten o'clock class to take her exam; but the exam had lasted longer than she'd anticipated, and on the way to Lynn's from the college she'd realized her watch had stopped. That was why she had asked Lynn what time it was the moment she arrived. It wasn't a soap opera program on TV she had been afraid she'd missed; it was the programmed call.

"I wasn't going to do it," Evans said after a time. "Kill her, I mean."

"No? Then why did you threaten her?"

"I wanted to hurt her even more. Inside, the way she'd hurt me."

"How did she hurt you?"

"She took Larry away from me. We were going together; I loved him and he said he loved me. We were going to get married. Then Lynn came along."

It was about what I had expected, but that didn't make it any easier to listen to. I quit looking at Connie Evans and looked out through the front window instead. You could see across the Great Highway to the beach and the Pacific beyond, and because it was a clear day the shapes of the Farallone Islands were outlined against the horizon. They were a long way from here, thirty-two miles west of the Golden Gate, and I wished I was a long way from here, too.

She said, "I tried to get Larry back, but he wouldn't have anything more to do with me. And I kept seeing Lynn around school, always around. I hated her, but I couldn't get her out of my mind. So I started talking to her, I got to know her; she thought we were friends."

"Why the obscene calls? Why pretend to be a man?"

"She told me once she hated that kind of thing, some man she didn't know talking to her like that. She said it scared her more than anything. I thought . . . I don't know what I thought. One night I just picked up the phone and called her, that's all."

And it hadn't been difficult for her to disguise her voice, I thought, or to make it sound masculine. She'd had at least some actor's training; Jud Canale had told me the Drama Club was where she and Lynn had gone yesterday evening.

I said, "Everything changed last night. Why?"

Sip. "It was Lynn's father. I was there when he came to see her. He asked me to step into the bedroom, but I listened anyway. He told her about Larry leaving her, going to San Diego; he called Larry a lot of bad names. At first I couldn't believe Larry would

do something like that. Then I hoped it was true. I thought maybe
I could talk him into taking me back, letting me go to San Diego
with him."

"Is that why you went to the boatyard?"

She nodded; her head bobbed as if it were on a spring, like
one of those little toys you see on the dashboards of cars. "Mr.
Canale said the name of the place. I went to Larry's flat first, but
he wasn't there; then I went to the boatyard. It was closed up
and I couldn't get in. But Larry drove up just as I was about to
leave. He let me in, and we went and sat in the boat. He had a
Big Mac and some fries that he'd bought, but he didn't offer me
any. He just sat there eating and drinking beer. I had to go out
to a machine by the office to get some Coke for myself."

I remembered the empty bottles and cans on the galley table.
Two people, Joel Reeves and the bartender at Elrod's, had told
me how fond Travers was of beer; so the empty bottles on the
table figured to be his. But beer drinkers never mix beer and soda
pop, which meant the soft drink cans had to belong to whoever
killed him. And Connie Evans was as fond of Coke as Travers
had been of beer.

"We talked for a while," she said, "and then he wanted to go
to bed. So we did. Afterward I asked him to let me go to San
Diego with him, but he said no. I begged him, I told him how
much I loved him; he just laughed. Then I saw how he'd used
me, how wrong I'd been about him and about Lynn. He was
running out on her just like he'd run out on me, and he would
keep on doing the same thing to other women if somebody didn't
stop him. I felt so ashamed. And I hated him."

Sip. "The gun . . . it was in one of the lockers. I saw it when
I first came on the boat; Larry told me it was for shooting sharks.
So I got it while he was getting dressed and I pointed it at him.
'This gun is for shooting sharks, Larry,' I said. 'Isn't that what
you told me?' Then I shot him. I don't know why I put the gun
in his hand afterward. I don't remember much about what happened after he was dead."

Her voice was still as emotionless as when she'd started speaking;
nothing had changed in her expression either. She took one last
sip of the Coke and then put the can down carefully on the carpet
beside her chair.

"I guess that's all," she said. "Except that I wouldn't have hurt
Lynn anymore. I really wouldn't have." She folded her hands in

her lap. "Are you going to call the police now?"

"Yes."

"That's all right. I don't care."

"They'll get you some help, Connie," I said.

"I don't care about that either. I hated him but I loved him so much longer. He's dead and so am I."

I looked away from her again, away from the emptiness in her voice and in her eyes. There was no anger left in me, not toward her; there was only pity and sadness. She wasn't to blame for all of this. Neither was Larry Travers, when you stripped it all to the bottom line. Blame it on the kind of animals we poor humans are, the things that drive us and obsess us. Blame it on a cosmos that might not be so benevolent after all.

I picked up the telephone receiver and called Jack Logan at the Hall of Justice.

9

FRIDAY MORNING, late January.

The weather was still good, clear and mostly warm. And people on the streets, I saw as I drove to my office, were still smiling over San Francisco's surprising Super Bowl victory on Sunday. But Lynn Canale, in seclusion at her father's home, wasn't smiling; and Jud Canale wasn't smiling; and neither was Connie Evans in her new home in a prison hospital. Death, like life, goes on—and so do mental breakdowns, and aberrant behavior, and pain and tragedy and grief—even in the midst of a week-long, city-wide celebration as jubilant as any San Francisco has ever known.

And that was why, on this clear and mostly warm Friday morning five days after the Forty-niners had won the Super Bowl, I still wasn't smiling along with everybody else.

EDWARD D. HOCH
City of Brass

I REALIZE NOW that Henry Mahon was a man who never really grew up.

He went through four years of college and three years of army life without appreciably changing his ways, and those who'd known him before were by degrees happy or discouraged that the "new" Henry proved to be the same as the old one. After the army he settled down in Baine City, where he'd spent his childhood, and wasted away the next sixteen months of life helping his friends get engaged and finally married, one by one—or perhaps two by two.

He ran with a crowd in which every third fellow already owned either a Thunderbird or some foreign sports car, a crowd that thought it great fun to spend the weekend between Christmas and New Year's at one of the nearby ski resorts each year. The fellows and girls always got to know each other better on such occasions, even if they didn't get in much skiing.

It was on one of these between-holiday weekends that Henry Mahon met the Clark sisters, most especially Jean Clark. They drank together on Friday night, skied together on Saturday, and slept together on Sunday. It was not the first girl for Henry, but Jean at least was convinced it would be the last. When they returned to civilization in the shape of Baine City, Jean Clark served notice on Henry Mahon that she expected him to make an honest woman of her. He laughed it off for a week, then tried to drink it off for a second week. Had he been more of an "adult" he would surely have found a way out of it, but as I said Henry Mahon never really grew up.

Cornered and run to earth at last, Henry consented to the sentence of marriage. And it took place at the first burst of spring, on April second in Henry's parish church. He joked at the time that he was lucky it was the day *after* April Fool's, but perhaps really it wasn't any joke.

Henry Mahon and Jean Clark were married, and the story had begun. . . .

I was passing through Baine City on the way back to New York, driving down from Buffalo where I'd been in hasty conference with our printer. It was one of those rare times when a couple of the major airlines were on strike and the others crowded to capacity, and since no one ever took the train any more I'd driven up to Buffalo on the Thruway—a fast nine-hour trip that wasn't half bad. I was figuring I could cut the return down to eight by stepping on the gas a bit, but as it happened I decided to stop off in Baine City.

It was a city of better than a quarter of a million people, with a lake at one end and a fairly wide river splitting it down the middle. Sometimes the Chamber of Commerce liked to call it the City of Brass, in recognition of Baine Brass, the single great industry that made the city what it was. Almost everybody worked for Baine Brass, or had relatives who worked for Baine Brass—there was no escaping it.

I don't really know just what made me turn off the Thruway for a pause at Baine City. Perhaps it was just that the long hours of driving were beginning to tell on me at last. Certainly it was not primarily to visit Henry Mahon and his bride, though he was the only person I knew in Baine City. We'd met some five years back, when he'd made a brief try at breaking into New York publishing, and for some reason I'd felt sorry for the guy. He certainly wasn't the type to make friends easily with his eternal attitude of a spoiled rich boy, but I guess I kept hoping there was something better underneath.

Anyway, we'd become friends of a sort, corresponding occasionally and seeing each other on Henry's semi-annual fun trips to Manhattan. He'd always been urging me to stop off in Baine City for a visit, and since I was feeling like taking a break just then I wheeled the car off the Thruway and into town.

His name was in the phone book, of course, and I wasn't too surprised when he answered himself. It was only four o'clock, but he would never be one for working a full day.

"It's not really you!" he greeted me with an overly friendly voice. "After all these years. . . ."

"I'm only passing through on the way back to New York, Hank. I have to be back on the road by six if I'm to get home by midnight."

"Well, hell, that's two hours, man. Zip down and have a drink with the bride and me. You've got the address."

I agreed to that and hung up. Fifteen minutes later I was parking my car before a rolling length of lawn that seemed to flow like a calm river from the house at its head. Not a big place, the home of Henry Mahon and his bride still had that modernistic look that put a $25,000 price tag on it. The house could have been the place next door to me in Westchester, but it wasn't a Thunderbird in the garage—only a last year's Buick.

Henry was waiting for me in the doorway, looking slick and neat with a drink the color of Scotch in his left hand. "Come in, old man. Damn but it's good to see you up here. Gotta introduce you to Jean."

He called to her and almost immediately a tall brunette appeared from the depths of the house. Her hair was caught back in some sort of knot, and she seemed quite relaxed in a knit sweater and tight black pants that showed off her long legs. She had the shape and gestures of a New York model, and I was a bit surprised at such class in a place like Baine City. Her mouth was a bit too wide and her eyes flashed a trifle too much, but these were minor complaints in a sea of near perfection.

Yes, she went with the place. She went with Henry Mahon and his crowd. She went with the story he'd told me about the weekend at the ski resort. She was the type of girl who lived that way—a few years of fun and then a quick marriage to a likely young rich boy who went too far.

"I've heard a lot about you," I told her. "Happy to meet you at last. This is certainly a nice place you've got here."

She smiled a slow, careful smile that showed years of careful practice before a mirror. "We like it, though I imagine you find it quite tame after New York."

"New York is a state of mind, full of sound and fury signifying nothing," I said with a smile. "Did you ever live there?"

"For a time I think every girl should spend a year there. It's like a post-graduate course in modern living. I wanted to be a model once, long before I met Henry."

Mahon interrupted with a jolly chuckle. "Come on, let's have a drink. Still like rum?"

"Anything, as long as it's wet. Those printers up in Buffalo are strictly a beer drinking crowd." I followed Mahon into the living room as Jean went off to the kitchen in search of glasses.

It was a rich man's house, without doubt. It screamed its wealth from the ornate gold clock over the fireplace to the tiny but expensive glass animals scattered here and there on coffee tables and window sills. I picked the most comfortable-looking chair and settled into it. "What are you doing with yourself these days, Hank?" I asked him. "Last I heard you were going to start your own public relations firm."

He waved his hand in a vague gesture of dismissal. "Didn't pan out. My partner got cold feet about sinking that much money into it. He's got a fine, safe, dull job with the local TV station and he's happy to keep it that way. You know, gotta have money to put the kids through college—all that sort of hogwash."

He was the same old Henry Mahon, I decided. He'd never change. Jean appeared at my elbow with a tray of drinks and I chose a light one that looked good and frosty. As she moved across the room to her husband her buttocks rippled under the tight pants.

"I understand you've got a sister," I said.

"Hasn't everybody?" she retorted. "Mine is just a little bit louder and livelier than most. Cathy Clark, the terror of every college campus from here to Cleveland. How's the drink—OK?"

"Best all week." I turned back to Mahon. "So what did you say you were doing now?"

"Oh, I'm just up at the University," he said, sipping his drink. "You know, foxing around the profs and such. Doing a bit of public relations for them, actually. Big fund raising drive coming up next month."

"Fund raising? I thought Baine Brass practically supported the place."

"Ah! A typical New Yorkish half-truth, my friend. Baine set up a trust fund for medical research and also several scholarship funds in the science field, but as far as the Arts College goes it's practically self-supporting. I guess old man Baine didn't hold much with liberal arts as a field of higher education, and his son just followed along in the same footsteps."

"But he likes it," Jean said. "Being around those college girls all day is his idea of heaven. I don't know when he ever gets his work done."

Mahon lit a cigarette and settled back with his drink. "I've got a little office squeezed in between the gym and the research lab. The money's good and the work is easy—high-class, you know."

"Yeah," I downed the rest of my drink.

"So how are things at Neptune?"

"The same. Hectic. We're putting in a new distribution system for our paperbound books." I went on to mention a few mutual friends and launched into some New York small talk.

"Say, it's almost supper time," Jean observed. "How about staying for a meal."

I shook my head sadly. "Still gotta make New York tonight— or Westchester, at least. The wife would never forgive me."

"Call her long distance," Mahon suggested. "Tell her you've decided to stay the night with us."

"Afraid not. Thanks for the drink and the conversation, but I've got to be back on the road now."

They insisted, and I was firm, and finally I won the battle and started down the walk to the car, with a final wave at Jean standing in the doorway. Henry Mahon followed me to the car and stood there a moment, wanting to say something.

"What is it, Hank? Something bothering you?"

"I . . . I didn't want to speak in front of Jean, but there is something. Sure you can't stay?"

"No can do. Can't you make it brief?"

"Well . . . it's the University. It's. . . ."

"A girl?"

"Nothing like that. This friend of yours—this Simon Ark you mentioned once—could he come here and help me?"

I shrugged my shoulders. "Simon Ark is a sort of investigator. He's interested only in the strange and unusual."

"Believe me, this is the strangest thing you ever heard."

"I don't know," I hedged. "Simon's been out of town. I don't even know if I could locate him. And I'd certainly have to tell him something."

"Tell him . . . tell him. . . ." He broke off as Jean came trotting down to the car.

"What's the big discussion? Exchanging phone numbers?"

"I'll write you," Mahon finished quickly. "Have a good trip back."

I said my goodbyes again and was off, heading south toward the Thruway. Actually, I didn't give a second thought to Mahon's questions about Simon Ark. People were constantly cornering me at cocktail parties and dinners to suggest a meeting with the fabled but all but unknown man who was my friend. I suppose they thought he was some kind of fortune teller, or latter-day prophet to work miracles in an age that no longer believed in them. But Simon was none of these things—he was only a curious wanderer across the earth, a man in search of truth and the evil that these days was sometimes the only truth some men followed.

So I thought no more of it, and concentrated on the winding ribbon of road ahead, chasing the lines of red tail lights headed south toward New York and home. . . .

But the letter came.

Just two days later it was sitting on my desk, waiting to be opened because the *personal* on the envelope had scared my secretary away. I delayed the act till well in the afternoon, because the press of business was squeezing me into a corner throughout most of the morning.

But finally I got to it, ripping open the envelope to disclose a fairly brief note typed on Baine University stationery.

"It was good to see you yesterday, and I'm only sorry we didn't have time to talk alone. The thing that concerns me— concerns several of us here—has to do with a series of experiments being carried out by Professor Kane Wilber here. The experiments, in the fields of heredity and evolution, are of a type that I'm convinced are harmful to present-day society. I can only hope that someone like your friend Simon Ark can get to the bottom of the thing before it's too late. Hope to hear from you by return mail."

Well, it meant nothing much to me and I tossed it down on my desk. What in hell was he getting at, anyway? A mad scientist at one of the country's largest universities? More likely it was something Mahon feared might damage his forthcoming fund-raising campaign. Perhaps a professor who drank too much, or was kidnapping neighborhood dogs to carry out his experiments. Nothing certainly that would interest Simon Ark.

I buzzed my secretary to dictate a reply but then dismissed her with a wave of my hand. Hell, what was there to say? I didn't want to hurt the guy's feelings by telling him he was just a rich spoiled kid with a ton of money who saw madmen behind every test tube. He belonged back at the ski resort, in bed with Jean, without a care in the world. He had Jean Mahon now, but he still needed Jean Clark.

I tossed the letter into a desk drawer and promptly forgot about it. . . .

Another week passed and we were into the summer sunshine of June. Simon Ark returned to New York on June first, as usual vaguely silent about his latest trip, and I had dinner with him in one of the little foreign restaurants off Sixth Avenue.

It was that night, on my homeward journey to Westchester, that the girl accosted me in Grand Central. "You don't know me," she said, making a firm statement of it.

"You're right there. I don't," I agreed, even though there was something not completely strange about her face. She was very blonde, with long hair caught back in a knot, and very young— probably not over twenty-two at best. Her mouth was a bit too wide, but—

Of course? She was Jean Mahon's sister. "My name is Cathy Clark," she was saying. "I think you met my sister a couple of weeks back."

"Oh! Up in Baine City."

"That's right. I must talk with you."

"Well. . . ." I shifted my weight on anxious feet, thinking of Shelly waiting for me at home. "How did you happen to find me here?"

"I . . . I followed you from your office, if you must know."

"What? All evening?"

She hung her head guiltily, managing to make it cute. "I'm afraid so. I was going to speak to you as you left your building, but you were with that strange looking man."

I mentally chuckled at her description of Simon. "How did you recognize me?"

"The elevator starter pointed you out. I told him I was a writer and wanted to meet you."

"Well, come on—I'll buy you a cup of coffee and listen to your sad story. That's the least I can do, I suppose."

"Thanks," she said, shaking her blonde head in gratitude.

We found stools at one of the countless Grand Central lunch counters and settled down over cigarettes and coffee. "It's about Henry and Jean," she opened.

"I expected it would be."

"He says he wrote you."

My first reaction was surprise that she even knew about it. Certainly Mahon had gone to some pains to keep this problem from his wife's ears, so why tell his sister-in-law all about it? "That's right," I admitted. "He wrote me about a week ago. But the letter was pretty vague—just general rumblings, you know."

"He needs help—badly!"

"Well . . . what can I say? He's a friend, but there's really nothing I can do, you know. First of all, I don't think I even fully understand the direct cause of all this anxiety. He vaguely mentioned a Professor Wilber at the University. . . ."

She ground out her cigarette and immediately lit another with nervous gestures. "It's not the kind of thing you can put into words."

"The nameless horror?" I asked with a chuckle.

But there was no responding laughter in her eyes. "Exactly."

"Well, I tossed down a quarter for the coffees, "if you want any help from me you'll have to name it." I amazed myself with the words. Now, suddenly, I was giving her a sort of backhanded agreement of aid. "And in a hurry, too," I added, to retreat a bit toward my former unyielding position. "I've got a train to catch."

She sighed. "It's not the kind of thing you can put into words. But believe me, it could rock Baine City to its foundations. If you're not interested in helping, or in telling this Simon Ark about it. . . ."

"I see Hank told you everything. Well, Miss Clark, it might interest you to know that the strange man you saw me with this evening was Simon Ark—in the flesh."

"It was! Where is he now? Where can I reach him?"

"He's not the kind of man you look up in the phone book," I told her. "And I'm afraid he'd be no more interested in your problems than I am."

"Then you won't help me?" Was the throb in the voice a little too intense?

"Look," I tried to explain, "I'm not a detective. I'm not even a lonely hearts advisor or a friend to the needy. Neither is Simon Ark. I happen to be the vice president of a publishing company, and it's a full-time occupation. If I ever have any free time— maybe in ten or twenty years—I'll be happy to take a run up to Baine City and see this Professor Wilber, but until then I can't help you. Sorry."

Cathy Clark gave her blonde head a defiant toss. "All right," she said. "We'll do something without you." She finished her coffee and slid off the stool in sudden haste.

"Sorry," I repeated, and I really was. But what could I do? There were times when you had to say no.

"Thanks for the coffee, anyway," she said, and was gone—out into the evening crowds headed this way and that in the eternal maze of Grand Central.

I watched her receding rear for a moment before it was swallowed up, then turned back to the dregs of a good cup of coffee. As I finished it and started to rise I found myself suddenly looking once more into the deep bright eyes of Simon Ark.

"Simon! What in the heck are you doing here?"

"Who was the girl?" he asked me with just a hint of a smile.

"You saw her?"

"She was following us all evening. I wondered why."

"You mean you saw her and didn't tell me?"

The smile broadened a bit. "She may have been a discarded love, or a current one."

"You decided she wasn't?"

He nodded. "But why was she following you?"

"Believe it or not, she wanted to see you—only she didn't know it at the time. She's Henry Mahon's sister-in-law. That's the fellow up in Baine City that I mentioned once or twice. Both of them have got some crazy idea that something pretty horrible's happening up at Baine U. It turns out Hank is running a fund raising drive for the University in a couple of weeks, and I guess he's worried about the bad publicity."

"What kind of a thing?"

"Huh? I don't know. Some guy named Professor Wilber is experimenting—probably got a drug to pep up the football team or something crazy like that."

"Do you think I should look into it?"

"What could it be to interest you, Simon? It's research being carried out on a grant from Baine Brass. They're surely not making hidden atomic bombs or anything like that."

"But if he's a friend of yours. . . ."

"Well, I'll tell you—maybe next week we can run up there. I may have to go to Buffalo again, and we can drive up."

Simon Ark frowned. "Evil often does not choose to wait, but perhaps as you say there is nothing in this but the overworked imaginations of a few people."

I'm afraid Henry Mahon is not the most realistic person in the world," I said. "Let's wait and see what develops. . . ."

So we didn't make the trip to Baine City the following week. Summer was upon us suddenly, and the New York heat made the beaches of Long Island the only fit goals for a drive. Simon drifted away without my even being conscious of his going, off to some other city or some other country half a world away. The days lengthened out into the glorious warmth of life that seemed suddenly so important to a man of forty, and I had the happy feeling that life was far from being over for me. There was Shelly, seemingly as young and lovely as when I'd first married her, and there was my job—more challenging but more rewarding with each passing year.

And so Henry Mahon and his wife and Cathy Clark were forgotten. They were people of a borderland at best, people who helped fill up your life without ever really being a part of it. And summer—a fortieth summer—was especially a time for being oneself. Shelly and I discovered the secluded little beaches that dotted Long Island's north shore, and there was only the sun to see us and approve as we basked in its warmth.

There was always the radio, filling the sand and the air with gentle music for a quiet mood, with occasional well-timed interruptions for the news of the world—just to remind one that men still plotted and schemed and lived and died, even on a sunny Saturday afternoon.

This day, the Saturday that marked the beginning of a long July Fourth weekend, we were alone together on a little strip of sand not far from the Eaton's Neck lighthouse. Shelly was reading a recent novel by Graham Greene and I was puttering around with the charcoal grill, trying to get a fire going for supper.

"Germany, China, Egypt." Shelly moaned. "We might as well be fighting a war already the way those newscasters talk." And then she fell silent as the droning voice of the announcer shifted to local matters.

"The upstate New York community of Baine City has a real murder mystery on its hands today with the discovery of the bullet-riddled body of a young girl." I sat up at the name of Baine City and dropped what I was doing. "The girl, twenty-two-year-old Cathy Clark, had graduated only last month from Baine University. Her body was found some miles out of the city on a side road where she apparently was shot to death while seated in her car."

That was all. Then he was off again to an oil explosion in Texas. "Baine City," Shelly said. "Isn't that the place. . . ."

"That's the place. And that's the girl who followed me the night I was late getting home. God, what could have happened?"

"She was the one who wanted Simon to help her?"

I nodded, running sand nervously through my fingers. "And I didn't listen to her."

"But what could you have done?"

"I don't know. Something. Apparently anything would have been better than nothing. Come on, let's pack up and get back to town. I want to get the details of this."

It took us the better part of two hours to reach the Triborough Bridge, battling the traffic of a hot holiday weekend every mile of the way. I bought all three Saturday afternoon papers on the way, but only one had the story. That was enough.

It was on page three, under a flash photograph showing a late model sports car with its door open on the driver's side. She was hanging there, half in and half out of the car, with her long blonde hair reaching down to the pavement. There was a stain below her head which might have been blood or perhaps only a random oil stain. The printed account carried little I hadn't already heard on the radio. A highway repair crew had found her in the early hours of Saturday morning while answering an emergency call. She'd apparently been seated in the front seat when someone had fired six pistol shots through the windshield and side window. There were no signs that she'd been attacked, the report concluded, meaning she hadn't been raped. I was mildly surprised to see no mention of her parents. Only Jean Mahon was mentioned as a survivor.

"I'd better try to locate Simon," I said when we reached home. "He'll want to know about this."

"I thought he was out of town."

"Maybe he's back for the weekend. There's always a chance."

I had a long list of telephone numbers Simon Ark had given me once, and I started through them. The Institute for Egyptian Studies was closed for the weekend and there was no one but the janitor to answer the phone. The little hotel on 84th Street hadn't seen him in weeks, and Father Toole at Fordham thought he was out of town. I tried a Long Island number and one in Jersey, but the answer was the same.

"Well, I'd better fly up to Baine City tonight," I told Shelly.

"Alone? Why in heaven's name? Why go up there? You hardly knew the girl."

"Well, for one thing, Hank Mahon might be in trouble too. If she was killed because of this Professor Wilber's experiments, maybe Mahon is next. They asked me to help—to have Simon Ark help—and now I've got to do something."

She didn't like it, I know, but I had to go. I caught an evening plane and was checking into the Baine City Hotel at midnight. . . .

Sunday morning in a city, any city, is a day set apart. It is a day of rest, and for those few who have to work it is a day filled with quiet activity. It is not a day for judging a city, because all cities have a certain charm in the peaceful quiet of a Sunday morning.

Baine City, on the third of July, was a city deserted by many of its residents. The three-day weekend had lured them away, to the nearby beach where many had cottages, or further a bit, to the mountains that could just be seen on a clear day from the tops of the taller buildings. The city could have been mine that morning as I stood at my hotel window seeing the sweep and flow of it. The streets shot out like empty arrows before me, and I realized after a time that the hotel was located at the point of a wide V. Far at the end of one set of streets was a great factory that I took to be Baine Brass. In the other direction, down the left arm of the V, I could see a typical college bell tower rising behind the buildings.

Baine Brass and Baine University, linked together by the network of streets that was Baine City. I wondered about this man whose name they bore, this man Baine who had carved his city in the heart of New York State and put his stamp on everything in it.

I called Mahon from the hotel. "I was sorry to hear about Cathy," I told him. "It was a shock."

"Believe me, it was a shock for us too. Jean is in bad shape."

"Can I come out?"

He hesitated a bit. "What for?"

"Well, you asked for help once. About Professor Wilber, out at the University."

"Oh. Well, I don't think you could do anything now. That's all blown over."

"But Cathy is dead," I insisted.

"I know, but that had nothing to do with Wilber. It—it was a wild crowd she was running around with."

"Mighty wild, to pump six bullets into her."

He sounded somehow different to me, troubled, unsure of himself. He cleared his throat and went on. "Well, there's nothing that can be done about it now. I appreciate your calling."

"Look, Hank, I flew up here last night just to see you. I'm trying to locate Simon Ark and get him up here too. If you don't want any help, just say so."

"I thought I'd said it, fella. The police will catch Cathy's killer. There's nothing for us to do."

"What about Professor Wilber's experiments?"

"I told you—there's nothing to it. My imagination got the better of me."

"Cathy saw me in New York. She was upset about Wilber too."

"Oh for God's sake! There's nothing to it, forget it, can't you?"

Another thought struck me. "Your fund raising drive—is it on now?"

"Yeah, all this month. And I don't want you and Ark stirring up a storm. Not this month. I'm getting one percent of everything I bring in, and it's tough enough as it is. You wouldn't believe there could be so much resentment against old Baine in this city."

"So the fund raising goes on, and Cathy Clark goes unmourned."

"What can I do? What can *you* do?"

"Maybe nothing," I admitted. "I'll be seeing you, Hank."

And I hung up.

Henry Mahon was a damned spoiled fool who loved nobody but himself and never had. This much I knew, but of course I'd known it for a long time really. The only problem now was my own course of action. I could catch the next plane back to New York and forget all about Mahon and Jean and Cathy and the mysterious professor, or I could stay and putter around on my own.

On my own, there was no real choice. I reached for the phone to call the airport, but it jumped into life as my hand touched it. "Hello?" I questioned softly, half expecting it to be Mahon calling back to say he was sorry.

"This is Simon," the familiar voice answered. "I'm downstairs. Shelly told me about the trouble. . . ."

We ate breakfast downstairs, and over coffee I told him about my phone conversation with Henry Mahon. He settled back in the chair to think about it for a moment.

"What do you say? Should we retreat under fire, or should we look into the doings at Baine University?"

"Do you think we'd really find something, Simon? Do you think we'll find Professor Wilber crouched over a rack of bubbling test tubes, changing himself into a Mr. Hyde?"

Simon Ark smiled. "I hardly think a true mad scientist would find it necessary to resort to bullets for his murders. Perhaps Mahon was correct about this wild crowd."

"Well, let's take a run out there anyway," I suggested. "Out to the University. We can at least look around."

Simon shrugged in agreement and we finished our coffee. Outside the hotel we found a single taxi with a sleepy driver who was happy to find a fare on a Sunday morning. "Nobody at the University, you know," he volunteered. "Summer courses don't start till the fifth. That's Tuesday."

"We know."

"Just don't want to steal your money. Here we are. Want me to wait?"

It was only a half-mile walk back to the hotel, so I paid him and sent him on his way. Then Simon and I set off on foot across the rolling green of the campus, toward the distant stone buildings where familiar ivy was beginning to creep up the walls.

"What do you think of it, Simon?"

"They are all alike, your American colleges. Space and air and the feeling of youth and age somehow combined. Places for fun, perhaps for too much fun."

"There's a lot of knowledge mixed in with the fun, though," I said, pausing a moment to study a sign that directed us left for the science building. "Our colleges today are the backbone of a vast educational system that promotes knowledge in every possible field. You're no doubt aware that much of the work on the atomic and hydrogen bombs had its beginnings in our universities, in science buildings not too much different from this one."

But Simon only sighed. "Education for destruction. You would certainly not argue that the world is a good place for all of that."

"I wouldn't argue anything with you, Simon. You'll probably still be around when I'm long dead."

"No doubt."

"Come on—this door is open. It must lead somewhere."

He followed me into the science building, down a whitewashed hallway that seemed to take us only deeper into the bowels of the place. And as we walked a queer chattering sound reached our ears—the sound of many creatures, animals, birds, something.

"What do you make of that, Simon?"

"We shall know in another moment, my friend."

We turned the final corner and found ourselves before a pair of open glass doors. Beyond was a laboratory, with rows of cages lining the walls. Monkeys, mostly, with occasional rabbits and birds—and at the far end great cages that held four good-sized apes. And in the midst of it all was a little man wearing a white coat and thick horn-rimmed glasses.

"Professor Wilber?" I asked, a bit uncertainly.

"Yes, I am Professor Wilber." His voice was like the rest of him—small and withdrawn, with only a bare hint of power and authority behind it.

"You work even on Sundays?"

He waved his arms vaguely. "My work is never done here. Just what can I do for you gentlemen?"

We introduced ourselves and I made some bumbling comments about the possibility of doing a book on Baine City and the University. "We heard you were engaged in basic research on the subjects of birth and heredity, with funds from Baine Brass."

"Oh, correct, correct, but hardly complete." He bustled about as he spoke, giving more the impression of being absent-minded than mad. Behind him a monkey screeched in its cage. "Yes see, I am looking into the very nature of life itself, looking into the mysteries of all creation. I plan to publish a paper on my findings."

I remembered some experiments carried out in Mexico some years back. "Are you trying to—create life?"

"No, no, nothing like that. I do not picture myself as God,

gentlemen. Not yet. Tell me, how is the weather outside?"

"Warm."

"Summer." He opened one of the rabbit cages and seemed to inject the beast with a small hypodermic needle. "Summer is the best time of all. Perchance next summer I will be out of this filthy clean room and into the warmth of the sun. And tomorrow is a holiday too!"

Simon Ark had been standing in the very center of the room, well away from any of the cages. But now he moved a bit toward the apes at the end of the wall. "You even work tomorrow?" he asked, contributing to the conversation.

"Every day, every day, because I never know which day the thing might go wrong. All a lifetime's work could go in a moment's time."

My thoughts went back to Cathy Clark. "Tell me, Professor, do you ever have some of the science coeds assist you here?"

The idea seemed to shock him. "No, no, no such thing. You see these large apes? This baboon is of the species that Burton once saw attempt to rape a girl in Cairo."

He was over my head but I stuck with it. "What?"

Simon interrupted. "Richard Burton—I believe in his writings he mentions an attack on a woman, in Cairo—1856. The beast was killed before he could do any damage.

"And because of that you don't have women assisting you? What about a girl name Cathy Clark?"

If he knew the name his face did not show it. "Clark? Clark?"

"She was killed yesterday," Simon said.

"Oh, I read something in the newspaper. Too bad, too bad."

"We have reason to believe she was connected with you in some manner, Professor Wilber."

"With me? With me? Impossible! I may have seen her about the campus, but nothing further. I spend sometimes sixteen to twenty hours a day in this room, and as I have said no women work here."

"But your researches are supported by Baine Brass?"

He bowed his head to one side in a gesture of assent. "The entire science program here is financed by the worthy donations of Foster Baine."

I pressed on, certain there was something to uncover here. "This Foster Baine is the president of Baine Brass?"

"Correct, correct. Grandson of the founder. Carrying on in a great tradition."

"But I understand he contributes nothing to the Arts College. Isn't that strange?"

Professor Wilber tossed his head. "Why strange? The Baine family stands for technological and scientific advancement. Thus that is the field of their endowments."

"One more question, Professor. . . ."

He gave me a queer look. "Are you people detectives or what? So many questions!"

"I was just wondering if you knew a young fellow named Henry Mahon. He's a public relations man who's handling the current fund-raising drive."

"Don't know him," Wilber answered shortly. He was convinced now that we were investigators of some sort, and he was clamming up.

There was nothing more to gain there so we left him, returning outside to the summer warmth. "Well, Simon, what do you think?"

"A strange man, but hardly a sinister one. More dedicated than anything else, I think. Your friend must have been imagining things."

"So where does that leave us?" I watched a flight of pigeons lazily circling the campus bell tower.

"It leaves us only with the murder of Cathy Clark," he said. "That much is real."

"Too real. Let's find the funeral parlor where she's laid out. If nothing else we can at least pay our last respects. . . ."

It looked like a great marble tomb, set suddenly in the very midst of the city to remind one of the immediacy of death—and perhaps that wasn't such a bad idea for an undertaker after all. We knew it was the right place because a police car was parked in front, its silent red light flashing meaningfully.

And inside all was thickly carpeted silence, respectful of the waiting dead. A black felt signboard carried only the white lettered name of *Catherine Clark,* with an equally white arrow directing us through a low alcove.

And there she was, strangely beautiful in death, her hands meeting across her chest, her hair magnificently blonde and young. Only twenty-two.

I looked down at her and felt I'd known her for many years. There was a subtle difference about her in death, but if anything it was a glorious difference. She seemed older, more worldly-wise, more ready for what life held. I only hoped she had been ready for what death held. I turned away, thankful now only that none of the bullets had ruined the simple beauty of her face as they were taking her life.

"Hello," someone said behind me, and I turned to see Jean Mahon standing there, all in black, a veil covering her forehead and eyes.

"I was awfully sorry to hear about your sister."

"Thank you."

"This . . . this is a friend, Simon Ark." They shook hands with solemn silence and brief nods. "Is your husband here?"

"No. Henry is home. It's hard on him—she was so much like me."

"You have no other relatives?"

Jean Mahon shook her head. "Our parents were killed in an auto accident three years ago. There was just Cathy and me, and now. . . ." The tears were very close and she broke off with a cracking voice.

"Do they have any idea who could have done it?"

She motioned toward a tall slim man holding an unlit pipe in his left hand. "That man's from the police. He's been questioning me about it."

The tall man had already started toward us, and my first impression was that surely he was not the type of detective to leave his car outside with the red light flashing. He was young and handsome and might have stepped out of *Esquire*.

"I'm George Quinn," he said, and the voice went with the rest of him. "Baine City Police. Were you friends of the deceased?"

"Not really," I answered. "I'd met her just once, briefly, about a month ago."

"An odd case," he said.

Simon had moved near enough to hear his quiet comment. "Odd how?" he asked. "Isn't all murder odd?"

Quinn obviously did not want to strike up a lengthy conversation in the presence of the victim. He motioned us into an adjoining room, and I noticed Jean give him a curious glance. When he had us alone he closed a sliding door and offered a cigarette. I took one but Simon declined.

"She was a strange girl, really," he began. "Not that I knew her personally, but I'd heard stories. There was some money—

thirty or forty thousand dollars according to the rumors—and it all went to Jean with the stipulation that she provide for Cathy's education."

"So Mahon married money," I mused. "Interesting, interesting."

"The part about Mahon and Jean Clark was a little bit surprising," Quinn continued, being unusually talkative for a detective on a case. "She was always the quiet one of the pair—the older sister in every sense. Cathy on the other hand was as wild as they come, running with the hotrodders when she wasn't busy at fraternity beer parties."

"Strange," I said, "she didn't impress me that way at all."

"She was a girl of many moods. That's what makes this case so difficult right from the beginning. It might have been one of the college crowd that shot her, or one of this hotrod gang, or somebody else entirely."

"It said in the paper that she hadn't been raped."

He shook his head. "Not even touched. But for all of that she was no virgin."

"Pregnant?"

"No, but no virgin. Not a surprising bit of news, really."

But it was surprising to me in my innocence. I always thought of promiscuous women as the other ones, the ones I did not know. All unmarried girls were virgins to my mind, and I still remembered the shocked surprise I'd felt in high school when the cute blonde kid down the street had left school three months before graduation to have her illegitimate baby in some private hospital fifty miles away. I'd never seen her again, and I'd spent endless weeks afterward speculating on which of my classmates had been guilty of the deed. Some years later I learned that any one of six boys could have been responsible, and that only added to the sense of shock.

And it was somewhat the same feeling that was inside me now—not that I'd really known Cathy Clark that well, because of course I hadn't. But, maybe, it was just that somehow she reminded me of that lost blonde girl from my youth. Lost, and never found again.

"You think the killer will turn up here?" I asked. "You think it was one of her boyfriends?"

"I don't know," he said, his voice carrying a trace of that eternal pessimism that seemed the lot of all true policemen. "Maybe a boy, maybe a jealous girl, maybe a wandering hobo no one will ever see again. Sometimes, as hard as we try, these things stay unsolved."

Simon Ark murmured something I didn't catch, and Quinn gave him an odd look. He put the pipe in his mouth for a thoughtful moment, then removed it and asked, "What did you say your name was?"

Simon scowled and told him. "Ark. Simon Ark, sir."

"Simon Ark. You knew the girl too?"

"I never met her."

"You people from New York?" His policeman's suspicions were being awakened now. "You come all the way up to see this girl you hardly know?"

"Did I say we were from New York?"

"You talk like New Yorkers. Not Mr. Ark, maybe, but you sure do. I like to study people's speech habits. Mr. Ark here is foreign, though I'd guess he's been in this country a long time."

"A long time," Simon agreed with a smile.

George Quinn leaned back against the wall, chewing thoughtfully on the pipe stem. "Baine City is an odd place. We like visitors, especially New York visitors. We appreciate your interest in this poor dead girl. We're friendly—you can see that. But all the same. . . ."

"All the same what?" I asked.

"All the same, don't go playin' detective or anything like that. I get paid to catch murderers—you don't."

"You get paid whether you catch them or not."

There was a tiny flicker of steel in his eyes. "I'll get the man who killed Cathy Clark," he said quietly, and I knew he meant it. The face behind the pipe relaxed quickly into the familiar smile and he slid back the folding doors. "Anyway, thanks for listening to me," he concluded. "Sorry to take up your time."

"Not at all," Simon said. I followed him back into the room with the casket and the jumbled mountains of flowers. He paused for a moment and I thought he might be praying. Then we left the place and walked across the street to a little triangle of green that was a park.

"It's a city," I said.

"A city," Simon nodded. "We must stay, my friend, and look beneath the surface of this city. It has a heart, if only a brass one."

"You think Wilber knows something about her death?"

"A possibility. But I think it is time we visited your friend, Henry Mahon. . . ."

We found him in front of the house, strangely puttering with his rose bushes. It seemed an odd action for a man who had just lost his sister-in-law. He looked up as I parked our rented car, and I thought I saw a flicker of uncertainty on his face.

"Hello, Hank," I said, leading Simon up the easily spaced steps.

"I told you there was nothing for us to do," he said. Then, "I see you brought Simon Ark." He made it a statement, not a question, and I wondered how he could be so sure. Simon's face was anything but well known, and I'd told Mahon I was having trouble locating him. And yet he knew this was Simon. Had somebody called to tip him off? His wife, or Quinn or even Wilber? Anything was possible, I supposed.

"We were out to the University," I said. "We talked with Professor Wilber. He seems a nice sort."

Mahon grunted. "I understand you were at the funeral home too." Apparently it had been his wife who'd called him.

"We stopped by," I admitted. "After all, I did know her in a way." I wondered why I was bothering to apologize to him.

"Come in," he said suddenly, his manner changing in an unaccountable way. "How about a drink?"

We agreed, and I flopped into the same chair I'd occupied on my last visit. The house hadn't changed much, actually, though I noticed that a small framed picture of Mahon and Jean was missing now from its place of honor on the coffee table. The drink tasted good after the day we'd spent in laboratories and funeral homes, and I for one was willing to devote the rest of Sunday afternoon to investigating the rest of the bottle.

Mahon, too, seemed intent on being the perfect host, producing a large poster from somewhere for our inspection. "How do you like it?" he asked. "I had two thousand of 'em printed up."

It was a gaudy thing, done in black, yellow and fluorescent red, bouncing its vivid message out at you with uncompromising fury: GIVE! DOLLARS FOR SCHOLARS!

"That headline was my idea," he said proudly. "Like it?"

I grunted something meant to be affirmative. "How's the drive going?"

"Well, hell, considering the time of the year and everything, not too bad at all. You know, people are up at their summer cottages and stuff—they don't like to be bothered with fund raisers. Some of them don't even have phones and I have to write them if I can track them down."

"Do you approach Baine Brass on something like this?"

"Well, not officially, though of course I sent a letter to Foster Baine. He graduated from the place back in '40, you know. Granddad was still alive then, throwing his money around like he had an endless supply—and maybe he had. Foster Baine has the whole works now, at a fairly young age, and I suppose he's doing a good enough job. You know, this is an odd city in a way. I can't think of another place in the country with a population as big as ours that is so completely dominated by one industry—one single company. Baine City and the University and our largest theatre are all named after the original Baine. The family is the social leader, the business leader, the cultural leader. When the city needs a new hospital, or a park for the kids, the mayor just calls up Foster Baine or his wife, and there's usually a fat check in the morning mail. And a fine spread in the following morning's newspaper. That's life in Baine City, and I suppose there's nothing really wrong with it."

"There was something wrong with it," I reminded him. "Something in Professor Wilber's laboratory."

He sighed and sipped his drink. "You're really persistent, aren't you? All right, I'll tell you everything I know—but I warn you, it isn't much. The whole thing was Cathy's doing, really. She came to me in May—nearly two months ago—with a story of being in Wilber's lab one day and glancing through some of his secret notes. She told me, or rather she didn't tell me, what it was all about—though she hinted that he was going against orders and doing some basic research in a forbidden field. We were both afraid that the news might break just at the start of my fund-raising activities."

Simon Ark cleared his throat to give warning of an impending interruption. "The good Professor Wilber led us to believe that women were never allowed in his laboratory."

I nodded in agreement. "Something about being afraid the apes would attack them."

Mahon snorted. "I think that Wilber's really nuts. Anyway, all I know is what she told me. And now she's dead."

"You think Wilber had a hand in it?"

"I don't really know what to think," he said. "I'm baffled. I can only suppose she took up with a bad crowd—those hotrodders from the end of town."

"Do you know any of their names?" Simon asked.

"No. . . . Zenny was one of them. Zenny something. There were others too. She seemed to think she was learning about life or something, hanging around with that wild crowd. At times she even talked about writing a book on sociology, but I don't think she was ever serious. Jean couldn't do a thing with her."

Quite suddenly Simon Ark was on his feet, thanking Mahon for the drink and making it obvious he wanted to leave. It was an odd action for him, but I had no choice but to follow. I shook hands with Mahon and assured him I'd be talking with him.

"Are you staying for the funeral Tuesday?" he asked.

I hesitated, not knowing what Simon had in mind. "We may, though I should be back at Neptune Tuesday morning. I'll see."

We went back to the car, and Mahon went back to his flowers. I headed in the general direction of the hotel, waiting for Simon to say something, but for a long time he was silent. Finally he said, "I think this situation is worth looking into further."

"You want to stay?"

"I think so. Until tomorrow, at least."

"Well, maybe I can get you a room at the hotel. What are you going to do?"

He thought about it. "Two fields must be investigated a bit. The University and the hotrodders. Do you have any preference?"

"Look, Simon, it's like Quinn said—we're not detectives. Why not stay out of it? There's nothing here to interest you. No witchcraft or ghosts or anything."

"Still. . . ."

"You want to stay. All right, we stay, but just overnight. I've got no reason to stick around for the funeral of a girl I hardly knew. But if you're going to do any sneaking around you can do it on your own."

Our route had taken us back toward the funeral parlor, and I swung the car around the grassy triangle to see what might be going on.

"Interesting," Simon said.

"What? Did I miss something?"

"Professor Kane Wilber, just going in. Since he said he didn't know her it's interesting that he should leave his work to come here."

"Maybe he wanted to make sure."

"Perhaps," Simon mused. "Please leave me off at the next corner. I will probably see you at the hotel later tonight."

There was no talking to him when he got in one of those moods. I dropped him off as he'd requested and circled the block to the hotel. But my curiosity got the better of me. I parked the rented car and went back around the corner on foot.

Simon was easy to spot, even with the late afternoon's sun in my eyes. Tall and black against the brighter colors of summer foliage, he was a man apart. I watched a moment and saw the door of the funeral home open. It was indeed Professor Wilber, and now he was leaving, walking with a quick firm pace back in the direction of the campus. Simon waited silently and then fell into step about a block behind him.

Well, where did that leave me? Should I go take in a movie or pick up one of the competition's books to read in my hotel room? I certainly wasn't going to fall in line behind Simon and add to this crazy procession. The door of the funeral parlor opened once more and a young fellow, maybe nineteen or twenty, came out. He was well dressed, more or less, but even the clothes seemed somehow uncomfortable. I could make a good guess that this was one of Cathy's hotrod friends, possibly even the one named Zenny. Anyway, he was heading my way, and I figured I had nothing to lose. "Hi, Zenny," I said, making it friendly. He twisted around at the sound of the name, going into a modified fighting crouch.

"Whoreyou?" Like that. All one word. It sounded like a dirty word.

"A friend of Cathy's. She told me about you."

"Cathysdead. I seen her." Was he sorry or just resigned?

"Could I come with you a ways, Zenny? Just to talk?"

"You a cop." He made it a statement, not a question. And he made it obvious he didn't like cops.

"No, I'm a book publisher. From New York."

"Huh! New York."

"Some people like it, Zenny. Mind if I call you Zenny?"

"Call me anything you like." He seemed resigned to my presence now, and he'd settled into a slower speech pattern.

"You were a friend of Cathy Clark?"

"I knew her. She wasn't one of these damn stuck-up college kids who think they're too good for you. She came around with the gang. She was lots of fun.

"What kind of fun, Zenny?"

"You must be a cop. Go get lost."

"She must have been two or three years older than you. Why did she hang around with a crowd of young toughs when she probably could have had her pick of the college crowd?"

"Damn!" he snorted, his face reddening. "You get lost, mister, or I'm goin' to flatten you, cop or no cop. I was just as good to Cathy as any damned college bastard."

I was silent for a moment, trying to decide on the best course of action. "Look," I said finally, "I'm no cop, I told you. I want to talk about Cathy, to meet some of her friends."

"Quinn's already talked about Cathy. You know Quinn, don't you?"

"I know Quinn, but that still doesn't make me a cop. I know the mayor of New York but I'm no politician. Besides, Quinn seems like a good enough guy for a cop.

He snorted and fumbled for a crumpled pack of cigarettes. "There are no good cops. If they were good they wouldn't be cops." He seemed ill at ease in the suit jacket and I figured he was anxious to get back to wearing his regular clothes, whatever they might be—probably blue jeans and a soiled sweatshirt.

"What's the matter with Quinn?"

"Oh, he's always suckin' around. One time about a year ago, when Cathy first started hangin' around with our crowd, he comes stormin' in one night to rescue her or somethin'. I guess he thought there was goin' to be a gang rape. She told him off good, I guess. You know, he went for her himself."

"Quinn?" He'd told us at the funeral parlor he never knew her personally. I turned that thought over in my mind but said nothing.

"Sure Quinn. Who you think I'm talking about? Hell, you're nowhere. Get lost, mister. There's the gang waitin' for me." He left my side and darted off toward a battered blue Ford that looked to be seven or eight years old. A dark girl in sweater and tight jeans stood by the door waiting for him, and there was another couple inside.

"Zenny! Wait. . . ." He turned a moment as if to stop, but the girl held open the door for him. She never looked directly at me, only almost through me as if I didn't exist. Perhaps for her I didn't. If she was Zenny's girl this was probably a big day for her, welcoming him back from Cathy Clark's coffin.

The Ford took off with a roar as soon as Zenny was inside,

and I could tell from the sound that there was something special under the hood. Then they were gone, and all was quiet again in the early evening.

In the lonely silence that settled around me I heard somewhere the familiar pop of a firecracker, and I remembered that the Fourth of July was now only hours away. Tomorrow.

A girl hurried by, her heels tapping out a sort of melody on the concrete, and somewhere mixed with the fireworks was the distant tolling of a church bell. It was six o'clock. I walked, heading nowhere, wandering in a fairly straight line that I soon saw would carry me near the towering stacks and low structures of Baine Brass. Well, that was as good a goal as any.

I wondered where Simon was now. Maybe lurking outside Professor Wilber's lab, watching him inject monkeys with the deadly serum that would turn them all into King Kongs. Hell, this whole trip was fantastic, and I was crazy to even be here, alone on a street I never knew, walking toward the twin brick towers that now reflected the dying sun back into my eyes. As I drew nearer, I saw that the sun was reflecting off two giant webs of neon tubing, forming the letters BB.

There was activity at Baine Brass tonight, and I guessed there must be a shift that finished up at six. Men, mostly, tired but joking, glad the long Sunday was over.

And also a few women, in slacks that were the badge of the girl production worker, lighting their cigarettes and glancing around to call out to friends. I stood by a tree for a time, watching them waiting for their buses, watching many of the men and a few of the women wandering across the street to the little bar. There was always a little bar across the street from factories, I decided, to purge the men of their paychecks and their troubles.

BB. Baine Brass.

After this there was no place left to go. There would be nothing beyond Baine Brass, so I turned to retrace my steps. Behind me, two of the home-bound workers were casually discussing the murder.

"What do you think of that killing?"

"You know how these rich girls are. Probably her boyfriend got her pregnant and then shot her."

"They claim it was nothing like that."

"Who claims—the papers? They're all in Baine's pocket. If his son or any of his friends got the girl in trouble the papers would sure keep it quiet. That's what happened all right. Foster Baine owns this damn city. I don't think they'd even commit a murder without his OK."

It was an interesting if somewhat narrow theory, and the other man didn't bother to reply. I figured it was just the eternal war between labor and management being carried on at a more personal level. They turned off into one of the side streets and the evening was silence again.

I was back almost to the funeral parlor when I glimpsed Simon Ark headed down the next block in the same direction. I stepped up my pace and caught him. "Learn anything?"

He didn't look at me, but rather kept his eyes fixed at an alley leading around the rear of the funeral home. "I learned that our Professor Wilber is indeed quite strange. Come—quickly!"

"What. . . .?"

"Wilbur is in there. He came back for some reason."

But it's the dinner hour. No one will be there now."

"No one but Cathy Clark," he reminded me.

We went down the alley to the back door. It was open except for a battered screen door that didn't quite close. "He went in this way?"

Simon nodded and signaled me to silence. Very carefully he pulled the screen door open, hesitating every few inches lest a squeak should give us away. Then we were inside the familiar hallway, creeping into the room where we'd spoken to Quinn. The place was empty, with only the dim funeral lights casting a glow over mounds of flowery anthills. The white folding door was half open, and through the crack we could see the coffin of Cathy Clark. We could see that, and something more.

The dim but certain shape of Professor Kane Wilber, bending over the casket like some fiend from hell. Bending over the casket and *running his fingers through the corpse's hair.* . . .

For a long moment that seemed like an hour we were frozen there, unable to move or utter a sound before this scene of sheer horror. Then, shaking myself free of the icy chill that gripped me, I started forward—intent on stopping him from this deed of darkness—but Simon held me back with a firm hand.

"Not yet," he whispered. "Wait—and watch."

Presently Professor Wilber rose from his task, his back still toward us, and rubbed his hands together. Then he seemed to be rearranging the ruffled hairs, covering the signs of his deed. And in the madness of my mind just then I wondered if somehow he had cut out her brain for use in some half-imagined monster. No, that was not possible, but his real task must have been no less sinister.

Then, while we watched, he was gone, slipping as silently as he'd come back through the screen door to the alley. The undertaker had heard nothing, the dead girl was undisturbed. He had only run his fingers through her hair.

"Strange," Simon said. He pulled back the folding door and went quickly to the coffin, bending over it much as Wilber had done. But he did not touch the glistening blonde hair. He only looked, at the hair, and face, and body of Cathy Clark. "Why?" he asked, more of himself than of me. "Why?"

"He's crazy, that's why. What else could it be?"

"I don't know," he answered slowly, "but I intend to find out. The ways of genius are sometimes strange, and we must not leap to conclusions."

"Did you discover what he's doing in that lab—what Cathy Clark was so upset about?"

Simon sighed and turned away from the casket. "No, I discovered nothing. It is a curious matter."

When we were outside once more I told him of my meeting with the boy called Zenny, and my stroll past Baine Brass. He listened intently but had no comments to offer. His mind seemed somehow far away, listening but not hearing. Somewhere distant another illegal firecracker exploded but there was no other sound to intrude our silent thoughts. The city was lonely again, but I couldn't help wondering where Professor Wilber had gone now. . . .

Strange, city strange, darkness settling slowly like fog over streets so quiet. A Sunday evening, July third, lonely July. I sat in my hotel window, on the ledge, smoking a cigarette, watching what might have been a bat circling high above the buildings, looking, seeking—what? The same as me? The cigarette was good in the night air, cooling from the heat of day, but still there was a certain odor about the city—not the Manhattan odor of exhaust fumes and pizza parlors, but rather perhaps the smell of hot brass if hot brass had a smell.

Still the lights burned bright in the factory at street's end, still the activity seemed to center there in this city at sleep. Still still. July third. Below me a girl hurried along, her blonde hair gleaming, and for an impossible moment it might have been Cathy Clark risen from the coffin for a last walk through this city of dreams. The night was like that.

Simon Ark sat across the room from me, twisting the dial of the quarter-an-hour radio until he found a program of symphony music from a New York City station. Then he settled back in the chair and closed his eyes.

"Why do they do it, Simon? Why do men kill?"

"Why do men love, why do they hate? Why do they journey through life's great adventure as individuals rather than a self-helping group? I sometimes think, my friend, that if all the peoples of earth could look beyond this life to the hereafter, they would end warfare and hatred forever—end it and spend their years in peaceful preparation for the beyond."

I grunted. "There'll always be evil in this world, Simon. You've found it yourself in almost every possible place—even monasteries."

"Evil, yes. Because evil is the devil's product. As long as Satan walks the earth, evil walks with him. Even here, in this quiet city of brass, someone has held hands with the devil, and fired those deadly bullets into a poor girl's body."

"Who?" I asked.

"The eternal question, but sometimes not so important as *why*. That is the most important question in the entire universe. *Why* is there evil? *Why* did Cathy Clark have to die? *Why* was Kane Wilber running his fingers through a dead girl's hair? *Why?*"

I lit another cigarette, watching a couple of hotrods dragging down the main street of town. Even the police seemed on holiday tonight, and I wondered if the youth called Zenny was in one of those cars. I wondered too if Cathy Clark had ever ridden there by his side. A dozen, thousand, images leaped up to confront me—images of Cathy beside the boy Zenny, naked and hot beside him. Images of Foster Baine, a man I'd never met, ruling this city with a brass fist. Images and dreams.

Nine o'clock. There were fireworks in the distance now, skyrockets lighting the night air with glistening colored sparks. They would be coming now from the lake resort area, a few miles to the north. The rich of Baine City would be there this weekend, just as the rich of Westchester would be out on the Sound with their boats.

"Simon, is there something about water that attracts wealth?" I asked casually, putting words to my random thoughts.

But suddenly I realized that Simon was no longer in the room. He had gone silently off somewhere, leaving me alone in the semi-darkness, with only a flashing red neon sign for company. And then the phone rang, and I answered it.

"This is Jean Mahon," the voice said. "Can I talk to you?"

"Certainly. Where are you?"

"In the lobby."

"I'll be right down."

She was the same, but still a little different, as she seemed every time I saw her. She had been a different girl at the funeral parlor, beside her sister's coffin, and now she was a bit different again, perhaps a bit more alive.

"Hello," she said. "Thank you for coming down."

"It's nothing. You must have put in a rough day—can I buy you a drink?"

"I shouldn't," she hesitated, but only for a moment. Then we were off to the hotel bar, a depressing place of phony tropical plants and overly polite waiters in red jackets.

"You look pretty good, considering," I told her over drinks. "Didn't Hank come down at all?"

She shook her head. "He can't stand to see dead people. Something about the shock of seeing his grandfather dead years ago. Of course that makes it harder for me."

Here, under the pale lights of the bar, she looked more than ever like Cathy. I remembered the night of our brief talk in Grand Central, and in the dimness this might almost have been the same girl. She had the wide, too-wide, mouth I'd noticed before, and the same habit of tilting her head a bit when talking or listening intently. I could see how she would have appealed to Mahon, especially on a cold ski weekend.

"Do you know anyone who could have wanted to kill your sister?" I asked.

"Now you sound like the police. No, no one. Cathy was a lovely, likeable girl."

"She was younger than you?"

Jean Mahon nodded. "By almost two years. She was still a bit wild, but we all go through that stage."

"There was a fellow named Zenny. . . ."

"I've heard her mention the name, but I never met him."

"He was at the funeral parlor this afternoon."

"Oh? There were so many of her younger friends. . . ."

I lit a cigarette. "What was it you wanted to talk about?"

"Well, nothing really. Henry mentioned that you were checking on Professor Wilber, out at the University."

"You know him?"

"Slightly, from when I attended the arts college. He was always scampering around, acting crazy. I . . . do you really think he might have a connection with my sister's death?"

"I don't know," I answered honestly. "I'm no detective, you realize. I understand she was hanging around with a pretty wild crowd."

"Oh, Zenny and those others! I suppose they were a bit wild, but everyone goes through that stage, I think."

"You said that."

She smiled. "I am repeating myself, aren't I? Time to head for home, I guess."

I thought she was kidding, but she wasn't. She downed the rest of the drink and rose to leave. "You're really going?"

"Yes. Thank you for the drink. Good night."

I watched her leave the place, her strong, youthful beauty still drawing stares from the line at the bar. Well, she'd called me up and said she'd wanted to talk. We'd had a drink, she'd said nothing at all of any importance, and then she'd gone off. What in hell did it mean, if anything? Was I crazy, or had she had some secret motive in her brief conversation with me?

I thought about it as I downed my drink and wondered vaguely where Simon was. Was the whole world crazy tonight or just me, just this place called Baine City? "I'll have one more, bartender," I called out. At least it was better than returning to the window sill in my room to stare out on the vacant city. I stayed there nursing my drink, and it was there that Simon Ark found me, a half-hour later.

"Get out the car, my friend," he greeted me. "We have traveling to do."

"Where? Back to New York, I hope."

"No, to the lake nearby. I have learned that Foster Baine and his wife are spending the weekend at a summer home there."

"What in hell do you want to see Foster Baine about? And at this time of night? It's ten o'clock already."

Simon nodded. "I know, but I believe we have an increasingly dangerous situation here. I think it narrows down to two possibilities—either Cathy Clark was slain by Professor Wilber or someone connected with his experiments, or she was killed by someone from the personal side of her life, someone like this Zenny. It is most important that we learn once and for all just what experiments Wilber is carrying out. In spite of your friend Mahon's insistence that Baine knows nothing about the experiments, I feel certain that he must have at least a general knowledge of them. In a city like this, someone like Foster Baine would know everything."

"All right," I said. "I'll drive you out there—but you go in by yourself. He'll probably have the police on us for getting him out of bed."

"Hardly, my friend. Today's newspaper reports a giant midnight fireworks display on the lake to welcome in the fourth. Surely the Baines will be up for that."

He was probably right, and I really didn't feel like bed yet anyway, so we got out the rented car and headed in the general direction of the lake. The night was a lively sort, with a brisk breeze blowing blue clouds across a bluer sky, and it was almost a pleasure to drive beneath it, even bound for so questionable a destination.

The lake we sought was named Iroquois, after the Indian tribes that had long ago claimed the region for their own. It rested like a great blue puddle in the lap of a valley, surrounded on all sides by cottages big and small. Now, even at night, there was a certain beauty about it all, and we swept down the lake road like a winged dragon coming for the conquest. One end, or side, of Iroquois Lake was given over to the mammoth summer homes and boat houses of the wealthy, and there we found the sprawling fenced-in grounds of Foster Baine's place of play.

The gate was open, and a number of cars stood in the cindered drive. We parked behind them and started off on foot for the house. Simon looked at me and smiled. "I thought you were staying in the car."

"I changed my mind. OK?"

"OK, my friend. No need to be upset."

"It's almost midnight. I suppose these fireworks are going to blast off pretty soon."

"Soon," Simon nodded. "It would appear that Mr. Baine is entertaining house guests for the display."

We went up silently onto a cobblestoned terrace, seeing through partly opened French doors the laughing, talkative crowd inside. There were perhaps a dozen or more men and women, all in the late thirties-early forties age group, and dressed in that casually expensive look of the very wealthy. A colored houseboy was serving a tray of cocktails and all was very, very proper. These were the rulers of the city of brass.

"Can I help you?" someone said behind us.

I turned and stared into the muzzle of a .38 revolver held tightly in the hairy hand of a smiling little man. "What?" I was startled by the sight of the gun, though Simon seemed almost not to notice it in the dim light.

"Pardon me," the man said, keeping the smile in place, "but there've been a number of robberies lately. Could you state your business?"

Simon Ark cleared his throat. "We wish to speak with Foster Baine. It's very important."

The little man put away the gun but kept the smile. "Wait here." Then he vanished through the open doors, into the midst of the party.

"What do you make of him?" I asked Simon. "Special guard?"

Simon shrugged, and we turned to look out at the water, its little wind-driven waves beating at the stony shore. There were men along this shore now, shadow men, standing every twenty or thirty feet, waiting at their posts like soldiers guarding against invasion. They would be watching the glowing dials of their watches now, waiting for the midnight stroke that would signal the start of the fireworks. The lake soon would seem a sea of fire, and somehow I supposed it would reflect the passing of another year of independence.

A tall, not unhandsome man in a summer jacket stepped onto the porch, closely followed by the guard who'd greeted us. Apparently Foster Baine didn't interview strangers alone. "Good evening, gentlemen," he said, his voice surprisingly mild. "May I be of assistance?"

"Foster Baine?" Simon asked, and when the tall man nodded slightly he went on. "I am Simon Ark. You do not know me, but I have come some little distance to speak with you."

The man waved his hand with irritation. "You see I'm entertaining. Can't it wait till Wednesday? I'll be back in the office then."

"It can't wait," Simon said quietly. "It concerns the murder of Cathy Clark."

If Simon's statement surprised him he didn't show it. Rather he seemed just the least bit annoyed, chewing nervously on his lower lip. "The girl who was murdered? What has she to do with me?"

"She was a recent graduate of Baine University."

Foster Baine snorted. "Am I now to be held responsible for every person who passes through the portals of that place? I never met the girl, or heard her name, before this weekend when she was killed. . . . Just who are you gentlemen, anyway?"

He looked down on me with a decidedly superior attitude as he spoke, but Simon was his equal in height and more than his equal in staring people down. "Mr. Baine," he said, bringing into play the full range of his startlingly powerful voice, "we have reason to believe that the death of Miss Clark may be in some manner linked with a series of experiments being currently carried on at Baine University by a Professor Kane Wilber."

"Am I supposed to know about those, too?"

"We thought you might, since you support the various research programs of the University."

His eyes broke with Simon's gaze and he turned away, toward the water. "I know Professor Wilber. I've known him for a good many years. He is without doubt one of the finest brains in the country in the field of heredity."

Simon moved a step closer to the man. "And what is the nature of the experiments being currently carried on?"

At that moment a flare fizzled into life across the lake, then another, and another, until the entire lake seemed ablaze in a matter of seconds. Rockets screeched through the black and blue night, bursting above us to litter the area with the sudden, already dying, brightness of a thousand suns. Almost at once we found ourselves surrounded by the rest of Baine's party, and for the moment further talk was impossible. We were all simply an audience now, held captive by the spectacle of color that bathed so briefly the lake before us.

What was the last question Simon had asked? The nature of the experiments being carried on? I thought about it as I watched the constantly changing brightnesses reflecting off the face of Foster

Baine. No, he was not a man to make monsters—he was an empire builder, a pioneer for all of his inherited riches. He was Baine Brass, as surely as his father and grandfather had been.

Another rocket burst far overhead, sprinkling colors like lights on some animated Christmas tree. Christmas in July. From inside the occasional music of a stereo phonograph drifted through to us over the sound of the bursting fireworks. It wasn't Christmas music—maybe rather July music, music for a summer night. Something from the twenties, dreamy.

The lights flickered and changed again, and I was looking at a face somehow familiar. A blonde girl, standing next to, and a little behind, Foster Baine. A girl who for one crazy instant could have been Cathy Clark in Grand Central Station, over a cold cup of coffee. I knew her, I knew this girl, from somewhere far in the past. Further back than Cathy Clark. . . .

It had been a summer, like this one, at a lake like this one, perhaps only because as one approaches forty all summers and all lakes seem much the same. I had forgotten everything about her—even her name—many years ago, because after all it had been summer at a lake. I remembered only that in those days, she'd looked well in a bathing suit, that she could do a Charleston like some imagined image of Clara Bow, and that she kissed me one night on the sandy beach, with little pebbles pressing into my back.

Now, as she turned, aware somehow of my questioning gaze, the same sort of half-remembering expression passed over her face—passed and was gone, all in an instant. "Pardon me," I said. "Don't I know you?"

A bit of a smile played about her lips as she answered. "Do you? I am Mrs. Foster Baine."

Yes, his wife now. A rich man's wife. "It was a long time ago," I began.

The smile stayed on her lips, but not in her eyes. "I think you must be mistaken."

"Perhaps," I replied, because there was nothing else to say just then.

We watched the fireworks for another ten minutes, until finally the bursts grew a little less frequent, the flares a little less bright. And the music from the stereo swelled up around us again, with a dreamy instrumental of an old song called *Dancing On the*

Ceiling. The party was breaking up now, with guests and their ladies saying courteous good-nights to Mr. and Mrs. Foster Baine. It was not the kind of gathering where half-drunk friends lingered till daybreak, dancing sensuously to unheard music. These were the proper people of Baine City—they had seen their spectacle and now it was time to go home.

And even as I watched them go I wondered at that strange quirk of modern society. Sometimes the rich and powerful were also the lawless and sinful, but there was a certain point of wealth and power that precluded all this—as if when a man reached a certain goal he ended his public sinning and started practicing it in private.

Then we were alone, Foster Baine and his wife and Simon and I, and we went back to the living room of the beach house. It was a room to be appreciated, a room to be studied and savored like a fine painting. There were trimmings of brass, of course, everywhere you looked. Brass fireplace screen, a huge brass clock on the mantel, even brass legs on all the furniture.

"Well," Foster Baine said, taking up a position on one side of the great open fireplace. "Where were we?"

I tried to catch Mrs. Baine's eye, but she wasn't having any. Like her husband, she was concentrating on the tall, commanding figure of Simon Ark. "We were discussing the current experiments of Professor Wilber," Simon said. "And the murder of Cathy Clark."

Her eyelids may have flickered at that. I couldn't be sure. But her husband might have been a block of brass. "Well, as I said, he has one of the finest brains in the entire country. As to his present work, I'm afraid I can't enlighten you there."

"Can't? Or won't?"

He gave us a hard smile. "What you will. The experiments are of a confidential nature. At the proper time full data will be released."

"I have been told that these experiments are of a somewhat startling nature," Simon said.

Baine shrugged his shoulders. "These days life is startling. Rockets circle the moon, planes fly the ocean in a few hours. Professor Wilber and others like him are only working for an even better tomorrow."

Simon Ark frowned. "Tomorrow seems only better because it is not here. Today's evil will never bring tomorrow's good."

"The experiments are not evil," Baine retorted.

"You know their exact nature?"

Baine hesitated a moment and then nodded.

"But you refuse to reveal them?"

"What good would be served by it? They are in no way connected with the death of Miss Clark. Why should I speak of such matters with two perfect strangers?"

He was beginning to get annoyed at Simon's persistence, and I noticed that the little guard had returned, standing casually just inside the door. It was time to go.

Simon apparently realized this too, for he rose and said, "We must be going. I am sorry to have kept you up like this after midnight, but we felt it was important."

Baine gave a wave of his hand. "Perfectly all right."

When we were outside in the dark I led the way back to the car. "What do you make of it, Simon?"

He looked up at the stars for a moment before replying. "I don't really know, my friend. A man like Baine is always difficult to figure out. He is a ruler here, like some feudal prince. The problem is whether his goals are the good of the people or merely his own selfish fame."

"I think I used to know his wife," I remarked, starting the car and heading back toward Baine City.

"Oh?"

"She wouldn't admit it, but I think I knew her one summer down on Long Island. It was a long time ago."

"A girl friend?"

"Not really. Not at all, in fact. That's why I can't quite figure out the cold shoulder I got. I never saw her or heard about her again, after that summer. She meant nothing to me."

"Perhaps that's why, my friend. Women like to mean something to a man."

"Well, she found her man, anyway. She found Baine Brass."

Simon cleared his throat. "Were you aware that a car was following us, my friend?"

"What?" My eyes shot to the rear-view mirror, picking out the twin headlights cutting through the night behind us. "Are you sure?"

"I'm sure," he said quietly. And even as he spoke the car picked up speed and began jockeying to pass us. "Be careful."

"Damn!" I twisted the wheel as the lights moved along side.

"If I had my own car I'd run him off the road." He was next to us now, edging us over, crowding us toward a blackness that could only be a ditch. I took my eyes off the road an instant to concentrate on the shadowed figure bent over the steering wheel. I wanted to see what death looked like when he came for me.

But it was not the bone-smooth face I'd half expected to see. It was the face of the youth named Zenny. There was someone beside him, a girl whose face I couldn't see. Just as I looked he swerved the wheel of his car, crowding me and bumping my fender. I slammed on the brakes and stopped with my right front wheel already on the edge of the ditch. Zenny brought his car to a halt some dozen yards ahead.

"This looks like trouble," I said. "That's Zenny, the Clark girl's boyfriend."

"Would you prefer that I. . . . ?"

"No, I'll handle it." I slid out from behind the wheel and stood there waiting for him. "Hello, Zenny. You wanted me for something?"

He halted a dozen feet away, sizing me up like a fighter about to move in for the knock-down. "What you want, anyhow, mister? You're workin' for Baine, aren't you?"

"No."

"I see you leavin' his place just now. Baine and I aren't exactly friends." He moved a step closer.

"That's too bad. Did you and the girlfriend follow me all the way out here just to tell me that?"

"We weren't following you. We just seen you." Behind him the girl had gotten out of the car. I thought it was the same girl who'd been waiting for him that afternoon at the funeral parlor. She wore the same tight sweater and jeans, but now her lipstick was smeared. He glanced at her and spat, "Get back in the car, Bun."

"God, Zenny, don't try nothing! There's another one in the car watching you. If they are cops they probably got guns."

He thought about this, sizing me up all the while. "I'm not going to hurt him, not yet. This was just a warning. Hear that, mister?"

"What kind of warning? I don't think I understand."

He stepped in closer, only an arm's length away. "This kind of warning. You tell Baine he's not framing me for Cathy's killing. You can tell him he'd better lay off or his wife will wish he had."

My left arm shot out and I felt my fingers catch his shirt collar.

"What do you mean by that?" I asked angrily, yanking him off balance. I thought I had him, but he was too experienced at that type of fighting. Before I knew what was happening his right hand was coming up under my arm, a sudden switch-blade catching the gleam from my headlights. It was only the girl's scream of fright that warned me in time.

We broke, and then the girl was on him, pulling the knife arm back. "No, Zenny, you damn fool! Let's get out of here."

Apparently he was convinced, because he started backing away, letting himself be dragged back to the waiting car by the girl in the tight jeans. He flung back only one shout. "Remember it, mister. You and Baine both remember it."

Then they were in the car, and it was jumping to life with the familiar cough of a souped-up engine. I watched until the red tail lights vanished around the curve and then went back to Simon.

"Tough guy," I said.

"My friend, Shelly would not like the thought of mixing with knife-wielding thugs. You're much too old for it."

I started the car, carefully backing away from the ditch. "I was never the right age, believe me. I think I'll head back to New York, where there's nothing to kill you but the traffic."

"We must stay another day, now. Things are moving to a head."

"Sure they are. I'll get knifed by Zenny tomorrow sure."

"Perhaps not, my friend. Perhaps not. We will wait to see what tomorrow brings."

And he would say no more. We drove slowly back to town, in silence. Behind us the night was dark. . . .

Fourth of July.

Dawning bright, crackling with the odor of burnt powder, singing with the distant sound of a parade. A picnic, a walk in the park, a familiar political speech. Midsummer day—holiday time, vacation time. I rolled out of bed just before ten and stood looking out at the city of brass, watching great white clouds chart a brief path across the sky, past Baine University, past Baine Brass. They were like some unknown islands in the sky, always there, yet changing with every tide of wind that blew across them.

It was so in Paris and London, Los Angeles and Washington, and here in Baine City. Just another place under the sun, where men lived and died, and life went on because it had to. Even today there'd be shifts at the brass plant, running the great forming and polishing machines. There'd be men standing around, taking a cigarette break, cursing the foreman, reliving the previous night's date with the well-stacked blonde. It was life.

And I wondered what life ever was to men like Simon Ark. Did he have a woman somewhere, anywhere, to rest him when the burden got too tough? Even as I thought it, there was a knock on the door and he was standing there, looking the same as yesterday, the same as when I'd first seen him twenty years ago.

"A pleasant morning," he said.

"Pleasant." I started dressing, turning over the random thoughts that were running through my mind. "Simon?"

He'd settled into one of the hotel chairs and crossed his hands as if in prayer. "Yes, my friend?"

"Have you ever had a woman, Simon? I've known you for all these years, and yet I really know so little about you."

I don't know what reaction I'd expected, but I was surprised when he dropped his eyes to the carpeted floor. "A woman? Well, now it has been a long time. . . . I am very old, you know, so very old. . . ." And then his eyes lifted, and he went on. "Did you know, my friend, that in ancient Greece the women of the streets—prostitutes—sometimes carved messages on the soles of their sandals, so when they walked along they imprinted messages in the sand or dirt of the streets?"

"What kind of messages?"

"Usually something like *follow me* or words to that effect."

"It's a queer world."

"Yes, and perhaps there is always a woman at its center. Perhaps woman is the real ruler of man. At least they need each other, and always will."

I nodded and put on my shirt. "Until someone comes up with a foolproof method of artificial insemination."

I'd said it mostly as a joke, but Simon didn't smile. "Most methods of artificial insemination are quite immoral," he said, and then fell silent a moment, as if deep in thought.

An idea struck me and I turned away from the window. "Simon, we know that Wilber has been working on experiments concerning birth and the life process. Is it possible that when we saw him bending over the coffin yesterday he was really studying Cathy's skull? Is it possible he intends to attempt to bring her back to life?"

Simon smiled a bit at that. "All things are possible in this world, my friend, but I fear you are being overly influenced by the current offerings of movies and television. I doubt very strongly if Professor Wilber is contemplating anything like that."

"So, where do we go from here?"

"It's a holiday. Why go anywhere?"

"Seriously, Simon, who do you think killed her?"

"If I told you, I doubt if you'd believe me. I hardly believe myself."

"Then you know!"

But he shook his head. "I have a suspicion, nothing more. A suspicion that cannot yet be put into words."

The phone buzzed and I picked it up, wondering who'd be calling us on this holiday morning. It was Henry Mahon, downstairs in the lobby and waiting to come up. I told him to come ahead.

"Mahon," I told Simon.

"Interesting."

"Very."

He came, a few moments later, looking somehow worn and red-eyed. I wondered if he'd been drinking the night before. "Good morning," he mumbled, sitting gingerly on the edge of the bed.

"Hello, Hank. What brings you down here at this early hour?"

"I . . . well, I thought you might have gotten the wrong idea about our conversation yesterday. I do care about my sister-in-law's death, really! I don't want to give the impression that I'm more interested in raising money for the University than in tracking down her killer."

He was nervous today, even more so than the last time we'd seen him, and all the familiar wildness seemed gone from him. Perhaps Cathy's death had hit him harder than we'd thought. Perhaps, but I doubted it.

"We have some leads," Simon told him. "Despite our reluctance to act as detectives, we have uncovered a few interesting facts."

"Oh, have you?" He was interested now, and I couldn't help feeling that this information had been the real purpose of his visit. I sat back and let Simon take it from there.

"Yes," he said, like a cautious hunter laying out the bait, "we've learned quite a bit concerning Professor Wilber, for instance. We followed him yesterday and saw him return to the funeral home during the supper hour. Amazing thing—he was in there all alone with the body."

"Alone?"

Simon nodded. "He was running his fingers through her hair."

Mahon was in the act of lighting a cigarette when Simon spoke the words, and his fingers faltered. "What? Why would he do that?"

"My friend here believes he might be planning to bring her back to life."

He looked at me as if I were crazy. "You really think that?"

"Well, not really. It was sort of a joke."

"Is this whole thing a joke? Do you know who killed her or don't you?"

"Sometimes life is a joke," Simon answered, "but we know who killed her."

"Who?"

Simon closed his eyes. "The murderer will be at the funeral tomorrow morning."

"That's all you'll say?"

"That is all I'll say."

Mahon sighed as if disappointed and got up to leave. It was obvious that he was unhappy with the state of the interview, but there was nothing much for him to do about it. After mumbled thanks and promises to see us later he departed.

"There's a guy who's really changed," I observed. "He's certainly not the rich playboy type any more."

"Men change for a reason," Simon said. "Find the reason and you learn much."

"I gather from your conversation with him that we're staying for the funeral tomorrow. Right?"

"Right. One extra day might make a great difference. I want you to do certain things for me while I am busy elsewhere today."

"What kind of things?" I always hated chasing around on missions for him like some third-rate Doctor Watson, but I could see I had little choice.

"You must contact Quinn, the detective. Tell him to be at the funeral tomorrow morning. Tell him he must have some of his men in the crowd."

"He'd probably be there anyway," I said. "Why do I need to tell him?"

"Just so he'll be prepared. Do it, will you?"

"OK. Where are you going to be?"

"At the University, with Professor Wilber. I believe a conversation with him might clear up the last of the haziness."

We went downstairs for breakfast and then separated. I was sorry to see him go, especially since I had only a vague knowledge of my real mission. Was it possible that Simon somehow suspected Quinn of being mixed up in the affair and wanted to scare him into the open. I'd met the man only briefly, but now I remembered the conflicting stories about his acquaintance with Cathy Clark. Well, stranger things had happened. Maybe Quinn was involved in some way.

Baine City Police Headquarters was an old sandstone building badly in need of a cleaning. Outside, flanking a short stretch of steps, stood two battered brass lamp posts surmounted by green glass globes. It was the police station of the twenties brought strangely back to life, and as I entered I half expected to see a chorus line of flappers being booked for indecent exposure, or a bootlegger paying his token fine. All was dusty with neglect, like a library in a country of the blind. Maybe that was it—maybe there just wasn't any crime in Baine City. No crime but murder.

Is Captain Quinn around?" I asked the man behind the desk, taking a wild guess at his rank.

"You mean Sergeant Quinn?" he asked with a slight smile. "Yeah, he's around somewhere. Have a seat."

I lowered myself onto a long dusty bench to wait. Presently one of the distant doors opened and I saw Quinn approaching with a well-dressed woman. It was Mrs. Foster Baine.

"Fellow's waiting for you, Sarge," the man at the desk said.

If Quinn was surprised to see me he didn't show it. He said goodbye to Mrs. Baine and came over to me with an outstretched hand. My eyes followed her out of the place but she purposely avoided glancing my way.

"Well," Quinn said, "good to see you again. Can I help you?"

I was still puzzled by Mrs. Baine's strange appearance, but I tried not to show it. Obviously Quinn wasn't planning to discuss her visit with me. "Simon Ark asked me to talk with you," I said. "He has a lead on the Clark killing."

"Ark? The man who was with you yesterday?"

"That's right. He said to tell you the killer will be at the funeral tomorrow morning. You should be there with some men."

Quinn made a noise somewhere between a grunt and a sigh. "Is your friend Ark going to unmask the killer at the funeral— pull him like a rabbit out of the hat? Maybe get the corpse to stand up and point an accusing finger like in Poe?"

"I don't know. I've seen Simon do stranger things."

"I'll be there, don't worry."

I started to turn away and then paused. "Say, didn't you tell us you'd never met Cathy Clark?"

Quinn's eyes narrowed. "Why?"

"I just heard from somebody that you knew her."

I'd tried to make my tone casual, but he wasn't having any. I was like a fisherman who finally gets a bite and finds it's a whale. "Who?" he rasped, seeming to tower over me as he spoke. "Who told you that?"

"A kid named Zenny."

He nodded. "Cathy's friend. You know him?"

"We've met."

"He's a nut. Be in trouble someday. Know why they call him Zenny?" I shook my head. "He's trying to be one of those beat characters like you have in New York. You know—Kerouac and all that. He reads books about Zen Buddhism and stuff, so his gang started calling him Zenny. He liked it and it stuck."

"He said you rescued Cathy from them one night. Took her home or something."

He shrugged. "Maybe I did. I usually try to get a girl out of their clutches, unless she's asking for it. Cathy Clark might have been one of them."

It was hard to decide whether or not he was telling the truth. Certainly he was an honest, educated man—and probably a good cop as well. I was inclined to take his word for it. "Then you'll be there tomorrow—at the funeral?"

"I'll be there."

With that he turned back toward his office and I left him, heading for the street. My mind was still on the conversation with Quinn when I saw Mrs. Foster Baine waiting for me outside. It startled me so that I couldn't be certain she was really after me until she spoke, calling me by name.

"Could I talk to you?" she asked.

"Any time. This is a surprise, after last night."

"I'm sorry about last night. I can explain it."

She was edging me toward a cream-colored convertible I'd noticed on my way in. It was parked in a striped *No Parking* zone not twenty feet from Police Headquarters, but I suppose that didn't bother people like Mrs. Foster Baine. "Your car?"

She nodded. "Want a ride?"

"Where to?"

"Just around. While we talk."

"What will your husband think?"

"There comes a time when it just doesn't matter much any more," she answered, opening the car door for me.

"And this is the time?"

"Maybe. I thought about it all night, I couldn't sleep." She went down the main street, in a direction I didn't know, driving with a skill that surprised me.

"It's been a good many years," I said. "What have you been doing?"

She twisted her lips into a sort of smiling sneer. "I got married."

"And pretty well, too—Baine Brass isn't just the corner drug-store."

She sighed a bit. "Ten years of it now. That's a long time for anything. I'll bet even Adam and Eve got tired after the first ten years. That's probably why it was so easy for the serpent."

"I didn't think anyone ever tired of money. Baine must be worth a cool hundred million, and it's family owned—no stock-holders to get in your hair."

The warm breeze caught at her hair and pulled it free behind her, billowing out in a beautiful way I remembered from the first time I'd seen her. She was still a pretty girl, though some others might have now considered her a beautiful woman. She was Mrs. Foster Baine. . . . I searched my memory for her first name and finally came up with it.

"Betty."

"What?"

"Betty Baine. They go together."

"Yes," she answered seriously, "I suppose they do."

"Tell me about it?"

"What is there to tell? He was charming, rich, and in love with me. I was past twenty-five and beginning to look over my shoulder at my youth. One night I just sat alone in my room thinking about it, and I guess I decided to marry the first man who came along. Foster Baine was that man."

"Too bad I didn't come back." I didn't really know if I meant it, but it was something to say.

"You're marrried now?"

I nodded.

"Children?"

"No. Shelly—my wife—well. . . ." I stumbled to a lame halt. There was no reason to discuss personal matters with Betty Baine. She'd only been the briefest of shadows in my past, a girl whose very name I'd had trouble remembering.

"Where did you meet her?"

"Out west. In a little town called Gidaz. It's a long story. That's where I met Simon Ark too."

"That strange man who was with you last night. . . . Who is he?"

"So many times people have asked me that question, and to tell you the truth I still haven't got the answer. At least I haven't got an answer that satisfies me. He's a man, a wanderer, a searcher. Perhaps in a way he is all men, seeking the ultimate truth that can never be found."

"Only fools seek truth," she said. "Others are content with appearances. Life is too short."

"It has been longer for Simon Ark," I said. "He has the time to seek truth."

She turned down a narrow street that seemed to be leading out of the city. Gradually the houses grew further apart and soon here and there a farm appeared on the landscape. A cow grazing in a field of high grass, the stalks of corn just beginning their annual spurt of growth. . . .

"What's your interest in Cathy Clark?" she asked suddenly.

"No interest in the girl personally. I only met her once, very briefly. But I've known Mahon for several years."

"He's got money," she said. "So's his wife. The Clarks were a wealthy family once, and Jean got it all."

"You know her?"

"Not really. She's a bit under my age group, you know. But of course I've heard of her. The whole city knows how she trapped Henry Mahon into marrying her."

"They seem happy."

"She is a beautiful, wealthy, intelligent girl. He has no complaint."

"What about Cathy? I understand she got shortchanged on the money end."

Betty Baine gave a slight shrug. "Her sister took good care of her. She always got everything she wanted."

It was all country now, with acres of rolling farmland in every

direction. I'd always admired upstate New York for this virtue—
it could be agricultural when it wanted without the intruding glare
of wheat fields by the mile that were so typical of the midwest.

I was beginning to get restless, though, riding like this toward
nowhere with a woman I hardly knew any more. "Would you
mind telling me where we are going?"

She half turned her head toward me. "If it was anyone but you
I couldn't do this. But I feel you'll understand."

"Understand what?" Was she about to seduce me?

"Foster—my husband—has a great many problems, personal
problems. I think it would kill him if they were made public."

"I'm not interested in making trouble for your husband, Betty."

"You're interested in Cathy Clark, aren't you? And in Professor
Wilber?"

"Yes," I admitted.

"And don't you realize that in a city like this all roads of
scandal lead directly to our doorstep? Don't you realize that if
Cathy Clark's killing involves Professor Wilber it also involves
Foster Baine and me?"

"You're worried about the scandal? You're apparently not worried about being seen driving around town with an old boyfriend."

"That kind of talk never worried me," she answered smugly,
and turned the car onto a bumpy dirt road. "Hang on, we're
almost there."

"Almost where?"

"To the Baine family secret. The skeleton in the closet."

"Does your husband know you're taking me out here?"

"It doesn't matter," she said. "Some things have to be done.
You want to know about Professor Wilber's work and I'm going
to tell you. Maybe then you'll be convinced it doesn't concern
Cathy Clark's killing."

I sat back in the seat, trying to relax, and presently we topped
a ridge to look down on a rambling old house that might have
been something out of Hawthorne or Dickens. Certainly it was a
house from the past, a house that had seen a good century of life
and death. Yet some small attempts had been made to modernize
it—a bright brick chimney contrasted sharply with the drabness
of the faded gray sideboards. We passed a single wooden name
sign bearing the simple word *Baine,* and this too looked somehow
old and faded.

"The family homestead?" I asked her.

She nodded. "Foster was born in this house."

"But his parents are dead, aren't they?"

She pulled up and parked behind a black Ford, the only other car in sight. "Most people think so. You lose track so easily of widows after their famous husbands pass on."

"You mean Foster Baine's mother is still living—in there?" I asked, but she didn't answer. She was already out of the car, heading up the front steps with quick, sure strides. I followed, a bit uncertainly.

The door was opened to her ring by a dumpy, middle-aged woman who could only have been a cook. "Hello, Gerta," Betty Baine said. "How is she today?"

The woman shrugged. "The same. She's always the same."

"Has Father Fox been here today?"

"Sure. He comes every morning, sometimes before I'm up."

I'd figured Mrs. Baine for some rare illness, but this mention of a priest threw me for a loss. What type of illness required the daily ministrations of a priest?

"We want to see her," Betty said. "Just for a moment."

The woman called Gerta eyed me suspiciously. "Does the mister know about *him?*"

"It's all right. I'll take full responsibility." She turned to me. "Come on, this way."

I followed her toward the front of the house, until we reached a locked door. Betty motioned to the woman and she produced a key from somewhere, inserting it in the gleaming lock that was like a sleeping eye to the heavy wooden door. Inside, all was semi-darkness. Blinds were tight on the windows and there was only the dim glow of dying embers from the fireplace to cast a flickering fire over the room. But my eyes went first to the woman who sat upright on a straight-backed chair in the very center of the room. Her eyes had been closed, but now she opened them, gazing out at us from a wrinkled yet strangely peaceful face. She was not a young woman, and I would have guessed her age at near seventy-five. That was Foster Baine's mother I had no doubt—the face bore the Baine look, as little of it as I'd seen.

"Hello, mother," Betty said. "I brought you a visitor."

The old woman focused her eyes on me. "Who?" she asked, nothing more.

"Just a friend, Mrs. Baine," I answered. "You don't know me."

A shadow seemed to pass across the face and the old head

nodded a bit. Then her eyes flickered shut. "She's sleeping," Betty Baine said.

"What's this all about, anyway?" I asked her.

"Look." Betty walked over and opened one of the blinds a bit, so that a ray of sunlight fell across the room and onto the woman's sleeping figure. Then she came back and reached for the two wrinkled hands lightly clasped in Mrs. Baine's lap. I bent over to see what she was trying to show me.

In the palm of each hand was a dark area, like a wound yet somehow different. I'd never seen anything like it before. "What is it?" I asked.

"Stigmata. The wounds of Christ."

"What?" I wasn't sure I'd heard her clearly.

"Mrs. Baine carries the wounds of the crucified Christ on her body. On her hands, her feet, and her side. In addition, she subsists solely on Communion given her each morning by Father Fox. She has eaten nothing in over five years."

I let out my breath in a low sigh. "That's fantastic."

"Nevertheless, it's true. Foster Baine's mother is a living saint."

"And you keep her here like this, locked up in this room?"

"There's no room in Baine City for a saint, especially when she happens to be Foster Baine's mother."

"You're Catholics?"

She shook her head. "No, but Mrs. Baine was—is."

"And this Father Fox—what does he say about all this?"

"Nothing. He comes, every morning, to give her Holy Communion, but he never talks about it. I get the impression he doesn't believe his own eyes."

"What do the doctors say?"

"Only her family doctor has seen her since it started. He's at a loss for any normal explanation. And Professor Wilber, of course."

I'd forgotten about Wilber. "What's his connection?"

She closed the blinds again, leaving us with only the fireplace glow. "He's investigating it. He has been out here and carried on several experiments."

I had to admit I could see no connection between this sainted woman and Cathy Clark. But why would Henry Mahon have thought this shocking? Odd, curious, fantastic—yes. But shocking? There was still something—many things—I didn't understand.

The old woman stirred again in her chair. Her eyes opened and focused on me. "Are you a friend?" she asked.

"Yes."

"They keep me here. I am alone with my God."

"Are you a prisoner?" I asked, and caught a sharp look from Betty.

"A prisoner, yes. I must go out, into the world, and spread the word of God. She waved her hands with their ghastly wounds.

"Come," Betty said, urging me out. "We must leave now. She's getting excited."

There was nothing more I could do. But I knew that Simon Ark would be most interested in this strange woman with the wounds of Christ on her body. I followed Betty out of the room, and we drove back to Baine City in tight-lipped concentration. Very possibly Betty was beginning to regret her action in showing off the family secret. . . .

Surprisingly enough, Simon Ark was sitting in my hotel room, staring at the city. He turned as I entered and smiled a greeting. "My friend, the pieces of the puzzle are now complete."

"That's what you think, Simon. I've got a whole new bag of puzzles—enough to baffle even you."

"Oh?"

"Did you learn anything about Professor Wilber?"

He nodded. "I learned the nature of his experiments."

"So did I."

This seemed to surprise him. "About the animals?"

"Animals? No, this is something else." And I quickly told him about my visit to the country house of Mrs. Baine.

When I'd finished I saw that he was profoundly moved by the events I'd narrated. "You actually saw the markings on her hands?" he asked. "There was no trickery with the lighting?"

"They were there," I insisted. "What point would they have in faking it? No one ever sees her."

"Stigmata is rare, almost unheard-of in this country," he mused. "And yet—perhaps. . . ."

"What about the animals, Simon? What did you learn?"

"That can wait," he said. "We have much to do before morning."

"I'm tired."

"There will be time to rest later. Right now—we may still be in time to prevent another murder. . . ."

* * *

Then we were in Professor Kane Wilber's laboratory once again, with the afternoon sunlight filtering through high windows. He'd been surprised to see us again, and now he was cautious—a man at bay, backed against one of his own monkey cages.

"What is it this time, gentlemen?" he asked.

"You work long hours on a holiday," Simon observed.

"There is much to do."

"With the animals?"

He looked away. "That and other things."

"We know about old Mrs. Baine, Professor," Simon said quietly.

"You do?" He made no effort to hide his surprise.

"What we want from you now is an account of these experiments we're told you carried out."

He was still on the defensive but he'd advanced from the cages now. "That information you'll have to get from Foster Baine. I can tell you nothing."

"You can tell us nothing about Cathy Clark, either?"

"Nothing."

Simon moved a step closer, until he towered over the man. "You know much about this matter, Professor. You are too deeply involved."

But Wilber only shrugged. "I can say nothing."

"Very well," Simon said. "Perhaps then I must release to the newspapers the information about the exact nature of your experiments with those apes."

Wilber's eyes narrowed. "You're bluffing."

"Am I? Should I mention the name of Mirza Ali Akbar to you?"

Whatever the name meant, it had its effect on Wilber. He seemed to shrink a bit inside. "Very well," he said. "What do you wish to know about Mrs. Baine?"

"Is she really a stigmatic?"

Professor Wilber shrugged. "I have discovered no other explanation. They called me in some time ago to investigate the thing, but of course it's a bit out of my field. I do know that she bears strange wound-like markings on her hands, feet and side. And she apparently needs no food or liquid nourishment to live. I have conducted careful searches of her room for any hiding places where food might be kept, but I have found nothing. It would appear to be a supernatural thing, from start to finish."

Simon Ark was growing more interested by the minute, and I

figured he'd already forgotten the Cathy Clark case and his promise to Quinn to reveal the murderer in the morning. Now he was filled with an excitement I'd rarely seen before, and as quickly as we'd arrived he was ready to depart.

"We will meet again, Professor," Simon told him. "Until later, thank you."

I followed him out and across the campus to where we'd parked the rented car. "What was that name you scared him with, Simon? And why didn't you ask him some meaty questions while you had him on the run? Why didn't you ask him what he was doing running his fingers through Cathy Clark's hair?"

"There was no need of that last question, my friend, I already know the answer."

"Great!" He might know but I surely didn't. "So now what?"

"Now you take me to the house of Mrs. Baine."

"The old lady? Nothing doing! Besides, that Gerta dame would never let us in alone anyway."

"There are two ways of getting by her."

"Yeah, but you've never seen her. Besides, you won't get a thing out of the old lady. I tried."

"Still. . . ."

We'd just reached the car when we saw the flashing red of a police vehicle heading toward us. "Now what?" I muttered. The squad car pulled up ten feet away and Sergeant Quinn climbed out. His face was grim and there was no humor in his eyes.

"One of my cars said you were up here," he said. "You'd better come along with me."

His eyes were on me, not Simon, and I asked him what it was all about.

"You were with Betty Baine this afternoon?"

"For a short time, yes," I admitted.

"Well," he said, "she's disappeared. And you're the last person seen with her."

"Disappeared? That's crazy!"

"Sure it is," Quinn agreed. "But she's Foster Baine's wife, and if she doesn't turn up right quick you've really had it, man. . . ."

Baine City, twilight, July Fourth. Monday madness, quiet groups standing in the street corner, the word spreading from one to the other. Mrs. Baine missing. Mrs. Baine kidnapped.

Mrs. Baine raped and murdered?

In a ditch somewhere?

A city alive, a city with a small town mentality, alive now with the scent of sensation. Betty Baine, the social leader, the woman in the cream convertible. Gone now, in trouble. No longer to be envied but only prayed for.

Past the funeral home where I could see Jean Clark Mahon standing by the curtained window, past the hotel, to the familiar police station with Quinn.

"Where do the boys go in the evening?" I asked.

"Huh?"

"The boys with the fireworks. I haven't heard one in hours."

"All out, I guess," Quinn answered absently. "Against the law, you know."

From the window of his office I could still see Baine Brass, where the second shift would be working now. I wondered if the word had reached them yet, at their machines. Probably.

". . . found her car, the white convert, in a ditch on the way back to the cottage. When did you leave her?"

"She dropped me at the hotel maybe two hours ago."

"Where were you with her?"

"For a drive."

"In the country? You were seen on the East Road."

"So what?"

"You went there for a little loving? Foster Baine thinks you knew his wife before."

"I knew her. When I was in college. Is there a law against that?"

"There's a law against kidnapping."

"Go to hell."

Quinn had been silent through much of the questioning, interjecting only an occasional comment. Now he came forward and pulled up a chair facing me. "Man, you're in bad trouble, don't you realize that?"

"Ask Simon Ark. I was with him all the time."

"You lie and he swears to it. Where did you and Mrs. Baine go this afternoon?"

"Get Foster Baine in here and I'll tell him. I can't tell anyone else."

Quinn slapped his knee. "By God, we'll do just that."

He went off somewhere and I looked around the bleak office for some sign of Simon. But he was gone, perhaps to one of the

other offices. The cop who'd been questioning me offered a cigarette. "Get up and stretch your legs," he said, sounding friendly
enough.

"Thanks."

Outside the grimy station window the night was gathering its
forces. What had they called it during the Middle Ages—the Blind
Man's Holiday? The period of day just before the candles were
lit? And even as I watched, the lights of Baine City were going
on, in silent response to some far-off electrical impulse. Their
yellow glow fell on people, standing, talking, waiting. It was a big
night in Baine City. Their queen had disappeared.

"Queens have died young and fair," I quoted, half to myself.

"What?" the detective asked.

"Thomas Nash. A quotation."

"Oh."

"You think she's dead?"

The detective looked up quickly. "Who?"

"Betty Baine."

"Mrs. Baine? No—her kind lives forever. They'll find her, unless
you did something to her yourself."

I grunted and turned back to the window. A car full of curious
teenagers went by and I was reminded of Zenny.

Zenny!

Of course! The half-veiled threat to get Mrs. Baine. He'd said
something like that, just the night before. There was no reason,
only madness, but perhaps people like Zenny didn't need a reason.

Quinn came back into the room, with Simon Ark behind him.
"You two sure got your stories down pat," he grumbled. "Maybe
too pat."

I ignored him. "Simon, remember when Zenny forced us off
the road last night? Didn't he say something about Mrs. Baine?"

Quinn looked surprised. "Zenny?"

"Zenny," Simon Ark repeated slowly. "Do you know where he
can be found, Sergeant Quinn?"

Quinn scratched his head. "Cathy Clark's old friend, huh? I
figured this would all tie in together."

"Where can we find him?"

"Should I believe you guys?"

Simon sighed. "You must believe somebody, someday, Sergeant."

"OK," he decided, "let's go—but no tricks. Joe, bring up a

squad car in front and clear some of those people away. We don't
want an audience. . . ."

Screaming through the night, screaming silently so our siren
would not give us away. Quinn and Simon and another and I.
Through the black bright dark of Baine City.

"The funeral's tomorrow, tomorrow at nine."

"Better to be hers than mine."

"Better. . . ."

Around a corner, bright headlights picking out the sights and
sounds of a sleeping city. Cathy Clark's neighborhood. Where the
Cathys prowled, through black alleys, searching searching. Zenny,
here Zenny, come quickly and quietly. Simon tense at my side,
Quinn intent on the twin beamed targets.

"See Zenny?"

"Not a sign."

"Keep driving."

"Zenny?"

"Zenny?"

"No Zenny."

Then—"There, it's his girl, Bun!" Quinn barked an order and
the car rolled to a stop. "Bun, where's Zenny?"

"Don't know." A summer night's dream in tight red shorts,
very short. Ready to take on the toughest of the boys.

"You'd better tell us, Bun. He's in big trouble."

"Big."

And Simon gazed up at the antique buildings around us. Brick
apartment houses topped with a Bronx-like forest of TV antennas.
Babes in the woods.

"Where?"

"Don't know."

People, crowds gathering even here. People all the damned people
in the world staring at me here and there and everywhere and.

"He snatched Mrs. Baine, didn't he, Bun?"

She shifted her bare legs, showing off the round smooth buttock
cloth of her shorts. "Don't know a thing."

"Take her," Quinn said. And into the car with us, in the rear
seat between Simon and me, with her hot bare legs pressing against
my pants. And on further, slowly now, deeper into the night that
was like some long dark cave.

A jazz joint, shouting its praise to the world. Brassily announcing that life was eager and gay. The corner drugstore because there always was one. The neoned bar with the red sign flickering for lack of money. Tired, like its people.

"That's his car," I spotted. "Parked there."

She went for my eyes, twisting and scratching like a wildcat. Simon was on her, pulling her away, muffling the scream of warning already forming in her throat.

"This is it," Quinn said. "Hold her down."

"Take the riot gun, Sergeant."

"Hell, man, that's Baine's wife. No guns."

Up the stairs, Quinn, Simon, me, with the other detective hanging fast to Bun. "Which apartment, Bun?"

"You figure it, copper!"

Quinn figured it. "Let her go."

"What?"

"Let her go."

She broke free, looking up and down like a trapped tiger as her mind tried to comprehend the snarl of the trap. To warn him or not? To run with him or without. Quinn had guessed right—she headed up.

"Zenny, they're here—*run for it!*"

And like a crazy fool he threw open the door to see what the yelling was about. He had a six inch switch-blade and Quinn had nothing, but the detective took him with one quick blow to the neck. He toppled like a hundred-year-old tree.

"You killed him," she sobbed.

"No such luck."

Inside was a dull and dusty mess of confusion. The unmade bed and dirty dishes told their own story, but there was no sign of Betty Baine. "Struck out," Quinn murmured.

"Third base," I said, pointing to a scattered handbag open in one corner of the room. Simon was already going through the connecting door to the next apartment.

And there she was, tied to a wooden kitchen chair with her skirt pulled up to her hips and her stockings shredded with runs. Quinn undid the gag and tried to sound sorry. "Are you all right, Mrs. Baine?"

She made a sour face and worked her jaw to loosen it. "I guess so," she answered, "but it's been one heck of a holiday. . . ."

Quinn's office at ten-thirty that night was crowded to overflowing. The mayor himself was there, expressing the city's concern and sorrow to Foster Baine. Quinn was there, and a handcuffed Zenny, and a sobbing Bun, along with Simon Ark and myself, and the center of all the attention, Betty Baine.

"Get this guy out of here," Quinn ordered, indicating Zenny. "I'll take care of him later."

Foster Baine had his arm around Betty's shoulder, comforting her, and Simon Ark was standing quietly in one corner, as if trying to pass unnoticed. As soon as Zenny and the girl Bun had been led away, Quinn went over to Mr. and Mrs. Baine.

"Did he . . . say anything at all when he forced your car off the road, Mrs. Baine? Anything as to why he might have done it?"

"I don't know," she answered thoughtfully. "I got the awful impression he was doing it to get back at Foster somehow. He said something about Foster trying to frame him for the Cathy Clark murder."

Quinn sighed deeply. "It all leads back to that, doesn't it?"

And that was when Simon Ark stepped from his corner. "If you would allow me the interruption, I could name for you the killer of that girl."

"Then you really do know?" Quinn asked, half doubting still.

"I believe so."

"Then name ahead."

But—"No!" It was the firm voice of Foster Baine, speaking up over the hush of expectant breath. Quinn turned questioningly toward Baine, but he didn't have to ask him the reason for the outburst. Baine was all too willing to continue. "This . . . this whole thing is closing about me like a web. First some young punk kidnaps my wife and now this mental wizard here is going to try to implicate me in a girl's murder."

But Simon held up a peaceful palm. "Not at all, my friend. I intend only to implicate the guilty."

"You're implicating Professor Wilber, aren't you? That's as bad as me. It's almost the same thing."

I thought I saw the dark shadow of Foster Baine's mother pass across his face as he spoke, and Simon must have had the same feeling. He said, "It is the country house you really fear, is it not, Mr. Baine? And its occupant?"

If the words surprised him he didn't show it. "That does not even enter into the discussion," he answered coldly.

"Ah, but it does, my friend," Simon insisted. "At times the ways of the gods are indeed strange. Take me there this night, let me spend a few lonely hours with your mother, and perhaps I can help this too."

"No one can help this too. Not the priest not the policeman."

"We shall see."

"No one," Baine repeated.

Quinn interrupted with a puzzled voice. "Your mother's still alive, Mr. Baine? I thought. . . ."

And then Betty spoke. "Heavens, Foster—it had to come out someday. Let this man see her. Perhaps he can help."

"Perhaps, perhaps! You're sounding like him now! And what were you doing driving with this other one this afternoon?" His finger jabbed accusingly at me.

"If you must know, I took him out there to see her."

It was the last blow to an already crumbling Foster Baine. "You took him out . . . ?"

"They have to *know,* Foster. It's time *everybody* knew!"

He wiped his forehead with a damp handkerchief. "Why? Why is it time? She'll be dead and gone in a few years. So little time. . . ."

Quinn had wisely stepped aside now. It was between Baine and his wife, with Simon Ark waiting for his moment. Finally he decided it had come. "I make you this promise, Mr. Baine. Let me see her tonight, let me speak to the priest, Father Fox, and by morning your problems will be solved."

And the man of brass seemed slowly to shrink within his shell. "What else is left now?" he murmured. "Very well, we will go tonight. She doesn't sleep."

Quinn made a move to follow, but Simon restrained him. "Tomorrow will be your day, Sergeant. Tonight is mine. . . ."

It was close to midnight before I once again topped the ridge and saw brief burning lights that told me somebody still stirred in the great old house. Simon and I were in the car alone, with Foster and Betty Baine bringing up the rear in their own car. Quinn had stayed behind, grumbling but convinced that he would not be needed.

Now, as I saw the house once more, I said to Simon, "It's late."

"It's always late, my friend. Always a little too late."

"Why do you think Zenny did it? Kidnapped Betty Baine like that?"

Simon thought about it a moment and then replied. "Perhaps it is one of the paradoxes of modern times, my friend. Each man strives for the fleeting thing called fame, yet most men secretly detest the famous. Thus the youth named Zenny rebelled against imagined wrongs by striking out at the city's most famous man. And perhaps in this manner he hoped for some slight fame himself. John Wilkes Booth is never remembered as an actor—only as the man who shot Lincoln—and even his brother Edwin seems sometimes in danger of being only the brother of the man who shot Lincoln. Of course such is not always the case. Herostratus destroyed the Temple of Diana, one of the seven wonders of the world, solely to achieve everlasting fame. Yet today his name is but a forgotten footnote to history."

I parked in the familiar space behind the black Ford, which I decided must belong to the woman named Gerta. The Baines were right behind us and there was another car coming over the rise. I guessed it would be Father Fox, whom Baine had called before leaving.

"This is the place?" Simon asked, studying the towering reaches of the old house.

"This is the place." I went over to meet Baine and his wife. He was still looking unhappy at the prospect, and I could see it was only Betty that kept him from changing his mind about the whole business.

"That would be Father Fox," Betty said, and the black figure detached itself from the last car in line. It was indeed a priest, a short, squat man with a kindly yet firm face. He spoke not a word about the lateness of the hour, but shook hands all around like a pastor greeting his flock on a Sunday morning.

"Ark, Simon Ark," he repeated, when I'd introduced them. "I have read that name somewhere."

Simon I knew would be smiling slightly, though I did not turn to look at him. "I have traveled," he told the priest. "You may have seen my name in the papers, or perhaps even read a brief little book I wrote on witchcraft."

"Yes," the priest nodded vigorously. "That was it."

We entered the house in a group, and the woman named Gerta appeared from somewhere to greet us. "You come late at night," she mumbled sleepily.

"We come to see my mother," Baine said. "Tell her we're here."

Simon and I had fallen back with the little priest and now I spoke to him. "Father, do you believe this business about the stigmata?"

The priest shrugged. "I believe what my eyes tell me, with some reservations."

"Have you reported the case to your bishop?"

"Of course. But that is all. I certainly have not recommended any official church action. As long as the woman remains here, in seclusion, what harm is done?"

Simon's eyebrows raised a trifle. "You are implying . . . ?"

"I imply nothing," the little priest said. "Let us go in."

We entered the room, and to me it was much as I'd left it that afternoon. There was even still the wisp of a fire in the grate, and the old woman sat upright in the same stone-like position. "Why do you all come here by night?" she asked with a little gasp. Then she saw Father Fox and said, "Is it time already, Father? Is it morning?"

Simon Ark knelt in silence by the woman and carefully examined the palms of her hands. For a long time there was no word spoken in the room. We simply stood and watched, and I think even the priest was wondering about this man who was still sometimes a stranger even to me. And as we watched, Simon spoke to her.

"Mrs. Baine, Mrs. Baine, can you hear me? My name is Simon Ark. I have come a long way to speak with you."

"Yes," she answered.

The flickering glow of fireplace embers danced on their faces, and they might have been in a world apart. "When did you last eat, Mrs. Baine?"

"It has been many years now. I need only the Communion of Father Fox now. I am very close to my God."

Foster Baine sighed and would have stepped forward to end it, but the little priest held him back with a touch on the shoulder. We stood and listened as these two before us continued their strange conversation.

"Is your God a good God, Mrs. Baine?" Simon asked quietly.

"He is all good, all powerful."

"Then why do you use such trickery to gain the glory of Heaven? Why do you live this great lie, Mrs. Baine?"

She turned on him with old eyes flashing. "How dare you question the wisdom of the Lord!"

But Simon would not retreat. "You do not eat, yet even now there are cracker crumbs on your lap."

The eyes closed, the body shuddered, and we waited. "Go," she said. "Go."

Simon stood up and looked around the room. "Professor Wilber said he'd searched this place. But perhaps. . . . Get me water—a pitcher of water. Quickly!"

"Simon, what are you looking for?"

It was Betty Baine who produced the requested water from the kitchen, while the rest of us just stood there transfixed. Simon pulled open the fireplace screen and hurled the water onto the glowing embers. There was a sizzling puff of smoke as fire and water met.

Then Simon was clawing the soggy logs out of the way with a poker, feeling around till the metal tip caught on something else of metal beneath the ashes. "A new fireplace," Simon said, half to himself. "I thought it would have a trap door for ash disposal. And . . . here's a little bundle wired to the inside of the trap."

The woman in the chair gave a sobbing scream and sprang forward. She was almost upon Simon when suddenly she gasped and clutched at her breast. "Catch her someone," I shouted, and they all made a grab for her at once. It was Father Fox who stood up finally, gave a little shake of his head and began to pray over her.

And as they covered her old face with a sheet from the bed I thought the look on Foster Baine's face might have even been one of relief. . . .

"She was injecting turpentine under the skin of her hands and feet with a syringe," Simon told us later. "It causes the appearance of stigmata, and of course with the look of a saint about her it was easy to persuade old Gerta to slip her occasional food. She kept the turpentine and syringe in a small bag in the ash chute at the rear of the fireplace, where even Wilber never thought to look."

We were back in Quinn's office now, with the Sergeant sitting in unofficially on the conversation. Baine and his wife were gone now, off somewhere with the body of the old lady at last free from her room in the old house. "But how did you know, Simon?" I asked him.

"The turpentine trick has been used before. I came across it in

France some years ago. And the fireplace just struck me as the most likely hiding place."

"But why? Why would she do it?"

"Why do any of them do it? Sometimes, especially in older women, religion can be a driving force that becomes too much for the mind to bear. I think Father Fox suspected something, but of course he had no real evidence."

"And now she's dead," Quinn said.

"She's released," Simon corrected. "I'm certain there will be a degree of forgiveness for her actions."

"Was she implicated in the death of Cathy Clark?"

Simon sighed. "No, my friend, she was not. But the chain of circumstances that seems to link everyone in Baine City reached to her as well. Perhaps it would be best if I told you a little about it."

Quinn rolled a pencil between his fingers. "I'm just interested in who killed the girl, that's all."

"Well," Simon began, "you see, I am not the only one to discover the murderer's identity. Professor Wilber knows, and has known all along."

"He knows and wouldn't tell?"

"He couldn't tell, for two reasons. Foster Baine feared that the involvement of Wilber would lead to the discovery of his mother's supposed condition. So he was bringing pressure to bear. And the real murderer was blackmailing Wilber with the threat to reveal still another activity of the Professor—a series of experiments that even Baine knew nothing about."

"The ones Henry Mahon mentioned!" I said, beginning to see the pattern.

"Exactly," Simon nodded. "But now that Baine's problem has been removed I think we can get Wilber to talk."

Quinn glanced at his watch. "There isn't much time for anything any more. The funeral's in four hours, you know."

Simon Ark stood up. "That will be all the time I need. I will be there, with Wilber and with our murderer. . . ."

Funerals are always sadder on a sunny day. Somehow you expect it when the skies open up to pour down rain, but the restless beating of the sun on the covered casket is more than a sensitive soul can sometimes stand.

This day, as I followed the six men with their burden down

the steps of the funeral parlor and to the edge of the waiting hearse, I had the distinct feeling that a climax was near. It was the end of a life, but it was also the end of something more. Perhaps it was even the end of a city.

I was watching the curiously tense Henry Mahon leading Jean into the third car, just behind the hearse, and for that reason I didn't really notice the car with Simon Ark and Professor Wilber fall into line at the end of the procession. My eyes were busy counting out the detectives in the crowd, seeing how many I could spot.

Quinn was there, of course, because this was his day. But there was no evidence of Betty Baine and her husband. They would have a death of their own to contend with this day. I wondered vaguely what those people would say at the news of Mrs. Baine's final death—those people who'd thought she'd been dead for years.

The graveyard was small and detached when we reached it, nestled in a niche between two groves of trees, behind an old country church that had somehow made its way into the city's outskirts. We'd weaved our way around, past Baine Brass, past Baine University, finally pausing here at the final resting place of Cathy Clark.

I knelt with the others for a moment by the grave, as a minister spoke the usual saddening words. Then we crowded nearer the casket as it was placed over the open grave, the noonday sun reflecting off the brass nameplate. Yes, there would be Baine Brass even at the end of it all.

And then Simon Ark spoke up, stepping through the crowd with Professor Wilber at his side. "Wait!" he spoke commandingly. "Don't lower that coffin yet!"

They turned, men and women, to stare at this fantastic interruption. And with the sun still beating down upon us Simon turned to Wilber. "Tell them, Professor."

Professor Kane Wilber cleared his throat. "I'm sorry about this all, but I feel I must speak now. The. . . ."

The sentence was never finished. From across the grave I saw a brief streak of light, the sun reflecting off a sudden gun barrel. It was a gun in the hand of Henry Mahon, as I'd somehow known it would be, and even as I watched it spat a single simple shot.

Wilber grabbed at his side and went down, and somewhere in the crowd a woman screamed. I never knew what madness Mahon planned next. They were on him, of course, in an instant, battering

him to the ground while they wrestled the gun away from him.
I saw that Wilber was only nicked, and Simon was helping him
to his feet.

"Mahon killed his sister-in-law?" Quinn asked, somehow not
wanting to believe it until Simon himself spoke the words.

I looked to Simon for the familiar slight nod, but it wasn't
coming. Instead he slowly shook his head. "Henry Mahon never
killed anyone. He's just someone who never grew up."

"What?" Quinn released his grip on Mahon's shoulder. "Hell,
if he didn't do it then who did kill Cathy Clark?"

And Simon in his moment of glory pulled himself up tall in
the sunlight, like an ancient figure of an avenging angel. "That
is just the point, my friend. No one killed Cathy Clark."

"No one. . . .?"

"The girl in the coffin is Jean Clark Mahon, and Cathy Clark
is standing right over there. *Stop her, Quinn!*"

And that was the end of it. . . .

I suppose, in some fantastic manner, I should have known. I
should certainly have known as quickly as Simon Ark knew—
Simon who had never even met Cathy Clark before the murder.
I should have known when Jean (or Cathy) came to the hotel
that night to have the drink with me and then quickly depart. Of
course she'd wanted only to make certain I hadn't penetrated her
disguise.

And there were a thousand other things, too. Even I had
commented on the similarity between the girls. Even I had noticed
that the color of their hair was the major difference between them.
But their parents were dead, and the dead girl's two closest kin—
her sister and Mahon—were ready to swear she was Cathy Clark.
Zenny never noticed the difference, nor did I. But Professor Wilber
did, of course, and returned to the funeral parlor to run his fingers
through the dead girl's hair searching for evidence that the hair
had been bleached to its blonde color. He found the evidence,
and then he was sure. Jean's hair had been bleached after death,
just as the real Cathy had dyed hers black to assume her sister's
role.

Motive? Cathy's motive was the small fortune her parents had
left to Jean instead of her. And Henry Mahon's motive in going
along with it was resentment at being trapped into marriage with
a girl he'd never really loved. For someone like him, Cathy would

probably have seemed a great improvement over Jean. So he'd stood aside while Cathy killed his wife and stole her identity. He'd stood aside then, and later at the end had even tried to shoot his way out of it for her. When he'd heard about Wilber examining the dead girl's head and hair, he'd known Wilber knew—but he'd counted on the blackmail to keep the professor shut up.

But even after it was all over I still had a few questions for Simon. "Why did they try to get you and me up here last month, anyway? Was that part of it?"

"At the time it must have been," Simon replied. "They must have had some other plan for killing Jean and possibly framing Wilber. But then they failed to hook us and changed to his plan— which certainly didn't call for our presence. We almost spoiled things right from the beginning by arriving so suddenly."

"And that was why Mahon wuldn't come to the funeral parlor? Because he couldn't face seeing his wife there, in her sister's coffin?"

"Exactly. It was a twisted crime, one with very little chance of success, and yet they really did almost get away with it."

And so we left them all behind. Baine City and Baine Brass and the so many twisted lives. And I really didn't think I would ever go back there again.

"Simon?"

"Yes, my friend?"

"What was Wilber's secret experiment?"

"I fear that must remain a secret. He tells me it was a failure anyway, and certainly I cannot help but feel that too was for the best."

"Do I have to paw through reference books till I find out who Mirza Ali Akbar was?"

And Simon smiled a bit. "You remembered the name."

"I remembered. Who was he?"

And he looked away, far away, as if peering into another world. "Can't you ask me something else? Like whether or not Cathy and Wilber were once lovers? Because they were, you know."

"I guessed that," I lied. "Otherwise how would he have spotted Jean in the coffin when everyone else missed it. But to get back to the subject. . . .?"

"There is no subject. The experiments are at an end."

"Mirza Ali Akbar?"

And finally Simon Ark sighed in surrender. "He was a man

from India. A hundred years ago, who was interested in the possibilities of breeding large female apes with human males. . . ."

I remembered the ape in Wilber's laboratory, and his conversation with us that first day, and I asked no more questions. Whatever the truth of the matter was, I felt I already knew too much. . . .